MESSIN' WITH THE KIDD

MESSIN' WITH THE KIDD: 3 Killer Fashion Mysteries (#1-3)

A Polyester Press Publication

© Diane Vallere

e-ISBN: 9781939197177

Print ISBN: 9781939197733

Includes:

DESIGNER DIRTY LAUNDRY

BUYER, BEWARE

THE BRIM REAPER

Solving crime through style & error

MESSIN' WITH THE KIDD

3 Killer Fashion Mysteries!

Designer Dirty Laundry
Buyer, Beware
The Brim Reaper

DIANE VALLERE

Polyester Press
READING, PA

DESIGNER DIRTY LAUNDRY

KILLER FASHION MYSTERY #1

1

IT ALL STARTED TO GO WRONG

WHEN YOU WEAR FISHNET STOCKINGS TO THE GROCERY STORE, PEOPLE tend to stare. Women look at you like you're affiliated with the sex trade. Men pretend they're not staring, doing so all the while. It's probably because they're thinking the same thing.

The last time I wore fishnets to the grocery store was weeks ago. It was then I met the man who changed the course of my life. Because of him, I'd traded in the title of senior buyer of ladies designer shoes at Bentley's New York to become the trend specialist at Tradava, the family-owned retailer in Ribbon, Pennsylvania. I'd given up an apartment in Manhattan to buy the house where I grew up. And now, because of him, I sat in a police station explaining my actions to a homicide detective.

I still couldn't pinpoint exactly when it all started to go wrong.

A WEEK EARLIER . . .

I changed clothes six times, then ultimately settled on the fashion uniform of black: satin motorcycle jacket cinched at the waist over a lace camisole, pegged pencil skirt, fishnets, and stilettos. Elsa Klensch meets Catwoman. Patrick, the fashion director and my new boss, was bound to approve. I topped off my look with a finishing blast of Aqua Net, powered up with coffee and a donut from a newspaper kiosk by my house, and headed to work earlier than I remember ever going to work before.

I arrived at Tradava and followed a trickle of other employees into the building. A petite Latina woman in an oversized pink sweater and black leggings struggled to carry a box through the door marked "Loss Prevention."

"Let me help you," I called out. I raced forward with my arms out. The woman pivoted and I grabbed ahold of the side of the box just as she was about to lose control. She inched her way backward and together, we got it through the door.

"Set it on the floor," she said. We both bent down, her in the manner How to Lift Properly posters advised and me in a way that would surely make my back stiff in an hour. The box thumped onto the exposed concrete floor. The woman straightened and smiled. "Thanks," she said. "That box just about killed me." She studied my face. " Are you a vendor? Let me get the sign-in log."

"I'm Samantha Kidd," I said. "Patrick's new trend specialist. Do you know if he's here yet?"

"He's here, but he didn't say anything about you." Her brow furrowed, and she picked up the phone and dialed an extension. When no one answered, she hung up.

"He's not in the office. You'll have to sign in like a visitor."

"But I'm not a visitor. I'm staff. Today's my first day."

The friendly vibe we'd shared after I helped her with the box that almost killed her had waned, but she *did* seem conflicted. "Do you have ID?" she asked hopefully.

I reached into my handbag and pulled out a quilted leather wallet, then held it open to show my driver's license through the plastic window.

"I meant a store ID."

"No. Not yet, anyway."

"That's a New York license," she said.

"You're right, I moved. But it's me, see?" I held the wallet up to my face and smiled at her in the way only a half crazy person brimming with caffeine and adrenaline over starting a new job might.

The woman reached her hands up and gathered her long, wavy, brownish-orange hair on top of her head then wound it around several times until it resembled a doorknob. She pushed the sign-in log toward me and held out a red ballpoint pen. "I'm sure you'll get it all straightened out today."

"Right," I said. Look at me, already making friends! I signed my name with a flourish then added *Trend office, 7:37.* I snapped my wallet shut and put it in my handbag then hopped out of the way of a flatbed filled with merchandise and headed into the store. Aside from security and shipping, the store was quiet.

I wasn't a morning person. It was day one of a new job and a new life. Full of potential. My early arrival had less to do with my natural inclinations and more to do with my need to make a good impression. I was determined to be the best trend specialist Patrick had ever hired.

I wandered through the shoe department on my way to the elevators, pausing by a round marble fixture that displayed a purple suede platform pump. My index finger traced over the black and white designer label that decorated the sock lining.

"Of all the shoes, in all the stores, she had to walk up to mine," said a husky voice behind me. I turned and faced the man whose name was stitched onto that label. The man I'd once fantasized about during a layover in Paris. The man I'd almost kissed after a business dinner that involved a good deal of Sauvignon Blanc and a serving of lemon meringue pie. My judgment is not to be trusted around lemon meringue.

Nick Taylor was a shoe designer. His showroom was charged with electricity, hot looks, and devastating style. His shoe collection wasn't bad, either. He was one of the few people I thought I'd miss after leaving Bentley's, that is, until I caught him flirting with the buyer from Bloomingdales and realized the only special thing we had was a gross margin agreement.

"You're a long way from New York," I said. "What are you doing at Tradava?"

"Same thing as you, probably."

"I doubt that. I'm here to start a new job." I cocked my head to the side and crossed my arms, the plum-colored laptop bag that hung from my shoulder now banging against my hip.

"First day? Let's get you into practice." He stood directly in front of me and held out his hand. "I'm Nick Taylor. Shoe designer and all around good guy."

I pursed my lips and took in his dark curly hair and his brown eyes, the exact shade of the three root beer barrels I ate in the car after finishing the donut. I met his outstretched hand with my own.

"Samantha Kidd. Former shoe buyer. Former angry New Yorker." I pumped his hand twice to emphasize the word 'former.' "Current trend specialist for Tradava on the cusp of a new life."

He pulled me in, converting our handshake to an embrace. I lost my balance and fell against him. "I thought I might never see you again," he whispered in my ear. "So, Tradava?" He looked to his left and right as if making sure no one was listening. "From the big city to the small town. I knew you'd land on your feet, but I didn't expect you to land here."

"You make it sound like I vanished into the night," I replied, blowing at a strand of hair that had gotten stuck in my lipstick. My cell phone buzzed from the depths of my handbag, and I pretended not to hear it.

"You did vanish in the night. Out of my life, out of my dreams . . ." He reached out an index finger and freed the lock of hair. A trace of red lipstick transferred to his fingertip. "And now I find you haven't even missed me. That hurts."

"So you took it upon yourself to stalk me. Good to know."

"C'mon, everybody needs at least one stalker in their life. It's good for the ego," he said.

Nick Taylor had captured the eye of more than one female at Bentley's, and rumors of his love life often permeated the otherwise work-heavy market weeks. More than once I'd wondered what would have happened if I'd given in to my post-pie impulse to kiss him after that innocent business dinner last May.

"You didn't answer my question. What are you doing at Tradava this early?"

"I have some outstanding business with the shoe buyer," he said. "The only time he had available was this morning."

"Did security make you sign in?" I asked, nodding toward the back hallway.

"Sure. They make everybody sign in before the store is open."

The elevator bell sounded. The doors attempted to open, then jerked shut. Nick stabbed the button with his index finger, and the doors repeated their spastic motion. I had the other option to take the stairs but with a breakfast of highly concentrated sugar, fat, and root beer barrels coursing through my veins, that wasn't going to happen.

The doors jerked open again, and I jammed the laptop between them. They beat an irregular rhythm against the plum nylon case but left a resulting opening large enough for my fingers. By now I had exerted more energy than I would have on the stairs, but I was determined to get on the thing.

I quickly changed my mind.

In the elevator was a well-dressed man. His jet-black hair was held perfectly in place with pomade, and his mustache was neatly trimmed. He wore a taupe suit with a violet windowpane pattern, a brown and purple paisley ascot knotted around his neck, and a crisp white shirt that no doubt had been laundered and starched by a team of professionals. Even though his body lay crumpled on the floor, the shirt was barely wrinkled.

Patrick.

My new boss.

I yanked the laptop out from between the doors. When I stood back up, the room spun. I put a hand out to steady myself and lost my grip on the computer bag. It fell from my shoulder and landed on its side.

My knees buckled, and I followed the laptop to the floor.

2

IS HE DEAD?

WHEN I OPENED MY EYES, I WAS SITTING ON THE SOFA IN THE SHOE department leaning against Nick. I blinked several times and tried to focus. My fishnets had torn over my left kneecap, so I crossed my legs to hide the tear. A pile of catalogs and magazines sat on the table in front of us. After spelling out V-O-G-U-E, I figured the worst had passed.

Nick pulled his cell phone away from his ear. "Are you back?"

"From where?" I asked, confused by more than his question. "What happened?"

"You passed out when you saw Patrick's body."

"Is he—he's dead?"

He nodded. "I couldn't find a pulse."

"Did you call nine-one-one?"

He nodded again. "Take a couple more minutes to relax. You went down like a ton of bricks."

Considering I was on a sofa about twenty feet from the elevator doors, the analogy was more humiliating by the evidence that he'd probably carried me to my present location. Mental note: lay off the donuts.

"I'm fine now," I said, feeling anything but.

The second elevator bell rung, and I turned back around. The doors slid open, and a thin woman in a navy uniform stepped out. She carried a collapsible gurney under one arm. She stopped in front of the elevator with Patrick's body and inserted a key in the control panel. Her hat was low on her forehead, obstructing her face. The reflective letters EMT on the back of her nylon jacket were more jarring than white shoes after Labor Day. I wondered how long it had taken her to get there, which made me wonder how long I'd been lying on the floor like a ton of bricks.

"It's my first day. If I'm going to be late, I should call someone." I rooted around in my handbag for my phone.

The EMT adjusted the bill on her hat. She coughed twice. "Today's your first day?" she asked in a scratchy voice. "What department?"

"His," I said, pointing toward the elevator. Reality hit like that cliché ton of bricks Nick had introduced into our conversation. I turned to Nick. The room spun again, and I leaned down, dropping my head between my knees.

"You go in and out fast, don't you?" Nick asked. His hand, warm through the fabric of my jacket, gently stroked my shoulders. I'd never fainted before in my life.

The EMT stared at us for a couple of seconds then knelt on the floor. She grabbed Patrick's ankles and pulled them so his body was straight. It looked like too big a job for one person, and I stood up. "Do you need help?"

The EMT didn't answer. She log-rolled Patrick's body onto the gurney. She snapped one end up, then came around and raised the other to make it level. She rolled it into the elevator that she'd arrived on and jabbed a gloved finger at the control panel.

"Wait! The cops are on their way. They'll want to talk to you or find out about the cause of death." I looked at Nick. "They will, right?"

"Heart attack. Textbook." She pulled out a tissue and blew her nose like a foghorn. "I'm taking him out through the sub-basement. They can talk to me there."

"Nine-one-one routed the call to you that quickly?" Nick asked.

"Nah, he must have called us from his office." She held up a cell phone then put it in her pocket and coughed again. She tossed a brown sheet over Patrick's body, covering the cuff of his taupe and violet windowpane pants and his purple cashmere socks. Until he was covered, I hadn't been able to look away, and I knew, long after he was wheeled off, his image would stay with me.

I turned back to Nick. "I should tell security."

"They know. They let me in," said the EMT. She kept one hand over the elevator door to keep it open.

"The executive office, then." I dialed zero on the phone that sat in the middle of the shoe department. Several rings indicated the operators had no reason to show up hours early as I had. "There has to be someone around here. I'll go to the executive offices and let them know."

"You'll have to take the stairs," the EMT said. "I'll have the elevators tied up for a while," She turned the key on the control panel and the doors closed.

"Are you sure you're going to be okay?" Nick asked. He looked concerned.

This wasn't how my life was supposed to start over, but Nick didn't have to hear that. "I'll be fine," I said. "But I should notify someone." I turned toward the hallway through which I'd come.

"Hey Kidd," Nick called after me, "Do you want me to come with you?"

"No. I mean, I can do this myself. Keep your appointment." I found the stairwell and started climbing.

Nick followed me. Halfway up the third flight, his footsteps stopped.

"You said you're working in the trend office, right?"

"Yes," I turned to face him, but he was looking down the stairs.

"They're on the seventh floor," he said.

"I know. I already told you, I can get there myself," I said between short, shallow breaths. My thighs were starting to burn, and I needed a gulp of air. Mental note: reintroduce exercise into my life.

"I'm going back to the shoe department to wait for the cops and let them know what we saw. I'll send them up when I'm done." He jogged down three steps, turned back in my direction, and jogged up five to where I stood. "Only five more flights, then your heart rate can go back to normal," he whispered in my ear. Without a trace of breathlessness, I noticed.

"Four and a half," I said.

"Good to see you again, Kidd, even under these circumstances," he said, then jogged back down the flights we'd already covered.

I scaled the rest of the stairs and only barely avoided hyperventilation before entering the trend offices. Fluorescent tube lighting illuminated the space and cast distorted shadows on piles of notebooks, slides, and posters. Two desks were covered with action figures, fabric, colored markers, drawings, and a few other items I didn't recognize. Posters of Marilyn Monroe dabbing on perfume, Warhol's tribute to Jackie O, and a concert poster of Madonna lined the walls. I wasn't sure what I'd expected of Patrick's office, but eighties pop culture wasn't it. My interviews had taken place on the phone and outside of Tradava, and I was starting to think Patrick wasn't at all what he'd seemed when someone cursed behind me.

I turned around. A green-eyed blond man stood in the doorway. His skin flushed red against a glowing tan.

"Did you say something?" I asked.

The stranger scratched the side of his head and left a chunk of hair sticking straight out above a wireless earbud. "I didn't realize anybody was here."

I sat down at the desk with the Wonder Woman action figure. "I'm Samantha Kidd. The new trend specialist." I waited, wondering if he was going to say anything. "Today's my first day. And you are . . . ?"

He leaned against the doorframe and smiled casually. My first impression was skateboard dude, but he had an air of maturity lacking in the guys I watched on ESPN extreme sports. His scruffy hair seemed more chlorinated than salon-dyed, and his Eighties concert T-shirt looked like it came from a pricey vintage-reproduction store. Either that or the laundry pile, I couldn't tell which.

He remained silent, with a lopsided smile on his face, while I tried to find a spot for my handbag. I finally leaned it against my ankles and folded my hands. I was on edge already, and his presence unnerved me even more. I didn't know where I should be, what I should be doing, or who I should be talking to.

"Don't you need to be getting to your department?" I asked.

"I can't get to my desk right now," he said.

"Why not?" I asked.

"You're sitting at it."

"Isn't this the trend office?" I hopped out of the chair as if it were wired with a shock device. The chair knocked over my bag. Four tubes of near-identical pink lip-gloss rolled out by my left foot. I bent down to collect them and felt my skirt split over my right hip.

"No, that's down the hall. This is the visual office. I'm the manager. Eddie Adams." He pulled the Bluetooth device from his ear and tossed it onto the desk. It rolled in a semicircle until it bumped into Wonder Woman's red and white boots.

"I'm sorry. I made a mistake," I said. I looped my handbag over my arm.

Before I had a chance to leave, we were interrupted by an exotic blend of black pepper and hyacinths. A reed-thin redhead in an off-the-shoulder leotard, black harem pants, and geometric earrings swept past us.

"Patrick?" she called out. "Patrick?"

"Patrick isn't with us," I said tentatively. It was an understatement, to say the least.

The woman disappeared into an office further down the hall. Moments later she returned to the hallway, stopping by a small desk. She flipped through a couple of cards on a Rolodex with one black fingerless-gloved hand while the other hand fiddled with one of her earrings. Her designer hobo bag overflowed with files and fabric swatches. She ran her fingertip along the card in the Rolodex, then left the desk and approached me.

"When Patrick gets here, tell him we're overdue for a meeting. The competition is right around the corner. I need to know where he stands."

I studied her face. Her red hair was bone straight, cut into an asymmetrical bob. A smattering of freckles peeked out from under a dusting of powder. She looked more effortlessly stylish than I had in any of the five outfits I'd considered wearing on my first day.

"Patrick isn't here," Eddie said.

"Never mind the message. I'll call him later." Before I could tell her that her efforts would be wasted, she left. "Do you know who that was?" I asked Eddie.

"One of the Patrick parade. There's a steady stream of designers coming in and out of here all day. Write 'Red was here' on a message pad, and he'll either figure it out or she'll come back."

I picked up a pen. I even went so far as to write the R from Red, before I set the pen down. "I'll be right back."

I left the office, hoping to find Patrick's visitor and let her know what had happened. I wasn't sure where I was going, but halfway through the lingerie department, my cell phone screen lit up with an incoming call from the number I'd avoided earlier.

"Hello?" I answered.

"Samantha Kidd?" said a female voice.

"This is Samantha," I replied.

"This is Brittany Fowler. From Full Circle Mortgage? We reran your mortgage application this morning, and there's a problem. It seems you don't work for Bentley's New York anymore?" She had a way of ending her sentences with questions that made me want to answer automatically.

"I changed companies. I have a new job. At Tradava, in Ribbon, Pennsylvania." I said, slowly circling a fixture of nightgowns. "Someone from the store was supposed to fax a letter to you a couple of days ago."

I'd been so wrapped up in impressing my boss at the new job that, for the last couple of hours, I'd forgotten about life outside of Tradava. Even though I gave my notice to Bentley's I still cited them on the mortgage paperwork. Gray area, I'd figured, since I knew I was about to start a new job. Seems gray was not the mortgage lender's favorite color.

"Hmmmm," she said, in a tone that suggested she wasn't happy with my answer. I reached the end of the fixture and headed toward a display of pantyhose. "How long have you worked there?"

"I just started today."

"Perhaps we could clear this up now if I could talk to your supervisor?" she asked.

"That's not going to work. He can't verify anything." I heard a sound behind me and turned. Eddie stood next to the nightie fixture with a middle-aged man in a baggy, western-cut suit.

"That's the woman you're looking for. That's Samantha Kidd."

The man stepped forward, and I stepped back. He scowled. "Ms. Kidd, I'm Detective Loncar. Get your things and come with me."

3

———

MIXED UP

"Detective?" I repeated. My cell phone fell to the carpet.

The man in the suit stepped forward and showed me a badge. "Ms. Kidd, I have a few questions about this morning. It's important we talk. Now."

"Can we talk here?"

"No." He turned on his heel, took a step, then turned back to face me. Red-faced, I scooped the phone from the floor and hung up on the mortgage company. I returned to the trend office for my handbag and followed the detective out of the store. Employees milled about the parking lot. The humiliating walk past people I hadn't yet met would be hard to overcome. It was like the first day at a new high school; No matter what I wore tomorrow, I'd never get another chance to change this first impression.

"Do you want me to follow you somewhere?" I asked.

"I'll drive," the detective said. He unlocked a sedan and held the door open.

It was hot. I unzipped my satin motorcycle jacket and exposed the black lace camisole I wore underneath. When we arrived at the police station, I followed the detective through the front doors, where a small group of cops eyed my Aqua Netted hair, my camisole, and my torn fishnets. I zipped my jacket back up and dealt with the sweating.

In a small office, with dirty windows and a checkerboard linoleum-tiled floor in shades of gray, gray, and gray, Detective Loncar grilled me "Ms. Kidd, what were you doing at Tradava this morning?"

"I work there. I'm about to work there. I just moved back to Ribbon."

"You're new in town?"

"Not new-new but new by your standards."

"And you're new to Tradava?"

"Yes, though technically I haven't started working there yet."

He made a note on a lined notepad. Pieces of torn-off paper stood out at a jagged edge from the binding. I leaned forward to read his handwriting upside down. He shifted the notepad so I couldn't.

"Tell me about this morning."

"What do you want to know?" I asked. I wasn't trying to be flippant. I was scared, which, I've learned, prompts me to act unnaturally obtuse.

"What did you see?"

"Patrick, in the corner of the elevator."

"Patrick who?"

"Just Patrick. He only has one name. Like Cher."

He stared at me. I fought every instinct to look away. "What else?"

"An EMT arrived in a separate elevator. She took him out of the store through the sub-basement."

"How do you know that's where they went?"

"That's where she said she went."

"Did you follow them?"

"No, but it makes sense, doesn't it?"

He made another note. "Did you notify security?"

"No, the EMT did."

"Did you call nine-one-one?"

"No, Nick did."

"Who is Nick?"

"Nick Taylor. He was there too."

"Does he work for Tradava?"

"No. He's a shoe designer."

"And he was with you?"

"He was with me, but he wasn't with-with me. Did you talk to him? Did he tell you about me? We should have planned this better." I uncrossed my legs, revealing the tear in my fishnets. My left leg started hammering the floor, and I crossed the right leg over it to keep it under control.

"Planned what?"

"This morning. I mean, this. Now. Not this morning. We didn't plan anything this morning."

"Ms. Kidd, do you and Mr. Taylor have a history?"

"Yes, well, not a history-history, but I know him."

"And do you know what Mr. Taylor was doing at Tradava this morning?"

Nick had said he had a meeting with the shoe buyer, but I had no evidence that was true. And it seemed Loncar didn't like that I'd blanketly accepted what the EMT had said, so to show I was paying attention, I simply said, "No." The detective waited for me to elaborate. I didn't. I was mixed up, and the answers to more than one of his questions eluded me.

"How did you get to the trend office?"

"I climbed the stairs." He glanced at my feet. "Yes, in these shoes," I added.

"Why?"

"Because they go with my outfit."

"Why did you climb the stairs?" he repeated without missing a beat.

"Because that's where I was supposed to be."

"The job you claim you were about to start."

"I don't claim it, it's true. Ask Human Resources."

"Mr. Adams told us he never saw you before this morning when he found you at his desk."

"I didn't know it was his desk. I'd never been there before."

"But you claim you were supposed to be working there."

Ah, we were back to that.

"Ms. Kidd, can you tell me anything else about this morning?"

"What exactly *did* happen this morning?" I asked. The detective didn't answer. "I can't help you with details. I always thought I worked well under pressure, but, um, I passed out."

"Do you have a habit of passing out?"

"No. I don't know. I mean, not usually, but I'm not in the habit of finding my boss dead in an elevator. This is new territory for me."

He leaned back in his chair and flipped the pen upside down. He tapped the end of it on the table in front of him. *Tap, tap, tap. Tap, tap, tap.*

Our conversation continued in circles, arriving close to where it had started. Nowhere. Despite a month of the kind of planning that filled notebooks by day and Post-its by night, I was about as far from my new life fantasies as I could have been.

"Why am I here? The EMT told me Patrick had a heart attack. She took him out of the store through the subbasement and said she'd talk to you there." Detective Loncar sat very still. After an awkward amount of time, I started to count. He shifted his weight when I hit seventeen but didn't speak until I reached twenty-two.

"Ms. Kidd, there was no EMT. There was no body. You keep telling me a man died, but we don't have a corpse. You're here because I heard about a nine-one-one call from Tradava, and when I got there, I found out you're the only person who was at Tradava who has no reason for being there."

"What about Nick?"

"This Mr. Taylor you mentioned?"

"Yes, him. Did he tell you why he was there?"

"For now, let's focus on why *you* were there."

"I work there!" I said.

He didn't have to say it this time. I knew what he was thinking.

Despite my forthcoming attitude, I left as in the dark as when I arrived. Three missed calls on my phone from the mortgage company. Their messages nagging at me like a bad song I couldn't get out of my head.

It was after eleven when I returned to Tradava. All the energy I'd put into impressing Patrick was gone. Ever since our first meeting in the parking lot outside of the store, I'd been looking forward to working with him. But now that would never happen.

Eddie met me before I reached the entrance. "You want to tell me why you left here with a detective?" he asked.

"Patrick," I said.

"Patrick isn't here."

"He's not going to be here. Ever. He's dead." I didn't care Eddie was a relative stranger. I had to tell someone. Complete silence. They're right about that pin drop thing. And then—

"Patrick? Dead? How? Where?" A gust of air lifted his blond hair straight up, and, for a moment, made him look like a startled chicken.

"In the elevator. Didn't you notice they were out of service when you got here?"

"I take the stairs."

Great. I needed comfort food, and this guy was probably going to bust out in yoga moves in the middle of the parking lot.

"How about we get out of here, and you tell me what's going on?" he asked.

Crowds of people milled around the store entrance and pieces of their conversation floated to my ears. *Who's she? Some new girl.* I hurried in my stilettos to keep up with sneaker-clad Eddie and separate myself from the staffers eager to gossip. For the moment, "some new girl" hadn't been identified, though by the way a few of the associates looked at me, torn fishnets and all, I was climbing the list of candidates. By the time we returned, that phrase would probably be embossed on my nameplate.

"I'd rather not walk through the store again today. Not until everybody leaves."

"Even if you wanted to, you can't. The police made us all leave the building. Come on," he said and led the way to a Volkswagen Beetle.

I followed Eddie to a diner that sat at the edge of the mall parking lot. Minutes later, Eddie bit into an egg-white omelet while I considered whether or not my stomach could handle the four pieces of bacon I'd ordered.

"I can't believe he's dead," I said as I lined up the strips of meat.

"Have you known him a long time?"

"No. Why?"

"You sound, I don't know, shaken up."

"He's Patrick. He was very influential in the fashion industry."

"You sound like he meant something *to you*."

"He did mean something to me. He was my boss."

"Today's your first day."

I didn't know how to explain the Starting Over Plan to Eddie. How do you tell an almost stranger you voluntarily gave up a coveted, high-profile job in the fashion industry because you weren't sure that's what you wanted out of life? That you had done your job so well you became the problem solver for everyone, but when your problem became the fact that you weren't happy, you had no one to solve that problem for you? That when your parents announced they were moving to California, you did the craziest thing you'd ever done and put in a bid on your childhood house without telling your family you were the buyer? It sounded nuts to me. I couldn't imagine what it would sound like to him.

An all-consuming sense of what-have-I-done kept me silent while Eddie flagged the waitress down for more coffee.

"I don't know where to start," I said.

"Start at the beginning."

While 'the beginning' was slightly ambiguous in terms of my life, I needed to talk to someone. I gave Eddie the highlights of the morning and wrapped up my story with a vague comment about the position of Patrick's body. My cell phone rang, and I recognized the mortgage officer's number. As I weighed the pros and cons of answering, the waitress returned to our table.

"You two work over there, right?" She tipped her head toward the window that faced Tradava. Eddie nodded. She topped off our coffee. "Crazy what happened this morning. A couple of officers said a call came in about a dead guy in the store, but when they went to check it out, there wasn't a body. Crackpot nine-one-one call, they thought."

"There was a body," I protested for the second time that day. "He had a heart attack." Like the detective, she didn't seem to believe me. My phone stopped ringing, and I dropped it back into my handbag. "I'm not making this up," I finished.

"Sounds fishy to me." She rubbed the back of her hand across her forehead. "Think what you want, but I bet there's more to this story than any of us know."

"Like what?" I asked.

She set the coffee pot on a nearby cart and put her palms face down on the table. "Routine heart attacks don't make bodies disappear. If you saw someone take a body out of the store, then I'd be willing to bet somebody was trying to hide something. Nothing routine about that."

"Are you saying you think Patrick was kidnapped?"

"I'm saying I think he was murdered."

4

____

SOLE CRACKPOT

THE WAITRESS WALKED AWAY WHILE HER WORDS RESONATED IN MY head. *Murdered?* It sounded implausible. "Murdered?" I said to see if it sounded any better as a part of a conversation. It didn't.

"You said you weren't alone when you found the body," Eddie said. "Who was with you?"

"Nick Taylor."

"The shoe designer?"

"You know him?"

"We carry his collection." Eddie's eyebrow twitched slightly. "So Nick saw Patrick's body too. I hope for your sake he talked to the cops. Otherwise you'll be the sole crackpot."

The sole crackpot. Another title I wasn't itching to add to my resume. Instead of asking the detective why Nick was at Tradava I should have demanded they get him to verify my statement. They'd do that anyway, wouldn't they? For the first time since moving out of New York, I wished I'd paid better attention to the crime in the city so I knew what to expect from the cops.

Eddie paid our check, and I followed him to his car. He nestled his to-go cup of coffee into the cup holder, and I pulled my cell phone out and listened to the latest message.

"Samantha Kidd, this is Brittany Fowler. We were cut off this morning? When I called you? We need to finish our conversation. Please call me back as soon as possible."

Eddie glanced at my phone. "If you want to make a call, make it out here. No cell reception in our part of the building."

"I have to talk to Human Resources first, straighten a couple of things out."

He pointed to the store, where people still stood outside. "I don't think they're letting people back in yet. Go home. Take a bath. Pretend the last twenty-four hours never happened."

As much as I would have liked to do just that, Logan would have been mad if he didn't get a gourmet meal. Logan has a bit of a temper and has been known to punish me by, well, getting funky in my shoes when I don't feed him on time. Logan, of course, is my cat. My second favorite thing besides my cat are my shoes, which says a lot about me and my priorities.

It didn't matter that the stuffy air in the police station had long since turned my Aqua-Netted hair to frizz, or that the events of the morning had left me looking more vice squad than fashion police. I drove to the grocery store and endured the silent judgment from the cashier that suggested black lace and torn fishnets weren't *de rigueur* in the fifteen-items-or-less lane. I was in need of a magnum of wine, a box of pretzels, an hour-long shower, and a do-over.

"I'm a very respectable person, you know," I said as I handed over a twenty-dollar bill. The cashier counted out my change but said nothing. I bagged my groceries while a couple of older customers stared at me. I wasn't sure if my fashion sense was helping or hurting my new life. If nothing else, it was getting me noticed.

As I carried my bag, I couldn't help remembering the last time I'd been in that parking lot. It was the day I met Patrick.

It had been the last day of my vacation. I spent it in Ribbon, helping my parents pack a lifetime of belongings into recycled cardboard boxes before movers came to empty the house and transport the boxes to California. My parents caught the shuttle to the airport the night before, and I'd planned to drive back to

Manhattan the previous night, but nostalgia had kicked in. I stayed behind in the empty house by myself.

The following morning, I stopped off at the grocery store before driving to New York. After loading the groceries into the trunk, I unloaded Logan's carrier and walked with him to the park bench in front of the store. We sat side by side, staring at the empty parking lot of a shopping center anchored by Tradava. The parking lot was set off by the marquee of a ninety-nine-cent theater, the same theater where I'd gone on my first date. The awareness that everybody else's lives were moving on and mine wasn't was hard to ignore.

Logan yowled periodically in solidarity of my life crisis or in protest of his blue plastic cage (it's sometimes hard to tell with him).

"It's not often you see a woman in tweed and fishnets outside of the market," said a proper voice behind me. I turned, and there stood the most nattily dressed man I'd ever seen (and working in fashion, I'd seen my share). Navy blue suit with a chalk stripe through it. Pink shirt, pink ascot, pink pocket square. Pencil-thin mustache, black pomaded hair parted on the side.

I dragged my index fingers under my eyes to eliminate any possible mascara smudges. "I'm a bit of a mess," I said.

"That's impossible. You cannot be a mess when wearing Chanel. It's the rule." He smiled, and the tips of his mustache pointed up with the corners of his mouth. "Patrick," he said, extending his hand.

"Samantha," I replied in like fashion, but it felt incomplete. "Samantha Kidd," I finished.

"And who do we have here?" he asked, peering into the cat carrier.

"Logan." As if on cue, the little devil started to purr.

"Tell me, Ms. Kidd, what brings a fashionista like yourself to my corner of the world?"

"I'm thinking about moving here." I surprised myself with the words. "My parents are selling my house. Their house. The house where I grew up."

He studied me.

"It's not even a great house. It has wood paneling and shag carpet."

"How very 1974."

"I never remembered it that way."

"What way?"

"Nineteen Seventy-four."

He tipped the cat carrier back and looked down his ski-slope nose into Logan's cage. A black paw pressed against the inside of the door and Patrick gently stroked it with his index finger.

"Seventy-four was a good year. The maxi skirt. Wide ties and Qiana shirts."

"Platform shoes and bell bottoms."

"The Russian peasant look."

"And Halston," I added with a smile.

Patrick picked up Logan's carrier and joined me on the bench. "What do you do, Ms. Kidd?" he asked while he and Logan played the finger equivalent of patty cake.

"I'm a buyer. Bentley's New York. Ladies Designer Shoes." I pulled a crinkled business card out of my breast pocket and held it out as if to prove something. He placed it in his suit pocket without looking at it.

"Are you serious about moving to Ribbon?" It had surprised me to realize that I was, but I simply nodded. "Ribbon is not New York," he replied.

"I know."

"Are you trying to find something you lost along the way?"

I considered his question before answering. It wasn't that I'd lost something, but that what I had didn't feel like it was mine. "I'd like to find my own corner of the world, I guess."

He pursed his lips and nodded as if he liked my response. "See that store?" he pointed to the department store that anchored the strip mall. "That's Tradava. I'm their fashion director. As it happens, I'm in need of a trend specialist."

I knew the store. It's where I had gotten the red cotton jumpsuit I wore on the first day of eighth grade. It's where my mom bought the charcoal gray and neon pink outfit for my first real date. It's where I picked out my white eyelet prom dress. I didn't tell Patrick any of this. Instead, I said the only I could think of.

"How soon can I start?"

He threw back his head and laughed. "Samantha Kidd, I like your style. Call me tomorrow and we'll work something out." He stood up and the creases fell effortlessly from his trousers. "It's been a pleasure meeting you."

He crossed the parking lot. I waited until he was all but a moving dot that disappeared into the doors on the side of the building.

"And so goes either my savior or some nutcase," I said as much to Logan as to myself. I stood and carried the cat cage to my car. I started the drive to New York, not knowing we'd be back in a couple of weeks.

WHAT PATRICK HAD OFFERED me was a fresh start. My life was like fabric in the clearance bin. Sure, some of my yardage had already been used, but there was still some left on the bolt. With a little planning, and if I cut corners, it wasn't too late to make something fabulous out of it.

My new life was about four days old, counting last Friday when I celebrated in the empty house with a large pizza and a bottle of pink champagne. Saturday the boxes arrived, along with the reality that I lived in a seventies split level house with avocado appliances and shag carpeting. Yesterday I dug through the attic to see what treasures Mom and Dad left behind while a *That Girl* marathon ran in the background.

And today I found my boss dead in an elevator.

A pre-autumn breeze washed over me as I pulled into the driveway. Crabapple trees in the front yard had blossomed and discarded soft papery white flowers that covered the ground. Miniature apples lay scattered around the base of the tree, produce cadavers to be pecked at by birds and squirrels and chipmunks running through the yard.

Inside the house, I peeled off the outfit I'd so carefully selected when the biggest crisis in my life had been what to wear to my new job and kicked it into a corner. After a hot shower, I pulled on a silk kimono and headed to the kitchen. I checked the messages on the answering machine that sat on the counter next to a stained Mr. Coffee. The only call was from Brittany Fowler at Full Circle Mortgage, and it was almost exactly what she'd said on my voicemail. There was nothing for me to tell her until I straightened things out with Tradava. I deleted the message.

While Logan swatted a felt mouse across the linoleum floor, I flipped through the mail, past catalogs, credit card applications, and an offer for customized stationery addressed to RESIDENT. I tossed the mail on the counter, unable to focus.

What if what the waitress said was true? Patrick's body had been at Tradava. I'd seen it. But if his body had gone missing, what happened was anything but routine. She'd said murder. Why would someone murder the fashion director? And how? Patrick had a heart attack. The EMT confirmed it before she wheeled Patrick away. She said it was textbook and I believed her, although it was my first experience with a dead body, murdered or otherwise, and it occurred to me I didn't know what textbook was.

If it weren't for my desire to change up my life, I'd still be sitting at my desk in New York, recapping the previous week's business, fielding calls from my vendors about what sold and what didn't, planning my next set of appointments to look at new shoes, and working on budgets for upcoming seasons. I'd still be Bentley's number one employee, working sixty-five hours a week, trading my personal life for an extra percentage of gross margin. If life had seemed difficult then, in all my years at Bentley's, I'd never found a dead body.

Finding Patrick's body complicated just about everything.

While the shower had taken off the vice squad stench, it provided little in the way of comfort. I reached for the ice cream and then put it back. I needed more than comfort food. I needed answers. I called Nick's number.

While the phone rang, I looked out at the backyard where my dad had taught my older sister Sasha how to mow the lawn with the riding mower. She was twelve at the time; I was eight. I'd watched them drive in ever-shrinking rectangles over the backyard. It looked like fun. I asked him to teach me too. *You're not ready yet," he had said, laughing at me. "You're just a kid."* To this day, I over-planned everything, making sure I was ready before I did anything.

You're just a kid. The four most defining words of my life. It was why I'd moved to New York in the first place and become such an overachiever at Bentley's, all to prove I was an adult.

Nick answered. "Hi," I said. "It's Samantha."

"Kidd. I was just about to call you."

I wound the curly phone cord around my finger until I came to a point where a kink interrupted the coil. I unwound to my starting point and repeated the pattern, stopping at the kink each time.

"Are you still with me?" he asked, reminding me that phone conversations generally require words.

"Do you want to meet me for a late lunch?" I asked abruptly.

"What did you have in mind?"

The clock read one-thirty. I was in a kimono, no makeup, wet hair. I could have spent the night with Logan, a carton of ice cream, a vat of wine, and an old movie. Nobody would have been the wiser.

"Meet me at Briquette Burger in twenty minutes," I said.

Eleven minutes later, the doorbell rang.

I know it was eleven minutes because it takes me four minutes to apply makeup, two minutes to run the requisite amount of serum through my hair, and five minutes to blow dry my natural curls into something I can live with. That's why I was still in my kimono when there was a knock on the door.

"Hey, Kidd," Nick said. "Can I come in or are you going to keep me out here like a Peeping Tom?"

"That implies you were peeping." I checked to make sure the sash on my kimono was secure and opened the door. I looked at him suspiciously. My brain was already filled with questions, so you'd think it was full, but, apparently, there was room for things like "How long have you been watching me?" and "Since when does 'Meet me at the restaurant' mean 'Show up at my house?'

I went with question number one. "How do you know where I live?" I asked, trying to make my voice sound casual.

"You told me all about this house last May. Remember, we went to dinner at that little French restaurant off 57th Street? You wrote the address on the back of your business card, and I kept it. I always knew you were good at your job, but that night was the first night I think I ever saw you come alive."

"It was the pie," I said quickly and turned to the refrigerator to get the magnum of wine. Truth? I never expected Nick to remember that night and here he was standing in the middle of my kitchen.

I splashed a bit of wine into two Flintstones jelly glasses left behind in the cabinet and handed him Dino. "Did you talk to a detective this morning?" I asked.

"Briefly. He wanted to know what I saw. If you think about it, neither one of us saw much of anything."

"I saw Patrick. Dead. I saw him. You saw him too. Don't pretend you didn't, Nick."

"Kidd, Patrick's corpse never made it to the morgue. And since we're the only two people who claim to have seen his body, the cops think we're the likeliest two people to be involved in whatever it is we're saying happened. And since we don't know what happened, the whole thing is a little unclear."

I put the wine back into the refrigerator and shut the door. "So then, what's the problem? If nothing happened, why do I feel like a criminal? And if something happened, where is Patrick's body?"

"I mentioned you were there, but you had passed out. I assumed they thought talking to you would be useless."

"Useless?" That comment, though accurate, was the icing on the cake that had already fallen. I swirled the wine around in my Bam-Bam glass and set it on top of an existing countertop stain. *Useless.* A new word to layer into the soundtrack playing inside my head.

"Kidd, you've had a heck of a transition in the past couple of weeks." He reached his hand out to the satin collar of my kimono and loosely ran his fingers inside by my collarbone. "I can take your mind off things if you're open to suggestion . . . " As his voice trailed off, his touch ignited my skin, like an unexpected spray of grease from a pan of frying breakfast meats.

"Bacon," I said, then felt my face grow hot. His hand fell to his side. I stepped away, trying to think straight. I picked up the glass of wine on the counter and swallowed a gulp.

"Bacon?"

"Comfort food. Let me change. You're driving." I went upstairs to put on clothes. Regardless of what I felt, this was one night where I didn't want to be alone. At least not yet.

BRIQUETTE BURGER WAS a small restaurant about a mile from my house. It had been renovated since I was last there, but the yellow and red sign on top of the building was as I remembered it. Inside, the first thing I noticed was a refrigerated case of freshly baked pies. I looked away before I did anything rash. We took an available booth and I ordered a cup of coffee. Nick ordered the Briquette Burger Sampler. Neither one of us mentioned bacon.

"I keep thinking I know something about this morning. That we know something. But I can't figure out what it is."

"Leave it alone, Kidd. The cops will figure it out."

"But we were there. We saw Patrick before anybody. And the EMT came from nowhere, and she had a key to take the elevator down to the basement. She seemed so, so *normal* I didn't pay attention to her. Did you?"

"I noticed you passed out. I noticed you never thanked me for carrying you to the sofa."

"I noticed that Patrick was dead. But nobody believes me because *his body is missing*. That doesn't bother you?"

"It's not your business. It's not my business."

The waiter interrupted our conversation with hot plates of food. We finished most of the sampler platter, leaving only the fried eggplant. Nick paid before I could reach for my wallet, and we walked to his truck in shared silence. He opened the door for me and I stepped up onto the sideboard, then hopped back down to the loose gravel of the parking lot. I stood to my full five feet seven inches and looked up into his soft brown eyes.

"I could have walked, you know. To the sofa. After I passed out. I don't faint. I'm not a fainter. I would have gotten up in a second and walked to the sofa. You didn't have to carry me."

"You're not very good at accepting help, are you?" He grinned and walked to the driver's side of the truck.

When we reached my house, he escorted me to the front door even though I said I could make it. I was crashing fast despite all the coffee. All I wanted was for this day to end. I wanted to collapse in my bed, wake up, and realize it had all been a dream.

"Thanks for meeting me," I said. "I sure hope my second day at Tradava is better than my first."

Nick fidgeted with the remote to his truck. "Kidd, I think you should forget about going back to Tradava."

"I can't exactly quit after one day."

"You'd be smart to stay out of it."

I turned to face him. There was more to what he wasn't saying than what he was. "You know something, don't you?"

"I know what's happening at Tradava is none of your business."

"Jobs don't grow on trees, Nick. If you don't recall, I left behind a *very* nice job in New York with this as the anchor to my future. The man who hired me is gone. But Patrick wanted me to work on his team, and that's what I'm going to do." Across the street, a light went on behind closed curtains. "Thanks for dinner. See you around." I wrestled briefly with the locks then went inside and slammed the door behind me. It was a solid twenty minutes later when I realized Nick hadn't told me to quit my job. He'd told me to stay out of what was going down at Tradava.

And that told me Nick knew more than he'd let on.

5

DAY TWO

MY ALARM WENT OFF TOO EARLY. I SLAPPED A HAND ON THE SNOOZE button, vaguely considered reasons not to get up, and shivered as images from the previous day assaulted me. Worse than the reality of what had happened at the store was the realization that I *had* to go back. Today was day two.

If day one is the day friendly co-workers escort you to your destinations and you're not expected to turn in any projects, day two is the day you try to prove your worth and accidentally walk into the broom closet. Day two is never better than day one, but compared to what I had to face today, the usual Day two issues were just the tip of the iceberg. *My* day two would put me face to face with a whole store of people who knew I'd left with a detective yesterday. Which reminded me of that troubling issue with verifying my employment.

I'd fallen asleep with the window open. The heat had broken overnight, and the air was crisp. Logan curled up on my pillow while I dashed from the warm bed to the hot shower. Fifteen minutes later, my curly brown hair was tamed into submission thanks to the blow dryer and a couple of pumps of serum, and my pale skin glowed under makeup. My reflection stared back at me from the bathroom mirror. I mugged to the left, then to the right, then stared directly at my reflection and stuck out my tongue.

I pulled on a pair of soft gray and lilac glen plaid pants and belted a gray tweed cape over an ivory turtleneck. Dark purple patent leather pumps. Matching handbag. I drove to Tradava and sat in the parking lot outside of the store. This time I knew there would be no familiar face waiting to welcome me to the trend department.

This time I was on my own.

The façades of old department stores are impressive. They tower several stories over street level, promising unique and exciting merchandise within their walls. The illusion is shattered once you've walked through a store's employee entrance. You'll never anticipate the appeal of new merchandise again.

This particular door had been painted gray at one time. (It looked like it had been painted gray many times.) I could guess the routine: touch-up paint slapped on every couple of years when top-level corporate executives were expected for visits. The kick plate at the bottom of the door showed the dings and divots of flatbeds, handcarts, and maybe the toe print of a few disgruntled employees. Inside, one bulb flickered overhead. It was a decorator's picture of Dorian Gray; this dismal passageway for the staff counterbalanced the goods showcased inside the store.

I approached Loss Prevention. The same Latina woman who. I'd helped with the heavy box was behind the desk. I held both hands up in an "I surrender" gesture. "I know, I know, I have to sign in." I scribbled my name with less fanfare than yesterday. "I'm going to Human Resources right now."

"They're not here yet," she said. "Most of the executives don't get here until after nine." Today her hair was flat-ironed and fell in an orange-brown sheath over her shoulders.

We shared a conspiratorial-yet-judgmental look over the tardiness habits of the executive team. I checked the clock on the wall. Again, I was too early. So far, being a morning person hadn't paid off.

I left Loss Prevention but didn't bother with the elevators. I took the stairs up seven flights, exited near intimate apparel and walked through the doors that housed the trend offices. A hush fell over the small group of people who milled around the hallway. This time I bypassed Eddie's desk and two doors later, entered a stark space that split into two offices. One housed a purple velvet sofa and one was stripped clean. I'd lay odds the empty one was mine.

It was quiet in this part of the store, but I didn't mind the solitude. A stack of pink While You Were Out messages accessorized my desk. *We need to talk to you. Contact us at the precinct.* A few phone numbers followed: office, pager, and cell. The next message read Brittany at Full Circle Mortgage. Urgent. Three more messages followed. All were dated with yesterday's date. I crumbled them up into small pink balls and lobbed them at the trashcan. Two of the five made it.

I was thankful the trend offices were in a separate part of the store from the other corporate offices. Outside the heavy glass doors that marked the entrance to this wing, the buzz of gossip would soon turn to a roar. I was still a stranger in a strange land, and until I could figure out how to feel as though I belonged, I was fine on my own. A knock on the doorframe interrupted my thoughts. A wood sprite in a mustard yellow velvet blazer that hung down to his knees met my startled stare. Matching yellow earbuds and iPod fed tunes directly into his head. His gravity-defying hairstyle hinted at a heavy gel dependency.

"Hi. I'm *Michael*." He bounced back and forth between his feet, as though he could barely control his energy while standing still. A ketchup-colored scarf hung around his neck. He could have been anywhere from fifteen to twenty-five, and I envied him the ability to project that range.

"I'm Samantha," I offered.

"I'm a *designer*. Did Patrick tell you about me?"

"Patrick and I haven't had a chance to go over things yet." What? It wasn't a lie. "How can I help you?"

"I'm here for my *portfolio*."

I looked around the office. I hadn't seen any portfolios and wasn't sure where Patrick would have kept them if they were there. "I'm sorry. Patrick didn't have a chance to teach me his filing system." Also the truth. I could do this all day.

"I know where it's at." He bounced away toward Patrick's office.

"Wait!" I jumped up and followed. "You can't go in there," I called to his back.

"Here it is," he said. He held a flat black folder zipped shut around three of the edges. He reached into his pocket and lip-balmed himself while I tried to figure out whether the portfolio really was his. "Are you one of the judges?" he asked.

"Judges of what?"

"The *competition!*" I must have looked confused. "Never mind," he said and bounded toward the heavy glass doors. I stepped into Patrick's office to see if anything seemed out of order even though I didn't know what to look for.

I hadn't questioned Patrick's desire to meet me outside of Tradava. Our first conversation had been in the parking lot, and our subsequent interviews had taken place over the phone and at local restaurants. When I'd asked if he wanted me to meet him at his office, he'd been evasive.

"I like to keep things less formal," he'd said. "There will be plenty of time at Tradava once I've made my decision." And when I'd pressed him about that decision, he smiled. "I chose the wrong words. Once my decision is official."

"Your decision has been made?" I'd asked.

"Let me be candid, Ms. Kidd. I need someone like you at the store, someone who loves fashion for fashion's sake. Designers must look to the past to envision the future, but many are in such a hurry to show their point of view that they fail to learn from those who have paved the way."

It was that night my plans to move to Ribbon felt real. Patrick had all but told me I had the job. The next day he called with an offer which I accepted. We discussed start dates. I gave notice to Bentley's. Patrick must have notified Human Resources and gone through the proper channels unless he was a person who felt like the rules didn't apply to him. I didn't know if he did or not. From those few meetings,

I didn't know much about him at all. He'd maintained a public presence throughout his career, but who was he?

Idly, I opened and closed file cabinet drawers and thumbed through piles on his desk. I found a set of keys by his monitor and tossed them from one hand to the other three times before I buried them in my handbag. A Rolodex like the one on the desk in the hallway sat on the corner of his desk. It was open to a card from a local fabric store, Pins and Needles.

It didn't surprise me to find the spinning business card holder on Patrick's desk. He was part of what we at Bentley's called the old guard, the generation who preferred their contacts to be at their fingertips versus at the click of a mouse. Names of designers now famous were scribbled on dog-eared pieces of paper along with people I'd never heard of. I flipped through additional cards and wondered about each name. Who were these people? What had they meant to Patrick's career, to Tradava, to fashion?

I left Patrick's office and went back to mine. A cardboard carton stamped with a fancy bottled water logo lay in the corner, now filled with obsolete office supplies: a battery-operated pencil sharpener, carbon papers, and three-ring binders with the covers falling off. Faded empty walls surrounded the room, bright squares of paint showing off where pictures had hung. The shelves behind the desk held fashion magazines and catalogs that were a couple of years old. I doubted I was going to get any valid information from them. Unless, of course, they had been there a couple of decades, since fashion tends to repeat itself.

Next, I checked out the file cabinet. It was a monstrous gray fixture with four deep drawers and stood inside the wall of the office. The first drawer was filled with files, old army green hanging folders so stuffed with paper the metal rods were barely able to support them. Plastic labels had cracked with age and paper that had started out white was now yellow. Handwritten titles on the labels read *Spring, Summer, Prefall, Winter, Runway.* The name in the upper right corner was Aries, and I wondered if my predecessor had identified herself by her astrological sign. (Fashion people were quirky.)

The next drawer was in much the same state of disorganization, though the folder titles were years past. The reports were the same format; this time LESTES was written in standard block letters. The third drawer contained more folders like the second. There was no name on the corner of the page, but the author had not minced words when critiquing a collection.

Expecting no surprises, I opened the fourth drawer. Surprise! It was empty. I moved to behind the desk and flipped through an issue of the *Style Section,* the fashion industry's weekly rag, that had been left in my inbox. I stopped at a page marked with a lilac Post-it. The newspaper copy read *First Ever Design Competition. Winner receives $100,000 grant to fund start-up collection, guaranteed order from Tradava, six pages featuring collection in Tradava catalog, and unparalleled recommendations in the fashion industry.* Patrick's name appeared at the bottom as one of the judges, along with Maries Paulson, noted icon in the industry. The Post-it said: *This competition is our number one priority. Let's make it fabulous!*

I wondered who the note was for.

A few pages later a *Where Are They Now?* article quoted Patrick, whose name was circled in red marker, speaking about designers who defined previous decades and renewed interest in their labels. I flipped back to the ad for the contest. Michael, the young designer who had collected his portfolio earlier, had mentioned it. So had the redhead from yesterday. It was as good a project to sink my teeth into as any. I went back to Patrick's office and flipped through his Rolodex until I came to a phone number for Maries Paulson. Four rings later my call went into voicemail.

"This is Samantha Kidd, trend specialist at Tradava. I was hired by Patrick, and I want to offer to help with the competition. You can reach me at—" I stopped. I didn't know the Tradava number off the top of my head. I rattled off my home and cell numbers just as Eddie rounded the corner to my office. He set two cups of coffee on my desk and slammed his finger down on the phone, disconnecting the call.

6

———

THE MATH TEST

"WHY'D YOU DO THAT?" I ASKED.

"You are a wanton woman," he said.

"I am not!"

"Yes, you are. People are looking for you. The cops, some mortgage company, and the head of Human Resources."

"They think I'm easy?"

"What?"

"You said I was a wanton woman."

"Wanted, not wanton." He sat down. "Who were you calling? What are you doing here?"

"I'm trying to do my job." I tapped the paper with my index finger. "Patrick was one of the judges of this competition. I thought I should do something, you know, on behalf of Tradava. The show must go on, and all of that. Why did you disconnect the call?"

"You don't work here." He glanced at the open Rolodex, then to the phone, then back to me. "You're calling people from Patrick's contact list and giving them your home number? That's stealing company resources."

"I do work here, and I would have left Tradava's number only I don't know it. I have it written down, somewhere, but it wasn't in front of me, and I thought I should give my number instead of nothing. Now I have to call back and explain why I hung up halfway through my message. Are you going to give me a hard time?"

"The standard response to someone bringing you coffee is 'Good morning' or 'Thank you', but yours works too. Less expected." He pushed one of the cups in my direction.

"Why did you bring me coffee if you thought I wouldn't show up today?"

"I was hoping you'd show even if I didn't think you would."

I pulled one of the cups toward me. "I haven't decided yet if it's a good morning."

"Have any cops showed up to talk to you?"

"Not yet."

"Sounds like a good morning to me."

Eddie wore a version of yesterday's outfit. Black and white checkered Vans, paint-spattered jeans, and a Devo T-shirt. Now that I had more time to take in his total look, I realized this creative surf dude didn't end up in retail fashion by accident. He had an eye for details. (I'd bet his longboard matched his wetsuit.)

"You don't remember me, do you?" he asked. He sat back in his chair and watched me watch him. He crossed one checkered sneaker over the knee of his other leg and pulled his ankle up until it rested mid-thigh.

I studied his face, his body language, his demeanor, all the while repeating his name inside my head. *Eddie Adams . . . Eddie Adams . . . Eddie Adams . . .*

"We graduated high school together." He raised his coffee cup toward me as though in a toast. "I was only there for the end of senior year. I didn't get to know many people. Check your yearbook."

I studied him. There was something familiar . . . . "The math test?" I asked as a memory clicked into place.

He nodded. "The math test."

Eddie had been the new kid at school, starting halfway through senior year. There was a test in Calculus, and he scored the highest score. As had the captain of the football team who sat to Eddie's left.

Rumors that Eddie cheated started almost instantly. And, being the new kid, there was no one to come to his defense.

That was the year I sat in the back of the class. I'd been stumped on the seventh question. Instead of concentrating on my exam, I'd been staring out at nothing, watching everyone else scribble numbers and math symbols on the pages in front of them. And I saw him copy the answers from another student's test.

Not Eddie. The captain of the football team.

He'd just gotten a full scholarship to college. Getting caught cheating would have cost him his future. He did it anyway and got away with it. Eddie got suspended.

I went to the principal's office three days later and told him what I saw. I demanded something be done. The school readministered tests to both boys.

There was no question that Eddie knew the material. The jock did not.

Eddie came back and finished out the year and went on to art school. I'd asked the principal to keep me out of it. I remember not knowing if Eddie had ever suspected I was the one who came forward with the truth until months later when I read what he'd written in my yearbook. The football player failed. And though I never told a soul, I'd gained a lot of satisfaction in doing the right thing. You work hard, and you get what you deserve. You cheat, you get what you deserve. That lesson followed me my whole life.

"You stood up for me," Eddie said. Miniature Sharpies dangled from a turquoise D-clamp he'd hooked to a belt loop on the side of his jeans. He jiggled the foot on his knee and the Sharpies clacked against each other like a set of plastic janitor's keys. The yellow one popped off and landed on the floor.

"Have you been in Ribbon since high school?" I asked.

"I landed this job out of college. I've been here ever since." A part of me wanted to push aside thoughts of Patrick's murder, the cops, the mortgage company, and Human Resources to get lost in our reunion, but before I could word the questions in my mind, Eddie tapped my cell phone with the bottom of his coffee cup.

"Weren't you listening yesterday? No reception." He glanced toward the ceiling. "These offices were never meant to be anything more than temporary. You won't get a signal. And store policy says you can't have one on the selling floor. Looks bad to customers."

I chucked my phone back into my handbag and peeled the top off my coffee. With full knowledge it was too hot to drink, I took a sip. Burned my tongue. (Patience is not my strong suit.) Finally, I spoke. "Are you sure you want to be seen talking to me?"

"It's better than talking to Patrick's assistant, if you know what I mean."

"Who is Patrick's assistant?"

He gestured toward the balls of pink messages that were littered on the floor surrounding the trash can. "Who do you think took those messages?"

"I don't know."

"Michael. Michael Dubrecht. The little guy who was here this morning."

"He was here yesterday too? I never even saw him." I sighed. "That's probably something the cops should know."

"They do. They came around yesterday, talked to everyone who was here. Anybody who came to work before eight thirty was questioned. They closed the store so nobody could get in after that, and store management was mad when they heard it was a false report. Significant loss of business."

I'd angered Store Management. I wondered how regularly they checked in with Human Resources about this sort of thing?

"Do you remember anything?" he asked.

"Nothing more than I remembered yesterday."

He shrugged out from under the messenger bag still hanging across his shoulder and set it on the floor next to the errant yellow Sharpie. "I think you know more than you think you know."

"I can't see how."

Eddie sipped his coffee. I waited for his questions to start. He set his cup down, leaned back, and folded his arms across the Devo logo on his shirt. "Are you going to tell me why you're really here?" he asked.

I froze, mouth filled with hot coffee, barely able to swallow. I coughed a few times after choking it down and glared at him with wide, water-filled eyes. My twice-burnt tongue clumsily formed a retort.

"Here, where?"

"Here. Tradava. Today of all days."

"I told you. This is my job. Patrick hired me. Just because he isn't around doesn't mean I'm not going to show up for work. Maybe hiring me was the last decision he ever made."

Eddie bent down to retrieve the yellow Sharpie. "What's your background?" His voice came from somewhere by my feet.

"Shoe Buyer at Bentley's New York."

He sat back up and whistled. "Nice. You travel much? Go to runway shows?"

"Some."

"Did you get fired?"

"No!"

"I'm not buying it." He tapped his palms on the rubber elbow rests of the desk chair.

"I'm not trying to sell something."

"You're telling me you left behind a buying career in New York to move to Ribbon? You traded twice a year trips to Paris and Milan for this? We're not the fashion capital of eastern Pennsylvania, and Tradava is not in the same category as Bentley's." He gulped from the coffee cup. "Nope, I'm definitely not buying it."

"Wait a minute." I leaned forward and grabbed my cell phone.

"No, seriously, people don't just up and leave jobs like that without good reason."

"Not that, this!" I held up my phone. "You said there's no reception in here."

"You're a quick one, aren't you?"

"The elevators are right outside the office. If Patrick had a heart attack in here and tried to call nine-one-one from a cell phone, the call wouldn't go through."

"True."

"Yesterday the EMT held up a phone and said Patrick called emergency himself. She was lying!"

Eddie slammed the palm of his hand down on the desk. "I knew it. I *knew* you knew more than you thought! What else do you remember?"

"I don't know." I stood up from the chair and paced around the office. "After I realized Patrick was dead, I sat in the shoe department with Nick. The emergency tech put a brown wool blanket over Patrick's body and wheeled him out through the basement."

"How much time passed?"

"I don't know." I stole a glance at him.

"Estimate."

"I don't remember." Because I passed out. Which I didn't particularly want to admit.

"You'll remember. You remembered that cell phone bit. You better tell that to the cops." Eddie finished his coffee; I pretended to let mine cool. I wasn't eager to field more questions, especially now that I had information to share with the police.

"How long have you known Nick Taylor?" he asked next.

"Years. I bought his collection for Bentley's. We were kind of friendly until recently."

Eddie gave me a knowing look. "Friendly? Is that code for 'We were sleeping together' or 'we had a flirtatious business association'?"

"That's a little personal, don't you think?" My face grew hot. Nick and my business relationship precluded anything other than dinner and the occasional two-cheek kiss. Romances between vendors and buyers were frowned upon at Bentley's so regardless of what I'd daydreamed about on that flight over Paris, I had accepted our relationship for what it was.

"Okay, you had a flirtatious business association and thought about sleeping with him. What was he doing here?"

"He said he had a meeting."

"With who? The shoe buyers are all in New York for market week."

Eddie was right, and I should have known that. If I were still at Bentley's, I'd probably be in the middle of a tight schedule of showroom appointments trying to cull together next spring's assortments. That life felt more like a distant memory than something I knew.

"Besides, Tradava dropped Nick's shoe collection based on poor reviews. I heard the advertising team talking about it at a meeting last week."

"He didn't mention that. Would Patrick have written those reviews?" I asked, wondering again about Nick's cryptic warning.

"Maybe," he said. "But back to my earlier question, how well do you know him? Have you spent time together outside the office? Do you know what kind of person he is?"

I wasn't sure where Eddie was going with his line of questioning, but for now I went along with it. "Occasionally we went to dinner together, but it was always business related." Ish, I added to myself. "I don't know his deep dark secrets or anything."

"You think Nick Taylor has deep dark secrets?"

"Everybody has deep dark secrets."

"Does he know your deep dark secrets?"

"No. I mean, I don't have any. I mean . . . " I paused, then gave up trying to defend my secret-less life. "What's your point?"

"What was he doing at Tradava yesterday morning when most people weren't even at work yet? Was it a coincidence he was with you when you found Patrick's body?" Eddie pulled a bottle of water out of a cargo pocket and downed half. "How much time transpired between you passing out and him calling the cops?"

"You're implying Nick had something to do with Patrick's death." I shuddered when I heard my words. "Why do you think that?"

Eddie sank his head into his hands. Chunks of blond hair stuck out between his fingers. Eddie had serious issues containing his hair.

"I don't know." He leaned forward with interest. "You were at the scene of the crime. You were on hand for vital clues and important details no one else saw except Nick."

I remained silent. *It's only your second day on the job*, I told myself. *Don't get involved.* I wanted to finish out the rest of my day without unexpected hitches, straighten out the hiring situation, and discover some trends. But what Eddie said made sense. "I keep thinking I should remember something, but I don't," I finally said.

"Are you sure nothing was out of the ordinary?"

"It was my first day of work. I found a dead body. Belonging to the person who hired me. Whose body is now missing. What part of that is ordinary?"

"Good point."

I stood up and shook my left leg until the creases in my pant leg released. "I can't think about this now. I have to go to HR and get the hiring straightened out."

"You better have a cover story for why you cost the store business yesterday. It's going to come up." He tapped the desk. "Go through what happened one more time."

I launched into my story for what felt like the millionth time: the elevator doors, the body, the EMTs, the cell phone, and the whisking away of Patrick's body to the sub-basement. And then I remembered something else.

"The computer."

OLD-SCHOOL

"WHAT COMPUTER?" EDDIE ASKED.

"Patrick loaned me a computer," I said. "A laptop. It's in a plum nylon case."

"Patrick didn't have a laptop. Patrick wouldn't know what to do with a laptop. He took notes. Longhand. Michael transcribed them."

"Who doesn't use a laptop?" I glanced at the desk. The answer was in front of me. The same person who kept their contacts in a Rolodex. Can you say old-school?

"Why did Patrick loan you a computer?" Eddie asked.

"He wanted me to get a briefing on his current projects. He handed it off to me in the Tradava parking lot."

"Why didn't you come to his office?"

"I don't know. Patrick specifically said he preferred meetings that were out of the store. It's starting to sound like he didn't want me be here. This was two days before I was supposed to start."

We stared at each other, processing what this might mean. I wasn't willing to accept the obvious answers. "How do you know Patrick didn't have a laptop?"

"He might have had a laptop, but it didn't belong to Tradava. Everybody in corporate got new desktop computers six months ago."

He jerked his thumb in the direction of the office, "There's a PC and a BlackBerry. All the directors and veeps got them. Anyway, people like Patrick aren't tech savvy. Did you look at it? What was on it?"

My breakfast of cold Pop-Tarts flipped over in my stomach. I'd read Patrick's newsletters and checked out his calendar, but other than that, nothing had struck me as odd. What if there was something else on the hard drive that he'd wanted me to discover? And where was that laptop now?

I pulled Detective Loncar's card out of my wallet and dialed.

"Loncar," he answered.

"Detective, it's Samantha Kidd. You said I should call you if I remembered anything else, and I remembered something else."

"Ms. Kidd. Where are you?"

"I'm at Tradava."

"What are you doing there?"

"I work here." Why was everyone having such a hard time with that fact? "Detective, Patrick loaned me a laptop that I had with me when he died, but I don't know where it went. I put it between the malfunctioning elevator doors, but I'm not used to having a laptop, so with everything that happened, I forgot about it." I waited for his response. "Until now. I remembered it. So I called you like you asked." Still nothing. "Hello? Are you still there?"

"Ms. Kidd. First, you said there was a body which we haven't found. Then you said there was an Emergency Technician, who we haven't identified. Now you say there was a computer that went missing. Plus, you claim to have employment nobody can verify."

"I'm not making this stuff up, Detective. I'm trying to be helpful."

"Hold on, ma'am," he said. Instinct told me now was not the time to tell him I was too young to be called ma'am. "Ms. Kidd, why don't you come down to the Human Resources department on the fourth floor? Maybe we can clear things up."

"You're in the store?" I asked. That was fortuitous. I hung up and told Eddie, "I'm going to HR. I'll be back in a sec."

I took the stairs. Detective Loncar stood talking with a woman with a gray pixie haircut. A chunky blue necklace hung around the neck of her Nehru-collar shirt. Perfect timing, two birds, one stone, and all that. I stepped around the side of the escalators and caught part of their conversation.

"She's on her way down," Loncar said. "She said she works here."

"I don't know what she wants or why she keeps returning, but we have no record of her interviewing here, let alone working for us. These awful things she keeps saying about Patrick, about him being dead—I don't know why a person would say such a thing. It's disturbing. Her presence yesterday morning seems as suspicious to us as it does to you."

The ground shifted under me in an unexpected bout of vertigo. The detective checked his watch, then scratched his head behind his ear. "I'll take her to my office, and we'll see if we can't figure out what's going on. Let's wait inside your office. I don't want to scare her away."

Too late for that, detective. As soon as they stepped into the office, I sidestepped to the escalator, picked up the stairs on the third floor, and bypassed the security entrance for the customer doors that faced the lot where my car was parked.

I broke all kinds of speeding laws driving home. I sat in the driveway with the windows down, breathing the scent of withered lilac buds that barely clung to branches on the bushes alongside the house. Did no one believe me? This was bad. This was like C. Thomas Howell in *The Hitcher* bad. Well, maybe not that bad—but it was close.

I called Nick. The one person who knew I wasn't lying.

My call went into voicemail, and I left a message. "It's Samantha. It's—" I pulled the phone away from my ear to check the time but couldn't see it because a second call was coming through. Brittany Fowler needed to get a life. I put the phone back to my ear. "It's important. Call me when you get a chance. I need to talk to you."

I went into the house and pressed the play button on the old answering machine.

Beep! "Hey Kid, it's your mom. Just wanted to check in on you and see how you're doing. Things are good on the west coast. We're going to the beach now so don't try to call us back. Love you!"

Beep! "This is a courtesy call is for Samantha Kidd. This is the video store. You have an overdue rental. Please bring the movie back to avoid accruing late fees."

Beep! "Ms. Kidd? This is Brittany Fowler from Full Circle Mortgage? Can you call me back today? I have to talk to you about this application?"

A lot of people wanted to check in on me. Aside from my parents, they were people I'd rather avoid. And the best way to avoid their calls was to avoid the phone. I grabbed the overdue movie, left my cell phone on the counter on purpose, and locked the door behind me.

I needed something familiar. I drove to the strip mall with the video store and left the car running while I dropped the DVD case into the wall slot. I got back into my car, but instead of pulling out of the lot, I meditated on the scent of lunch meat coming from the hoagie store three doors down.

The most serious relationship I'd had during my years in New York was with the deli guy at my local market. The breakup affected me on a deep, lunchmeat-starved level. But New York smelled like New York and Ribbon, Pennsylvania smelled like my childhood. Capicola, Provolone cheese, and lilacs.

I turned off the engine and followed the scent to the counter of the sandwich shop where I ordered a hoagie big enough for two: twelve inches of hard roll seasoned with oil and oregano, filled with four different kinds of lunchmeat and assorted cheeses, lettuce, and onion. I snagged a large bag of Utz potato chips, a carton of Icy Tea, and stepped to the register to pay. My appetite may have been slightly larger than my stomach, but more than anything in my life, I needed that sandwich. It might clog my arteries, but it would clear my brain. No distractions like missing bodies or untimely police visits or angry mortgage companies—

"I see you got your appetite back," said Nick from beside me.

I turned and searched my crowded mind for a comeback but didn't want a repeat Bacon incident, so I kept my mouth shut.

He looked as good in a crisp white shirt and jeans as he did in a suit. Before he could make another comment on the size of my lunch, the cashier reclaimed my attention with the total. The twenty in my wallet would barely cover it. I hoped against hope the flush warming my face was not apparent.

"Looks like if I want to spend some quality time with you I'll have to kidnap you from the hoagie store."

"Wouldn't want you to commit a felony," I said. (Perhaps too quickly.)

"Fine, then I'll kidnap your lunch." He snatched the bag from the cashier who thought he was being playful. "Play along, and nobody gets hurt," he hissed out the side of his mouth. He placed a firm grip on my elbow and steered me out of the sandwich shop before I knew what was happening.

8

———

INSURANCE

"WHAT DO YOU THINK YOU'RE DOING?" I ASKED WHEN MY SENSES returned.

"You're coming with me." He held up the bag. "Insurance."

We left the store, Nick holding my lunch hostage. He turned to the right. We walked down the sidewalk in silence, approaching the video store. For a brief moment, I wondered if he was about to turn me in for harboring stolen movies, but when we passed it, and his grip didn't let up, I wondered something worse.

We passed three additional storefronts before he stopped in front of a vacant one. "In here. This place looks deserted." He handed me the food and pulled a credit card from his wallet. "You keep a lookout. I'll pop the locks. Nobody will know we're here."

Panic set in. He was right. Not only would nobody know we were there, but nobody knew where I was. (Was that the same thing?) I tried to stay calm on the outside, but inside I freaked out. What did I know about Nick aside from what I'd picked up when we worked together? I mean, how many shoe designers who know how to pick out a decent Sauvignon Blanc know how to pop open a locked door with a credit card? And how many have the guts to do it during business hours?

His choice of words hammered an ominous refrain inside my brain. No one will know we're here. I'll kidnap you. You're coming with me. Insurance.

The lock gave him trouble. Daydreams while flying over Paris notwithstanding, I knew if I were going to get away, it would have to be now. My weapons for defense were limited: a carton of Icy Tea and a hoagie.

I pulled the tea from the bag and stepped back on the sidewalk. My foot hit the edge of the curb. I lost my balance. I fell backward and dropped the food. Nick turned and grabbed me, his bear-claw hand circling my wrist. He held tight while my feet sought stable footing. The carton exploded on the sidewalk and instantly the air was scented with lemon and sweet tea. I planted one foot, then the other, underneath me. Nick's grip relaxed. He bent over and picked up the bag of food. A puddle of brown liquid seeped onto the sidewalk and headed for the toe of his oxfords. He sidestepped the stream and handed his Visa card to me.

"Kidd, relax. If it bothers you that much I'll use the key." He fumbled around with the change in his pocket, pulled out a key, and unlocked the door.

Color me confused.

Nick held the door open, but I didn't move. I did lean forward for a view inside the vacant store so I could describe it to the cops at a later date, but all I could see were stacks of shoe boxes along the back wall.

With Nick's logo.

"They're not going to bite, you know," he said tentatively. He seemed more nervous than I was.

I looked inside again. I still wasn't 100 percent sure we should be there, but I was at about 85 percent. Before I dropped the tea, I was only at about 35 percent, so things were heading the right direction. Nick's expression had changed since we left the hoagie store, or were at Tradava, or even on the sidewalk out front. He turned away and looked at the walls, the floor, the ceiling. His empty hand jiggled change in his front pocket. "Well? Your opinion means a lot to me."

"My opinion about what?" I asked.

"My new showroom."

He guided me inside. It dawned on me (slowly) that there were a lot of things about Nick I didn't know, not the least of which was why he was in Ribbon. When the door was closed behind us, the time seemed right to start asking questions.

"Your new showroom?"

"Yes. Satellite showroom. Satellite showroom slash store. Imagine it like this," he said and stepped forward. "A desk up front, white laminate." He walked to the middle of the room. "Tables here and here," he waved his hands to either side, "so buyers can work the collection. I picked up two dozen frames from an art supply store. After I paint them, they'll go on the walls around shelves to display my samples."

"White?"

He nodded. "Yellow rod lighting. I can't decide about the floor. White carpeting, which might be a nightmare, or exposed cement."

"Hardwood. Whitewash it."

"Tom Sawyer-style?"

"Why not?"

He stared at the floor. "Not a bad idea."

I joined him in the middle of the room. "Why Ribbon? Why now?"

"A lot of reasons. It's cheap. It's not that far of a drive from New York City. I show at the market center in Manhattan, so I'll save money on office space. My collection has always done well in Ribbon, and now that I've scaled back my distribution, it seemed a natural decision to start small. Thanks to stores like Tradava, there's name recognition and a built-in customer base."

"Did Patrick know about this?"

"Yes." He looked back and forth between my eyes and his brows pulled together. I waited for him to elaborate, but he didn't. He covered a bare patch of carpet with sheets of white tissue paper, then set my lunch in the middle like a picnic. "It was his suggestion. Some people think I'm making a big mistake." He took his Visa card out of my hand and tucked it back into his worn brown leather wallet. "Even when I use the keys I feel like I'm breaking and entering."

I stepped closer and squeezed his hand. "I think you made the right decision. You're a talented designer. There's no way you won't succeed."

He squeezed back. "I had a feeling you'd like it." My stomach rumbled again, removing all sentiment from the moment. "Enough about my business. Let's get you fed. I don't want to stand between you and that hoagie."

We sat down on the floor and split my sandwich in half. Nick didn't seem concerned that his showroom was going to smell like potato chips and cured meat.

Countless business dinners had taught me Nick favored a martini during the social hour and vacationed in Hawaii once a year, but they left me short on his creative aspirations. But now, I saw one thing clearly. Nick was starting a new life just like I was.

"This is it," he said. "A showroom of my own."

"That you are incapable of breaking into."

"I guess I'm not cut out for a life of crime."

"So you say." I raised an eyebrow.

"Seriously, I felt bad about last night when I told you to stay away from Tradava. It might have sounded like I was lecturing you."

"It did." I waited for him to explain, but he didn't. I bit into a potato chip with a snap. "Are you nervous? About starting something new?"

"Nervous? Sure. But excited too."

"But what if something goes wrong?" I was knee-deep in my sea of self-doubt and wanted to know if what I felt was normal.

He looked down at my hands which were now crumbling the other half of my potato chip. "If something goes wrong, I'll fix it. I know there'll be challenges along the way, but I'll deal with them or move on. That's what you should do."

His words hit me harder than I expected. My throat tightened, and my face flushed. I stared down at the chip bag, letting my hair fall forward. *Move on.* I didn't want to move on. I wanted to make this work. Why didn't he understand that?

"Do you have a restroom?" I asked abruptly.

"Sure. Back of the store, to the right."

I stood and smacked my hands against each other, showering the tissue paper with tiny potato chip flakes. I passed piles of shoe boxes and a closet-sized reception nook and entered an office that smelled like cookies. I scanned the desk and found a Vanilla-scented plug-in air freshener. A blue blazer hung from the back of a chair. There were no signs of a restroom around. I started to backtrack when I spied a familiar plum laptop bag on the floor of the office next to the desk chair.

Nick had Patrick's computer?

I bent sideways at the torso, in the kind of limbering-up waist exercises that were common on eighties aerobics videos and checked that Nick was still out front. He was. I extracted the laptop from the bag and looked around for a way to smuggle it out of the store.

"Kidd?" he called out.

Crap. I flipped my tweed cape up and shoved the flat computer into the back of my waistband. My pants, now fighting both stolen office equipment and an unhealthy amount of lunchmeat, dug into my waist. When I rounded the corner, Nick stood in the doorway, talking to a striking brunette in a clingy purple wrap dress and beige heels. I pressed myself against the wall and strained to overhear their conversation.

"Will I see you tonight?" she asked.

"Not tonight. Tomorrow?"

"I don't know if I can wait that long. You can't change your plans?"

"I don't think it would be a good idea. She doesn't know about us yet, and that's a good thing."

Behind me, a door slammed shut thanks to an unexpected cross breeze. Nick and the brunette turned toward the noise. I ducked into the reception area. The laptop shifted into my tights. I had to get out of there—Lycra only stretched so far.

When I returned to the showroom, Nick was alone. "You okay?" he asked.

"You have a lot of nerve, Taylor," I said. "First you warn me to quit my job, then you take my lunch, then you pretend we're all friendly, but clearly, we're *not*."

He leaned against the wall and smiled. The crinkles in the corners of his eyes made him look infuriatingly cute. "What did I do this time? Put the toilet paper on the roll the wrong way?"

I was in no mood for his playfulness. I stormed past him to the makeshift picnic and loosely wrapped the rest of my hoagie in wax paper. I shoved it into my handbag and stood. Whereas I would have liked to depart on a highly witty note, brevity and the computer in my pants won out.

"See you around." I headed toward the door.

Nick jogged past me and blocked my path. He looked confused and hurt. "Did I miss something?" he asked.

"No more than I did," I replied cryptically. I was *thisclose* to confronting him, but it was more important to find out what Patrick had wanted me to see in the first place than to let Nick know I was onto him.

He held the door open for me. I concentrated on the tea stain on the sidewalk out front until I was out the door.

"So, when I see you at the Tradava Gala on Sunday, will we be past this?" he called behind me.

I froze on the sidewalk and then turned. "The what?" I asked.

"The Designer's Debut Gala at the museum. You're going, right?"

"Wouldn't miss it for the world," I said.

Now, I just had to figure out what he was talking about.

9

———————

A VERY TIMELY DEADLINE

BACK AT MY HOUSE, THE LEFTOVERS WENT IN THE FRIDGE AND THE laptop went on the dining room table. The beauty of the hoagie is that, unlike a new job, it's just as good on Day Two. The answering machine blinked with a second round of messages and I considered throwing it in the trash compactor.

Beep! "Hello, Ms. Kidd, this is Maries Paulson. Please call me at your earliest convenience."

Beep! "This is a courtesy call for Samantha Kidd. This is the video store. You returned an empty box to the store. Please bring the movie back to avoid accruing additional late fees."

Beep! "Yo, it's Eddie. Hit me back when you get a chance." He left his number.

Beep! "Ms. Kidd, this is Brittany Fowler. If you don't contact me to resolve the issues regarding your mortgage, I'll have no choice—" I pressed delete mid-sentence.

I returned Maries' call first, and almost immediately a sultry, scotch-and-cigarettes voice answered.

"Ms. Paulson, this is Samantha Kidd," I said. "I work in the trend office with Patrick. Worked," I corrected myself, cringing. Good thing she couldn't see my face.

"Ms. Kidd, yes. You called me earlier. How may I help you?"

"In light of Patrick's—in light of what happened, I wanted to offer my help with the design competition." I hesitated, and then added, "and with the gala at the museum."

"You mentioned you work with Patrick. Do you know where he is?"

"You don't know?" I asked, shocked. But of course, she didn't know. According to everyone but me, there was nothing *to* know. But I knew. I knew what I saw. I didn't want to talk about it anymore, but it was a fact, nonetheless.

"We are facing a string of very timely deadlines and I've been unable to reach him for the past three days. The finalists are all expecting answers. Are you acting on his behalf? Did he share his thoughts on the competition with you?"

"Only briefly," I said, looking at the computer on my kitchen table.

Patrick had a file at Tradava and notes on the computer. Surely, I could fake my way through being in the know. And if Maries treated me as though I worked in the trend office, then Tradava would have less reason to doubt my claims of employment, right? (It was a sad display of self-negotiating. I wasn't proud of myself, but I needed a break.)

"I'll be working from home for the next few days, but I'm available to help with whatever you need," I finished. I gave her my address and phone number and promised to be in touch.

I draped my cape over the back of the kitchen chair and turned on the laptop. Patrick had mentioned the competition when he loaned me the computer. I thought back to that conversation.

"Tradava has indulged me with an annual design competition, and it's my top priority. This will be the first time we've attempted something on this scale. We've invited residents within a sixty-mile radius of Ribbon's epicenter to show us what they're made of, or rather what their wardrobes are made of."

"Do you want to brief me on the competition?"

"I don't want to bore you with the mundane details of this project.

My hope is to discover a talent within our city and put Ribbon on the map."

"Do you think the industry will pay attention? Ribbon is not New York, you know," I said, repeating the same thing to him he had said to me in the parking lot outside Tradava the morning we met.

"The hundred-thousand-dollar prize will make the industry pay attention." That's when he handed me the computer.

I cued up the File Manager. A series of folders lined the left side of the screen. The first folder contained old files of Patrick's trend newsletter. I'd read them a few nights ago but perused them again in case I had missed something. I discovered little more than Patrick's droll take on the demise of couture, and his commentary about controversial subjects like the hemline to high heel ratio advisable for the modern woman.

The second folder was titled RUNWAY, and, as expected, contained slides and background information for different runway shows. I sifted through additional files for travel expenses and budgets for the office, along with a few spreadsheets that projected how much inventory Tradava owned in different trends and how much volume they projected from these of-the-moment categories.

As I clicked around the excel file, I wondered what it would have been like to work for Patrick. We'd talked for close to an hour about fashion week and going to "market," the frenzied window of time when designers showed samples of their collections to buyers to place orders. He lit up when we talked about the fast pace of the New York fashion industry.

Patrick had been a fixture on the east coast runway circuit until sometime in the eighties when he left the Big Apple and took the position as Fashion director at Tradava. Though he didn't share his reasons for changing his life, he was the first person who appeared to accept my decision to change mine no questions asked. I selfishly wished I would have had the chance to be part of his team.

The doorbell distracted me from my research. I closed the laptop and pulled a couple of newspapers over it. An elegant woman draped in black stood on my front porch. I recognized her immediately and opened the door.

"Ms. Kidd?" she asked. I nodded. "Maries Paulson." She swept past me, a cloud of cashmere and Chanel No. 5. Oversized black sunglasses obscured most of her face. She did not take them off. Her head was covered with a turban that looked so chic I wondered if it were time for the style to make a comeback.

"I hope you don't mind the face to face. I'm more troubled by Patrick's absence than I led you to believe. I can't believe he'd leave me, our competition, our designers, with so many details left—"

"Ms. Paulson, Patrick didn't abandon anybody. At least, not by choice."

I explained what happened on Day One at Tradava. Out loud, it sounded crazy. Maries didn't act like I was insane. She pulled a white monogrammed hankie out of her quilted Dior handbag and dabbed at her eyes under the large black sunglasses.

"May we sit?" she asked. I gestured to the kitchen and she led the way.

"Patrick was a dear friend of mine. He was an amazing man. I'm sure you knew that."

"I didn't know him well. You—you believe me, don't you?" She nodded. "May I ask why?" She looked confused. "Nobody else does."

"Ms. Kidd, Patrick anticipated something like this would happen. He received a couple of threats and alerted the police."

"What threats?"

"Threats to cancel the design competition, that something would happen if he didn't." She pulled the glasses off, and for a moment she focused on me as if seeing me for the first time. Her eyebrows were drawn on, and her lipstick was as red as a tomato-shaped pincushion. Her bright blue eyes were filled with tears that pooled in her lower lids. I'd place her in her seventies, but I bet she'd deny it vehemently.

"The police paid him little mind." She adjusted her cashmere wrap. "If the police kept that information from you, it only means they are worried about how they will look in the eyes of the public when your statement becomes common knowledge."

I remained silent while she composed herself. I offered her a glass of iced tea, which she accepted.

"He saw himself in you, you know," she said.

"He talked to you about me?"

"You impressed him, and that's not easy to do."

I looked at the pile of newspapers on the kitchen table. Thankfully, the laptop was out of sight. I didn't want Maries to know so soon after her friend's death I was trying to break into his files, especially after learning I'd impressed him. I set the glass of tea in front of her and dropped into a vacant chair. We sat in silence for upwards of a minute.

Logan entered the kitchen and meowed at her. "Sweet cat," she said. She bent down and ran her hand over his shiny black fur. When she sat up, she studied me. "I wonder if you would consider looking into Patrick's murder?"

"Don't you think that's a job for the police?" I asked.

"Simply put, the police don't understand the intricacies of the fashion world like we do."

"What makes you believe he was murdered? As far as I know, the police haven't found his body. Maybe they're right. Maybe he orchestrated the whole thing because he needed to get out of town."

She reached inside her handbag and pulled out an interoffice envelope. "What happened to Patrick is only the beginning." She removed a stack of applications from the envelope and set them on the table. "You already know Patrick and I are judges of a design competition. These are the applications and profiles of the contestants. I have reason to believe the killer may be one of them."

"Then you have an obligation to turn this over to the police," I said, pushing the pile back toward her. We were like two kids trying to get out of eating Life cereal.

"Ms. Kidd, you're being myopic." She pulled her glasses down a second time and touched the inside corner of each eye with a tissue. "I suppose, if I want you to see the big picture, I should share with you a bit about Patrick's past. About what brought him to Tradava."

She leaned back. Her black cape flowed over the arms of the

chair. For all her presence, she appeared exhausted. "Patrick was a legend for a very long time, until one day, he was not. There came a point when his opinion was no longer relevant. He sensed it. He knew he was becoming a dinosaur."

"Is that why he moved from New York?"

"He chose to re-envision his role in the industry he loved. By moving to a smaller town, to Tradava, he chiseled out a new home for himself. No one with his credentials had ever worked for Tradava. He was a big fish in a little pond, and at that point in his career, it suited him."

Big fish, little pond. Patrick and I had talked about the same thing during one of our interviews. Find a way to remain relevant and you can live the life of your dreams, he had said.

"When Patrick first dreamed up the competition, it was a way for him to be a voice again. To help the next generation of designers. I've been asked to judge many a competition over the years, and I've always said no. The only reason I said yes this time was because of Patrick. I owe my career to him."

She paused to take a sip of tea. The ice cubes clanked around in the glass. "He approached Tradava and they agreed to underwrite the competition expenses and the reward. He convinced them it would be a great way to get out from their current reputation as a mass-market retailer and claim a portion of the fashion trade he so loved. Part of the reason they hired him was to bring his cachet to the store, and I'm sure he felt pressure to deliver on the promise of his connections and establish a legacy."

"But what happened?" I interrupted.

"As the economy took its toll on the store's business, the board of directors determined they couldn't foot the bill for what Patrick had in mind. They pulled their funding. He procured sponsorships from another source, and Tradava agreed to underwrite the gala. He considered it a win-win." She paused again and swirled what was left of her tea. Beads of condensation trickled down the outside, forming a wet circle on the faded cotton placemat in front of her.

"Last week, I received an anonymous phone call demanding we cancel the competition," she said.

"What exactly did they say?"

"'Kill the competition before it's too late.'"

"Too late for what?"

"I don't know. I told Patrick about the call, and he advised me to tell the police. That's when he told me he'd received similar phone calls."

"What did the police say?" I pictured Detective Loncar, in his western-cut suit, being asked to take seriously a threat over a design competition. The image was anachronistic at best.

"As I told you, the police have paid no attention to Patrick's concerns. This morning, I received a second call. A demand for one hundred thousand dollars, the competition prize, to be delivered by me at the Designer's Debut Gala. The caller said, 'What happened to Patrick was a message.' Without knowing more, I'm afraid we might both be in danger."

"We?" I asked.

"You and I," Maries said. "The last thing the caller said was a warning. 'Go to the police again and the trend specialist is next to die.'"

10

BEING PUNISHED

"I don't understand," I said. The overwhelming evidence pointed to the fact that I *wasn't* the trend specialist. Maybe it was time to stop telling people I was?

"I admit I don't understand either," Maries said. "I don't know who Patrick was involved with or where the money was coming from."

"Do you know where it is now?"

"In the bank, I imagine. I'm beginning to think he turned to an unconventional source. Whatever information he kept hidden, he would have kept at Tradava. With him gone, you represent the trend office and have access to his files." Her gloved hand fingered the clasp on her cape. "Someone doesn't want us to proceed. Without more information, I don't know which way to turn."

"Are you going to cancel the competition?"

"This competition is Patrick's legacy. I will not be bullied into canceling it. I owe Patrick that much." She stood from the table and pushed the chair underneath. I followed her into the living room.

"Ms. Paulson, there was a designer in Patrick's office the morning he . . . that morning. I didn't catch her name, but she was tall, thin, with bright red hair—"

"There are always designers around Patrick. She's insignificant in the grand scheme of things." She waved her hand as though shooing a fly. "Ms. Kidd, will you help me?"

I looked down at the shag carpet to avoid making further eye contact. "I'm sorry about Patrick, but I'm trying to start a new life in Ribbon and have had a couple of challenges of my own. I think it's best I concentrate on doing the job I was hired to do and put what happened at Tradava behind me."

In my head, I politely tacked on another suggestion that she go to the police, but I couldn't speak the words. Maries seemed firm in her belief that the police wouldn't help. She left as abruptly as she arrived.

What was I doing? There should have been nothing keeping me in Ribbon. Screw the fact that I'd grown up in this house. I'd always heard you couldn't go home again, and because I tried, I was being punished. But where was I going to go? If I couldn't make the mortgage payment, I would be little more than a squatter on the property. My rent-controlled apartment was now going for three times what I'd paid while living there and moving to California to crash on my parents' sofa wasn't an option. Something told me skipping town wasn't going to help me in the credibility department when it came to my new friend Detective Loncar either. After what Maries had told me, my path was bound to cross with the detective's sooner rather than later.

After Maries left, I turned my attention to the folder she'd given me. There were two stacks of paper inside, each secured by a binder clip. The first was thick. I flipped through it with my thumb. The second pile held only four pages. The letters A through D were carefully printed in purple marker on the upper left corner of each page, circled with Giotto-like precision. A Post-it on the smaller pile read FINALISTS. I fanned the finalists out over the table. Four names, along with answers to questions on inspiration and experience, stared back. Amanda Ries. Clestes. Michael Dubrecht. Nick Taylor.

Nick Taylor?

Nick was a finalist in the competition? There was more wrong with that than right. He was already a professional designer. He hadn't mentioned any of this on the opportunities he had to tell me, and he'd been the one to take Patrick's computer.

I'd forgotten all about Patrick's computer!

I pushed the newspapers aside and opened the laptop. I double-clicked a file named DESIGN COMPETITION. The computer prompted me for a password.

Curses.

I didn't know enough about Patrick to crack his password in the first seventeen tries. I thought, not for the first time, if I wanted to understand why Patrick had been murdered, maybe it was time for me to get to know Patrick better. And the best place to do that was at Tradava.

I changed into faded jeans, a black turtleneck sweater, and rubber-soled black booties with chains hanging down around the heels. Investigative style, I might have called it, if I were writing an exposé instead of planning a B&E on Patrick's office.

There's a certain skill set common to retail buyers. Sometimes you have to be creative. Sometimes you have to be analytical. The problem with this mental makeup is sometimes you lack the common sense normal people take for granted. When it came to creative, analytical problem solving, my cup runneth over. When it came to common sense, my glass was half full.

The late September heat wave had broken with an unexpected thunderstorm, and raindrops pelted Tradava's empty parking lot. An occasional flash of lightning illuminated the lack of activity around the store's exterior. Aside from a woman in mommy jeans running toward a minivan, a hunched-over lady pushing a stroller through the lot, and a mall employee hoisting a lumpy bag of trash into the dumpster, the lot was deserted. The store staff had probably dwindled to minimal coverage on the selling floors. I wondered if Eddie was anywhere in the store.

I ran as fast as my impractical but sassy boots would allow and entered through the main customer entrance. I took the elevator to the fifth floor, ducked into the stairwell, and hiked up two additional flights to the trend offices (where I was pretty sure I wasn't supposed to be). I felt like a criminal with every passing step. I pulled the keys I'd lifted out of the bottom of my handbag but kept them hidden in my palm.

After a deep breath, a couple of sideways glances, and three keys that didn't fit the locks, I found a match. The door swung open. I went to my office, set my handbag down, and wondered what to do next.

I'd searched the file cabinet yesterday. I'd been through the files on the floor as well. In fact, all the items in the office had been given my once-over, and I'd learned nothing. But according to Maries Paulson, someone connected me to Patrick, and the only tether between the two of us was Tradava and a job I probably didn't have.

Outside his office sat a small yellow desk with a phone, a lava lamp, and a bundle of purple number two pencils stamped with the name Michael. A sketchpad lay next to a tear-off calendar featuring quotes by tough-talking women. I slid open a drawer and found a manila file folder that contained clippings on different designers along with a copy of the *Style Section*. I flipped it open a couple of pages and found a picture of Nick and the brunette who had come to his new showroom. The caption read *Nick Taylor and Amanda Ries: compatible competition?*

Amanda Ries. I recognized her name; she was one of the finalists.

Dark, smooth hair that matched the shine of her lip-gloss hung in a delicate waterfall to her impossibly small waist. Porcelain skin set off by arched eyebrows and a low neckline that revealed nothing but perfection. She filled out the gown she was wearing, a chic halter that plunged to her navel, revealing the intangibles of life: great cleavage and no sign of tummy rolls, tan lines, or stretch marks. She was not the type you invite for a picnic with hoagies and chips.

She was exactly who someone like Nick would date. Why wouldn't he? He was a talented shoe designer, attractive, funny, and full of charm. This woman—Amanda—could wear bias-cut fabric without Spanx and her hair was frizz-free. Somewhere between noticing her ability to accessorize, a fat tear hit the newsprint and distorted the copy.

Seeing this woman, looking perfect, next to Nick, was too much. Not only did I not have the guy, but I also didn't have a job or a paycheck. What I had were two new friends: a homicide detective and a mortgage officer. I imagined a conversation between the two of them: *Why no, detective, we didn't know she was involved in a murder investigation. Did you know she lied on her mortgage application? I think that speaks to character, don't you?*

I wasn't here to read about Nick's social life. I was here to learn about the man who should have been my boss. I shut the newspaper and moved into Patrick's office. Vintage *Vogue, Bazaar,* and *Elle* covers hung on the walls. Photos on the shelves above the desk showcased a younger Patrick in various settings with various, then-starting out, now-legendary designers. Outdated outfits helped identify the decades, but Patrick was like a fashion Where's Waldo, wearing some version of the same outfit in every photo. His black hair, neatly parted on the side and his waxed mustache, seemed to have become his trademark in the early seventies and remained a constant, much like the plaids and checks and stripes I had recognized when I saw his body crumpled on the floor of the elevator.

I reached out to the Rolodex. It was still open to the card for Pins and Needles. I wasn't sure if this was what Red had been looking at when she flipped through the card file yesterday or not, but it was worth investigating. This time I pocketed the card. Next, I rifled through Patrick's inbox looking for something, anything that would clue me into his personality. Midway through the stack, I noticed a mini-fridge in the corner next to the purple sofa. Leaving no stone unturned, I abandoned the inbox to see if it was stocked.

The mini-fridge held a pitcher of lemonade, about a dozen small bottles of Pellegrino, and several somethings hand-wrapped in gold foil. Further investigation exposed individually wrapped chocolate and caramel sweets, neatly piled in stacks: two stacks: one of six and one stack of four. A sucker for symmetry, I ate two from the stack of six to even them out.

I poured a glass of lemonade and searched Patrick's desk drawers, eventually finding a folder labeled DESIGN COMPETITION. I opened it and a small piece of paper fluttered to the floor. Written on a page from a monogrammed tablet with an elaborate P in the center was a note in Patrick's fluid handwriting. I read slowly at first, then again, and again.

I'm wracked with guilt over my recent behavior. This is not what this business is about. New talent needs a proper home, and I fear I won't be around to protect my legacy. I leave it to you to look in vogue. This is not about the money. It is about the creativity. Friendship and loyalty do not have a price, and I was foolish to think otherwise. If this is the new business of fashion, it will go forward without me. My only regret is that I turned to the wrong people to achieve my final goal.

I set the paper on top of the other pages in the folder and thought about what this meant. Patrick had left behind a note that indicated his guilt about . . . *something.* But what had he done? And one sentence gave me the chills. *I fear I won't be around to protect my legacy.*

Maries was right. He'd been expecting the worst.

I scanned the note again. Words like *money, regret,* and *the wrong people* stood out like bandanas on a display of silk scarves. He was trying to tell me something.

Unexpectedly, my vision blurred. My heartbeat whooshed in my ears, loud and rhythmic, making it hard to hear anything other than the pounding of my pulse. I stood and felt along the corners of the desk for balance as my vision swam, distorting the details of the office in sideways, stretched images.

Something was wrong with me.

The heel of my boot caught on the edge of the carpet and I grabbed at Patrick's inbox, pulling it off the desk and scattering the contents over the floor. I sank onto the pile of papers, closed my eyes, and faded into blackness.

I AWOKE WITH A START. A yellow Post-it fell from my cheek and fluttered to the carpet. I was on the floor of Patrick's office. I blinked several times and tried to figure out how I'd gotten there. My head throbbed.

I crawled to Patrick's chair and planted my hands on the soft black leather. After a few motivating breaths, I pulled myself into it. The office was dark, illuminated only by emergency lights from the hallway. I pulled the desk phone close enough to read the display. One thirty-seven.

I was trapped in the store.

I was in the one place I wasn't supposed to be. If caught by the wrong people, this would not look good. Considering I was trying to find out details about a murder during off-hours in a store where questions surrounded my employment, the wrong people were numerous.

My paranoia kicked into overdrive. Having worked (or not) for this store for about twelve hours I realized this might not be behavior they encouraged. Not only that, but I didn't know vital facts about their operation, things like what overnight security they had. I strained my ears to listen for the sound of bloodhounds sniffing out intruders and became aware of my movements, wondering if the store had invisible light beam laser grids like Catherine Zeta-Jones had trained to beat in *Entrapment*.

Think, Samantha, think.

I rubbed a sore spot on my temple and while my vision adjusted to the darkness. This was the second time in two days I'd blacked out. But this wasn't like seeing Patrick's body in the elevator. This had been different. My mind was fuzzy, like fleece after it's been laundered. I fished my cell phone out of my handbag, but Eddie was right. No signal. Still groggy, I moved to the purple sofa and curled up under a pashmina someone had left draped over the back.

Someone shook me awake. I opened my eyes and saw purple velvet. Immediately, my body went rigid, and I whirled around, ready to strike. Eddie caught my fist. When I relaxed, he did too. With effort, I sat upright. The office was light. I had spent the night asleep in the store.

I rubbed my eyes, accidentally smudging my (probably already smudged) mascara. I searched for the words to explain how I'd come to be asleep on Patrick's sofa behind the doors of a previously locked office.

"You've been here all night?" Eddie asked before I worked out my explanation. I nodded. "Then you don't know." He averted his eyes.

"I don't know what?" I asked.

"Someone found Patrick's body in a dumpster behind the store."

11

———

NO RUNNING INVOLVED

Eddie ushered me out of Tradava, past store security, and to his car. I didn't put up a fight. He drove to the diner and led me to a booth in the back by the kitchen. We flipped our coffee cups over and a waitress filled them. Before either of us spoke, we each drained our mugs. Me from a need to snap out of the zombie-like trance I'd found myself in, and Eddie, probably, from caffeine addiction.

"Who found him?" I asked. Eddie had been patient with me, allowing me time to wake up, collect my wits, and try to feel normal, though the idea of Patrick's body being discovered in the dumpster would keep me from ever feeling normal again.

"Michael Dubrecht. He said there was a meeting scheduled for the design competition but nobody else showed up. It's on page four." He pushed a newspaper toward me. I took another swig of coffee then told Eddie what had happened since he last saw me. "I went to talk to Detective Loncar, just like I said, but he was with the head of HR, and I got the very strong feeling neither one of them was going to hear me out."

He stared at me. "You ran away from a detective?"

"There was no running involved." I paused. "I took the escalator."

"Dude."

"That's not the worst of it. I went home and then left and ran into Nick. He's—he's involved in this, I just don't know how."

"Nick's a boy scout."

"He had the laptop. I found it."

Eddie set his coffee cup down. "What did he say when you asked him about it?"

"I didn't ask. I took it and left. And then I talked to Maries Paulson, and she brought over the applications for this design competition Patrick was coordinating, and it turns out Nick is one of the finalists. So's this Michael person."

I detailed her visit, including the part about the funding, the extortion, and the threats about going to the cops.

"She's probably right about the murder being connected to the competition," Eddie said. "You know what killed him?"

"Heart attack," I said, though I already suspected this to be untrue.

Eddie shook his head. "He was strangled with seam binding."

My stomach flipped. Eddie waved the waitress over and ordered plain wheat toast. She turned to me and I waved her away.

"Where'd you hear that?"

"Store gossip."

"Reliable?"

He leaned back against the vinyl booth. "Michael ran into the store and told a guy in security. The security guy is dating the counter manager for Clinique. One of my staff members was working on a new fragrance display next to the Clinique department." He shrugged. "Most reliable source of information in the industry, if you ask me."

Eddie's news left me at a loss for words. Last night I'd thought nothing about going to the store. Now I find out Patrick's body had been dumped less than fifty feet from where I'd parked my car. Talk about too close for comfort.

Eddie continued with other facts I didn't know.

Point A: Because of the thunderstorm, the building had been close to empty. The skeleton crew of managers had most likely left as quickly as possible, making it an ideal night for someone to do something illegal like dumping a body. (I'd suspected as much.) (Not the illegal activity part.)

Point B: There were no laser beam grids in the store, but the killer had managed to get in there once before and might very easily have been there again. (Yes, I asked. Seemed worth knowing for next time.) (Scratch that. Why did I think there would be a next time?)

Point C: Patrick's candy bars and fresh-squeezed lemonade were as legendary as he was. Visitors to his office scheduled afternoon appointments when they were guaranteed an offer of a snack. (I asked that too. Don't judge.)

He didn't mention point D, but it hung in the air: I'd been sneaking around Tradava during the night when Patrick's body had turned up. Some folks might find that suspicious.

And the worst thing of all: I'd learned nothing. I was no closer to unlocking Patrick's files or finding the money. I still didn't know why he'd died or who had killed him.

I told Eddie about the designer profiles on my dining room table. "Patrick was strangled with seam binding, and I can't think of anybody who walks around with seam binding except for maybe a fashion designer. Somebody who entered the competition was going to win one hundred thousand dollars. If you were a finalist and you thought you had a chance of winning, why kill the judge? That makes it seem like it's one of the people who had no chance of winning. Maybe one of the designers who wasn't a finalist." I slouched down in the booth. "And that's the bigger pile of candidates. Worse, nobody knows where Patrick got the money or where he put it. Maybe someone already took the money and skipped town."

"Then figure out who skipped town."

"Sure. We can systematically track down over a hundred different designers who may or may not hold a grudge because they did or didn't final in the competition. That won't be difficult at *all*. And as soon as we find out who is missing, we'll tell the cops." But there was something wrong with that logic. Everything I'd taken to Detective

Loncar had to do with what couldn't be found. Patrick's body, the laptop, and the EMT.

Patrick's body had been found, and I had the laptop, which ironically corroborated my statement and made me look guilty at the same time. To introduce a hundred thousand dollars that couldn't be found along with a missing designer would do little more than encourage the detective to file me under C for Crackpot or P for Person of Interest. My best bet was to steer clear of the police. All the way around.

The waitress returned with Eddie's food. She set a small plate with two strips of bacon in front of me, then smiled and held a finger up to her mouth and tipped her head toward the man by the cashier. I assumed he was the manager and she was the angel of mercy who had delivered me the unexpected bounty of breakfast meat. I picked up a piece and snapped it off between my teeth.

"Remember Red? She said something about the competition. I asked Maries about her and she said she was insignificant." I thought for a second. "And don't forget, she's just one of the strange people who was traipsing around that morning."

"What strange people?"

"Red, Michael, Nick," I ticked off, then bit into my second piece of bacon.

"Red came in asking for Patrick. Michael was Patrick's assistant, and as far as I can remember, Nick didn't come into the office."

"What are you saying?"

"That there's nothing strange about any of those people being at Tradava. The only strange person is you."

"I resent that."

He changed the subject. "What else did you find last night? Anything in Patrick's desk or files?"

"No. I found nothing in Patrick's desk."

"How can you find nothing?"

"There was a space in his desk drawer where something had been but wasn't there anymore. How much space do you think a hundred thousand dollars cash would take up?"

Eddie shrugged. "What else was in the drawer?"

"Desk drawer stuff. Old calendar pages, mechanical pencils, paper clips, flu medicine. And a big empty space."

"Bigger than a breadbox?"

"Big enough for a lot of dough, that's for sure."

"You think he kept the prize money in cash in his desk drawer?"

"I don't know what to think."

"Here's what I think. You need to go home and sleep. You aren't looking your best right now."

"Sleep—that doesn't make sense either. How did I fall asleep at Tradava? Before two days ago, I've never passed out. Is there something special about the air quality in Ribbon since high school? Is it thinner? Infused with Lithium?"

Eddie ignored my questions. "Go home. Take a shower. Lay low. This will all blow over."

We slid out of the booth and he threw a twenty on the table by the bill. I fished two ones out of my wallet and tucked them under my coffee cup. I liked knowing, in the middle of everything else that was rapidly going wrong with my life, that there existed a waitress in a diner who was willing to slip me some bacon when I most needed it. I gave Eddie a head start and ignored his advice to lay low. Instead, I drove to Pins and Needles, the fabric store from the card I'd swiped out of Patrick's Rolodex.

"I'LL BE with you in a minute," said a plump woman measuring fabric on the cutting table. She wore a red taffeta smock buttoned up the front over a white cotton shirt and black pencil skirt. A pair of gold scissors hung from a chain around her neck. A white plastic nametag that said Florence was pinned to her shoulder.

The shop was long and narrow, and the walls were lined with bolts of fabric sandwiched tightly on high-gloss white shelves. Bust forms around the store were draped with silk, chiffon, and cashmere, secured with little more than an array of pins. The entire interior was like a time warp; I half expected Edith Head to step out from the stockroom.

"How may I help you?" Florence asked while attaching a small hand-written price tag to the yardage of fabric she had measured.

"Where I can find the seam binding?"

She pointed across the store. "Notions are with zippers and thread. Past the fixture of gabardine."

I eased past the cutting table and followed her directions. A small fixture about the size of a doghouse was pushed into a corner and stocked with the item I'd come here to find: seam binding. I pulled a package out and turned it over in my hands.

"Are you finding everything okay, dear?" asked Florence, who had silently reappeared next to me. I glanced at her feet, in sensible shoes with rubber soles. If I were going to take up sneaking around, I might need to find out where she bought them.

"I'm not sure. I think this is what I'm looking for."

"You don't know?"

"Not really."

"Not a lot of people still use it, though it's been a hot seller lately."

This piqued my interest. "Why would that be?"

"I imagine because of the competition. A few of the designers have been in here to purchase it."

"I didn't realize the competition was so well known."

"Don't let the smock and the sensible shoes fool you. I run this fabric store, and I have a longstanding love affair with fashion. My business is based on it. If I didn't know about the competition, people would question my expertise."

"Do you know the designers?"

"Of course! Most of them are regulars."

"Is Michael Dubrecht a regular?"

"Oh, that Michael is such a nice boy. Always shops the remnants. He has grand ideas but not a very large budget."

A bell rang at the front of the store and Florence excused herself. I doubted Florence would gossip with me if I'd simply rattled off names of suspects. I needed a better plan. Lost in my thoughts, I left the store and started the drive home.

Two traffic lights away, I saw a small BMW turn right at the intersection. It could have been black, it could have been gray, or it could have been dark blue. I was less interested in the color of the car than the color of the hair of the driver. Red.

I did an illegal U-turn when the light changed and hoped the Ribbon police force was out trying to catch murderers and not watching for traffic violations. I weaved through traffic, looking for a black, gray, or dark blue sedan. I spotted it just as it made the left-hand turn into the Pins and Needles parking lot.

Red parked in a space close to the front door. I parked by the rear of the lot. Aside from her license plate number and the fact that her car was black, gray, or dark blue, there wasn't much I would learn by watching her parked car, so for the second time that day, I headed inside.

"Back so soon?" called out Florence as the bell chimed overhead.

"I forgot my list," I said, waving an old receipt I'd grabbed from the center console. I returned to the Notions aisle. When I rounded the corner, Red stood by the seam binding, filling her basket with packages.

Her brilliant hair hung to the side of her face. Her ankle-length dress bore the asymmetric lines of Japanese design, but she'd cinched it at her waist with a leopard-printed patent leather Obi belt.

"Stocking up?" I said as I approached.

She was noticeably startled by my voice. "I didn't realize anyone was there. What did you say?" She looked at her basket. "Oh, seam binding. This is the only store that carries the kind I like."

"I didn't realize seam binding varied that much. What's so great about that brand?"

"Most of the newer ones are rayon but this one is polyester. I like the feel of it in my hands. You'd be amazed at what you can get away with when you use it."

Interesting choice of words. "You stopped by Patrick's office two days ago. Are you a designer?"

"I own a boutique at the Designer Outlet Center." She reached into her handbag and pulled out a business card. I glanced at the name: Catnip. Underneath, in a neat cursive font, was "Ribbon Designer Outlets," followed by an address, phone number, email. There was no name on the card. As I took it from her hand, she stared past me, across the store. "I have to leave," she said abruptly, abandoning her basket by my feet.

She ducked out the door that faced the back alley, leaving door chimes tinkling in her wake. I still didn't know how she was connected to Patrick but this time I knew where to find her. I picked up a package of seam binding and turned it over. One dollar and thirty cents.

Seemed like a small price to pay for a murder weapon.

12

———

DISCLOSURE

I DROVE HOME AND POWERED UP THE LAPTOP. THERE HAD TO BE something in there that I'd missed. I called to Logan, but he didn't appear. A noise came from behind the door to the basement. When I opened it, a bolt of black fur shot past me. Food or litter box? Logan bee-lined for the food bowl, which meant there was probably a small mess in the basement. I headed down the rickety stairs to find the spot he had chosen to leave his mark. A sickening smell hit me, and I turned on the light switch, gasping at the sight.

Only a few days ago, I had sat in front of the house gazing fondly at the crabapple trees. Recalling summer nights, sitting on the porch swing with my dad or baking pies with my mom. I'd managed to edit our leaky basement from my memories, had forgotten that a storm of any magnitude would turn the concrete floor into a murky indoor swimming pool, ruining anything not at least two feet above floor level. A night of thunderstorms brought me back to reality. Rising water claimed paperback books, back issues of fashion magazines, and broken TV sets left in a state of disrepair ages ago.

I wondered, not for the first time, why I was trying so hard to make this fresh start. *Just pick up the phone and call your old boss,* said a voice inside my head. *Ask Bentley's to take you back. Better yet, call mom and dad. Tell them you need their help.* But as I watched my childhood belongings swirl around in the muck, I knew I wouldn't make that call.

Thoughts of the sixty-five-hour work weeks, the daily battles with my landlord and dry cleaner, the inconvenience of paying to park in a garage where I couldn't get my car when I needed it flooded my mind like the water flooding the basement. The thoughts made up a patchwork maxi-skirt of reasons why I'd been so willing to leave that life. This move was about a fresh start. I wasn't going to throw it all away over some soggy cardboard boxes.

I had a flashback to my childhood and knew what I had to do. My dad's rubber fishing waders were propped along a wall in the garage and I pulled them on, even though they were a few sizes too big. Time to find a bucket.

Several hours and inventive curses toward the previous owners later (I suspended familial loyalty within the first half hour of work; there was a little thing called 'disclosure' mom and dad had ignored when they sold me the house), the water level had waned from feet to inches. Autopilot replaced exhaustion. The rancid smell of decades-old memories and waterlogged mildew turned my stomach. I'd done what I could, for now. I left the basement.

Logan sat at the top of the stairs licking his paw and running it over his head. He made a lazy attempt at a meow, as if to say I should consider cleaning myself up too. I peeled off the wet everything: boots, socks, clothes, and underwear, and left them in a trail up the stairs to the bathroom where I showered. The last thing I remembered was collapsing into my bed naked, oblivious to the sun shining through the curtains.

I woke with Logan swatting at my head. I pulled a Go-Gos T-shirt over a fresh set of undies and went to the kitchen. The doorbell rang. My mind filled with warnings not to open the door to strangers, and I armed myself with a bread knife.

"Kidd, it's Nick Taylor. I know you're in there. I can hear you walking around. Will you open the door already?"

For the second time in as many days, I covered the laptop in a pile of newspapers on the table. I opened the door, forgetting I held the bread knife. Nick stepped back. His eyes darted to the hand holding the knife then grew darker as his gaze shifted to my lower half.

"What are you doing here?" I asked.

"May I come in?"

"No." *Don't trust him*! sounded in my head. I stood in his way, one hand on the door, the other on the frame. I was a one-woman bouncer in a T-shirt and cotton panties.

Oh no! I was in my panties!

My face flushed. "Wait here," I said, jabbing the air between us like a swashbuckler with the world's smallest sword. I slammed the door and ran upstairs, grabbing the wet clothes and underwear I'd strewn about before showering. I jumped into a pair of jeans, grabbed the breadknife, and went back downstairs. "What do you want?"

He scanned my body before looking me in the face. "I forgot to give you this when you were in my store." He held out the plum laptop case. At least one of us knew it was empty. At least one of us chose to keep that fact to ourselves in pursuit of more important information.

"Where did you get that?"

"You left it behind at Tradava the morning we found Patrick. After I walked you to the stairwell, I went back to the shoe department. That's when I saw it."

I searched his face for an indication he knew it was empty. I got nothing. "Thank you," I said. I took the bag and set it on the end table.

"It occurred to me that maybe you saw it in my office and that's why you were so mad when you left. But then I thought if you had seen it, you would have asked me why I had your laptop. So, I still don't know why you stormed out of my store."

I needed to distract him, and for a brief second regretted not being able to play the T-shirt-and-panties card. He leaned closer to me, close enough that we were sharing the same air. He brushed his finger under my chin and tipped my head back. "I heard about what happened last night. Are you okay?"

I looked directly into Nick's root-beer barrel brown eyes and lied my heart out. "I'm fine." I walked to the sofa. He followed. We both sat down. Nick was waiting for an explanation and there was the smallest possibility I owed it to him.

"I'm curious. Were you this crazy when you were a kid Kidd? Or when you worked for Bentley's?"

"What's your point?"

"I'm not sure I would have trusted your strategic thinking if I'd known," he said.

"I don't recall you complaining when I wrote your orders."

"Back then I just thought it was good business. I had no idea you were nuts."

I sank deeper into the green velvet cushions, ignoring the broken spring that dug into my left butt cheek. "Do you ever think about your childhood? About whether or not you're the you you started out to be?"

"I'm not sure I follow."

"I worked at Bentley's for nine years. I started as a sales associate and left as a buyer. I was promoted every two years into some great positions. None of them made me happy. I mean, sure, I celebrated every time I got a promotion, and for the first six months, I was so busy learning my job I didn't have time to think about my slowly deteriorating quality of life, but I should have been thrilled to get up and say I was a buyer for a store of Bentley's New York's caliber. I wasn't."

"Is that the real reason you changed your life?"

"I was about to drive back to Manhattan after helping my parents move. I didn't want to leave. I met Patrick that morning, in the parking lot outside of Tradava. He told me about the trend specialist job and, well, here we are."

I leaned against the cushions of the sofa and stared at my fingers, wrinkled from dealing with the water in the basement. "I didn't expect it to be easy to start over, you know? But I thought it would be fun." The phone rang in the background. I expected Nick to ask if I was going to answer it. He didn't. After four rings the machine clicked on.

"Ms. Kidd, this is Brittany Fowler from Full Circle Mortgage. We need to talk."

I went to the kitchen. I hit the delete button and switched off the machine. "I have to get some new things around here," I said to Logan, who stared at me from the floor.

Nick followed me into the kitchen. "Can I do anything? To make things easier for you?"

"There is one thing," I said. Before he had a chance to answer, I continued. "The gala? With everything that's been going on, I misplaced my invite. Can I go with you?"

"Not that you don't have a charming way of inviting yourself, but I already have a date."

"I didn't mean to imply it would be a date," I said quickly.

"Good, because I'm going to be busy that night. You'll have to find your invite."

"You're one of the finalists!" I blurted out. We stared at each other for an intense couple of seconds. "Can't you get me in?"

"Kidd, maybe you should sit this one out."

Unwelcome tears coated my eyes. I wanted to blink them back, but blinking might have caused them to spill down my cheeks and I wanted that even less. I tipped my head back and stared at the ceiling, doing little more than establishing tracks of tears that ran from the outside corner of my eye into my hairline.

"Something else is bothering you," Nick said. "What's wrong?"

"The house. The basement floods."

"I find it hard to believe you ended up with a flooded basement after one thunderstorm."

"You don't believe me? Come on," I said. He fell into step behind me. My dad's hip-waders sat in a puddle in the garage next to the door that led to the cellar. I pulled the door open and hit the light switch, shocked to see the water level had risen again.

It couldn't be!

I had spent too many hours lugging water up the steps and

outside. I stepped halfway down the staircase. The water-logged boxes of vintage fashion magazines my mom had left stacked by the walls of the basement had busted open. The issue that glided past me had the same cover as the one Patrick had hanging on the wall of his office. It, like dozens of other issues, floated across the floor like dead fish. I watched it bump up against the wall. That's when I saw a green garden hose, dangling through a broken window, pouring water into the room.

"I'll be right back." I pushed past Nick, through the garage, and around the side of the house. A green hose was screwed into the outside spigot by the back door and the water was turned on to full force. I closed my palm over the round metal valve and turned it off. I followed the length of the hose to the back of the house, only to find the other end threaded into a broken window at ground level. It all meant one thing.

My flooded basement wasn't an accident. Someone had wanted me out of commission.

13

VANDALISM?

Vandalism? On top of everything else? That just made me mad. I returned to the garage. Nick stood by the cellar door. I would not make eye contact with him. I should have seen the broken window and the rubber hose earlier. And because I didn't, I was going to have to deal with a flooded basement.

Again.

Nick's attitude changed. If it weren't for the crinkles in the corner of his eyes, I'd have broken down. The crinkles kept me in check. Because I didn't believe a person like Nick, with root-beer-barrel eyes that crinkled in the corners, would be laughing at me if things weren't going to be okay. He draped his arm around my shoulder. "It's just a house, Kidd. It isn't a sign. It isn't a message. Sometimes with old houses, things go wrong."

I only wished I could believe him.

Hours later, my cell phone chirped from the nightstand. How did I end up in bed? Nick had come over to check on me. I remembered that much.

He'd helped me drain the basement for the second time that day. After we were done, he'd guided me up the stairs to the bedroom. A glance under the sheets at my undies confirmed Nick had seen me in my panties two times in one afternoon. A flood of more important thoughts pushed that one to the side. The broken window. The garden hose. The vandalism.

The fact that the person who would do these things knew where I lived.

I climbed out of bed and followed Logan to the bathroom. My reflection matched my condition: gray around the edges. I dressed in jeans and a heavy cowl neck sweater. After pulling on navy blue Wellies, I went outside to the back of the house.

When I first saw the broken window from the inside the basement, it was like my vision had a zoom feature. All I could focus on was the break, the jagged edges, the hose snaked through the opening. Now I wanted to find something else.

The window was about two feet wide by one foot tall and broken in the corner. A window well framed out a semi-circle of ground around it. The inside ground of the well was covered with pebbles and leaves. A rock sat to the side. Maybe it had been used to break the glass. Maybe not. At this point, it was hard to say. The surrounding ground had been tamped by footprints, probably my own. They wouldn't tell me anything.

I returned to the kitchen and sat at the table, staring out the back window. Someone had been right outside that window while I was passed out at Tradava.

I should call the cops. Report the vandalism. Maybe it wasn't connected. Maybe it was a prank, kids messing with their new neighbor. That would be a totally acceptable reason to call the police. I would not mention the competition. I would not mention Patrick. I'd say enough to get a patrol car assigned to my street. Detective Loncar probably wouldn't even learn of it.

I went back inside and called nine-one-one.

By the time the sedan pulled into my driveway, I was convinced I'd made a mistake. It wasn't an act of vandalism by bored high schoolers. Someone was sending me a message. I prepared to lie like a rug when Detective Loncar knocked on my door.

"Why are you here?" I asked, looking behind him for a couple of fresh-from-the-academy cops.

"Ms. Kidd, did you call the police?"

"I did."

"What seems to be the problem?"

"Isn't this a little minor for you?"

"When a person of interest in a homicide calls the police, word gets around. Especially when that person appears to be avoiding us." He pushed his elbows behind his back and tipped his head from side to side, as though he had cramps from spending too much time in the car. Come to think of it, he'd arrived pretty quickly. Had he been staking out my house? Had he picked my call up off a scanner? Was this tantamount to illegal entry?

"Person of interest? I'm a suspect?"

"You've been acting like one," he said. "May I come in?"

"I'd like to wait for back-up."

The detective stopped his limbering-up routine and coughed. He covered his mouth with a balled-up fist, then patted down the outside of his windbreaker. From an inside pocket he pulled out a cough drop and bit the end of the wrapper then used his teeth to extract the lozenge into his mouth.

"Back-up?" he said.

"You're not going to force your way in, are you?"

"Ma'am, that's not the way this works. You called me. I'm here. If you have a problem, you have to tell me. I'd suggest you do, because the call's been documented, and I don't think you should make a habit of reporting bogus crimes."

"Boy who cried wolf, and all that," I added, to show I was following. "It's a waste of department resources."

"Making false nine-one-one calls is a misdemeanor."

"Follow me." I walked the detective around the side of the house to the broken window. "When I came home this morning, the basement was flooded. I know it rained but not enough to flood it like it did. After I drained the basement, I noticed the hose dangling through the broken window."

Loncar stooped down by the window well and looked at the broken glass. He stood back up. He shielded his eyes even though he wore sunglasses. A breeze ruffled his crew cut and for a brief second, I thought he was taking me seriously. *He's going to help me. Calling the cops to report the vandalism was the right decision.*

"You said 'when I came home this morning.' You didn't spend the night here?"

And then I thought, *crap.*

"I, no, um, well, I didn't say that—"

"Ms. Kidd, if you were here, I'm guessing you would have heard the glass break, or you would have heard the water in the basement. I'm assuming you didn't hear it because you weren't here."

"I wasn't here."

"What time did you get home?"

"I think it was around nine."

He looked at his watch. "It's four thirty."

"I drained the basement, had a visitor, drained the basement again, and took a nap."

"And then you called in your emergency."

I nodded.

"Ms. Kidd, may I suggest in the future if you feel something is an actual emergency, you rearrange your schedule and make the call on a timelier basis?"

"I didn't know it was an emergency until it flooded a second time."

"And then you took a nap."

"You don't believe me, do you?" I asked suddenly.

"Your credibility is not at stake here."

He took a couple of pictures of my broken window and garden hose and jotted something illegible (from my upside-down perspective) in a small flip-top notepad. "Anything else you want to tell me? Are you going to say this is connected to Patrick's murder?"

"Absolutely not," I said in a voice that suggested I'd greatly improved my lying skills. "But I do think it's a good idea to send a patrol car around regularly. You know, in case whoever did this comes back."

Detective Loncar flipped the notepad shut. "Be smart, Ms. Kidd. Lock the doors and get that window fixed." He tucked the notepad into his coat pocket. "And if you suddenly determine this was related to Patrick's murder, call me." He handed me a business card. I was amassing a collection, but I took it anyway. It was the polite thing to do.

I followed him to the front yard. I wasn't up on the protocol for nine-one-one-slash-homicide-detective house calls and wasn't sure if I should offer him a cup of coffee while lying to his face. I stood by the garage door while he backed his car out of the driveway and drove away.

I pulled the sleeves of my sweater over my hands and wrapped my arms around my body. As the sun dropped, so did the temperature, leaving a chill in the air that rivaled the one in my bones. I went back inside and double-checked every lock on every entrance. I angled the green velvet sofa against the front door and sunk into the well-worn cushions.

Someone was making my life difficult. Why? I rubbed my hands over my face. When I dropped my hands and stared into the kitchen, I saw the pile of newspapers that hid Patrick's laptop. That laptop held the key. It had to. It was the only thing I had that someone else might want. And for some reason, Patrick had given it to me. Those conversations with him were starting to haunt me.

Patrick had asked me to meet him in the parking lot outside of Tradava the day before I started.

"I would have come to your office," I said.

"I enjoy the chance to get out every now and then." He handed me the plum messenger bag. It had a cross-chest strap and I couldn't imagine Patrick in his dandy attire ever wearing it.

"A colleague's idea of a gag gift," he said dismissively.

"Is there something specific you'd like me to review?"

"My current projects are saved on the computer. I'll expect you to be versed in them and offer your opinion when asked."

I took the bag and fought the urge to duck under the cross-chest strap in his presence.

"Samantha, there is something I need to discuss with you before you start." He sat on the bench next to me and we looked out over the sea of cars in the lot. "Working at Tradava will be different for you after life at Bentley's. Are you prepared for that?"

After all our talk about choosing our paths, his question surprised me.

"Different, how?"

"At a large store you can become somewhat invisible. At Tradava, people will see you. Our store team looks to us to give them a taste of the glamour of our industry, even if we don't always see it ourselves. Your problem-solving skills and creativity will serve you well here. You will be noticed."

"That's the question, isn't it? Be someone in a smaller environment or be no one in a larger environment. Big fish, small pond, or small fish, big pond."

"The eternal argument."

"Have you argued that argument?" I asked.

"Countless times."

"Have you won?"

"To myself, I have. To the industry, I can't be certain."

"Does that bother you?"

"Only on rare occasions." He stood from the bench and shielded his eyes, then turned to face me. "I look forward to seeing what you bring to the trend office, Ms. Kidd. I trust you'll be able to figure things out on your own."

I stood up and shook his hand.

That was the last time I saw Patrick alive.

I CARRIED the laptop bag from the kitchen to the sofa and looked inside. Aside from a stack of business cards wedged into a pocket, the interior was empty. But the more I thought about that conversation in the parking lot, the more I knew Patrick had expected me to figure something out. I pulled the stack of cards out and dealt them one by one onto threadbare sofa cushion. When I flipped them over, on the back of the last one, was written pw: LiVo72.

I went to the kitchen and typed the code into the password field.

The protected file opened!

It was the easiest thing I'd done in two days. And now it was time to discover what was so important that Patrick had hidden it in the first place.

14

DISQUALIFIED

THE FILE ON THE DESIGNER COMPETITION SPRUNG TO LIFE IN FRONT OF me. The first column said ENTRANT. Under it was a list of names. The first name was *CLESTES*, followed by fragmented commentary: *This is the work of a stylist, not a designer. The addition of a textile artist does not carry the collection. There is no DNA. Maries likes use of color and architectural elements.*

I continued down the page. *MICHAEL DUBRECHT: Needs time to develop. Interesting ideas. Is this talent or a fluke? Maries disagrees. Thinks there is nothing there.*

AMANDA RIES. *Fresh perspective. Innovative use of fabrics. Strong sense of design, proportion, color. New. Commercial. Ageless. Timeless. ORIGINAL. Shows much promise. This collection will be BIG. Maries says this collection could rewrite fashion history. I suspect she is right. Keep separate from Clestes to avoid clash.*

The last line on the file said *NICK TAYLOR: disqualified.*

Patrick had gone to great lengths to keep these notes hidden. His opinion of each designer was obvious, but that wasn't what struck me. I already knew he and Maries were the judges. So did everyone else. Of course there would be criticism of the collections.

The real question was why had Nick been disqualified? And what was he doing in the competition to begin with?

I looked over Patrick's notes one more time. If what I thought was right, one of these people had a lot to gain if they knew they weren't going to win the competition. I had to find out which one. A hundred thousand dollars would go a long way in helping someone disappear. And hiding Patrick's body for a couple of days would have given them a head start before the police started looking for them.

I pushed stacks of unopened mail and newspapers around the table until I found the envelope Maries had left behind. Inside were profiles on each of the designers. Four finalists, and a thick sheaf of papers for those who hadn't moved to the final round. I looked at the top application on the larger pile. The upper right corner was stamped with a grid. Dates and notations had been filled in: *Application fee processed. Collection sketches received. Feedback supplied with thank you for entering.*

Next, I looked at the pile of finalists. Nick's application was on top. The same grid was stamped in the same place. *Application fee processed. Collection sketches received. Finalists notified.* I flipped past Nick's page to Michael's. *Application fee waived. Collection sketches received. Notified.* A small, hand-drawn smiley face was next to the last word.

Michael hadn't paid his entry fees. I didn't know what to make of that. Had his position as Patrick's assistant earned him a free pass? And had that free pass included finalist status?

I flipped through the other applications. There had to be a clue in here, but I couldn't help wondering, seriously, if I was in the middle of a hoax that had gone awry. This was fashion. Outside of Gianni Versace, the words "homicide" and "high style" didn't belong in the same sentence. It was a stretch to think someone whose name was in this file had killed to keep it from being seen.

I set the pages on the table and looked back at the screen. If I were looking at what Patrick had wanted me to see, then the message was lost on me. I clicked around on a few different cells, then discovered a hidden tab. I unhid it and stared at a new page of information.

It was a list of Italian designers. Ten of them. The first eight were male, the last two were female. They were each listed by one name only, and I doubted a person without a passing knowledge of fashion would have known who they were.

I knew who they were. I just didn't know why they were in a file on Patrick's computer. What was he using them for? Why were they on a hidden tab in a protected file on his computer? The more I discovered, the less I knew. It was a frustrating place to be.

I called Eddie and asked him to bring me food. I returned to the computer. Twenty minutes later, Eddie pounded on the door. I closed the file and shut down the laptop, then spent a couple of minutes moving the sofa away from the front door. Eddie leaned in and looked around before entering. One hand held a Tradava shopping bag, the other carried a stack of white takeout containers. He set the Tradava bag on the sofa.

"Are you okay?" he asked. "You seem so calm."

"Calm? I'm freaking out. After I left you, I came home. Somebody vandalized my house."

"Dude—" Eddie started, but I cut him off. The amount of information I had to share was in direct relation to the caffeine I'd had, leaving him no opening into the conversation. "I called the cops to report the break-in, and the homicide detective came over. What is this, Chinese?" I asked, taking the containers from him and moving into the kitchen. He remained in the living room. "Can you imagine if I were here last night instead of Tradava? Somebody was *at my house.*"

"Dude, sit down and be quiet for a second."

"Sorry, sorry." I pulled an eggroll from one of the containers and bit into it. "Thanks for coming over. I'll make it up to you after I figure this thing out."

"I think you should move on."

I set the eggroll in the lid of the take-out container. "Move on?" I said calmly. "You want me to move on too?" He didn't speak, which was smart on his part because I wasn't done. "I moved here under the illusion that Tradava was going to be my source of income. Now my boss has been murdered, I'm a suspect, and I'm going to lose my house if I can't prove to the mortgage company that I have a job. Yesterday somebody broke a window and flooded my basement. I used to live in an apartment overlooking, well, overlooking a bunch of other apartment buildings, but the windows were made of glass. Now my window is made of duct tape. Why does everyone think I can move on?"

When he spoke, his voice was low. "Dude, the detective was back at the store. He knows Patrick was murdered and now he thinks Tradava was the crime scene. Somebody tipped him off that you went there last night, and his team found your fingerprints all over Patrick's office."

I balled up a paper towel and threw it at the trash can. It bounced off the rim and landed on the floor by a muddy footprint. Logan swatted it under the oven.

"Enough with the bad news. That's all there is. Right?"

"Not exactly."

"What else could possibly have happened?"

"They found an EMT jacket stuffed in the bottom drawer of the file cabinet in your office."

15

NO AMOUNT OF PRETENDING

"I looked in that drawer," I said. "It was empty." The memory felt like a lifetime ago.

He pulled a newspaper clipping from a cargo pocket on the side of his pants and held it out. "You need to be careful. If that drawer was empty, then that jacket was planted. Recently. It doesn't look good for you."

I took the clipping and scanned the story. *Fashion Director Murdered* was the headline. Lines like, "suspicious character in the store on the morning of the murder," "overwhelming class evidence," and "closing in on a suspect" gave me chills.

"Even if you're not guilty, you keep coming close to the killer. Sooner or later the cops are going to find the actual murderer. Until then you have to watch out. Okay?" When I didn't answer him, he spoke again. "I brought you a one-month supply of the *Style Section* to catch you up on the fashion world, since you're supposed to be a specialist." I ignored his attempt at humor. He pulled a mini bottle of wine out of the bottom of the bag. "I don't want to encourage you to drink alone, but this might help you forget what happened."

"But it did happen, Eddie. No amount of wine can make it go away."

"Dude," he said quietly.

I sat back, no longer hungry. By telling the detective about the vandalism, I'd told him I wasn't home last night. Worse, someone else knew I wasn't home last night. The someone who had left Patrick's body in a dumpster. The someone who had vandalized my window. The someone who was out to frame me.

"Do you need this?" Eddie asked, holding a receipt.

"For what? Dinner? Just tell me what I owe you and I'll give you the money."

"No, the food's on me. This was on your floor." He set the receipt on the table.

"Where's it from?"

"The fabric store." Logan hopped onto the table and I picked him up and put him back on the floor. He yowled and walked away. "Did you buy out the store? Is your strategy to wipe out the inventory, cut off the murderer's supply?"

"What are you talking about?"

"How expensive is that stuff anyway?" He pushed the receipt toward me with his elbow.

I picked it up. The receipt was from Pins and Needles. It was damp and smudged with mud.

"Seventy-four dollars of seam binding." I flattened it out with the side of my hand. "I must have tracked this in from behind the house." I set the receipt on the table.

Eddie stood. "You sure you're going to be okay?"

"Sure. As long as the sofa's up against the front door, I'll be fine."

"I'll call you tomorrow. Every hour on the hour. I'll give you until 11:00 to sleep in."

"Dude," I replied.

After Eddie left, I examined the receipt. Someone who'd been in my backyard had spent seventy dollars on seam binding. I suspected the talkative store manager at Pins and Needles would remember such a sale. I located the business card I'd swiped from Patrick's Rolodex and called the store.

"Thank you for calling Pins and Needles. This is Florence," said a friendly voice.

"Hi, Florence, I was in the store earlier today, and I was wondering if I could ask you a few questions about seam binding?"

"Who are you?" she said, her voice suddenly flat.

"Samantha Kidd."

"No! What are you doing? No!"

"Excuse me? Florence?"

"Get away from me!"

"I—Do you know who I am?"

"I'm going to call the cops if you don't leave!"

"Don't call the cops! Wait—leave where? I'm at home. What's going on?"

Muffled sounds filled my ear and then I heard *clunk.* "Florence?" I said. There was no response. "Are you there? Florence!" There was no reply.

I disconnected and redialed the number. Busy signal. I tried three more times with the same result.

I called the operator and asked her to ring the store. Within five seconds she was back, confirming my suspicions. The phone was off the hook. By now I realized why the brief conversation with Florence sounded off. She hadn't been talking to me.

I hung up then started to dial nine-one-one. I stopped before the second one. What if I was wrong? This would be my third call to them call in less than a week. I grabbed my handbag, and ran to the car. Traffic on the highway was light enough to get me to Pins and Needles in a matter of minutes. I parked by the entrance and ran to the door. It was locked, and the store was dark.

I slapped my palm on the front door. "Florence? Florence! Are you in there? Can you hear me?" I pressed my ear to the door. The only sound I heard was a faint tinkling of chimes.

Chimes. Like the kind I'd heard over the back entrance the last time I was here.

I raced around the other side of the store. Red taillights glowed at the edge of the parking lot then disappeared onto Penn Avenue. It was too far away for me to make out necessary details and I wasted no time trying. I yanked the door open and ran inside.

"Florence! Are you okay?"

It took a couple of seconds for my eyes to adjust to the darkness. As quickly as I could, I moved through the store with my hands in front of me. A body jumped out. I screamed. It fell over and I tripped. It was a bust form draped in fabric. I kicked it out of the way and stood back up. Slower, I moved to the cutting island where Florence had been earlier that day. I put my hands on the counter and made out the appearance of the phone base. Movement from the ground startled me. I peeked over the counter. On the floor, bound, gagged, and blindfolded, sat Florence.

"It's okay now. I'm here to help you," I said.

I crawled over the counter and knelt next to the store owner. I pulled a wad of fabric from her mouth, then took the blindfold from her eyes. She looked scared at first. "I'm not going to hurt you. I was on the phone when whoever did this to you did this to you."

"Scissors," she whispered and held up her wrists. I froze in place when I saw the tight lilac seam binding biting into her flesh. "In the drawer by the register."

I cut through the cords on her wrists and ankles. "Can I get you anything?"

"You can hand me the phone. I'm calling the police."

"The police—" If Florence called the police, she could tell them she was on the phone with me when she was attacked. They would know I couldn't be in two places at the same time. I shifted to all fours and felt around for the phone.

"What are you going to tell them?"

"I'll tell them who attacked me."

"You know who it was?"

She leaned to the left and reached under the counter. "Whoever it was dropped this." She held out a business card. I leaned close to read the details in the dark. It was one of Patrick's cards, only Patrick's name had been crossed out.

Unfortunately for me, my name was written in its place.

16

YES, THAT SAMANTHA KIDD

"Florence, that's me. I mean, that's my name. I'm Samantha Kidd, but I didn't do this to you."

"Hand me that phone, young lady," Florence said.

I handed her the phone and watched her dial nine-one-one. I stood up and looked around the store to make sure Florence's attacker was gone. Aside from the army of bust forms that I'd tripped over, we were alone.

"This is Florence Ingram. I am at Pins and Needles on Penn Avenue. Someone came into my store and threatened me and tied me up. Please send a police car." She stopped talking for a moment. I waited, not sure if I should stay or go. "A nice young woman, Samantha Kidd, came in to help me. Yes, she's still here with me. Yes, I'll do that." She hung up the phone.

"Samantha, the police will be here shortly, and it seems they'd like to talk to you."

I'm sure they would.

Avoiding Detective Loncar was high on my priority list but not as high as abandoning an innocent woman who had been attacked. Besides, I reasoned internally, if I stuck around, I might be able to learn something from Florence's statement.

I helped Florence into a folding metal chair and handed her a paper cup with water, then settled in next to a bolt of green paisley cotton and waited. Eleven minutes later swirling blue and red lights illuminated the windows of the fabric store. Florence tried to stand, but I could tell she was still shaking. "I'll let them in," I said.

I braced myself for whatever Detective Loncar was going to say when I opened the door, but he wasn't one of the two uniformed men in front of me.

One was about half a head taller than the other, with a smattering of freckles across his face. The other was Mexican, with dark curly hair and the beginning of a mustache.

"You called nine-one-one?" asked Mustache.

"The owner did. She's waiting inside." I led the two uniformed officers to the center cutting table. Florence wasn't there. I looked around in the darkness, not sure where she'd gone. The lights came on. The sudden change blinded me. I shut my eyes, then blinked rapidly until my sight adjusted. Florence appeared from a door in the back of the store.

"Hello officers, I'm Florence Ingram. I'm sorry if I startled you, but I don't like sitting around my store in the dark."

"Ms. Ingram, can you tell us what happened here?" asked Mustache.

I stood to the side while Florence described the attack. I wanted to listen, but Mustache and Freckles kept me from hearing much by standing between us and keeping their voices low. I picked up only the essential facts: she had been straightening the store before closing when the phone rang. She answered, and the lights went out. Someone grabbed her from behind, shoved a wad of cotton batting in her mouth, and blindfolded her, then bound her wrists with seam binding.

"Were you here with Ms. Ingram?" Freckles asked.

"No, I'm the one who was on the phone with her. I thought she was talking to me when she was talking to the person attacking her."

"You heard the attack?"

"I heard her asking what someone wanted. I thought she was talking to me."

"Maybe she was."

"No, she was talking to the person in the store, weren't you, Florence?"

"I'm a little mixed up between the phone call and the attack. I'm sorry, but I don't remember much about your phone call."

"I told you who I was, and your voice changed. You said 'Get away from me' then you said you would call the cops if I didn't leave." I turned to Freckles. "but I couldn't leave because I wasn't here. She had to be talking to her attacker."

"Ms. Ingram, can you corroborate that?"

Florence held out the business card she had shown me. "The person who attacked me left this behind." Freckles took the card and rubbed his thumb over the edge of it.

"I'm sorry, ma'am, I didn't catch your name," he said to me.

"Samantha Kidd. Yes, *that* Samantha Kidd," I said, pointing to the card. "But I didn't drop that card and I didn't attack Florence. I came to the store when I realized what happened and I waited until you arrived to make sure she was okay. Would I do that if I had attacked her?"

"Ms. Kidd, what's your contact info?"

I gave him my phone numbers, home and cell. Considering I'd switched off my answering machine and stopped carrying my cell phone to avoid contact with the mortgage company, there was no risk. I suspected I'd hear from Detective Loncar shortly but didn't tell them that. They were getting paid to make those deductions, and I was unemployed. I had a stronger sense of people needing to work for their paychecks these days.

My mind was abuzz while I drove home. For now, the cops were treating the attack on Florence as a burglary. But it was her card, the one Patrick's Rolodex had been open to, that had led me to her store, and it was my name handwritten on a Tradava business card left behind at the scene of the crime. There was a connection, I could feel it. I had to find out what it was. Because the cops would be looking for a connection too, and even I had to admit I was in the middle of something. If the cops were looking to connect the dots between the murder, the attack, and me, there were dots aplenty.

When I got home, I pushed the sofa in place in front of the door and wedged two wooden dining room chairs between the sofa and the hall closet. Tracks from the feet of the sofa were starting to tear at the shag carpeting. I closed Patrick's laptop, moved the competition applications to the junk drawer, and drank a juice glass of wine (Pebbles). I finished it in three swallows.

In my former job, the one I'd left behind, I'd demonstrated I was a problem solver. It was on every review I received. My problems these days were as big as they came, and it was time to see if the executives at Bentley's were right about my skill set.

Logan rubbed against my ankles and I scooped him up, held him close, and nuzzled my face into his shiny black fur. He licked at my fingers. The warmth of his body vibrated against me. I carried him to the bedroom and set him on the comforter. I changed into pajamas and dove between the sheets. So far, my move to Ribbon had been a disaster, but tomorrow was another day. Logan crawled on top of my chest and stretched out his paws so they touched my chin.

"The only person who can take care of me is me," I said to him. "Starting tomorrow, I'll show the world what a risk taker I am." I closed my eyes and failed miserably at sleeping until the sunlight told me to stop trying.

As promised, Eddie started calling at eleven. I didn't tell him about the fabric store. I told him I was laying low. I told him not to worry. I told him all of this while sitting in my car in the parking lot of the Ribbon Designer Outlets. And after I hung up, I turned off my phone and stashed it in my glove box.

Ribbon was neither a booming metropolis nor a small town. It was somewhere in the middle. The population had been on the decline since sometime in the thirties, but it had its own Pagoda on a hill overlooking the city. Ribbon had the fifth highest crime rate of cities its size and marginal Mexican food, but the pizza was excellent. Ribbon wasn't known to many people outside the Tri-state area, but those who do think fondly of it for two reasons: the pretzels and the outlet malls. Pretzels were a staple in Ribbon, ready to snack on at basketball games, picnics, and quilting bees. (I've never been to a quilting bee, but if I did, being raised in the eastern Pennsylvania region, I'd be upset if they didn't offer me pretzels.) We proudly call ourselves the pretzel capital of the world, providing an unparalleled assortment of the salty snack.

As proud as we are of our pretzels, we are even prouder of our outlet malls.

The off-price outlet mall can be traced to Ribbon. The first of their kind in the country, discount shopping venues on Moss Street and Penn Avenue offer everything from jeans to home furnishings to Japanese fighting fish. You could pay a couple hundred dollars to get a discount Ralph Lauren ensemble that originally cost closer to a thousand, or you could pay ten bucks for a velvet portrait of Elvis. I wanted neither a velvet Elvis nor a Japanese fighting fish. Today, I wanted information. I consulted the mall directory and located Catnip in the grand maze of retailers. I ducked into a few shops along the way and charged a respectable amount of merchandise to create the appearance of a non-threatening customer. Three return policies (confirmed) and one phone call to the credit card company verifying someone hadn't stolen my Visa, I reached my destination.

Catnip had softer lighting and far fewer customers than the other stores in the mall which indicated two things: exclusive merchandise and higher prices. Designer clothing, even severely discounted and bought off-season, cost more than most people were willing to pay. Red stood by a fixture, adjusting a display of leather skirts so the hangers were each an inch apart. She moved to a table of cashmere twinsets and refolded the lavender stack.

Her striking red hair framed her face. She was either less than one percent of the population or had a great colorist; I couldn't tell which. Tall and lean, with a body less curves and more angles, she approached me with confidence. She didn't acknowledge we'd met before. With an armload of packages, I looked like the perfect customer, and on a slow day, she wouldn't want to risk offending me. She offered to hold my bags behind the counter and I took her up on it because it would be easier to focus if I weren't bogged down with merchandise I already knew I couldn't afford.

I headed for the designer racks, trying to hatch a plan to chat her up.

"You look like you're losing your steam," she said.

"I think my last cup of coffee has officially worn off," I said as I flipped through satin blazers marked 75 percent off. "All that's left is a desire to accessorize."

She laughed. "A desire to accessorize can provide a lot of fuel. I know that first hand."

She motioned to the racks by the front of the store. They were peppered with signs identifying their creators: Donna Karan, Gucci, Escada, Nina Ricci. Other, smaller fixtures surrounded them, a mixture of merchandise from lesser known names.

"Your assortment is fantastic," I commented. "I'm not familiar with a few of your collections. Is this one new?" I asked, pulling an olive green satin army jacket from a fixture signed "Clestes." It was one of the names in the design competition.

She took the hanger and held the jacket in front of her. "One of a kind, handmade couture." She brushed her hand against the fabric twice, smoothing out invisible creases.

"Clestes," I said slowly. "Is that a man? Woman? "

"Both. It's a male-female team. Mostly unknown. He designs the textiles. She designs the patterns. I don't think their timing is good, but I do love the clothes. Would you like to try it?"

"No," I said a little too quickly. "Olive green isn't my color," I added.

"Perhaps this is more your style?" She held up a pinstriped suit from a neighboring rack.

I took the hanger from her and ran a finger down the black satin piping that set off the lapel. It was fabulous. A menswear-inspired jacket cut for a woman. The subtle feminine touches made it sexier than a sheer black lace dress. There was no label inside, only a couple of threads to indicate that one had been removed. "Who designed it?"

"I don't know. This came from a lot of designer apparel I bought sight unseen. The price for the lot was worth the gamble. What size should I pull for the pants?"

I played the role of enthusiastic shopper. She stayed by my side. Every time I got close to bringing the conversation toward Patrick she redirected my attention back to her merchandise. I finally admitted I was too tired to try anything on, and she took that as a cue to direct me to the register. I wished I'd met her under different circumstances, where I could invite her to lunch and we could talk about fashion instead of murder.

"You know a lot about the industry," I commented, looking for a way to bring Tradava into the picture.

"I was thinking the same thing about you. Where do you work?" she asked.

"I'm the trend specialist at Tradava," I answered in a what-the-heck moment. "Remember, I was there when you came looking for Patrick."

The color drained from her face. "Did you see the hat display? They're seventy-five percent off." She pointed to the rack next to me.

I wasn't going to fall for that. Hold on—was that a fuchsia fedora?

She turned around, put my selections on a small fixture, and punched a code into the register. For all her great customer service, she was now violating Rule #1 by keeping her back to me. If her behavior up to now had been any indication, it seemed my last statement had shaken her up.

I grabbed the bright pink hat from the rack and set it on the counter. "Add this," I said. She had to turn around to ring up the hat, and when she did, I was direct. "What do you think about Patrick's murder?"

She straightened her shoulders and lifted her chin slightly. With the back of her hand, she pushed her hair off her forehead and looked toward the stockroom doors then looked me dead in the eyes. "You want to know what I think? I can't say I'm surprised. Sooner or later, if you make that many enemies, the odds turn in favor of something like this happening."

17

FINAL SALE

THE BRAKES SLAMMED ON MY SHOPPING TRIP. IF IT HADN'T BEEN A metaphor, the store would have smelled like burnt rubber. "How well did you know Patrick?" I asked.

"Well enough to know he probably had it coming," Red said.

Our conversation was interrupted by a tall muscular man with tattooed forearms and sideburns who called out to her from the stockroom. "Yo, sis! That detective you called is on line two."

"Excuse me," she said to me and walked away.

She'd called Detective Loncar? When? And why? Maybe she *had* recognized me. Maybe she'd been chatting me up the way I thought I was doing with her. But no matter what, if Loncar was coming to her store, I wasn't going to be there when he arrived. He would have learned about my involvement in the attack at Pins and Needles by now and might not understand my reluctance to return his calls. I wasn't ready for that face to face conversation but despite five or six shopping bags of merchandise, I hadn't yet gotten what I came for.

The shop owner returned quickly. "I'm sorry about what I said. I've never been Patrick's biggest fan." She twisted her fingers in the long strand of pearls around her neck. It was the first nervous habit

I'd noticed, and it had started at the mention of the police. "Can I get you anything while you continue to shop?"

I couldn't leave without getting information. "You were at Tradava the morning Patrick died," I said, pushing the conversation in the direction I wanted it to go.

"Fashion's a big industry but a small world."

"And how did Patrick affect your world?"

"I'd rather not talk about Patrick," she said. By now the necklace had become a knot. We stood facing each other, separated by a table of clearance cashmere and the kind of static you get by rubbing a balloon against your sweater. "I know Patrick has a great reputation, but I'm not part of his fan club. My assortments are better than Tradava's, but I have to play the game just like everyone else. Right now, the name of the game is respecting the deceased."

I wondered where she'd put my purchases and if she'd notice if I fled the store and left everything behind.

"Do you need help carrying everything out to your car?" she asked, switching gears.

I couldn't leave yet. I needed a plan. "That would be great." She picked up the packages behind the counter and walked ahead of me to the back door. I jogged a few steps to keep up with her, then pointed to my car in the corner of the lot. When we reached it, I popped the trunk and took the bags from her.

"Thank you. I'll definitely be back."

She reached up to the lid of my trunk and slammed it down over the bags. "I don't know what game you think you're playing, but I don't want your business."

"Excuse me?"

She turned to look at her store, and then back at me. "I know you're not the trend specialist at Tradava, and I know you spent the last hour trying to get me to talk about Patrick. I heard you inserted yourself into the design competition and I don't like it. The cops are on their way, and if you don't want to talk to them, you better leave." She stepped away from the car. "Consider that merchandise final sale and find yourself another place to shop."

In stunned silence I drove home. It wasn't until I sat in front of my house that I questioned her unwillingness to talk.

IT TOOK me four trips to get my packages into the house. Well, three to get the packages inside, and another to round up Logan, who had decided the open door was a chance for him to test his freedom. Fortunately for me, when Logan escaped, he only got so far before the options confused him. Kind of how I felt these days.

It was late afternoon, and it was time to process what I knew. Time to think. I checked the answering machine before realizing I'd turned it off. I switched it back on and was halfway up the stairs when the phone rang.

"Dude, where have you been?" Eddie said. "You haven't answered either number."

"I turned off the machine and locked my cell in the glove box. Nobody good calls me. I mean, except you."

"You might reconsider when you hear why I'm calling." He was silent for a beat. "Loss Prevention called a meeting of the Tradava executives. We've been instructed to notify them if you show up or claim to work there."

I wasn't sure I heard him correctly. Of course, the (Wilma) glass I dropped when he said that shattered on the floor, which might have affected my hearing.

"Say that again?"

"I don't think I have to."

"No, I don't think you do."

I hung up. Three days ago, I'd optimistically thought my first friend in the store worked in Loss Prevention. Today, her department had put a target on my back. I wondered if she'd stood up for me: "She can't be all bad. She helped me carry a very heavy box."

Who was I kidding?

I crossed the kitchen to the pile of *Style Sections* Eddie had dropped off yesterday. The copy on top was the issue I'd flipped through during the night I spent at Tradava, the one with the picture of Nick inside. I used it as a dustpan, rounding up the broken glass shards from the floor, then threw it away and went upstairs to escape.

My thoughts ran in an abstract pattern, moving from question to question. Who killed Patrick? Would I look as good as Nick's date at the Designer's Debut Gala? Did I need to look for another job? Should I cap off my night of pampering with a glass of wine?

The answers were simple. I didn't know, unlikely, probably, probably not. I lined my purchases along the wall of my bedroom. Until I worked out the job situation, I had no business shopping. I showered and changed into a robe and went downstairs.

I fished the *Style Section* out of the trash and set it on the table. Nick wasn't the only one whose picture was in there. Amanda Ries was in there too, and it was time for me to learn how she was connected to all of this. I tapped one finger on the models in red coats on the cover and called Nick's now familiar number.

"Nick Taylor," he said.

I forced pleasantries into my voice. "It's Samantha," I said. "Kidd," I added, to match his professionalism. "Who is Amanda Ries?"

"Leave it alone, Kidd." He hung up.

I called him back.

"Nick Tay—"

"Why won't you tell me?" I demanded.

"—lor. With whom am I speaking?"

"What are you trying to hide from me?" There was a long stretch of silence. "If she's your date for the gala, just say so. And if she's involved in a homicide, I'll find out."

"I'll see you at the museum." He hung up a second time. I tried to crumble the newspaper up into a ball, but it was too big. I threw it across the room like a Frisbee.

Next, I called Tradava and asked for the visual department. Eddie answered on the second ring.

"When do you get off work?"

"I've been trying to leave for the past two hours."

"Can you meet me for dinner? Brother's Pizza, my treat."

"Be there in twenty."

I picked the *Style Section* off the floor and smoothed it with my hands, then rolled it up and stuck it into my handbag and added the stack of applications for the competition. I changed into a tweed tunic, jeans, and black boots, pulled a matching tweed hat over my ponytail, and left.

When Eddie arrived, he walked right past me. I waited until he doubled back, then lowered the newspaper I held in front of my face. "Psssst. Over here."

He dropped into the booth across from me. His eyes moved back and forth between my face and the hat. Blending in was new to me and apparently, I'd failed.

Chianti bottles dangled over our heads and velvet-flocked paisley wallpaper cocooned us from the twenty-first century. The flame of the candle between the oregano and crushed red pepper threw off an eerie red glow, thanks to the faceted glass dome around it. The original wood tables had remained in place since the seventies; kids probably came here to find their parents' initials carved inside a heart. If they ever tore out the interior for a renovation I could redo my basement in retro pizza chic.

I pulled the *Style Section* out of my handbag and pushed it toward Eddie. Coffee grounds smudged the face of the model on the left of the cover. "Page seven."

He unfolded the paper and flipped the pages. "It's a good thing my picture never ends up in here," he said.

"Why?" I looked across the table and gasped. Amanda the goddess's face, no longer a picture of beauty, had been creatively defamed with doodles. Her perfectly whitened teeth had been blacked out and a set of horns had been drawn on her head.

Somebody didn't like Amanda. And considering I was the one in possession of the newspaper, it seemed like that somebody was me. Embarrassing as it was, I reasoned to myself, it could be worse. I could have cut out a picture of my head and pasted it on her body.

I slammed a hand down over the doodling. "She's a finalist in the competition, and except for a chance sighting at Nick's showroom, I haven't seen or heard from her. That's suspicious, right?"

"Is that what you're all hopped up about? I would have thought it was the fact that she—"

I cut him off with a wave of my hand. "I'm not that shallow. Nick can date whoever he wants."

"You didn't let me finish. I thought it was because she used to have your job."

18

———

A BIG BLOW-UP

"Amanda worked for Patrick?" I asked. I remembered the word
ARIES on files in the cabinet. *A. Ries.* It was so obvious now. "When? Did you know her? Are you two friends?"

Eddie glanced around Brothers. "Dude, keep your voice down. Yes, she worked for Patrick. No, we weren't friends."

A waiter approached our table with a pizza. Eddie pulled two slices apart and slid one onto a paper plate, shaking crushed red peppers and oregano on it. He paused briefly to acknowledge my stare and tipped his head to the side. "I called ahead and ordered. If I left it up to you we'd never eat." He tore off a piece of the crust and bit into it, letting his slice cool on the plate.

"Amanda worked for Patrick for a couple of years. I don't think they got along. I don't think they *didn't* get along either, but there wasn't a real connection. She covered the accessories market and a few of the smaller designer shows Patrick didn't want to attend. I heard they had a big blowup when he wouldn't listen to her critique of a major runway show. She even went over his head to the executive committee, but they sided with him. She didn't show up for work for two weeks and everybody thought she abandoned her job."

"That's how she left?"

"No, she came back like nothing happened. It was weird. People used to talk about her freelancing but after she came back, there was an unspoken rule: don't get caught talking about Amanda. Nobody knows what she did during that time. I think Patrick gave her an ultimatum. Like, it was Tradava or whatever she was doing on the side, but she had to make a choice. Conflict of interest, I think. There was no room for advancement at Tradava if she kept working for Patrick."

"But if Patrick was out of the picture, she'd be in line for a promotion?" That could be motive, right? I wouldn't have minded if we found a tidy way to hang the murder on her, since it would clear me of all wrongdoing, get my job back, and leave Nick available for ten to fifteen years. Maybe less for good behavior. (Maybe I *was* that shallow.) "Why didn't you tell me this before?"

"Before when? Before two days ago you were a signature in my high school yearbook. Besides, I don't spend a lot of time in those offices. My home base is in the workshop with my staff. They actually work when I'm around."

"Doesn't this make her a legitimate suspect? She had means. She had opportunity. And Nick won't tell me anything about her."

"What's her motive?"

I pulled the stack of designer bios out of my handbag, flipped to Amanda's, and slapped it onto the table. "There's her motive." I jabbed the paper.

He looked over the information. "She says here Patrick is the one who encouraged her to enter. Explain how that would give her motive?"

"She's in the competition and she could have come and gone. No one would have suspected her. Why do I have to find a better motive? *I* don't have a motive! How come I'm under suspicion and she's not?"

"She used to work there. Any evidence of her presence was probably written off as normal."

"She doesn't work there now, and I bet nobody bothered to see if she skipped to Canada with a hundred G's in small bills." I slumped down in the booth and stared at my slice of pizza. I wasn't even hungry. "Whoever killed Patrick didn't seem like the murdering type." I continued. "Otherwise Patrick would have known who was threatening him. It must have been someone who didn't seem out of place at Tradava. And the EMT jacket in that bottom drawer, that's weird. Who could have gotten into my office without being noticed? Employees, that's who. Amanda. Michael. Both on the list of designers." I bit into the tip of a slice and immediately chugged water to cool my burnt mouth. "My money's on Amanda."

Eddie had a faraway look in his eyes, and I could tell he was looking for flaws in my logic. Gone were the jokes and sarcasm. Spread out in front of us was the assortment of designer bios, and pieces of the disjointed puzzle were coming together like panels on a quilt.

"What about security at Tradava? Don't they keep track of who comes and goes from your wing?" I asked.

"Security is there to protect the merchandise from being stolen from the store. They don't watch the corporate offices. It's our responsibility to lock the doors if we don't want people to walk in."

"Nobody seems to take that seriously."

"Michael took the responsibility very seriously, but he said his keys are missing."

"When did he say that?"

"This morning. He came in and I asked him."

"But they were in the office the day I started."

"How do you know that?"

"Because I took them."

"Dude!"

I tore a piece of crust from the pizza on my plate and dabbed it in a pool of grease. "Get this. Michael's entry fees were waived. And Florence, the woman at the fabric store, says he only shops the remnants because he's broke. He was there the morning Patrick was murdered, he was there when the body was found, and you said he was there today. That's a lot of coincidence."

"I never saw him as homicidal."

"It's always the ones you don't suspect."

"Okay, so we have another person with means and opportunity. What does his bio say?"

I flipped through more applications until I found Michael's. "Wait here," I said. I left Eddie at our table and went to the restroom. After locking myself in, I pulled my cell out and called the number on the application.

"MD designs," answered a high-pitched male voice.

"Michael, this is Samantha Kidd. We met a few days ago at Tradava. In the trend offices."

"Um, yes. I remember." His voice quivered, but I couldn't tell if he was nervous or if it indicated a residual note of puberty he'd never outgrow.

"I need to talk to you about the competition."

"You have nothing to do with the competition."

"That's not entirely true," I said. I paused for the briefest moment. When no counter-point followed, I continued. "I've reviewed Patrick's files and I have a few questions. Where and when can we meet?"

"What do you want?"

"I want to talk about the money."

"The money is in a safe place, and the person who is entitled to it will get it."

"You know where it is!" I said, perhaps a bit too enthusiastically, as indicated by the click on the other end of the phone. "Hello? Hello?"

This was news. Big news! Michael knew something nobody else did. Which bumped him up several steps on the scales of suspicion. I noted the address listed on his application and headed back to the table to share the news with Eddie. Problem was, he was no longer alone. Nick sat across from Eddie with a slice of my pizza on a plate in front of him.

"Fancy meeting you here," he said.

"Didn't we already talk about you stalking me?"

He shrugged, as though it was a possibility, which made me wish I hadn't joked about it.

I looked back and forth between the two men. Nick, in a camel hair blazer, white shirt, plaid scarf. His curly brown hair was slightly disheveled which made him look younger than he was. Eddie sat across from him, in a nylon windbreaker over a Green Lantern T-shirt. He'd shaved the side of his head on one side, not unlike his yearbook photo. Both looked comfortable in their skin even though they couldn't have appeared more different.

"Have you two been formally introduced?" I didn't wait for an answer. "Nick Taylor, Eddie Adams. Eddie, Nick. You guys should chat. You probably have a lot in common." They looked at me like two straight men who'd been set up on a surprise blind date. I grabbed the *Style Section* and designer applications off the table and shoved them into my handbag. "I gotta go."

I used my GPS to get to the address on Michael's application. It wasn't far. I passed several gas stations, one roller rink, and a beverage distributor before the numbers on the buildings came close to Michael's address. A small shed that sat back from the road. The mailbox out front said MD Designs in black plastic letters.

I parked next to the mailbox and got out of the car. The shed was the kind you could buy at Lowes and place on the back of your property line to store your lawnmower and tools. It wasn't a residence. I knocked on the door, but no one answered. There were no cars around. I walked to the back. A small blue Gremlin pulled up behind my car and Michael got out. I clutched my keys tightly and returned to my car. There was no way to hide now.

"What are you doing here?" he asked.

"I told you we needed to meet to discuss the competition."

"I don't believe you."

I thought quickly. His response, though argumentative, was not the same as saying he knew I was lying. I ran with it. "Patrick had your name on his calendar for today along with your address. I think he wanted to review your ideas."

"Patrick was a judge. The judges don't see the collections until they're done."

"Who sees them first?"

"Ms. Ingram, the consultant."

"Florence? From Pins and Needles?"

"If you were part of this competition you'd know that."

"Michael, we both know Patrick must have seen your collection. You worked for him and you're a finalist. I have a hard time believing you were able to keep everything secret from your boss."

He balled up his fists. "I knew someone would say I cheated! That's why Patrick didn't want me to know about the bank account or the sponsors."

"But you do know about them, don't you?"

"I'm not telling you anything." He looked at my fist. "Keys." I raised my hand and spread my fingers with the key ring hooked over my thumb so he could see I wasn't holding anything threatening. "You told Eddie your keys were missing, but I found them in the office."

"They were missing. After I get to work I put them in the bottom drawer of my desk. Always. When I couldn't find them, I told security. I told the detective too."

"What-who-when?"

"When he questioned me about you being at Tradava."

"What did you say?"

"That I never heard of you."

"But you were Patrick's assistant. He had to have told you about me."

Michael's deer-in-the-headlights stare relaxed into a smile. "You would think so, wouldn't you? But he's not around anymore so it looks like you're on your own."

"I'm not the person the police are looking for."

Michael snapped his fingers. "The police, that's right. Detective Loncar asked me to call him if I saw you again." He pulled out his phone. I didn't stick around long enough to find out if he made that call. I hopped into my dirty car and drove home.

Unfortunately, I had company.

19

──────────

PATRICK'S ENDORSEMENT

"I DON'T REMEMBER INVITING YOU OVER," I SAID TO NICK.

"You didn't." He rose from the porch swing and followed me into the house.

I headed directly to the freezer and pulled out a half-gallon of ice cream. "Make yourself useful," I said and pushed the carton and a couple of bowls toward him. When he wasn't looking, I shoved the *Style Section* into the trash and hid the computer. Nick tore a paper towel off the roll and wiped a blob of ice cream from the counter and then carried the soiled paper towels to the trash.

"You threw out the newspaper with my picture in it." He pulled out the *Style Section*. "I find that personally insulting. I'll forgive you if you tell me you didn't know my picture was in it."

I snatched the issue from his hand. Play dumb? Yeah, sure. I could stall him for oh, about ten seconds at best. "I didn't know your picture was in it," I said dutifully.

He snatched it back. "Let me show you. It's not every day the paparazzi takes my picture."

He opened the paper and pointed. You would think for all the times I'd looked at that picture I would have had a hard time faking surprise, but it came pretty easily. Largely because I wasn't faking.

The picture was unmarred by black ink. I gasped, which Nick misinterpreted as mild infatuation with celebrity.

"I had no idea you'd be so impressed," he said.

Where were the black teeth? Where were the horns? "When was this taken?" I asked.

"A couple of months ago. I was lucky to step in front of the press photographer at the right time. That photo got me a lot of exposure."

I wanted to ask him about the caption that identified Amanda but it felt like I'd be commenting on the elephant in the room. We stared at the newspaper in front of us, scooping ice cream into our mouths. I tried another approach.

"Do you attend a lot of benefits?"

"Not really. Now that I'm opening my boutique it's going to be more of a priority to attend industry events. You know, see and be seen. You never know who you're going to run into, or what could potentially be discussed at events like this. A lot of times it's just food, drink, and entertainment but sometimes you get lucky and end up seated next to a CEO, or a magazine editor is wearing your shoes, and you have a natural conversation waiting to happen."

"Has that happened for you?"

"A few times. I've had my collections in major retailers for a while. I already have connections in the industry but now that I'm limiting my distribution, I need to cultivate a different set of relationships. It's not all about market week, potential department stores, and buyers anymore. Now it's about editorial coverage in magazines, a loyal client base, and capital."

"How exactly did you go about getting the funding to go solo?"

"It wasn't easy and it's still not a done deal. Getting referrals from people in the industry, especially at a store like Tradava, helped. Without Patrick's endorsement, I might have been looking at an entirely different set of circumstances. You have to find backers willing to invest in your business plan but let you follow your vision. Sometimes these backers have ideas of their own, and the designer's vision gets lost. Best case scenario, you find a way to get the money with no strings attached."

I thought about the hundred large attached to the design competition and wondered again about the strings Patrick had pulled to get the funding. "A large windfall could help a new designer."

"For designers starting out, yes. Being in the right place at the right time doesn't hurt, either. Publicity, getting people to know your name." He gestured toward the newspaper picture. "That's what Amanda was hoping, at least."

"Could winning the design competition help you?" I asked tentatively, immediately wondering if I'd blown the only opening I had to get him to talk about Amanda. But Nick had never mentioned his connection to the competition, and I didn't know if there was bad blood there.

Nick looked at me sharply. "Why would you ask something like that? I'm not in the competition."

"But you entered. I saw your application."

"Amanda entered me without asking. Technically it's a design competition and I'm a designer. A couple of interns processed the paperwork and I got lost in the shuffle. When Patrick saw the candidates, he was afraid it would look bad to say there had been a mistake, so we agreed he'd disqualify me. Stop guessing at things that have rational explanations, Kidd. If that's what's been bothering you, you should have asked me."

My mind wandered to the money. The contest. The contacts. The guaranteed order from Tradava. It would have been easy for an insider to gain favor from the judges by being closer than the competition. Amanda would already have friends on that judging panel. If her history with Patrick was less than favorable, his vote might not have gone in her favor. That might be something worth killing for. And Nick's behavior, while temporarily explained, was still off. There was a reason he'd told me to stay away from Amanda and I still didn't know what it was.

Suddenly I wasn't feeling so great. I carried my empty bowl to the sink and ran cold water over my wrists. "Do you know how I can get in touch with Amanda? If I want to ask her some questions?" I asked.

Nick's spoon clinked against the bottom of his bowl. "I don't think that's a good idea," he said without looking up.

"Why not? She used to work at Tradava. Maybe she can give me some tips."

He pushed his bowl away from him with a shove. "I'm warning you, Kidd, keep Amanda out of this."

It was like a slap in the face. "Keep Amanda out of what?"

He leaned back against the kitchen counter and glared at me. "She's moved on and you should too."

"Yeah? I'm trying to move on but the world, life, isn't cooperating!" I leaned forward and waved my arms around. "That's what this whole move to Ribbon was about—moving on. Only I can't, Nick. I can't move on because there are walls all around me, closing in. I can't move forward or backward or sideways."

His expression softened. "Come here," he said and opened his arms. I kept my distance. His arms dropped to his sides. "I guess the transition to Tradava has been tough on you."

"Things at Tradava are fine," I snapped.

"Are they?" He stared at me. Long enough for me to wonder how much he knew about my predicament. Long enough for me to crack under the pressure of his eye contact and look away. Long enough to realize how that must have looked to him and to look back.

He picked up his jacket. "I'll show myself out." I followed him, my nerves fraying as we walked. When we reached the door, he turned around, catching me off guard. "You're not as alone as you think you are, Kidd. You're the one who's building those walls." The sweetness of his smile was disarming.

I stared into his deep brown eyes, this time not breaking the connection. A few seconds later he turned around and left. I shut the door behind him and triple-locked it.

I didn't waste time pushing the sofa in front of the door. I raced to the newspaper on the table to figure out what was going on. I checked the cover, then flipped through the pages one at a time. When I got to the page with Nick and Amanda, a round stain on the opposite page stared back at me. No horns. No blacked-out teeth.

That meant there were two newspapers. These newspapers had come from Tradava. This could mean only one thing.

Someone at Tradava disliked Amanda more than I did.

I SPENT the balance of the evening reviewing what I knew. None of this would be an issue for me if I hadn't met Patrick. But now, no matter which way I turned, all roads led to him. Aside from my observations during our interview, what did I know about him?

Were there people who missed him? Did he leave behind family? Was anyone sad he was dead besides me? Was there going to be a memorial service? To find the real killer, I had to know more about the victim. More than I'd learned from our interviews or from sleeping under his desk. I had to study his life, his patterns, and his history like I was following a seam to figure out how best to alter a dress. If I followed the stitches I'd eventually come to the starting point and ending point, hopefully without fraying my nerves in the process.

I went to work, writing up notes. *Who was Patrick? Critic. Mentor. Judge. Boss. Tastemaker. Famous. Fashion Insider. Powerful.* I scribbled over the preprinted blue lines on the blank page. Next: *Eliminate clues that lead to me.* That made me sound guilty. I lined through it and wrote: *Find other suspect(s). Why kill Patrick? Career advancement. Blackmail. Revenge. Inherit his 'power of the pen.' Falsify his recent reviews. Information on laptop. DESIGN COMPETITION.* Other thoughts flowed from my mind. *Strangled with seam binding? Seam binding—fabric store—Florence. How does she tie in?* I wondered about the ally I thought I had in Nick and realized I still wasn't sure of his innocence. *What is Nick hiding?* He had a relationship with Amanda, who had a lot to gain by Patrick's untimely death. *Find out truth about Amanda.*

I underlined that last part twice.

I didn't need Nick's permission or blessing to talk to Amanda. I had her contact information in the file of applications. I hit *67 to hide my return number then called her. She answered on the third ring.

"Could I speak to Ms. Amanda Ries, please?"

"This is Amanda."

I paused and scanned the bookcase looking for an alias. "This is Donna Parker calling from the *Style Section*."

"Donna Parker? Like the children's mystery series?"

Crap. "Um, no. Donna Poker. Like the card game." Stop babbling! "I'm checking facts for a story on Patrick." I let my voice trail off. "I understand you worked for him at Tradava?"

"That's correct."

"And you're a finalist in his design competition?"

"That's true too."

"Can you tell me anything about the competition?" I asked in a sudden bolt of ingenuity.

"Ms. Poker, if you're interested in talking about this, we need to meet face to face to talk. I know a few things that might help you out."

20

CHICKENS IN A CAGE FIGHT

I made arrangements to meet Amanda at the public library. I didn't care what Nick had said. I wasn't letting this opportunity go to waste.

The library stood in the downtown district and inspired happy thoughts and a fascination with the concept of trust since childhood. Information coded in a small plastic card told the staff behind the desk that I could take things for free and be trusted to return them.

Amazing.

An eerie silence, more so than the usual library quiet, cloaked the building. Scruffy men in need of a shower read the newspapers and magazines to the left of the circulation desk, but the research terminals to the right were empty. I wandered the aisles and found a copy of *Who's Who: Fashion Edition*. Balancing the book on my knee, I flipped to the R's. There was nothing where Ries, Amanda should have been. I shut the book harder than intended and a puff of dust fluttered in the sun's rays. I mouthed an apology to the librarian.

A brief search of the library's database led me to several back issues of fashion magazines that referenced Patrick. I keyed the articles up, one by one, and read through *Mirabella, Mademoiselle,* and

Glamour. Vogue carried a featurette on him as part of their "People Are Talking About . . ." series.

It was the cover that was blown up to poster size and hung on Patrick's wall. The Patrick that smiled at me from the picture accompanying the article was a much younger man than I'd interviewed with weeks ago. One picture showed him standing next to Halston. The caption read: *Jersey? Sure!* Another showed him clinking champagne flutes with a woman with white hair and trademark black glasses. The caption read: *Celebrating Carrie Donovan's "29th" birthday.* Patrick had hung out with fashion royalty, that was for sure.

After reading the articles from the magazines, I moved my attention back to the *Who's Who.* Patrick's reputation blew me away. He had had an eye for talent. He was credited with being one of the first American tastemakers, calling attention to stateside artisans once anonymous but now common knowledge. Article after article called him a friend to the unknown designer, encouraging those with talent to go out on their own and not let their careers be defined by the powerhouse labels that gave them their start. I saw what Maries had meant when she said the design competition was Patrick's legacy. Establishing a forum for new designers was a big deal, and the success of the first competition would allow for subsequent contests.

I read on. These journals painted a picture of someone who had impacted the lives of young students of fashion. Patrick had been in the industry for decades, so it was possible his encouragement could have motivated a newcomer to go solo years ago and now be successful. Tradava was probably filled with assortments from people he'd discovered, those indebted to him for giving them their foot in the door. Recipients of glowing reviews had probably moved on to bigger and better collections, leaving behind nothing more than a few leftover markdowns on a clearance rack.

Patrick had a reputation for exposing new talent, but from what I'd read, he hadn't discovered anyone recently. The changing face of the industry had left critics like him behind while reality shows and celebrity endorsements "discovered" the next big thing. The industry he loved had moved on without him. But then, he had decided to create a local competition.

This year.

Coincidence?

He had joined Tradava years ago to be a big fish in a small pond. Was that all there was to his move? A high-profile fashion director could exist comfortably at Tradava. A family-owned department store wouldn't challenge him, an industry legend, to make or break anyone's career but rather would hope his reputation would lend them credibility. It was the perfect co-dependent relationship until Tradava pulled the plug on Patrick's plans for the competition.

When Patrick turned elsewhere for funding, he made a statement that he was still relevant. If only I knew where he had gotten the money. Or where it was now.

Other than this competition, Patrick seemed to live a quiet life. He had no enemies. Greed seemed to be the best motive for murder I'd discovered, and my research solidified the fact that the finalists in the folder at home represented those with the most to gain.

The librarian approached me with a thick, bound journal under her arm. "Would you prefer this copy?" She said. "It was returned while you were reading." Met with my confused silence, she continued. "Another patron finished with it."

"Thank you," I said automatically, while I craned my neck to see the figure who had left the library. The windows were smudged, restricting my view. A flash of red punctuated the gray figure but from this distance, I couldn't make out the details. Was that red hair peeking out from under a hat, a red scarf knotted around someone's neck, or just a red herring?

I turned the new volume of *Who's Who* to the 'R' section and looked up Ries, Amanda. There she was.

Amanda Ries was indeed listed as a new designer. She had schooled at I-FAD, the Institute of Fashion, Art, and Design, had won design awards in local competitions, and had shown a capsule collection from a hotel room in New York a few years ago. It was the only collection cited.

There was nothing about her time at Tradava, which didn't surprise me. Our position was an assistant to the director, so it wouldn't merit a mention in *Who's Who*. The thing that stood out was even though she had been the trend specialist at Tradava there were no unaccounted for years on her design history. The journal wrote of time at school and her scheduled collection debut this year.

I reread the last line.

A collection debut this year.

The same year Patrick had decided to launch a competition.

Patrick's endorsement might have made a difference in her success, but an unflattering review would have killed those opportunities. Amanda was a finalist in the competition that he would have reviewed, and he wasn't around to give his opinion. The timing seemed suspicious.

I flipped to the T's and read about Nick.

Instead of following the well-trod path of most designers, design school and internships, Taylor interrupted his schooling to gain experience working for local cobblers, to understand how to construct footwear like a couturier constructs a garment. He spent his nights pursuing a double major in fashion history and business, graduated with honors, and licensed his name.

While his schooling could easily have landed him a sought-after position at an established fashion house or director of fashion at a respected retailer, he chose instead to partner with financiers to produce his shoe collection. His knowledge of the ins and outs of fashion and the business acumen gained in college put him a clear step ahead of other designers vying for editorial attention and orders from retailers. Uncredited, he collaborated with several ready-to-wear designers to produce shoes for their runway shows, building a solid network in the business, and believes these contacts led to his early success. After years of successful partnership between Taylor and his financial team he stunned again in a bold move to buy back controlling interest in his name, scale back distribution of his collection, reposition his line at a more attainable price point. It is unknown if this risk will pay off.

The article mentioned details of his graduation from the same fashion institute Amanda had attended. The same year. And knowing he and Amanda met in college disturbed me more than that photo in the *Style Section*. There was something about college friends that allowed them to drop in and out of each other's lives. Those bonds withstood just about anything. I wondered if the same applied to Eddie and me. Could I count on his loyalty if I needed it?

I approached the librarian at the checkout desk. "Can you tell me who returned this?" I asked in what I hoped to be a conversational tone. She looked at me suspiciously, then shook her head.

"Nobody returned it. It's reference material and can't be checked out." She took the volume from my hand and set it on a shelf behind her. "Another patron had been reading it, much like you were."

"Who?" I asked. "Was it a man or a woman? Can you tell me anything about them?"

She stared at me for a few seconds. "That would be a violation of privacy. Why are you so interested?"

"I'm new in town and just started a job in fashion. I thought maybe I'd find someone with the same interests as mine."

The librarian fingered glasses that hung on a chain around her neck. "Fashion, you say?" She bent down and pulled a manila file folder from the trash. "A man called a couple of weeks ago and asked me to run copies from our stacks. He said he would send his assistant to pick them up. I threw the file away this morning while I was cleaning." She handed me the folder.

I flipped it open and discovered copies of magazine articles from back issues of *Vogue*. The top one was the "People are Talking About . . . Patrick." The following articles were on each of the designers listed in Patrick's protected file. Each copy was dated on the upper right corner in cursive handwriting.

"Are you sure it was a man who asked you to make these copies?"

"Quite sure."

"May I have them?"

"Five minutes ago, they were in the trash, which is where I'll return them if you don't take them with you."

I doubled the folder over and stuck it into my bag. As if to prove she was telling the truth about the trash bit, a smudge of ketchup smeared across the corner and left residue on my thumb. I looked around for a tissue box but found none. Instead, I found myself standing face to face with Amanda.

Perfectly straight jet-black hair, a lilac wool tunic belted over brown tights and boots, and a stunning lavender handbag. While I would have known her anywhere, the recognition wasn't two-sided. I put on my best poker face, fitting, for more reasons than one, and held out my hand. "Amanda Ries? Donna Poker. From the *Style Section*."

"You? You asked me here to talk about Patrick?"

"Yes." I stepped away from the librarian who had evidence in the form of a library card application that I was lying about my name. "Can I buy you a cup of coffee?" I asked.

"You can stop the charade, *Ms. Poker*," she said. I didn't like the way she emphasized my alias. Made it sound fake. She glared at me and I forced myself to maintain eye contact. Looking away would have been too obvious of a tell. "I don't buy your cover story for a second. Are you a spy for Clestes?"

"Clestes?" I blurted. "Your competition?"

"You might want to check your facts a little better." She leaned in and I smelled peppermint on her breath. "I don't know who you are or what you want, but you work for the *Style Section* about as much as I do. If you're looking for facts, let me tell you one thing." She flipped a lock of black hair behind her shoulder, glanced toward the librarian, then back to me. She leaned in, well into my dance space, and I pulled back involuntarily, then immediately regretted the move and leaned forward too. I had the feeling that, to anybody watching, we looked like a couple of chickens in a cage fight.

"Patrick and Maries have given me consistent encouragement and Florence has been impressed with everything I've done so far. Don't get in my way. I *will* win that competition." She stormed past me and pushed against the heavy wooden doors. I followed.

"Florence Ingram was attacked at the fabric store," I called out behind her. "You know anything about that?"

Her hand reached out for the banister and her knuckles went white as she gripped it. Her left foot dangled over the step long enough for me to notice she was shaking. She continued her descent down the concrete stairs to the sidewalk.

More slowly, I descended the stairs too, then unlocked my car and flipped through the articles in the folder. I could think of only one man who would take the time to have a file of articles copied and never pick them up. The same man who had a list of designers on his computer in a protected file. The man who may have had every intention of sending his new assistant to the library to pick up the file.

Patrick.

I drove to Tradava. I needed to get into the gala and the Tradava connection was my best shot. It wasn't until I sat in the parking lot outside of the store that I questioned my motives. Was this yet another in a cumulative string of bad decisions? Was my judgment completely in left field, or was I getting closer to figuring out who killed Patrick? I didn't know but now didn't seem like the time to question my instincts. After all, I'd recently bought a fuchsia fedora for seventy-five percent off and there was no lemon meringue in sight. Clearly, my judgment was fine.

I found a driving glove in the glove box and dug its mate out from under my car seat. After snapping them on and disguising myself oversized sunglasses and the pashmina I'd swiped from Patrick's office, I went into the store and headed straight to the trend offices.

There was a strip of yellow tape across the glass door, but it had already been sliced through. I pushed on the door and it swung open easily.

Someone else had been here. Recently.

The desk had been cleared of Patrick's inbox and the papers I'd left behind and set up with a sewing machine. A mess of fabric cuttings, lace, and trim covered the purple sofa. A bust form stood half-pinned with origami folds of taffeta in shades of lavender, orchid, and black. Pieces of chartreuse lace lay on the floor along with a long strip of lilac seam binding. The color palette was rich and sophisticated.

I crossed the hallway to Michael's desk and called Eddie. A black and white photo peeked from the base of the phone. I freed the picture, immediately recognizing the two people in the photograph, even though one of them had been covered with horns and a mustache. It was a picture taken outside the diner Eddie and I frequented the day I found Patrick's body. The Devo logo was legible on the front of Eddie's T-shirt. But the person he was talking to, the person with a knife drawn stabbing her in the heart, with blood droplets drawn down her gray tweed cape, pooling around her purple patent leather pumps was me. The words GET HER were scrawled on the side of the picture, and the handwriting was undeniably the same as that on Michael's calendar of tough-talking women.

I slipped the picture in an envelope and put it in my pocket. Eddie's machine picked up. "Eddie, it's Samantha. I'm at Tradava, and I'm freaking out. I think I stumbled onto something"—I heard noises out front. "Call me."

I hung up and hurried into the hallway. Just as I rounded the corner, I felt a blow to the back of my head. I fell to the floor and blacked out.

21

CREEPY GAME

"KIDD? YOU WITH ME?" ASKED A VOICE THAT SOUNDED LIKE IT CAME from the other end of a tunnel. "Yo, Kidd, come on, wake up." Somebody jostled my shoulder repeatedly. "Samantha?"

I moved a little. My head pulsed with pain. The voice saying my name got closer, and when I finally opened my eyes, I saw a very unfocused Nick. He joined me on a sofa outside the customer restrooms.

"Are you okay?" he asked.

"What happened?" I tried to remember. "Why are you here?" I looked at him again. I wasn't supposed to be at Tradava. I had to get out of there before someone recognized me. I tried to stand. Nope, not ready to walk just yet. I touched the back of my head, felt a lump, and dropped my hand to my lap.

"I found you sitting here by yourself. I said hello a couple of times and you didn't answer me. I was going to give you a hard time, but when I sat, you slumped against me. You gave me a scare, at least until I felt your pulse. What are you doing here?"

"I-I don't know." I had been in Patrick's office, but now I wasn't. My fingers returned to the lump at the back of my head. I'd been knocked out. But how had I come to be sitting on a bench outside of the ladies' lounge on the fifth floor? "Work," I said. Paranoia was back, and I was in a distrustful mood. I needed more time to think about what had happened when I was in the office. "Get away from me," I said, pushing his arm.

"Calm down." Two short, round ladies in hats walked out of the ladies' lounge and smiled at us. Nick put his arm around me and smiled back.

"Let go of me," I hissed.

"Kidd, I don't know why you're mad at me, but I didn't do anything." He smiled his eye-crinkling smile, and I wanted to believe what he said more than I didn't. His phone rang and he glanced at the screen. "I have to take this. Wait here."

"Okay," I lied. As soon as he turned the corner, I stood up on shaky legs. Dizziness overcame me, and I reached out to the wall to steady myself. I could leave. I could go right now before Nick returned.

I fingered the envelope in my jacket pocket then pulled it out. On the back was a hastily scribbled note. *You are wasting your time. I can prove you murdered Patrick if you get in my way.*

I sank back into the sofa. Someone had been in the trend offices. Someone had deliberately knocked me out. The envelope was empty, the photo I'd found on Michael's desk was gone. If I had any doubts about being watched, set up, or knocked out, they'd just been erased. And it wasn't bad luck that made me look guilty. Someone was orchestrating all of this. The magnitude of the situation hit me. Was I scared? Sure. But I was pissed off too. Someone was making a mockery of my fresh start in Ribbon, tearing out the seams of my carefully planned new life and throwing bleach on the vivid colors of possibility. Everyone around me wanted to stop me from discovering who that person was.

Nick returned. I stuffed the envelope back into my pocket before he could ask about it and stood back up.

"I didn't think you'd wait," he said.

"I told you I would."

"I assumed you were lying. Come on, I'm getting you out of here."

I begrudgingly accepted his offer.

When we reached the parking lot he directed me toward his white truck, against my constant claims that I could drive myself home. "I don't know what happened to you back there, but you're in no shape to operate heavy machinery. Get in."

"I don't want to leave my car at the store."

"You don't have a choice."

"I'm not drunk, and I didn't take prescription medication."

"Exactly. But you were passed out on a bench and you won't tell me why. I'm taking you home so you can rest." Our standoff ended when Nick picked me up and threw me over his shoulder.

"Put me down!" I said and pounded on his back. He ignored me until we reached his truck. I could have elbowed him in the ribs and tried to run away, but even I knew I wouldn't have gotten far.

Nick drove to my house in silence. Our relationship had taken a weird turn a couple of days ago and was still in uncharted territory. I didn't know if we were better or worse for all of the changes. By the time we reached the house I was too tired to function. I tossed my coat on the sofa. The envelope fell out of my pocket and landed on the floor by Nick's feet. He bent down to pick it up and tapped it against his thigh a couple of times before tossing it on the table. A nagging voice at the back of my head said I needed to get him out of my house. I think it came from the same area as the bump.

"May I have that?" I asked, nodding at the envelope.

He folded the envelope in half and thrust it at me. "You're not still going to the gala, are you?"

"Of course, I'm still going. It's an industry event, right? I work in the industry."

"It's going to be boring. And I'll be there, so if anything happens, I'll let you know."

Heat flared up around my neck. "Look, Nick. Just because we had a moment over lemon meringue pie doesn't mean I'm blind. If you're trying to string me along while you date your girlfriend, that's not going to happen. I appreciate you helping me out today, but don't think you can tell me what to do. I'll go where I want, when I want. With who I want. Got it?"

He leaned forward, his forearms resting on his thighs. "I'm worried about you," he said.

I hated not knowing his motivations. On one hand, I wanted to show him the threat on the envelope, tell him about the suspects, and ask if I could be a third wheel on his date with Amanda. On the other hand, he knew something and was keeping it from me. And if Amanda was the one guilty of murder, that made him an accessory, and not the kind you coordinate with your shoes.

"You look like you want to talk about something," he said.

Fight the temptation to tell him what you're thinking. "I'm tired, that's all."

"Then get some rest." Unexpectedly, he kissed me on the forehead, then stood up and left. I threw the locks shut behind him and turned off the lights. As I drew the curtains, I saw the outline of a man detach himself from a bush in front of my house.

Someone was outside my house. Right now.

And I was alone.

A flashlight would have been handy, but I was unprepared for this emergency. Mental note: leave flashlights everywhere.

The last time I lived here and had to rely on my senses in the dark was when I was ten years old playing hide and seek with my older sister. She'd turn off all the lights and give me a head start. In the pitch-black house, she would try to find me, while I either stayed hidden, or moved from spot to spot to stay unnoticed. In hindsight, it was a creepy game for a ten-year-old to play.

But creepy or not, it had left me with the knowledge of how many steps it took to get from one room to another. The statistics were burned into my memory. Nine steps would get me to the kitchen. Eleven to the counter. Twelve to the phone.

At the ninth step, I ran into the stool tucked under the counter and knocked a stack of metal mixing bowls onto the floor. They rolled in a circle, sounding an aluminum alarm to anyone in a five-block radius. The phone fell to the floor and an insistent beep replaced the dial tone.

I guess my legs were a little longer than when I was ten.

A shadow approached my front door. I pressed my body to the base of the counter. Slowly I extended my right leg, pointing my toes like a prima ballerina, and tried to snag the cord of the phone with my foot. The man moved from my front door to my bay window, his silhouette distorted by the curtain. He reached inside his coat for— what? A knife? A gun? A lead pipe?

From the living room, my cell phone ring pierced the silence. The man out front returned to the door again. I moved, fast, scrambling from the kitchen to the living room for my phone. The ringing stopped. I switched the ringer to mute. A few seconds passed, and my phone vibrated. I sent silent messages to the caller. *Leave a message. Come check on me. You should think it's weird I'm not answering the phone.*

The man out front rapped his fist against the living room window. "Dude, I know you're in there. I just saw you. Let me in."

Eddie.

I unlocked the locks and pulled the door open.

"Took you long enough. Where have you been? I've been calling you since I got that message from you at Tradava. What happened?"

"Follow me," I said. I righted the kitchen phone and restacked the metal mixing bowls. I poured two glasses of water (Fred Flintstone and Barney Rubble) and handed one to Eddie. "There was a photo on Michael's desk. A picture of you and me outside the diner. Someone drew a knife stabbing me in the heart. And blood droplets and a pool of blood around my boots. It said 'get her' along the side of the picture. I put the picture in an envelope and took it, but someone knocked me out. I woke up on the fifth floor next to Nick. Empty envelope, bump on my head."

Eddie gulped half of his water. He leaned against the kitchen table. Logan buzzed his ankles. "You have to call the cops. This is beyond detective games."

"You think that's what I'm doing? Playing detective games?" I drained my glass and considered refilling it with vodka. "Think about it from my perspective. Someone is out to get me." I picked up the driving gloves I'd worn to Tradava, lined up the fingers, and set them in a neat pile on the countertop.

"Can I see the envelope?" Eddie asked.

I tossed it on the table between us. He turned it over and read the threat, then set it on the table. "Dude, I'm telling you, go to the cops."

"I don't think so."

"Don't be stupid. That's a threat. I mean it's a clue. I mean, it's both."

"Is it? Loncar hasn't believed one word of what I've said so far. If I take this to him now, what's to make him believe me? I could have written this myself. And it's not just Patrick anymore. A woman was attacked at the fabric store. The owner. She was the consultant to the finalists of the competition. She might have been killed if I didn't show up. But Loncar doesn't believe that either."

The phone rang. We stood in the dark, staring at it until the machine clicked on. "This is Brittany Fowler from Full Circle Mortgage. If you don't return my call in twenty-four hours, we're going to start foreclosure proceedings." She hung up.

"What am I going to do?" I said.

"If you don't go to the cops, I will," Eddie said.

"Give me a day." I looked at the phone and then back at him. "Give me the same twenty-four hours the mortgage company is giving me. Let me get through the gala and see what I can find out."

"I don't feel good about this." He stood up and crossed the room to the front door, then turned back around. "Twenty-four hours," he said.

22

LEMON MERINGUE PIE

Eddie didn't understand my reasoning for not calling the police, and I didn't waste time trying to explain. I shuffled him out the door, then filled Logan's bowl with vanilla ice cream. He sniffed it, patted it, then licked his paw. I lowered myself to the floor, opposite him, and scooped a mound of ice cream from the carton into my mouth. After it melted on my tongue I swallowed, then reached my hand out and stroked Logan's black fur. "If the cops take me away, who's going to take care of you?" I asked him. He turned his yellow eyes toward me and yowled. Traces of ice cream coated the tips of his whiskers. I pulled my hand back, ate another scoop, and let him eat in peace. My mind, hopped up on Breyer's, wandered to Nick.

His presence at Tradava. The ride home. The right place/right time coincidences.

When I was a buyer and Nick was a vendor, he needed my relationship—the professional one—to ensure his success. From the moment I met him, years earlier, I felt an attraction to him and if I read the signs right, he felt it too. But getting involved with one of my vendors was strictly verboten. I'd had to remind myself of it on more than one occasion, especially on those nights when he took me to dinner after a long day of appointments.

From that first night, when he offered to walk me back to my hotel before learning I lived in the city, to the night in May when we capped off the evening with lemon meringue pie, I knew there was the very real possibility of ruining our working relationship by trading it for something fleeting. Had the chemistry I'd felt been an act? Had the flirtation been about business? Nick didn't need anything from me anymore. I had absolutely nothing to do with the success of his solo venture unless you counted future shoe sales. What I'd read in Who's Who detailed a talented designer driven enough to stand out from the pack. What I didn't know was the depth of his drive.

Nick was on the verge of jumpstarting his career without the benefit of financial backers. Could that make him go from the charming person I had been attracted to in the past—heck, was still attracted to—to a person with homicidal tendencies? I couldn't see it. But was he willing to look the other way if someone he knew did? What did Amanda know about Nick that I didn't? Nick and Amanda weren't the only two people on my radar. There was Red. And there was Michael. And there was Clestes, the mystery entry to the competition. Not to mention employees of Tradava who could have gotten into the trend offices, or Maries Paulson, who was the other competition judge, or Florence Ingram, the consultant to the designers. There was whoever funded the contest prize that Patrick had kept secret.

It came down to one thing. The person who killed Patrick was either the person with the most to gain by him being dead, or the most to lose by him remaining alive.

Patrick had taken measures to tell the world something was wrong. Going to the police. Loaning me the laptop with the protected file and hiding the password in the laptop case. Leaving his Rolodex open to the card for Pins and Needles. Having copies of articles left in a file for me at the library. But as charming as his cryptic methods might have appeared once, now they frustrated me. Why not just spell it out in an email? Because that wasn't his style.

I thought back to our last meeting.

"As arbiters of fashion, we have an obligation to honor the past and encourage the future. Every piece of fashion before us was important. Claire McCardell. Pierre Cardin. Steven Sprouse. Patrick Kelly. Every fabric means something too."

"Even double-knit polyester?" I joked.

"We are not here to judge, but to guide and educate."

"I'm excited about this job," I'd told him.

"I see that in you. You'll make a fine addition to my team, Ms. Kidd."

"Is there anything else I need to know?"

"I don't email." He thought for a moment. "When you want to say Thank You, send a note. When you want to communicate, come to my office. And always remember, in our business, it's important to look the part. I expect you to be on time, but if you must be late, I'd prefer it to be because you were putting on lipstick or choosing the right shoes. When all else fails, Ms. Kidd, look *en vogue*."

At the time, I'd liked that expression. It was like a sentiment lifted from *Working Girl*. I liked thinking my sense of style would help me do my job. But now, I was as frustrated as ever. I looked at the ceiling.

"Patrick, why did you waste your time telling me how to dress? Why didn't you tell me what was happening in your department? This business, your fashion office, was not as important as your life, and now you're gone and I'm the only one trying to figure everything out." I stared at the ceiling for a few more moments, wishing he would speak to me from beyond the grave. Logan jumped up on the table and sat on top of the folder I'd brought home from the library. I scratched between his ears before scooping him up and flipping open the folder.

There was one article in the folder for each designer listed on the hidden tab in the password-protected computer file. Patrick wanted to make sure someone paid attention to that file. I turned on the laptop and opened the file and stared at the list of designers. Until now, I'd been approaching the mess of my life in reactionary mode. The killer had been one step ahead of me, and I'd barely been keeping up. But what about those years of experience I had, the problem solving, the analytical sense? What about the ability to walk into a showroom filled with samples and edit a collection into a cohesive assortment for Bentley's? What if I relied on that to figure things out?

My years of working in a buying office had left me with above-average skills when it came to manipulating a spreadsheet, and I couldn't get past the idea that what I needed to know was staring me in the face.

I clicked around the other pages in the workbook.

Nothing.

I scrolled down.

Nothing.

I hit control/ end, to go to the last cell used on the page.

The cursor bounced to v61472. Patrick's notes had ended on row 657.

It seemed I'd found upon something.

I clicked the button between the row numbers and column letters and set the font to black. Cells that had appeared empty now filled with data. Patrick had set the text to white on white so the page appeared blank to the naked eye. Virtual invisible ink.

I scanned the list of Italian designers that I'd seen before. This time each name was followed with two columns of information. The column to the immediate right was a second name, and to the right of that was a dollar amount. The first eight names had ten thousand dollars listed. The two female designers were marked as "Pending." Two additional rows were visible below the list. *Entry fees: $10,400. Total: $90,400.*

I'd recognized the list of designers the first time I'd accessed this file, but it wasn't a passing knowledge of fashion that helped me recognize the second set of names. It was a passing knowledge of quote/unquote businessmen. Names that had been in and out of the papers for suspicion of illegal acts for years. I didn't know what they had to do with the list of designers or why Patrick had hidden the info.

But that wasn't all.

Below the names was another section of text. It was addressed to me.

Dear Samantha,

I'm wracked with guilt over my recent behavior. This is not what this business is about. New talent needs a proper home, and I fear I won't be around to protect my legacy. I leave it to you to look in vogue. This is not about the money, it is about the creativity. Friendship and loyalty do not have a price, and I was foolish to think otherwise. If this is the new business of fashion, it will go forward without me; my only regret is that I turned to the wrong people to achieve my final goals.

I felt a chill down my spine. It was the same note I'd found in Patrick's drawer the night I spent in Tradava, but this time it was addressed to me. There was no doubt he'd intended me to find this file.

But why? What did a list of known Mafiosi have to do with his murder? Had he gone to them for the money? How had he planned to pay it back? I didn't know what to make of it, but it was clear this was more than the minor leagues. Eddie was right. The cops needed to know about this, although they didn't need to hear it from me. After working up my nerve, I called the detective.

"Loncar," he answered.

"I have infor—" I panicked, fearing he'd recognize my voice. I dropped it lower and disguised it. "Invormazon. Deeteective, zhere ist more to ze Patreek case zan designers," I continued, immediately embarrassed. Instead of reporting important information to the police, I sounded like I should be plotting big trouble for Moose and Squirrel.

"Who is this?" he asked.

"You need not know my identitee." This was going poorly. I had to get him the info and get off the phone. "Ze monee ist from ze mob." I dropped the accent but kept my voice low, then quickly rattled off a list of the names in the file. When I reached the last one, I paused for a couple of seconds, considering the least suspicious way to disconnect the call. I finally hung up without saying goodbye.

Patrick had reached out to me, and telling the police was the right thing to do. Loncar had the information now. He had to investigate it. Whatever it meant, he'd figure it out. That was his job.

The phone rang. I jumped and knocked over Logan's bowl. He scampered into the living room. My heart pounded until the machine picked up. "Ms. Kidd, this is Detective Loncar. I need to talk to you about some information we received from a call made from this number." He paused, as though he knew I was screening his call, then left his number and disconnected.

That was impossible! I'd dialed—no I hadn't. I'd forgotten to *67.

What was wrong with me? Why was I unable to fully embrace my situation, to act like an adult, to turn what I knew over to Detective Loncar and move on with my life? Because being back in Ribbon, back in this house, made me feel like a kid despite any professional success I'd achieved in New York.

I wandered the living room, straightening pillows on the green velvet sofa, rubbing the toe of my shoe against the tracks in the carpet from moving the sofa. I wasn't the only person dealing with the situation. Maries Paulson was too. I went to the kitchen, searching the piles of paper on the dining room table for the interoffice envelope she'd dropped by. When I found it, I called her.

"Ms. Kidd? I was starting to think I wouldn't hear from you. The gala is tonight. I assume you're calling me because you found the money?"

"Ms. Paulson, I think Patrick went outside of the fashion industry to get the money. I don't think you're going to find it."

"What are you suggesting?"

"I found some password protected files on Patrick's computer and I think—I mean, I'm not sure, and I don't want it to sound like I'm accusing him of anything, but—"

"Get to the point, Ms. Kidd."

"I found a list of, um, businessmen."

"It's quite possible that Patrick did approach a team of businessmen. Financial types are often looking for a return on their investment. This competition, if it discovered a new talent, would be worth much more than a hundred thousand dollars in publicity. Plus, it could give someone a foothold in the fashion industry, instant status as part of the new wave of tastemakers."

"Ms. Paulson, I don't mean businessmen like the kind who look at portfolios and crunch numbers. These men are all . . . " I stopped talking. What were they? They were all Italian. When had I become guilty of racial profiling the same nationality credited with bringing the world my favorite foods? Regardless of my instincts, of the familiarity of the names, and the conclusions I'd drawn from their collective associations, I had nothing. "Maybe I'm wrong," I finished quietly.

"My dear, Patrick's reputation in this industry is spotless. If I understand what you're implying, no one would believe you."

Once again, I found myself twisting the phone cord around my finger. This time when I reached the kink I kept winding. The tip of my finger turned purple. "That's what I thought you were going to say."

"Tell me the names," she said.

I rattled off a few of the names from the top of my head. Maries laughed, at first a low throaty laugh that grew. Uneasily, I waited, wondering what was so funny.

"My dear, those are garmentos!" Her laughter continued.

"Garmentos?" I repeated.

"Businessmen, like you said. In the garment district. Fabric wholesalers who depend upon the fashion industry's success for their livelihood. Oh, but you gave me a laugh."

"Ms. Paulson, these men each gave a ten-thousand-dollar donation. Would those men have cut Patrick a check? The entry fees to the competition totaled ten thousand, four hundred dollars. How would that be collected? Wouldn't he have deposited the money in the bank?"

"I don't know, but at least now I know where he obtained it. I'll make a few phone calls and find out."

I thought about what Michael had said. "I'm not sure the money is safe. I think he might have kept it in the office and one of the designers in the competition found out."

"I highly doubt Patrick would have kept the money in the office."

"If he caught someone in the act of stealing it, he would have tried to fight them. That might be how he died."

"If someone stole the money, they wouldn't be pressuring me to deliver it to the gala, would they? No, I don't think anyone has gotten their hands on the money. Not yet. This can all be over if I make it be known I'll deliver the money as requested. You haven't called the police about any of this, have you?"

"Not exactly," I said. The room felt hot, and I opened the sliding doors behind the kitchen. A breeze caught the long vertical blinds and blew them into the room, then sucked them out as quickly, snapping the plastic against itself. "Are you still attending the gala?"

"Of course."

"And you're taking money for a payoff?" I asked in a tentative voice.

"I've already met with my financial advisors and made the withdrawal. I see no other choice," she replied. "Too many lives, including yours, are at risk. I can't see how I can ignore this request."

"What about the police?"

"I've followed the instructions given to me, in deference to you, but I have asked the museum to make arrangements for heightened security. I have a few trusted people who will be monitoring everything. If all goes as planned, this will soon be over."

"Someone killed Patrick over that money. If someone believes you have the money, you might be in danger too," I said.

"Ms. Kidd, I have a plan to draw out the murderer at the gala, but it will only work if he or she thinks I am complying with the instructions left to me. That is imperative. Now it is your turn to do as I say. Keep this information to yourself. I'll speak to the executives at Tradava this afternoon, and we'll turn the event into a memorial for Patrick. If one of the designers is the guilty party, this change in plans will cause them a misstep, one that might give the police the break they need."

"Ms. Paulson, the police think I'm involved in Patrick's murder," I said.

"My dear, when this settles down, let me see what I can do about finding you a position in my showroom. I like your style."

If it weren't so bittersweet, it would have almost been funny.

I SHOWERED and looked in my closet for something to wear. There was no chance of me going far from the house, short of lugging the recycling to the corner for pick up the next day, so I pulled on a pair of lavender cashmere pajamas and wandered around, tidying up messes that had accumulated in the house. As I tucked several errant shoes into the closet I rediscovered the garment bag from Catnip. Now seemed as good a time as any to try on what I'd bought.

The pants slipped on easily, with a low-slung waistband and a flared leg. I turned around and checked out the fit from the back. The flattering cut concealed evidence of my recent comfort eating. But the suit needed shoes, and I had a good idea where to find the perfect pair.

Back when I landed the job as senior buyer, after my first appointment at Nick's showroom, he'd sent me a package. Samples. Nestled snugly in the cardboard shipping container were four crisp white shoe boxes, all marked in my size. It was against company policy for me to accept a gift of this value from a designer, and I wasn't the type to break policy. Yet there had been something about Nick's generosity that touched me, and I didn't have the heart to make the phone call to tell him to take the shoes back. I folded the flaps of the shipping container inside of each other and tucked the box away in the back of my closet. I had never thanked him. Never acknowledged his gift. Never worn the shoes.

I'd rediscovered the carton when I cleaned out my closet before moving. No longer an employee of Bentley's, I owned the shoes outright. I packed them up with the rest of my wardrobe and put them where they'd been all along, in the back corner of my closet, sight unseen.

I knelt on the floor, reached past my turquoise suitcase, and found the carton. With two hands, I lifted it over the suitcase and set it in front of me. I tore it open. Inside were the four white shoeboxes, labeled in black with Nick's logo.

I eased one of the shoe boxes out of the packing crate and lifted the lid. Inside the tissue was a pair of black and white Dalmatian-printed mules. I held one shoe in my lap and traced my finger over Nick's signature like I had at Tradava before I found Patrick's body. There had been so much hope and anticipation that morning. I had been on the verge of something new. I had been energized by the idea of working for Tradava in their trend office. And then, in seconds, the opportunity vanished.

I slipped the shoe onto my foot and held it up. A perfect fit. I stood, slipped into the other, and looked in the mirror. My reflection showed the image I wanted to project at the Gala. Confident. Stylish. Someone who belonged at the event. But looking the part was only a portion of my strategy. Knowing the details, as many of the details as I could, before arriving on that red carpet was part two. I was going to attend that gala and figure out a few things or my name wasn't Samantha Kidd.

23

GOOD GIRL

The doorbell rang while I was admiring my outfit. "Kidd? It's Nick. I have food."

The scent of tomato sauce and mozzarella trumped the warning bells ringing in my ears. I stripped off the suit and pulled my cashmere jog suit back on, then descended the stairs and let Nick inside. I did not comment on his tuxedo, or the carryout bag in his hand or the bottle of wine tucked under his arm. He set the bag on my kitchen table and handed me a couple of paper towels, then poured two glasses of wine. After he unwrapped a pair of meatball sandwiches, I pulled one over to my placemat and started without him. He eased himself into the wooden chair across from me, watching with an amused expression on his face.

"Are you going to come up for air?"

A meatball dislodged from inside the roll and fell on my lap, leaving a round stain on my thigh before it rolled off and landed on the floor. I scrubbed at the stain with the paper towel, turning it into a trapezoid.

"I trust you're in for the night?" he asked.

I was going to the gala whether he thought it was a smart idea or not, so I decided to avoid the subject and the lectures of the

Samantha-be-careful sort. "I'm going to relax tonight, forget my worries, and watch a movie." Usually I was pretty good at vaguely answering questions and not committing to actual lies, so I made mental notes to put on a movie and relax when I got home. Aside from a frontal lobotomy, there wasn't much I could do about the forgetting my worries part.

"Good. I was afraid you were still thinking of going to the gala."

I glanced down at my stained pajamas. "Do I look like I'm going to the gala?"

"No, you look like you're ready to sit this one out." He refilled my wine glass, though it was far from empty. "Good girl."

I cringed. I can't stand that language.

"I need to tell you something," Nick said, ignoring his sandwich.

"Mkayf," I replied, which was supposed to be "Okay," but I was chewing a particularly large glob of mozzarella. He picked up the oregano shaker and spun it around in his hands, then set it back down on the table.

"I'm taking Amanda to the gala tonight."

I wasn't sure where he was going with this but the timing, when coupled with the golf-ball sized amount of meat and cheese and in my mouth, was unfortunate. I swallowed a too-big lump and, with no other options, guzzled from the glass of wine to force it down my throat.

"You're telling me this why?"

"I don't know. There's absolutely no reason in the world I should worry about telling you. Except . . ." His voice trailed off, and I would have paid good money to get him to finish that thought, if I didn't need all my good money to pay the mortgage. "Except I can't get you out of my head."

His brown eyes were the colors of melted Milk Duds, all chocolaty and caramelly and sweet, and . . . STOP IT, SAMANTHA!

Nick waited for my response, but I didn't know what to say and, for once in my life, that translated into not saying anything. He finally broke the silence. "You sure you're going to be okay by yourself?"

"I'll be okay. This is one night where I'm happy to be by myself."

"I brought you a movie," he said and set a DVD case on the sofa. *How to Steal A Million.* A movie about a woman who plans a museum caper and some undercover work. Perhaps a glimpse into Nick's sense of humor, or worse yet, an indication he was on to me.

I ignored the reference. "One of my favorites. Thank you." I held the door open for him and leaned against the frame. "Don't have too much fun without me."

"Deal." He reached his hand out and I took it. Our fingertips kept contact while neither of us spoke. Maybe the lemon meringue pie had nothing to do with that moment Nick and I shared at dinner last May. He raised my fingertips to his lips and kissed them and then dropped my hand and left.

Nick may have had my best interests at heart, but a part of me, the paranoid part that felt like my ankles were being pulled down into a pit of quicksand, still wasn't sure.

After he left, I caught my reflection in the bay window and realized I hadn't needed to do much to convince him I wasn't planning to leave the house. I looked and smelled like I'd spent the past few hours in a pizza oven and I had only about half an hour to get ready. I called information for a taxi company, then reserved a pick-up in thirty minutes. Time to get glamorous.

Twenty minutes later, I was dressed in the designer pinstriped pantsuit from Catnip. Designer Dalmatian shoes. Designer attitude marked down to half price. If ever there existed a reason to wear an outfit I couldn't afford, this was it. I knotted a vintage black and white scarf over my head like a sixties film star and topped off the look with the fuchsia fedora. A spritz of perfume masked any lingering meatball sandwich smells. I twirled in front of the mirror. Not bad for an unemployed ex-fashion industry employee suspected of murder.

From the driveway, the taxi driver laid on the horn. I called out the front door I'd be ready in a couple of minutes. The taxi driver called back he was starting the meter.

Nick's visit put me behind schedule, allowing no time for second thoughts. I grabbed my already assembled handbag filled with essentials for the evening, locked the door behind me and pulled on a pair of gloves. I slid into the back seat of the cab and told the driver where to go.

The day had moved from dusk to dark, helpful for my clandestine activities. My nerves rose in direct proportion to the distance we were from the gala. I asked the driver to drop me off at a coffee shop within walking distance of the museum. He pulled over and I held out his fare plus a generous tip. "If anyone asks, you never saw me. Got it?" I said. I didn't know if it was the fedora or the pinstripes making me act like Humphrey Bogart.

He eyed me up and down and took the money from my outstretched hand. "If you don't want to be remembered, you shouldn'ta worn that hat."

Inside the coffee shop I bought a bag of chocolate covered espresso beans and a latte while trying to ignore the fact that everyone in the shop stared at me. I was a roadside attraction in the middle of Starbucks.

I finished my latte and stood to leave. On my way to the door, a group of high school boys asked where the costume party was, and I succumbed to the pressure of conformity. I took my hat off and gave it to a little girl playing on the floor by her parents. "Enjoy it, honey," I said and patted it onto her head.

I popped a few espresso beans in my mouth and approached the museum. The air was crisp and cool, and if it weren't for the fact that I was out looking for a murderer, it would have been a perfect September night. Shiny luxury cars pulled onto Museum Drive; people in eveningwear mingled outside. I sat on a bench by the duck pond, close enough to watch but maintaining distance of anonymity. I was looking for something—anything–unusual. I just didn't know what.

In a fashionable crowd, "unusual" was defined more by the poseurs than the socialites. Women who had dressed for the event shivered in the evening air, unprepared for the drop in temperature. They looked out of place next to women in full-length fur coats. A flash of red hair caught my attention, and I watched the owner of Catnip move through the crowd.

She cut a chic picture in a black pencil skirt and a fitted jacket with a nipped in waist. The jacket reminded me of the outfit I'd worn that first day at Tradava less than a week ago. Silver chains dangled from her lapels, which coordinated nicely with the long silver earrings she wore. A silver leather clutch, flat as a pancake, was tucked under her arm.

I followed her figure until she entered the museum, passing a large black and white portrait of Patrick displayed on a wooden easel. A woman blocked my view but when she turned, I recognized Amanda Ries. Her dress, a high cut halter with a plunging back, fell to the floor like black oil and oozed onto the ground around her feet. Light from the almost-full moon bounced off her creamy skin. Her hair was held back with chopsticks, and a beaded handbag rested in her left hand. She waved at someone on the steps.

Nick.

Even though I knew they'd be attending together, I wasn't prepared for the sight of them as a couple. A pang of jealousy trumped other, more practical, emotions. I studied their body language: her laughter when he whispered in her ear, his hand casually resting on her arm. Her hand tucked into the crook of his elbow, his on the small of her back to guide her inside the building. I felt played. Nick's admission earlier amounted to little more than a ploy to keep me home. This was clearly the body language of a couple in love, or a couple of conspirators, not a couple of college chums.

Well, that's just great. No invitation, no man, no hat. This gala wasn't good for my ego or my wardrobe.

The crowd had thinned drastically. Smokers lingered on the balcony, but the festivities were about to begin. I didn't care I was missing out on dinner and a bad cover band for the night, but I did want to know what was going on under that roof. I wished someone would show up with a banner that said, "I killed Patrick and am prepared to frame Samantha Kidd if necessary so I can get away with murder," but if that banner existed it seemed to have been traded in for satin evening clutches and beaded shoes. Even murderers cleaned up well.

A limo slowed by the steps. The driver hopped out and circled the front of the car, opening the passenger door. Maries Paulson stepped out, and the driver handed her a small, flat briefcase. Bursts of camera flash illuminated her lavender fur stole. Her dark aubergine lace dress fit so well it appeared to have been sewn on her body. She paused at the bottom of the stairs, allowing the media to capture her better angles, and I knew this was my only chance to speak with her. "Ms. Paulson!" I called out. Her head turned toward me, and a thousand flashbulbs crackled. I stepped toward her, not sure she had heard me. "Maries?"

"You have no right to be here," she said in a hostile voice.

"I'm here to represent Tradava like I told you," I said, confused by her unexpected animosity. I dropped my voice. "I didn't tell anyone what we discussed." She pointed her manicured plum-black fingernail at me. "Don't pretend to know me or to be my friend. More than one person has contacted me about you. I trusted you and put myself in danger. You're no more the trend specialist than I'm the Queen of Sheba. I don't know what role you played in his murder, but I intend to find out."

I searched her face for signs she was acting for someone else's benefit, but Botox injections had made her face unreadable. I didn't know what had changed from earlier that day when we'd spoken. I looked at the briefcase she held, then, realizing what was inside, stepped forward again. "Ms. Paulson, wait!" I reached out for her arm and she flung off my touch.

"Don't–*Don't!*" her fingers fanned out aggressively and her voice dropped to a whisper. "I would rather throw this money in the stream than give it to a manipulative bottom feeder like you." She turned away from me and advanced up the stairs.

"But you said—I thought we—I'm trying to help—"

She turned back around. "Approach me again and I will make sure you never work in this industry again." She scanned my outfit from head to toe. "On you, that's a waste of six yards of fabric."

24

ALONE AND IN A TREE

Maries paused by a security officer standing by the door and pointed one finger my direction. I jogged to the bench by the duck pond and crouched behind it, watching the conversation between Maries and the officer. She handed him the briefcase, then lit up a cigarette. The officer disappeared inside. Her burning ember marked her presence until it went out. A high voice, from the bottom of the steps, pulled me out of my thoughts. "Ms. Paulson!"

Maries looked down. A scrawny figure in a purple velvet tuxedo bounded up the stairs to her. Michael Dubrecht, Patrick's assistant and self-proclaimed designer. Was this it? I wondered. Was this the moment when someone demanded a hundred thousand dollars from Maries, no police present, in exchange for my safety?

You're no more the trend specialist than I'm the Queen of Sheba. If Maries no longer believed I was the trend specialist, she was no longer concerned with my safety.

Michael said something to Maries. She smiled and shook his hand then turned away and left him behind. He jumped to grab the handles before the doors closed and narrowly slipped inside.

I swiped on another coat of lip-gloss then circled the museum, my heels puncturing the ground with every step. I made slow progress, avoiding dry leaves that begged to be crunched underfoot. I popped a few more espresso beans into my mouth and continued. The darkness cloaked me, and I dropped my guard. That's probably why I jumped when a beam of light shot through the darkness and the groundskeeper asked what I was doing.

Think fast, Samantha, and don't worry too much about telling lies or telling the truth. Say something to make him go away. My heart raced, and my hands grew sweaty inside my gloves.

The man waited for me to talk. His flashlight cast about two thousand degrees of heat in my direction. Like Detective Loncar's office, it wasn't the best circumstance for thinking under pressure.

"My cat ran up one of these trees and I'm trying to find him."

He flashed the light up into the trees and a few birds fly away. "Up there? Where'd he come from?"

Keep talking. "I live over there," I motioned to the houses behind the museum. "When I got home from work he bolted out the door and ran over here. I think he might have chased a squirrel and now I can't find him." I almost believed the words as I spoke them. They sounded plausible. Cats escaped and chased squirrels up trees all the time, I was sure of it.

He flashed the light around while I silently begged him to stop. He was drawing attention to us, and all my efforts to stay undercover would be wasted. I held my breath for a few seconds, not sure if he bought my story.

"I think he's up there," he said, motioning toward the tree beside me. "I have a ladder inside the shed. I'll help you get him."

"That's okay. I can get him."

He looked me up and down, scarf-wrapped head to Dalmatian-printed toes, then looked me straight in the eye. "Little lady, how do you think you're going to get a cat out of a tree dressed like that? I don't think those shoes were made for scaling maples." He shined the light on the path and walked toward the building.

I couldn't believe my luck. I tried my best attempt at cute, helpless female. I hated that routine, but it was the only thing to keep this charade going.

"Thank you so much. I don't know what I was thinking." I followed him to the building, hoping he would lead me to a door that would get me inside. We reached a separate building where he had the necessary tools and machinery to maintain the grounds, and my hopes fell.

"Try to be quiet, though, because there's a big event going on in the museum tonight."

"I noticed. But they can't hear us out here, right?"

"This shed has an underground passageway that connects to the museum. If we make sounds out here, they'll echo through the passageways and someone might come check it out. I was supposed to be gone long before this thing started tonight, and as much as I want to help you, I don't want to lose my job over a lost kitty."

His comments explained why he was speaking so quietly, and I think he attributed my newfound silence to what he'd said but I was contemplating phrases like "underground passageway that connects to the museum," and "I was supposed to be out of here long before this thing started tonight." I thought for a second about trying to pull the pins from the hinges on the door, but that might be an actual crime since it was on public property and I was not currently chaperoned by someone who could approve such an act. My newfound comfort with danger notwithstanding, I thought it best to avoid actively breaking the law.

He handed me a rope net. "Hold this." He gently closed the door to the underground passageway and inserted a key into the door to relock it. I hid my disappointment. He then walked to the exterior museum wall where a ladder leaned alongside the building. "Don't just stand there, missy, grab an end and help me move this thing. I can't do it myself."

I tossed my handbag on the dewy grass and grabbed the other end of the ladder, juggling it with the net. We maneuvered it against the tree. I knew we weren't going to find a kitten up there but was obligated to go along with my story.

"Do you see him?" he asked.

"No. It might not be this tree." I was getting antsy, wondering how

I was going to ditch the groundskeeper and continue my search now that he had decided to do his good deed for the day.

"Look. It's this tree or nothing. If the little guy isn't up here, you ain't gonna find him tonight."

"Okay, maybe he *is* in this tree."

"Well? You gonna climb up and check or not?"

"I'm not good on ladders."

The look on his face told me I didn't have a choice. "You said the little guy ran out the door and took off this direction up a tree. He probably climbed too high and now he's scared. I got a couple of cats at home myself. Once they're scared they won't come to just anybody. They want to hear a familiar voice. I don't plan to let you call out to him from down here while I go up and chase him further. You better get up there and call him. Take your shoes off first. You'll have better luck on these rungs." He pointed toward the net. "Once you get him, put him in the net and hang it down to me. He'll hang on tight until he's down, and you can come down to get him. But you better get a move on, 'cause I don't have all night."

I had no choice but to climb. The ladder bowed in the middle and might as well have been a hundred rungs high, neither of which bolstered my confidence. I kept climbing, soon becoming hidden by leaves, wondering if I would be lucky enough to find a random kitten trapped thirty feet up in a maple tree.

"You see him?" The groundskeeper called up to me.

"Not yet."

"Call his name a little."

I couldn't subject Logan to my lie, so I named my fake kitty. "Max, here Max," I called softly, and made kissing noises in the air. The stupidity of the situation was not lost on me.

Ten minutes and no kitten later I climbed back down. "No luck. I think it's another tree."

"I can't stay here anymore." He looked up at the sky for several seconds, moonlight bouncing off his full face. "It looks like it's gonna be a clear night tonight. The ladder will be fine if we leave it out. I'll be back in the morning. I'll help you move it to another tree but then, I gotta leave."

I became Johnny on the Spot, carrying the ladder to the next tree. The groundskeeper made his apologies and left me alone to conduct my rescue mission, ignoring the thanks I called to his back.

Again, I climbed the ladder. With a little maneuvering I positioned myself in a fork in a branch. I was temporarily distracted from the danger of looking for a murderer by thoughts of being found, unconscious, outside of the event, because the branch where I'd sat had broken under my weight.

I strained my eyes to take in every detail of the event. Round tables covered with white cloths took up much of the ballroom. Each table held an elaborate floral centerpiece arranged around a miniature bust form. Along the side of the room, on a raised, lighted platform, stood three mannequins draped, toga-like, in black fabric. Next to each mannequin was a sign holder that held a capital letter: A, B, C. Four spotlights shone down from the ceiling, three illuminating the mannequins and one shining on an empty pedestal next to the letter D. This event was called the Designer's Debut. My suspects were all present and accounted for, representing their collections. But the mannequins draped sloppily in black cloth lacked the originality expected in fashion.

I looked for familiar faces in the crowd, scanning the audience systematically, left to right, clockwise around the table, then moving on to the next seating arrangement. This would have been easier if 90 percent of the fashion industry didn't wear black.

Empty seats peppered the ballroom. I guess when nature calls, you answer. Better change that train of thought. I was trapped in a tree with literally nowhere to go. Three tables back along the far side I spotted Red's hair. I didn't recognize anyone at her table. I continued my search of the crowd. A few tables past her I saw Nick and Amanda at the back of the room. Watching them get along so well made me feel all kinds of alone. Alone and in a tree.

What was I doing? This was crazy. I wasn't going to discover anything.

At that moment the band stopped playing and a speaker came on stage. I couldn't hear what he said but watched as the crowd applauded politely. The man looked to the side, as if expecting someone to appear. A few awkward moments passed as he leaned into the microphone again but didn't speak. Heads in the crowd twisted at varying angles, looking around.

Something was wrong.

I started to lose my balance and grabbed a branch in panic. It snapped off in my grip and my earlier fears became a reality. I reached for another limb. Several leaves snapped off and fluttered through the air. The caffeine had made me jumpy. When I regained stability, I looked into the room and swore Nick was looking right at me. Was that possible? I was pretty far away from him, and he had no reason to look for me in a tree outside the event.

But Nick was starting to know me pretty well. He had lots of reasons to look for me in a tree. He glanced at the empty stage then back up to the window. I froze, hoping to blend in with the background and seem like a figment of his imagination. Anger shaped his face, with a crease between his brows and a firm, hard jawline. He stood abruptly, pushing his chair toward the table so hard the seat back bounced when the two collided.

Maybe he was going to check on Amanda, who now that I thought about it had been gone for a long time. Maybe he was going to come outside and check on what he thought he saw in the tree. He looked side to side before pushing through the swinging doors that led to the exit.

This was humiliating. I wasn't going to stick around and let him find me. I fled down the rungs of the ladder, grabbed my handbag, and slipped on my shoes. This had been a mistake. I was going home.

And then something—someone—stepped away from the shadows close to the back wall of the museum then receded into darkness. Someone had been watching me while I watched the gala.

For a moment I was as rooted to the ground as the tree I'd been sitting in. I heard the crunch of leaves under a foot—close. Closer than the shadowy figure had been. Someone grabbed at my arm. I tried to yell but no sound came out. I yanked my arm away and ran past the museum to the road. The heel of my left shoe stuck in the ground, but I kept running. I jumped into the first taxi in a line of several and pounded my open palm against the back of the driver's seat.

"Go, go, *GO!*" I shouted frantically, slapping the plastic partition with each word. The driver peeled away from the curb with a squeal of tires. I turned around at the first Stop sign and squinted through the dirty rear window. A figure stood in the middle of the road.

If he had wanted me dead right now, I would be.

IT WAS close to midnight when I got home. I triple-locked the front door, pushed a folding metal chair under the lock, and angled the sofa up against it. I carried Logan with me to the bathroom where he sat outside the shower doors while I stood under a jet of hot water. As the spray pummeled my head and pooled around my ankles I knew what I should have known all along. There was only one way out.

I turned off the water, turbaned my hair, and walked, naked and dripping, down the hallway, to the phone. The number was easy enough to remember.

"This is Samantha Kidd. I'm done playing games. We need to talk about Patrick's murder." By the time I hung up, I wondered if I'd just sealed my fate.

25

THIS IS NO JOKE

THE RAPID-FIRE ASSAULT ON THE FRONT DOOR JERKED ME UPRIGHT LIKE a limp puppet about to perform. Between stints of pacing and regret that had lasted until close to three in the morning, I'd tried, unsuccessfully, to fall asleep. Whenever I closed my eyes I felt the touch of the man who had grabbed for me at the museum. Exhaustion kicked in somewhere around four thirty and I'd crashed on a makeshift bed of cushions from the sofa that was pushed up against the front door. Now, foggy from being pulled out of a sleep I never thought I'd find, I struggled to wake up.

The pounding persisted. I pushed my feet into slippers and moved the sofa away from the door. By the looks of the sunshine, it was well into morning. Two men stood on my doorstep. One I recognized, the other I didn't. Neither looked pleased.

"Detective Loncar, come in," I said.

"Ms. Kidd, we need you to come with us."

"Let me make some coffee. I have a lot to tell you, but I'm not quite awake yet."

They looked at each other. Logan buzzed my ankles while we stood in the living room.

"Let me go upstairs and get dressed," I said. "If you want, I can follow you to the station—wait, no, I can't, because I don't have a car. Give me five minutes to get dressed."

"Ms. Kidd, this is no joke."

"I'm not joking. I really can be ready in five minutes." I turned around and let go of the door, thinking they would catch it or come inside or maybe didn't want to intrude and would stay on the porch. Detective Loncar reached out and snatched my thin wrist in his bear grip and everything about the moment felt wrong.

They weren't there to give me news about Patrick's murderer. And they weren't there to listen to what I had to say. They were there to take me in. As in, IN.

I looked at the wrist the detective was clutching, thinking he would realize I needed the wrist before starting that five-minute routine. He looked down at my wrist too, and the next thing I knew, he clamped a handcuff on me.

"Ms. Kidd, you are under arrest for suspicion of murdering Patrick … Patrick … " the new officer's voice trailed off and he looked at Detective Loncar.

"He only has one name," Loncar said, looking directly at me. "Like Cher."

"There have been some new developments in the case," said the unnamed man.

"Do I have the right to know what they are?" I asked.

"No. But you do have the right to remain silent."

Dizziness hit me. My knees went weak. To make matters worse, I was still in my bathrobe. The officers maneuvered me to the car with a yank on the handcuffs and a nudge between my shoulder blades. Loncar opened the back door. I slid in, and he clamped the other handcuff to the door. It wasn't like I was looking for a breakout or anything, but a girl likes to keep her options open. Now I didn't have any options to speak of.

Maybe if I'd listened to Eddie, I wouldn't be in the back of a squad car.

Or maybe the police didn't have any new details. Maybe the person who threatened me had hung me out to dry after all, or maybe I had been on their radar all night. They couldn't possibly think I was guilty. Could they? *Gather your thoughts, Samantha.* Being new in town, I didn't have a lawyer. I was left trying to reason this out myself (because clearly that strategy was working out for me). And still, one question nagged at me: what possible motive could I have?

As we walked from the car to the stationhouse, I tugged at the neck of my robe, painfully aware that underneath I was next to naked. It was a metaphor for the situation. Clothing was my armor. Without it, I was vulnerable.

The dynamic duo led me down a narrow hallway to a small room. Two chairs sat facing each other. A white laminate table sat next to the chairs. The walls of the room were the color of smog; the floor, harvest gold. Corners of the linoleum tiles had since come unglued and chipped, leaving murky pockmarks underfoot that matched the walls. Aside from a camera mounted in the corner above the door, the room was a box: no windows, no art, no distractions. Nothing to take me away from the fact that I was about to be questioned.

Detective Loncar unlocked my cuffs. The new officer introduced himself as Officer Smoot. I watched and waited. I was torn between keeping my mouth closed and spilling everything I'd discovered. I thought about things like unflattering orange jumpsuits and ankle monitors that would make me rethink my choices in footwear and decided right there to let them direct the conversation while I played it safe.

"Where were you yesterday?" Smoot asked, flicking his thumbnail against the underside of his wedding band.

"Home, most of the day. "

"What'd you have for lunch?"

"Meatball sandwich."

"From?"

"B&S."

"Did you do anything else?"

"Watched a movie."

"What movie?"

"How to Steal a Million." I paused. "It's a classic."

"Rented?"

"No. I mean, yes, I think."

"You don't know?"

"I own it, but the person who loaned it to me didn't know that so I don't know where he got it."

"He?"

"The person who brought me the food and the movie. Is that relevant?"

"In the afternoon?"

"Yes."

"But you said you ate at B&S."

"No, I said the food was from B&S."

"And you've seen this movie before?"

"It's one of my favorites." I kept my answers short, contained.

"Did you go out last night?" Loncar asked, drumming his fingers rhythmically on the splintered wooden table while perspiration marks appeared under his arms. When I didn't answer he repeated the question. Dangerous territory.

"I went to the museum last night. To the Designer's Debut Gala."

Smoot stood up and leaned against the wall. Arms crossed, he jumped in where Loncar had left off.

"You just said you didn't have a car."

"I took a taxi." I perked up a little. "My car is at Tradava. Can you tell me what this is about?"

They exchanged another look. Loncar spun his watch in a circle around his wrist. I wanted to reach across the table and tighten the band so he'd have to stop, but that was close to assaulting a cop, and considering my situation, I refrained.

"Why is your car at Tradava?"

"Two nights ago, I was knocked out in the store. Someone gave me a ride home, and I left my car there."

"You were attacked?"

"Yes."

"Did you file a police report?"

"No."

"Why not?"

"Because I wasn't supposed to be there in the first place."

"Are you confessing, Ms. Kidd?"

"To what? Being knocked out at Tradava two nights ago? Yes, I guess I am."

"What were you doing there?" Smoot asked.

"I was—" I didn't want to admit to rifling through Patrick's mail looking for the museum invitation. "I can't say. Will you please tell me what this is all about?"

"Why can't you talk about Tradava?" Loncar asked.

"I was with another woman's boyfriend," I said dramatically. If this were a *Lifetime* movie, it would have gotten a reaction. "He drove me home. I didn't want anyone to find out. End of story." Telling the truth wasn't so hard. That was probably the most honest thing I'd said since I arrived.

"Who's the guy?" Loncar asked, flipping through a file.

"What?"

"Who's the guy who gave you a ride home?" He shut the folder and looked at me. Smoot watched me closely too, gauging my reaction.

"Why does that matter?"

Loncar suggested this mystery guy might corroborate my story. That suggested to me someone was planning to tell Nick what I said. And that suggested I might want to clam up.

"I don't want to say."

"Who are you protecting?" Smoot said, leaning forward on his palms.

Duh. I was protecting myself.

Loncar sat back and stared at me. "Let's take a break. You want anything? Need to go to the bathroom? Want some coffee?"

I looked back and forth between their faces for signs of sympathy or pity.

I got nothing.

"No, thank you," I said automatically. The two officers left the room, presumably to make me think about my situation. A couple of minutes passed. I grew restless. More time passed. I went from restless to nervous. When I'd gotten home from the gala I was ready to confide in them but now something was off and I didn't know what. I wasn't sure how long they left me alone with my mounting paranoia.

All I'd wanted was a chance to get on that other path in life, the road peppered with dreams and hope and imagination. But who was I kidding? Even if I found that road, at this rate the entrance ramp would be closed for construction.

The door reopened and Detective Loncar came back in, this time alone. My hands were locked together in my lap. He set a bottle of water on the table next to me. After a couple of seconds, I reached for it and took a sip, then screwed the cap back on.

"Ms. Kidd, you work in fashion, right?"

"Yes."

He lowered himself into the chair in front of me.

"What do you think of my outfit?"

"Excuse me?"

"My wife says I shouldn't wear plaid."

I shrugged one shoulder, tipped my head to the side, and crossed my arms over my chest. "You can pull it off."

"What about these shoes?" He pushed a foot out in front of him, giving me a clear view of a pair of thick, round-toed black sneakers with black soles and black laces. Standard issue orthopedic.

"Do you have foot problems?" I asked.

"No. Why?"

"They're not particularly attractive."

"What would you suggest?"

"Tell me what you do in the course of a day," I asked. I uncrossed my arms and leaned forward. He stared at me for a couple of seconds, like he didn't understand my question. "Do you walk? Drive? Run? Sit?"

"All of the above. This isn't about work. My wife has been nagging me to update my style."

"Do you really want to know what I think?"

He nodded.

"She's right. Lose the plaid shirts. Go for something with a vertical stripe. Definitely a collar, and never, ever, ever wear a V-neck T-shirt. Keep your jeans dark. Have your suit dry-cleaned. And do something about those shoes."

"They're that bad?"

"They tell the world you've given up."

He looked down at his feet for a couple of seconds, then nodded. "I guess you're right."

As we sat there, him staring at his ugly shoes, me staring at the top of his head, working up the nerve to suggest a different hairstyle, I realized how easy it was to say what needed to be said and how hard it was to keep it all bottled up.

"Detective?" I said tentatively. "I'm ready to tell you about yesterday."

He looked up from his shoes and nodded, once. I told him about Nick, the meatball that fell from my sandwich to my lap, and the threat on the envelope. I told him about Patrick's computer, the password on the back of the business card, the file of quote/unquote businessmen. I described the sewing machine set up in Patrick's office, the bump on the back of my head, the person in the shadows outside of the museum, the photo under Michael's phone that said GET HER with an arrow pointed to me, and the message to me I'd found on Patrick's computer.

It felt good to clear the air. No one stopped me, and I wondered for the briefest moment why I'd been so scared to talk to the police, why I had ignored the voice of common sense that should have prompted me to confide in Detective Loncar days ago. I told him about the fabric store and my conversations with Red, Amanda, Michael, and Nick, Maries, Eddie, and Florence when he cut me off.

"What about the attack?" Loncar prompted.

"At Tradava? I told you all I can. I didn't hear anybody, didn't see anybody, but I was knocked out."

"Not that attack."

"The attack on Florence? I told you what I know about that too." I leaned back in the chair and crossed my arms over my chest, then immediately uncrossed them. I kicked my heel against the metal leg of the chair.

Loncar leaned forward, one elbow resting on the table to the side of us. His face was inches from mine. "We know you were at Tradava when the break-in happened, and we found your fingerprints all over the office. We want to know what you were looking for. We have enough to connect you with Patrick's murder, the fabric store, and last night's attack."

"What attack?" My chest tightened, my palms were sweaty, and the air I gulped didn't seem to reach my lungs. The room spun. I bent down to try to control the nausea.

Loncar picked up the water bottle and held it out to me. I waved it away. Where were they getting their information? I dug deeper into details that twenty-four hours ago I had hoped to conceal. About the taxi to the museum, the walk from the coffee shop, the surveillance by the duck pond. I told about hiding in the shadows and enlisting the help of the groundskeeper to look for a nonexistent kitten.

For every detail I provided he asked for something to corroborate my story. I had paid the taxi driver to forget I was his fare. I ditched the fuchsia fedora so as not to draw attention to myself. I had no hope with the groundskeeper since he had already said he was going to deny helping me. There was no kitten named Max; there was no taxi reservation to take me home. The chances of finding the high school kids from the coffee shop were slim to none.

I described the clothes I had seen at the event. I begged him to do the research to see if I was right. I personally thought the detail with which I described the outfits should have proven the accuracy of my story, but he seemed to think anyone could identify black tie ensembles with such precision. If only there were a way to prove I had been at that benefit—

"Talk to Maries Paulson," I begged. "She knows I was there."

"Oh yeah? You talk to her last night?"

"Outside of the museum. She was mad at me."

"You two fought?"

"She accused me of—" Loncar leaned forward and instantly I knew it wasn't wise to finish that thought. "Ask her. She'll tell you I was there."

"We would ask her if we could. We can't. She's unconscious in a hospital bed."

26

FREAKIN' FAIRYTALE

BEFORE I COULD ASK ANY MORE QUESTIONS, THE DOOR OPENED. A young woman in a white shirt and blue Dickies motioned Loncar into the hallway. I was in the middle of a very real, very scary crisis, and wanted to go back in time. I wanted to go back to New York, back to the sixty-hour work weeks and the monotony of primetime TV as my social life. I may have lived between muggers and crack heads in New York but at least I'd known what to expect every second of every day. Here? Not so much.

By the time the detectives reentered the room I was beyond exhaustion. Loncar's thick fingers were wrapped around a bulging mailing envelope, a stack of well-worn file folders, and a couple of videotapes. He dumped the pile on the table next to my elbow. I closed my eyes. It must have been hours since we'd arrived, though the passage of time mattered less than it ever had in my life.

"Tell us about Nick Taylor," Detective Loncar said.

"We used to work together when I lived in New York. I was the ladies shoe buyer for Bentley's and he was one of my designers."

"You still consider him a friend?"

"I don't know what I consider him," I answered truthfully.

"Do you consider him an enemy?"

"No."

"How did your relationship with Nick Taylor impact what you did yesterday?"

"Nick knew I wanted to attend the Designer Gala at the museum, but he thought it was a bad idea. He showed up with dinner and a movie and I pretended I was in for the night. As soon as he left I changed clothes and took a taxi to the museum."

"What were you planning on doing at the museum?"

"I don't know. I was looking for something suspicious. Someone wants me to look guilty and I'm trying to figure out who. Maries Paulson said she was being extorted for the prize money from the design competition. Whoever threatened her told her not to go to the cops."

"How long have you known this?" Loncar asked. I looked at my hands in my lap and didn't answer. "Ms. Kidd, if you had cooperated with us all along—"

"They threatened her and told her they'd kill me" I said in a small voice. "Somebody tried to grab me last night when I was leaving. If I cooperated with you all along I might be dead now." I didn't sob. I didn't wail. No one said a word for several minutes.

"Ms. Kidd? You've told us a lot of crap today."

"No, I haven't. I told you the truth. I even told you the truth about your outfit." Loncar didn't look away. "I didn't do anything wrong," I said. "If I'm guilty of anything, it's of being in the wrong place at the wrong time, and if there were a way to prove any of this, I'd do it."

Slowly, Loncar unwound the string on the bulging interoffice envelope and pulled out a dirty, Dalmatian-printed shoe. He held it between his hands for a second, then handed it to me.

"Put this on," he said slowly.

I set the shoe on the floor and slid my foot into it. Despite the clumps of mud caked to the heel and sole, it fit perfectly. I looked up at the detective, who scratched the side of his balding head. "Freakin' fairytale around here." He looked in a ratty brown folder that had been recycled once too often, then turned to the door. Before he left the room again, he turned back to face me. "Thank you for your cooperation. The police would like to offer an apology."

"That's it? I can leave?"

"You can leave."

The woman in Dickies reentered and told me to follow her. We walked down a narrow corridor to the front desk. The clock on the wall read ten forty-two. Nick leaned against the wall, talking to a pair of officers. He still wore the tuxedo from last night, though his bowtie was gone and his shirt was unbuttoned at the collar. He turned to me. I couldn't read his face. He picked up a sweatshirt and pants from the desk next to him and held them out to me.

"Put these on in the restroom and meet me out front. I'm taking you home."

I hobbled to him, off-balance since I was only wearing one shoe. I couldn't read his expression. I put a hand on the desk to balance myself before taking the clothes. He put his arms around me and I leaned against him, too tired to laugh or cry. He slowly pulled away and held my shoulders. I didn't know what strange trick of fate had brought him there at that exact moment, and I honestly didn't care.

His low voice whispered in my ear. "We'll talk when I get you home. Right now, you need to get dressed. Your robe is coming open and there's a pool going on whether or not anybody's going to see you naked."

I tugged at the collar of the robe and went into the bathroom to change. When I came out, Detective Loncar was waiting for me.

"Detective, why did you ask me about your outfit?"

"Ms. Kidd, you were all over the place in there, and you haven't exactly been honest with me. I had to figure out what you were like when you were telling the truth so I could figure out what you were like when you were lying."

I leaned in closer and dropped my voice. "And what about Nick Taylor? What's he doing here?"

"What, him?" He jerked a thumb toward Nick's truck in the parking lot. "Prince Charming's been working with us from the start."

27

———

BOOBY-TRAPPED

"WHAT DID THE DETECTIVE MEAN, YOU'RE WORKING WITH HIM?" I asked Nick as we walked to his truck.

"Get inside."

"Not until I get an explanation. You owe me that."

He unlocked the door and held it open for me. "Do you want to do this here, in front of the police station, or at your house? Because I can go either way, but I'm not the one wearing borrowed clothes of questionable origin."

I climbed into his truck and waited a whole half a block before prompting him for an answer.

"Remember when you asked me about being in the competition?" he said.

"Yes. You said Amanda entered for you, the application got processed and went too far and Patrick disqualified you instead of admitting the interns made a mistake."

"I wasn't entirely honest with you."

"Meaning what?"

Nick merged from Penn Avenue onto the highway. He didn't speak until after he passed a large truck with a grocery store logo on the side.

"I knew Patrick fairly well. He took an interest in me back when I was producing footwear for designers' runway collections. He introduced me to a couple of financiers who put up the money for my first collection and encouraged me to get out from under the hem of apparel designers, so to speak, and let my shoes stand on their own."

"When was this? "

"Ten years ago? Fifteen? I don't remember exactly. Before I met you, before you started buying for Bentley's."

"You knew Patrick." Why didn't I know that?

"He knew there was trouble with this competition. He asked me if I'd pose as a finalist to check things out from the inside."

"What did you find out?"

"Nothing. The morning I saw you at Tradava, the morning we found him, I was there to go over his concerns."

"But you're listed on his files as disqualified, and those files are from before he was murdered."

"One of the designers made a stink about me. Said I didn't meet the eligibility requirements since I already had achieved full collection success."

"Do you know which one?"

"Clestes."

"Who is Clestes?"

"Catherine Lestes and her brother. They do some interesting work, but she's a real firecracker. She threatened to go public with the news the contest was rigged if I wasn't disqualified."

"She—she who?"

"The redhead. Patrick, Maries, and I all knew I was a bogus entrant but there wasn't anything else we could do when she cried foul. Once I was disqualified, I lost my inside angle."

"But you didn't. Amanda is your—Amanda kept you connected."

Nick turned onto my street. Two blocks later he turned into my driveway and cut the engine. "I don't want to bring Amanda into this any more than she already is."

"But she's in it, isn't she? Be honest, Nick. Because if Amanda isn't your connection to the competition, then she could be as guilty as any of the other designers. What does she say about last night?"

"I haven't talked to her yet."

"Maybe you should. I bet she has a couple of secrets she's not telling you."

"Kidd, listen to me. The police are handling it."

I got out of the truck and slammed the door. Nick got out too. "Where do you think you're going?" I asked.

"Every time you tell me you're going play things safe, I trust you. And then I find out you lied. This time I'm going to make sure you play things safe. Now go inside, take a shower, lay down, and go to sleep."

"Are you going to tell me what's going on with you?" I asked with a yawn.

"We'll talk more when you wake up."

Hours later I awoke and stretched as far as I could, savoring the peaceful post-sleep state. Memories of the previous night, of the gala, the cops, and of Nick assaulted me and I sat up and looked around, expecting not to be alone. But the room was empty; the house was quiet.

Maybe I dreamt the whole thing.

I pulled myself to the corner of the bed, ignoring the clothes now folded and sitting outside of my bathroom. They strongly resembled clothes I dreamt I wore home from the police station. (That's why I was ignoring them.)

I approached the window and looked outside, not sure what I'd see in my driveway. Surprisingly, I saw nothing. Maybe I dreamt the drive home too.

I opened the bedroom door. A crash came from the hallway. Footsteps sounded downstairs. I shut the bedroom door and leaned against it. Who was here? Where was I to go? Someone knocked on my door. I froze. Footsteps walked away. I opened the door and tiptoed into the hallway and looked down the stairs.

At Nick. Surrounded by several dozen books, scattered in messy piles around his feet.

"What was that crash?" I asked.

"I booby-trapped your door so I would know if you tried to escape."

"You what?"

"You have a habit of lying about your whereabouts, and I wanted to make sure I knew if you tried something funny."

A rope was knotted around my bedroom doorknob. I followed it with my eyes, down the stairs, to the floor by Nick's feet. "This rope is rigged to my door. What if I tried to go out the window?"

"I had a different booby trap for that."

I stomped down the stairs until I was directly in front of him. "I don't need a babysitter, Nick."

As we stood in the living room, having a stare-off, a green VW Bug barreled down the street and swung into the driveway next to Nick's truck. I looked past Nick to the window and saw Eddie clutching a greasy paper bag to his white Frankie Say Relax T-shirt. He jogged to the front door and let himself in.

"What are you standing around for? Burgers are getting cold." He looked back and forth between us.

"What are you doing here?" I asked.

He raised an eyebrow. "I picked up food since it is a well-known fact that you are much more forgiving about people dropping by your house when they bring you food and honestly, how much pizza can one person eat?"

"I'm not talking about the food. Why are you here?"

Eddie looked at Nick. "You want to tell her, or should I?" Nick shrugged. "Dude, it was your plan."

I didn't like what I was hearing but the scent of onion rings from the greasy bag distracted me long enough to get past my annoyance. Eddie thrust the bag at Nick and let him pass us, then pulled me into a conspiratorial whisper. "Nick doesn't want you to be alone. I'm here to get your keys so I can get your car from Tradava." He followed Nick into the kitchen and sat down at the table.

"Your burger is getting cold," Nick said from the kitchen. I rounded the corner and watched him bite into his hamburger. A blob of mustard remained on the corner of his mouth.

"Get out of my house," I commanded.

Nick stood up with his burger in one hand. He took another bite, then set it on the table. "I can see there's no way you're going to eat while I'm here, so I'll go. Eddie, can I count on you?"

"No problem," Eddie answered between chews.

Nick wiped his mouth and headed toward me. I turned around and he followed me to the front door and tugged on my ponytail.

"Take it easy, Kidd."

I locked the door behind him. When I returned to the table, I stuffed two onion rings into my mouth and bit into a burger before swallowing. Eddie toyed with the onion rings on his plate.

I smelled something that didn't blend with dinner. "What's with the babysitter routine? I spent the day at the police station and now they know everything I know. It's over. Is it too early for champagne? We should be celebrating."

"You seem to be the only person who doesn't realize how dangerous it was for you to go to that gala. Nick saved you today, and he's worried you're going get in more trouble. He knew about everything: the threat on the envelope, the missing money, the notes in Patrick's file."

"You're right. Even though the cops are on my side now, I still don't have a job, and I'm still going to lose my house. I'm right back where I started, except the Patrick thing is over. Why are you looking at me like that?"

"Dude, the Patrick thing is definitely not over. Nick didn't want me to tell you this, but there was another attack at Tradava."

The burger and rings turned over in my stomach. "Who?" I asked, not sure I wanted to hear the answer.

"Maries Paulson."

"But she was at the gala."

"She must have left or been taken to the store. I don't know why. She was pretty badly beaten and bound with seam binding."

"Just like Patrick and Florence," I muttered. "The three people who controlled the outcome of the competition."

"She was found unconscious in the trend office. When the police swept the room, they found your fingerprints all over."

I didn't know what to say. The threat I received on the invitation said I would be set up if I kept digging, and sure enough, that's what happened.

"What are you thinking?" Eddie prodded.

That the real killer was still on the loose. That going to the cops hadn't finished anything. That trying to do the right thing had made things worse.

"Someone said they knew you were there. Turns out they only saw your car. When they talked to Nick, he told them he gave you a ride home, and that you left your car at the store."

"Nick saved my butt."

"He also told them you were at the museum event."

"Nick didn't see me at the museum event."

"Well, he may have made a few assumptions on that one. He saw a person outside of the event perched in a tree." He paused, closed his eyes and shook his head at the idea, and continued. "And he found a shoe stuck in the ground. A Nick Taylor shoe he claims he gave you years ago."

"I was saving them for a special occasion," I said.

"It's a good thing you wore them last night because they might have kept you out of jail. You know, another thing you might want to consider is Nick left the gala early and spent the last twelve hours making sure you were safe."

"Amanda was left alone," I said. "I'm telling you, it could still be her."

Eddie ate an onion ring while my accusation hung in the air. "What do you want to do?"

"They found Maries at Tradava. Patrick's body was at Tradava.

And I was attacked at Tradava. It's not going to end until we figure out why everything leads to Tradava."

It was time for another overnight stakeout.

28

IT WASN'T RIGHT

Undercover Fashion Chic, I might have called it, if I were writing editorial coverage instead of preparing for a date with doom. Phrases like "death wish" and "bad idea" filled my mind. Eddie ran home to change then returned to my house, giving me ample time to back out. I didn't.

We agreed on a uniform to keep me from being recognized. Black knit hat, black sweater. Black cargo pants, though his were canvas and mine were satin. We matched down to our Doc Martens, his buffed to a high polish, mine coated with a layer of dust. I didn't even wear lip gloss.

We arrived at the store shortly before closing time and planned to meet up in the trend office.

"If anybody asks, you're a freelance visual stylist. Don't get into a conversation. Just say you're new and you work for me," Eddie instructed. He unscrewed the cap from a bottle of tomato juice and took a swig, then tucked it into the side pocket of his cargo pants and got out of the car.

He used the employee entrance and I used the door by Juniors. I took the stairs, all seven flights, to the trend office. Using the key I lifted from Michael's desk days ago, I let myself in.

I headed for Patrick's office. It was in complete disarray. The framed cover of *Vogue* hung crooked on the wall above the purple sofa. The oversized *Harper's Bazaar* cover sat on the floor, the frame and the glass broken. The sewing machine was on its side. I tried not to disturb anything, tiptoeing through the mess to the back of Patrick's desk. Several sheets of white paper were scattered over the floor. I picked them up one by one and assembled them by page number.

It was Maries' speech for the gala, a fitting tribute from one legend to another. She started by acknowledging the lackluster mannequins draped in black, explaining her last-minute decision to use the display to indicate the designers' mourning for Patrick instead of showcasing their runway creations. Before I could finish reading, Eddie's voice interrupted me from outside the office.

"Michael's desk has been cleaned out." He passed the desk in the hallway and joined me. He went straight to the mini fridge and poured himself a glass of lemonade. "He took everything." As he took a gulp, I spun the knob on the side of the empty Rolodex on the corner of Patrick's desk. Someone had pulled every card from the spinner and left the stand behind.

A red scarf, the same one Michael had worn around his neck the day he picked up his portfolio, jutted out of the hall closet. I touched the wool and let the scarf trail through my fingers.

"Odd that he took everything but left his scarf."

"Do you think he's behind this?" he asked.

"He knew about the money and he worked close enough with Patrick to maybe know his password. He said something to Maries to make her distrust me. He was here all along, and he had access. But still, it doesn't feel right."

Eddie drained his glass and crawled under the desk. "How did you do this? It's not exactly comfortable," he complained. After a few minutes of watching him try to find the best position, I crawled over to help him figure it out. I was a little curious how I had slept there myself.

We sprawled out, side by side, staring at the bottom of Patrick's desk. It was pretty big but with two of us, it was close quarters. I folded my hands over my hips and made a steeple. Eddie drummed "We Got The Beat" on the bottom of the drawer above us.

"Why are you so willing to help me?" I asked somewhat tentatively. He stopped drumming. I wasn't sure how far I wanted to push the boundaries of our friendship. And I didn't realize it when I'd asked but the longer the question hung in the air, the more vulnerable I felt.

"That math test in high school. The accusations could have changed the entire path of my life. If you hadn't come forward, I would've been expelled. I had a scholarship to art school lined up. It would have disappeared. And that's what everybody, the principal, the teacher, the other students thought. I was the new kid, the troublemaker from out of town. Nobody would have been surprised."

"But you didn't cheat."

"Until you spoke up for me, nobody was on my side. I still don't know why you did it. We weren't friends before it happened, and we didn't become friends after either."

"Because we graduated."

"Why did you stand up for me?" he asked.

"Because I saw it happen. Somebody was trying to get away with something, and it wasn't fair. Not to me, who stayed up studying all night. Not to you, the person who knew the material. Not to anybody in that class who was being graded on the bell curve."

"It was high school. People don't go around sticking up for strangers."

I didn't speak right away. Eddie was right. I couldn't have been the only student in that class to see the captain of the football team copying Eddie's answers. But I was the only one who said something. I'd thought about that a lot since reconnecting with Eddie, and I knew exactly why I'd done it. "It wasn't right." I bounced my knees against each other and stared at the bottom of Patrick's desk. The office was silent. "You work hard to make your opportunities. You don't get breaks by stealing someone else's hard work. That's not the way life is supposed to go."

"I've stayed in Ribbon my whole life," Eddie said. "A few years ago, I had the opportunity to move to New York and take a risk. It was a great job, and I thought about it long and hard. But I didn't go. And here you are. You had that career and it didn't make you happy."

"What are you saying?"

"You're where you're supposed to be. But you can't appreciate it because someone made you doubt yourself. You'd be good at this job if you stuck around long enough to do it."

"Help me figure out who killed Patrick and I'll stick around long enough to tell you all about what you missed by never moving to New York."

I didn't use the words "I promise" because I wasn't sure I could. But I *was* sure I couldn't figure things out myself.

Eddie reached over and thumped his fist against my hands. I thumped him back. The seriousness of the moment hung in the air for a couple of seconds. "Dude, seriously, this is not comfortable."

"I think my body shut down that night. Between moving here, finding Patrick's body, the cops, the mortgage people—I don't know. I just collapsed and slept."

"Was this your view?"

"Pretty much." I pointed out the wad of Post-its, cold medicine packets, and crumbled business cards that belonged to employees who at one time occupied the chair in the trend office. I worked one of the business cards loose and looked at the name. *Cat Lestes. Trend Specialist.*

"Let me see that," Eddie said and snatched the card from my fingers. "This is an old card. At least six years. We changed our logo five years ago and this has the old one on it."

"Cat Lestes—Clestes. Red. She's the one who got Nick disqualified. She worked for Patrick? Did you know her?"

"Six years ago, I was on staff. Visual didn't move up here until three years ago, and even now the visual still works out of the office on the first floor."

"Wait here," I said. I inched my way out from under the desk, then flipped over and crawled on all fours until I had space to stand up. I went back to the trend specialist office.

Only days ago, I'd thought this office was empty because the person I followed had left on poor terms. Today I knew that wasn't true. Amanda had been my predecessor, and I wanted to explore a little more. There was something here in the trend offices, a connection I'd missed.

I scanned the vacant office, looking at it through the eyes of a stranger. The office held little more charm than a high school gymnasium the day after the prom, with remnants of life swept into the corners.

"There's nothing here," I said. "We're wasting our time." I returned to Patrick's office and froze as a dark puddle oozed out from under the desk and slowly stained the carpet.

My heart jumped into my throat. I put out a hand on the door and gulped deep breaths. Eddie's arm stuck out from under the desk, palm up, fingers curled. And a hand clamped itself over my mouth to keep me from screaming.

29

MORNING PEOPLE

I bit down on the hand. It let go. I whirled around. Nick.

The same Nick who had arranged for me to be at home under Eddie's watch. The same Nick who claimed to care about me. The same Nick who had been everywhere something had happened from the time I showed up expecting to start my new job. This time, there were no comforting crinkles surrounding his eyes. This time I was scared to death.

"Stay away from me. I don't know why you're here, but I'm calling the cops." I stepped backward, one hand out front, the other in back feeling for the desk. He reached his unbitten hand out to me and I smacked it away.

"Don't touch me! What did you do to Eddie?"

"What happened to Eddie?" he asked, looking confused.

I pointed toward the desk, to Eddie's feet jutting out from underneath.

"Eddie's—he's lying under the desk. You—you—while I was in the other office."

Nick looked first at the desk, then back at me. "Keep talking," he ordered, moving toward Eddie. The stain on the carpet grew.

"I didn't hear anyone. I didn't hear *you*. I came back to tell him we were wasting our time."

The sound of a snore from under the desk brought a halt to my babbling. Eddie's legs, the only thing visible other than his limp arm, repositioned themselves as he shifted. An empty tomato juice bottle rolled across the carpet, bumping against Nick's foot. He picked up the bottle and held it by the lid with two fingers. Dribbles of thick red liquid ran down the outside of the bottle. A fat droplet hit the carpet and seeped in. Nick set the bottle on the desk behind me and wiped red tomato-juice handprints on his jeans. He led me to the purple sofa.

"Why are you two here?"

My words came out in a rush. "Everything happens at Tradava," I said. I was shivering uncontrollably but not because it was cold.

"Have you learned nothing?"

"It's the only way to get on with my life. I needed Eddie because he could get me in here. I didn't think he would be in any danger." I didn't know if I made sense, but I couldn't stop talking.

"You saw a large puddle on the carpet and assumed he was dead. Then you saw me and thought I was the killer. That's why you bit me?" Nick massaged his palm. For all I knew he was wondering if I had rabies.

"You clamped a hand over my mouth. Biting was instinct." I lowered my voice to a reasonable level. "I know you want me to leave all of this alone, but I can't." Considering how loud the voices in my head were, my voice came out quiet and more than a little shaky. "I'm sorry you're wrapped up in this, and I'm sorry people keep getting hurt." I paused. "I just want to get on with my life."

"I called you at your house. You didn't answer. I called Eddie. I could hear enough background noise to know he was at Tradava. It wasn't hard to put two and two together, even if it doesn't add up to anything wise." I braced myself for the lecture I was sure Nick was gearing up to deliver. "Kidd," he said. He sandwiched my hand between his. "Look at me." I slowly raised my eyes from his hands to his face. "Amanda is my friend. She's mixed up in this, and I've been trying to help her."

"How?"

"She was about to debut her first collection under her name. It was an important step. She had a good chance of winning the competition and the hundred thousand dollars. For an emerging designer, that's a lot of money."

It *was* a lot of money. It was enough money to solve my problems, at least temporarily. I'd get the mortgage company off my back, tear out the shag carpet, and buy Logan a year's supply of the best brand of cat food on the market. But those were my problems, and this wasn't about me.

"Aside from the money, the contest came with connections. A guaranteed order from Tradava. Plus, Patrick met with the buyers regularly to advise on trends and emerging talent. His connections and endorsement could have opened a lot of doors for her. She needed him to validate her designs."

"But she worked for him. Wouldn't she already be able to count on his endorsement?"

"Stores are like little worlds. You get a job, and that's who you are. There's not a lot of room for someone to reinvent themselves, and for Amanda to have any credibility, she needed this. Something big to endorse her talent and let her be something other than what she was."

"But wouldn't there always be a question about her winning?"

"That's why she quit. It's why Patrick needed an outsider as his trend specialist. It's why he never had you come to the office—to make sure you had no preconceived notions about her when you started."

For the first time in days, things started to make sense. All along Nick had known more than I did, and he'd kept it to himself while looking out for me on the side.

Eddie rolled over again and knocked his head on the desk. He cursed, sat up, and looked around the room with glazed eyes. After he mumbled some unintelligible words he stood, the tomato juice caked to the side of his pants. He refilled his lemonade and drained the glass in several gulps, then squinted at us as though he couldn't make us out clearly. He stumbled to the sofa, plunked a pillow from under my arm, and returned to the floor behind the desk. His even breathing resumed.

"Morning people," I scoffed, shaking my head.

"I wouldn't criticize too much. Didn't you fall asleep in here too?"

He had a point. "Tell me about the gala. Something happened inside that room. What? And where's the money?" I asked.

"What money?"

"The prize money. The hundred thousand dollars. Maries Paulson had with her."

"Why would she take the money to the gala?" he asked.

It was my turn to pick up the explanation. "Someone was extorting the money from her. But Patrick never told her where he kept it. I found a list of investors on his laptop, and it looked like he had collected eighty thousand dollars, plus the entry fees. That was ninety thousand, four hundred. He was short. But Michael told me the money was safe, and the right person would get it."

"Michael Dubrecht?"

"Yes. He was at the gala too. I saw him talk to Maries. All the suspects were there."

"All?"

"The designers. Michael, Red—I mean Cat, Amanda, and you."

"Me?"

"You. You were there the morning Patrick was murdered. You were there when my house was broken into. You had access to the laptop—I found it in your store. And you tried to keep me from going to the gala."

His face clouded. "I tried to keep you away for your own good. This is a murder investigation, Kidd, not a game. People have been hurt."

I jumped up from the sofa. "Then why are you here now, Nick? If it's so dangerous for me to be here, why isn't it dangerous for you?"

"Because I suspected you weren't going to stay away. Patrick is dead. Two other people have been attacked. I don't want you to be next. Do you?" Nick stood up and gathered his jacket in his palm. "There's one way for me to prove I have nothing to do with this, and that's to leave. Wake Eddie and let's go. This isn't business for us. It's for the cops." He walked to the doorway before turning around. I stood rooted to the spot next to the purple sofa.

"Come with me, Kidd."

"No," I said, surprising both of us. "I can't leave. I can't let this go until it's over."

"I won't let anything happen to you."

I thought about Nick helping me with the flooded basement, about Nick driving me home after I was knocked out at Tradava, and about Nick saving me from the police interrogation. I thought about how often he'd been there to save me, and how it was time I saved myself. "I have to do this for myself."

"I can't watch you put yourself in danger." He walked out. Seconds later, I heard the heavy glass doors clunk into place.

How much truth was there to what Nick said? More than I cared to admit. In one week, I'd lived through some of the worst experiences of my life, and most of them were of my doing. Why was I forcing myself to stay? What did I really expect to gain?

I shook Eddie's leg until he woke up. "Let's get out of here."

He sat up and scratched the left side of his head. "Dude, where am I?"

"Tradava. Here. Take the keys. There's something I have to do before I leave."

He pulled himself out from under the desk. He opened his eyes as wide as he could and blinked repeatedly. "I'm not driving."

"I'll meet you in the car. Hang tight." I checked the clock. The store would be closing soon. This was it, my last chance to stand in these offices. Once I walked out that door, I'd be done with Tradava. This job had worked out for me about as well as a root canal performed by a sadist. Someone had done a number on me, one that exposed my weaknesses, my nerves, my doubts to the world. Then they'd drilled.

It was time to say goodbye to my fresh start.

Eddie took the keys and stumbled out of the offices. I rounded the corner from Patrick's office and turned into what should have been my empty office.

But it wasn't empty. Michael Dubrecht lay slumped in a corner.

His spiked black hair, gelled into a Mohawk, pressed into his forearm, leaving small red welts. His red scarf, the one I'd seen in the closet when we first arrived, was knotted around his neck.

I rushed to him and loosened the scarf. His eyes were unfocused and dilated. His mouth was open. I pulled off my gloves and felt along his neck. My fingers found a piece of seam binding knotted under his scarf. With shaking fingers, I fumbled with the knot until I was able to loosen it. I pressed on his neck and found a faint pulse.

"Help!" I called, but no one was there to answer.

"Can you hear me?" I asked, shaking him by the shoulders. His eyes opened slightly.

"Water," he choked out, then coughed a couple of times.

"There's no water. Stay with me, focus on me. There's lemonade. I have to leave you to get it."

"No!" he said, his hand gripping my wrist tightly.

"I'll be right back. There's not a lot of time."

"Not alone," he said.

"We are now. Nick and Eddie were with me, but they left. I'll be right back, and I'll get you out of here." I raced to Patrick's office for a glass of lemonade.

I flipped the light switch a couple of times, but it didn't work. I grabbed a glass and filled it. There was a heavy *ka-chunk* in the hallway, like a lock falling into place. Store security had taken to locking the offices to keep people like me out. But we had to leave. Otherwise Michael might not make it.

I raced back into my old office, sloshing lemonade over the brim of the glass. He hadn't moved. I tipped his head back and poured lemonade into his mouth. When I let go of his head, it lolled to the side, his neck muscles too weak to hold it up.

Footsteps sounded in the hallway. "Help! Help! We're locked in here!" I hollered. I reached for the desk phone. There was no dial tone.

Someone brushed against me. I spun around. "No," I said, staring into the one face I hadn't expected to see tonight. If only I'd been faster to figure it all out, so much could have been avoided. I should have known from the beginning, but now it was too late.

30

DELUSIONAL

I watched the designer push a stray lock of brilliant red hair from her eyes. Then, in a sudden gesture, she pulled a wig from her head and shook her head. A sheath of glossy black hair fell to her shoulders and I stared directly into the eyes of Maries Paulson.

"I thought you were in the hospital," I said.

"That's what you were supposed to think," she said. "It's that Ries girl in the hospital, not me. It only took a couple of bruises to her face to make her unrecognizable and a blow to her head to make her unconscious. I planted my ID on her and called nine-one-one. She wasn't conscious enough to tell them they'd made a mistake."

It had been easy for Maries to copy the signature hair of one of the finalists, as easy as it had been for her to impersonate an EMT or a grieving friend. It was a testament to her natural beauty, or at least dermabrasion and an expensive moisturizer, that with a two-hundred-dollar wig, she could pass for a woman almost half her age.

"You have a real talent for doing what I want, don't you, dear?" Maries joked. "It might have been fun to work with you if you didn't keep getting in my way. Now, where's the money?"

Any surgeries she'd undergone had been successful if success was judged by a vacant expression that gave away nothing. But her desperation showed through her eyes. They'd seen too much and hinted at her true age. The dark sunglasses she frequently wore had been the best defense she had against the truths her eyes revealed.

"I don't have the money. I don't know where it is."

"How predictable. Predictable people are nice to have around until they wear out their usefulness. You helped me figure out what Patrick had done. I didn't know about the file on his laptop, or that he'd gotten the money from the garment district. You told me all of that. And you made it very easy for me to make you look guilty. It's too bad you're going to wear out your usefulness in one night, sweetie," Maries cooed. Her attitude angered me, but she was right. I might as well have been following a script.

The gloves I had so carefully worn to avoid leaving fingerprints were on the desk next to Michael. Both Eddie and Nick were gone while I was in danger. I looked around the office for a way out while the walls closed in.

"Who do these kids think they are, entering a contest to get money to back their collections? That's not how it used to work. It took talent. Passion. Vision. I've been designing clothes since I was seventeen. I witnessed the beginning of American Design. I watched Dior launch the New Look when I was a child and realized how famous he would become—he'll live forever because of that! That's the industry I wanted to be a part of. And I was. I dated Halston!"

The woman was delusional. Everybody knows Halston was gay.

"But the industry changed. I've seen the genius of Courrèges copied so many times people think he's a boot and not a designer. I've seen true talent retire because fashion became less about creativity and more about marketing. This contest, this whole farce, is the problem, not the solution. Dangling a contract and money in front of a bunch of small-town designers is not the way to discover the future of style."

"But you're a judge. You were part of the contest all along," I said. "You're gaining as much publicity as any of the contestants."

"I don't need the publicity. I need money. My debts run deep. When Patrick said Tradava pulled the funding, that he had to raise one hundred thousand dollars to see the competition happen, I thought it was over. But when he secured the money, quickly, I had to know how he had done it. He wouldn't tell me details. That's when I knew I had to get the money for myself."

Her eyes glowed with rage and insanity, accented by the reflection of the fluorescent tube lighting. "He caught me going through his files. I suspected he knew, but he pretended not to. I discovered the bank and the account number. All I needed was the password on the account and I could have transferred the money and vanished."

"You framed me," I said. "You vandalized my house and attacked the woman at the fabric store and told her you were me."

"You were supposed to get scared and leave. But when you didn't go away, I knew I could use you."

My breath caught in my throat. "You killed Patrick for money. He was a better person than you. He went to businessmen who had a stake in the success of future designers. He remained true to the industry while you wanted to steal from it," I said.

"Don't be a child. Those men were loan sharks. I should know. I turned to them myself when I first had financial trouble. There's no getting away once you're in bed with them. This was my way out. Patrick knew I had turned to them once. He was the one who reopened that door, not me. And he wasn't going to stand in my way after the door was open."

"But you said—"

"Such naiveté. It's almost charming." She ran a gloved finger down the side of my face. I sat still, achingly still, clenching and unclenching my jaw. "When I came here, that morning, I pleaded with him to help me. He refused. He said he would find another judge and that I was no longer a part of the competition. When he hired you, he planned to train you to be the second judge. I couldn't allow him to do that. I couldn't allow him to tarnish my name, to cut me out, and I couldn't let you take my place." Her pupils dilated, and her spittle hit my cheek. "He put up a good fight. I didn't expect that. Now, I'll ask you again. Where is the money?"

"I don't know where the money is," I said. "I don't know anything about the money."

"You've been snooping around here for a week. You're the only one who had access to his files. Don't you understand? I have to have it!"

"Maybe there is no money," I said.

Her rage turned to disturbing calm. "Or maybe you demanded the money from me, money that would help you start over," she said. A chill settled onto my shoulders. "Solve your financial problems. If anything happens to me, maybe I've left enough evidence to lead back to you."

I moved away from her and bumped into Michael's foot. He made a gurgling sound. Maries stood up and we both looked at him.

"I know where the money is," he whispered.

"Where?" Maries asked.

"Water," he choked out.

Maries grabbed the back of my jacket and yanked me up. "Get him something to drink."

I picked up the glass of lemonade and held it to his head, beads of condensation transferring onto his bluish skin and running down the side of his face. My mind raced. I needed time to figure things out, but time might be the one thing Michael couldn't spare. I raised my eyes to the ceiling and silently prayed to the gods of footwear and designer clothes and everything I found holy. Who was the patron saint for fashion? *Yves St. Laurent, I need your help! Are you listening?*

Lemonade sloshed out of the glass. Maries grabbed my wrist. The glass dropped and shattered against the floor. I jumped at the crash. Maries picked up a shard with her other hand and dragged it across my cheekbone. My skin burned like someone had set it on fire.

I tried to pull away, but she was stronger than I'd imagined. She twisted my wrist until my shoulders and neck followed. The pain had doubled me over and my face was inches from the broken glass on the desk. She bent over me, pinning me down.

"Get more lemonade," she hissed in my ear. She let go and I tried to stand. My legs were shaking so hard I could barely walk. I couldn't speak. I leaned against the walls in the hallway and guided myself to Patrick's office.

I pulled the glass pitcher out of the mini-fridge. It was half empty.

Before all of this happened, I might have said it was half full.

My eyes darted wildly around the office. To the desk. To the sofa. To my reflection in the glass on the framed magazine covers that had fallen off the walls and now littered the floor. My cargo pants were disheveled from sitting on the floor. My undercover chic look had morphed into Satanic cheerleader hours ago, but what difference did it make now?

"I don't think he has a lot of time left," she called in the singsong voice of a murderer.

I walked back to the horror scene. Maries had moved Michael into the chair behind the desk. She was perched on the corner, close enough for me to see the roots of her hair.

She was crazy, of that I had no doubt. But unlike me, she had managed to keep her gloves on. She looked like she always looked: elegance personified. And here I was, sweating profusely and barely able to stand.

My mind swam with information. The design competition, the night I spent locked in Tradava, and the museum event. I thought of Eddie, asleep in the car out front. Of Patrick's password, and Michael's promise the money was safe, of the protected file, and the letter Patrick had written me on his protected file. I watched a smile spread across Maries's face as I tipped the pitcher to Michael's mouth. And then everything became clear.

31

ENJOYING THE SILENCE

Maries Paulson had doped the lemonade. That's why I'd slept under Patrick's desk. It's why Eddie had passed out too. And it was how she'd incapacitated Patrick, a man with a heart condition, enough to kill him.

She said I was predictable, so I did the most unpredictable thing I could imagine. I smashed the pitcher against the desk, crashing it into a thousand pieces and splashing the remaining lemonade on her. She jumped back, startled. Score one for me.

The door to the offices rattled. I heard my name called from the hallway.

Maries lunged for me. I jumped back, one step, then two, then turned around and raced for the door. She grabbed my jacket and threw me sideways into Patrick's office. I stumbled across the floor and hit the desk. My left hand connected with the arm of the purple sofa, but I was off balance. My right hand slapped against the wall. Maries grabbed the back of my head and pushed it forward, into the metal frame on the *Vogue* cover. Pain exploded behind my right eye. The glass shattered then fell to the floor. The poster curled from the frame exposing neat stacks of hundred-dollar bills.

"The money!" Maries gasped.

I spun to face her. I grabbed a long blade of broken glass. Maries lunged at me, her hands clawing on either side of my body at stacks of bills that had been hidden in the office all along. I closed my eyes and screamed. Her body fell against me, knocking me backward, into the wall, and onto the pile of cash on the floor. I kicked, screamed, and tried to move her off me. She went limp.

The doors opened, and a flood of people came in. That flood a swarm of uniformed officers, paramedics, and included dear, sweet Detective Loncar.

It also included Nick. He hadn't left after all.

Detective Loncar bent down and pressed his fingers into Maries' neck. "She's dead," he said. He extended his hand. I took it and he pulled me up. Nick cocooned me in a blanket and wrapped me in his arms.

We stood in the hallway outside Patrick's office. Through sweat, tears, and matted hair I watched paramedics move Maries Paulson's body from the pile of money on the floor to a gurney. It was the first time I'd seen her not look glamorous.

A blonde woman in scrubs offered me a cup of water. "Michael," I said and pointed to the other room. "He's hurt worse than I am." I held the blanket around me while they went to check on him. Minutes later the blonde pushed a wheelchair into the office, then Michael was pushed out.

Detective Loncar directed a team of police officers around the office. "Ms. Kidd, do you want to tell me what happened here tonight?" the detective asked. He ran the palm of his hand over his short crew cut while he looked around the room. A skinny man in a black leather jacket snapped photos of the damaged poster, the broken glass, and the money.

"Somewhere else," I said. My voice had turned raspy despite the water. Loncar and Nick guided me away from the trend offices, and I told him the story of Maries Paulson, the design competition, and the hidden money that had led to Patrick's murder.

IT MIGHT HAVE BEEN the birds chirping or the sun shining. It might have been the soft, fluffy down comforter on my bed, or Logan by my side. It might be the peace and quiet I'd earned after the night at Tradava when I'd narrowly escaped with my life. Whatever it was that allowed me to sleep, I didn't care. The drama was over, and I was free.

Tradava had been given enough information to exonerate me from wrongdoing, but no offer of employment had been extended. That meant I was probably going to have to interview for the trend specialist job all over again.

If I still wanted it.

My mind wandered to Cat—Catherine—Lestes, the owner of Catnip. In a parallel universe, she and I might have been friends, her owning a boutique that could fuel my passion for fashion. Everything she'd said had been true. Clestes was a collection of one of a kind items co-designed by her and her brother. She sold the collection at her store. Together, they'd been a legitimate finalist in the design competition. She had never believed the competition was fair. My arrival at Tradava and misguided partnership with Maries Paulson had done little other than lead Cat to believe I had something to hide.

The bags from my shopping spree were still lined up along the wall, ready to be returned. I didn't need a collection of unique choices I couldn't afford to endorse who I was. Even if I wore last season' clothes, fashion was in my blood.

Just not today.

I opened my T-shirt drawer and stuck my hands into the back. Under the stack of neatly folded white tank tops I found it. A faded black T-shirt that said The Kid. The adult XL that had once hung to my knees now fit like a security blanket, softened with repeated washings. The black had turned to gray and the fusible iron-on peeled up by the bottom of the decal. I pulled it on over Union Jack pajama bottoms and shoved my feet into a pair of white Moon Boots for warmth. Downstairs, I retrieved the newspaper and the mail from the front porch. There would, no doubt, be an account of the events at Tradava, as there had been every day since the showdown. It had been over a week, and the story was still going strong. I carried the still-bundled newspaper from the porch to the recycle bin.

Nick's truck turned into my driveway. I looked down at my outfit and sighed. I was tired of trying to impress people. The boss who'd been impressed by my resume was dead. So was the designer who appreciated my style. My closet was half full, but this was me too. Moon Boots and all.

I held the door open. Nick followed me to the sofa. "How's your hand?" he asked.

I held it up to show off the clean application of gauze across the cut on my palm. "I won't be playing handball anytime soon, but I'll survive." Logan padded into the room and jumped onto the window sill, staring outside. "How's yours?"

He held his up. "The toothmarks are gone." He smiled. "Have you read the papers?"

I shook my head.

"Do you want to talk about it?"

"I don't know."

We sat side by side on the green velvet sofa. It was back in place along the wall, facing the large bay window. I had stopped pushing it up to the door the day after the police brought me home from Tradava. I finally felt safe.

"Patrick wanted this competition to be his legacy," I said. "He believed, completely, that design talent doesn't have to come from a big city. He wanted to find someone with vision and put them on the map." I flipped my wrist over and stared at the gauze, then flipped it back and set it on my thigh. "He asked Maries to be his partner. I don't think it ever occurred to him what would happen."

"What happened when you were in there with her? Why did she snap?"

"She owed a lot of money. Money she borrowed from loan sharks to relaunch her collection. She was desperate. When she learned Patrick had raised the hundred thousand dollars, she saw a way out of debt. Add in that Patrick had turned to the same people she owed money to, and she freaked."

"But why did Patrick keep the money in the frame?"

"That wasn't him. That was Michael." It made sense after the fact. Michael heard Patrick talk to people about investing in an undiscovered talent. He knew where the money was coming from, and where the account was kept. Maries Paulson had asked to be a co-signer on the account, but it never happened. Michael thought Patrick was being secretive about the money because he was a finalist. But when Patrick died, Michael had all of Patrick's passwords, and moved the money out of the bank and hid it in Patrick's office—the office he thought would be vacant. What he wanted was the validation a contest could provide. He wanted to be announced the winner.

When Patrick and Maries first conceived of the competition, they both had ulterior motives. Patrick wanted to be relevant again. A new generation of designers barely knew who he was, and he wanted to be a part of the future of fashion.

"Patrick's password. Livo72. Look in Vogue 72. I misunderstood him. The note he left told me to 'Look en Vogue.' Michael saw the note and took it literally—'look in Vogue.' It was right there. His password was more than a password, it was a clue. I should have figured it out. If I had, Maries might still be alive."

"Kidd, Maries made her bed and now she's lying in it." Nick cradled my cheek, his thumb lightly tracing the almost-healed cut Maries had inflicted.

I tapped the toes of my Moon Boots together. "How's Amanda?" I asked, trying to change the subject.

"She's recovering from injuries. The doctors say there will be no long-term damage, but she's shaken up. I think she's taking an extended break from the runway circuit. Women like Amanda don't get over things like this easily."

"What about women like me?"

"Women like you are harder to find. That's why I'm here."

I turned to Nick and felt the same connection I'd felt during that business dinner last May. His eyes moved from mine to my lips and back to my eyes. Whatever I felt, I knew he felt it too.

We didn't kiss. I didn't know what Nick was thinking, but after everything that had happened, I wanted to savor the moment. We sat there, together, in comfortable silence.

Finally, Nick spoke. "What's next for you, Kidd? Are you going to stay in Ribbon?"

I didn't want to face how much that question had plagued me over the past week. Had this all been a sign I should never have moved back here? Was the house too much for me to handle? Would I be able to get my job back—or officially get it in the first place? Did I want to work at Tradava? Or did I want the job in New York that I'd left? Was I anywhere closer to knowing what I wanted to do with my life?

I'd changed. I wasn't the same person who had left Bentley's with the hopes of starting over. I'd grown up more since moving back than I had in the entire time I'd spent in this house in my childhood. I'd been interrogated by the cops. I'd risked my life. I'd watched a woman die.

"Kidd?" Nick's voice snapped me back to reality. He took my hand and entwined his fingers in mine.

"I don't know what's next," I said. It was the most honest thing I could say.

He stood and pulled me up so we were facing each other but didn't let go of my hand. The gesture was both innocent and intimate. "I don't want to say anything that's going to affect your decision, but as long as I'll be here, I wouldn't mind having you around too." He stepped back and scanned me from head to Moon Boots. "You bring a certain *je ne sais quoi* to Ribbon." I pushed him away. He pulled his keys out of his pocket. "Call me if you need anything. Lemon meringue pie, or bacon, or . . . anything. You know where to find me." He left.

I closed the door behind me and picked up the stack of mail from the end table. Absentmindedly I flipped through the envelopes. A postcard from Mom and Dad. Another form for customized stationary, like the one I'd received a week ago. A threatening letter from Full Circle Mortgage.

I carried the mail to the sofa. So much had happened. I'd given up a job and lost a mentor, but I'd gained direction. I grabbed a pen and filled out the form. *Name: Samantha Kidd. Address:* I paused.

I closed my eyes and remembered the details of the house I knew so well: the seventies shag carpet and built-in bookcase in the living room, the avocado green appliances in the kitchen. For all my recent questions, I had one answer. This was where I wanted to be.

My decision was made. A couple of phone calls were in order to straighten out the mortgage and the job. I'd do what I had to do, and it would be fine. Logan jumped on the sofa next to me, paws on the mail, nuzzling me for attention. It felt right, sitting on the sofa with my cat in my parents' house.

In my house.

Maybe I wouldn't call anyone just yet. Maybe I'd hang out with Logan while enjoying the silence.

BUYER, BEWARE

KILLER FASHION MYSTERY #2

PROLOGUE

This wasn't how I'd planned to spend my Saturday night. It was one thing to be home alone waiting for the phone to ring. The man I wanted to call was in Italy, and I'd gotten used to Saturday nights by myself. Maybe that's why I was hiding in a bathroom with a naked man. He quickened my pulse, shortened my breathing, and inspired thoughts that would make a more innocent woman blush. Never mind that he was made of wood and tucked inside my handbag. Never mind that five minutes ago I'd stolen him from his place of honor in the admissions hall of the local design school.

I'm not a thief, my inner monologue cried out. *I'm not a crook, or an opportunist, or the kind of person who breaks the law.*

Well, maybe, on occasion, I *was* the kind of person who broke the law, but only in very specific situations of the life-or-death variety.

I bargained with the patron saints of thieves and fashion: *If I make it out of here safely, I promise to never wear sweatpants in public again.*

From the hallway, I heard the resonant strike of leather soles on the marble floor. I promised myself if I could make it fifteen more seconds without breathing, I could have two bowls of cherry vanilla ice cream when I got home. If I got home. If I didn't get caught.

Not the best strategy for not breathing.

The footsteps faded, and I exhaled. The naked statue shifted lower in my handbag. I relaxed for a moment and rooted around, making sure my wooden companion was hidden inside the slightly worn Birkin handbag I bought on eBay back when I had a disposable income. At least if I was hauled off to jail, it would be locked up with the rest of my outfit, patiently awaiting my release. How long do you get for stealing art? Ten to twenty years? Good thing the Birkin was a classic.

The door to the bathroom creaked open. Before I could scream, climb through a vent, or adopt a really cool fighting pose, a man in a black turtleneck, black knit hat, black gloves, black cargo pants, and black Vans grabbed my wrist and pulled me toward the exit. It was Eddie Adams, my closest friend and occasional bad influence.

"Did you make the swap?" Eddie whispered.

I nodded.

"Good. The security guard is on the other side of the building. We have to go. Now!" He shoved me into the bright hallway. We raced past closed classroom doors and bulletin boards filled with colorful slips of paper that announced campus activities and tutor sessions. We burst out the exit, down the concrete stairs, to the parking lot. I dove into the back of the waiting getaway car, otherwise known as our other friend Cat's Suburban, and pulled an open sleeping bag over my body. Eddie disappeared into the night on foot. I snuggled against the backseat and remained curled in the fetal position around my Birkin while Cat drove to the edge of the lot.

The car stopped. Why did the car stop? There was no way we were out of the parking lot. It was too soon to stop.

"Can you tell me how to get back to the highway?" Cat asked in an innocent tone. I pictured her flipping her red hair over her shoulder and tipping her head to the side. A male voice described a series of exits and turns. She thanked him. A set of tires peeled out of the lot past us, the voices ceased, and off we drove, me clinging to the naked man like it was our third date.

And that describes my first premeditated robbery.

1

———

NOT A THIEF

THE NIGHT WAS A SUCCESS, IF SUCCESS CAN BE MEASURED BY THINGS like theft and clean getaways. We'd done it. We'd pooled our collective resources and talents and swiped a statue from the Institute of Fashion, Art, and Design, or I-FAD, as it was known in fashion circles. My careful planning had taken us from concept to execution, but success was a team effort. Eddie, visual manager for Tradava, Ribbon, Pennsylvania's oldest retailer, Cat, owner of Catnip, a discount designer boutique in the outlet center, and Dante, Cat's brother, had made it happen. Even more impressive than the success of our mission was the fact that I'd planned the whole thing less than a week ago.

Things had been quiet around my hometown of Ribbon, Pennsylvania. Life was normal, or as normal as it can be when you're in your early thirties, out of work, trying to figure out how to pay the bills. Six months ago, I'd given up my glamorous job as the senior buyer of ladies' designer shoes at Bentley's New York for a chance to move into the house where I grew up. Things hadn't turned out exactly as planned thanks to a murder investigation. I lost my job and my mentor and came darn near close to losing the house. I'd taken to obsessively reorganizing my wardrobe, first by color, next by silhouette, and finally by decade. With my savings account rapidly dwindling thanks to things like the new mortgage payment and cat food for Logan, I was a starving fashionista living off the contents of my closet.

And then the contest had been announced in the *Ribbon Times*.

Interested in a Heist?

Ribbon's hottest new store opens on July 14. Join us for the Pilferer's Ball to get a sneak preview of our unparalleled assortments at criminally low prices. Daring attendees are challenged to arrive with one of the following items in tow, "borrowed" from their current place of residency. Should you successfully lift said loot without notice, you can win a $10,000 shopping spree at HEIST. Rules and regulations listed below.

It was right up my alley.

Eddie, a high school friend I'd reconnected with during the aforementioned murder investigation, seemed the perfect person to help. Plus, safety in numbers and all that.

"The best time for the theft is in the early morning, like three or four o'clock. It'll be dark, the night guard will be tired, and there will be minimal traffic on the campus since the bars and parties shut down at two. Anyone wandering around will probably be drunk and not a credible witness," I had said to Eddie, while we hung out in my living room, discussing my plan.

When I first moved in, the house was a study in post-college hand-me-down. I'd painted an accent wall with a gallon of aqua paint from Home Depot's "Oops" rack and decorated the wall with fabric cuttings framed in black plastic document frames from the dollar store. Three rows of nine frames each filled the wall opposite the large bay window. A white afghan, crocheted by my grandmother, covered the back of the gray flannel sofa Eddie bought me from a prop sale at Tradava, the store where he currently worked (and I thought I'd be working—but that's a different story for a different time). Two black and white chairs sat opposite the sofa, set off by blue tweed fabric I'd found in the markdown bin at the local fabric store and fashioned into curtains.

"We need to not look suspicious around the campus, because

people might remember us if we seem like we don't belong," I added. "I think you should pretend to be a security guard. That way the real guard won't spend too much time watching the areas where you already are."

Eddie sat sideways in one of the black and white chairs, his knees bent over the arm, his checkered Vans bouncing on the outside of the fabric. His pencil flew over a pad of drawing paper, making sketches.

"I don't think I'll make a very convincing security guard."

I ignored him. "My new neighbor is the head of the fabric curriculum at I-FAD. I'll volunteer to talk to one of her classes or something."

I was interrupted by a knock on the door.

"Hold that thought," Eddie said. He spun to a sitting position and pushed himself out of the chair.

"You invited someone to my house?" I asked, shoving incriminating plans and schematics under the sofa. I followed him to the door.

Standing on my porch were a man and a woman. I recognized the woman as Catherine Lestes, the Catnip boutique owner. The last time we'd spoken, we shared a couple of not very nice words. (She'd accused me of murder, and I don't take well to that.) Next to her was a stranger, attractive in a bad-boy way. His outfit could have been assembled from the greats: black leather jacket from Brando, white T-shirt from James Dean, faded denim jeans from Paul Newman. His jet-black hair and sideburns looked like Elvis's in the 1968 comeback special. His scuffed and worn black leather boots probably protected his feet from snakes while walking through the jungle. Out of Africa, maybe. Redford. I looked back at his face. Dangerous and brooding. Not Redford.

"Are you Samantha Kidd?" he asked.

"Yes."

"I've heard a lot about you." He held out a hand. His black leather sleeve rode up, exposing flame tattoos around his wrists. "I'm Dante. You know my sister, Cat." He tipped his head to the side.

Not sure of the protocol to welcome a formerly hostile fashionista and a strange biker dude on my doorstep, I looked at Eddie. He stepped to the side and held the door open.

"Glad you guys could make it. Come on in," he said.

Not what I'd expected. I glared at him, communicating thoughts that he appeared able to tune out.

"I get the feeling you didn't know we were coming," Dante said to me.

"Eddie invited me. We're here to help with the theft," Cat added. "I invited Dante to join us. You don't mind, do you?"

"Sure, fine, no problem." I turned to Eddie. "Can I see you in the kitchen for a moment?"

Logan, my frisky black feline, slinked into the room. I turned to Cat and Dante. "Watch out for my cat. He's very selective about the company he keeps," I said. Logan crossed the room and sniffed the toes of Dante's boots. Fickle cat.

In the kitchen, Eddie said, "Before you say no, think about it. We can't pull this thing off by ourselves."

"Cat doesn't like me."

He waved my protest away like the scent of stinky cheese. "She didn't like you when she thought you were a murderer. Things change. Let them stick around and listen what they can do. Cat has connections at I-FAD, so she can be our person on the inside. And she tells me her brother has all kinds of hidden talents."

"Like what?"

"I don't know, sneaky stuff, by the looks of him. But listen, we might need another man besides me."

The problem was, I already had another man besides Eddie: Nick Taylor. Only, I didn't.

In terms of style, Nick was Redford. And Clark Gable and Cary Grant. He was Hamptons preppy with a side of early Duran Duran. Nick was a shoe designer I'd worked with in my former (glamorous, financially successful, emotionally draining) life. When I gave up that job for a lifestyle makeover and moved from the Big Apple to the small town—Ribbon, Pennsylvania—Nick's name moved from the "colleague" column of my life to the one labeled "you've got potential." And then, like all good shoe designers, he left for Italy, where he'd been for the past month. I was pretty sure that, in addition to keeping the secret about our planned theft at the museum, keeping the secret of the hot tattooed biker who had all kinds of hidden talents might be a bit of a challenge.

"Fine," I said, though it was anything but.

We returned to the living room. Logan was curled up next to Dante on the gray flannel sofa. Cat sat on one of the black and white chairs, flipping through the Halston coffee table book I kept on my glass and chrome coffee table. Her legs were crossed, and she bounced one patent leather lime green pump against her calf.

I sat next to Dante and retrieved the plans and schematics from under the sofa. I outlined my general plan to get them caught up.

"I'll come up with assignments for both of you tonight. In the meantime—"

"Dante will make a better fake security guard than I will," Eddie said. He pulled a piece of paper from his manila folder and held it out to Dante. "Plus, that will give me more time to work on the fake."

Cat chimed in next. "I'll set up a guest professorship with the college, Samantha. I've done it before and already have the contacts. The college probably won't respond to your offer to guest lecture since you're currently unemployed." She brushed a stray lock of vibrant red hair behind her ear. "Now we just need something for you to do." She leaned forward, her elbows on her olive pants, her fingertips tapping against each other while she thought.

"I got it!" Eddie said, spinning to the front of the chair and leaning forward. "You can go undercover as a student."

We all turned toward him. Expensive moisturizers and a box of Miss Clairol could only do so much, and I think the ship had sailed on "undercover student" ten years ago.

"Undercover *grad* student," he clarified. "What?" he said, addressing the doubtful expressions in the room (which numbered more than just mine). "Get her into a sweatshirt and jeans, and she'd look like half the students on campus." He looked at me and cocked his head to one side. "A tan, less eyeliner, no lipstick, some highlights ..."

"We get the point," I said.

"To make sure I'm up to speed," Dante said, "Eddie's going to make a fake sculpture. Cat's going to get inside the college and look around. I'm going to pose as a security guard. And Samantha's going back to school."

Everyone nodded but me.

"Eddie, how long will it take you to make the replica?" Cat asked.

"Not sure. I need measurements, pictures, specs. I need to conduct recon."

Dante pulled a folder of his own from inside his motorcycle jacket and tossed it on the coffee table in front of Eddie. Cat leaned forward, and Eddie opened the folder. I watched out of the corner of my eye. Eddie fanned a series of photos across the table. They featured every conceivable angle of the statue, along with newspaper clippings describing the material, installation, security, and measurements.

"Is that what you need?" Dante asked.

Eddie's eyes went wide. "Where'd you—"

"You guys aren't the only ones who read the newspaper. Just seemed easier to be part of your team than try to steal it on my own. How long?"

"With this info? I'll review it tonight and work on materials tomorrow. I'll take a couple of days off and can have it ready by the weekend."

"Good. We all know our assignments?" Dante asked.

The heads around the table bobbed. I pushed my chair away from the table and walked into the kitchen. Dante followed. I pulled a Fred Flintstone juice glass from the cabinet and filled it with tap water, pretending I didn't know he was there.

"You don't like that we changed your plan," he said.

"Doesn't really matter. It's not my plan anymore."

"Sure it is. The players may have changed, but the game is still the same. Just because people swapped parts doesn't mean you didn't design it. Besides, it's best everyone take the role they're most comfortable in."

I turned around and faced him. "You really wanted to try to steal the statue on your own?" I asked, leaning against the counter.

"The thought occurred to me. I like a challenge."

"How do I know we can trust you?" I asked, swirling the water around in the glass. "I know nothing about you."

"You can keep me under surveillance if you'd like."

"What do you mean?"

"I've got nothing to hide. Spend the next couple of days with me."

Heat climbed my face. "I—I can't," I said, cursing my shaky voice. "I have to stay on task," I added.

He shrugged. "I have to split. If Cat wants to stick around, tell her to call me when she's ready for a ride." He took my hand in his and flipped it so it was palm-side up. He picked up a pen from the counter and wrote a series of numbers across the fleshy part. "That's my number."

"You're her brother. I think she knows the number."

He capped the pen and set it on the counter. "I know she knows the number. That's for you."

He walked to the front door, calling good-byes to Cat and Eddie, who were flipping through the Halston book. As much as I wanted to dive in and show them the outfit on page 157, I followed Dante because it was the hospitable thing to do.

"You sure you can keep them focused?" he said. "Because this won't work unless everyone stays on task."

"I'll do my best."

He reached down, tipped my chin back, and stared at me for an uncomfortable couple of seconds. "This turned out to be a pretty good night," he said. He turned and left.

2

WOODY

Turned out, Eddie was right. Rarely do professionals move as quickly as beauticians who hear the phrase, "I need to look younger," and the professionals I'd chosen from the back of the yellow pages were no exception. My brown hair had been highlighted and layered into a tumble of curls that hadn't been allowed this kind of freedom in a decade. My blue-green eyes stood out against sun-kissed skin, the result of a week's worth of spray-on tanning and bronzer to achieve a post-spring break glow. I traded foundation for tinted moisturizer and lipstick for lip-gloss and fought my eyeliner habit. Cat bought me an I-FAD sweatshirt, laundered and dried a dozen times to give it a lived-in look. I drew the line at matching sweatpants, pairing the sweatshirt with a kicky pleated plaid skirt.

It was uncanny to look in the mirror and see a face that only slightly resembled my own. It was even uncannier to spend the next week wandering the college campus. Surprisingly, that's all it took. One week of surveillance to figure out what we needed to know to pull off our plan. The uncanniest part of all of it was that it worked.

After the theft, our hodge-podge team regrouped at my house for a celebratory drink. It was close to two in the morning, but we were hyped up by the fact that we'd gotten away with (sanctioned) thievery.

Dante popped a bottle of champagne, and we toasted our success. At least, Cat, Dante, and I toasted our success. Eddie was upstairs getting the shoe polish off his face.

I pulled the bundle out of my handbag and unwrapped it. A wooden Puccetti statue on permanent loan from the Philadelphia Museum of Art to I-FAD. It was one of the few known works by Milo Puccetti, a student of Brancusi. It had resided on the college campus for the past five years, and we'd managed to swipe it, all because of a contest in the newspaper.

"Who's going to be in charge of Woody until the party?" Dante asked.

"Woody?" I asked.

Dante pointed toward the Puccetti. "Woody."

Cat rolled her eyes. "You can't call him 'Woody.'"

"We can't call him Puccetti," Dante countered. "What do you suggest?"

"Allen. Get it? Woody Allen." Cat said.

"What about Steve?" I asked.

"Steve?" they answered/questioned in unison.

"Woody Allen—Steve Allen. Steve."

"We're naming him? Can I get in on this?" Eddie asked, towel-drying the side of his bleached blond hair.

"We went from Woody to Woody Allen to Steve Allen. Where do you want to go? Tag, you're it. You pick the final name."

Eddie repeated after me. "Woody... Woody Allen... Steve Allen..." He dropped the towel and shot two fists in the air. "Steve McQueen!"

I dipped two fingers into my champagne glass and dabbed the base of the statue. "I hereby dub thee McQueen."

We stared at all twenty-four inches of him. It was the figure of a well-sculpted man, and I knew size didn't matter, but his twenty-four inches were impressive. Now we just had to get him to Heist and present him to the judging committee. That was the last detail on our agenda, and it would happen tomorrow night at the Pilferer's Ball, the store's opening party.

Cat yawned. "Time for me to get home and go to bed. Dante, you want a ride?"

Dante looked at me. I was still wearing my college-girl outfit, and even though the outfit included a bulky oversized sweatshirt, it felt a little like he was seeing me in my underwear.

"Yes, Dante wants a ride," I said.

Eddie was back to his usual shade of surfer-dude. He tossed the damp towel on the end of the sofa. "You guys are leaving already? The party is just getting started."

With sound effects. Because that's when we heard the sirens.

3

THE PILFERER'S BALL

I GRABBED THE TOWEL FROM THE SOFA, WRAPPED UP THE STATUE, AND pushed the bundle under the cushions. The sirens grew louder. It was obvious they were headed in our direction. There was nothing to do but wait for them to come to the front door, announce themselves, and take us into custody. And, contest or not, we all knew we were guilty—guilty of theft from a public institution.

I fed my hand behind the blue tweed curtains and created an opening wide enough to look through. The cars didn't turn in to my driveway. They turned in to my neighbor Nora's. The sirens turned off, but the flashing lights pierced the darkness at evenly spaced intervals. We may have been tired fifteen minutes ago, but we were wide awake now.

"Should we leave?" Cat asked.

"At two o'clock in the morning, with the cops right outside the house? I don't think so," Eddie said.

Dante reached down and untied his shoes. "Those aren't police cars, they're campus security. They're parked in front of your neighbor's house, and they're going in."

Then he put his feet up on the ottoman and put his hands behind his head. "Looks like I'm staying after all."

"Eddie, can I see you in the kitchen, please?" I went to the kitchen. He knew the routine by now.

"I don't think Dante staying over is a good idea," I said.

"After tonight, I think you can trust him."

"It's not him I'm worried about," I said. I leaned forward and peeked into the living room. Logan sat in the chair with Dante. He stared right at me, and I felt myself blush. "Having Dante around is going to be a little distracting, if you know what I mean."

"What's wrong with a little distraction?"

I stepped backward, out of Dante's line of vision, and pulled Eddie with me. "I'm finally in a place where I can start a relationship with Nick. Just because he's halfway around the world right now doesn't mean I'm going to blow that chance. Cat can crash upstairs with me. You have to keep an eye on him. Can you help me with that?"

"How's Nick going to know? He didn't even call you tonight."

"Shoot." I scampered to the living room to get my handbag. Cat was asleep on the sofa, half-covered with the white afghan. Dante studied my face with an amused look on his.

"Looks like my sister took the sofa. Got anywhere else I can sleep?"

"The floor." I returned to the kitchen. When I powered on my phone, the missed message alert beeped. One message.

"Samantha? It's Nora. Your neighbor. Call me as soon as you get this. I need to talk to you about something."

"It wasn't Nick. It was Nora," I said to Eddie.

"As in next-door Nora?"

"As in the-professor-for-the-college-we-just-stole-a-statue-from Nora. As in campus-security-is-at-her-house Nora." We both looked at the wall between my house and hers. It would have made more sense if there'd been a window there.

"Find out what she wants," Eddie said.

"Not tonight," I said. "I'll call her in the morning."

I woke up thinking about that message. What was it Nora wanted to tell me? I called and left a message. I called two more times and hung up on the third ring. Around lunchtime I crossed the yard between us and rang the doorbell, but there was no answer. Her car was gone from her driveway, so I figured she'd gone out for the day. I'd try to call her later, but I had other things to think about.

Tonight was the party at Heist, and after succeeding in our small-time perpetration, we were juiced to collect our prize money. The last part of our plan had been to arrive at the new department store with the statue bundled in my handbag. And don't think it wasn't hard to find an evening bag that accommodated a twenty-four-inch tall Puccetti statue, either.

Scrub as I had, my new fake tan wasn't budging, so I based my evening attire around my new carefree seventies look. I pulled on an amber silk caftan with gold beading at the neckline and cuffs, gold shoulder duster earrings, and an armful of colorful bangle bracelets. The time I saved by not straightening my hair helped me still arrive on time.

Eddie waited for me in the parking lot. His black tuxedo jacket opened to a Frankie Say Relax T-shirt. He paced back and forth, looking nervous, despite the message on his tee.

"What's wrong?" I asked.

"Did you talk to your neighbor?"

"No. I tried to call her, but she wasn't home. Why?"

"I didn't want to tell you this, but I signed the fake statue that we used for the swap." He shrugged. "I guess it was a matter of pride. If anyone came along and stole the one we left, I wanted to prove they didn't have the real one."

"It's a priceless statue. They probably have better tests of authenticity than that."

"Okay, fine. I wanted to show off how well I copied it."

"So why are you asking about Nora?"

"You said Nora was a professor at I-FAD. We stole the Puccetti from I-FAD, and they'd know it by now. I keep thinking about the campus security at her house. I don't think we're home free. In fact, I have a very bad feeling about tonight."

"It'll be fine," I said. "We'll collect the prize money, and I'll be able to pay my mortgage for a few more months." And buy a new outfit, I added to myself.

Cat's Suburban pulled up behind Eddie. She and Dante got out. Cat, ever the fashion plate, wore a vibrant purple one-shoulder cocktail dress, layers of chiffon cut at a diagonal that ended halfway down her thighs. She crossed the parking lot on glitter-encrusted strappy platform sandals. Dante followed, in a gold Nehru collared shirt with a paisley ascot knotted at the neck.

He stepped close to me and slipped an arm around my waist. His hand was hot against the small of my back, even though there was a thin layer of silk between us. I tensed. He noticed. He moved his hand up and down in a small gesture of familiarity and then pulled his arm away. The heat from his hand had spread through my entire body, leaving me in need of air conditioning.

"You two are not allowed to stand together tonight," Cat said, pointing a finger back and forth between Dante and me. "It's like it's 1968."

Once inside the store, we moved to the accessories department where a young man in a tuxedo held a tray of champagne flutes. I took one. Cat and Eddie each took a pair of sunglasses from a top-of-the-counter carousel and tried them on. A second later they exchanged pairs and checked their reflections again. I looked at the visuals and the merchandise. Heist had certainly one-upped Tradava in the merchandising department.

Until Heist had announced they were moving to our town, Tradava had been the only other local retailer. Tradava was a family-owned chain of stores based in Ribbon. They'd shown interest in changing their image and staking claim to a more fashionable client base, but from what I could see tonight, Heist had steamrollered their attempts with an aggressive ad campaign and bold assortments. If Tradava was trying to change by whispering, "Come on in," to the fashion crowd, Heist was screaming through a bullhorn, and the message they projected was effective.

Images from Heist's catalogs filled the store. The walls in the cosmetics department were covered with mug shots of women of all ages in flawless makeup. Models in jeans stood with hands on the back of a squad car, a pose that showed off both their curves and the back-pocket stitching of each brand of denim. Still others stood behind bars in a jail cell, in the tiniest whisper of lacy lingerie. My favorite showed a model in an orange jumpsuit scaling a pile of designer handbags to break out of prison. Their creative director had run with their theme, using gritty, Helmut Newton-like photography to create the edgy ad campaign. It was creative. Fresh. Something completely different from what Tradava would have done, and it had been executed perfectly.

I wandered away from my team, into the apparel department, taking it all in. Heist's leather jackets weren't locked up to a lockbox with indiscreet cables like other department stores but were handcuffed to a ballet bar. I continued toward the shoe department, curious how their assortment compared to what I might have bought for Bentley's. A pile of shoes, some of the most coveted styles I'd seen in the past pages of fashion magazines, sat in the middle of the department. A mannequin was at the center of the pile, staring out between stilettos as if hiding from pursuit. I touched the display. The shoes didn't move; they'd been hot-glued together. Any store that was willing to install visuals like this must have an unbelievable amount of merchandise to back it up. I wandered through the department picking up samples at random intervals. The tagline on every price tag in the store said it all: *Our discounts are criminal!*

The world of fashion was one where I was comfortable, or I had been, once upon a time when I was on the industry's payroll. But being on a budget had put a serious damper on my shopping habits. I'd started wearing the clothes I found at the back of my closet. I was a walking exhibit of fashion through the ages, or at least the late seventies through last year.

Even if I didn't get depressed by the thought of waiting for last year's fashions to be discounted to 50 percent off, these days even 50 percent off designer apparel was too rich for my dwindling checking account. Wandering through Heist, ogling the merchandise, I couldn't help getting a familiar tingle. I wanted to try on these clothes. No, I wanted to buy these clothes and go out into the world, a renovated version of myself ready for anything, the way I was when I first moved back to Ribbon six months ago.

An attractive blond man in a black tuxedo stood at the rear of the handbag department flipping through a bin of colorful clutch bags. He didn't see me. His profile spoke of male models in underwear ads: that defined handsomeness that whispered of a confidence he'd known since a very early age. He was a pretty boy, with chiseled features and a square jaw line but with the certain hardness that comes from living your twenties to the max. My guess was that this man knew his face was his ace. He eased his way past a wall of Prada, looking to both sides. That's when I hit his line of vision.

"Who are you?" he asked.

"Just a partygoer." When he didn't move on, I held out my hand. "Samantha Kidd."

"Kyle Trent." His hand was warm and soft. He looked past me as though he was looking for someone else and then refocused his attention on my face. "What are you doing here? I thought the party was to be contained to the lounge area and the open bar."

"I couldn't help myself. I'm admiring the assortments." I fingered a teal-green, patent leather handbag that defied practicality. "It's simply amazing. Like nothing I've seen."

He scowled. "You should tell Emily."

"Who's Emily?" I asked, looking around for somebody else.

"Emily Hart. She's the handbag buyer." Again he looked past me and then behind him, as though he'd been chased. "Better yet, don't. Her head's big enough already. She's around here somewhere. Just look for a woman in a little black dress."

"That's everyone here."

"Not quite everyone," he said, eyeing my amber silk caftan.

"Anyway, I'd be willing to bet she's the only one wearing a five-carat yellow diamond ring."

He let go of my hand, which had been growing sweaty under his awkward, too-long handshake. My other hand clutched my personal handbag with the Puccetti statue was inside. I fought the urge to wipe my palm against the silk of my ensemble, knowing it would leave a mark.

"Emily thrives on compliments. If you see her, tell her what you think." He continued past the shoe department and back the way I had come.

As Kyle left, I moved farther in toward the display wall of handbags. Simple white pegboard had been hung against the wall. Utilitarian metal pegs held clear Plexiglas shelves, and a soft glow from behind the pegboard illuminated the display through the small holes, backlighting the colorful assortment.

The sign above the wall read "Vongole." The Italian design house was the latest to join the ranks of it-bag designers, their designs spotted on the arms of most celebrities these days. Heist carried more of their designer handbags than I'd ever seen in one place, and that included the time I'd spent working in New York. Heck, that included the street corners in New York that sold the not-too-shabby knockoffs, too. I gazed up to the highest shelf, where a yellow matte crocodile bag called my name.

I'll just hold it for a second, I thought.

The shelf was slightly higher than my reach. Fairly certain that the stolen Puccetti statue was not at risk, I set my clutch on a glass case that held a display of wallets and small leather goods and found a stepstool a negligent employee had forgotten to put away for the night. As I positioned the stool below the display shelf, I placed my hands on the pegboard for balance. I climbed up the three steps so I was within reach of the handbag, but I never got it off the shelf, because from my new perch about two feet off the ground, I saw something that made me forget about the yellow crocodile handbag altogether.

To the left of the display wall was a metal gate that secured the department back stock from customers. And behind the metal gate, a body lay sprawled across the floor. The case of small leather goods blocked my view of her face and her outfit, but the one thing I was able to see was the very large yellow stone gleaming from the ring on her left hand.

4

____

EXPLAIN HOW

EDDIE WAS RIGHT TO HAVE HAD A BAD FEELING. THE TINGLING excitement brought on from the merchandise in the store turned to panic. I jumped off the ladder. My bracelets clinked against each other like a windchime as I grabbed my gold clutch and ran back to the party. I found Cat trying on a pink headband with feathers. Eddie was next to her, straightening fixtures, even though this wasn't his store.

"Have you guys seen anybody in uniform?" I asked Eddie. "Police, security, Rent-a-Cop?"

Behind them someone sprayed on too many pumps of perfume and the sweet scent of lilies and sugar filled the air. Dante leaned against the scarf case, swirling his champagne around in the flute. I tugged on the sleeve of his shirt.

"Have you seen anybody who looks official?" I asked him.

"Define official," he said.

But I didn't. I pushed past the three of them through the crowd of strangers, a difficult task in a caftan. When I reached the front of the store, two men stood checking IDs.

"Are you in charge?" I asked one of them.

"I'm in charge," said a stout bald man in a black suit, white shirt, black tie. "What's the problem?"

"A woman—in the handbag department—she's—" I stopped. I didn't know what she was. "She might need help."

"Might?" said the security officer.

"Or it might be too late," I added. I turned around and pushed back the way I had come. But before I had a chance to get the officer to the handbag department, a bloodcurdling scream pierced the store.

Everyone looked in the direction of the scream. Everyone except for Dante, who stared at me. He held his champagne flute out. I drained it in a matter of seconds and set the empty glass on the counter.

AN HOUR LATER, I would have traded a sizeable portion of my anticipated prize money for another glass of champagne. We'd been told that no one could leave the store until after speaking to the police. The crowd had been separated into groups, and Cat and Dante had been shuffled along with a different audience. I kept telling myself we hadn't done anything wrong. We'd taken on the challenge Heist advertised in the newspaper. The theft we'd committed was part of a publicity campaign. Still, I felt guilt from the theft, from carrying around the stolen statue in my handbag, and from wandering parts of the store that were off limits. I wondered how that would translate when the police got around to talking to me. For the time being, I decided not to mention it.

A short, well-appointed man stood off to the side of our line. More than once our eyes connected. He drank a watery drink from a glass tumbler. His expertly tailored black pinstriped suit fit him well, though at a height shorter than my own I wondered where he'd found it. Custom? That costs money. Gold cufflinks punctuated with diamonds glistened from his shirt. I glanced at his shoes. Yep, money. I hadn't seen menswear like that since I worked at Bentley's. The man continued to watch me—that's exactly how it felt, like I was being watched—and I looked away, scanning the crowd, to hide my awkwardness.

The line crept slowly toward two uniformed police officers who were taking statements. There were too many of us to all be detained, so I imagined the cops were taking down names and contact information, checking that each person had a solid reason for being at this party, this night. Looking for someone who had infiltrated the fashionable happening for reason other than free champagne and a chance to shop the newest retailer one day early. Meanwhile, the advertising hanging around the store disturbed me.

This couldn't be one big publicity stunt, could it?

"Why didn't you just say you found a body?" Eddie whispered to me. "You could have told us."

"Because I don't want that to become my catch phrase," I answered, thinking of the last time I'd found a dead body and how it had complicated my life.

Six months ago, I'd moved to Ribbon looking for a fresh start. I'd found a fresh corpse instead. It was the man who'd hired me to work for him, which had raised all sorts of hard-to-answer questions from the police, the mortgage company, and the bill collectors. I managed.

Eddie bumped me with his elbow. "Look, there's your friend." He jutted his chin toward the man at the front of the line. He wore a rented tux that was too narrow in the shoulders. The sleeves were also too short, exposing the cuffs of his white shirt (no expensive cufflinks in sight). I scanned him down to his feet: round-toed oxfords with thick rubber soles.

Detective Loncar.

The detective was an older, graying man, thick around the middle, balding around the top. I've heard of women having an inexplicable attraction to police officers, something about the law and order, or the uniform, or the position of authority, but I didn't get it. Detective Loncar did his job without any hint of flirtation or sexuality. Our line advanced slowly, until we stood in front of him.

"Samantha Kidd." He turned to the young female officer to his right. "We already have her information on file." She nodded one quick nod. "What brings you to Heist tonight?"

"I'm a retailer. This is the competition. I wanted to see what they were all about."

He jotted a few notes on a tablet. "That's it? No undercover work? No extracurricular activities?"

"Pretty much."

"Still live in the same house?"

"Yes."

He jotted down a few more notes. "Okay. Sign here, please." He handed me a clipboard filled with names, addresses, and phone numbers. I set my handbag down, took the offered pen, and signed my name with a less than customary flourish.

"That's it? I can leave now?" I asked, clipping the pen to the clipboard in an efficient manner.

"Detective, look," the female officer said. She held my handbag. It had tipped on the counter, and a white bundle was exposed. Only the white bundle was no longer well wrapped, and the Puccetti statue peeked out of the top.

The detective stared into my bag for an uncomfortable duration of time.

"No, Ms. Kidd," he said slowly. "I don't think you can leave now. Follow me." He picked up my handbag and walked toward a small, dark hallway. Then he turned back to the female officer and said, "Meet us in five."

I trailed behind the detective until he reached a room, glowing with the particular blue that emanates from a Pepsi machine. "Soda?" he asked.

"Sure."

"Sit down," he said.

"Am I about to be interrogated?" I asked warily.

"Ms. Kidd, we've been through this before. We don't interrogate people in the employee lounge of department stores." He pumped some change into the machine, punched the button with a jab of his right fist, and then repeated the routine. I took the Pepsi he offered. "Have a seat," he instructed.

I pulled a plastic chair out from under the folding table. I'd been in more than enough employee lounges of more than enough department stores to know that this one, expertly decorated in black and white with punches of primary colors, would all too soon be spilled on and chipped, and the paintings would hang slightly askew. Despite the best intentions of the store to provide a nice spot for breaks, this room would show signs of employee angst in a matter of weeks, if not days.

I popped open my Pepsi and took a swig. Detective Loncar pulled a chair next to me and set his soda on the table, still unopened. He put his hands on his head, rubbing the sides, where there was still a ring of hair. Footsteps sounded in the hallway, and the female officer entered, only she wasn't alone. The short businessman in the expertly tailored pinstriped suit who had watched me earlier followed her into the room. The next person to enter was my neighbor, Nora.

From what I'd seen since she moved in, Nora fit the part of professor perfectly. On most days she even wore jackets with elbow patches. Today she was in a beige sheath dress and low-heeled pumps. She didn't look nearly as surprised to see me as I was to see her.

When everyone was seated, Loncar spoke. "Ms. Kidd, why don't you start by telling us about the statue in your handbag?"

"Heist had a contest advertised in the paper. The ad is right here." Now that the statue was out of my handbag, the only thing left were my wallet, keys, and a few pieces of paper. One of the papers was the original ad from Heist.

I handed Loncar the torn piece of newsprint I'd been carrying around since the day I first saw it. "My friends and I thought it would be fun to enter, so we decided to try to steal the statue."

"Fun," Detective Loncar repeated. The other people in the room remained silent. The Puccetti statue sat in the middle of the table like a centerpiece.

"Ms. Kidd, we know about the contest." Detective Loncar sat back in his chair. "That's not the issue here. We just want to know how you got this statue."

"I'm telling you how I got the statue."

"No, you're telling us why you have the statue. Explain how," said the businessman.

I turned to the cop. "You said I'm not being interrogated, right?" He nodded. "Then I want to know who everyone here is and why you're all asking me these questions."

Loncar scratched his head. "Fair enough. This is Officer Rachel McCord. Next to her is Tony Simms, owner of Heist. And Nora Black—"

"I know Nora," I interjected. I looked at her. She smiled.

"Your turn," Loncar said again. "How did you steal this statue?"

"It wasn't that hard. I assembled a team. I knew there would be a limited amount of time between stealing the statue and having the college discover it was missing, and I knew we weren't the only people who saw the ad in the paper. I came up with a plan. Replace the statue with a fake. Then our competition could steal the fake and get caught, which would throw suspicion off us."

"You came up with the plan?" Loncar asked. He had stopped taking notes, and that struck me as something of an insult.

"Yes, I came up with the plan. You don't believe me?" I leaned against the back of the seat and raked my curly hair into a low ponytail off my neck. When I let go, the curls fell down my back on the outside of the caftan. I scanned the faces at the table. And then I told them about the meeting that one night last week when Cat, Eddie, Dante, and I had congregated in my living room. I told them about the fake statue, the assigned roles, and my grad student makeover, blushing when I remembered the way Dante had looked at me before he left.

"Ms. Kidd, we're waiting," said the detective.

"Waiting for what?"

"You told us you figured out what time to hit the school admissions hall and your plan to duplicate the statue and replace it with a fake before anybody else got to it. And then you got quiet, and then your face turned red."

"And?" I asked. I wrinkled up my forehead and leaned forward. "Why am I here? My friends and I can't be the only people who took the contest seriously." I searched the faces that watched me. Under different circumstances, it would have felt like a poker game.

"Let me tell her what's going on," said Nora. She looked first at Tony and then at Loncar. Officer McCord was paid no attention. The men each nodded consent.

"That contest you mentioned, yes, the college agreed to participate, but they put me in charge of the original statue, which has been in a safe place since the ad ran in the paper. A replica was put on display at I-FAD, so the real statue wasn't at risk. I was notified last night that someone had stolen the fake."

"That's it?" I asked, relieved.

"Not exactly," Detective Loncar said. "You said when you stole the statue, you left one in its place."

"That's right. Why?"

"That's why you're here. Earlier this evening, your copy was used to bludgeon a woman to death."

5

———

UNIQUE SKILL SET

OH DEAR, I THOUGHT. ONLY IN MY HEAD, I DIDN'T USE THE WORD "dear."

"Samantha? Samantha?" Nora's voice sounded like it was coming through a tunnel. "Officer? I think she's going to pass out."

I held the Pepsi can up to my flushed cheeks. "Give me a second. I'll be okay," I mumbled. I chugged as much soda as I could without burning my throat with the carbonation. I suppressed a burp. "Where's Eddie?"

"I'm right here."

I twisted at the waist and saw him sitting in a chair behind me. I didn't know how long he'd been present. He leaned forward and said quietly, "They brought me in after taking my statement about the statue. They found my signature."

The room was silent. Eddie looked out at them. "You can see it right on the base if you look under a magnifying glass. It might have been a copy to everyone else, but to me it was an original."

———

WE WENT OVER ALL the details of the theft more times than I could count. By the fifth time it was hard to sound like I wasn't bragging about my plan and our—well, if I couldn't call it success, I didn't know what to call it. Finally, we were let go. There would be no climactic ten thousand-dollar prize money or free champagne from Heist in my future. Only a long, hot bath, a scowling cat, and a warm, comfy bed. And a phone call from Nick that I was going to try my hardest to miss, because no matter what role he played in my fantasy life, I wasn't sure how to explain my reality, and I wasn't sure tonight was the night to test out phone sex as distraction. I got home, turned off my cell phone and my answering machine, and dove between the sheets.

The next morning, I woke, brewed a pot of coffee, and fished the paper from the front yard. Last night had made the front page: *Buyer Murdered at Retail Gala*. I sat at my kitchen table reading over details that I both knew and didn't know. The victim was Emily Hart, the handbag buyer for Heist. Like Nora had said, she was bludgeoned to death with a replica of the Puccetti statue, which had been found a few feet from the corpse.

I still hadn't heard from Cat or Dante. The policewoman, Officer McCord, had gone to look for them after I'd implicated them as participants in my plan, but they'd both already given their statements and left the party.

After two cups of coffee and a shower, I dressed in a pair of pink satin cargo pants from the mid-nineties, a gray cashmere hoodie from a Barbie collector website, and a pair of high-heeled black canvas sneakers with white rubber soles. Logan trailed me around the house and jumped up on the newspaper that I'd left open on the table. I scratched his ears.

"See what happens when you let yourself get involved in hare-brained schemes?" I tried to flip the page, but he pounced on the article, attacking my hand from under the newsprint. We played this game for a couple of minutes. This should be my life. Me and my cat having fun. No homicides. No stress. No police detectives. I rested my hand for a second and Logan swiped at my arm.

"Ow!" I pulled back instinctively, but his claws had punctured the skin. I extracted them. He jumped down and started licking his paw like I'd given him cooties. Nice cat.

The doorbell rang. It could have been any number of people, but Tony Simms, the diminutive owner of Heist counted among the least expected. "Ms. Kidd. May I come in?"

"Yes, of course," I held the door open and allowed him to enter. "Would you like a cup of coffee?"

"Yes. Thank you." He followed me into the kitchen, where I poured him a cup.

"Cream? Sugar?" I asked.

"Black."

I handed him the mug and accessorized my own refill with a healthy amount of milk. (Third cup that hour.)

"Ms. Kidd, I have a proposition for you," Tony Simms said.

I sank down in a chair opposite him and half-wished I wasn't wearing a Barbie sweatshirt. I glanced at the newspaper in front of him. My name hadn't been mentioned in the article. In last night's activities, I was merely an innocent bystander. Ish.

"As you know from last night, I am the owner of Heist. I have a lot of money staked in the success of that store. Millions are already invested between the construction and the inventory. Heist cannot fail."

"Some might say last night's publicity was more than you could ever have planned on your own," I said.

"Last night's publicity was not the kind we want. And now we have a murder investigation happening under our noses, but the store must still open."

"What does this have to do with me?"

"You demonstrated a unique skill set with the contest. I asked around about you. I liked what I heard. I'd like to offer you a job."

I wasn't sure where he was going, and I wasn't sure I wanted to know. And we both knew that was a big, fat lie.

"You asked around about my background in retail? About my experience working for Bentley's New York?"

"About your short time at Tradava. Your involvement in the investigation of your boss's murder, specifically."

"That's not something I want to talk about."

"Samantha, I find myself needing to fill a job left vacant by a murder victim. I also find myself heavily invested in a store where a crime took place—a crime that could have been committed by any number of people, employees and customers included. Your recent experiences indicate you can work through the possible difficulties that may come with the job and, if I'm correct in my assessment of your recent history with Tradava, you'd be forthcoming with any suspicious behavior you may witness while on the job." He turned his coffee mug but didn't pick it up. "I'm prepared to offer you a generous compensation package if you say yes. Are you interested in a job?"

He wanted to hire me? No more mortgage worries. No more reading the want ads, or polishing my resume, or casing the unemployment office, or making piles of clothes to sell on eBay. All I had to do was say yes.

My dad told me once that this was the most common phrase from my childhood. "All you have to do, Dad ..." followed with my childish, simplistic ideas.

Can I have a tree house? All you have to do, Dad...

Let's build a soapbox racer! All you have to do, Dad...

I have a good idea for the science fair. All you have to do, Dad...

Dad had claimed those six words were the kiss of death. But this was different. Right?

"What did you have in mind?" I asked.

"Handbag buyer. You were a buyer at Bentley's New York for nine years, right? You have the experience."

It was unnerving, him knowing my background, but I hid my unease. "Yes. I know how to be a buyer. But if I'm going to do this, there are things I'm going to need."

"Name it."

"Clothing allowance. Expense account."

He reached into the inside breast pocket of his suit, pulled out a wallet, and extracted two pieces of plastic. One was a credit card. The other was an ID for Heist.

My name and photo were on both.

The words "job" and "offer" hadn't been uttered to me in a long time. At least not by a man who was fully aware of my history since moving back to Ribbon. All I had to do was say…

"Yes."

My dad was wrong. That had been frightfully easy.

"I GOT A JOB YESTERDAY," I said to Eddie. We were at Arner's Diner. It was seven thirty in the morning, and I was dressed in a navy eighties power suit complete with linebacker shoulder pads. It had been my interview suit upon graduating college and was perhaps an extension of the undercover college student identity I'd recently adopted. I was more than a little excited that it still fit.

I was going to show up at Heist on Monday morning, ready to be the newest handbag buyer in their corporate structure. I was pretty sure that a maniacal serial killer wasn't on the loose knocking off buyers, so the fact that I was about to assume the post of the dead woman didn't faze me much. The fact that I was about to work for a very rich man with a Napoleon complex who'd agreed to my pie-in-the-sky requests without batting an eye fazed the living daylights out of me.

Eddie's fork stopped halfway to his mouth, dangling a delicate bite of egg-white omelet. On his plate was an untouched piece of multigrain toast. I sliced through my last sausage link and raised the bite-sized piece to my mouth. Then I took a bite of my English muffin and chewed a moment, swallowed, and finished off my orange juice. If he wasn't going to respond, I was going to eat. But when his stare continued after I'd cleared my plate, I figured it was time to go ahead and let the second shoe drop on the floor.

"At Heist. I got a job at Heist."

"What job?" he asked suspiciously.

"The handbag buyer job."

"What?" he exclaimed.

"It's a job," I said. "What happened to Emily Hart was awful, but the store needs a buyer, and I'm qualified for the job."

The waitress appeared at the side of our table and asked if we wanted our coffee topped off. I said no and asked for the check. She pulled a pad out of the pocket, flipped a few pages, and tore off our ticket.

"My treat," I said, pulling the Heist credit card out of my wallet. Seemed as good a time as any to test it. I waved Eddie's wallet away. I handed the card to the waitress and sat against the back of the booth.

Eddie stood. "Dude, I can't in good faith allow you to rack up your charge card on breakfast when you haven't even started working yet." He signaled to the waitress to return.

I reached out to stop him, succeeding only in grabbing a handful of his Billy Idol T-shirt. I yanked him back enough to get his attention and then let go. "It's an expense account. I need to make sure it works," I hissed.

His eyes widened. When the waitress turned around, he flapped his hands in the air. "Never mind. We're good." He dropped into the booth. "Heist gave you an expense account?"

I had been debating whether to spill the details to Eddie. There was no way I could keep my new job a secret from him, though, so I told him what I had to tell. My name came up, from my work experience, and I was contacted by someone at the store. It had been too long since I had a job, and maybe Tradava and I weren't made for each other, but opportunities don't grow on trees, so I accepted the offer. I start Monday.

See? When said it like that, it sounded perfectly innocent. And it was good that I had a chance to practice, because I was going to have to tell that same story to Nick tonight.

Eddie asked enough questions to feel comfortable that I knew what I was doing, and we parted ways. But my instinct to tell someone what I was really up to led me in a very scary direction.

I headed to the police station.

6

A SITUATION

"Is Detective Loncar here?" I asked the portly man behind the desk.

"Yeah, he's here. Is he expecting you?"

"I don't know."

On some level, Detective Loncar might have been expecting me to drop in since the first murder investigation I'd been involved with. On another level, perhaps one laced with wishful thinking on both of our parts, he might have hoped to never see me again.

"Why are you here?"

"I have to talk to him about a situation that has to do with a homicide."

The cop looked at me sideways. "A situation, huh?" He tipped his head backward. "Yo, Charlie! You got a visitor!"

The door behind the portly guy opened, and Detective Loncar looked into the hallway. For three solid seconds, our eyes held, until he turned, looked back into the room where he had been, and then turned to face me again. "You're here to see me?" I nodded. "That's a first."

"Can we go somewhere to talk?" I asked, ignoring his cop humor.

"Follow me."

We started down a linoleum-tiled hallway that could have benefited from a once-over with a mop. At the end of the hallway, he made a right and turned the doorknob of a splintered door. The sign on the door said Questioning. I stepped backward.

"Isn't there another room we can use besides that one?" I pointed to the door.

"We're going to my office. It's through here." He held the door open until I took my first step, and then he turned his back to me and walked past a small wooden table. He opened another door and went inside, this time with me tripping over his heels. The door shut behind me, and I stood, uncomfortably, looking around the makeshift office of a homicide detective.

"Have a seat."

I sat in a worn chair with a maple frame and brown vinyl seat. The cushion made a *pfffffft* sound when I sat, like a whoopee cushion with motivational issues. Neither Loncar nor I commented on the sound.

I told him about the job offer from Tony Simms. Detective Loncar already knew about the dead body, and he already knew about my ability to insinuate myself into a murder investigation. What he didn't know was that I was capable of growing, learning from my mistakes, and partnering with the boys in blue.

After telling my story, I laid my cards on the table. Literally. I pulled the credit card and ID card out of my wallet and set them in front of the detective. He picked up the credit card and stared at it for a couple of seconds, leaned back in his chair, and then stared at the ceiling. He tapped the plastic card against his dimpled chin. When he put the chair back on all fours, he pressed a button on his phone.

"I need a credit check," he barked into the speakerphone, and rattled off the sixteen digits on the front of my card. He scribbled a series of numbers on a tablet and pushed it toward me. "Is that your Social?"

I looked at the paper. My Social Security number stared back at me. "Yes."

"Print it and bring it to me," he said back into the phone. He hung up and drummed his fingers on the worn wooden desk. His nails had been bitten to the quick, and the callused tips made a hollow sound against the wood. *Badarabam. Badarabam. Badarabam.*

"You already said yes to the job, right?"

"Right."

"You were hired to do a job, and you're going to do that job. But it's possible that you'll learn things that could help us with the investigation. Are you willing to cooperate?"

"I'm here, aren't I?"

"Who knows that you're here?"

"Nobody."

"You planning to keep it that way?"

"I think so."

His eyebrows shot up. "You think so? You don't know so?"

"Okay, sure. I plan to keep it that way." The fingers crossed in my lap countered the conviction in my voice.

"Good. I'll call you tonight with details."

"Do you know what time?"

"Why, you got something more important to do?"

I thought about Nick's impending call and what I was going to tell him. I'd rather talk to him before any more conversations with the cops—less to hide. But still ...

"Whenever is fine." Turning various shades of red, I left through the back door.

* * *

No matter how you looked at it, I was back in the fashion industry, so I had to look the part. I also had to snoop around and spy on people and somehow try to figure out why the last handbag buyer got knocked off. No matter how you looked at it, my life was about to change.

I headed home from the police station and took a very long shower. I wasn't sure if I was trying to wash off the memories of being in police headquarters or the common sense that had taken me there, but half an hour later I was scrubbed clean, with my hair up in a towel turban, a plush terrycloth robe covering my body, and fluffy pink slippers on my feet. I padded into the kitchen and searched the fridge for food.

Logan swirled around my ankles and swatted at the pompoms on the front of my slippers. I scooped him up in my arms and nuzzled my face into his fur. His front paws curled over my shoulder, and he head-butted me. The light on my ancient faux-wood answering machine—a relic of my parents' life before they'd sold me the house—was red. I pushed play, peppering the space between Logan's pointy ears with kisses.

"Samantha, this is Tony Simms. I've arranged for you to go to Heist tonight. Call this number"—he rattled off nine digits—"and make arrangements with security for what time you'd like to arrive. Gabe Gaithers is expecting your call. He'll give you a tour and some shopping time." He disconnected.

Logan wriggled away and jumped to the floor. He stretched, walked over to his food bowl, and meowed. I pulled the top off a can of moist cat food and emptied it for him.

I called the number that Simms had left. A deep voice answered after three rings, and I introduced myself, unsure what else I should say.

"Samantha Kidd, yes. Tony told us you'd be calling. Come by tonight if you want. Park by the south doors. I'll let you in."

I changed from terrycloth to a navy sheath dress that was slightly more in style than the eighties power suit. My newly cut hair would have taken too long to straighten, so I pulled the curls into a low ponytail and knotted a printed scarf around it. Jackie-O glasses covered my five-minute makeup routine, and I was off.

Heist was less than two miles from my house, and don't you dare say a word about how I could have walked there. The large bald man who I'd told about Emily Hart's body the night of the party opened a door. Tonight he wore a slate-gray, button-down shirt and pleated pants that didn't quite match the shirt.

"Are you Samantha Kidd?"

"Yes."

"I'm Gabe." He tipped his head toward the inside of the store. "Follow me."

We walked through the same store I'd wandered through two nights ago, but this time it was different. Instead of being mesmerized by the gritty photography or the merchandising standards, I thought about what it would be like to be a part of this team. It had been well over six months since I'd been a buyer, and even though I'd been a good one at Bentley's, I'd chosen to leave that life behind. I didn't doubt the skills would return once I understood the store's demographics, spreadsheets, and profitability standards, but there was a certain pressure that came with that job. That pressure was why I walked away from the job in the first place.

Hindsight and unemployment had glamorized my memories of being a buyer. More recently, I'd been the unwanted jobseeker. Despite the best well-wishes from my friends, both those who knew me in Ribbon and those I'd left behind in New York, I still wondered if it had been the right decision to leave a successful career behind to rediscover myself in my old hometown. I had set out to simplify. So far, I'd found one homicide and another had found me. Nothing simple about it.

"We just got in a truck of merchandise, and I have to get to the dock. You okay by yourself?" Gabe asked me.

"Sure."

He handed me a set of keys. "Mr. Simms said you're to bring whatever you want to our office. We'll write it up, and if there's an executive available to sign off on the forms, we'll process it tonight. These keys will unlock the fixtures and the fitting rooms." He left me in the middle of the designer sportswear department while he disappeared through the store.

The fixtures surrounding me were filled with clothes that begged to fill my closet, and I could have lost hours trying on 85 percent of their offerings. Instead, I wandered to the handbag department to see what kind of assortment decisions my predecessor had made.

"Samantha Kidd? Is that you?" asked a singsong female voice

from behind me. I turned around. The woman approaching me was familiar in a vague way. She had shoulder-length hair colored so blond it was almost white, blown into a fluffy style that framed her face and flipped up by her collar. On the bony side of thin, she wore a taupe jersey jacket and fluid pants with classic ivory pumps.

"Belle," she said. "Bell DuChamp." The lightbulb switched on. Belle DuChamp was the general manager for Tradava who I hadn't had a chance to work with. What was she doing here?

Belle held out a perfectly manicured hand and shook mine. A bracelet of gold links and aged antique coins clanged around her delicate wrist like chimes. "Welcome aboard our team."

"Our?"

"Heist. You'll be working with me. We never got the chance to work together at Tradava, and after what you did for them, I say it's a shame. You're a talented gal, and we're lucky to have you. Stole you out from under their noses, I'd say, even if that's not exactly the way it happened. But I believe"—she extended an arm in front of her, inviting me to join her walk through the aisle— "right place, right time. And no better time than the present." She winked at me. "Don't you agree?"

I was taken by her bravado, though I still wasn't entirely sure what we were talking about. "Ms. DuChamp?"

"Don't Ms. DuChamp me. Call me Belle. Tradava may have had those ancient political ideals and stuffy policies, but Heist is a young company. We're all on a first-name basis. Even Tony Simms."

She didn't seem to have fond memories of Tradava, and considering my spotty work history with them, I was wondering if I should suggest we start some sort of club.

"Come to my office. We've got a lot to discuss."

Belle Duchamp had the figure of a twenty-year-old and the attitude of a woman in her fifties. Confidence seeped from her like she'd bathed in it. We reached a glass door, which she pushed through, much like the glass ceiling I imagined she had hit at some point of her career at Tradava. I followed her down a carpeted hallway to the last office. It overlooked the parking lot. A wooden desk sat off to the side, and a glass-top conference table sat by the window.

"Have a seat." Again she gestured, this time to the red and brown plaid chair in front of her desk. The store hadn't even opened, and her desktop was in disarray. "Don't mind all this. They're still a little paperwork heavy around here, getting the store open and all." She pushed a pile of papers together, squared them off at the corners, and set them inside one of her drawers. "Tell me everything I need to know about you."

It seemed I'd misunderstood Tony Simms when he'd been at my house. "I didn't come prepared for an interview," I said.

She threw her head back and laughed the kind of full-on laugh that most women are too shy to release. I counted five fillings—three on the bottom, two on the top—before she closed her mouth.

"Samantha–Sam, can I call you Sam?"

I nodded. She reached over and patted my hand. "Relax. You got the job. I just wanted to get to know the newest superstar on the Heist team."

"In that case, I'll give you the short version." I launched into the highlights of my resumé.

She cut me off from the work stuff and interrogated me on the life stuff and dangled an awfully big carrot on trash-talking Tradava, but unlike Bugs Bunny, I didn't bite. It still felt too soon to burn that bridge, even if they didn't want me on the other side.

We talked for the better part of an hour. When she paused to look at the clock, she smacked her hands palm down on her desk. "Jesus! Look at the time. You came here to shop, and I'm holding you hostage in this stuffy office. I didn't leave you much time before they kick us out for the night. You'll be here all day tomorrow, so you'll have plenty of time. Go home, get some sleep." She stood from her desk and walked me back out to the security office. "We'll have coffee in the morning. Meet me here at quarter to nine."

She pumped my hand twice like businesswomen in movies from the eighties did and headed back into the store. I retraced my path to the security department. Gabe pushed a clipboard my direction.

"Sign out before you leave."

I jotted my name on the first available line and pushed the clipboard back. "Do you lock up the store this time every night?"

He looked at me oddly. "What makes you think we're locking up the store?"

"That's what Ms. DuChamp–Belle–just said."

"You must have misunderstood her. We won't lock up for another three hours."

I glanced at the now-vacant hallway. If there was something in the store that I wasn't supposed to see, I'd just been railroaded away from finding it.

CANOODLING IN THE BOARDROOM

Instead of braving the grocery store, I joined Eddie and Cat for dinner at Briquette Burger. We sat around a large booth waiting for our entrees. Cat dredged a piece of bread through the cruet of truffle butter that rested on the center of the table and took a healthy bite. After swallowing, she tore off another piece of bread and wiped the cruet clean. Must be good, I thought; it was the first time I'd ever seen her openly gorge on carbs.

When three glasses of wine arrived at the table, Eddie raised his to me in a toast. "To Sam. For landing on her feet."

"To Sam," Cat echoed.

I smiled a nervous smile, knowing what was in store for me, and raised my glass to clink theirs. We each took a sip.

Cat excused herself to the ladies' room, and I bit into the last piece of bread. I didn't need the excuse of fancy butter to accessorize a perfectly good hunk of dough.

"So you start tomorrow, right?" Eddie asked.

"Mmmhmm," I answered, chewing my way through a sourdough roll.

"The dead woman's job?"

A young couple two tables over stared in our direction.

"Keep your voice down. People are looking at us." I bit into the roll again and used both hands to tear it from my teeth. I swallowed a mouthful and washed it down with water. "I met Belle DuChamp today. Do you know her? Thin, perky boobs, chic clothes, blonde hair?" I added.

Eddie choked on his wine.

"People at Tradava call her Belle of the Balls. Because when her husband was around, she was known for squeezing them." Eddie lowered his voice. "She was the general manager of Tradava for the last eleven years. Always seemed like a pretty amazing woman but not the most politically correct, if you know what I mean."

"Actually, I don't," I said. If Eddie had dirt on someone I'd be working with, I wanted to hear it.

"I heard she had a couple of affairs during that time, with a couple members of the board."

"That's probably just the rumor mill. She was the only woman in a sea of men. Everybody says that kind of stuff."

"Well, maybe, but here's what I heard about why she got fired." He leaned in closer, dangling juicy gossip like the steak that was heading our direction. "She was caught canoodling in the boardroom."

"Who uses words like 'canoodling'?"

He ignored me. "She was on the fast track, too. Doesn't make sense, really, because she's a smart cookie. Why would you throw away your entire future, job security, all that, for a quick romp on a wooden table?"

"Maybe she was too dominant at home and her husband couldn't, uh, perform. Some men don't like their women to be that strong and independent."

"Speaking of which, what does Nick say about your new job?"

I glared at him. "Do not compare us with them. Nick and I are not even at the relationship stage. We aren't even in the same city."

"Maybe that's the problem."

"Who says there's a problem?"

"What does he have to say about all of this?"

"All of what?"

"The statue. The murder. The job." He made big circles with his hands. "All of this."

"He didn't really have anything to say about it. What's taking Cat so long?" I looked behind me at the restroom doors.

"That's not like Nick. Why do you think he hasn't said anything?"

"Seriously, she's been gone a long time." I stood. Eddie reached across the table and grabbed my wrist.

"Answer my question."

I shook him off. "Nick hasn't said anything because I haven't told him. Are you satisfied?

Eddie stared at me. His blond hair had been buzzed on the sides in a makeshift Mohawk, and the longer top flopped onto his forehead. "Why haven't you told Nick what you're up to?"

"I don't want him to worry."

"Why would he worry about you getting a new job?" he asked. Suspicion was written all over his face. "There's something you're not telling me."

"I have to check on Cat." I stepped away from the table and went to the bathroom. When I got there, I found her passed out on the ceramic tiled floor.

"Cat? Cat?" I untied my scarf and flapped it over her face and then ran tap water onto a wad of tri-folded paper towels and held the stack against her forehead. "Cat?" Her eyes fluttered open and closed again. When they reopened a third time, they narrowed and looked from side to side. I sat next to her on the cold tile and held her hand.

"Why are we on the floor?" she asked.

"I don't know. This is where I found you."

Her narrowed eyes widened. "I don't feel so good."

She didn't look so good, either. Green generally looks good on a redhead, but the shade Cat had gone under her normally porcelain skin wasn't her best. I helped her up and stood by her side while she propped herself on the sink. She ran her wrists under cold water and dabbed her fingertips against her hairline.

"Will you mind terribly if I don't stay? I want to go home."

"Of course I don't mind. Do you want me to drive you?"

"No, I'll be fine."

We walked back out to our table, where Eddie sat surrounded by three steak and potato dinners. Cat stopped a few steps short when the smell of food hit her. "I need fresh air," she said. She clamped her hand over her mouth and ran for the front door.

"What's wrong with her?" Eddie asked.

"She's sick." I leaned on the booth and watched Cat leave the restaurant.

He slid out of the booth. "Take the food to go. I'm going to drive her home. We'll celebrate another time, okay?"

"Sure," I said. "Call me when she's safe at home."

He nodded and left. The waiter came to the table and asked if something was wrong. "Change of plans," I answered and asked for a couple of to-go boxes. Logan was going to eat well tonight. And I had a second opportunity to use my new expense card too.

It was after nine when I unlocked the front door. The house was dark and silent. Logan was asleep on the sofa. Sweet cat. I was going to miss him tomorrow when I headed off to work.

I showered and changed into a silk nightgown and laid out my first day's outfit: a pink trench coat over a pearl-gray sheath dress and gray flannel stiletto Mary Janes with a black patent toe and heel. I transferred my handbag essentials into a vintage black patent clutch I'd scored at a sale in New York. After I finished, I sank down on the bed and started thinking about what I was about to get myself into.

Emily Hart, handbag buyer for Heist, had been found dead. I'd been tasked to be her replacement and keep my eyes and ears open to anything suspicious. It seemed that the actual store manager didn't know my true reasons for being there. Did that mean she was under suspicion?

Come to think of it, after what Eddie had said, I wondered about Belle DuChamp. She'd been on the fast track at Tradava, worked there for eleven years. At her level, that surely put her into pension category, and she probably felt she had some job security. Had she really been found canoodling in the boardroom? Seemed a stretch. But if Tony Simms didn't tell her about me, then there might be a reason. She *had* ushered me out of the store awfully quickly that very afternoon.

The comforter on the bed started ringing. I padded my hand around until I found the cordless phone twisted up in the sheets. It was early for Nick to call, but maybe he was making up for lost time.

"Hello there, Tiger," I said in my best sex-kitten voice.

"Samantha Kidd? This is Detective Loncar."

It was going to be a long night.

8

NO DISRESPECT INTENDED

"Here's the plan," Detective Loncar said, ignoring the way I'd answered the phone. "You go into work like you're expected to. We're not yet sure what we want you to look for, so take note of anything you think is suspicious. I'll call you tomorrow night to touch base."

"No disrespect intended, but that's a pretty vague plan. Don't you want to tell me who the suspects are so I know who to watch?"

"Ms. Kidd, may I remind you that you have volunteered to cooperate with us, but you are not a member of the police force."

"Okay, tell me this. Is working for Heist dangerous? Will something happen to me?"

"Ms. Kidd, you were offered employment by one of Philadelphia's most influential businessmen. You legitimately have a job."

I was starting to have second thoughts about the whole thing, and not just a little because of the homicide. The cops might think Tony Simms was on the up and up, but something about him spooked me. That he'd shown up on my doorstep with identification in my name before formerly offering me a job was only a part of it.

My cell phone started buzzing around on the nightstand, and I didn't even have to look to know it was Nick.

"Detective, can you hold on a second? I have another call." I couldn't remember which button on the cordless was mute, so I pushed it under the covers and answered my cell phone.

"Hello?" I said, using my sultry voice for the second time that night.

"Hey, Kidd," said Nick. His voice was low, gravelly. Sexy. I leaned back onto the pillows and hugged my knees. "What's going on in chez Kidd?"

"Not much, just getting ready for tomorrow."

"What's tomorrow?"

A muffled sound came from under the covers. I felt around with my left hand until I connected with the cordless.

"Hold that thought," I said to Nick. I set my cell on the nightstand and pulled the cordless out from under the covers. "Detective? Are you there?"

"Don't do that again, Ms. Kidd. Now, about tomorrow, just do what I said. Don't bring up the homicide, don't ask questions. Just go to work, keep your eyes open, and we'll talk at the end of the day. Same time as tonight." He disconnected before I had a chance to consent, though I guess I'd done that when I showed up at headquarters.

I picked up my cell. "Nick? Are you still there?"

"I'm here."

I pictured him in his bed, shirtless, half-covered with blankets, propped up against the pillow. Then I got a little turned on and thought it was better not to picture that. Not now, not when I had some very dreaded information to share with him. There was a very good chance that once I told him what I was up to, we were not going to be talking like one of those 976 numbers.

"You know, when you set the phone down, I thought I heard you say 'detective.' "

"I did," I said, trying to come up with a cover story. "Eddie's here. We're playing Clue."

"What's going on, Kidd?"

"Nothing! We, uh, made up new rules. Whenever someone lands in the library we have to say 'detective.'"

"You can't play Clue with two people."

I pushed my feet far under the sheet. Why hadn't I gone with Uno? "Nick, there's a new retailer in town, and I'm going to work for them. You probably heard about the store before you left for Italy. Heist?"

"I read something about them expanding into Tradava's markets. From what I've heard, they're pretty high concept, right?"

"Yes. Do they carry your shoe collection?"

"No, I never got into business with them. Now that I took back distribution of my label, I have to be careful about expanding too quickly. Besides, their discount agreement is a little too deep for me. What are you going to do for them?"

"I'm going to be the handbag buyer." I climbed out of the bed and went downstairs to the kitchen. I was going to need a side of ice cream to go with all this honesty.

"Did I know about this? That you applied there?"

I chose my words carefully. "No, I didn't say anything about it because I didn't expect anything like this to happen. Turns out they were very impressed with my, uh, experience." I opened one of the takeout containers and cut off a small piece of hamburger for Logan. I tore a corner off the bread and tossed it in his bowl, too. It was free bread that came with the meal, and I was totally within my rights as a consumer to empty the basket into my carryout container.

"Why shouldn't they be?" Nick asked. "You're smart and talented. Just because things never worked out like you wanted at Tradava doesn't mean things aren't going to work out for you in Ribbon. Just think, if you'd never moved to your old hometown for a job at Tradava, we wouldn't be having this conversation. You never know what's right around the corner."

Nick was right. I didn't know what was right around the corner. But something about this particular opportunity that I was embarking on was unsettling. Maybe it was the fact that, aside from Detective Loncar, nobody knew what I was getting myself into.

I'd had more than my share of excitement since I'd moved back to Ribbon, and Nick had seen me through a lot of it. I knew he worried about me. But the two thousand miles between us created a bridge too big for him to cross if I needed help again. Maybe that's why I'd partnered with the cops. I was learning. I was growing. And maybe that's why I found myself wanting to tell Nick everything.

"I have to tell you something. Something big." Silence. "Are you still there?"

"I'm here," he said, but something in his voice had changed.

I stood with the phone pressed to my ear, watching Logan. I toyed with the best way to bring up Emily Hart's murder and how it had led to my employment at Heist. Logan swatted at the piece of meat in his bowl then licked it a couple of times. He pulled away and shook his head side to side.

"When I said Heist was impressed with my experience, I wasn't only talking about my work experience."

Logan slinked into the living room. A couple of seconds later, he made a choking sound. I ran to the front room, where he hacked a few more times and then threw up. He took a few steps away from the nasty pile on the carpet and lay down on his side. His eyes went glassy and unfocused.

And I remembered Cat, passed out on the floor of the restaurant bathroom.

And the food that I'd just put in Logan's bowl.

"Nick, I'll call you back. Something's wrong with Logan."

I couldn't bear the thought of something happening to my cat. He was my little soldier, waiting for me every night when I got home. I wasn't ready for him to leave me. I'd never be ready for that but at the hand of a piece of tainted meat from dinner? That wasn't playing fair. I didn't know how that factored into his nine lives.

The vet agreed to see him after I called in panic mode. I trundled Logan in a light blue pashmina and held him on my lap while I drove. Being captive in a car is not Logan's favorite thing, but tonight, he was quiet. That freaked me out more than anything.

The vet's assistant took him from my arms. She instructed me to fill out paperwork while she took blood and other pertinent samples that would tell if I had an overactive imagination or if my cat had been poisoned. And to kill time, since I was alone in the waiting room, I knew there was one phone call to make.

"Loncar," the detective answered.

"I'm out," I said.

"Who is this?"

"Samantha Kidd. I want out of the arrangement. They got to my friend. They got to my cat. I can't do this."

"Ms. Kidd, slow down. where are you?"

"I'm at the vet's office. My cat is sick. And my friend was sick earlier, and they ate the same food but not at the same time. I mean, the food was for me, and I got it to go after Cat had to leave, but then I gave a piece of it to Logan. He's a cat, too, only not like my friend Cat, and now he's sick, and I think maybe someone poisoned my dinner, and I didn't know who else to call." I knew I sounded frantic, but frantic was about ten steps calmer than how I actually felt.

"Tell me again what happened."

I recounted finding Cat passed out on the restaurant bathroom floor and Logan's strange behavior when batting around the meat. But the question that hung in the air that Detective Loncar was nice enough not to ask was why someone would have poisoned me at the Briquette Burger.

"You said you found your friend on the bathroom floor. Did she eat the steak?"

"No. She only ate the bread."

"Did your cat eat the bread?"

"He licked it a couple of times, probably for the butter."

"Ms. Kidd, I don't know if we're looking at our first case of poisoning through butter, but I don't think this has to do with your job at Heist. I'll send someone out to the restaurant to check it out, but you should go home and get a good night's sleep."

"But what about my cat?"

"Call me back and tell me what the vet says."

Loncar disconnected. Already this partnership with the cops left much to be desired.

I wiped away the tears that had cut tracks down my cheeks. The door opened, and the vet came out cradling Logan. He made a sound, like a meow that had been recorded on a forty-five and played at thirty-three.

"He's fine. He ate something that didn't agree with him, but it's all out of his system now. Cats are funny that way. Better off than us, some might say. I gave him a sedative, but he'll sleep that off and be back to normal in the morning." He handed Logan to me, and I cradled him like a newborn.

I drove home, thinking about what was in store for me. It was after eleven when I pulled into the driveway. I set Logan on the kitchen table, next to my computer, and filled the Fred Flintstone juice glass with Merlot. One of these days I was going to update the house from early inheritance to modern woman. But before I could think about that, I had a few things I had to work out. I booted up the computer and started an e-mail to Nick.

The solitude of e-mail gave me the courage to confess my involvement in the homicide and the real reason I was working for Heist. It included phrases like *I'm working with the cops, nobody else knows about this,* and *I'm pretty sure I'll be okay, but I wanted you to know.* I signed it with a bunch of Xs and Os and prayed to the gods of internet communications that if this was the wrong thing to do, there would be a technical error and the e-mail would bounce. I turned the computer off so I couldn't see his response, turned off the cell phone so he couldn't call, and carried my now-snoring cat to my bedroom. Whatever it was that I was in for, it was only hours away.

9

—————

KNOCK 'EM DEAD

"ID, PLEASE," SAID A PETITE WOMAN BEHIND THE SECURITY DESK AT Heist. I handed her the card that Tony Simms had given me. She studied it for a moment and then handed it back.

"You're Samantha Kidd? Nice outfit. Welcome to the team."

"Thank you." I adjusted the belt on my pink satin trench coat. I followed a few other people into the store, snaking my way through the denim department to an aisle that led to the handbag displays. Tony Simms stood in by the escalators.

"Samantha." He nodded.

"Mr. Simms," I replied.

"Call me Tony."

That was better than calling him the scary small man that I wasn't sure I could trust, so I went with it. "Okay, Tony."

I hadn't expected to see Tony this morning. I got the feeling this guy would know every move I made and every breath I took. Good thing I'd brought the police into my life; they were singing my theme song.

We walked through the store, past the ballet bars of handcuffed leather jackets and the mug shots in cosmetics. In light of recent events, it was more creepy than edgy. But still, their accessories department rocked.

He led me to a small office, not much wider than the desk inside. "I'm on your speed dial, top button. Call me if you need anything. Otherwise, take today and get acclimated. Instructions on logging on to e-mail are under the keyboard, along with your passwords. Your assistant buyer will be in shortly, I imagine, and she can give you a briefing on your schedule."

After he left, I gingerly sat in the chair of a now-dead woman. I powered up the laptop and signed into e-mail. The unread ones were in red, and the first one's subject was *Welcome to the team!* It was my second "Welcome to the team" that morning, and already the phrase felt fake and automatic, like "May I help you?" sounded to thousands of shoppers programmed to answer, "Just looking." This welcome was from Belle DuChamp.

I read her brief note welcoming me aboard the Heist team. It had been sent on Saturday, probably after I'd left. She offered to give me a tour of the store at ten and wanted me to sit in on two meetings in the afternoon to get a feel for the store's promotional activity and upcoming advertising. I jotted both in an unused day planner that I found in the upper right-hand drawer of the desk.

The next note was from a Mallory George, whose signature line read *Assistant Buyer, Handbags. Heist—Our Prices are Criminal!* The note was brief and decidedly un-chatty and included details on an appointment with the account representative from Vongole, apologies for having a dentist's appointment that would cause her to be half an hour late, and no uses of the words "welcome" or "team."

I fussed around with the drawers and the notebooks and the catalogs, all of which bore a striking resemblance to my first day at Tradava so many months ago. Would I ever outlive this relatively newfound need to put myself in danger? Whatever it was I was seeking, besides the current task of identifying Emily Hart's killer, I wondered if I would find it.

The phone rang, pulling me out of my self-analysis. "Samantha

Kidd," I answered, not sure if that was Heist's standard method for answering the phone.

"Who? I'm looking for Emily?" said a perky female voice.

There are some things you just don't say on the phone to a stranger, and "Emily is dead" is one of them. (Insert any name for Emily, but still, it just isn't done.)

"I'm sorry, Emily isn't here. Is there something I can help you with?"

"Who are you again?"

"Samantha Kidd. Handbag buyer for Heist." It sounded weird out loud.

"Oh. Wow. I knew Emily wanted to leave, but that was quick!"

"I'm sorry," I said again, though I'd done nothing wrong. "Who did you say you were?"

"Andi Holloway. I'm the account manager for Vongole. Actually, I run the showroom Bag Lady. Vongole is my biggest account right now."

"I think I have an appointment with you today, but I don't know what time," I said.

"Fantastic. I have some new items that you will absolutely freak out over. Four o'clock?"

I checked the day planner that, at the moment, only had three things written down, but one of them was in the four o'clock timeslot.

"I can't make four. Can you see me any earlier?"

"That could be problematic." I heard her flipping pages on the other end of the phone and pictured her juggling buyers like men on a debutante's dance card. "Can you make noon? Twelve thirty? No, make it one. Can you make one? It'll be cutting it close, but I can do it."

Sounded like I didn't have much of a choice. "One it is. Where are you located?"

She read off a Penn Street address. "It's a renovated office with space for rent. Seven stories, big Art Deco building. You can't miss it. My Bag Lady offices are on the seventh floor."

We disconnected with the pleasantries of "see you at one" and "I look forward to meeting you." It wasn't a lie. She knew Emily had wanted to leave Heist, and if that was true, then she had more than a professional relationship with Emily. You don't tell your business associates you're looking to leave your job unless you consider them a friend.

A petite woman carried a large vase of flowers into my office. So large that the only way I knew it was a woman were the skirt and stockinged legs visible from the waist down.

"Samantha Kidd?"

"That's me."

"These were waiting for you at security." She set the vase on the corner of my desk. Striking orange flowers were nestled in a square glass vase that was lined with bamboo. A card was clipped to the side of the vase. It wasn't in an envelope.

Knock 'em dead!

Though a smattering of people knew I was starting this job, only one would take the time to send me flowers. Nick's sense of humor and level of support were off the charts on this one. Maybe I should confide in him more often.

"They're the most amazing calla lilies I've ever seen," the petite woman said.

"They are pretty, aren't they? What did you say they were?"

"Bronze Callas. He must be pretty special, whoever he is. That's not a cheap arrangement."

"He is," I said, adjusting one of the waxy-textured flowers to the left.

"They last a long time, too."

"Good. I'd hate to throw it away."

We could only focus on my flowers for so long before we exchanged introductions, and considering she'd brought me flowers with my name on them, I was the only one in the dark.

"You must think I'm rude," she said. "I'm Mallory George. Emily's —I mean, your—assistant buyer." She held out a hand for me to shake.

"Hi Mallory. Samantha Kidd."

Mallory's black bobbed hair had the rigid angles of a Louise Brooks bob and had been straightened with a precision that lent it a Japanese flavor, though her features were definitely not Asian. She wore a crisp white shirt tucked into a long straight pencil skirt. If she had any curves, her outfit kept them hidden.

"Do you mind filling me in on your background?" she asked.

"Excuse me?"

She stood in front of my desk with her handbag still draped over her arm, hands folded in front of her. "What is your work experience?"

I was taken off guard. I'd gotten this far without an actual interview, and now it seemed as though my own assistant was going to be the one to question my abilities.

"Don't you want to put your things down?"

"In a second." She stared at me, not with hostility, but with something that felt alarmingly like X-ray vision. And I was not in a position to have someone see right through me. "This is a big job," she said. "Emily had been in the handbag industry for ten years before landing here. I've been on the Heist team for fifteen. I relocated here when they opened this location. We have aggressive plans to outpace the rest of the store's sales and be the number one department. I don't think it's too much to ask what your qualifications are since you're now the buyer of the most important department in the store."

I glanced at the phone and saw the time was minutes away from ten o'clock.

"I have an appointment with Belle DuChamp at ten, so we'll talk when I return. Oh, and Andi Holloway rescheduled us for one o'clock at her Bag Lady showroom today. She said we should both come. We can talk on the way there. Does that work for you?"

Mallory looked surprised. She nodded her head, and her bobbed hair bobbed. She looked at my flowers one more time and then shuffled into her own office. I grabbed a notepad and pen, tucked my cell phone into my pocket, and traveled back to the executive offices to find the store manager.

Belle DuChamp's promise to give me a tour of the store turned out to be empty. She was tied up on the phone negotiating the price of a large purchase with a customer. She held her hand over the receiver and whispered to me, "He's so close. If I can close this, we'll blow away our opening numbers. Sorry about the tour. Tomorrow?"

I nodded. She scribbled something on a piece of paper and returned to her call.

WITH THE NEWFOUND available pocket of time, I left her office and wandered into the store. It was the perfect time to snoop. My snooping, not surprisingly, led to the handbag department.

A woman in a black nylon sheath dress accented with silver zippers was rearranging the assortment. Her dark brown hair was parted on the side and gelled back into a tight ponytail barely an inch long. Oversized silver hoop earrings weighed down her earlobes. A white can of RockStar Diet Energy drink sat just out of her reach.

"Isn't this bag fantastic?" she asked, holding up a nylon tote with the Vongole logo emblazoned on a leather piece attached to the middle.

"I like the yellow one better." I pointed to the crocodile bag I'd noticed at the gala.

"Omigod. I know. They're totally fab, right? I can't get enough of these. I have, like, ten of them in my closet, and it's not enough. Look at the blue one." She picked up a cobalt blue leather hobo bag. The color was magnificent. The logo was again stamped into the leather, in one of those very clean, linear fonts that are equally timeless and modern. "Here, try it on. It'll totally pop your outfit." She was referring to my gray sheath dress. I'd left my pink trench hanging over the back of my chair.

I took the bag from her and slung it over my shoulder. It was big enough to carry around a laptop and just about anything else I'd want to schlep back and forth to the store.

"Omigod, it's so you. Let me find someone who can ring it up for you." She looked around the store.

"Actually, I'll take it to my office. That way I can get it on my way out."

"You work here?" She was noticeably let down.

"Yes. I'm the new handbag buyer."

"Omigod! Are you Samantha? I'm Andi Holloway, from Bag Lady!" She hopped with enthusiasm and shook my hand. My eyes darted between her and the energy drink. "This is totally funny. We're still on today at one, right?"

"Sure."

"I was just at Tradava meeting with Kyle, and we finished up early, so I came over here to merchandise. He told me about Emily." She dropped her voice and moved in closer to me. "I get why you didn't tell me on the phone. Kyle said it was awful. Just awful."

"Kyle?" It was the only thing she'd said that stuck in my head.

"Kyle Trent. Your competition."

I must have still looked confused, so she continued.

"You know, the totally hot handbag buyer at Tradava?"

10

———

DOESN'T ADD UP

Now this was news.

Kyle Trent had been at the gala in the area of Emily's body. In fact, he'd been coming out of the shadows of the handbag department when I'd first noticed him. He had treated me like I was the one who didn't belong, and all things considered, I hadn't given him a second thought. Now I knew he worked for Tradava, Heist's biggest competitor in the city of Ribbon. That meant *he* was the one who'd been out of place. And what was it he'd said? Something about Emily, about her head being big. Had his comments been made to distract me from his presence, to make me more aware that I wasn't where I should be so I wouldn't take note that neither was he?

I was going to have to tell this to Detective Loncar. I wandered to the cosmetics department and asked a makeup artist for a tissue and a lip liner. I wrote KYLE TRENT on the tissue, handed the liner back to the suspicious employee, and balled the tissue up in my palm. It was just about noon. Mallory and I would be on our way to the handbag showroom in a short while, but I wanted to collect my thoughts, grab a bite to eat, and check on Cat, not necessarily in that order.

I stopped outside of my office when I overheard my assistant,

Mallory, on the phone. "Somebody sent her a pretty expensive flower arrangement. Guess it's her boyfriend or husband. I don't think she's going to fall for Kyle's tricks. She knows Belle, too, but I don't know how. I'll find out." There was a pause of silence, and then Mallory's voice dropped. "I can't talk. Call me later." The phone clunked against the receiver while I ducked into my own small quarters. I shrugged back into my trench coat and belted it around my waist, picked up my vintage handbag, and went to Mallory's doorway.

"What time do we have to leave to get to Bag Lady by one?" I asked.

"Twelve thirty should be fine, but Andi's cool if we're a little late."

"We'll be on time. I'm going to grab something to eat. Why don't we meet by security at twenty-five after? I'll drive."

It was clear that Mallory wanted to undermine me, but I wasn't going to let her. I didn't know her deal yet, but with the tight quarters of my Honda del Sol looming in our future, I'd have approximately half an hour to find out.

I bought a Snickers bar and a packet of peanuts from the newsstand in the corner of the parking lot and sat on a public bench. I bit into the Snickers and scribbled names into my composition notebook, munching without any trace of manners, completely absorbed in my candy bar and *Harriet the Spy* routine. That's why I didn't notice the motorcycle that pulled up in front of me until the driver got off.

Dante.

He climbed off the bike and put it on its kickstand. He wore a pretty close approximation of what he'd worn the night he showed up at my house. Black leather jacket, white T-shirt, jeans, black leather boots.

I slammed my notebook shut and wiped a ring around my lipstick with my index finger to remove any traces of chocolate that may have smeared onto my face.

"What are you doing, Samantha?"

"Nice to see you too, Dante."

"You're working here now?" He jerked a thumb behind him in the direction of Heist.

"It would appear that way, yes."

"But sometimes things aren't what they appear to be."

"Okay, I'm working here now."

He straddled the paint-chipped bench and faced me. "Doesn't add up."

"What?"

"If you knew you were going to be working at Heist, you would never have entered that contest. And you would never have gotten a job so fast if you hadn't applied before the contest. So somehow you got a job here, between the time that woman was murdered and today. And between that time, someone poisoned my sister. And I think it's related, and I want details."

It would have been easier to lie to Nick in Italy than to lie to Dante in front of me, but the irony was that I'd been honest with Nick despite the distance between us. I suspected what Nick would say about me being *thisclose* to a homicide investigation, but I didn't know Dante that well.

I did a little internal negotiating on whether or not I would feel better/want help/want Dante's help when something he said struck me.

"What do you mean someone poisoned your sister?"

"They found traces of poison in Cat's system. That's why she passed out."

"But we didn't have time to eat. I took the food with me when Eddie drove her home."

"She said she ate the bread."

"We all ate the bread."

"And you didn't get sick?"

"Nope." But Logan had.

"Dante, Cat's husband is on the road, right?"

He nodded.

"Are you going to stay with her, at least for now, to take care of her?"

"Yeah."

"Good."

I stood up from the bench. Dante stood too and turned me toward him. He leaned in, and I could smell cinnamon on his breath. "That doesn't mean I'm not going to keep an eye on you. I don't buy this whole 'new job' thing. I don't know what you're hiding, but if you're into something, I'm going to find out." His brown eyes bored holes into my head. "If this is about you feeling some kind of rush, you're risking too much."

He stepped closer. I tried to back up, but my calf hit the bench I'd been sitting on. There was no place for me to go, and parts of my body were telling my brain they didn't really want to go anywhere.

"Besides, there are better ways of getting a rush," he said, running the back of his index finger down the side of my neck and across my clavicle.

I flicked his hand away with a *Karate Kid* wax-on/wax-off maneuver. "I'm not looking for a rush."

"Good. Some things are better when you take them slow."

In the distance, I saw Mallory exit the store. "I have to be somewhere," I said, which seemed the safest of the things running through my head to say out loud. "Tell Cat I hope she feels better. I'll come by later this week to check on her." I walked past him to my car.

"Samantha," he called out behind me. "Be careful."

"Of what?" I said, turning around and walking backward for a few steps. "I'm just a buyer for a department store." I smiled and then turned away again, feeling the heat of his stare on my back the whole time.

IF MALLORY WANTED to know my qualifications, she was going to have to broach the subject again without my help. As far as I was concerned, I was fully capable of doing this job, even if "the job" involved a few things probably not spelled out in the description. I met her outside the security entrance and invited her to join me in the car.

She stopped off at a PT Cruiser, pulled a pair of tortoise sunglasses from the center console, and locked the door. She matched my stride to the car, no easy feat considering I was naturally taller than she was. Her posture was bent slightly at the waist, causing her to pitch forward awkwardly. She balanced expertly upon five-inch platform wedges and came darn close to towering over my five-foot seven frame. I did a double take when I saw the size of her feet. No wonder she could balance on those boats.

We settled into the car and I immediately turned off the stereo, not wanting to blast her with the greatest hits of Tom Jones. I drove from the parking lot to the access road to the highway in silence, wondering who was going to speak first. I side-glanced at Mallory and caught her staring at the compartment between our seats. When we stopped at the next traffic light, I followed her stare. Eddie had left the sketches of the Puccetti statue half-rolled up between the seats. I had to teach that boy to clean up after himself.

"Maybe I didn't ask correctly this morning, but I am curious to know what brings you to Heist," she said. Her approach was softer than earlier. I wondered what made the difference.

"I've been in the industry for more than a decade. I worked at Bentley's in New York. Just moved here recently."

"You were their handbag buyer?"

"Shoes."

"A lot of the same vendors, I suppose," she admitted. "So why did you move to Ribbon?"

"I grew up here. My parents wanted to move to the west coast, and it seemed like a good idea to buy their house. The one I grew up in." It sounded so insignificant when trying to explain it to a person who probably wasn't interested.

"Trying to go home again. Did it work?"

"The jury's still out." I changed lanes to let an aggressive driver pass.

"Why Heist?"

I wasn't sure if I should mention my brief work history with Tradava or not, but she could find out easily enough. "They recruited me after they found out I no longer worked at Tradava."

She seemed surprised. "Nobody told me you worked at Tradava."

"I was only there briefly." *Mental note: stay vague on the details.* "I'm still trying to figure out who gave them my name."

"It had to be Belle DuChamp. She's from Tradava, and she didn't leave on good terms. I heard she's very interested in crushing them."

"She was fired?"

"You didn't know? They caught her and the handbag manager getting it on in the board room. That's why it's so weird that you showed up. With Emily gone, I figured he was a shoe-in."

11

TO DIE FOR

I TRIED TO KEEP OUR CONVERSATION TO A MINIMUM FOR THE DURATION of the drive because I couldn't exactly stop and take notes. What was becoming apparent was that Mallory George was going to be a wealth of information if I played the situation correctly.

We arrived at Bag Lady and found Andi Holloway cradling her cell phone between her tipped head and hunched shoulder while she bought a diet RockStar energy drink from a vending machine in the lobby.

"Can't talk now," she said into the phone and raised her head. The phone dropped to the floor. She scooped it up and smiled at us. "Thank God! You just saved me from a lecture from my dad. You want one?" She held up the white can as if making a toast.

"No thanks. Mallory?"

"None for me, either."

We followed Andi past a couple of smaller rooms filled with crocheted hobos and patchwork tote bags. Finally, we reached a room merchandised with Vongole's collection.

Colorful handbags sat on perfectly lit shelves just like at Heist. The shelving features were a milky white Lucite, glowing from hidden lights behind them, highlighting colorful patent leather bags. Clutches with silver hardware in the colors of hard candy lined the wall, but Andi had taken advantage of the negative space on the shelves to break the assortment up into trend stories. I picked up the canary-yellow patent sample and unsnapped the clasp. Soft lilac suede lined the inside. I snapped it shut before it started whispering sweet nothings to me like a seashell from the Jersey shore. On a separate shelf sat a collection of bucket totes with chain link handles and the V logo formed out of Bakelite. Knowing I couldn't stock Heist with every bag they carried, my job got ten percent harder. And that was on top of trying to figure out who murdered my predecessor.

"I can tell you like what you see. I know. To die for, right?"

"They're gorgeous."

"They're totally freakin' hot. I mean, look at this. Look at this!" Andi's energy drink habit had turned her into a one-woman merchant machine. This was the kind of energy level not witnessed since I tried out to be a high school cheerleader. The same day I learned enthusiasm doesn't translate into a perfectly executed cartwheel.

"You don't need to worry about anything right now. This is just a review appointment, and Belle already called in an order for Heist. She'll be giving you the details later today or tomorrow or something." She waved her hand to shoo away a fly.

"Is that normal? That Belle would call in an order?"

"She totally knows what's right for Heist. You're sooooo lucky to have her with you. Kyle is probably freaking out over at Tradava."

"If Belle did my job already, what did you want to cover in our appointment?" I asked, not sure I liked knowing Belle had taken control of the handbag buyer responsibilities so soon after Emily's murder.

"We're supposed to be going over your growth plans for Vongole at the store, but Belle said she'd be working on them with you later today."

I felt my forehead crease with confusion. I stopped myself from pointing out that I was the buyer, not Belle, though she was the general manager of the store, and having worked there for less time than it takes a pie crust to rise, I wasn't sure I knew enough to challenge the situation.

Andi continued. "She knows the market so well, you know? Belle ran into me in the store, and we got to talking about the inventory. She called me about an hour ago and told me a couple of items that you needed. She didn't want to miss out on a delivery while you got up and running in the job. I had what she wanted—don't worry, if I didn't, I'd probably steal it from somebody else's inventory to keep you in stock—we have such a good partnership with Heist!"

She turned to Mallory, who had been standing to my left for the majority of the appointment, meek as a mouse. Not the confrontational employee I'd seen this morning at the store.

"I'll send you the order in an e-mail," Andi said. "You just have to get me a purchase order, and I'll ship. Okay?"

I honestly wasn't sure if it was okay, but it was too soon to know. This was not the time to pretend to be more in charge than I might be. Maybe Belle did have the ability to place orders without me. I knew of other retailers who allowed the general managers to supplement their stock with special buys. I wondered if Emily Hart had stood up to Belle and gotten in the way. Would that be cause for murder? And how much business could possibly be lost between Emily's death and my starting in the job? And had Belle been trying to hide something from me when she thwarted my efforts to see the store?

I apologized to Andi for not being ready with the Vongole growth strategy and asked if she would spend the balance of the appointment reviewing the upcoming deliveries. She agreed and walked us through the samples. Apparently everything in the showroom was already on order; Emily—or whoever had been writing the orders—didn't have much of an editorial eye. But considering how luscious these handbags were, I didn't think we'd have a problem selling them, especially at Heist's customary discounted prices. Occasionally I asked Mallory's opinion. With a little encouragement she offered up her thoughts, which were strikingly on target. She had a good knowledge of trends and of business, but I didn't think she would have said a word during the entire appointment if I hadn't point-blank prompted her.

Andi, on the other hand, seemed put off by my inviting Mallory to participate in the conversation. When the appointment closed in on an hour and a half, we had to leave. I had a meeting scheduled with Belle back at Tradava, and I was eager to ask her about the orders she'd placed.

Andi handed Mallory a shiny blue folder filled with line sheets and prices. "Here's everything you need on the collection. E-mail me the order tomorrow, and I'll ship."

Mallory glanced my way. I tipped my head ever so slightly, allowing her to answer for herself. I was curious.

"It's a busy week. I can have it to you by Friday."

"How about Thursday by noon? I can get the orders in the system by the end of the day, and we can ship on Friday. You'll have the merchandise by the following Monday."

"I don't know if Thursday is going to happen. I'll see what I can do."

"Okay, but you don't want to let this one slip. There are others out there that will snatch this up!" Andi's smile hid an undercurrent of urgency. Her casual haven't-we-been-friends-forever? attitude most likely took her a long way in selling the collections she represented, and judging from what we'd walked past, Vongole was the shining star in her showroom. The other collections mirrored what I'd seen in junior shops and flea market warehouse venues, the kind that cost pennies on the dollar to produce. I wanted to hear how she'd landed the Vongole account, but that was a conversation for another day.

"Don't forget to calculate the forty percent discount off cost," Andi said as we were leaving the showroom. I wasn't sure I heard right.

"Forty percent from cost?" I repeated, halfway through tying the square knot on my trench coat belt. "Industry standard is five."

"I know. It's sooo much better than what everybody else offers. But like I said, we have such a great partnership with Heist that we totally want to make sure you have room to sell at those criminal prices and still make high margins. Belle negotiated the whole thing with the owner. It's insane but good for her. And you," she added as an afterthought. "Bye!"

Mallory and I walked to the car in silence. I wanted to take notes, but there wasn't time. I needed to plan for these things better. I needed a pocket tape recorder or a solo trip to the bathroom or something. I started the drive back to Tradava.

"So, what did you think?" I asked Mallory.

"I don't know that we need everything in the showroom, but I'm sure everything will sell once we slap that discount on there."

"Is that the discount we get from everyone?"

"No. Vongole is by far the highest."

"I thought Vongole was the new It-Bag designer."

"They are. They have lots of press from the celebrities carrying them. It's the kind of word of mouth that Marc Jacobs and Chloe bags used to get."

I'd read enough magazines to know that the perfect storm of new product plus hot celebrity endorsement could launch a marketing frenzy. Witness Jennifer Lopez and the Manolo Blahnik Timberland bootie—the one from the "Jenny on the Block" video. When I was buying shoes for Bentley's, we couldn't keep it in stock, and a pair sold on eBay for eighteen hundred dollars while we were waiting on our reorder. Madness.

"I can't figure out why they would be willing to give us such a big discount when their product is in such demand. It's not the smartest strategy. You would think if they were the hottest thing going, someone would have the business sense to pull back on their discount and milk us for whatever they could get. I'm not complaining, because it's good for Heist, but still, it doesn't make sense. Right?"

She was right. The Heist deal was out of the ordinary, and Mallory recognized it. Any number of assistant buyers would be so blown away by the low prices on Vongole's handbags and how great they were for anybody with an employee discount. Mallory had a way of seeing through the promotional tactics of Vongole and pointing out the imperfections, even if those imperfections were to our benefit. The discount troubled me, and I wanted to find out how Belle had negotiated it, but right now, I wondered what else Mallory had picked up on, regarding Heist, Vongole, or Emily Hart.

"What did you think of the assortment?" I asked.

"They've got the best range of color I've ever seen. That showroom is like a candy store."

"That's what I thought, too."

"The bags look better in there than at Heist."

Again, she was right. Heist's assortment looked good, following the same minimalist merchandising standards as the showroom, but not as good as the samples had looked. Andi was selling the product, and Heist was selling the discount.

I stole a quick glance at Mallory. She was looking at a spreadsheet in the three-ring binder on her lap. On more than one count, she'd demonstrated her value to the office. I wondered, could she do my job? Was she in line for it? I felt a pang of guilt, knowing I not only hadn't applied for the job, I wasn't even doing it for the sake of doing it well. My time at Bentley's had trained me how to be a successful buyer, but I'd also learned that the job took more than a skill set. It took passion and dedication and instincts.

I'd already acknowledged once that being a luxury-goods buyer for a large retailer wasn't my passion, but there was something about the ever-changing world of fashion that was in my blood. I was still trying to find my place in the industry. Did Mallory have more passion for this position than I did?

We returned to the store and went into our separate offices. I had a few spare minutes before meeting with Belle and used them to scribble the questions that remained. Well, right after I buried my nose in my very attractive calla lilies and thought about what I would say to Nick later that night.

I popped my head into Mallory's office and told her I'd be in meetings with Belle for the next couple of hours. That should give her the time to work on the Vongole orders.

"Do you think you can get the orders to Andi by Thursday, or is that going to be a problem?"

"I can 'totally' get the orders to her by Thursday." She used finger quotes around "totally," and I laughed. "I just don't think the vendors should get into the habit of thinking we're at their beck and call. We're the customer, not them. I think Andi sometimes forgets that."

12

———

PR CAN SPIN ANYTHING

THE EXECUTIVE OFFICES OF HEIST'S MANAGEMENT WERE ONE FLOOR above mine and down a carpeted hallway. Belle's secretary was busy tapping at the keyboard of her computer. Before I could introduce myself, she said, "Go on back, she's expecting you."

I thanked her and walked down the hall to the large corner office.

Several men and women in professional attire sat around a rectangular glass table by floor-to-ceiling windows. Belle sat at the end, with a notebook by her side, a calendar in front of her, two cell phones, and a BlackBerry next to them. This was a woman who didn't want to miss a beat.

"Join us," she said. She waved a hand toward a chair behind two of the men. "This is the store's team of executives." She gave me a blanket introduction to those assembled at the table. "This is Samantha Kidd. She's someone to watch. I asked her to join us so we could get her up to speed on what Heist is all about. It's a crash course on our identity," she joked.

For the next hour I listened to the team that ran the store. A blonde in a too-tight suit and too-tan cleavage brainstormed with Belle about upcoming events and ways to keep people coming back to the store. Another woman, in a black polo shirt and jeans, made a few comments on the store's opening expenses. And a man in a wrinkled linen shirt and faded khakis brought up the store's promotional contest, the event that had brought me to them in the first place.

"That was a great contest. It's almost a shame that there wasn't a winner," I said.

They turned in my direction. "Well, there was a winner, but we decided not to announce it because of what happened. We're on the fence on how we should proceed with that."

"Who was the winner?"

"Only one group succeeded in getting away with one of the challenges."

"Which one?" I asked.

"The statue."

I sat up straighter. "That was me." I studied their expressions. "I mean, I had help. I didn't do it alone."

Wrinkled Linen Shirt looked at me with open admiration. Tan Cleavage looked skeptical, and Belle looked shocked.

"You were the one who stole the Puccetti statue?" she asked.

I nodded. "It was a great contest, only I don't think Heist got the kind of publicity you wanted."

Cleavage cocked her head to one side. "Are you kidding? That publicity was a wet dream."

Three of the men chuckled. Wrinkled Shirt leaned toward me. "PR can spin anything."

"Well, I guess that gives us our answer about what to do," said Belle, reclaiming everyone's attention before the meeting got out of hand. "The rules clearly stated that no employees of Heist were eligible to win. Since Samantha is now an employee, the contest becomes void. We can make an announcement that there was no qualified winner and move on."

Her secretary crossed the office with a pink phone message in her hand. She set it in front of Belle, who glanced at it then looked at me. She tucked the message into the spine of her desk calendar and slammed the book shut.

"When should we make the announcement?" asked Cleavage.

Belle reopened her calendar, and the pink message floated out from the inside. It landed in front of Wrinkled Shirt. He slapped it down on the table and held it out for Belle. *Call Mallory.*

Belle tucked the pink paper back inside her notebook and ended the meeting. "Samantha, can you stay with me for a couple of minutes? I want to talk to you."

The rest of the staff left her office, huddled in their own conversations about visuals, publicity, merchandising, and gossip. When the office was empty, Belle closed the office door, leaving the two of us secluded.

"I want a person like you on my team. Here."

"But I am on your team."

"I don't just mean Heist. I mean here. Running the store. You pulled off that statue prank very well, and it's a shame that you weren't allowed to win, because you deserve it. I'll see what I can do about a prize."

Guess she didn't know about my new clothing allowance.

"People don't stay in jobs for long at Heist. It's a fast-moving company, with lots of opportunity. Talent gets recognized, and I think you've got talent. I want you helping to run the store."

"I'm flattered, but my experience is in buying, and I'd like to see what I can do with the handbag job first," I answered slightly mechanically. It was starting to feel like my career at Heist was a train on tracks that had no brakes, and the rails were getting shifted underneath me. "Thank you for thinking of me." I stood, thinking the meeting was over.

"I'm a determined woman, Samantha, and I'm willing to fight for what I want. I want you by my side. I think you're a risk taker. Now, I have to return a couple of calls, but meet me back here in about ten minutes, and I'll give you that tour of the store I promised. And don't worry about the handbag job. I've got plans for that, too."

My hand was on the doorknob, but her last words halted my exit. I turned back.

"Belle, is there something you want to tell me about Kyle Trent?"

13

WE HAVE TO TALK

BELLE'S EYES AND MINE REMAINED LOCKED FOR AT LEAST SIX SECONDS, assuming my pounding heart was keeping a beat-per-second rhythm. She broke the stare, looked at her calendar, and then sank into her chair.

"I forgot about a late appointment. We'll do the tour another time." She picked the phone off the cradle and without looking at me dialed a number from memory. And with that, I was dismissed.

I wandered through the store. Something was up at Heist, but I didn't know what. Mallory had intimated that Kyle wanted the handbag job. And Mallory had called Belle. Maybe Belle didn't know Tony Simms had offered me the job, and this was her way of opening the position back up for the looker from Tradava. Sure, it felt good to be praised, but there was no way the attention I received had anything to do with my eight-hour performance on the job.

When I finally returned to my office, Mallory was working on the Vongole order. I considered asking her about the message on Belle's desk but didn't. I wasn't sure how to interact with Mallory just yet. I didn't know how to interact with anybody, and until I felt a little loyalty from someone, I was going to stick to myself. I went to my desk and checked my e-mail. One note, marked urgent, was from

Tony Simms: *I noticed you haven't had time to shop. I'll have a few things sent by your house tonight.*

Yep, something was definitely up.

I left early, knowing I was being watched. There was no other explanation for Tony knowing whether or not I'd selected a few items to fulfill his agreement with me. And though I'd been the one to demand such a greedy perk, his insistency that I claim my due felt more like bribery than part of my compensation packet.

I needed to sort my thoughts. Logan met me at the door, still lethargic from the sedative. He grazed my ankles and purred. I carried him to the kitchen and set him on the counter. A wave of paranoia washed over me. Was I being watched right now? I carried both my laptop and Logan to my sister's old bedroom. Logan settled into a beanbag chair, and I sat at Sasha's eighth-grade desk, feeling only slightly less vulnerable.

The usual e-mails greeted me: coupon from the bookstore, discount offer on shoes, promotional code for the latest as-seen-on-TV item. And one from Nick: *We have to talk.*

Nothing good ever came from the four words he'd used as his subject line. I ignored his e-mail and went downstairs to check the answering machine.

Beep! "Ms. Kidd, this is Detective Loncar. Call me when you get in."

All things considered, the men in my life were a little too demanding. Between Nick's "we have to talk" and the detective's message, I wondered what was behind door number three. I dialed the detective's number anyway, wanting to get this part of my day over with.

"Detective? It's Samantha Kidd."

"Ms. Kidd. You done with work?"

"I left early."

"You didn't get fired already, did you?"

"No, I didn't get fired."

Rustling papers. A clunk. A curse word. "Can you come down here? I have a couple things to go over with you."

"Sure. When?"

"Now," he barked. "Unless you have other plans."

Considering my only other plans included reading Nick's note, my schedule was wide open. "I'll be there in twenty minutes." I grabbed my notebook and a few items that needed the detective's attention and headed on my way.

Detective Loncar was waiting for me by the front desk. "Ms. Kidd. Follow me."

I followed him down the linoleum-tiled hallway. A janitor pushed a dark gray mop over the tiles, barely changing the color. I hopped over the wet spots where dirty water pooled on warped tiles and moved past the questioning room to his office. I sat by the wooden table.

"Nice outfit," he said, eying my pink trench coat.

"Thank you."

"That your undercover spy look?"

I didn't answer, largely because it was. Every self-respecting fashionista knows you wear a trench coat to spy.

I filled him in on everything I could remember. I won't bore you with the details because you were there the first time, but before long he knew what I knew about Andi Holloway, Belle DuChamp, Mallory George, and Kyle Trent. I consulted my composition book a couple of times when he prompted me with questions and even remembered to share that my team had won the Heist contest, though we weren't eligible to claim the prize. I couldn't tell anyone else, and I had to tell someone. I expected him to at least say congratulations. He didn't.

"When you go into work tomorrow morning, move your flowers to your assistant's office."

"Why?" My eyes darted to the left and then the right and then back to the detective. "How do you know about my flowers?"

"They're from us. They're bugged."

"I thought they were from—" I stopped.

"Who?"

"The card was signed with Xs and Os."

"Nice touch, don'tcha think? Figured it would keep the riffraff away if they thought you were taken. You're a pretty girl, Ms. Kidd. We don't want you to have any distractions while you're at Heist."

"That is so wrong."

"It's for your own good. We think we might learn something from your assistant, so we want you to move them in there."

"On one condition." I pulled a Tupperware container out of my handbag and set it on the detective's desk. "Have someone at your lab analyze the butter on this roll."

"Are we back on your sick cat?"

"My friend was poisoned, and my cat was poisoned, and this is my only link between those two things."

"Are you trying to negotiate with the police?"

"I'm having second thoughts about helping you."

"Too late."

I put my index finger on the top of the Tupperware lid and pushed it across Loncar's desk calendar. "Find out about the butter, and I'll play ball."

"Ms. Kidd, I really wish you'd start talking like a normal person."

"Is it a deal?"

"Yes, it's a deal."

"Are we done here?"

"Yes, we're done. Unless you got something else?"

I stood to leave. "Yes, one more thing. Mallory will think it's strange that I'm giving away my flowers, especially if they're from the man in my life. I'll expect another arrangement tomorrow."

It's a good thing I had the cops sending me flowers because by the looks of Nick's subject line, the prospects of our ever being a couple were slim to none. I stared at my inbox for seven and a half minutes before I opened *We have to talk.*

Samantha, There's a problem at the factory and it won't be fixed for a couple more weeks. I'll call you tonight, and every night, at nine o'clock your time, to make sure you're okay. Be on the other end of the phone, or else. -N.

It wasn't the response I'd expected.

By not mentioning my e-mail, I had no context for his note. Was he mad? Concerned? Interested? Or did he simply not care?

I picked up my phone and dialed the first half of his number in Italy before I hung up. What would I say? That I wanted to know what he thought about my involvement in a homicide? I already knew what he'd say about that. No, I wasn't going to sit around worrying about what Nick thought of my life. Despite our attraction, he was there, and I was here. Fine, I thought. I can take care of myself. I turned off the computer and relaxed into the chair.

Until I heard the front door slam downstairs.

14

CLOTHING ALLOWANCE

"Sam? Sam! Are you here?" Eddie called from downstairs.

Aside from the near heart attack-inducing surprise of having someone wander unexpectedly into my house, Eddie's arrival wouldn't have bothered me if I didn't have something to hide. I left the room, closing the door behind me.

"I'll be right there," I called before descending the stairs.

Eddie stood in my living room. His cargo pants carried three different colors of paint, two of which (lime green and cobalt blue) were repeated across the ironic quote on his T-shirt, one of which was smudged by his hairline (orange). A large cardboard wardrobe box with black arrows on the side indicating which end was up stood between the coffee table and the black and white chair closest to the door.

"What's that?"

"Dunno. It was sitting on your front porch. Has your name on it. Says it's from Heist."

Apparently Tony Simms had been serious.

"Aren't you going to open it?"

"No, I'll wait till later."

"You're not curious," he said.

"Not really?"

"It wasn't a question."

"Mine was."

Eddie crossed the room and disappeared into the kitchen. He returned with the kind of knife that most people kept for carving turkeys. "I want to see what you got."

"I'm sure it's nothing. Just stuff I need for the job."

"I've worked in retail for fifteen years and have never, ever heard of or seen a box this size show up on someone's doorstep on their first day on the job. And you sit here and say you're not curious." He set the knife on top of the box. "What's going on with you?"

"Nothing. I'm just trying to focus on my new job." That wasn't so far from the truth.

We both heard the muffled meow at the same time, followed by scratching. "Logan! He's probably trapped in the bedroom."

"I'll let him out. You mind if I check my email?" He jogged up the stairs without waiting for my answer. Then it hit me that Nick's e-mail might still be open. I scaled the steps two at a time but was still too late. Eddie sat in my chair, staring at the screen. I pounced on the mouse and closed the browser.

"Sorry, that was an e-mail from Nick. Kind of personal."

"Speaking of Nick, we never got around to him the other night. What does he have to say about the job? Or the cops?"

"Nick's proud of me."

"Interesting. What did he say about the homicide?"

"Nothing."

"I'm pretty sure Nick would say something you being this close to a homicide. What gives?"

"Nothing gives. You know Nick—he'd worry."

"So you aren't confiding in him either?" His gaze hadn't faltered since I entered the room.

"It's not like he could do anything from Italy."

"Dude, if something's going on, you should confide in your friends. As in me."

"I don't know what you're talking about," I said.

He looked at my trench coat for a second, down to my shoes, and then back up to my face. I was starting to wish I wasn't dressed in cartoon spy fashion.

"I may have contacted Detective Loncar after the night of the murder."

"You're confiding in Loncar, now?" He pushed his grown-out Mohawk back, away from his forehead. When he let go, it flopped to the side of his head. "The detective is a one-way street. He's going to take your information and use it to solve the homicide, but he's not going to keep you in the loop. Don't expect him to. That's not his job."

"Yeah? Well, my job is handbag buyer. For Tradava's competition, and since you work for Tradava, I'm not going to tell you what I do at Heist. It would be a conflict of interest. Even though Nick's in Italy, I can talk to him."

"Nick's two thousand miles away, so he's safe."

He sat in my chair, twisted at the waist, watching me with his intensely green eyes.

I fidgeted with the belt knotted on my trench coat and then shoved my hands into my pockets. Eddie stood up.

"I thought you wanted to check your e-mail?"

"Nah, I can do it from my place."

I followed him down the stairs to the living room. I had met Eddie in high school but didn't really get to know him until six months ago, after I'd moved back to Ribbon. He'd seen me through a murder investigation and had been the only new friend to stand by my side as my life fell apart. I wanted to tell him what was going on. I wanted to tell him we'd won the contest but weren't eligible for the prize. I wanted to tell him about Tony Simms and Belle DuChamp and Detective Loncar and Andi Holloway and Kyle Trent...

"By the way, Cat's doing much better," he said. "I thought you'd want to know. She's going back to her store tomorrow."

"Dante stopped by Heist today and told me." I thought back over what Dante had said. My face grew hot.

"She'd probably like to see you if you can manage a visit."

"Dante's staying with her, right? I'd rather avoid him."

"Why? Is there something he knows that you're trying to hide?"

We stood in my living room, Logan swirling around Eddie's purple Vans, occasionally licking the paint smears on his pants. He slinked over to the wardrobe box and ran his head against one of the corners. Then he eyed up the distance to the top of it, leaned back, and easily cleared the four feet to the top. Eddie reached over and scratched Logan's ears.

"I'll get out of here so you can open your giant package. You might be trying hard to not act like yourself, but curiosity is killing your cat."

Logan flopped onto his side and pawed at the brown packing tape that sealed the box.

"Eddie, are you busy for lunch tomorrow?"

"Why?"

"I thought I might stop in."

"Come to my office around noon."

"Deal. I'm buying."

For the first time since he'd entered my house, he laughed. "I know."

Eddie was right; I was bursting to open the giant package from Heist. I shooed Logan from the top of the giant box and sliced through the tape.

Inside, hanging from a metal rod, were four plastic garment bags. I pulled each one out and set them on my sofa. Then I pulled the blinds and locked the front door.

Each item carried the Heist price tag. The first bag contained a black skirt suit not unlike the one Tan Cleavage had worn earlier that day. The second held a black zip front dress like Andi Holloway's. The third contained a boxy menswear-styled black vest and matching trousers. Tony Simms didn't have an active imagination. He also didn't have any idea of how I wanted to dress. He was sucking the fun out of the clothing allowance one piece of dismal black apparel at a time. At least he got the sizes right.

The phone rang after I'd zipped up the pants and buttoned the vest over my bra. I flopped on to the sofa and answered.

"Are you alone?" Nick asked.

"Yes."

"What are you wearing?"

This conversation was starting off better than I'd expected. "A pair of black pants and a vest."

"Good. That means you're not dressed up like a spy in a trench coat. That means you're acting normal, at least for now." His voice softened. "Now tell me about this thing at Heist."

Truth time. I filled him on everything that had happened since my e-mail last night: the contest, the murder, the visit from Tony Simms, and the partnership with Detective Loncar. I went into detail about my first day, how busy it was and how little I'd done that was handbag related. Actually, that wasn't true. Most of what I'd done had been handbag related, and it had been related to Emily Hart's murder too, which meant if I kept doing what I was doing, I might find a motive.

"I don't think I like this, and I definitely don't like that I'm not there," he said when I finished.

"What happened at the factory? Why won't you be coming back as soon as you want?"

"The factory somehow ran out of the leathers I bought for my collection. They can't tell me what went wrong; I placed the orders six months ago, and they confirmed them, but now they're short. I'm going to have to use these designs in another fabric, find another factory, or scrap the whole thing and start over. None of the options are very appealing."

"So how long does that mean you're going to be there?"

"Easily another month. Maybe more."

I pouted and shoved my now-cold feet under the white afghan. A horn beeped out front, and I moved to the window to see who it was.

Dante was walking up my driveway, carrying a large box under one arm.

"Nick, I have to go."

"Are you okay?"

"Yes. Cat's brother just showed up."

"Does he know anything?"

"No, but like everyone else around here, he suspects something."

"Be careful. And call me tomorrow morning before you leave for work. Okay?"

"Okay."

I tossed the phone on the sofa after saying good-bye. It wasn't until after I opened the door that I remembered the vest I was wearing over my black lace bra. One of the bra straps fell from my shoulder and dangled by my upper arm.

"First a schoolgirl, now Madonna. You don't make it easy, Samantha," he said.

I hooked my thumb into my bra strap, pulled it back up, and crossed my arms over my chest to hide the plunging neckline. "What are you doing here?"

"My sister sent me over with this." He handed me the box. "She said you might need it for your new job. Something about bringing you back into this decade? I don't remember the exact quote."

"She was probably delirious at the time." I took the box and turned. "Do you want to come inside?"

"Yes, but I'm not going to."

"Why's that?"

"Because you have a man in your life who is out of town, and I have a sick sister back at the house, and I think it's better that we focus on those two things instead of how cute you look in your black lace bra."

I pulled the afghan off the sofa and wrapped it around my shoulders like a superhero cape.

"Good night, Samantha." He leaned in and kissed me on the cheek. A hint of cinnamon lingered in the air. I turned my head slightly. He didn't move away. I felt the bristle of his unshaven cheek dust my face.

I took a step backward and forced a smile. "Good night, Dante."

He closed the space between us. My back was against the sofa. He tipped my chin up and looked me straight in the eyes. "I have to go out of town for a few days, but whatever you're trying to hide, I'll find out when I get back."

The afghan fell from my shoulders. He looked over my body, turned around, and left.

15

TREADING DANGEROUS WATERS

I took a long shower after Dante left, washing and conditioning my hair three times and shaving my left leg twice. To say I was distracted was an understatement. For someone who liked to plan and anticipate everything, I never saw Dante coming.

I'd certainly dated during the nine years I lived in New York. My Saturday-night suitors had come in the form of Wall Street bankers, pastry chefs, and at least three deli counter employees who satisfied my need for cured lunch meats and provolone cheese. The problem with all of those dates was simple.

Nick Taylor.

From the minute I'd met Nick on a dirty, slushy street in New York City, him in a *Rocky* T-shirt and me in yoga clothes, ponytails, and a knockoff Vuitton bucket hat, I'd felt an electricity I hadn't otherwise known. Where other men had either fawned on me too soon or made other intentions clear, Nick kept me on my toes. Every time I thought I knew where I stood with him, he pulled the rug out from under my sample-sized feet.

It wasn't until I gave up my job, moved to Ribbon, and left my career and connections behind that I learned he felt the attraction too. But discovering Nick's interests exposed his warmhearted, protective nature. He was an old-fashioned guy, and part of me liked that, but another part of me needed to prove I could take care of myself. Only now, with him halfway around the world, it seemed I could use a guardian angel in a *Rocky* T-shirt. And even though I knew that, and I recognized I was treading dangerous waters, I liked the way it felt. I liked taking chances, and I didn't know if Nick could deal with that side of me.

Dante, on the other hand, seemed to accept that side of me. From what I'd seen so far, he encouraged it.

I changed into pajamas and attended to Cat's gift. A heavy ivory envelope was tucked under the satin ribbon that held the lid on. I pulled a piece of monogrammed stationary from the envelope.

It's from last season, and that's as vintage as I'll let you go.—Cat

The box held a mint-blue knit dress and coordinating tweed topper with an oversized collar. Deeper in the box was a pair of black suede boots with three-inch heels. Catnip, her store, was a designer outlet, and often last year's looks were this year's new arrivals. I'd loved this outfit from the first time I saw it in the pages of *Vogue*, but without a job the price had been too steep. It brought tears to my eyes to think Cat was thinking of me while I was shutting her out of my world. I punched her number into the phone to say thanks and arrange a time to visit.

"I love it. I'm going to wear it tomorrow," I said when she answered.

"Is that a promise?"

"Yes. Temporarily, thanks to you, I'll be the height of style, give or take six months. How are you feeling?"

"Better. I'm going back to the store tomorrow."

"How about dinner after?" I asked.

"Sure. Come over to the house. I can't seem to shake Dante, but you don't mind if he joins us, right? He makes a mean meatloaf."

"Sure, that's okay. But I might have to leave early," I said, thinking about my nine o'clock phone call.

"Nick can call your cell phone," she said, laughing.

"Okay, tomorrow night. I'll be there around seven thirty."

That phone call was going to prove a problem if Dante was still suspicious of my activities, but there wasn't much I could do about it now. I carried my new outfit (the one I liked, not the boring black ones from Heist) to my bedroom and curled up in bed.

When you're trying to make a long-distance relationship work, you tend to fall asleep with your cell phone. You never know when late-night texts will come through, and you want to catch every last one of them. That's why I woke at four thirty, something buzzing next to my thigh.

I fished the glowing blue screen out from under the covers and rubbed my eyes until I could see clearly. The text message was from Nick. *What is new work e-mail?*

I texted back.

Seconds later a second text appeared. *Have idea.*

THE NEXT MORNING there were two arrangements of flowers on my desk: the bronze callas from yesterday and a vase of flaming orangey-red Hawaiian stems. This time the card was inside an envelope. *Thank you for last night.—DL.* The Xs and Os were gone, but it was charming how the detective had signed the card. Since he'd kept up his part of the bargain, I kept up mine and carried yesterday's arrangement to Mallory's office.

"I'm sharing the wealth," I offered and set the square vase on the corner of her desk. "How's your workload look?"

"Okay. I came in early and finished off the Monday recaps. They're in your inbox. I'm going to work on the Vongole order next."

I glanced at the clock. "What time did you get here?"

"Don't worry. I always get in early. I like having quiet time to get stuff done. Before the phone starts ringing."

I was going to have to remember that Mallory had free rein of my office when I wasn't around. If there was snooping to be done, and I mean snooping that wasn't done by me, I'd have to cover my tracks.

I shrugged out of the tweed jacket, hung it on the back of my chair, and booted up my PC. My email was full of unread messages. Amongst the company announcements was one note from Nick.

Dear Samantha, You may remember working with my shoe collection while you were a buyer for Bentley's NY. With my recent plans to expand the Nick Taylor collection, I am adding a limited edition collection of handbags to the fall line. Attached are the line sheets of the items. You always were a great partner in the development of my shoe collection; I am eager to hear your feedback. Regards, NT.

Well, what do you know. Nick was going undercover too.

I wrote a brief reply thanking him for thinking of me first and saying I would happily consider his collection of handbags. I finished with a few details about our current assortment, vaguely disguised information for him to have while running amok in Milan handbag factories.

"Mallory?" I called out. "Do you know what factory Vongole uses?"

"They use two. Luta and Lussuria."

"Why two?"

"Their basics are done at Luta, and their fashion is at Lussuria."

"Got it." I pecked at the keyboard, suggested Nick visit these two factories, and clicked send.

For the next couple of hours, I looked over files in Emily Hart's—I mean my—office. Every time I'd been promoted in my past life—the successful life as a buyer for Bentley's, not the recent past that had stalled out at Tradava—I'd taken the first day to acclimate myself with my predecessor's information to get a sense of the job. To Mallory, or anyone else who might come along, what I was doing looked perfectly natural. And it's a good thing, too, because Tan Cleavage from the executive meeting showed up unexpectedly in my office.

I was highlighting numbers on one of Mallory's spreadsheets and comparing the information to a file of sell-through expectations I'd found on the computer. I wasn't so much hoping to find a clue but to get a sense of the business. It felt natural having a job again, especially one I knew I could do. Homicide notwithstanding.

Tan Cleavage entered the office, acknowledged me with little more than a nod, and disappeared into Mallory's office. I heard her and Mallory talk in low voices.

When Cleavage left, it was with Mallory behind her. She paused in the doorway. "Is it okay with you if I take my lunch now?"

"Sure, fine." I calculated the time on the clock and realized it was my turn to snoop. "I have a lunch date myself. I'll probably be gone when you get back. Are you fine on your own this afternoon?"

Mallory's eyes darted to the flowers, and Cleavage snickered in the hallway. "Of course."

I called Eddie and left him a message that I was running late and would be there by one. Then I moved into Mallory's office and jotted down her computer's IP address. I returned to my desk and used a couple of tricks to find her on Heist's network and connect to her drive. Now I could cruise her files without having to ask.

Under the guise of leaving behind additional information for her, I created a fake spreadsheet and printed it out, using Post-Its to instruct her on what I wanted. It was a dummy project, but it gave me another excuse to go through her desk.

Sitting on the corner was a red folder labeled Orders to be Approved. I opened it and flipped through the papers. There were five outstanding orders to Vongole, totaling more than a million dollars at cost. Odder still was the note scribbled across the sheet of paper: *Mallory, our Vongole inventory is too high. Don't write any more orders until we sell through at least 30% of our current stock.*

The note was signed EH.

16

SMART AND TALENTED TOO

EMILY HART HAD PUT THE KIBOSH ON FUTURE ORDERS OF HEIST'S hottest handbag line, and I wanted to know why. No, that's not true. I could respect why she'd halted orders. What I wanted to know was why Belle DuChamp was writing and approving orders if the store really was in an overstocked position. Did this have something to do with Emily's murder?

A million dollars' worth of orders would translate into a hefty little paycheck for Andi Holloway, and a surplus of inventory would provide Belle DuChamp with a lucrative opportunity for sales above and beyond her forecasted goals. I still couldn't see how Kyle Trent figured into this whole thing, but I was about to. Lunch with Eddie wasn't the only thing on the agenda at Tradava.

I found Eddie at his desk like he said, but the half-empty carton of Chinese takeout that sat on the corner told me he hadn't waited.

"I have to go to the fabric store today," he said. "Last-minute plans. I could've had lunch with you if you'd been on time but not now."

"What's the project?"

"What?"

"What's this last-minute project?"

"I can't tell you."

"Why not?"

"Because, like you said, you're the competition. You shouldn't even be in my office right now."

"Are you kidding me?"

"Dude, you can't just waltz in here and expect me to tell you Tradava's business plans now that you work for Heist."

"I didn't ask you to tell me business plans, and you know what? We never talked about business plans before. Why would we start now?"

"I don't know. Maybe that's how you work?"

"Are you suggesting I don't have any ethics?"

He put his hands up in front of him in a defensive manner. "I don't know. When you first started at Tradava, you were knee-deep in some serious shit, and you trusted me. But ever since you got this job at Heist, you're being private. Maybe you were using me when you were here at Tradava. I don't know. But a lot of people are concerned that you're on Belle's team now. She signed a non-disclosure agreement stating she wasn't going to recruit from Tradava, and then you showed up there."

"You've got to be kidding. Tradava hasn't exactly made it known they want me on the payroll. You're right, I trusted you, so you know I moved to Ribbon to work *here*. The reason I don't work here has to do with the store, not with me."

"Apparently that's the reason they're not able to legally go after her."

"Because they don't want me?"

"Not exactly. They just can't clearly qualify why you no longer work here and whether it was your decision or theirs."

It was my turn to throw my hands up in disgust. "And this is the company you want to be loyal to? You should hear them talk over at Heist. They're so passionate about what they're doing. Their executive meetings are like a think tank. They brainstorm and listen to suggestions and try new ideas. They want to stay on the cutting edge. Tradava *should* be worried about them but not because of me."

I stood up and tugged the hem of the knit dress Cat had given me.

"I thought we were friends, Eddie. But lately it sounds like my friends don't want me to succeed." I tucked my handbag under the crook of my arm and turned to leave.

He didn't say a word until I got to the doorway. "Nice outfit. Where'd it come from?"

Bastard.

Eddie was right about one thing. It would have been highly unethical for me to masquerade around Tradava as a random stranger and find my way to Kyle Trent's office. That's why, when I found him sitting by the coffee bar on the first floor, I invited myself to join him.

Kyle's male model looks weren't even slightly diminished by the lack of tuxedo or event lighting. If anything, he looked even more attractive today. He wore a crisp, textured ivory shirt, paisley tie, and grey suit. The lapels on the jacket were narrow and notched, a trend that was among the latest sartorial details to differentiate men's suits from season to season.

"Is this seat taken?" I asked.

He looked up from the catalog he was reading. I could tell he recognized me, but it appeared as though he couldn't figure out why. I left my hand on the back of the tall barstool and pasted an I'm-not-threatening expression on my face. It took about eight seconds for recognition to hit. When it did, he closed the catalog and sat back on his stool. With an ever-so-slight shrug, he indicated it was okay. Or possibly the shrug told me to go to hell. Sometimes shrugs are hard to read.

I gingerly perched atop the blue leather swivel stool and set my handbag on the table.

Kyle stood. "Wait here," he said.

I was not giving him this easy a getaway. I spun to the side and slid myself off the stool.

He stopped me. "You want a cup of coffee? My treat. And why don't we move to one of those tables over there?" He glanced at one surrounded by a pair of modern wooden chairs. The padded stool was certain to be more comfortable, but when I added in the privacy factor, the table and chairs won.

"Sure. Thanks." I moved to the table and watched Kyle. I'd place even money he had been fast-tracked early in his career and now held an enviable job that he'd keep for the next decade if he was smart. A few sales associates stood in line behind him, openly giggling when he smiled their direction. I bet girlish giggles followed Kyle Trent a lot. He was no stranger to attention and probably didn't spend a lot of nights sleeping alone.

He set two cups of black coffee on the table and pushed one in my direction. "Not sure how you liked it."

"This is fine," I answered.

"You're the new handbag buyer at Heist, aren't you? Samantha Kidd?"

"I am," I answered, mildly surprised he knew that much.

"What brings you to Tradava today? Are you shopping the competition?"

"I was supposed to meet a friend for lunch." I considered, not for the first time, Kyle's possible reasons for being in the handbag department at Heist the night Emily died. "Much like you were probably meeting a friend at Heist."

"I don't want to be reminded of that night, if you don't mind." The brown cardboard ring that kept his coffee from burning his hands sat at the base of his cup on the table. He spun his cup in circles. He was concentrating too hard on such a mundane task.

"You get noticed a lot, probably. You're an attractive man."

"So I've been told." He picked up his coffee and drank. I was thrown by his emotionless acknowledgement of a fact most people would take as a compliment. "I'm smart and talented too, in case you're interested."

"Interested in what?"

"In finding out what's below the surface."

I felt like a ball of yarn being swatted about by a frisky cat. I had no desire to be Kyle Trent's ball of yarn. "I'm not interested," I said, perhaps too quickly. "Besides, you could probably get any woman you want."

"Not any woman."

"Belle DuChamp? Is she the woman you want?"

"Belle's different from the others."

"Why? Because she's married?"

"Because she saw the smart and talented part."

"Did Belle get fired because she was caught"—I tried to think of an appropriate word and gave up and settled on Eddie's—"canoodling with you in the boardroom?"

"Is that rumor still alive and well?" He laughed, and for the first time in our conversation, it felt like he'd let himself go. "You should check your sources. Besides, some people think Belle is still on the Tradava payroll."

"What do you mean?"

"I've heard things about you too, Samantha. You're smart. Tenacious. You'll figure it out." He slapped his palms down on the arms of the chair, elbows pointing out. He hoisted his lean body out of the chair like a swimmer heaving himself out of a pool. "Pleasure talking to you. Good luck at Heist. You've got some big shoes to fill." He picked his cup off the table and walked away, leaving me staring at the back of his very trim double-vented suit.

As long as I was at Tradava, I figured I actually would shop the competition. No reason not to, especially after two different people had made it relatively clear they didn't want to be sitting around talking to me.

I sweet-talked the creamer away from a nice old couple sitting one table away and diluted the coffee to a drinkable shade of camel. After I finished, I went to the handbag department.

There was noticeably less foot traffic there than at Heist, partially because of the hype of a new store coming to town, I'm sure, but still, it had to be hurting Tradava's business. That was how it went with new stores—big opening, big hoopla, and then how to keep up that level of interest and shift the customer loyalties from the stores they always shopped at to the new one, long term.

It was a delicate time for both competitors. Tradava had to put their best face forward: charming customer service and a familiar setting had to trump deep discounts. The history of Tradava, a family-owned fixture in Ribbon, needed to cling to its loyal customer base to counter the novelty of Heist. Tradava would suffer in the short term, and no one knew what would happen in a couple of months, let alone a year.

I picked up a black and white fur handbag and turned it over in my hands. It was connected to the fixture with a thin wire that disappeared into a small locking system, much less obtrusive than the in-your-face theft deterrents at Heist. But somehow Heist owned their concept so completely that Tradava's hint at protecting their profits against shoplifters seemed more of an insult. I was able to open the clasp and pull the tissue out, inspecting the powder-blue suede lining and interior pockets trimmed in black patent leather to match the handle. It was such a pretty color combination, and the lining would be tarnished shortly after the wearer loaded in the assorted items she needed to get through the day. My own handbag carried a three-inch ballpoint pen mark, a smudge of cranberry lip liner, and a grungy corner from where a small bag of pretzels had emptied.

I snapped the bag closed and placed it in the crook of my arm so I could admire my reflection in the full-length mirror. It was lovely. An associate headed my way with a smile on his face, and I sensed I was in for a compliment and a sales pitch. I put the bag on the table and stuffed the tissue back inside. That's when I noticed the small gold metal vendor tag affixed to the interior cell-phone pocket. VONGOLE. My split-second moment of awareness gave the closest sales associate the time needed to reach my side.

"She's a beauty, isn't she?" he asked.

"She sure is," I replied.

He held the bag in the light. "One of the best bags they've done recently. We used to carry a lot of Vongole's bags but lately not too many."

"Is that because of Heist?"

"No, they have good prices but don't carry the same quality of merchandise as us."

"They carry Vongole, though," I said.

"Yes, but Vongole's collection is big, and our buyer keeps our assortment streamlined. We don't need to carry every bag they make, just the good ones. Like this." He smiled, letting the black and white fur bag rock side to side from his index finger not unlike a hypnotist dangling a watch. "What do you think?"

"I think I'm going to have to start packing my lunch so I can treat myself soon." I smiled graciously and checked my watch. "I'm already running late. Thank you." I turned to leave before he had the chance to hit me up with a new charge application, but my path was blocked. Kyle stood in front of me, fidgeting with the knot in his tie.

"Samantha, a word of caution. I'd watch my step around Heist if I were you."

It sounded like a threat, and I wanted to laugh but didn't. "I don't think I have to point out that I know you were at Heist the night Emily was murdered."

"Of course I was with her the night she was murdered. It was a big night for her. Why wouldn't I be there?"

Something about Kyle's attitude coupled with the knowledge of Emily's death and the memory of how he'd spoken about her did not compute. As I stood there, trying to make sense of the three incongruent pieces of information, Eddie stepped out from behind a fixture. He put his hand on my elbow and squeezed. "Dude, Kyle was at the gala as Emily's date. They were engaged."

17

SUGAR CUBE

"Engaged?" I said. I shifted my attention from Eddie's expression to Kyle's and felt the weight of his sorrow. He nodded. "I'm so sorry," I said. "Can we talk, like talk-talk? Away from the store?"

Kyle nodded. We left Tradava together. I was fairly sure Eddie wanted an invite, but if I was going to stay true to my word, work with the cops, and not bring anyone else into this mess, I was going to have to shut Eddie out.

I had absolutely no idea what was on my schedule for the balance of the day at Heist, but I doubted it would be more important than talking to Kyle. We walked in silence to a diner in the corner of a parking lot at Tradava.

It wasn't until we were seated at a booth in the back, empty seats all around us, that I spoke. "Is that true? You and Emily were engaged?"

"Yes. I proposed two months ago. I wanted her to work at Tradava. She'd been with Heist, the store in Center City Philadelphia, for a long time. I thought it would be a good step for her. She saw things differently. She wanted me to leave Tradava and work for Heist."

"How did you meet?"

"Market week, years ago. We were both handbag buyers. No

matter how hard the vendors tried to keep us on opposite schedules, it was inevitable. Every couple of months we'd run into each other in New York or Milan. Last year we got stuck at the airport together. Our flight was canceled, and we sat up all night and talked. By the next morning I was calling her my girlfriend."

"Your stores didn't mind the conflict of interest?"

"We tried to keep our relationship a secret at first. When Tradava found out, they thought it was unethical. Belle DuChamp had always been a mentor of mine, but that was a turning point for us."

"She was angry?"

"She actually warned me my job was on the line if I didn't reconsider how I spent my spare time. That's one of the reasons Emily and I were keeping the engagement a secret. We knew it would complicate our work situations."

"But what about that rumor?"

"I never said I was a saint. I had a life before Emily, but that's all I'm saying. Anything I say now impacts how people will remember her, and that's not fair. I loved her. I was ready to spend the rest of my life with her." His eyes turned bloodshot, but no tears appeared.

The waitress approached our table and asked for our order. Kyle suddenly stood. "The lady is going to dine alone. It's on me." He peeled a twenty out of his wallet and tossed it on the table.

"Kyle—wait," I said.

He stood by the table and looked down at me.

"Is there a way I can get in touch with you? If ..." My voice trailed off.

Kyle reached inside his suit jacket pocket and pulled out a small leather business-card case. He slid an ivory card out and tossed it on top of the twenty. "My cell is below my work number," he said.

I slid the card across the table and tucked it into my wallet next to my library card.

"Did you want to order something, ma'am?" the waitress asked.

"Yes," I said. I leaned sideways and looked out the door, making sure Kyle had left. "I'll have a BLT to go." I dropped my voice so the people in the next booth couldn't hear me. "Hold the bread, lettuce, mayo, and tomato."

———

IT WAS five o'clock when I pulled back into the Heist parking lot. The only thing calming my nerves from being gone four hours was the fat from five pieces of bacon and the knowledge that my job offer from Tony Simms came with a fair amount of job security. I speed-walked through the store to my office but stopped short when faced with the assortment of flowers on my desk.

An orange bromeliad sat next to a square vase lined in bamboo shoots—similar to yesterday's floral arrangement. The card, clipped to the vase, said REPLACEMENT FLOWERS. There was no doubt in my mind. This arrangement had come from the cops.

Two arrangements of flowers were overkill, which meant the earlier arrangement wasn't from Detective Loncar. I texted Nick's phone: *Thx 4 flowers.*

A couple of seconds later I received a response: *???*

Uh-oh.

Mallory came into my office as I was sticking my phone back into my handbag. Her bag was over her shoulder. "He must be quite a guy."

I cocked my head, shaking it in a you-don't-know-the-half-of-it manner. My cell phone beeped with a text message. I ignored it. "Sorry I was gone so long. Did I miss anything here?"

"You didn't miss anything, and nobody missed you. And considering you took a four-hour lunch on your second day, I'd say you were pretty lucky."

"Let's get something straight. It's not my job to report to you."

She glared at me in a manner not unlike the kid from *The Omen*. I stood my ground even though my left boot pinched my toes, and I really, really, *really* wanted to sit. My cell phone buzzed again before I had a chance to say anything else.

"I was here early this morning, and I'm going home now. You'd better check your phone. Sounds like someone's looking for you," she said.

She left without looking back once. I pulled the cell phone out and keyed up the text message: *turn your flowers around before you leave.* Honestly, Detective Loncar was turning into a high-maintenance fake boyfriend. I was ready to chuck the cell phone and cut all ties with him when I noticed who had sent the message.

Dante.

Mallory had left for the day, and I had to use the facilities. I palmed my cell phone and went to the ladies' room. Once inside, after checking under each of the stalls, I called the number.

"You got my text," he answered in lieu of hello.

"What are you doing sending me flowers?"

"What are you doing working for Heist?"

"We already covered this. They offered me a job, and I took it."

"Samantha, I know something's up with you. Just like I wrote on the card, I'm here if you need me."

"You're DL?"

"Those are my initials. How many other DLs do you know?"

"Just one—I mean, next time you should be more clear. I mean, there shouldn't be a next time. You shouldn't be sending me flowers."

"This isn't about the flowers."

"That's what I'm afraid of."

"There's a camera inside the arrangement."

"Dante, I might not have been very easy to read the other night, but—what?"

"There's a camera inside the flower arrangement. A sugar cube."

"Which is it? A camera or a sugar cube?"

"The camera *is* the sugar cube. That's what it's called, because that's roughly the size of it."

I already knew I was going to regret the next question. "Why are you sending me flowers with a camera inside?"

"Because you're up to something and nobody knows what, but considering a woman was murdered, I think you're in danger. And you're pushing your friends away, which is not the smartest thing to do."

"Maybe there's a reason for my acting the way I'm acting," I said, wondering if I should just open up and confide in him. He didn't know me that well. Maybe he'd see my side instead of siding with Cat and Eddie.

"Sure. Maybe you're trying to figure out Emily Hart's murder?"

I stopped wondering. "What is so wrong about me trying to have my own life?"

"If that's all you were doing, sweetheart, there'd be nothing wrong with it. Only I'm having a hard time believing it."

"Well, believe it."

I would have liked to sit down for a second, but I was in the ladies' room, and the only place to sit was, well, not where I wanted to be sitting while having a conversation with Dante. I thought about making crackly noises and pretending we had a bad connection.

"Can we call a truce on this? I'm coming to Cat's house tonight, and I don't want us getting into a thing around her. I think she's totally fine with me having a new job and wouldn't appreciate your accusations that I'm hiding something."

"Are you kidding me? Who do you think told me to send you the sugar cube?"

18

EZ MART

Cat and I may have started out on rocky terrain owing to the murder investigation six months ago, but from what I'd seen since, she was a nice, normal woman. This piece of information put her in an entirely different light. Oh, sure, I was still going by the house to check on her after work, but I was going home and changing out of the fabulous mint-blue and tweed ensemble she'd given me and into something polyester that would offend her fashion sensibilities first.

Logan sat in the middle of the laundry basket watching me change. He was nestled on top of a pink four-hundred-thread-count sheet. He was rapidly returning to his normal self. The cat had good taste. I scooped him up, planted a kiss between his ears, and set him back down. He turned around in a circle until he ended up in pretty much the same position he'd started in.

I scribbled the notes I could remember from the day and wedged them into my handbag. Letting my hair air-dry shaved five minutes from my getting-ready routine, and the tan—even if it was fake—opened up the door to a whole palette of colors that washed out my normally fair skin.

It was a warm night. I took the top off my convertible and let the wind have its way with my curly hair. When I pulled into Cat's driveway, I was more relaxed than I'd been in about a week. Even having Dante meet me at the door only ratcheted up my pulse the amount any totally hot and slightly dangerous biker would. Good thing I was holding a chilled bottle of champagne to cool me down.

He stepped back and scanned my orange double-knit polyester scooter dress from the mod era. "I was hoping for the knit dress you had on earlier. I only got a glimpse of it through the sugar cube, but it seemed to hit you in all the right places," he said.

"I didn't want anything to happen to it."

"Shame."

The door opened behind me, and Eddie walked in carrying a pizza box. "It's about time you got here. Follow me."

We traipsed, parade-like, through the house to the den where Cat sat on the sofa, tucked in beneath an ivory chenille blanket.

"Aren't you hot?" I asked after saying hello and hugging her.

"It's chilly in here."

"It's so not chilly! It's totally warm!" I said, holding the champagne against my forehead.

"You're only hot because you're wearing a plastic dress," Eddie said.

"It's not plastic, it's polyester."

He unscrewed the cap on his bottle of water and dumped what remained on me. The water beaded up and ran down the front of my dress. Cat dabbed at the carpet with a couple of paper towels. "That is not how good clothes react to water, Sam."

"Can't a girl just come for a friendly visit without getting a fashion criticism?"

"You're the fashion person, not me," Eddie said. "At least you were." He looked at my dress and wrinkled his nose. "I'm not sure who you are anymore." He set the pizza on the card table in the middle of the room and walked out.

"I wish everybody would stop acting like me working for Heist is such a big deal," I said half to myself, half to Cat.

"I know it's not a big deal," she said.

"You don't agree with him?"

"Sam, you were a buyer in New York, right? And you've been looking for a job. And you got one that you're obviously qualified for."

"Yes. That's right." I processed her words. "That's right!"

"The only person acting like it's a big deal is you."

"Am not!"

"Are too." She leaned back against the sofa cushions and tucked the chenille blanket around her legs. "If you thought you had a chance of working for Heist, you wouldn't have entered that competition. You would have said something first."

"You and Dante have compared notes."

"Either Heist rejected your application, and you wanted to get back at them by winning or you never even applied, and they came to you because of your job qualifications. None of that is out of the ordinary. The only weird thing is that you kept it a secret. That's why Eddie's angry. His feelings are hurt."

"His feelings?" I asked. The idea that his reaction to my job at Heist came from something other than suspicion had never occurred to me. I looked at the doorway where Eddie had disappeared. Dante leaned against the doorframe, watching us.

"I didn't realize you were still here," I said.

"I'm leaving now. You need anything, sis?"

"Celery and peanut butter." She looked at me. "Are you going to stick around?"

"I'm all yours."

"Bring Samantha some ice cream."

FOR THE NEXT two hours we ate pizza and played Monopoly while *The Big Sleep* played on TCM. The bottle of champagne had been opened, but I barely touched it. Considering a visit with Detective Loncar was in the near future, I thought it prudent to take it easy. Cat claimed to be nauseous and sipped at a glass of club soda. After Eddie's earlier dig about my fashionista standing, I considered it a personal victory that the words "Heist" and "job" didn't come up the rest of the time I was there. I stood to leave shortly after Eddie acquired Boardwalk.

It was quarter to ten. The police station wasn't far from Cat's house, and I made a couple of turns through her neighborhood, hopped on and off the highway, and pulled into a visitor space. It still gave me chills to park between a squadron of black and whites.

Detective Loncar stood inside the front door with a black mug in his hand. "Thought you bailed on us."

"I had other things to do tonight. Important real estate transactions."

"Follow me."

We trekked along the now-familiar path, over the might-be-dirty, might-be-clean gray linoleum tile, into the room that led to the room that was his office. I was starting to not notice the dinginess. I wondered if that's how it was for him. Maybe he'd long ago tuned out the monochromatic shade of bland surrounding him.

The detective poured me a mug of coffee without asking if I wanted it. I took a sip and gagged. No wonder he didn't ask first. He was just trying to finish off a bad pot so he could start fresh.

"I found something out about Kyle Trent," I started.

"Calm down for a second. Today I'm telling you something instead of the other way around. Remember those flowers?"

"Yes." I thought about the card. "You'd better start editing those cards before you send them."

"We told the florist to write whatever he wanted." He hammered a couple of keys on his computer and pulled up an audio file.

"Listen to this," he said, while his knobby finger punched the enter key. The words were clear. "I happen to know there's going to be an opening in shoes." The background of the recording popped and fizzed like an Alka-Seltzer dropped into a cup of water, but the voice was unmistakable. Mallory George.

"That's the assistant buyer," I said.

"You know who she was talking to?'

"No, but I wasn't in the office much today."

He sat forward in his chair and narrowed his eyes at me. "Why's that?"

"I was looking into something at Tradava."

"You're supposed to be looking into things at Heist. There's more." He punched the enter key again, and Mallory's voice continued. "Either the job is mine, or there's going to be another opening in handbags."

I pointed to his computer. "Is it my imagination, or was she just threatening to take me out? She said she would make another opening in handbags. Did she mean me? I think she means me—"

"That's what we thought. You'd better watch her. She's obviously blackmailing someone. We think she knows more than she's letting on, and we need you to find out what it is."

When this whole thing started, I'd accepted the job on the basis that:

a) I needed a job, and

b) There was a pretty good chance someone wasn't going around knocking off handbag buyers.

Only now I wasn't so sure. And, because of point A, I was a handbag buyer, so if point B was in fact not true, then I was in the line of fire. That in itself was unsettling.

I started the drive home, lost in my thoughts. It wasn't until halfway to my house that I noticed a pair of headlights directly behind my car.

I pulled onto the main street and turned left and then made a sudden right at the next intersection. The sedan followed me. It was dark, and the car had tinted windows. Maybe it was just my imagination, after what Detective Loncar had played for me. Surely this was all in my head.

I circled the neighborhood twice, unsure where to go. The car stayed on my tail. I shot through a yellow light and made an aggressive left turn, then a right, then pulled onto the highway's access ramp. The signal changed behind me. I peered down from the circular ramp to see the pursuer caught at the light. I sped up, putting distance between myself and that intersection, and pulled into a gas station half a mile up the road. The wind whipped my hair around my face. My polyester dress was cool against my skin. I got out of the car and ran inside the EZ Mart, repeatedly looking over my shoulder.

The clerk stood behind the counter talking to a pretty teenage girl. I crouched next to the Slushie machine and peered out the window. The highway was relatively quiet. This wasn't the busiest stretch of it, just beyond the mall, and it was late enough that I could track every car that passed. A red sports car sped by, easily over the speed limit. Then a minivan.

I wandered the aisles, keeping an eye on the road out front. There were no other cars in sight. I approached the counter, thinking I'd lost my tail—or that maybe Loncar was right and I needed to stop watching thrillers—when a dark sedan approached the entrance to the gas station.

Considering my Honda del Sol hadn't been produced since the eighties, my car wasn't the most undercover vehicle in the world, but it was too late to think about that now. The sedan passed the first entrance but hooked a hard right into the exit. It circled around toward my car.

I rushed to the counter. "I think I'm in trouble. Do you have a restroom?"

He glanced at my Slushie. "Most people say that after they finish one of those."

"No, I'm being followed. Can I hide somewhere?"

"Restroom's outside." He pushed a large wood block keychain toward me.

"I can't go outside. Do you have a stockroom?"

"I don't think you should help her," the girlfriend said. "Are you wanted by the cops?"

The clerk pulled the keychain back before I could grasp it.

It was too late to answer because the chimes sounded over the EZ Mart door.

19

TRAIL OF BREADCRUMBS

"You could make this a little easier, you know," Dante said, taking a couple of steps toward me. He was wearing the same uniform he'd worn when posing as a security guard the night we robbed I-FAD of the statue. I'd almost forgotten this had all started with the statue.

"What are you doing? Besides scaring me to death?" I asked. I had half a mind to throw my Slushie at him and make a clean getaway.

"Come with me." He put his hand on my arm and steered me toward the exit.

"I haven't paid yet," I said, stalling, turning back to face the clerk.

"Everything okay, officer?" the teenaged twerp asked.

"Okay, now, son. What does she owe you?"

"It's on the house," the kid said.

Dante looked at me and grinned.

"Thank you," I called behind me. I left with Dante close behind.

"Sit in my car," he instructed. He kept his hand on my elbow while we walked to the navy sedan.

"Don't you drive a motorcycle?"

"This is a rental."

"Why did you rent a car? You could have borrowed Cat's car. She's your sister. I don't think she'd mind."

"You would have recognized her car."

"I'm the reason you rented a car? You did this to follow me?"

"You went to the police station after you left my sister's house. Why?"

"That's why you left, isn't it? You waited until I left and followed me to the police? Is that why I never got any ice cream?"

"Why?" he repeated.

I ran my fingertips over my forehead a few times. This was not good. Deep breath in, deep breath out. I looked at Dante, who was waiting for my response.

"I'll talk once we're in the car."

He unlocked the doors, and I slid onto the blue fabric seat. The teenagers in the Quickie Mart were watching us. "Do we have to do this here? I feel like I'm half of a peep show."

"We could go back to your place," he said.

"On second thought, this is fine."

"Samantha, what were you doing with the police?"

"I can't talk about that."

"You're working with them, aren't you?"

I repositioned myself on the front seat of the car, my back to the window. "Why do you expect me to talk to you? I barely know you."

"Compared to you, I'm an open book."

"Written in invisible ink," I muttered.

"Ask me anything."

"Okay, for starters, what do you do? Why are you here? Where did you come from? When are you leaving?"

"Those are the starter questions? I'd hate to see how you end."

"It doesn't feel good to be interrogated, does it?"

Dante relaxed, one arm around the back of the seat, the other bent, resting on the dashboard.

"I'm a photographer. Freelance. I take jobs where I get them. Sometimes that means a fashion shoot. Sometimes it means following someone around for insurance purposes. Sometimes it means catching people doing things they don't want to be caught doing."

I waited, not sure if he was going to say more.

"I live in Philadelphia. My sister lives here, and I come to visit her from time to time. I'm here now because of the contest. I'm not leaving until it's all wrapped up." He stared intensely at me. I suspected he was waiting for a response. It would take longer than the time I intended to spend in the front seat of the car with him to absorb what he'd said, so I tucked it away for later.

Dante may have made a good confidante. He was close to Cat, who was close to Eddie, who rounded out the list of people I didn't want to get involved. I couldn't explain why I'd been so willing to take Tony Simms's offer, but I had. Working with Detective Loncar gave me a sense of importance. It wasn't a joke, and I wanted to keep it that way. I wanted to prove I could do this.

"Here's what I see," Dante said when I didn't speak. "You got yourself mixed up in something. I don't know who talked you into it, but you're shutting everybody out." He shrugged. "Maybe you're telling your friend in Italy, I don't know, but that's still pretty safe since he's in another country. You're not good at letting people in, are you?"

I didn't like that he'd hit the nail on the head after knowing me less than a week.

"Is this about the police or about my character flaws?"

"Samantha, I know I just met you, but I think I 'get' you. You don't want to ask for help, and you don't want to let anyone in. It's like you have something to prove." He leaned back against the seat and rubbed his hand across the bristly top of his hair, now a couple weeks past the buzz-cut stage.

Like it or not, I couldn't deny his accuracy. "What are you trying to say?"

"Something happened to you after we stole that statue, but I can't figure out what. You're following a trail of breadcrumbs that didn't start out with the loaf of bread."

"Yes it did. The breadcrumbs started at Heist," I said, before realizing I was admitting to following the trail of breadcrumbs. Instead of shouting "Gotcha!" like I expected, Dante didn't even flinch.

"What took you to Heist? The murder?"

"The statue, but that's because of the contest."

"Seems to me like there's some kind of tie-in between the statue and the murder."

I sat for a couple of minutes, my hands wrapped around the forty-eight-ounce plastic Slushie cup. Water had condensed on the outside and coated my fingers. A few drops landed on my polyester dress and beaded up like Eddie's water had earlier that night.

"The owner came to visit me. He said I had a unique skill set and that he wanted to hire me. At first I thought he was talking about my history as a buyer, since he was in need of a buyer, but he asked me to look around, to see if I noticed anything out of the ordinary. The store was trying to shut down the bad press they got. That night at the gala, someone murdered Emily Hart with our statue. When the cops found the statue in my handbag and pulled me aside, Tony Simms was in the room. He knew everything I knew."

"You think he doesn't trust the cops?"

"No, that's not it. Detective Loncar is a good cop. He's going to do what he can to find the murderer. He's not concerned with how Heist comes off looking through this whole thing, or whether they're going to still be able to open their doors for business in Ribbon without any lasting implications. I think that's what Simms cares about. Not who killed his handbag buyer."

"Does Tony Simms know every move you're making?"

"No, at least I don't think so. I never told him I went to the cops."

"Why not?"

"I don't know. It just seemed like a good idea to keep that part to myself."

LOGAN MET me at the front door, meowing for cat food. I filled his bowl. I hadn't wanted to confide in Dante, and truth be told I really didn't, much. But what he'd said had got me thinking, and once I get to thinking, there's really no stopping me. There was one person who knew something about the statue but was unconnected to Heist, and that was Nora. I hadn't seen her since the theft, but now seemed like a good time to visit. It was much too late to show up on her doorstep, but I could see her silhouette through the window, and that meant she was still awake, so what was the problem with a phone call?

She picked up after the fifth ring. (I probably should have hung up after four.)

"It's next-door Samantha. Did I wake you?"

"No, I'm grading papers." She stifled a yawn. "What's keeping you up?"

"I'd like to talk to you about what happened with that statue."

"I don't know that I want to end my evening by discussing a murder. Why don't you come by the college tomorrow afternoon, say, around five?"

"Is that when your classes end?"

"My last lecture ends at four forty-five. That'll give me a chance to talk with the kids who have questions before they dash back to their dorms."

Nora really was a noble professor. I agreed to meet her, because what was so wrong about cutting out of work early another day?

THE NEXT MORNING, I dressed in the black trousers and plunging vest Tony Simms had sent over to my house, only this time I wore a white cotton shirt with French cuffs under the vest and topped it with a long strand of pearls knotted like a necktie. I arrived at the store at eight o'clock. If Mallory was going to show up early, I wanted her to know she couldn't count on being alone in the office.

I spun Dante's flowers around, this time fully aware Mallory was worth watching. By the time she arrived at eight thirty, I'd already reviewed a portion of the recaps she'd put in my inbox and had caught a couple of errors, too, which always helps to level the new boss/tenured-assistant-with-attitude playing field.

"You're here early." She seemed surprised.

"I wanted to get a jumpstart on the day."

Mallory left for her adjacent office. For the next hour there were no sounds except for the clicking of keys on her keyboard.

Heist's offices may have been nice for professionalism and privacy, but at the moment I missed the old, un-renovated offices at Bentley's, where all of us were crowded into one room about ten feet square. You couldn't get away with anything in that situation.

The phone rang, and Belle's name flashed on my caller ID.

"Sam, Belle DuChamp here. I'm with Tony. We want to have an impromptu meeting to discuss the Vongole strategy. Can you come to my office in about fifteen minutes? Bring whatever history you have on their business: sell-through reports, profit analyses, and pending orders. Thanks. Bring Mallory too. I'd like her to sit in on this." She hung up before I had the chance to respond. But if Tony Simms was in the building with her, it wasn't like I had much of a choice about attending.

I knocked on Mallory's doorframe to announce my presence. "Belle just called. She wants to go over the Vongole strategy. Do you have it?"

"There isn't a Vongole strategy, as far as I know."

"Then I guess we're making one up today. She asked for all the information we have on their history. I don't know where we keep that, aside from the recaps you put in my inbox."

Mallory pulled two overstuffed three-ring binders from a shelf. "Whatever you need should be in the first one, but if not, take the second one so you're prepared."

"That's all on Vongole?"

"No, this is the history of all our vendors. She'll probably want a comparison, and you don't want to not have the information in front of you."

"Okay, let me get my stuff, and we'll head down."

"We?"

"Yes. She specifically asked for you to sit in." I paused for a second before adding, "Tony Simms will be there too."

The color drained from Mallory's face. She dropped the overstuffed binders. One popped open, and recaps of business spread across the floor. When she reached out for them, her hands were shaking.

Something I'd said had thrown Mallory off-kilter.

20

TIME FOR A TAKE-DOWN

"Come in, sit down," Belle said.

She and Tony sat at the large glass conference table. How much Windex did it take to keep the fingerprints off?

I sat to Belle's right, and Mallory sat to my right. Tony sat across from me. If this were a game of Red Rover, Mallory, Belle, and I would have the advantage. We were down to one notebook, thanks to Mallory's shock-and-drop maneuver minutes earlier. I hoped it had the information we needed.

"Tony and I were talking about opportunities for Heist," Belle said. "Accessories are an exploding category, and we need to identify a key vendor now and negotiate accordingly."

Tony jumped in. "Handbags are like shoes. Women crave them. It's crazy what women will pay for a handbag. Doesn't matter if they need to lose ten pounds, if they're having a bad hair day, if they're getting over a breakup. Plus, the handbag business is a no-brainer. You don't have to think about sizes like with apparel. Our markup structure was at the industry standard, so we took the category and tinkered with the formula. The margin exploded."

"Tinkered with the formula how?" I asked. I was trying to keep up. Mallory was scribbling notes on a yellow legal pad.

"We get a forty percent discount from the cost, so we dropped the retails by thirty percent. Nobody else can touch our prices. The bags sell themselves. Customers come to us first because of our pricing and stay loyal because of our assortment. Every market we've entered, we've stolen Tradava's client base overnight."

"But Tradava has a whole assortment of Vongole's bags on sale right now," I offered. "Fifty percent off."

Mallory looked up, surprised. Belle and Tony didn't say anything. I looked between their faces.

"I was shopping the competition yesterday," I finished, hoping they'd see that as an entrepreneurial spark and not a goofing-off streak.

"Those are last year's bags. We bought out Vongole's entire inventory this year so they couldn't fill any orders for Tradava," Tony said. He folded his hands behind his head and leaned back in his chair. It was the cocky body language of a college student who had just one-upped a competitor at a debate match, and with his boyish looks, he kind of looked the part. I was willing to bet he'd won plenty of battles in the boardroom, even if other executives towered over him.

We spent the better part of an hour reviewing the profit analysis for Vongole. Aware that Mallory was watching me, I didn't point out the errors I'd caught that morning. Even if it was the perfect opportunity to correct the boss-employee dynamic, I took the high road.

More than once, Belle asked Mallory's opinion, calling her out of her silence, forcing her to participate in our discussion. It was a humble, almost shy Mallory who spoke when spoken to, offering up valid points about Vongole's past performances. Belle and Tony brainstormed an aggressive strategy to keep Vongole on our shelves and out of the hands of Tradava. Belle showed a devilish pleasure in plotting to shut down her former store's business. I wondered again what had happened to turn her away from Tradava and what her relationship had been with Emily.

When the meeting was over, Mallory grabbed the unused

notebook and stormed back to the office. I may not have known the answer to every question asked, but I'd more than held my own in the strategy meeting. I should have earned her respect by now.

"That went well, don't you think?" I asked when we reentered the office.

"I'd hardly say that," she spat and disappeared into her office.

Okay, time for a take-down. I followed her to her desk and crossed my arms over my pearl necktie. "What exactly is your problem with me?"

She glared at me, slowly shaking her head. "Don't play stupid. I know all about you."

"Then why don't you tell me all about me, because clearly I don't know what's going on."

"Don't play dumb. I'm friends with the PR manager, and she told me you told a room full of strangers that you made the weapon that was used to kill Emily. Then you show up here in her job. I don't know why it doesn't look suspicious to anyone else, but it sure looks suspicious to me."

"You think I—" I didn't finish the sentence. "You're joking, right?"

"Why do they love you so much?" Her eyes widened, and her voice raised.

The scent of the calla lilies, pleasantly fragrant yesterday, now caused the back of my head to throb. Mallory's verbal attack didn't help. I put my hands to my head to massage my temples.

Mallory continued. "I'm here on my merit. I've got a drawer full of performance reviews to prove it. But clearly you have some kind of relationship with Tony Simms that trumps experience and hard work. Maybe I'll be hearing about *you* in the boardroom."

"That's enough," I said. "Whether you like it or not, I'm your boss, and I don't appreciate what you're implying. You have two choices: get on board with me as your new buyer, or don't."

We stared at each other. The office felt like someone was pressing a large balloon on top of us. I didn't care what Mallory did next. I was done with her attitude.

When she didn't speak, I took my hands off my temples and put them palm side down on the Monday morning vendor recaps in her inbox.

"I didn't want to bring this up in the meeting today, but you made a couple of mistakes on the Vongole profit analysis, mistakes that significantly overstated their margin."

"What mistakes?"

I pulled out the form and circled the blank fields in freight, theft, and markdowns. "You didn't fill out all of the components of the margin calculation, so the profit is coming in overinflated."

She glanced at the paper and then pushed it back toward me. "You don't know what you're talking about."

I fanned out six other recaps on the desk. "These are all complete."

"Vongole is different. We get such a high discount from Andi that we don't take markdowns, not even coupons. It's in the disclaimer. The bags are locked up so there's no shortage."

"What about freight? Freight expense runs at three to five percent of the cost of an order. That alone will change their profitability."

"Vongole uses Simulated Trucking, and they don't charge us."

"Why not?"

"I have no idea, and that's not my job. The reports are correct. Now, if that's all you wanted to address with me, I have other work to do." She turned to her computer and pretended I wasn't there. Before I left, I remembered one more thing. "Mallory, if this is such a high-margin business, why didn't Emily want you to approve any more orders?"

She stopped typing. "How do you know about that?"

I pulled the red folder marked Orders To Approve out of her inbox and opened it up. Inside was the note that I had seen last night. She took the folder from me, the animosity gone, replaced with a furrowed brow and eyes that stared off to the corner of her desk while she appeared to think.

"I told Belle about that yesterday," she said in a normal voice. "I called her to find out why she wrote those orders when we were overstocked. If we bring in the inventory Andi has on hand, we'll risk our entire profit structure, and if we have that much inventory, we'll throw off the supply and demand. We'll have to take markdowns to liquidate. And I don't understand how Vongole even has that much inventory. Four months ago, we bought every bag Vongole had available so they couldn't ship to anybody else." For the moment, her animosity toward me had dissipated.

"Have you ever asked Andi about this?"

"With Andi, everything related to one of her vendors is a great opportunity. 'Omigod, like, totally!'"

She was right; Andi was not going to do anything to make Vongole look bad. But if Andi was able to play the "Omigod, you're, like, totally my new best friend" routine, then so was I. I returned to my desk and dialed her showroom number.

"Andi? Samantha Kidd, from Heist."

I finagled a session of after-work cocktails and girl-talk. Mallory looked impressed, but before she had a chance to compliment me outright, we heard a male voice in the hallway. "Samantha Kidd?"

"That's me," I called and stood up.

A deliveryman in a brown shirt and shorts carried a vase of pink roses into the office. "Where'd you like me to put these?" he asked, noting the two arrangements that already occupied the front of the desk. It was starting to look like Birnam Wood in here.

"I'll take them," I said and transferred the vase from his grip to the bookcase behind me.

"You must be quite a woman." He held out an electronic device that I signed with a plastic stylus.

I pulled the card out of the tiny white envelope after he left. *Don't know who sent you flowers yesterday, but here's hoping mine are better. Miss you.—NT*

I went to my desk and answered with a professional-sounding e-mail:

Dear Nick, Your sketches look amazing, would love to see the real thing. Have you had a chance to meet with either Luta or Lussuria factories? Regards, Samantha.

I received a response almost immediately.

Dear S, Have not had time yet but they're on my schedule. —N

I KILLED the rest of the afternoon with buyer-related tasks. At four thirty, I shut down the computer and slicked on a coat of lip-gloss. I pulled my sleeve over my hand and polished the fingerprints off my patent leather handbag.

Mallory stood in my doorway. "Before you meet up with Andi, you should know Tradava cancelled a bunch of Vongole orders, and that might be where the surplus inventory came from."

"That sounds like confidential information. How do you know that?"

"I overheard Kyle and Emily arguing the night of the gala. They didn't realize I was in here. I heard him say he'd cancelled his entire Vongole order, and he couldn't believe she'd bought all of this crap, and she yelled at him that he had no right to tell her how to do her job. They were pretty mad at each other. He said she had to pick one or the other, and she didn't answer. The last thing I heard him say was he couldn't take it anymore and was going to end it."

"What happened after that?"

"I don't know. I bolted. I didn't want to be around if they decided to make up, if you know what I mean."

"Did you tell any of this to the cops?"

"No. When I said I bolted, I mean I bolted from the store. I wasn't here when she was... found."

"How did you hear the news?"

"Belle called me the next day to let me know."

I nodded calmly. Did I believe her? I wasn't sure. As far as workplace personalities went, Mallory seemed a little unstable.

I thanked her for the info and left. In the past eight hours Mallory had insulted me more than once, and then she made a concerted effort to confide in me. Those two actions seemed at odds with each other, but neither action changed two very important facts:

a) Last night, Detective Loncar had played a conversation for me where Mallory had threatened someone for a promotion, and

b) Today she confessed to being right here the night Emily Hart was murdered.

And whether she realized it or not, she also told me she really didn't have an alibi.

21

BOYFRIENDS

There was a limited window of time before cocktails with Andi, and I used it to meet with Nora at I-FAD. I parked in a visitor space near her lecture hall. The only other car in the lot was a highly polished silver BMW. The college was either paying more to their professors than I thought or there were some very spoiled students. When I went to school, I got around on a one-person motorized scooter that capped out at thirty-five miles per hour unless I was going downhill.

An irregular breeze wafted past me, blowing green whirlybirds from the trees. They spun in circles as they descended, landing in soft piles on the grass, to be trampled by students between classes. I picked one up, held it in front of me with two fingers, and let go, watching it spiral its way as it fell.

Students trickled out of the lecture hall, holding beat-up backpacks on one shoulder. I didn't want to waste any more time, so I pushed through the door and followed the mustard-colored carpet runner to the front. Nora stood, leaning against a marble table, talking to Tony Simms. Surprised, I stepped backward and put one hand on the door to leave, but it was too late.

"Samantha! Perfect timing. I told Mr. Simms you were coming here today, and he wanted to talk to you."

"Hello, Samantha," he said, extending his hand. I grabbed it and shook, trying to anticipate the squeeze-and-pump manner he'd used the first time we'd been through this routine.

"Hi, Mister"— I caught myself—"Tony," I finished lamely.

"What brings you to the college today?"

"Nora," I answered, opting for vague over lying.

"Aren't you two neighbors?"

"Yes," I said, not sure how he knew that. "With the hours I'm putting in at Heist, I barely see her anymore." It was meant to be a joke. I hoped he saw that.

"Speaking of Heist, that's the reason I'm here." He checked his watch. "I'm late for an appointment. Nora, do you want to fill her in?"

"Be glad to, Tony."

They shook hands as a good-bye, though Nora didn't appear to care about the business squeeze-and-pump. She looked a lot more natural than I did during the whole process. The small businessman left through a side door marked only by a red neon exit sign.

"I didn't expect to find him here," I said, this time opting for the truth over vague.

"Neither did I."

"What's this thing he was talking about?"

"Tony has been very generous to I-FAD. As a thank you, the college is dedicating a building to him. It wasn't going to happen for a month, but he wants to bump up the agenda to divert attention from the negativity that's surrounding Heist."

"Can he do that?"

"When you've given as much money to the college as he has, you can pretty much write your own ticket."

Interesting. "What do I have to do with this?"

"He wants a team from Heist here at the dedication. Turn it into a story about the store, the professionalism, the career path. Help tie it to the community. He was here to meet with the academic chair on possible internships for students and a guest professor program using Heist staff. Your name came up."

I didn't point out that I'd worked for the store for a total of three days. It was quickly becoming a moot point. "Heist is new to the area. Why isn't Tradava getting this kind of treatment? They've been in Ribbon forever."

"Tony Simms is trying to get people to connect him with the city, to give him goodwill," she said.

"If it didn't seem like such a political move, I'd say it was a good idea."

"I get the sense that Tony Simms doesn't have bad ideas, and if he decided to run for mayor, he'd probably get a lot of votes."

I turned around and looked at the door through which he'd vanished. "I'm starting to get that sense too."

"Now, what was the reason you wanted to talk to me today?"

Tony's knowledge of my whereabouts unnerved me, and I changed my mind about sticking around to talk to Nora. I told her I was running late and made plans to have dinner at her place tomorrow night. I took the next ten minutes to sit in my car to transcribe what I remembered from my encounter with Tony.

WHEN I ARRIVED at Andi's showroom, I was surprised to find Kyle there. I could tell he was on his way out, based on the dual-cheek air-kiss he and Andi exchanged. Nick used to give me those, back when he was my vendor and I was his buyer. I wondered if we'd ever get past that, if we'd transition from texted Xs to the real thing, or if the distance between us was insurmountable in terms of starting a relationship. I hated to admit that even air-kisses were better than text messages.

Andi waved to me while Kyle nodded a greeting and caught the elevator. Today she wore a black knit sleeveless dress with a cowl neck, no stockings, and flat sandals. She bounced over to me.

"Omigod, I'm sooooo happy you called. It's been a long week

already, and it's only Wednesday. We can totally hit happy hour if we leave right now." She grabbed a purple handbag and tossed in a notebook, a BlackBerry, and a laptop. "I know, most people would carry a briefcase, right? Let's get out of here," she said and locked the showroom door behind us.

We walked across the parking lot to a restaurant overflowing with the after-five crowd. Strong tubes of neon framed the entrance. Andi shimmied her way past several of the tenants to the bar, where she perched on a stool. She thumped her hand on the top of the one next to her. "Have a seat, girlfriend!"

The bartender came over, drying a glass with a white towel. "Your usual?" he asked Andi. She nodded. "What'll you have?" he asked me.

"I'm not sure. What's your usual?" I asked Andi.

"Diet RockStar and pomegranate vodka."

"Oh. I'll have a—" I tried to think of something that sounded adult and serious. "A Manhattan."

"Oooh, fancy!" Andi said.

While the bartender disappeared to make our drinks, I wondered how I was going to keep up this newfound best friend routine. Turns out that didn't matter, because I was sitting with a pro. Andi started a nonstop stream of chatter, about the totally perfect weather, the restaurant's totally awesome calamari, the totally horrendous outfits the waitresses were forced to wear, and the totally hot hunks working behind the bar.

"Don't you just love bartenders? I married one once. Turns out the best thing about him was his name. We split up after a month, but he didn't mind that I wanted to keep it."

The bartender set our drinks in front of us, and she continued. "Thanks, babe. This is Samantha. Sam, this is Cal. He's one of my boyfriends." She tipped her head back and smiled at him while running an ice cube down her throat. The bartender chuckled.

"I have boyfriends all over now. They take care of me. And I take care of them. Right, Cal?" She flipped a credit card out of her wallet and handed it to him.

"Wait, I'll get these," I said, fumbling for my own credit card while searching for a way to steer the conversation to Emily Hart.

"Absolutely not! I can expense this," she said.

"At least let me get the first round."

"Don't worry! You have no idea how many receipts I have that are time-stamped after midnight. Besides, you're my top client these days. I'd do just about anything to make you happy." She giggled.

It seemed she'd delivered me my opening.

"Then let's toast why I'm your top client." I raised my glass to hers. "To Vongole."

"Abso-freakin'-lutely. To Vongole."

I took a sip of my drink and recoiled at the taste, heavy with vermouth. How did Marilyn Monroe drink these? I looked at Andi. She'd finished more than half her drink on our toast. Good sign. That meant it might not be too hard to keep her talking. I sipped again, fighting the taste. I was in the middle of phrasing and rephrasing different prompts in my head when she spoke.

"It's so great to have you at Heist. I mean, it's totally sad what happened to Emily. Kyle's miserable about it. But business is business, and you're going to rock that job, I can already tell."

"I think I'm lucky to have such a strong team of supporters."

"Oh, you mean Belle? She's awesome. Such an inspirational woman. You know, when she went through her divorce, it was pretty nasty. She totally pulled herself back up and reestablished who she was, and now she's even more respected than ever." She finished off her drink. "You ready for another?"

"Not yet," I said, swirling the stem of my martini glass. "What do you think of Mallory?"

She rolled her eyes. "She's a little too by-the-book, if you ask me. We all want to be successful, right? So there's got to be a little wiggle room in the numbers and orders. One time she had Heist hold a payment from us for six months because she said the collection wasn't going to be profitable, and they'd have to send back the orders. She claimed it was Emily's strategy, but I know it wasn't."

"What happened?"

"That's the season we started giving Heist the discount. Suddenly, everything was coming up roses, and we were getting paid within a week."

"I bet it wasn't coming up roses for you," I nudged, playing the new-found BFF confidant. "Fifteen percent of the discounted order is a lot less than fifteen percent of the original, even if Heist bought more."

"Can you believe they totally took that into consideration? It went all the way to the top of Vongole, too. The owners agreed to pay me fifteen percent on the original orders or twenty-five percent of the discounted orders. Either way, I win."

In all of my years in the industry, I had never heard of such a lucrative arrangement.

"Now I just have to get Tradava back into my client base," she said. She raised her hand to cover her berry-stained lips. "Oops! Shouldn't have said that in front of you, right?"

"I thought Heist negotiated an exclusive?"

She spit her drink out in a spritz of surprise and then mopped it up with a couple of promotional Bud Light napkins before the bartender could get to us.

"No, Heist bought out my inventory so we couldn't fill anyone else's orders. But Tradava's such a big account that we put together something for them, and Kyle ended up returning it. Something about the quality not being up to standard." She drained her second drink and motioned for another round for each of us. "Poor guy, he can't get over what happened at Heist. He keeps saying it's his fault."

"Why? Because he and Emily had a fight?" I prompted, still wondering about Mallory's version of that night.

"Couples fight. That's reality." Andi waved at the bartender and pointed to our drinks. When he nodded, she turned back, suddenly very serious. "Kyle doesn't feel guilty about fighting with Emily. He feels guilty because of what they were fighting *about*."

22

———

RUMORS

I was surprised Andi knew they were fighting about Vongole. "I didn't think anyone knew," I said.

"Yes, Kyle does a good job hiding how much he hates her."

"Her? Her who?"

"Belle."

"Kyle hates Belle? But people say—"

"That's why he hates her. With a passion. She won't let that rumor die."

"That's what Emily and Kyle were fighting about?"

"Yes. He was always defending himself against that stupid rumor."

"That he and Belle were caught canoodling in the boardroom?"

She laughed raucously and drew the attention of several patrons near us. "'Canoodling'?! You're funny. Yeah, that's the rumor, but I can't see it being true. He was way too devoted to Emily." She sighed. "He used to send her flowers when they were at market and room service breakfast in bed. Belle investigated him too. Accused him of expensing it to Tradava. Turns out he paid for all of that stuff himself."

"Did Belle apologize?"

"Heck no. Kyle wanted to leave Tradava and work at Heist with Emily, but then everyone was shocked when Belle was fired, and even more shocked when she was named Heist general manager a few weeks later. Kyle thought he'd have an in if he applied to the store, but then that nasty rumor started. Even if there was an open job that he was totally qualified for, he couldn't apply. Everyone would have said he got the job because he was sleeping with Belle. He kept trying to make sure Emily didn't believe the rumor, and I don't think she did, but it just kept following them around. Belle didn't exactly deny it."

I thought about that for a second. "It's not a bad rumor to have floating around about you, if you're Belle. I just can't figure out why Kyle told me some people think she's still working for Tradava. Like there are people who think she's taking everything she learns about Heist and reporting it back to someone at her former store."

"What? Girlfriend, I hear everything, and I never heard that one. She's smart enough to do it though." She reached out for her third drink. "I'm so thirsty tonight!" she said. She pulled the red plastic sword out of the glass, set it on her napkin, and took another drink. "But let me tell you, Kyle hates her. Haaaates her."

"Andi, do you have any pictures of Emily?"

"Sure." She pulled her BlackBerry out of her handbag and pushed the small buttons with blood red-painted thumbnails. "Here." She tapped a few more buttons and handed me the phone. It was a picture of Kyle Trent and a blonde with their arms around each other. Large, toothpaste-commercial-worthy smiles covered their faces.

"When was this taken?"

She took her phone back and looked at the screen. "Last year. The night he proposed to her." She stared at the screen. Her expression was less joy than jealousy.

It got me thinking that something didn't make sense. I needed to talk it through, and there was only one person I could count on for that.

"It doesn't make sense, right?" I asked Detective Loncar. He'd agreed to meet with me on the basis that I had information for him, info that might lead to a break in Emily's case. At least that's what I told him when I called, because it seemed the detective wanted to determine for himself how important my info really was.

I recounted Andi's gossip, though while I was repeating it, it felt more like I was in the middle of a high school love triangle and less like a murder investigation.

"I mean, it sounds like a bunch of rumors." I sat back in the folding chair and stared at Loncar, who sat behind his desk.

"How well do you trust this Andi?"

"Oh, as much as anyone else, I guess."

"She seems to know a lot of dirt on the people we're watching."

"A lot of sales reps do. It's a subtle form of blackmail. They hang out with you until you trip up and do something you'd rather not get around. It's pretty standard in the fashion industry."

"Nice industry," the detective said.

I thought about her RockStar and vodka shooters. "I thought I was going to have a hard time getting away from her, but when I said I had to leave, she said she had other plans too. Until she said that, I thought she was going to stay there all night."

"You sure she wasn't playing? Sales reps have been known to close business deals over drinks."

"Did you get that from *Glengarry Glen Ross?*"

"She might have thought you were a party girl," Loncar continued as though I hadn't interrupted him.

"Do I look like a party girl?" I asked.

Loncar looked down at my pearl necktie over the white shirt and black-and-white pinstriped vest and then back at my face. "No, Ms. Kidd, you look like an upstanding citizen," he said in a robotic voice.

"This is a very nice outfit," I said. I waited a few beats before adding, "Menswear is hot."

"Ms. Kidd, do you have anything else to tell me?"

"When Andi was talking about Kyle and Belle, her eyes turned very focused. It was like staring into the eyes of the Cheshire Cat at first, all zoned out and loopy, and then when she stood, she was completely in control."

"How many drinks did she have?"

"Three."

"She didn't get in a car, did she?"

"No. The bartender called her a cab. It was no big thing to either of them, like she does this every day. I think *she's* the party girl."

"Then maybe it is no big thing to her. People are allowed to blow off steam, Ms. Kidd."

I couldn't help thinking the detective wasn't putting the proper importance on my new information.

***

I PULLED AWAY from the police station, circled the block a few times to make sure Dante wasn't following me, and headed home. Halfway there I pulled into the parking lot of an ice cream store and parked in the far corner under a light. I went inside and ordered two scoops of black raspberry ice cream in a cup, carried it to my car, and ate it slowly while I thought about what I should do next. When I was finished, I pulled Kyle's card out of my wallet and called the number.

"Kyle, this is Samantha Kidd." I hesitated, not entirely sure what I wanted to say. "I know it's late, but I was wondering if I could talk to you."

"Samantha Kidd. I didn't think you'd call. Funny thing is, I was just thinking about you."

"You were?"

There was a pause on the other end of the phone, and then Kyle continued in his languorous voice. "I have something I think you might like. Something I wanted to give Emily the night we were at Heist. I think you'll find it interesting."

I wasn't sure what he was talking about, and for a moment I wondered if he was coming on to me. "I—I'm not looking for companionship tonight."

"I don't know what it is you think I'm offering you, but the only 'companionship' I want right now comes from a bottle."

"But you said—"

"I know what I said."

"I'm confused. Do you want to give me something, or do you want me to leave you alone?"

"Where are you?"

I hesitated. "The Tastee-Freez parking lot."

"Are you going to be there long? I can be there in ten minutes."

Considering he was seeking companionship from a bottle, I didn't want to be the reason he got into a car.

"I have a better idea. Why don't I come to you?"

"Fine. Here's my address."

I felt around the floor of the car for a pen and came up with a mauve lip liner. I scribbled his address on the bottom of the empty ice cream bowl and hung up.

Kyle Trent lived in the Woodgate Apartments, a secluded set of buildings not far from the on-ramp to the highway. I parked by his building and glanced in the rearview mirror, wiping a smudge of black raspberry from my lower lip before getting out. The door to his apartment opened as I scaled the stairs out front.

"Come on in," he said. He wore a gray bathrobe over light blue pinstriped pajamas and held a glass tumbler of something amber. He left the door open, and I followed him inside.

His apartment was sparsely furnished. A burgundy leather sofa faced an unlit fireplace. There were no pictures on the mantle. A collection of Chinese food takeout containers covered the maple coffee table, along with two empty beer bottles and an empty bag from McDonald's. The polished, professional Kyle Trent I'd first met at Heist and conversed with at Tradava was gone, and in his place was a man who reeked of desperation and a couple of days without a shower.

"Thanks for meeting me. I wanted to ask you about Belle and Emily—"

He waved his hand in front of me. "I don't want to talk about any of this."

"But you said you had something for me?"

"I do. I have a question." He sat down on the burgundy leather sofa and pointed at me with the index finger of the hand holding the glass. "Why do you care so much about this? You didn't even know her."

I didn't know what I expected from my meeting with Kyle, but I didn't expect him to question my motives. I looked at this man, who days ago could just as easily have graced the pages of a retailer's catalog as he could be the buyer behind the merchandise. Kyle Trent, for all of his good looks, his confidence, and his ace-in-the-hole charm, was me. He was a buyer who did his job well, who was attracted to someone in his industry. Only, unlike me, who had accepted that buyers don't date vendors, that companies don't like romances that threaten the business, Kyle risked his job for his relationship with Emily, and the two had fallen in love. And look where it had gotten him.

I sat on the far end of the leather sofa and leaned forward, propping my elbows on my pinstriped pants. "I didn't have to know her to see she was special," I said softly.

Kyle stared into the glass he held, swirling it around a few times. He leaned forward, set the glass on the coffee table, and held his head in his hands. His shoulders shook like he was crying.

"I'm sorry. I'm sorry I came over here, and I'm sorry for your loss. I'll let myself out." I stood and walked toward the door.

"Samantha, wait," Kyle said.

I turned around and saw him pull a white envelope out of his bathrobe pocket. It was folded in half. He held it out to me.

"I sealed it so nobody else would see it. I was planning to show it to Emily, but I never got the chance."

"What is it?"

"It might explain a few things."

I took the envelope. If it had to do with Emily or Vongole or Belle, then he was right: I'd probably find it interesting. If it had to do with Tradava, he was risking his job to give it to me.

"Do you want me to open it now?"

"No. Please go. I want to be alone," he said.

At home, I triple-locked the front door, undid my pearl necktie, and tore open the envelope. Inside was a printout of a spreadsheet: Vongole Gross Margin Recap, with the season and year as heading. It was Tradava's version of the profit recap I'd seen on Mallory's desk. I didn't have the Heist version at home, but I didn't need it to remember that Vongole was a very profitable vendor at Heist. That's why it struck me that on Tradava's recap, for one season, Vongole's "profits" were a hundred and seventy-five thousand dollars in the hole.

A hundred-and-seventy-five-thousand-dollar loss in one season? That's not a growth strategy. That's a business about to go belly up.

23

OBLIGATIONS

I woke at six the next morning. I'd been up half the night, my mind abuzz with questions about the Tradava/Vongole recap. Profit and loss statements—or P&Ls, as they're called—were standard spreadsheets in the industry, recaps that indicated gross sales and backed-out expenses to let a retailer identify whether or not a business was good for the bottom line. I had questions about what I'd read, questions that could only be answered once I compared the Heist profitability against the Tradava one. My best bet was to get into the store before it was filled with employees, customers, and Mallory.

I had two cups of coffee and filled the rest of the morning with anxiety-ridden accessorizing. I stepped out of the house in a black and white polka-dotted blouse and flouncy ivory and black silk skirt, a pair of pointy-toed black patent leather pumps, and a black satin headband with a white camellia above my left ear. I knew I'd kissed off my attempts at undercover investigations.

Worse, Dante sat on his motorcycle in the middle of my driveway.

"You might want to go back inside and change. That's not exactly appropriate for the back of a motorcycle."

"Why are you offering me a ride?"

He held up a small metal thing with wires sticking out of it. "Cars don't run without this."

"You vandalized my car?" I asked.

I marched past him in my pointy-toed shoes and polka dots. I popped the hood of my car. Having used up most of what I knew about cars other than checking the oil, I stared at the engine, torn between touching things so I looked like I knew what I was doing and stepping away to keep the car dirt off my outfit.

Dante watched me from his motorcycle. I felt exposed. I slammed the hood back down and glared at him, trying to think of something snappy to say. Black car grunge had gotten on my fingertips, and I held them away from me like I'd just had a manicure and was waiting for my polish to dry.

"I'm not going to let this go." I turned around and went inside.

Ten minutes later, I returned wearing black skinny pants, pumps, and an ocean-blue taffeta jacket cinched at the waist. I carried a pair of futuristic silver sunglasses and accepted the helmet he handed me. Helmet hair. My morning was going from bad to worse.

"Where do you want to go?" he asked.

"Heist," I said. "I don't know where you thought I'd be going, but I'm due at work."

Dante leaned in close. "You could play hooky with me, if you want. We can drive to the Jersey Shore, make a day of it. Forget your troubles. Nobody has to know."

I flushed. "I have obligations, and now I'm going to be late."

"Hop on. I'll get you there in no time."

I climbed onto the back of his motorcycle and tried to figure out how to hold on. He gunned the engine, and the bike lurched. Out of panic, I wrapped my arms around his torso and flushed. I was glad he —or anybody else—couldn't see my face.

At Heist, I went to my office and located the Vongole folder on Mallory's desk. I laid the two recaps side by side and compared the information. Both stores had achieved the same sell-through. Tradava had higher sales than Heist. So why was Heist reporting profits of two hundred thousand dollars while Tradava was almost the same amount in the hole?

I heard Mallory enter the office. She dumped her oversized handbag on the floor and sat down, cueing up her computer screen. I knew I needed the notebook that was shelved over her head, the one with the Vongole strategy, but before I could get it, she pulled it down, flipped a few pages in, and tore several sheets out of the binder without opening the rings. I leaned forward, watching her elbow propped on the outside of the notebook as she sorted through the pages. I stood up and pretended to get something from the closet so I could get a better view. She wadded the paper up and put it in her trash can. Seconds later, she stood up with her trash can and carried it into the hallway, where the trash crew would soon come to empty it.

I needed to see what she'd thrown out.

I pulled three business-sized envelopes from a drawer and scribbled addresses on the front: Cat, Eddie, and Logan (my cat is a very convenient undercover operative). Security went through our handbags every time we left the building, and I couldn't risk being caught with company information. I tossed promotional postcards into the envelopes to Cat and Eddie and shoved the Tradava/Vongole recaps into the envelope addressed to Logan. I stood up and walked past Mallory, waving the envelopes. "I'm heading to the mailbox. Got anything?"

"No."

"I'll be right back."

Once in the hall, I scanned the three matching trash cans lined up outside of the office, zeroing in on the crumpled piece of paper that sat on top of the can closest to our office. I palmed it and walked down the hallway and through the store. As I walked past the handbag department, I smoothed out the paper, tri-folded it, and shoved it into the envelope addressed to Logan. I sealed the envelopes and carried the lot to security.

"What time does the mail get picked up?" I asked Gabe.

"Three thirty." He looked at the top of my envelopes. "They're stamped? There's a mailbox on the corner of the parking lot. They pick up in the morning too. You're early enough to make it."

I jogged to the mailbox, clutching the wad of envelopes. After dropping them into the box, I wondered if I'd done the right thing. The only actual piece of paper that proved anything until now was in the hands of the mailmen. Let's hope today wasn't the day they went postal.

Back in my office, I closed my working spreadsheet and checked my e-mail. There were four unread messages from Nick.

Samantha, I have a meeting set up with the Luta factory this afternoon. I was unaware that Lussuria was an extension of Luta's production. I will keep you posted. Regards, Nick Taylor.

SAMANTHA, I won't be meeting with Luta after all. They are under investigation for producing merchandise that is not acceptable to export quality standards. Again, thank you for the recommendation.–Nick Taylor.

SAMANTHA, If memory serves, you mentioned quality concerns when we last spoke. That last piece of information might prove interesting to your boss. I could be wrong but I believe his name is Loncar? –Nick

S, My initial sample collection of shoes has been flagged and is being inspected by customs. In order to focus on the shoe collection, I'm going to postpone any handbag ventures indefinitely.–N

NO DOUBT NICK had been busy, but of all the information in my inbox, the e-mail that struck me the most was the last. He was halfway around the country pursuing his own passion, the production of his shoe collection, and yet he was researching factories for me. If his collection was indeed tied up in customs, and he had to deal with the Italian government to get it back on track, then I had no right to involve him further.

But Nick was right. I had to share this info with Detective Loncar. I called the police station.

As the phone rang, Mallory came into my office. She stood by my desk, clutching a large binder to her chest.

"I'll be just a second," I said to her.

"I'll wait." She sat in the chair across from my desk just as the detective answered. I watched Mallory open the binder and pretend to study a spreadsheet. She wasn't going anywhere.

"Hi—honey," I said. Pause. "I never got a chance to thank you for the flowers you sent to Heist."

There was silence on the other end of the call, and I couldn't tell whether Loncar knew who he was talking to. "If you keep sending me flowers, the other buyers around here are going to get jealous."

Mallory looked up at me, and I smiled, pointed to the receiver, and mouthed the word "boyfriend." She looked back at her notebook.

"What's this about, Ms. Kidd?"

Okay, good. He knew who I was. "I was wondering if you could meet me for lunch? I have a surprise for you."

Mallory stood up and left. I turned away from the door and dropped my voice. "I'm sorry. The walls have ears."

"Ms. Kidd, not that I don't enjoy your company, but if you have something to tell me, then tell me."

"You know what I could do? Write notes on a brown paper bag and throw them out in the trash can at the edge of the Heist parking lot, say, around two? You could pretend you're going through the trash and take my notes—"

"Two o'clock. Heist. I'll meet you there."

"I think my plan's more covert."

"Is there a place to sit?"

"Yes, but that's not the point."

"Ms. Kidd, I'll expect you to meet me at two o'clock, Heist parking lot, with whatever information you have for me. Is that clear?"

"Crystal."

———

FOR THE NEXT few hours I kept myself busy with the actual functions of being Heist's buyer: familiarizing myself with the rest of the assortment, reviewing the seasonal budgets, and reading countless e-mails dictating the company's position on color, trend, accessories, and silhouettes. Where Tradava had seemed to use the throw-spaghetti-at-the-wall approach to merchandising—buy a little of everything and see what sells—Heist had a clear vision of who their customer was and how they expected her to dress for the upcoming season.

Mallory nibbled on carrots from a plastic baggie in her office, the occasional snap and subsequent series of crunches the only sounds except for the click of her mouse. I was surprised she didn't take a lunch break, until it occurred to me that maybe she didn't want to leave me alone in the office.

At five till two I picked up my handbag and left the office. Detective Loncar was in his car, drinking from a red aluminum travel mug with Kutztown University's logo on the outside. He got out of the car before I had a chance to tap on his window.

"Hi, Detective. Are you hungry? Can I buy you lunch?"

"Ms. Kidd, you said you had information for me?"

"Oh, yes, sure. There's a pizza place at the other end of the strip mall. Are you sure you don't want to talk there? It's my lunch break."

He stared at me.

"I guess you already ate." I sat next to him, hoping my stomach wouldn't growl during our meeting. "So here's the thing. Kyle Trent gave me a spreadsheet from Tradava for this handbag business, Vongole. When I got into the store, I looked at the same information for the business at Heist. It's not easy to understand someone else's spreadsheet, but once I figured it out, I realized there's a huge discrepancy in how Vongole sells to each store."

"I'm no retailer, but it seems to me it's up to each store to determine how to run their business."

"Under normal circumstances, I'd agree. Only, this isn't normal, you know? The buyer here was murdered. So I'm thinking maybe it's about business."

"Do you have these spreadsheets with you?"

"Um—no. I will, though, in five to seven business days."

Loncar's forehead wrinkled.

"Never mind that. I shouldn't even have the spreadsheet for Tradava. The important thing is that Tradava is showing a six-figure loss on the Vongole handbag line while Heist is showing a profit. For some reason, Heist doesn't factor in freight, theft, or markdowns. Doesn't that seem weird to you?"

"I'm sure this means something to somebody, but unless you tell me you found a note that says, 'Kill Emily Hart because of Vongole handbags,' I don't think it matters much to the case."

"No note. Not a note in sight."

"I've got means figured out and opportunity," he said. "Now I'm looking for the motive."

"That's what I found! Listen to me," I said, slapping him on the arm for emphasis. As soon as I did, I froze, not sure if I'd overstepped my boundaries.

Loncar didn't move, didn't say a word.

I took a deep breath and ticked points off on my fingers. "Here's how a retailer figures out their bottom line. They take their sales, and then they subtract the costs of doing business. Merchandise, markdowns, shipping and transportation costs, theft. Like, if you had a lemonade stand. After you counted out what you made selling lemonade, you'd have to subtract out the cost of lemons, the gas you used driving to the store and back. If some kids from the neighborhood stole a pitcher when you weren't looking, that would be theft. If you started selling for three dollars a cup and weren't moving it, you'd mark down to two dollars a cup, but that one dollar would be a markdown. Are you following me?"

"I get the general concept."

"Heist doesn't use any of those expenses. For some reason, they don't pay for shipping, they don't mark down their merchandise, and nobody steals anything. But Tradava is the other way around, and they're showing a pretty big loss."

"What do you think this means, Ms. Kidd?"

"I don't know yet, but it's too big of a red flag to think it doesn't matter."

"You say Kyle Trent gave you the Tradava information?"

I nodded. "Last night. He invited me to his apartment."

"What time was this?"

I felt my eyes roll up for a second as I thought. "Let's see. I was at happy hour with Andi, then I went to the Tastee-Freez, and then I went to his house. Probably around seven."

"Did you stay there long?"

"No, only about ten, maybe fifteen minutes. He wasn't in very good shape."

"This information he gave you. Tradava would consider that confidential, wouldn't they?"

"Yes. He risked his job to give it to me."

The detective scribbled something in his small spiral-bound notebook and tucked it back inside his wrinkled blazer. I fought the urge to suggest a local tailor who could make his suit fit better. It didn't seem like the time for fashion advice.

"Are you going to move on this?"

"Ms. Kidd, I appreciate the information." He clicked his ballpoint pen and stuck it into his breast pocket. "If you think of anything else, call."

I wasn't sure, but it sounded like he was less sincere than he'd been at the beginning of all this.

I grabbed a slice of pizza and went back to the office. Mallory had left a note taped to my phone that said she'd be back by a quarter after three. I had seventeen minutes to snoop. I ate the pizza and used the remaining sixteen minutes (I was hungry!) to figure out Kyle's motivation. He'd cancelled Tradava orders based on quality issues. It seemed the new lot of available inventory wasn't up to Vongole's usual quality standards, and Belle's interest in pushing through orders quickly and stocking the shelves suggested she knew this.

It was a well-known fact in retail circles that salaries were only a portion of a vice president's income, but annual bonuses, based on statistical performances, were pretty lucrative. I pulled out a calculator and ran a few what-ifs. At the industry standard, Belle's possible bonus for the year was in the fifty-thousand-dollar range.

Not too shabby.

And there was another perk in it for Belle. By bringing in the inventory—a seemingly unlimited supply of the hottest it-bag vendor—she could exceed the sales plan and secure her future at Heist. She'd be celebrated in social circles, a veritable celebrity among fashionistas. Andi had mentioned Belle's divorce. Belle was a ballsy woman, tough, and smart and driven. I wondered who'd divorced who in that scenario, if Belle's nature had been the reason for the split or the by-product of it. If she'd been left in the dust once, she wasn't going to allow that to happen again. By driving home the largest profits that Heist had seen, she would earn raises, bonuses, and stock options.

It all made sense. Kyle must have figured out Belle was manipulating the system for her own personal gain. He'd see Emily would be responsible if the strategy failed. It explained the fight Mallory had overheard and the animosity between Kyle and Belle. Belle would have started the rumor about the two of them, causing a rift between Kyle and Emily and giving herself the distance she needed. Regardless of business, Emily wouldn't have wanted to actively grow the Vongole business, which explained the note to Mallory. Belle must have ultimately determined Emily was a threat to her plan, and she eliminated that threat the night of the gala. Nobody would have questioned her presence on the selling floor of Heist because she was the general manager.

And the next day, Belle would have rushed to secure the last-minute orders with Andi before anybody could ask questions.

I glanced at the clock on my computer. I had about seven minutes before Mallory would return, seven minutes to call Detective Loncar. Seven minutes, as long as Mallory didn't come back early.

I made the call. "Detective, I think I figured it out."

"Make it fast," he barked. "We got some information of our own."

"Belle DuChamp–she's the one. She—" I looked up as Mallory entered my office and passed through to her own. I lowered my voice. "She had the means and the motive and the opportunity. That's what you needed, right? I have it all here. She had to be one who killed Emily."

"Ms. Kidd, thanks for playing detective with us, but we'll take it from here."

"So you're coming here to arrest her?" I asked.

"No, we're not coming there to arrest her."

"Why not?"

"Because Belle DuChamp's body was found in the parking lot outside of Tradava this morning."

"What are you saying? That she's above suspicion?"

"No, Ms. Kidd. I'm saying that Belle DuChamp is dead."

24

———————

DONE

While I was apparently the first to know, word about the general manager's murder spread quickly through the store. A member of the store's senior staff came around to each of our offices, telling us the store was going to close for the day.

I collected my things and popped my head into Mallory's office. Her back was to me. "Mallory, are you ready to leave? I'll walk out with you."

When she turned my way, her eyes were red and angry. "I don't trust you. I don't know why anyone else won't listen to me, but I know you're up to something," she said, spittle flying from her lips.

The part of the unduly suspected employee had already been played once by me at Tradava, and I wasn't rushing to reprise my role at Heist.

"You're upset. Anyone would be. Let's walk out together."

Mallory took a few deep breaths and powdered her face from a compact that was slightly more orange than her natural skin tone.

"Leave me alone," she said and clicked the compact shut.

I walked through the store, past the handcuffed jeans and pile of shoes with the mannequin inside staring out. I couldn't help wondering how real events were going to affect the future of the store that proclaimed its prices were criminal.

It wasn't until I reached the parking lot that I remembered Dante had dropped me off. I called him. "I need a ride home."

"Be right there," he said.

When Dante's motorcycle blazed into the parking lot and stopped in front of me, I straddled the seat and buckled the spare helmet over my head. And when we reached my house and I saw a cop car parked in my driveway, I thought about telling him I'd changed my mind about us heading to Jersey.

Detective Loncar sat on my front porch with two younger men in uniform. Dante let the bike idle behind the cruiser before I hopped off the back.

"You want me to stay?"

"This doesn't concern you," I said.

"It concerns you?"

"It shouldn't, but it does."

"I'm coming with you." He turned the ignition off.

"You're waiting outside."

We crossed the yard to the porch. "Detective," I said cordially, nodding once while freaking out inside.

"Ms. Kidd, we need to talk to you."

"Okay, I'll just be a second," I said, fumbling with the keys to unlock the front door.

"Ms. Kidd, there was a shootout in the Tradava parking lot last night."

"I wasn't anywhere near Tradava last night."

"Nobody said you were." He folded his hands in front of him but pointed his index finger and thumb out like a shadow-puppet of a gun. "You've been forthcoming with information regarding Heist, Tradava, and the recent murder of Emily Hart."

"I have more to tell you too."

Loncar cut me off. "We appreciate your help, but we have a suspect in custody."

"Will you tell me who you arrested?"

"No."

"So that's it? No more flowers at work?"

"No more work. You're done at Heist."

"But Tony Simms hired me to do a job."

"Mr. Simms hired you to help figure out why his handbag buyer was murdered. That question's been answered. Thank you for your help." He held a hand out to formalize the end of our working relationship.

"What about the poison?" I asked suddenly.

"What?"

"The poison? From the restaurant? I brought you samples from takeout? My cat?" My voice rose with each question.

Detective Loncar retracted his hand. "The mushrooms they used in the truffle butter were poisonous. Somehow the supplier got a few of the bad kind mixed in with the regular delivery. They're in the process of changing their supplier, and we can't pinpoint whether the bad mushrooms came from the old delivery or the new one. Unfortunate accident. Couple of people got sick—nothing serious. They tossed their supply and started fresh. No truffle butter for the restaurant for a while."

"But my cat and my friend—"

"You shouldn't be feeding your cat human food. Your friend is a different story. No one else reported passing out. Maybe she should eat more."

This time the detective let well more than a minute of silence pass before he offered his handshake and left with the uniformed officers. I didn't know what I expected from working with him, but it was more than this—and more than this and two bouquets of surveillance flowers too. I shook his hand, but the voice inside my head screamed, *This isn't over!*

I was scared the voice was right.

Dante followed me into my kitchen. The light on my machine blinked.

"Can you wait out front?" I asked. "I don't want you to hear my messages."

I hit the playback button the second the screen door slammed.

Beep: "Sam, it's Eddie. Call me."

Beep: "Sam, where are you? It's Eddie."

Beep: "Dude, you're freaking me out."

Beep: "You didn't have something to do with this, did you?"

Beep: "Are you okay?"

Beep: "I'm calling the cops."

It's nice to be loved.

I called Eddie. He answered on the first ring. "I'm fine, and I didn't do anything," I said.

"But you know about Kyle?"

"I know about Belle. What happened to Kyle?"

"The police arrested him half an hour ago."

25

STARING AT THE SHEETS

THE NEWS SUCKED THE WIND OUT OF ME. THE PHONE CLATTERED TO the floor, and I reached for the edges of the counter to steady myself. "Dante?" I called out.

He ran inside and guided me to a chair. "Put your head down," he instructed, his hand hot on the back of my head.

I bent forward and held my head in my hands, trying to shake the sound of voices in the distance. Then I realized the phone hadn't disconnected when it landed on the floor, and Eddie was still talking.

Dante noticed it too. He scooped up the phone and said, "She'll call you back."

"Dante, is Cat still going stir crazy?"

He nodded.

"You think she'd like to come over?"

FOR THREE DAYS I did little more than sleep. There were two lessons to be learned from my short time at Heist:

    a) Love doesn't conquer all, and

    b) I was borderline unemployable.

Twice a day my friends checked up on me. At first I tried to make small talk, but it didn't last. I dug into the pile of discarded clothes on the floor and pulled out a black polyester tunic with green and yellow trees embroidered on it. There was a hard spot on the right thigh where someone had accidentally melted it with a cigarette back when flammable polyester clothes were in style. You didn't find cigarette holes in clothes anymore. Those were simpler times.

It was like my life. Moving to Ribbon had been about giving up the pressures of a job I knew I could do in order to retrace the steps of my life and figure out what it was I was meant to do. I hadn't sought out the handbag buyer job at Heist; the job had found me. I'd been in a vulnerable enough position that I took it. And now, I was back where I had started: unhappy and unemployed.

It wasn't the crimes that left me unsettled either, though they didn't help. It was the feeling of failing, repeatedly, that made me sick to my stomach. That's what kept me from joining my friends downstairs, even if they took turns staying at my house.

Cat brought me a tray of food on Friday. She tapped on the door. "Are you awake?" she asked softly. "I brought you grapes and cheese."

She carried the tray to the bed and sat it next to my leg. The weekend edition of the *Style Section,* the industry newspaper, was folded and tucked under a silver bud vase with a flower from the front yard. Logan stood up and walked over my knees to sniff the cheese. Cat held out her hand and set a kitty treat on the blanket. Logan lost interest in my cheese.

"You couldn't have known it was a crime of passion, Sam," Cat said. "Nobody would have believed it."

"It doesn't fit. Nobody ever mentioned Kyle being the jealous sort. I can't see him killing his fiancée. All I ever heard was how well they got along."

"Sometimes it's the ones you least expect."

"Sometimes..." I said.

"Do you want to come downstairs and join us?"

"Not yet." I stared at the ceiling.

"Do you want me to stay?"

"No, I'd rather be alone."

EDDIE DELIVERED my tray on Saturday, bringing his homemade macaroni and cheese. An origami monster sat on the corner by a glass of lemonade.

"Dude, time to rise and shine." He set the tray on the foot of the bed and pulled the cord on the curtains, flooding the room with unwelcome sunlight.

"I don't want to rise and shine."

"Then consider taking a shower."

I rubbed my eyes and blinked a few times to adjust to the brightness. Eddie fluffed a pillow from the chaise lounge that sat in the corner and rearranged the frames lining the top of my dresser. He picked up the pearls I'd worn to work earlier that week and tucked them into my jewelry box, along with a couple errant earrings.

"The police really arrested Kyle?" I asked.

He turned to me. "Seems that way."

"But he was your friend."

"Sometimes you think you know people, but you don't really know them at all." He picked up yesterday's pajamas and tossed them into the hamper. A pair of my panties were on the floor in front of it. He stood there looking at them before shutting the hamper, leaving them where they were.

"Dude, you can't stay in bed forever."

"I'm not ready to acknowledge what a colossal mess my life is."

He looked up. "Seems to me if you were really 'just a buyer for Heist' like you keep telling me, nothing's really changed. You get up, you go to work, you do your job. Only you're acting like you don't have a job to go to. Why is that? Why would Kyle's homicidal tendencies have anything to do with your job as buyer for Heist? As far as I know, you haven't even called in sick for the past two days. And nobody's been calling here looking for you either."

He stood in the doorway, one hand on the doorknob. Inside, I knew if I said I wanted to tell him everything that had been going on, he'd sit on the edge of the bed and listen. He'd forgive me for not confiding in him all along. He'd be what I needed. A friend.

Only I couldn't. Not yet. I didn't believe Kyle was guilty. And if I was right, that meant this wasn't over.

"I don't know what you want to hear," I said.

We looked at each other for a few more seconds before he let himself out of the room. I pulled the curtains shut, took a half-hour-long shower, and crawled back into bed. There was something I wasn't seeing, and I needed to take notes, to reason it out.

I opened the drawer to my nightstand and pulled out a wad of take-out menus I'd moved from the kitchen in an effort to cut down on my junk food delivery habit. I found a Sharpie on the floor by the closet and wrote the names of each player on top of the listings over my favorite comfort foods: Kyle Trent, Tony Simms, Andi Holloway, Mallory George, Belle DuChamp, Emily Hart. I rearranged the menus in different order, trying to see the connection between them but succeeded only in giving myself a craving for cheap Chinese food.

The house remained silent for the rest of the night. I stared at the ceiling. Eddie was right. I couldn't stay in bed forever. I pushed the covers back and opened the bedroom door. The serving tray sat on the floor. An Atomic Fireball rested in the middle of a small, white saucer, next to a note. *It's just you and me.*

I belted my silk kimono and went downstairs.

"Hello?" I called.

"The kids went to get something to eat," Dante said. He folded a newspaper on his lap.

"I got tired of staring at the sheets."

He held out the newspaper. "Want to read the details?"

"Sure," I said, taking the bundle. I felt him watching as I unrolled it and scanned the front-page headlines of the *Ribbon Eagle* and *Ribbon Times*, respectively: "Respected Businessman Endangers Life in Hostage Situation" and "Fatal Showdown at Tradava Ends Murder Investigation."

I went with the *Times* article first. It detailed Belle DuChamp's visit to Tradava and her suspected love triangle with Kyle Trent and Emily Hart. "Ironically, the designer handbag collection that brought these three people together will most likely go bankrupt. Tradava has already distanced themselves from Vongole and, according to a statement from Simms, Heist will remain closed indefinitely to restructure their business model."

I flipped open the *Ribbon Eagle* and scanned the newsprint, a basic afternoon rehash of the information that had appeared in the *Times*. "Sources close to DuChamp and Trent confirm their business relationship but maintain the couple kept their private dalliances private. According to local entrepreneur Tony Simms, 'Belle DuChamp was a smart woman, too smart to risk her career for a one-night stand.' Other sources report when Trent proclaimed his love for DuChamp, she denied reciprocating those feelings, and threatened to turn him in. People were concerned for her safety. 'I confronted him and told him to back down, to leave her alone, but he was too upset. He pulled a gun and shot Belle. I was able to detain him until the police arrived.' "

It was hard to fit these pieces of the puzzle into the thought patterns I'd been playing with for the past few days. First Emily met Kyle. Then he killed her. He professed love for Belle, and she denied him. When he tried to kill her too, Tony Simms saved the day.

I still didn't like it.

"Dante? When did you say Cat and Eddie would be back?"

"About five."

"Do you think you could give me about an hour alone?" He studied my face. "I want to take a long shower and make a couple of phone calls to tell everyone I'm okay."

"If that's what you need." He left with not much more than a good-bye, his motorcycle kicking up gravel as he peeled out of the driveway.

True to my word, I made those calls. To my parents in California. To my sister in Virginia. To Nick in Italy. Nobody answered. I left messages for all.

And then I called Tony Simms.

I needed to know what was to become of my future at Heist, though with a three-day tenure, my imagination had already served me walking papers.

I caught Tony in his office and asked him to come to my house. He agreed to come in about twenty minutes. It wasn't a random amount of time. It was the minimum I required to look at least part human. Eighteen and a half minutes later, dressed in the black pantsuit Heist had delivered earlier in the week, I descended the stairs as a silver BMW pulled into my driveway. I didn't need to see the vanity plates to know it was the store owner.

My cell phone buzzed with a new text message from Dante: *10 more min.* Here's hoping Tony Simms could talk fast.

I held the door open for him before he had a chance to ring the bell.

"I heard about what happened. I'm sorry," I said.

"We're all sorry. Thank you."

I was about to invite him to sit in my living room but changed my mind and had him follow me to the dining room. We sat in opposite chairs across the table from each other. A small wooden napkin holder my sister had made in seventh grade sat between us, holding a stack of plain white paper napkins. Tony turned down my offer of iced tea, so I sipped my own while he spoke.

"Samantha, we're going to close down the store indefinitely. Regroup and restructure. If we intend to have a future in Ribbon, we need to let the bad publicity pass. The other Heist stores shouldn't be hurt by the press; in fact, it might help them. But that means we no longer need your services. In light of the recent deaths connected to Vongole, we are dropping their line. We're also moving the buying offices for all of Heist from each individual store to a central office in Philadelphia. Thank you for taking on such an important role at the store."

"It was nothing," I said.

"We're still planning on hosting the dedication at I-FAD, and I'd like you to be there. Can you do that?"

"You just said I don't work for the store anymore."

"I need you to be there as an ambassador of Heist. A liaison between the store and the college."

"What about Nora?"

"She'll be there too, but I need someone with your skill set to back me up. Someone who knows the score."

"Wouldn't it be better to have more tenured people from Heist there instead of me?"

"I'll have plenty of tenured people there. You represent the kind of new Heist blood we want. If you wanted to move to Philadelphia, I'd find a place for you in the Center City store. But since you don't, consider this your last job assignment. Representing the store. You can do that, can't you?"

"Sure. Yes. I can do that." I felt backed into a corner.

He pulled an envelope out of a pocket inside his suit jacket and slid it across the table. "Consider this payment for your time at Heist."

I didn't want to look in the envelope because, after all I'd done, I didn't know if I could allow myself to accept it. I didn't want to know what I was turning down. I pushed the envelope back.

"You've more than earned it," he said. "I've written a letter of recommendation for you should you choose to pursue employment elsewhere in Ribbon. I understand you've had difficulty holding on to a job around town, and you're not to be faulted for what happened. You were no more involved in the Vongole situation than I was."

A letter of recommendation from a Tony Simms would go a long way in offsetting my career cooties. He stood and held out a hand.

"Samantha Kidd, I enjoyed having you on the payroll."

I stood too. "Tony Simms," I mimicked, "I enjoyed being there." We shook hands, me finally matching his two-pump handshake.

"If there's anything else I can do for you, don't hesitate to call." He held out his business card. I thanked him for the offer and watched him walk away.

See, now, that should make me feel good. Right? A noted businessman recognized my worth to the tune of—I glanced in the envelope he'd left behind—wow.

That was a lot of cash.

I pulled the stack of bills from the envelope and counted ten thousand dollars in hundreds. There had to be some kind of mistake. I'd worked at the store for three days, and no way had I earned that kind of dough. Even if I had put myself at risk by working with a couple of greedy, homicidal sex fiends, if the papers were to be believed.

I ran to the door with the cash in my hand to see if I could catch Tony and ask if this was a mistake. Instead, Dante stood on my doorstep. I put my hand behind my back.

"Give me a minute," I said, and shut the door in his face.

I put the money inside the front cover of the Halston biography on the coffee table, but the cover wouldn't close. I moved it to the back of the book, ignoring the fact that the book was no longer flat.

"Come on in," I said, as though slamming the door in his face was routine.

"Got your mail. Couple of days' worth." He held a business-sized envelope between his fingers but pulled it away when I reached for it. "Something addressed to your cat?"

I snatched the envelope from Dante and tore it open. Two recaps, just like I remembered. I would have done better to mail the recaps to the cops. If nothing else, it would have been evidence that I was working with them, but who was to know that this whole thing would go down before I could offer up my discoveries?

Still, I called Detective Loncar. "Hi Detective, Samantha Kidd here."

"Ms. Kidd, like I told you, we're all done here. No need for you to keep checking in with us."

"I know. I just, I have that information you needed. The spreadsheets I told you about? Remember, Kyle Trent gave them to me before he... you know... and I thought it might be important."

"You can bring them by if you want, but we already got a witness and a pretty solid case against him."

"Did he confess?"

"Do you have anything else to tell me?"

"You'd look good in blue," I said.

The detective hung up on me without saying good-bye. I stared at the recaps, wondering if Kyle had been playing me when he gave me this info. Maybe he'd been the one trailing the breadcrumbs I'd been following.

I thought it through again. Kyle had killed Emily at Heist, probably minutes before he'd run into me in the handbag department. A crime of passion. I could have easily overheard something, or seen something, and that was one thing he didn't know. So he figured out a way to keep an eye on me. Plus, he was the one who fed me information about Belle. Once he confided in me about his engagement to Emily, I wrote him off as a suspect. I never saw this one coming. And when I'd floated the rumors past Andi Holloway....

I'd forgotten about Andi. She had benefited financially from the apparent feud between Tradava and Heist's buyers, and she had a relationship with each of the buyers. In fact, even she said she didn't believe the rumor about Belle and Kyle. The romantic stories she'd told me about what Kyle had done for Emily when they were at market were the stuff of chick-lit novels, not murder mysteries. It didn't make sense.

Unless Kyle had been playing her too.

26

NOT A TOTALLY IN SIGHT

"Dante, I have to get out of the house. I'm going for a drive." I grabbed my keys but stopped before reaching the front door. "Is my car back to normal?" I asked.

He nodded.

I took off, only slightly surprised he didn't follow.

It was a warm spring day. The wind whipped through my curly hair, just what I needed to clear my mind. I snaked around a couple of suburban streets while deciding where I wanted to go, turning onto Perkiomen Avenue behind a delivery truck. I blasted the Go-Gos from my stereo and cruised a couple miles without a specific destination. I ended up in a parking space in front of the renovated building where Andi rented her Bag Lady offices. I entered the showroom and found Andi slumped in a chair surrounded by opened boxes of handbags.

"Andi?" I hopped to the side so I had a better view of her.

"Yes?" She spun her chair toward me. The normally peppy RockStar-fueled woman was like a deflated balloon. "Oh, hi Samantha," she said, not standing up. "Did we have an appointment?" She stood awkwardly and used her instep to push one of the shipping boxes out of the way. Her eyes were bloodshot and puffy, and her nose was dry from too much dabbing with a tissue.

"I heard, and I thought I should... I mean..." Suddenly my visit seemed calculated, and I didn't know what to say. "Are you okay?" It was the only sentence that felt right.

She slumped back into her chair.

I stepped around the boxes and sat across from her in silence.

"I don't get it. I just don't understand. It doesn't make sense. I've known Emily and Kyle forever. They seemed so in love. I thought they'd found it. Made me believe that I might find someone too but not living this kind of life," she tossed a shiny red wallet on the table. "The only thing keeping me from a total breakdown is the Xanax I took this morning. I don't see it. I can't see him doing it. I know that's just denial speaking, but I completely, utterly, wholly can't see it."

She must be upset. Three adverbs and not a "totally" in sight.

My eyes strayed to the paperwork on the table. It was an invoice for the shipment she was unpacking, and the letterhead said Ace Trucking Company. I pointed to it.

"Did Vongole change their delivery service?"

She pulled the invoice toward herself but made no effort to hide it. "No, Ace delivers my samples. Simulated delivers the store's inventory." Her index finger had poked the invoice by the Ace Trucking Company logo, and she pushed it back and forth in a nervous gesture. "Only someone screwed up this time." She reached down to the box on the floor and pulled out a yellow patent leather clutch. It was the same one I'd drooled over when Mallory and I were standing in the showroom only days ago. "Here, take it."

"No, thanks," I said.

"Seriously. The factory screwed up, and these clutches accidentally came in with my samples. I'm just going to end up selling them in a sample sale. I might be selling it all." She waved her hand around the showroom. "After Kyle and Emily and their association with Vongole, both stores are dropping the line to protect their reputations. I might as well cut ties too."

"How will that affect you?"

"I've been looking for a reason to cut back on my travel and try to have a real life. I can focus on my other vendors. Most of them are local." We both looked around her showroom at samples of striped cotton pajamas, sachets shaped like hearts trimmed in lace, and a collection of glass *objects d'art* shaped like hard candy. Vongole had been the shining star in her assortment.

I didn't know what else to say, so I hugged her and said good-bye. She insisted I take the yellow patent handbag, so I did. I could give it to Loncar as evidence. Then again, maybe I wouldn't.

I started the drive home and got caught behind a large delivery truck. Traffic was bad enough that I couldn't get past him. Through seventeen traffic lights, I stared at his "How am I driving?" sticker until he pulled off the road into the Briquette Burger parking lot. That's when I noticed it was a Simulated truck. I called Nick with little regard for the Ribbon/Milan time conversion.

He answered on the third ring. "'Lo?"

"I just followed a Simulated truck, and it's pulling into Briquette Burger. That's the trucking company that delivers the Vongole handbags. Don't you think that's weird?"

"S'mntha?"

"Hi, Nick. Sorry if I woke you, but I didn't know who else to call."

"Are you in trouble?" His words were becoming clearer as the suspicion of imminent danger to me hung somewhere over the Atlantic Ocean.

"A Simulated truck pulled into Briquette Burger. Why would he do that?"

He yawned. "Maybe he's hungry. Is that really why you called me?"

The way he phrased that question led me to believe that wasn't a very good reason for calling. "No, I just wanted to hear your voice."

"That's sweet." His breathing turned even.

"Nick?"

"Mnh."

"Go back to sleep."

I parked in the ten-minute takeout space next to the restaurant.

The Simulated driver jumped down from the cab, went around back, and opened the doors. I couldn't see inside, but in a matter of minutes he'd removed three cardboard cartons and stacked them on a dolly. He pushed it to a door in the back of the restaurant. Minutes later he returned and repeated the routine.

Before he had a chance to push the second dolly load to the back door, I approached. "Can I talk to you a second?"

"Sure, little lady, whaddya want?" He uprighted the handcart and leaned against it.

"What are you delivering to this restaurant?"

He looked nervous.

"I mean, is this a regular stop for you?"

"Yeah. Restaurant supply stuff, for what it's worth."

"How long have you been delivering to Briquette Burger?"

"Couple of weeks now."

"Did you deliver some mushrooms here recently?"

"Why does everybody want to know about them mushrooms?" He pulled the mesh John Deere hat that had probably been standard issue when he got his trucker's license off his head, scratched his bald spot, and pulled the hat back over it. "We don't normally deliver produce, but when it came time to unload the delivery for this address, the crates were there."

"Doesn't Simulated deliver to Heist? The new department store?"

"Yeah, the owner's got us running all over town these days. Guess we're makin' him some money somehow."

"Who's your owner?"

"Local big shot. Tony Simms. Hey—you okay?"

The last question, I was most certain, had to do with the sudden bout of vertigo I felt at the mention of Tony's name.

"Yes, I'm fine. Thank you for your time."

I raced to the car where I'd left my cell phone in the cup holder. First call, Detective Loncar.

"Ms. Kidd, what do you want now?" He didn't seem happy to hear from me.

"Did you know Tony Simms owns Simulated Trucking?"

"Yes, Ms. Kidd. Tony Simms owns half of Ribbon."

"And that doesn't concern you?"

"That we have an entrepreneur in our midst? No, that doesn't concern me. Especially when he risked his life to come forward and pinpoint the murderer in a recent homicide investigation. Is that it?"

"Yes." I was about to hang up when I remembered the mushrooms. "Wait! Simulated was the trucking company that delivered the mushrooms too."

"Ms. Kidd." I could hear the lecture in his voice. "The Ribbon Police Department appreciates your interest in helping us. I would never want to say anything to deter you from working with us again in the future, but I think we got about all we need this time. Thank you for doing your civic duty."

The worst thing about cell phones is that there is absolutely no satisfaction in punching the hang-up button.

I called Nick again.

"Mmmmmmmh."

"Nick, it's Samantha. This is important. Are you awake?"

Silence and then a grunt.

"Tony Simms owns Simulated Trucking. Don't you think that's weird?"

"Mmmmmh."

"Nick, I'm being serious. You're the only person who knows about what's been going on, and if we're going to do this relationship thing, then we need to be able to talk to each other. I need someone to talk to. Okay?"

He yawned audibly. "You want to know what I think? Maybe a homicide investigation isn't a good basis for a relationship. Good night, Kidd." He hung up before I had a chance to argue.

I threw my phone in my handbag and turned to my car. Dante stood next to it, arms crossed, flame tattoos in full display.

"Did I hear you're looking for someone to talk to?"

27

FAKE-BUSTING

DANTE FOLLOWED ME BACK TO MY HOUSE AND PARKED HIS MOTORCYCLE in the driveway behind my car. Neither of us said a word until we were inside the living room. I shared the gray flannel sofa with Logan. Dante took one of the black and white chairs.

"Here's what's really been going on," I said. "Tony Simms owns Heist, and when he offered me the job, he said, 'Heist cannot fail.' And, aside from the way he produced ID with my name and picture on it, I remember his eyes boring through me when he said that. Now, he's an intense man, I know that." I held up a palm to stop Dante from interrupting me. "And he's a successful man. But don't you think it's weird that he's connected to everything that's going south? Heist, Vongole, Simulated Trucking, the mushrooms that poisoned Cat and Logan?"

Dante leaned forward. "Keep going."

"Simms had big plans for Heist, which is why he wooed a very successful general manager away from Tradava to run it. Think about it: he owns the store, and he owns the fleet of trucks that deliver to the store. If Heist had been successful in its initial opening, they would have put a big dent in Tradava's business."

"And with their prices, they could have continued with the momentum long after opening too."

"Right. Their entire success was staked on their pricing structure." I pulled the two Vongole reports out of a folder. "Kyle Trent gave me these."

Dante leaned back and held his hands in front of him. "I'm not a spreadsheet guy."

I laid them on the table facing him just in case the red numbers made him curious. "The basic components of a product's profitability are the same from any retailer. This is Tradava's recap of the Vongole business. They're showing close to a hundred-and-seventy-five-thousand-dollar loss in one season, while Heist was projecting a two-hundred-thousand-dollar margin surplus off discounted prices. It doesn't make sense."

"Could Tradava be mismanaging their business?"

"Vongole sold the same amount of merchandise to both Heist and Tradava, but Heist got a forty percent discount off of the cost of the merchandise. They only passed thirty percent of that on to the customers, so they made more money on every bag that was sold than Tradava did. What I can't figure out is why Tradava can't move their inventory at fifty percent off." I leaned back against the flannel sofa. Logan climbed onto the afghan and sat behind my head. He flicked his tail, and it swatted my ear.

"When I went to Tradava the other day, there was this giant table filled with marked-down bags. Something about that pile of markdowns was off. The bags looked cheap."

"Maybe it's the merchandising?" Dante asked.

I shook my head.

"You have another theory?"

"I think the sample bags are high quality, and the bags at Tradava aren't. That's why Kyle wanted to cancel the Vongole orders. He told me the quality suffered when their business exploded."

"What about Heist?"

"The assistant buyer said something interesting. Four months ago, Vongole didn't have enough merchandise to fill their orders. Now the store is overflowing with merchandise."

I sat back, waiting to see if Dante was going to connect the dots in the same manner that I had earlier, or if I'd been reasoning a murder investigation on a sleep-deprived mind and a handbag-hoarding mentality. "I think the quality suffered because the bags are being mass produced with poor-quality leathers."

"You think the bags at Heist are knockoffs."

I nodded. "I found out today that Ace Trucking Company delivers the samples to the showroom, but Simulated delivers the inventory to the store. At least to Heist."

"So there's a different trucking company that carries inventory, which could mean the stock production comes from somewhere other than the sample production." Dante followed along.

"And look at this." I pulled my yellow patent leather clutch out from inside a dingy white pillowcase where I'd kept it wrapped since coming home.

The front door opened, and Eddie and Cat walked in. I had an idea. "Cat, what do you think of my new handbag?" I held the yellow patent leather clutch out to her.

She turned it over in her hands, opened up the magnetic closure, checked the lining, sniffed inside it, and snapped it shut.

"I hope you didn't pay too much for this," she said. "It's a fake. A good one, but still."

"Is that your opinion?" Dante asked.

"It's a fact." She handed the bag back to me. "I'm surprised you couldn't tell."

"I could," I said.

Dante crossed his arms over his chest, and Eddie leaned forward.

"How can you be so sure?" Eddie asked.

Cat leaned on the arm of the chair Dante sat in, swinging her left foot back and forth. The heel of her bottle-green bootie bounced off the worn fabric on the side.

I looked at her, not sure which of us would answer.

"Take it away, Sam," she said.

I opened the bag. "Look, the lining is pink. Vongole makes it a point to only line their bags with the literal opposite color on the color wheel. A yellow bag would be lined in purple. A red bag would be lined in green. A blue bag would be lined in orange."

"What about a pink bag?" Dante asked.

"Any bag that isn't a primary or secondary color is lined in powder-blue suede," I said, thinking of the black and white bag I saw at Tradava.

"You're hanging your entire assessment on the color of their lining?" Eddie asked. Dante stood up and went into the kitchen. I stared at his back and considered a comment about his lack of enthusiasm for my fake-busting skills.

"I'm not done. See, the label is metal. Vongole's labels are all silver, and they're sterling silver at that. If you look closely, you can always see the '925' stamp on real silver, and it's not here. And the pull-tab along the zipper closure is too short. It's supposed to be six inches long."

"How do you know that's not six inches? Looks close."

I turned the Halston book upside down and pulled a flattened hundred-dollar bill from the back. I held it next to the pull-tab. The tab ended right around the first zero on the crisp green bill. "US currency is six inches long."

"What's this all about, Sam?" Cat asked.

"The cops arrested the wrong guy," I said.

Eddie was still staring at the book on Halston (or more likely at the bulge where the stack of hundreds were inside the book on Halston). He folded his hands across the Union Jack on the front of his T-shirt. "It sounds good enough to us, but I think you're going to need more to make the detective take you seriously. Like proof from the factory."

"Nick checked into the two factories that claim to produce Vongole."

"Vongole doesn't have two factories. Their bags are produced at Luta," Cat said.

"That's what I was told when I started. Basics from Luta and fashion from Lussuria. But when Nick heard his factory couldn't produce his samples, he checked out these two." I waited a couple of seconds for effect. "Lussuria doesn't even exist."

"So Nick's been helping you all along?" Eddie asked with surprise. "What does he think about your current theory?"

I thought about Nick's reluctance to keep talking about the homicides. "He thinks it's time I left it to the cops." I looked from face to face, trying to decipher their thoughts.

Dante returned from the kitchen with a steaming mug of coffee. "Does this guy even know you?"

EDDIE AND CAT LEFT, but Dante stayed behind. I dug through the newspapers and mail piling up on my kitchen table and found Tony Simms's business card. Office, home, and cell numbers were listed below his name. I went with cell, hoping it was the easiest way to catch him.

"Tony Simms," he answered.

"Mr., um, Tony, this is Samantha Kidd."

"Samantha Kidd. I got two minutes."

"I, um..." This was no way to sound believable to a businessman. I took a deep breath and cleared my throat and matched his cadence. "I don't think I can make the college dedication."

"Impossible! I need you there. We've already covered this. Liaison to the store, goodwill. I thought I made myself clear."

I thought about the money in the Halston book. "You did."

"Good. The dedication is at eight. Meet me there at seven."

"But—"

"Time's up. See you at the college." He disconnected, leaving me with more questions than I'd started with and fewer opportunities for escape.

"What was that about?" Dante asked.

"The college is dedicating a lecture hall to Tony Simms next week. He asked me to go to represent the store, or act as a liaison to the store, or something like that. I tried to cancel, but he won't listen."

"Tell me again what he said when he offered you a job."

"That he valued my unique skill set."

"So that's it." He leaned back against the sofa, knees apart and wrists resting on his lap. "You're the one link between all these people. He didn't hire you to investigate from the inside. He needed a shortcut. He asked you to keep an eye on everybody else, but he's the one keeping an eye on you."

28

___

TALK, SCHMALK

Dante left with the others, and I suddenly felt very much alone. If I was right, and the killer was still out there, I was going to have to figure out a way to prove that and figure out a way to keep myself in one piece too. That was a tall order for someone in my size seven shoes. I didn't want to be a part of this anymore. It wasn't fun, it wasn't fulfilling, and it might get me dead.

In short, I wanted out.

I needed another person close to the situation, another ace. Nick wasn't due to come home for another two weeks, and based on our most recent conversation, I probably shouldn't count on his willingness to discuss it. Then I remembered the way Andi had looked at Kyle on her cell phone picture. There was no way she believed him to be guilty, and if I wasn't mistaken, that look spoke volumes of her feelings, even if she'd chosen not to speak of those feelings out loud. I had a good sense that I knew where to find her too.

I parked in the lot outside the bar. Her shiny black Miata was parked by the front door. When I entered, I scanned the interior. There she was, perched on a spinning barstool, dangling a maraschino cherry and cleavage in front of the twenty-something mixologist. Maybe I'd been wrong. She didn't look like the kind of woman pining away over another woman's man.

"What'll it be?" the bartender asked. Andi spun on her chair and recognition hit.

"Girlfriend!" she shouted, and hopped—or should I say slipped, because she didn't seem to have control of her faculties enough to hop—off the barstool. She threw her arms around me.

I hugged her back, knowing I had to play into our BFF routine again. "I'll have what she's having," I said.

"RockStar and pomegranate vodka martini?" the bartender said.

"You go, girl!" she proclaimed, struggling to right herself on the stool.

The bartender set a frothy pink drink in front of me, and Andi clinked my glass. "You are so smart. Hey, Steve, this is Samantha, and she's, like, the smartest buyer in all of Ribbon. No! In all of Pennsylvania. No, wait! In the whole tri-state area!"

Not that I didn't enjoy the compliments, but I was starting to wonder if I really had it in me to pull Andi out of this moment of escapism and drag her back to reality and her unspoken love for a man suspected of killing the last two women he'd been involved with.

"Um, Andi, have you read the news today?"

"Screw the news. Have a drinkie!" She picked up her glass, shook the ice cubes around, and drained what was left. I caught Steve's expression. He was watching her with interest too. Only our interests were obviously of different natures.

I nursed my drink while she started on another that had appeared before her without even ordering. Steve leaned in front of her. "That one's on the house."

"Ohh, honey, you know the way to my..." She dragged her finger over her lower lip and let the tip draw a line down her neckline. This was going nowhere fast. There was no way I was going to have a real, meaningful conversation with her tonight.

"Andi, when's a good time to talk?"

"Talk, shmalk. Let's party!"

"Seriously. I mean, I need to have a serious talk with you."

"Screw serious! I just wanna have fun tonight! No worries! You with me?" she asked Steve the bartender.

He picked up an ice cube and tossed it down her cleavage.

"Oooohh! You nasty boy. Now who's going to help me fish that out of there?"

I couldn't take any more of this. I unfolded a Bud Light napkin and pulled a pen from my handbag. I jotted my cell phone number down after my name and folded it carefully. When she wasn't looking, I tucked it into her handbag. She was too preoccupied to notice.

I opened my fake Vongole clutch and pulled out my keys. When I looked up, I spotted a woman with a jet black bob sitting in the corner booth. It was my assistant buyer, Mallory George. She buried her head in a large menu, but I wasn't fooled. She'd been watching me from the second I'd walked in.

THE SUN WAS HALFWAY visible above the horizon as I drove home. Was it possible that I was making too much of a situation that was already resolved? No. Definitely not. Two people were dead, and something was still not right. And just when I thought I was out on my own, I was pulled back in for the dedication at I-FAD. Heist was like the retail mafia. And even the envelope of money I'd moved from the Halston biography to between my mattress and box spring did nothing to comfort me.

The lights were on at Nora's house. I parked in my driveway and crossed the lawn, pushing a couple of crabapples out of my path. "I've been expecting you," she said, holding the door open.

She wore a Mercersburg sweatshirt pulled over a turtleneck and jeans. Blucher moccasins, standard issue at most prep schools, adorned her feet, and a stained white cotton apron dangled loosely over her clothes. She was the best candidate I'd ever seen for a makeover, but if given the chance, I wouldn't change a thing. Some people just know who they are.

"I saw you through the window. I was hoping you were heading my way. Care to test out a new recipe?"

"Sure." I followed her to the kitchen. Her house was laid out much like my own if you held the floor plan up to a mirror. She used an ice cream scoop to measure out a perfectly round dollop of rice into a bowl and scooped something vaguely orange over it. "Thai curry. It might be a little spicy. Want some bean sprouts?"

She handed me a fork and set a bowl of sprouts on the counter. I scooted up onto one of her bar stools and dug a forkful into my mouth. Exotic flavors of basil and coconut hit me a split second before the heat.

"Water?" I choked out.

"Milk will be better. Is it hot? I wasn't sure. I may have added too much liquid pepper. You're okay with mushrooms, right?" She filled a glass with milk from the refrigerator and handed it to me. I drained it and toyed my fork around in the rice for a while, not sure if I wanted any more.

"Nora, with everything that's been happening around town, do you think it's good timing for the dedication at I-FAD? Don't you think it should be postponed?"

"Tony was on the fence, but I convinced him to go for it."

"He was going to cancel?"

"He was concerned for everybody's safety. I think it's wise that he arranged extra security."

"Detective Loncar?"

"The detective on the Hart case? No. Well, I didn't ask for him specifically. The college is hiring extra security officers to work for the night, Heist security guards will be there, and we'll have a large presence of campus police. Between that contest and the matters at Heist, there's bound to be some kind of activism. I admire that the students want something to protest, because it's good to stand up for things, but in the event their activities get out of hand, someone's got to be there to keep things under control."

"You think the students are going to riot against Tony Simms?"

She laughed. "I've gotten beyond the age when I can predict what the students are going to do. What I do know is that several of the students participated in the promotional activities of the Heist contest and were not happy when there was no winner announced. You know, Simms owned each of the landmarks mentioned in the contest, and in each case there was really no chance for anyone to actually win."

"My team won. We swapped the Puccetti statue for a fake."

A knowing smile crept onto Nora's face. "Wait here," she said. I sampled another scoop of curry after she scaled the stairs and refilled my glass with water to wash it down. The water ignited the heat in my mouth, and I ran to her fridge for milk.

When I turned back around, she was coming down the stairs holding a locked metal strongbox. She set it on the counter and pulled on a pair of white gloves, the kind a magician wears while waving his hands as distraction before the *voila!* moment. She spun the dial on the padlock until it opened and pulled out a bundle wrapped in white sheets. She unwound the fabric and exposed a wooden statue that bore a striking resemblance to the one I'd swiped from the college only a week before. I swallowed a mouthful of milk in one gulp and pounded on my chest until the pain went away. She pulled the statue away from me to prevent me from tainting it with DNA evidence.

"This is the real Puccetti." She kept one hand on the base of the man while the other gently patted him on the head.

"You've had this one the whole time?"

"Yes." She kept a finger on the head of the statue and spun him around to face her. "It's been killing me not to tell you."

"But Tony Simms told me we'd won the contest. In fact, the team at Heist said one team succeeded in pulling off the stunt, and Simms said he would see to it that my team was paid the prize money. Why would he say that if we didn't actually steal the original like the contest wanted?"

Nora's eyes flicked from my face to my bowl of curry, now virtually untouched. "Come into the living room with me. I can finally tell you the backstory."

29

THE REAL MCCOY

“Heist wanted a massive publicity event,” Nora said. “One that would have a viral word-of-mouth feel that would energize shoppers. The idea was to be so different from what this town has seen that it would instantly feel cool.”

“How do you know all this?”

“Once Simms heard the concept from the PR manager, he wanted to go full force with the idea. Originally it was a much smaller scale, like a scavenger hunt, but Simms knew he had the unique option of using his own holdings around Ribbon as the bait, and that would accomplish two things. He’d instantly connect Heist with landmarks from Ribbon, and he’d get the kind of publicity he wanted.”

“So Tony owned all of the prizes,” I said mostly to myself.

“The Puccetti has been in his family for generations. His father donated it to the Philadelphia Museum of Art decades ago. It’s been at I-FAD for about five years now. There was a nice amount of publicity that went into the exhibit, and he wanted to leverage that publicity by naming the statue as one of the objects for the contest.”

“I get it. He fooled the public by using a fake at the museum, so the real one was never at risk.”

"That's when I came in. The college appointed me keeper of the real statue. No one was ever going to know."

"Nora, that statue has to be worth millions. You kept it in your house?"

"Of course not! It's been in my safety deposit box. Just yesterday Tony asked me to make sure it was back in place for the dedication. I picked it up today and am delivering it to the school tomorrow morning."

"Who else knew the statue had been replaced with a fake?"

"Simms, the PR manager of Heist, the dean of the college, and me. We didn't tell campus police because we wanted them to take the protection of the statue seriously. When you stole it, they came to my house to deliver the news."

"We saw them that night. We were celebrating. At least we were until we heard the sirens. We thought they were coming for us."

"They weren't happy when they heard they'd been duped."

I peered closely at the little wooden man on her counter. "So that's the real McQueen."

"Don't you mean McCoy?"

"We called him—never mind."

"For what it's worth, yours spooked a lot of people. You must know some talented people to have come up with a knockoff that good on such short notice."

I did. I thought back to Dante, showing up at my meeting with a folder of surveillance photos of the statue, and Eddie, who'd taken those photos and made the fake. I remembered our assignments: Cat as executive professor, Dante as security guard, me as undercover student. Undercover grad student.

"You can't repeat any of this, you know," she said. "I shouldn't have told you at all, but I've wanted to tell you the truth since you showed up at the Pilferer's Ball with our fake."

My mind was abuzz. In addition to the people I'd been watching at Heist, Nora's information now made me think I-FAD could be involved. She'd been at the party, so who else? The killer, who had bashed Emily Hart's head with Eddie's copy of the Puccetti statue, would most likely be at the dedication. And while the press had reported about the murders, news of the statue as weapon had been kept quiet. The only people who knew were those in the inner circle: my friends, colleagues, and the killer. Whether or not the killer knew the statue would be at the dedication was one thing, but if he—or she—knew what I now knew, he—or she—would expect the real statue to be in place.

I was short on both time and ideas, but in the brief moments, when I ignored the fear of trying to trap a killer who had escaped the police, one fact remained consistent. The killer had used the fake statue to murder Emily Hart, and I could trick him—or her—into thinking I had evidence to prove that. I excused myself from Nora's house and all but ran home and called Eddie.

"Can you make another fake Puccetti statue?" I asked.

"Consider it done."

"How long will it take?"

"Seriously, consider it done."

"I know it's no big thing, but I need to know the timetable."

"I made an extra when I made the first one."

"I know you—what?"

"I needed a prototype, and I thought it might be a cool little item to remember our adventure. Meet me at Arner's tomorrow morning. Seven thirty."

"Okay…" Rarely did my plans go so smoothly.

THE NEXT MORNING I dressed in a sequined tank top, a pair of navy chiffon harem pants, and a cropped white denim jacket with frayed edges. I buckled on blue T-strap sandals on a two-inch heel, grabbed the yellow handbag, and headed for the local family-owned diner. Eddie was already in a booth when I arrived, even though I was seven minutes early.

"You're up to something," Eddie said while munching on a piece of dry wheat toast.

"What makes you think that?"

"There's no way you'd agree to a seven thirty meeting if you didn't really need this. And by the way, MC Hammer called. He wants his pants back."

"One more crack about my clothes, and I'm taking scissors to your Frankie T-shirts when you're not looking." I poured a cup of coffee from the pot on the table and waved at the waitress, pantomiming my order of bacon and scrambled eggs. "Speaking of weird accessories, what's with the bowling bag?"

"I couldn't exactly walk in here with a wooden statue that looks a lot like a piece of art that was recently used in a homicide, could I?"

"Yeah, but a bowling bag? At seven thirty in the morning?"

"I've seen the handbags at Tradava. Bowling bag, doctor's bag, knitting bag. That's what they all are. Someone else's bag. Pretend it's Chanel and call it a day."

"Chanel never made a bowling bag. Vuitton did. Chloe, too. But not Chanel."

"Whatevs." He washed the dry toast down with coffee. "What's with all the questions? According to you, you just wanted a keepsake."

I'd slept on Nora's information and on my theories and kept returning to the statue. I shrugged. "It was nice knowing we pulled it off."

"I had my doubts, but your plan worked. Is that what you did at Bentley's before you moved here?"

"I told you what I did. I was a buyer. There's a lot more to it than picking out pretty shoes. There's plans, projections, strategies for three months, six months, one year, three years. Then there's the constant what-to-do-when-things-don't-sell pressure. You don't get to make one strategy and call it a day. Sometimes trends don't hit, and you're stuck with merchandise. That's when you have to figure out a new way to drive your business and liquidate your inventory."

"Trends. That's what you were supposed to be doing at Tradava. Trend specialist."

"Yes."

I could almost feel the heat from the light bulb over Eddie's head. He had now seen my natural planning and problem-solving abilities firsthand. "What's next for you?" he asked.

I felt the conversation shift. I knew he was taking about my work history and lack of job leads, so regardless of my suspicions that I wasn't ready for what was next because I was still dealing with what was now, I answered the question on the table.

"I don't know. Temporarily I'm at a standstill."

I thought again about the money Tony had given me. It made me uncomfortable. In the past twenty-four hours I'd moved it from the Halston book to my mattress to the never-used salad crisper. If I deposited it in the bank, I could pay my bills for a few months and figure out my next step. Only, depositing it indicated I was keeping it, and as much as Tony Simms claimed I'd earned it, I still wasn't sure what he was paying me for. A few days on the job or my silence?

"I'll do the thing at the college for Heist, and then I'm officially unemployed again," I finally said. "Maybe I'll call Andi, see if she has any contacts." I checked my watch. "Better give her a couple of hours to sleep off that hangover, though."

Eddie looked suspicious. "You really think a party girl is going to have a job lead for you?"

"It seemed pretty clear to me she was looking for an escape last night. So maybe she knows how I feel."

"I hope for your sake she does."

"For what it's worth, she told everyone in the bar that I was the smartest buyer in the entire tri-state area. Too bad I didn't have a tape recorder with me."

"You are smart, dude. That's why we listen to you."

"Since when do you listen to me?"

"The gala? Swiping the statue? Your genius plan?" I stared at him, stunned by his frank compliment. "Seriously, you're way too hard on yourself. Just because you can't keep a job around here doesn't mean people aren't in awe of what you've accomplished. Even yesterday I overheard a couple of the Tradava executives talking about"—he made air quotations with his fingers—" 'that trend specialist we used to have. The one with the great personal style.' And you know as well as I do that fashion people can be a little judgmental."

I perked up. "People from Tradava said that? What else did they say?"

"Let's just leave it at that, shall we?"

"What else did they say, Eddie?"

He averted his eyes, cleared his throat, and mumbled. "They said too bad corpses followed you wherever you went."

"They didn't."

"Those weren't the words they used, but they kinda did."

"What about Belle DuChamp? She was killed at Tradava, and I was nowhere near the store. I was out having drinks with Andi."

"No one really understands that one."

"What do you mean, no one?"

"Just saying, you've made yourself quite a reputation around these parts."

"Sometimes I wonder why I hang around you."

"Because I don't buy into the gossip? Because I like you for who you are? Because I'm willing to stare death in the face and hang out with you, knowing that just being in the same room with you might increase my chances of impending doom?"

I reached out and whapped his arm.

He rubbed his bicep with the other hand and smiled. "The same goes for Cat, you know. When this whole thing started, she was in it for the shopping spree. Now that she's seen what you're capable of, she's impressed. She put her life at risk by associating with you. Probably Nick too. He must be proud on some level."

"Nick would rather not talk about Heist anymore." I thought about that last conversation we'd had.

"It's probably not going to get any easier," Eddie said.

"What?"

"The long-distance thing."

"Nick's coming back in a couple of weeks."

"Dude, he's a shoe designer. He's going to spend half the year in Italy. I know you know that. I just don't know if you *know* that." Eddie tipped his head and scratched the short blond hair that had grown in on the side of his Mohawk. "There is one person you could talk to."

"You mean Dante?" I leaned back into the red vinyl booth and stared up at the ceiling, trying to figure out what to say. "He's different from Nick, that's for sure. It's almost like he encourages me to get involved."

Eddie leaned forward and propped his elbows on the table. "Can I ask you a personal question?"

"Shoot."

"You moved here to start over, to leave your old life behind, right?"

"Yes, but that didn't exactly work out—"

Eddie cut me off with a raised hand. "Nick's somebody from that life. That former life."

"You're from my former life."

"That's different. We know each other from high school. That's like the you you were before you became the you you are."

"Sure, that's clear."

"What I mean is, we got to know each other when we were still figuring out who we were. You took a side street after that—the one that landed you in New York. That's where you met Nick. He doesn't know the person I knew at Ribbon High School, the person who risked her own reputation to save me from a cheating scandal that would have impacted my future."

I pushed the fruit around on my plate for a couple of seconds while the memory came back to me. Eddie as the new kid in high school. The football player who copied off his test. The accusation that Eddie had been the one to cheat. And me, in the principal's office the next day, admitting in confidence that I'd seen the whole thing. Eddie's scholarship to art school was safe after that, and until I read what he wrote in my yearbook, I didn't know he knew what I'd done for him.

"I think Nick sees that part of me too."

"Sure, but he met the professional out to prove something to the world. Who you are today, the Samantha who moved back to Ribbon to start over, came second to him, not first. Dante's like a breath of fresh air—"

"—that smells like cinnamon—" I interjected.

"You know what I mean. You're here in Ribbon, and in your first six months you did something nobody believed you could do. Maybe you should run with that."

"But Nick—I can't explain how I feel about Nick. Since the first time I met him, there was something there. A spark. And for all that time I worked at Bentley's, we never acted on it. Now we can." I speared a slice of pineapple from Eddie's plate and took a bite.

"What I don't get is Nick's behavior." He popped the last piece of crust into his mouth and washed it down with coffee. "He knew you were involved. He wouldn't tell you to leave things to the cops unless he knew the cops were already involved something. Why back away now? And why not want to talk about it? I think you're just trying to bait me again. Unless Dante's right about Nick not knowing you at all."

He got a second slap for that.

"Samantha? This is Andi Holloway. "I just found your note in my handbag. I'm concerned. Call me."

I ran to the phone on my counter. "Hello, I'm here," I answered breathlessly. "You got my note?"

"Yes. I'm not sure what it means."

"I wanted to talk to you last night, but you had a couple of distractions." I trailed off, not sure the best approach was to tell her that I'd watched her get sloshed, or ask how it felt to wake up next to a different bartender seven nights a week. Actually, I kinda did want to know about that last one.

"Oh, those boys, we just like to have fun. It was nothing. So, what did you want to talk about?"

"Kyle Trent." There was silence on the other end of the phone. "Andi? Are you still there?"

"What do you know about Kyle?"

"I don't think he killed Belle DuChamp."

"Who do you think killed her?" she asked.

I took a deep breath and then exhaled. "Tony Simms."

"Give me your address. I want to hear your plan to get that bastard." This time there was no mistaking the click on the other end of the phone.

30

——————

CONFLICT OF INTEREST

By the time Andi arrived, I'd fleshed out my thoughts on the take-out menus. I held them in my hand like a fan, ready to make my case for her. My denim jacket hung from the back of a dining room chair. Three sequins had fallen from my tank top and landed on the table next to a dusting of pretzel salt.

"Are you ordering food? I already ate," she said, glancing at the menus.

"These are my notes." Andi pulled a chair away from the table and sat. I'd been sitting for too long and instead paced back and forth on the other side of the table. "You told me Simulated Trucking delivers Vongole handbags to Heist. Right?"

"Right."

"That's the key." I looked down at what I'd written on the menu from B&S Sandwich Shop. "Tony Simms owns Simulated Trucking."

"Tony Simms owns a lot of things," she said.

"Why is everyone so willing to accept that? It's a conflict of interest. Tony owns Simulated, and Tony owns Heist. Simulated delivers the handbags to Heist."

"I never thought much about it."

"There's more." I flipped the menu over. "Heist has a growth strategy in place for Vongole, but didn't Tradava cancel orders because they felt the bags weren't up to the appropriate quality standards?"

Andi sat up straighter. "How do you know that?"

"Kyle told me. He thought it was suspicious."

"He was right to be suspicious." She sat back in her chair, plucked a small pretzel out of the bowl I'd set in the middle of the table, and tapped the pretzel on the placemat. "Last season, Kyle brought it to my attention. I contacted the factory in Italy. They said the leathers came from a new source, and they weren't using them anymore."

"Did they offer to take the bags back from Tradava?"

"Better. They offered to pay all markdowns if Tradava liquidated them."

I thought about the pile of Vongole handbags on the Tradava selling floor. The pile-it-high, let-it-fly merchandising certainly didn't improve the appearance of the bags, but if Vongole was paying markdowns, Tradava probably encouraged the bargain-basement mentality.

Andi leaned forward. "What else do you have?"

I tossed the sandwich menu onto the table and flipped open the Chinese menu. "Emily was trying to exit the Vongole business. She must have known something was up."

"But that doesn't make sense. Belle bought out my inventory."

"I know, right? I thought that was weird too. That's when I realized Belle had some additional interest in the Vongole business." I held the menus in my right hand and flapped them against the fingertips on my left. "But before we get to how Belle ties in, let's follow this." I squinted to read my writing over the fried rice options. "Kyle and Emily were engaged. No doubt, their loyalties were to each other and not to their respective stores."

"Which would have pissed off their respective stores," Andi interjected.

"I think that's when Belle started the rumor about Kyle, to get between them—"

"—So Emily would stop listening to him—"

"—and get back onboard the Vongole gravy train."

Andi's eyes lit up. We were finishing each other's sentences. She wasn't pointing out any flaws with my logic. She saw what I saw.

"Tony ultimately pockets the profits from Heist," I added.

She crushed the pretzel in her fist. "Between Tradava's cancellations and Heist dropping the line, Vongole wouldn't be able to recover. We have a lot tied up in those two accounts."

"How would it affect your showroom?" I asked.

"I'd be fine, if that's what you're wondering. Vongole is my biggest account, but I rep other lines. I could pick up another handbag line and use my contacts to fill the void. I never did because I'd have a conflict of interest between two different vendors." She brushed her palms together, sprinkling pretzel crumbs like pixie dust over her placemat. "How did you put all of this together?" she asked.

"It started with the contest."

Her brows pulled together, and three small wrinkles appeared between them. "What contest?"

"Heist had a contest." I told Andi about the ad in the paper, the Puccetti statue, and how it had tied us to the murder of Emily Hart. "If Eddie hadn't knocked off the statue, I wouldn't be sitting here talking to you right now. The publicity contest is the key."

"How so?"

"Tony Simms owns the statue. He's the only one who would have had access to the knockoff we left the night we stole it. That statue was what he used to kill Emily. Tony probably knew the statue was a fake and our fingerprints would be all over it."

The three wrinkles between her eyebrows marked her thought processes, and her eyes stared into mine in a manner at odds with the vacant party girl from the night before. She was thinking about what I had said. She was gauging if she should confide in me. My plan needed her, and she needed a push.

"Andi, I saw how you looked at Kyle in that picture on your phone. I think he means a lot to you, more than just a buyer/designer relationship. And I know how that feels. The guy I'm—Nick Taylor—he was one of my vendors when I was a buyer at Bentley's. We had to be professional because of our jobs. But that didn't last forever, and now there's no conflict of interest, and even though he's in Italy and I'm here, we're trying. Just like you and Kyle could try if he was clear of this mess and had a chance to move on. You can help him get that chance, if you want, but he's never going to move on if he's suspected of something he didn't do."

She sat back against the wooden chair. I surprised myself with the personal information I'd shared, and part of me wanted to take it all back. But it was true. And if it helped convince her to clear an innocent man and trap a guilty one, it was worth it.

"Here's what I think has been going on with the handbags." I sank into the chair opposite her. "The showroom has the real samples, produced in Italy by quality factories. After the orders are written, a different factory produces the bags with imitation skins and cheap hardware. Somebody in that equation is pocketing the difference."

"You think Kyle knew. Tony framed him to keep him from talking."

I nodded. "I think Belle knew too."

She lobbed questions at me, questions I answered deftly, having recently spent a week reasoning out these very same conundrums from a cocoon of down comforting and stuffed animals. By the time the sun went down and the air grew chilly, we were on the same page.

Unfortunately, that page indicated one very scary thing. I was about to meet the killer at the dedication at I-FAD, and with the exception of a handbag rep with a happy-hour habit, nobody believed me.

"The thing is, Tony Simms didn't get to be Tony Simms by accident," I said. "He's a smart guy. We have to make him think we know everything. We have to get him so worried that he's about to be caught that he trips up. We probably aren't going to have any backup from the cops either, considering they have Kyle in custody."

"Let's hear your plan," she said.

I studied her face and took a deep, steadying breath. "He murdered Emily with the statue, right? So we make him think the cops have the wrong statue, meaning that we pulled another switch and the one we have has his fingerprints and her, um, blood."

"That's going to take some doing."

"True, but it can be done."

"And you? How are you going to protect yourself?"

"I'm going to call in a favor from a friend." I made my apologies—some prior commitment I pretended I'd missed—then triple-locked the front door and found my cell phone in the bottom of my handbag. I stared at the keypad for a solid twenty seconds before I called the only person who had the skills to help.

31

UP AT NIGHT

"I NEED YOU," I SAID WHEN DANTE ANSWERED.

There was a long pause on the other end of the phone. I stood very still, not sure if I was on the verge of a bad decision. Finally, he spoke.

"What time does your man call?"

I blushed even though he couldn't see me. "Nine. Ish."

"Ish?"

"Nine. Exactly at nine."

"I'll be there at nine twenty."

"See you then." I exhaled a long breath I didn't know I had been holding.

If I were a different kind of person, I should have been able to walk away from it all myself, but I'd gotten involved too far, and the only way I knew to make sure I came out of it alive was to get the person that I believed to be a killer behind bars. I had learned that, somewhere in me, under the fashionable exterior and the business savvy that had launched my career, that there was also a need to see justice done.

I couldn't explain it. I wished I could. Truth be told, since Kyle

Trent had been arrested, I couldn't sleep at night, I couldn't eat during the day, and I'd lost my desire to accessorize.

I couldn't live like this.

When the phone hadn't rung by nine thirteen, I called Nick.

"Hey," I said. "It's me."

"What's going on?" he asked. His voice was cool.

I knew he didn't want to talk about the homicide. But with the meeting at I-FAD in my immediate future, there wasn't much else I could think about. The best way to maintain a truthful conversation with Nick was to tell him everything. That I knew to be right. Only I wasn't ready to hear what he had to say, even though he'd been remarkably supportive until recently. I was on the verge of doing something really, really dumb—or genius, depending on how you looked at it—and I didn't want his reaction to sway me from my plan. I adopted what I knew to be a successful manner of communicating the truth, without sacrificing my privacy. I finished all of my sentences in my head.

"Just hanging out." I glanced at the wall clock and climbed on a dining room chair to mark the time Dante was going to arrive with a yellow Post-It note.

"Are you glad that whole mess is over?"

"I'm not exactly sure it's over," I said without thinking, distracted by the Post-It that had only partially stuck to my clock and now dangled by a corner.

"Kidd, why do you do this? Why can't you just let it go?"

"You sound like you're judging me."

"I just want to understand how your brain works."

"My brain works like it's always worked. I like to solve puzzles. I like to figure things out. I like resolution."

"Is it the fact that the cops figured it out without you that's keeping you up at night?"

"How do you know I'm up at night?"

"It's just an expression. You're up at night?"

"No, not really,"

"You just said you were."

"Okay, so I am."

"Kidd, what's going on?"

The doorbell rang. "Nick, I gotta go." I hung up without saying good-bye.

I opened the door for Dante. He pushed past me and strode into the kitchen. I followed Dante. He opened a few cabinets, pulled out the canister of coffee, and made a pot before facing me. "That Simms guy was right about one thing."

"What's that?"

"You possess a unique skill set."

"He was talking about my background as a buyer at Bentley's."

"Sit down, Samantha," he ordered. I noticed the brown nylon duffle bag that sat on one of my chairs. "I agree with him. You do possess a unique skill set." The pot of coffee was only half full, but Dante pulled it out and filled two mugs. He pushed the pot back into the machine and carried the mugs to the table.

He set one of the mugs in front of me and moved the duffle bag from the chair and sat down. The bag landed by his feet.

"You're not planning on staying over, are you?" I asked.

"We'll get to the bag in a second." He drank from his mug. "I'm going to tell you a couple of things tonight, and I don't want to hear that you repeated them. Got me?"

"I, um, I don't want to agree to anything until I know what I'm agreeing to," I stated in a sentence that started rather tentatively but ended with conviction.

"You still don't trust me, do you?"

"You're Cat's brother, so yes, technically, I trust you. Only I don't completely trust you for other reasons."

He raised an eyebrow.

"But we're not getting into those reasons tonight. In fact," I stated, gaining spitfire momentum, "I don't think we should be getting into anything tonight. In fact," I repeated, because it seemed as though my little speech was for me as much as it was for him, "I think after this cup of coffee you should be going. Because I have a very nice man in Italy, and just because he's not here is no reason I should entertain you in his absence."

"You called me."

"Maybe that was a mistake."

"Samantha, I'd be lying if I said I wasn't jealous of your very nice man in Italy, but that's not why I'm here."

"It's not?"

He reached down to the duffle bag and unzipped it. I tried to look inside but didn't recognize anything. He pulled out a square metal object with wires sticking out of the top.

"Did you take that thing from my car again?"

He set the contraption on the table. "This didn't come from your car."

"Whose car did it come from?"

"One at the junk yard."

"What are you saying?"

"There was nothing wrong with your car the morning I showed up here."

"You tricked me?"

"I knew you were up to something. So yes, technically I tricked you, so I could see where you were going and what you were up to. Once I followed you to Heist, I figured you'd either come out with files or paperwork that I could read, or the sugar cube would pick up something you did. And it did. You got very excited about a couple of papers."

"The spreadsheets I mailed to my cat."

"Why did you do that?"

"I knew they were important. Kyle was going to give the recap to Emily, but she was murdered. He gave it to me because he thought it was suspicious."

"Why'd you mail them?"

"Heist might not have liked it if they saw me taking recaps on their profit margin out of the building, especially considering what happened to Emily, but I was pretty sure Vongole was at the middle of the whole thing. I thought about putting the recaps in my shoe or my bra, but I was too scared they would fall out or somehow someone would find them."

"Who did you think was going to look in your bra?"

Considering Nick was in Italy, it was a good question. Considering I was talking to the only other person I found myself inappropriately flirting with, I chose not to answer.

"So your instincts told you to mail them to yourself—your cat."

"Yes, and I mailed two other envelopes at the same time so security wouldn't be suspicious when I waved a stack of hand-addressed envelopes in front of them. And I ran them out to the mailbox on the corner of the parking lot so they wouldn't be sitting around in the store. They were delivered a couple of days ago."

"Addressed to your cat."

"That's because I was afraid of addressing them to myself."

"I know a lot of women, and I know how a lot of women think. And I don't know a single other woman who would do what you did in that situation."

"What can I say? I'm special," I said, not entirely sure he'd intended what he said as a compliment.

"Remember I told you I sometimes get hired to take photos for investigations?"

"Yes."

"I learned stuff. How to get information, how to trip people up, how to hide things. I have a knack for it."

"I'm sure you do."

"You have a knack for it too, only the opposite. People think you're going to zig, you zag. You're unexpected." He studied me for a moment. "The problem is you have no idea what you're doing."

I set my coffee cup back on the table with a bang, letting the brown liquid splash out of the mug and onto the placemat. "I got this far, didn't I?" I asked.

"And some people might say it's a wonder, but I won't, because, like I said, I agree with Tony Simms. You possess a unique skill set."

"Dante, if there's something you're trying to say, just come out and say it already. It's getting late."

"For all I know, Kyle did kill those people."

"That's a load of crap, and you know it."

"Let me stay tonight and teach you a couple of things to help you."

"I—I'm kind of in a relationship," I said with less conviction than I should have.

"Assuming this Nick guy cares about you, I'm sure he'd appreciate knowing I'm going to arm you with knowledge that will protect you when you go off tilting at windmills."

He might have had a point. Whether or not it held water was a different issue.

"You think someone else is the killer. That's a big accusation." Dante sat forward and propped his elbows on his thighs. "Not that I don't follow you, but you're going to need a solid set of connectors to get anyone to buy it. Why don't you spell it out for me one more time?"

I let out a big sigh. I didn't want to be mocked or shot down anymore. "It's going to take a lot of time for me to go through what I know and try to convince you."

Logan entered the kitchen and nuzzled his head in the duffle bag. We watched him pull his head out and then step his front feet in and circle a few times. Less than a minute later he was curled up inside, purring.

"I hope your entire lesson plan isn't under my cat," I said.

"Drink your coffee. I'm going to check out a couple of things."

He left his mug on the table and walked upstairs. Logan raised his head and watched, stretched, stepped out of the bag, and followed him. I reached down to the bag and dug through it. But before I could determine what Dante brought, his tattooed arms reached down and grabbed the nylon webbed handles and hoisted the duffle away from me.

"Bring the coffee." He turned back toward the stairs and disappeared.

"Where are you going?" I asked with a little more than mild alarm. My bedroom was up there.

"My sister's not the only one around here who knows how to accessorize."

"Accessorize?" I called behind him.

"Yeah." He stood at the top of the stairs, staring down at me. "You're getting another makeover. This time on my terms."

32

***

MAKEOVER

I CLIMBED THE STAIRS AND WENT TO MY BEDROOM. DANTE WASN'T there. Not sure if this was his idea of a prank, I whipped the closet doors open, expecting to find him staring back at me. He wasn't. I dropped onto all fours and bent my head down, peering under the bed, butt in the air.

"Do you want to tell me what you're doing?" he asked from behind me. I pulled my head out and looked up at him propped against the doorframe, holding Logan and scratching his ears.

"This isn't a bedroom kind of thing. I'd prefer to do this in the room over here." He jerked his head back and to the right.

"What exactly do you prefer to do?" I asked, scooting to my feet and dusting a few cobwebs off my harem pants.

"Luck has brought you further than anyone expected."

"It's not luck. Everything I've done has been completely reasoned out."

"Like I said, not a single woman I know would jeopardize her job and send her cat confidential paperwork from her place of business."

"But it was—"

"Not a one."

"But–"

"You have some kind of talent for this stuff, but you also have a knack for finding trouble. I can't in good faith send you out there to the world at large thinking luck is going to protect you."

"What do you plan to do? Outfit me in Kevlar and wire me with a camera that looks like a tube of lipstick?"

Dante looked at my tank top for a second and then back at my face. "No, I kind of like the way you dress." He pulled a couple of things out of the duffle bag and placed them on the old wooden desk in the room. A Bay City Rollers poster hung on the wall, one of the few things left from when it was my older sister's room. My parents had never tossed the last of her high school belongings, and I had yet to figure out what I was going to do with the room, so I'd left it empty.

"What do you call this room?"

"My sister's old bedroom."

"You might want to start calling it your crime lab." He pulled a few items from the duffle. "I've been doing some digging. I'm not one hundred percent sure you're making this whole thing up."

"Really? You believe me?"

"Not entirely, but I'm not going to discount your suspicions, either."

This was it. This was the time to flat-out tell Dante what I thought. I was bolstered by the fact that I'd shared this very knowledge with Andi, and she hadn't balked.

"I think Tony Simms is the killer."

Once again, our eyes held for several seconds. Even Logan, who had followed us into the room, sat as still as a Puccetti, waiting for the inevitable reaction.

"So that's the real reason he wants you there. If he can keep tabs on you, you can't get to him."

I stared at Dante while he made his point. There was more, and I knew it, and I wanted to know if he would go far enough to say it out loud.

"But if he's keeping tabs on me, then I can keep tabs on him too."

"Simms' plan isn't just to watch you, sweetheart. If he's the killer and thinks you know something, he'll kill you too."

"What am I thinking?" I jumped up from my chair and spun around, not wanting to face the tough guy who was listening to me and leveling with me, because my inner tough girl had run screaming for the hills. "Why am I doing this? What is wrong with me?"

I started to leave the room, feeling hot tears on my cheeks, feeling desperation obliterate my confidence. I wanted to get out of there before Dante saw me break down. I tripped over his duffle bag and fell toward the door.

He caught me with both arms and spun me around. I buried my head into his T-shirt and took deep breaths. "Shhh. Breathe. Calm down," he said, one strong arm holding me and the other stroking the back of my head. I was shaking.

"All I wanted was a job where I could wear nice clothes. And instead I'm a failure."

"Look at me." He gently pushed me away from him and took my face in his hands. His thumbs swept the tears from under my eyes like wiper blades. "You are not a failure. Get that? You are... not a failure."

"You're not the person whose cotton I should be using," I muttered. Clearly this was not a time to be worried about grammar.

"Does your guy in Italy wear cotton?"

"Sometimes."

"Then pretend I'm him."

It was such an innocent statement said with no ulterior motive. If ever Dante had an opportunity, he had one now. He didn't go there. Aside from the heat from his arms, there was nothing hot about the way he held me. In that one second, Dante got more personal than he had in my fantasies.

I excused myself and went to the bathroom. I splashed cool water on my face, put drops in my eyes to offset the redness, and delivered a pep talk to my reflection.

"Why are you doing this? Why can't you just let it all go? You're going to be all alone if you can't stop doing this. Alone or dead." Nice options.

There was a tap on the door. "Samantha? You're not going to be alone. I'll be there too."

I dried off my face and opened the door. "You're going to help me?"

———

BY THE TIME DANTE LEFT, it was well past one o'clock in the morning. The pot of coffee had kept us going for hours, but the emotional rollercoaster I'd ridden had left me drained.

True to his word, Dante taught me a couple of tricks of the PI trade, and true to my word, I promised not to repeat anything he'd said. He was right. It was crazy to think I'd gotten this far on instincts alone. After triple-locking the door, I changed into pajamas and crawled into bed. I had a daunting task ahead of me. Tomorrow morning, stage one of our plan, I was going back to Heist.

33

EVERYTHING GOES

I wanted to get in and get out. If I timed everything well, no one would know I had been there—well, besides the security team I'd have to walk past. But I was ready for them. I flashed my ID to the glass window that separated us.

"Sign the sign-in sheet." Gabe, the portly security guard, was working. He waved toward the clipboard and the pen connected by a dirty white string. His swivel chair squeaked under his weight as he spun away from me.

"Here's my ID," I waved again.

"Store's closed, and no one goes in or out without signing in."

"Fine." I scrawled my name on the first available line and scanned the names above mine. Only about half a dozen were on the sheet, and none looked familiar.

I rested the pen on the top of the clipboard and went to my office. The store was glowing with light, and if it wasn't for the lack of employees, you'd think it was open for business. As I rounded the corner from the contemporary department to the handbags, I found the stock team throwing merchandise in giant plastic garbage bags.

"What are you doing?" I asked.

"Everything goes," said the shortest guy of the bunch.

"Where?"

"To the Heist in Philly. We're transferring as much of this inventory as we can." He hoisted a full bag onto his shoulder like Santa Claus and bent at the waist to counter the weight. Many of the handbag shelves were empty, though scads of the inventory had been dumped on the selling floor. Other members of the stock team were scooping up the inventory and dumping it into the plastic bags too.

"Wait! Those bags aren't cheap!"

They looked at me like I was nuts. "There's a cloth bag inside each one. Put the bag in the cloth and *then* throw it in the plastic." I opened a purple clutch and pulled a Vongole-stamped felt bag out from against the yellow suede lining, placed the bag in the felt, and pulled the drawstring shut. "See?"

"We don't have that kind of time, lady," said another member of the operations team. "We have an hour to pack up this department before we move on to shoes."

"Fine. Just don't let anybody else see how you're treating the merchandise." I stepped over a pile on the floor, hopped to a narrow pathway through the mess, and continued through the store.

Honestly, what did I care at this point? I already knew the bags were fakes. And I knew if there was a loss to be had from the mistreatment of these bags, it would fall on Tony Simms's shoulders. I wasn't the buyer anymore. I wasn't connected to the store in the least. I wasn't going to drive to Philly to buy one of the patent leather creations at eighty off, or whatever ridiculous discount they were going to pass off to get rid of them.

To get rid of them.

Those bags weren't going to make it to Philly.

No wonder no one cared how the bags were packed. These bags, these fakes, were part of the bigger picture, part of what would make sense of the killings. Once this evidence was destroyed, no one would be the wiser about Simms and his activities.

I had to get Detective Loncar to the store, to get him to see the merchandise, and to see the inventory was being moved. If he could follow the truck, he would know the truth. I dumped my bag on my desk, picked up the receiver, and called him.

But before he answered, I heard a noise in the office next door.

34

STEALING FILES

I set the receiver back on the cradle. If the stock team was packing up inventory, there was no reason for anyone to be in the buyer's offices. As quietly as I could, I crossed the carpet between my desk and the doorway.

Mallory was filling a large canvas tote bag with files. She didn't notice me at first, but when she did, the files fell to the floor. Manila folders spilled out recaps and past orders and photo sheets with selling information.

"What are you doing here?" she asked. I had been one second short of asking the same question.

"I came for my personal things."

"You haven't been here long enough to have personal things. You came here to steal files."

"I'm not the one rifling through the file cabinet."

"You don't know this business like I do. I've taken too many chances, and you're not going to ruin this opportunity for me."

"What opportunity? The dedication tomorrow night?"

She turned pale. "Tomorrow night? But I won't be ready."

"You shouldn't go. I wouldn't if I hadn't been asked by Tony. I'd be as far away from there as I possibly could get."

"Tony asked you to go? I thought you didn't even work here anymore!"

"How do you know that?"

"It's not about what I know, it's about what you think you know. I've worked too long and too hard to get noticed around here, and some nobody isn't going to get all of the credit that I deserve. I don't care what you have on your resume. With everything I've been through, *I* deserve the recognition, not you!"

"I don't know what you're getting at, but I think you've got the wrong idea about me, Mallory," I said. "I just came here to get my flowers."

I went back into my office and picked up the arrangement Dante had sent. I didn't know if the sugar cube was still working or picking up anything she had said, but I didn't want to take any chances. The arrangement from the cops was sitting on her desk, and I wanted that one too, if only for the wireless mic.

"Stay home tomorrow night, Mallory. Please. Listen to me. Nobody's going to notice whether or not you're there. It's not going to be a big deal."

"Are you kidding? None of this would have started if it wasn't for me and I'm darn sure going to see that it's finished." In her anger she took a few steps toward me, closing the gap. She shook a balled-up fist in the air as though she was claiming to never go hungry again.

I stepped backward, but the toe of my shoe caught on a piece of paper that had fallen from the files, and I slipped. I let go of the flowers and grabbed for the desk to right myself. The vase landed on the floor, the flowers still secured in the green sponge at the base. The miniature camera fell loose, lying inches from Mallory's foot. We both stared at it for a tense couple of seconds.

Mallory looked up, her face red in splotches that continued down her neck. "I don't care how you got this job or what you plan to do after this, but I am going to finish you. I intend to be at that dedication, and I'm going to make sure Tony Simms knows you're up to something."

She picked up the camera and stormed out of the office.

I WASN'T LOOKING FORWARD to telling Dante I'd lost his camera, or that in doing so I may have tipped off a murderer to the fact that I was on to her, even if she wasn't the suspect I'd been figuring out how to trap. I was mixed up. The only thing clear about my thoughts was that I was barely making sense.

Mallory. Was it possible? Had I misjudged her so much during my short time at Heist? She'd done a good job of pulling the wool over my eyes, but I mentally ticked off my checklist. She had admitted to being around Kyle and Emily the night of the murder. I'd overheard her threaten Belle DuChamp. She had done little to hide her open displeasure when I'd started working at Heist and I didn't know why. This couldn't all be about a promotion or a career path. Unless ...

Could it be?

There was one simple answer I hadn't wanted to see, and that answer was yes.

Yes, Mallory knew I was doing more at Heist than replacing the murdered handbag buyer.

Yes, if Mallory had murdered Emily over the Vongole knockoff scheme, she'd be threatened when I showed up unexpected.

Yes, Mallory was going to be at the dedication. She had said it like a threat, not a fact.

And yes, it was entirely possible Mallory was the killer.

I sped home. I parked in the garage and pulled the door down to hide my car. Logan stood guard over his empty food bowl, yowling for dinner. I snapped open a can of gourmet cat food and spooned it into the bowl. He buried his head, and I sank down on the linoleum tile floor, legs splayed in front of me.

"How can you eat at a time like this?" The sounds of wet cat morsels being gulped down answered me. He pulled his head up and stared at me for two long seconds. Then he walked over and head-butted my forehead. I scooped him into my arms and held him close for comfort. The phone rang. I held Logan to my chest and stood. I answered on the third ring.

"Ms. Kidd, this is Detective Loncar." Long pause. "I know Tony Simms asked you to be at the event at the college, but I am strongly suggesting you don't go. Do you understand?"

"But you said everything was over. If everything is over, then I'm free to do what I want, right? Your case is closed. Unless you want to admit you have the wrong person in custody and you have some questions for me. Do you have any valid questions for me?"

"Just one. Do you want to explain to me why Mallory George wants to file a restraining order against you?"

35

____

WHO'S IT GOING TO BE TOMORROW?

GOOD THING CATS ALWAYS LAND ON THEIR FEET, BECAUSE WHEN I processed the detective's question, I knocked Logan off the counter.

"She what?" I asked.

"I don't know what you did to her, but she was clear that she doesn't want you to be anywhere near her or the dedication."

"Because she's the killer."

"Ms. Kidd, a week ago you said Belle DuChamp was the killer. Yesterday it was Tony Simms, and today it's Mallory George. Who's it going to be tomorrow? These accusations are borderline defamation of character."

"The only person I haven't said was the killer is Kyle Trent."

"I'm sending a car over. If you leave your house, we'll know. It is my very strong recommendation that you stay away from I-FAD for the next forty-eight hours."

"Why? The dedication is tomorrow, right?"

"And the dress rehearsal is tonight." He hung up.

I looked out my window. A gold PT Cruiser drove slowly down the street. That was Mallory's car. I remembered it from the day I drove her to the Bag Lady showroom. Considering she claimed she wanted to keep a distance spelled out in a restraining order between us, her presence in my neighborhood was suspicious. I called Dante.

"Are you close? How close? Can you come get me now? Right now? I have to be gone from my house like really, really, really fast."

"Samantha, slow down."

"I don't have time to slow down. Please. I'll tell you everything when you get here."

A motorcycle pulled into my driveway. We weren't going to talk about how fast that actually was. I scooped Logan up and kissed him. "I'll be back soon, I promise." I took the stairs two at a time, grabbed Dante's duffle bag, and ran back downstairs and out the front door. I straddled the bike while buckling the helmet on. Dante peeled out of the lot just as I wrapped both arms around him. He circled the block, and a police cruiser passed us. I gripped tighter.

He turned his head around to me. "Are they headed for you?"

I nodded. He revved his engine and shot through the intersection. I closed my eyes and leaned my head against the orange and red flames on the back of his jacket.

He sped past most cars and pulled onto a narrow drive that took us up the side of Mt. Penn. We passed basketball courts and kids playing hopscotch. The road was narrow and windy like the Autobahn. We slowed by a white iron gate.

"We're here."

I didn't know where "here" was, but I was vaguely certain no one else who might be looking for me would know where "here" was either. Safe enough for me.

I took off the helmet, and he locked it to the back of his bike. "Follow me."

He pulled the handles to the duffle bag out of my grip and started up the concrete stairs that wrapped around a porch that led to a wood-and-glass-paneled door. He unlocked it and entered a room no bigger than a small hotel room.

A wooden, fold-out futon sat under a window facing a flat-screen TV mounted on the opposite wall. Tall, metal bookcases that held books on their sides flanked the TV, and an oblong piece of marble sat on two concrete blocks below them, holding magazines on cars and photography. Next to the futon was a desk with a computer and chair. Silver cups filled with colorful markers lined the back of the desk. Blues, greens, and purples in one cup, oranges, yellows, and reds in the other.

Dante dropped the bag next to a turntable and opened a small fridge. When he stood, he held a beer out. I took it and drank a fair amount, even though I'm more of a wine girl.

"Sit."

I collapsed on the sofa.

"Talk."

"I, um, may have been wrong about Tony Simms being the killer."

Dante demonstrated great patience after I made that statement, allowing me to gulp my beer, supplying me with a second one when the first ran low. In fact, it wasn't until my cell phone started going crazy from inside the pocket of my pants that he prompted me with questions. I muted the phone and started talking.

I recounted what had happened at Heist that morning, barely believing that less than a day had passed since Mallory had caught me–or vice versa. I ended with her reaction to seeing the camera on the floor.

"I'm sorry. I'll pay you back whatever it cost when I get a chance."

He waved my apology away with his hand. "That's not important. You said the cops told you she filed a restraining order against you?"

"Yes. And that can only be to keep me away from the dedication. But there's no way I can stay away now. She's going to murder someone else. Maybe Tony Simms. Maybe Nora. Maybe she'll take out a bunch of students. Who knows how far she'll go?"

"Calm down. None of this makes any sense."

"I know."

"No, you most likely don't know." He set his beer on the table and leaned back against the futon.

"What most likely don't I know? I mean, what don't I know most likely? I mean, what do you mean?"

"Do you need some kind of sedative?"

Mental note: chill out. "Tell me what you mean."

"There's no way this Mallory person can get a restraining order in a couple of hours. The cops would know that. They would also know you've been working with them. And they would know you've been saying the real killer is still out there. So if this Detective Loncar wants to talk to you so badly that he sent a car to your house, it might be because he finally has reason to listen to what you have to say."

"Detective Loncar has already shown up on my doorstep once before." I didn't add that he'd read me my rights, handcuffed me while I was in my bathrobe, and taken me to the police station. It wasn't a happy memory. "When he said he was sending a car to get me, I wasn't going to hang around for a repeat fashion intervention a la Copper."

"The handcuffs were copper?"

"Copper, like James Cagney. You know, 'Come and get me, Copper!'"

"You seriously learned everything you know about the police from old movies, didn't you?"

"I resent that." I said. I fidgeted with my hands, crossing and uncrossing my arms, sitting on my palms, trying to find a position that didn't look or feel completely vulnerable. I looked around the interior of the room. "What is this place? A safe house?"

"This is where I live." A smile crept along Dante's face and then blossomed into a full-blown grin. "At least when I'm not at my apartment in Philly."

I immediately looked around for insights into Dante's personality. While I watched, he reached out to a small metal box that sat on the table next to the futon. Inside was a stash of Atomic Fireballs. He pulled one out, bit into the plastic, and popped it into his mouth.

"Do your parents have any idea how badly they screwed you up by naming you Dante?"

"You might offer me an apology."

"For what?"

"That 'safe house' crack. Just about confirmed what I thought about your knowledge."

He was right, and I knew he was right, but I was full of pride and indignation. I stood up and marched across the room to the one interior door that had been shut.

"What's in here?"

"Bathroom."

I went inside and shut the door behind me. This was as good a place as any to let the steam cool down from behind my ears. I sank to the white tiled floor and started thinking.

Within five minutes, I knew I had to talk to Loncar. Someone's life was at risk. I still didn't know whose. It could be mine. Or Kyle's, or Tony's, or Andi's, or Nora's, or any unrelated person who came into contact with Mallory.

I won't let you ruin this for me, she'd said. *After all I've done, I'm taking what I deserve.*

I stood up and opened the door. Dante stood directly on the other side, one hand up, ready to knock.

"Can I use your phone?" I asked.

He handed me my cell phone. The number was already on the screen. I punched the connect button and waited.

"Ms. Kidd, where are you?" Loncar demanded.

"I'm at the grocery store," I lied.

"I want you to listen to me carefully. Mallory George wanted to file a restraining order against you. I explained that unless the two of you were lovers living in the same house, what she was seeking didn't pertain to your 'relationship.' Now I want to know what you did that makes her think you're a danger to her, and I'd feel a lot better about this conversation if we had it in my office."

"No disrespect, Detective, but that's not going to happen. And I'm going to hang up every twenty-nine seconds so you can't trace this call."

He sighed heavily. "Ms. Kidd, that's not necessary."

"I'll call you right back." I hung up.

Dante reappeared in front of me. "Done so soon?"

"I don't want him to trace the call."

"You have to stop giving me ammunition."

I held my hand up to silence him and hit redial. "Detective Loncar? It's Samantha Kidd."

"Why does Mallory George want a protective order issued against you?"

I stared at the blond hardwood floorboards and traced a line between the seams with the toe of my shoe. "I've been thinking about that."

"Give me the abridged version. Try to keep Hollywood out of it."

Dante and Detective Loncar probably would have a great time hanging out over drinks.

"She told me she was at Heist the night Emily was murdered."

"What's she stand to gain?"

"I don't know for sure. She's the assistant buyer. You're the one who played back the recording of her threatening me. I also heard her threaten Belle DuChamp. At first I thought she just wanted a promotion, but this is too crazy. Nobody wants a job this badly. At least, not this job. Not at this level. You don't kill to be a buyer. CEO maybe, or something like that, but not buyer. The perks just aren't that great."

"You don't hear about people killing to be CEOs either. I've heard of a lot of motives. They pretty much boil down to love, family, money. You don't see the connection to any of them?"

I shook my head.

"Ms. Kidd? You still with me?" the detective asked over the phone, since I hadn't answered him out loud.

"The answer is no. I don't see the connection to any of those motives. But she's trying to keep me from the dedication."

"You feel pretty positive something's going down at that dedication?"

"I do." I waited for him to order me to stay home, or to tell me my active imagination had run away from me into a fourth dimension.

"This Mallory George said you've been secretly filming her in the office. That's a violation of privacy."

"You were secretly recording her! How is that any different?"

"Where'd you get the camera?"

"A friend who is looking out for me."

"I thought that friend was in Italy."

"Different friend."

"What's his motivation?"

My eyes flickered to Dante, who stood in the kitchen watching a pot of water. "Same as yours."

"Put him on the phone."

"No can do. I'll have him call you."

Dante locked eyes with me, and I snapped the phone shut.

"Detective Loncar wants to talk to you. Here's the number." I scribbled it on a paper towel and tossed it into the sink. "Call him, don't call him. It's up to you."

Dante snatched the phone and dialed the number with his thumb.

"Detective?" he said into the phone. I couldn't hear the other side of the conversation. Then Dante dropped the hand that held the phone to his side and told me to go back into the bathroom while he finished the conversation without me.

And just in case you're wondering, I knew Dante was purposely keeping the tone light, and Detective Loncar wouldn't be listening to me if he didn't believe maybe I was right. And having two men converse secretly over how to best protect me while a potential killer orchestrated one last hit did nothing to calm my nerves.

So I called the other man who would have something to say about my current situation.

36

TIME'S UP

After I left a message with Nick that included phrases like, "I need to talk to you," "Things have gotten out of hand," and "Please don't think I am a drama queen needing attention, but even the cops are starting to listen to me now," I hung up and waited.

And stared around Dante's bathroom.

And at his shower.

A shower would feel good. A shower would go a long way toward cleaning my aura, or at least the smell of fear that had begun to travel in small circles with me.

I opened the door to the bathroom. Dante was still on the phone, making notes on a lined steno pad. Fine. Let them figure out I was right. For the next half hour, it was going to be their problem and not mine. Yes, I said half an hour. For once it wasn't my hot water bill.

I locked the door and peeled off my clothes, tossing them into a pile next to the sink. The water sprayed the walls of the shower, producing a cloud of steam. I climbed in, dunked my face under the spray, and doused my hair. It felt good. It felt better than good. I rested my forehead against the walls of the standup shower, and the insistent pulse beat down on my shoulders and back. Tensions calmed. Muscles relaxed. I lathered the bar of Ivory soap into a foam of suds and washed my face and body like I was exorcizing a demon.

I repeated the routine with Dante's shampoo and conditioner and then sat on the floor and let the water wash over me like a tropical rainforest. I could sit here for hours. I could sit here all night. I didn't have to ever come out of here again, except maybe for the occasional serving of pretzels. For the first time in days, I was totally relaxed.

Then a shadow appeared on the other side of the shower curtain, and a deep voice broke my trance. "Time's up."

The water suddenly shut off, and I was left sitting in the middle of a shower. Naked. With Dante on the other side of the flimsy plastic curtain. I jumped up, and in an attempt at modesty, turned my back toward the curtain. A fluffy white towel hit me on the head.

I wrapped the towel around my torso. Dante pulled the plastic curtain aside as I secured the corner by my bust line. "Detective Loncar thinks there might be some truth to what you're saying, but he's not ready to admit Kyle is the wrong guy. It appears as though your new 'evidence' started a ticking clock on the amount of time they have to tie everything together with a big bow."

"So we're going to the college tonight? I don't have anything to wear."

"This isn't a date."

"That's not what I mean. I bolted from the house, and all I grabbed was your duffle bag. I don't have anything to wear to shake down a killer."

"Your term papers must have been fun to read."

"I majored in the history of fashion. I didn't need to use phrases like 'shake down a killer' when writing about Emilio Pucci."

He shoveled his hand under a neatly folded pile of clothes. "Put these on. They should work."

I flipped through the pile. White shirt and work pants. "Are these your clothes?"

"Let's not get into where they came from. Hurry up and change."

I turned back into the bathroom and dressed. The button-down, collared, short-sleeved shirt was part of a uniform. The name Doris was embroidered onto a red patch sewn over the right breast. The pants were a men's flat front boxy cut, narrow fit through my hips and ridiculously full at the waist.

"Hand me the duffle bag," I said through the cracked door.

He handed it to me. I unclamped the black nylon shoulder strap, adjusted the length of it, and clamped it over the waistband of the pants like a cinch belt, creating the kind of paper-bag waist that made Isaac Mizrahi famous. I rolled the cuffs of the pants up until they were slightly above my ankles and then buckled my feet into my blue patent leather T-strap sandals.

"I'm ready," I said and left the bathroom.

He walked toward me and reached his hands on either side of my head, flipping the collar up.

"Good idea. The flipped-up collar works," I said, catching my reflection in the glass of a framed pin-up girl on the wall.

"Put this on." He lowered a skinny blue necktie, already tied, over my head like a noose.

"That might be a little much."

"These people are going to expect you to have on some kind of weird getup."

"Why? It's not a costume party."

He stood back, eyed me up and down, and tightened the necktie. "Because they know you, and you always have on some kind of weird getup."

"I resent that."

"The tie is wired with a transmitter. If you speak clearly, I'll be able to hear everything you say or anyone close to you says."

I fingered the blue fabric. "This tie is bugged?"

"Yes, and it cost more than two hundred dollars, so don't spill anything on it."

WE ARRIVED at the college about twenty minutes later. Dante spun the bike around the mostly empty parking lot and then pulled under a couple of maple trees that kept us out of sight.

"Get off."

"You could be a little more polite, you know," I said, stepping down on my right foot and hopping backward so my left leg could swing over the back of the motorcycle. I unbuckled the helmet and hooked it onto the clip.

"This isn't the time to joke around, Samantha. Are you scared?"

"Yes, I'm scared."

"Good. You'll be more careful if you're scared."

"Where are you going to be?"

"I don't know yet."

"Then why did you tell me to get off?"

"I'm not coming in with you." He handed me the duffle bag. "McQueen's in here. You need to put him on the platform where the real statue was."

"I don't think this is going to work."

"Listen to me. You need to have a reason for being here. McQueen is your reason. If anybody says anything, you say you're there to replace the statue. If things get hairy, you put him on the pedestal, and you leave."

"Okay, sure. I can do that."

"I'm going to be able to hear whatever you hear, but if you stand too close to something with background noise, I'll have a harder time. So try to stay away from general noise."

"But I'm the bait."

"McQueen's the bait."

"So I'm what dangles the bait. I'm the fishing wire?"

"Try not to get tangled up." His eyes held mine for too long. I couldn't read his thoughts, and I wasn't sure I wanted to.

"Can I pretend you're Nick again?"

He looked at me for a couple of seconds and then touched my cheek. "You can do this." He revved the motor and pulled away, scattering pebbles over the toes of my shoes.

I hoisted the duffle from the ground and scaled the steps to the business school. Nobody else was around. I pulled McQueen from the duffle and stuck him on the pedestal and then left out the front door. After descending the stairs, a shiny red sports car sped into the lot and shot directly toward where I stood.

37

NOTHING IS GOING TO BRING HER BACK

Kyle got out of the car and slammed the door. His eyes were glassy and unfocused, shifting his male model looks into fallen pop star territory. "Where is he?" he yelled as he ascended the stairs. He stumbled halfway up.

Andi followed more slowly. She grabbed my arm, her eyes wide with fright. "The police couldn't charge him with the crime, so he was released. I was watering his plants at his apartment when he walked in. I told him what you figured out, and he freaked. You have to stop him. I'm afraid he's going to do something bad."

I pulled away from Andi and ran after Kyle. "He's not here, Kyle. Nobody's here."

"How did that get here?" he asked, staring at McQueen.

"Tony wanted it here for the dedication." I moved closer to the glass case of trophies and then took a step backward, into the hallway that led to the lecture hall.

He stood, rooted to the marble floor, staring at the statue as if he'd seen a ghost. "That bastard. He must have the police in his pocket if he got them to release evidence for his event."

"That's not the one that he used—" I cut myself off. Kyle had been in love with Emily; she'd been his future. Whether or not the statue in front of us was the one that had been used to bludgeon his fiancée, it hardly was a point worth mentioning.

"You put this here, didn't you?" he asked. "He asked you to put it here, and you did."

"Yes."

"What are you trying to prove? She's dead. The love of my life is dead, and nothing is going to bring her back. Not taking on Tony Simms, not shutting down Vongole, not a single thing you, or Andi, or anybody else can do. I have to try to move on, to learn to get up and go every single day without her. Can you imagine that? Learning to live without the love of your life?"

Kyle was not in a good place. His eyes were bloodshot, more so than they'd been when he arrived. A vein pulsed alongside his eyebrow. He spoke carefully, like he needed to make extra effort to get the words out clearly.

Andi remained in the parking lot. She looked scared. I made a face at her and waved her closer when I thought Kyle wasn't looking.

"Kyle, why don't you let Andi drive you home?"

I walked Kyle to the door and guided him to the steps out front. It seemed like yesterday that Eddie and I ran down those steps with the Puccetti statue hidden in my handbag. I held Kyle's arm as he descended the stairs. He walked to his car in a trance. I didn't know if he had tuned it all out up to this point, if seeing the statue had triggered something that he'd been able to keep buried behind emotional walls, and I was afraid to ask.

Andi looked at the keys, at me, and then at Kyle. "I can't drive stick."

Kyle aimed his remote at the car and sat in the driver's seat. He didn't start the engine. He draped his arms over the steering wheel and bent his head, his shoulders shaking with sorrow.

As I stepped away from the car, I realized the one thing I'd wanted by bringing the fake Puccetti here was to elicit a response from someone. There were too many suspects. I knew the person who had used the statue to murder Emily would have a hard time with the sight of it on its pedestal. From the looks of Kyle Trent, he was the definition of "hard time."

Had Detective Loncar been right all along? Had something I'd said or done released a killer from custody?

I had to talk to Dante. I backed away, up the stairs, and into the admissions hall. After the door closed behind me, I looked at the pedestal.

The Puccetti was gone.

I glanced back at the parking lot. Exhaust puffed from the tailpipe of the red car. As I turned to my right, something wooden and solid swung at me and connected with left cheekbone.

The momentum knocked me down. A foot connected with my midsection. I curled onto my side and wrapped my torso with my arms—the same way I'd curled up in the back seat of Cat's Suburban the night we stole the statue. Pain yielded tears that blurred my vision. Something fell to the floor next to me.

Twenty-four inches of wooden man.

I forced myself onto my hands and knees, fighting each movement like a battered Rocky Balboa. I slowly crawled down the hallway to the bathroom where I'd hidden after stealing McQueen a week ago. I pulled myself into a standing position. After I opened the door, I moved across the black and white checkerboard floor and bent over the closest sink. I splashed cold water on my face. Pink water, tinged with blood from the strike on my cheek, trickled down my face into the basin.

A rock smashed through the small glass pane of the crank window in the tiny lavatory and landed in the sink next to me. "What just happened?" asked Dante's voice through the now-shattered window.

"Somebody hit me."

"What? Speak more clearly. Your voice is muffled."

I glanced down at the tie, now wet in patches thanks to the water I'd splashed on my face.

"Samantha, I can't hear you anymore. Get out of there. I don't have a good feeling about this."

"Kyle's here. He's drunk. He freaked out when he saw McQueen."

"I can't hear you. Move closer to the window."

I stepped around the broken glass on the floor and looked for Dante through the metal frame. "Kyle. Red sports car. He shouldn't be driving."

"I'll try to catch him. Meet me out front."

A toilet flushed behind me. The stall opened, and Nora stepped out.

She caught my eyes in the reflection of the mirror above the row of sinks. "Samantha! What happened?" She grabbed a handful of paper towels, ran them under cool water, and turned around and held them gently against my face.

"I-I'm fine." I pushed her away. "I'm not sure what happened."

"Let's get you out of here. I'll take you home."

"Not yet." I backed away from her into the rose-pink metal door to the stall.

"What's wrong?"

My face throbbed, and I couldn't think straight. When I looked at Nora, I felt like someone was hurling neon Frisbees at me. I was having a hard time standing up.

"Can you give me a couple of minutes? I'll meet you out front."

"Sure, if that's what you need." She tucked her sandy blond hair behind her ear and left.

I smacked the tie a few times and moved closer to the window. "Dante? Are you out there?" There was no answer.

I splashed more water on my face and dried off as best as I could. When I pulled the door to the bathroom open, I looked up and down the hall. There was no sign of Nora, no sign of anybody.

I couldn't risk going out the front door. Not when I didn't know where Dante was, or if someone was waiting out there to ambush me. I crept the other direction to the lecture hall and ducked inside the heavy doors.

"Samantha, I was starting to think you weren't going to make it," Tony Simms said. He was the picture of calm, or, he would have been, if he hadn't been tied to a folding metal chair.

The door closed behind me. "Watch out!" Tony called.

Someone pushed me into the back row of seats, but I threw my arms out in front of me and broke my fall by landing in the velvet-covered theater seats. I heard the sounds of metal clanking against each other. I sat up and saw Andi feeding a padlock through a heavy chain that secured the lecture hall doors.

"What are you doing?" I asked.

Andi turned quickly and dropped the padlock key. Her normally slicked-back hair had come loose, and pieces hung in spikes around her face. Dark circles colored her under-eye area, and she was missing an earring. I mentioned none of this, and she didn't mention the trail of blood that dripped onto the collar of my borrowed shirt once owned by a woman named Doris.

"Tony is going to pay for what he did."

"This is crazy. Call the police. Let them arrest him. This isn't our job."

She stared at me as though she didn't understand me.

"He has to pay," she repeated. "I'll never have a life until he pays."

"I'll help you," he said. "Let Samantha go."

"You've done enough!" she spat at him. She stormed down the aisle and screamed at him. "You can't control me. You can't touch me!"

"Andi, calm down," I said.

She pulled a gun out of her pocket. Something wasn't right. It was as if the plastic game pieces had popped from the game of Concentration, and everything I thought fit didn't. But as the pieces fell into new and different arrangements, the scattered information pointed me in an entirely different direction.

"Andi?" I said, approaching her.

"Shut up!" she screamed. I didn't know which of us she was yelling at.

Could Dante hear us? Or anybody? Where were Nora and Kyle and the cops?

"Why couldn't you let me live my life?" she asked. Touches of white saliva spotted the corners of her mouth. "I killed her. I should have let it go, but you tried to protect me. Now two people are dead."

"Nobody has to know what you did. It'll be our secret," Tony said.

Detective Loncar's words resonated in my head. Love-family-money. The Concentration game pieces snapped back into their slots, and suddenly I knew why Andi Holloway drank so much, why her father would never let her leave the family business, and why she was so desperate to take down Tony Simms.

"You never let me try to achieve anything for myself. If you had believed in me, just once. If you had let me fail, let me learn about hard work, about what it feels like to succeed on my own, everything would have been different." Andi kept the gun aimed at Tony. "But you didn't, and now there's no way out."

"I worked hard to succeed so your life would be easy. I can get you help."

I fell to the floor and crawled the last few feet to the door. The key had landed somewhere around here. I padded my hands across the carpet in search of it. My fingernail snapped in half. I stifled the instinctive cry of pain, not wanting to draw attention to myself.

"I know all about your 'hard work.' You were never there for Mom, and you were never there for me."

I flipped my cell phone open and powered it back on. The screen glowed neon blue. I cued up the text screen and typed "Simms daughter Andi Holloway need help" and then hit send. Who could think about verbs and apostrophes at a time like this?

I had to keep Andi from doing something rash until help arrived. There was a chance Dante had heard the argument and called the cops, which meant there was a glimmer of hope, a chance the good guys would burst through the door. If I could just stay alive until then.

"Andi, I made mistakes with you. I see that now. I should have been there for you, but it will all end tonight. I can help you. Put the gun down."

"I'll never get away from you. If I'd have been caught, it would be over. But now I'll never have a normal life. You did this to me. You made me this way." Snot bubbled out of her nostrils as she sobbed and screamed.

"You won't have to live with the memory of killing Emily Hart if you let me help you."

"You're right. I don't have to live with the reminders, but you do."

A gun fired.

Tony Simms shouted.

I screamed.

Sirens blared.

And Andi Holloway collapsed on the cold marble floor. Her body toppled like the Puccetti statue had from its pedestal, and a puddle of blood seeped out of the self-inflicted gunshot wound that ended her life.

38

OUT OF MY SYSTEM?

THE DAY NICK WAS SCHEDULED TO ARRIVE IN RIBBON WAS SPENT cleaning, showering, and changing into outfits from at least five different decades. I may have worn my best underwear and changed the sheets on my bed. I'd rather keep that to myself.

I didn't know how I would feel when I saw him. The last time we spoke, things had been strained. I braced myself for what I would get when I opened the front door, whether it be lecture or hug.

I opened the front door. Nick stood on my porch, dressed in a cream knit turtleneck and plaid pants. He held a dozen pink roses wrapped in butcher paper tied with twine in one hand and a shoebox in the other. His curly brown hair moved with a breeze that passed over us. His eyes, deeper brown than I remembered, sparkled with the reflection of the waning sun, highlighting golden flecks in the middle of their normal root-beer-barrel shade.

We stood there for a second, not talking. I was close enough that I saw his eyes go from mine to the fading bruise on my cheek, to my lips, and then back to my eyes. All of the flirtation, the innuendo, the chemistry from life before he'd gone to Italy flooded back.

"Kidd," he said.

"Taylor," I said back.

"These are for you." He held out the roses. "This too," and extended the shoe box.

I took both. "Do you want to come in?" I asked.

Nick stepped forward. I stepped back. He stepped forward again and I tried to step back but the door to the hall closet behind me made that impossible. Nick put his fingers under my chin and tipped my face up to his. His lips brushed against mine once, twice, and then pressed down in our first kiss. I dropped the flowers and the shoebox and buried my fingers in his hair, and his hands moved down my neck, shoulders, and body.

When the kiss ended, he pulled away and touched his fingertips to my bruise.

"Does it hurt?" he asked.

"Not anymore."

"Do you want to talk about it?"

"Not anymore."

I took his hand and led him to the sofa. We sat next to each other. I tucked one bare foot under me and faced him. He reached out and twirled a lock of my hair through his fingertips.

"I didn't expect the curls and the tan."

"I didn't expect the..." I looked at the front door where we'd kissed. "Roses."

The lid had come off the shoebox when it fell, and one pale pink strappy sandal had fallen from tissue paper, resting on its side. The twine had come undone, and stems of roses scattered across the hardwood floor.

"I should put them in water." I stood up. Nick caught my hand and pulled me back to the sofa.

"Leave them," he said. We kissed again, like two teenagers with five minutes left before curfew. "I hated that you were in the middle of a dangerous situation again and I couldn't help you. It helped knowing you were working with the cops."

I thought about my frustrating partnership with Detective Loncar. I'd expected something from him after the dust had settled on his investigation, maybe a thank-you note, maybe the key to the city. At minimum, I thought I deserved a third bouquet of flowers.

I was still waiting.

Nick had helped me. From across the world while he was working on his own agenda, he'd taken time out to do what he could. He deserved to know the details the rest of us knew. "Andi Holloway was Tony Simms's daughter. She resented him, resented that he wasn't a part of her life other than handing her job opportunities and money. He wasn't a father to her. Andi was desperate to find someone who cared about her, to treat her like a full, visible, valuable human being. She saw how Kyle treated Emily and thought if Emily was out of the picture, that could be her."

"She killed Emily at the gala?"

"Yes. That's how I got involved. Andi took the statue from I-FAD. She knew it was part of Tony's art collection. She didn't know we'd replaced the one that was there with the fake Eddie had made. I think she thought she was killing Emily and framing Tony. The cops found it, and I got called in to explain it all to Detective Loncar."

"And Belle?"

"The working theory is that Tony killed Belle to protect Andi. Tony's not saying anything, but he's definitely not innocent. He's the one who started the rumor about Belle DuChamp and Kyle Trent. He wanted Andi to think Kyle was a rat. He'd also been the one to funnel knock-offs into the two stores that carried Vongole, knowing that eventually the business would go belly-= up and he could offer his daughter another job."

Tony Simms had kept his daughter in his pocket, the way I'd put the Puccetti statue in my handbag, and Andi had carried that anger and resentment around with her like a purse filled with baggage. She'd been in and out of psychiatrists' offices dealing with abandonment issues. Just like she'd told me, she'd married a bartender early, divorcing him quickly but keeping his name.

Her hatred for her father ran much deeper than I ever could have imagined. If he'd been more of a real dad, not a mere figurehead, maybe this would have worked out differently. Instead of knock-off handbags and false success, Andi Holloway might have had a real life with ups and downs, failures and successes, highs and lows. But desperation to have her own identity forced her into a declaration of her own independence. Some might say she punctuated the declaration with a bullet.

"What about Kyle?" Nick asked.

I picked up a postcard I'd received a few days ago. It pictured a forest in black and white, with one small tree in the middle. The leaves on the tree were green. The message on the back was short and sweet: *Thank you for believing in me. Life goes on.—Kyle* After his signature, there was a PS: *There's an opening at Tradava if you're interested.* I handed the postcard to Nick, who read it and then set it down on the table.

"So that's it," I said.

"Is that it?"

I leaned against the sofa cushion and thought about what I hadn't told Nick.

Mallory George did not apologize to me face to face but sent me an arrangement of bronze callas to rival the bouquet Detective Loncar had sent me at Heist. Her note was simple: *I learned a lot from you.* I taped it to my bathroom mirror and read it every morning before restarting my job search.

I finished cleaning my closets and donated half of my wardrobe to charity.

I didn't apply for Kyle's job.

A week after the showdown at the college, I went to Cat's house for dinner. Eddie was there, but Dante was not. After dinner, I drove to Dante's apartment with the freshly laundered clothes he'd loaned me to wear to the college. The necktie lay folded on top of the pile.

I hadn't seen Dante since the night at the college when everything went down. And with Nick back in town, I didn't know if I was ready to analyze the way Dante made me feel. I carried the clothes to his front door. The lights were out, so I left them with a note. *Thanks for the education.*

When I got back to my car, I looked up the stairs. Dante leaned against the wooden banister in front of his door. I waved, and he tilted a bottle of beer in my direction. The next morning, there was a note under my windshield. *I don't meet many women like you, Samantha Kidd.*

I tucked that card in my underwear drawer.

Nick pulled me close and kissed the tip of my nose. "I'm glad you worked this out of your system," he said. "It is out of your system, right?"

I looked behind him to the small crystal bowl that sat on the end table, now filled with Atomic Fireballs. Things were different now. Different-good or different-bad, I didn't yet know.

"Kidd, you didn't answer the question. Is it out of your system?"

I smiled and kissed him again.

THE BRIM REAPER

KILLER FASHION MYSTERY #3

1

———

STOP SIGNS AND SALE SIGNS

It was hard not to overhear the argument. Two deep male voices shouted at each other from the office of the art museum. I stood at the back entrance of the Ribbon Museum of Art by a rotating exhibit of influential fashions. I wasn't sure if I should continue inside or pretend I hadn't arrived yet.

Across the exposed concrete floor was a flight of stairs that led to the main display space. I could cross the floor, get up the stairs, and pretend I'd been there all along. If I didn't need to check in with someone in the office, I would have tried to do just that.

"I don't care how much publicity it will bring. I'm not doing it!" one voice said.

"You might own your store, but you're not in charge here," said the other.

I took a tentative step onto the concrete.

"I'm here because of my experience and connections. You want them; you let me do things the way I see fit."

"That wasn't the arrangement."

"If you'd been up front about the arrangement from the beginning, we wouldn't be having this conversation."

Had there been clothing on the naked mannequins placed

around the cavernous gallery, the sound might have been muffled. Instead, the voices reverberated off the walls and magnified like a conversation yelled across the Grand Canyon.

"You don't need to know everything I have planned."

"You're right. I don't need to know *anything* you have planned. I quit."

The man who stormed out of the office was red in the face, an unfortunate color combination with his royal blue glasses. He was bald but had a sculpted white mustache and beard, and he looked like a patriotic ad for blood pressure medicine, or at least the "before" photo for someone who might need an intervention. He wore a black suit with a white T-shirt underneath, no socks, and shiny black wingtips. The leather soles of his shoes made a snappy sound as he crossed the marble foyer. He pushed both palms on the inside of the entrance doors, but it was Monday, and the museum was closed to the public. The doors flexed outward a few inches and then, bound by the heavy chain and padlock on the opposite side, snapped back toward the man, knocking him in the head.

"Are you okay?" I rushed to him, my sandals making their own staccato clacks across the floor.

He cursed and slammed his balled-up fist into the back of the door. "Who are you? My replacement?" he asked over his shoulder while massaging his hand.

Since I wasn't sure what my role at the museum was other than showing up to help a friend, I answered with an introduction. "I'm Samantha Kidd. I'm here to help with an exhibit of vintage movie costumes. Is your head okay? The doors whacked you pretty hard."

He fanned his fingers out and looked at the back of his hand, and then he touched his forehead, where a red lump was already forming.

"That man is an idiot."

Before I could answer, the injured man's cell phone rang. He scowled at the display and dropped it back into the breast pocket of his jacket. On the sixth ring, he fished it back out, answered the call, and held the phone out to me.

I put my hands up and shook my head, but he nodded and held it closer.

Before I decided to take—or not take—the phone, a voice came through. "Engle? Are you there?" Pause. "I want you and your stuff out of here by midnight."

The bald man pulled the phone away from me and put it to his head. "Midnight is too late for me. I'm out of here now." He shoved the phone into his pocket without hanging up. He looked at me. "If you want to help, tell your friend to get as far away from this exhibit as he can."

He strode off in an angry path to the back door.

I counted to ten before realizing I had to approach the man in the office, presumably the other side of the conversation. I kept counting and reached twenty-seven. When no other angry people appeared, I click-clacked my way back to the office and tapped on the door. There was no answer. The door was cracked, and I pushed it open.

"Hello?" I called. The office was empty. "I'm Samantha Kidd, and I'm here to help with the exhibit. Hello? I need a museum pass."

I stepped inside and looked behind the door and behind the desk. As far as offices went, it was bigger than I would have imagined. A row of white bookshelves filled with coffee table books about costume design, fashion history, famous designers, and art filled the back wall. A steel desk sat in front of the bookcases, and an olive-green ergonomic chair was pushed away from it like someone had stood up quickly.

"What are you doing in here?" a voice behind me asked.

I spun around and faced a thin black man. He pushed past me to the desk. A silver plaque bearing the name Thad Thomas sat by the back of the computer monitor. Like the angry man earlier, this man was bald, though his baldness was worn as a style choice, not an inherited trait. His bright green eyes were trained on me. I'd never seen eyes so green before. My money was on colored contacts.

"I'm Samantha Kidd," I said for the third time that morning. "I'm here to help with the exhibit."

"The exhibit is upstairs."

"I was told to check in with someone in this office."

As he looked past me to the desk and around the office, presumably to see if I'd pocketed anything while in the office alone, I took in his outfit. Blue-and-white-checkered shirt with a yellow bowtie. Dark denim jeans. Frye boots.

Frye boots?

"Why didn't I hear you?" I asked.

"What?"

"Your boots. They should have made noise on the marble floor. Why didn't I hear you?"

"Rubber soles."

"Frye boots don't come with rubber soles." He stood straighter and focused on me. For the briefest second, I regretted my black strapless jumpsuit, my silver leather blazer, and my lime-green obi belt. I stood by the pink shoes.

"Tell me again why you're here?" he asked once his full-body scan was complete.

"Eddie Adams asked me to help with the exhibit."

"You're here to help Eddie?" His condescension deflated. "Go on up. I'll get you a pass this afternoon."

The Ribbon Museum of Art had been part of the city's history since the late twenties. As a child growing up in Ribbon, I'd been on more than one field trip to the imposing building during elementary school. I discovered "Jazz Under the Stars" during my teens and had a few dates at the planetarium across the parking lot.

The building was one of my favorite places in Ribbon. A spacious foyer, with admissions on the left and the gift shop on the right, gave way to a flight of wide marble stairs. Ten steps up was a landing, above which was a massive window that looked out over the manicured grounds. The staircase split into two additional flights, one to the left and one to the right, both leading to the upstairs gallery space where I found Eddie.

Eddie Adams, visual manager for the local retailer Tradava and extender of the invitation to work for zero pay, was knee-deep in Styrofoam peanuts and bubble wrap. His hands were wrapped around a white armless mannequin that he was trying (unsuccessfully) to anchor onto a chrome pole base. Behind him stood an army of similar limbless mannequins. At least two were headless.

Beads of sweat dotted his forehead. His bleached-blond hair, left uncut for the past several months, was tucked behind his ears. He planted his black-and-white-checkered Vans on either side of the mannequin and tipped it to the side.

"This place smells like garlic and mothballs," I said, wrinkling my nose.

"Give me a hand."

I waved my hand in front of my nose to dull the smell and walked to where he stood. I picked up a long white leg and snapped it onto the torso, and then I tipped the chrome pole and poked around under the butt of the mannequin until the pole slid into the opening. All in all, it was an embarrassing display of, well, visual display.

As the base slid into the figure, Eddie shifted the weight of the mannequin toward me. I wrapped my arms around her slight waist, and my strapless jumpsuit dropped a couple of inches. I dropped the mannequin and hoisted up my neckline.

Eddie grabbed the torso and staggered backward under the weight of it. He pushed it back to a standing position. "Dude?" he asked.

"I had to adjust."

He scanned my outfit. "I thought I told you to dress appropriately."

"What's inappropriate about my outfit?" I turned away and faced the mirror that was propped against the wall. Any regrets I'd momentarily thought when the man downstairs had given me the once over vanished. The jumpsuit had been left over from my J-Lo phase in the early millennium. Every piece had been rediscovered after a recent closet purge, which resulted less in a purge and more in fashions-through-the-ages.

I grabbed the base of the column, helped Eddie move it a few feet to the left, and then backed away as he righted it and lined the straight edge of the base to a perfect parallel with the wall behind him.

"How's the job search going?" he asked.

"How much do you think I could get for a dozen satin cargo pants from the mid-nineties?"

"That well, huh?" Eddie flopped down on a pile of bubble wrap. A burst of popping sounds shot from under him.

"The main problem is my recent work history. I was a buyer at Bentley's for nine years, which was great, but it feels like another lifetime ago. After that, I moved here and worked at Tradava for a week. Six months later I worked at Heist for something like that too. So basically my resume makes me look like a flake."

"I might have a lead for you. That's why I wanted your help. I can't pay you, but I thought I could be a reference. Give you something to fill in the gap in your employment until you find a job." He kicked his feet out in front of him. "But it doesn't really matter, I guess. This whole project has been trouble from the start. You showing up looking like an extra in a hip-hop video is just the icing on the cake."

"Why would my outfit have anything to do with your project?"

"Because my project could very easily become your project."

"I'm not following."

"Your major was the history of fashion, right? This exhibit encompasses that. We're getting loans from some of the best private collections of clothing in the tri-state area, along with a couple of local hat stores and one designer from Hollywood."

I leaned forward. "The museum's putting on an exhibit on the history of fashion? Here, in Ribbon? You're in charge of it? The whole thing? I would *love* to be involved with something like this, except my experience is in retail buying, not visual."

"That's where the opportunity comes in. I'm in charge of the installation. I'm giving you a foot back inside the door."

"So why's my outfit a problem?"

"I need you to be my liaison with the sponsor."

"Who's the sponsor?"

"Tradava."

Tradava. The local department store that had promised me a job but delivered a homicide investigation—and then sent me a very polite letter that said they were dismantling the very department I'd been hired to work in.

As soon as I heard the name of the store, I tensed. I turned away from Eddie and pushed my fingers into my long dark brown hair, boosting the roots. "You're the curator of the exhibit?"

"Guest curator. More like exhibit merchandiser. Last year the museum sponsored a visual competition between a few different retailers. Tradava won. The prize was the chance to guest curate an exhibit. It took a while for the board of directors to agree on the exhibit concept and for the director to obtain loans from collectors, but once they green-lighted it, I've been on an almost impossible deadline. If you're looking for something to tear you away from your job search, I could use your help coordinating the exhibit. You never know what it could lead to..."

"Maybe I should forget about Tradava. Maybe what happened is a sign that I shouldn't work for them."

"Sign-schmign. You need a job. They're hiring. Sounds like a match to me."

"You don't believe in signs?"

"I believe in stop signs and sale signs. Everything else is woo-woo."

"Oh yeah?" I asked, turning to face him, my hands on my hips.

Eddie's normally unfazed expression was suddenly fazed to the max. I looked down to make sure my jumpsuit hadn't accidentally left me exposed.

"Dude! Move!" he cried out. He jumped out of the chair and came at me with the force of a cannon, catching me off guard and knocking us into a shipping container of Styrofoam peanuts.

A crash sounded behind him. I lifted my head and looked at where I'd stood. A beam of track lighting had fallen from the ceiling, landing on the white mannequin Eddie and I had assembled. She lay crushed on the floor, a pile of broken plaster and limbs.

2

AT A STANDSTILL

THE BOX COLLAPSED UNDER OUR WEIGHT. EDDIE ROLLED OFF ME. I yanked up the top of my jumpsuit.

The thin black man from the office scaled the staircase. "What happened?" he asked. His eyes went from the light fixture in the middle of the room to me in the middle of a squashed shipping container of foam peanuts to Eddie.

I struggled to get out of the box with little success and even less decorum. "The light fixture fell."

Eddie and Frye Boots looked at the ceiling. Eddie's arms dangled by his sides. Frye Boots crossed his over his chest. They studied the mess on the floor. The track sat, bent at an unfortunate angle, in the exact space where I'd been standing. The head of the mannequin rolled back and forth. Eddie put his sneaker against its cheek to make it stop.

With a little momentum, I flipped the box onto its side and rolled out. I got on all fours and pushed myself up, dusting residual Styrofoam bits off my tush. When I stood, a spear of pain shot through my ankle.

"I'm okay. Thanks for asking," I said.

"Let's try a formal introduction here," Eddie said. "Thad Thomas, meet Samantha Kidd. Samantha's here to help with the exhibit. Sam, Thad's the assistant to the museum director."

"We met downstairs," he said, ignoring my outstretched hand. Thad turned to Eddie. Afternoon light from the museum windows glistened off his almond-colored, clean-shaven cheeks. "Milo Delaney is on his way with his collection. You'll have time to unpack everything and start setting up today."

"Already?" Eddie said.

Thad handed Eddie a janitor-sized key ring on a lime-green D-clamp, which Eddie fastened to the waistband of his already-low jeans. "Keep working as long as you like. Drop the keys off in my office before you go." He turned his back to us and left down the grand staircase without saying goodbye.

"Is everybody around here so rude?" I asked.

"Never mind him. Are you okay?"

"I think so." I looked up. "Has that ever happened before? A light fixture falling from the ceiling?"

"Not as far as I know." We stared at the ceiling for a few more seconds.

He tapped the ring of keys, so they bounced against the palm of his hand. "Remind me to put these in the admissions office before we leave tonight."

"I don't think there's much of a chance of you forgetting, considering they're compromising the waistband of your pants."

He looked down. A band of elastic with Joe Boxer stamped on it rested below his washboard stomach. The weight of the keys pulled the right side of his pants two inches lower than the left. He tucked his index fingers into the belt loops and hiked them back up. As soon as he let go, they fell again.

"Who's the extra in a hip-hop video now?" I asked under my breath.

He made a face at me and let the keys dangle. "The engineers were trying to figure out a way to remove the track lighting yesterday. Maybe they started the job and nobody told me, which is possible, since I'm not even supposed to be here right now. Either way, until somebody moves this thing, I'm at a standstill."

I bent down, wrapped my hands under the steel track of the light fixture, and then lifted with my back the way most chiropractors tell you not to do. The beam barely budged.

"This is not good." He dropped to the floor and bent forward with his head between his knees. His hands were on his head, and after sitting there for upward of a minute, he mussed up his hair and pushed his hands out front. I joined him on the pile of bubble wrap.

"I get the feeling the light fixture is only part of the problem," I said. "Do you want to talk about it?"

"What's there to talk about? Tradava has been trying to build their reputation as an affordable fashion retailer. Somebody on the board thought it would be a good idea to host events every market week, to give the city of Ribbon something 'fashiony' to participate in and connect back to the store. I'm working with the head of the history of fashion curriculum at I-FAD and the director of the Ribbon Museum of Art to put together an exhibit that Tradava's sponsoring."

I-FAD was Ribbon's answer to Parsons, FIT, and FIDM. If you couldn't afford the move to New York or Los Angeles but wanted a creative background to help break into the fashion industry, I-FAD was your college. Half the buyers at Tradava graduated from there. I'd recently spent some time on the campus posing as an undercover student. The reasons for that had started out innocently and ended in death. I wasn't rushing to return to the campus.

"You really think my helping you will lead to a job for me?"

"Who knows? I heard they're putting the trend department back together. You could get that job you moved here for."

That job was trend specialist, a job I could do with both hands tied behind my back with last year's must-have scarf. I wanted—no, needed—a job. In the past year I'd burned through the majority of my savings account. I'd moved to Ribbon for a chance to change my life. Well, to change my life and buy the house my parents vacated and establish my own identity and prove I was a grownup and—

"Earth to Sam," Eddie said, snapping his fingers in front of my face.

"What?" I asked again.

"Pay attention."

I looked around the open gallery at the naked mannequins and the boxes and the bubble wrap. "Unless the exhibit is called the Emperor's New Clothes, it seems you're missing a vital element of this 'fashion exhibit.'" I used the first two fingers on each hand to make air quotes around "fashion exhibit," just in case Eddie missed the sarcasm in my voice.

"That's the thing. With the current interest in all things retro, Tradava wanted the exhibit to be both art and merchandise. The head of fashion merchandising from I-FAD is connected to local money. Apparently, the closets in those Main Line houses are better than the archives at the Met."

"The entire exhibit is on loan?"

"Most of it. Tradava signed a licensing agreement to produce an accessories collection. We'll showcase the originals in the exhibit and have knockoffs for sale in the store and here the day after the exhibit opens."

"Whose idea was this? It doesn't sound like the kind of exhibit the museum usually puts together."

"Christian Jhanes, the guy from I-FAD, arranged it."

"I think I met him. Bald guy, blue glasses, suit, T-shirt?"

"No, that's Dirk Engle. He's the hotshot curator."

"He *was* the hotshot curator. The way he stormed out of here proclaiming he quit makes me think he isn't coming back."

"Dirk Engle quits once a day. He'll be back."

"Even if he changes his mind, some other guy told him to be gone by midnight."

Some of the color left Eddie's face.

"Believe in signs yet?" I asked the top of his head.

As he sat there staring at the floor under the soles of his Vans, I stood and wandered around the gallery space. Small pedestals, flashlights, wire, and a large plastic bag filled with mannequin limbs sat along the back wall. A flatbed with the fixture that had crashed to the floor and the trail of foam peanuts occupied the center. I knocked a few peanuts to the right with my instep.

"Fine." I sighed. "I'll help you. Tell me what I need to know about the exhibit, and I don't mean what you already told me. Tell me everything. The good, the bad, and the ugly."

He adopted a stuffy tone of voice and spoke down his nose. "The exhibit is being pitched as 'a juxtaposition of film and fashion.' The general manager told me if this was a success, there's a promotion in it for me. Director of visual merchandising."

Not too shabby. Tradava had very few directors, and a promotion like that would put Eddie squarely in a place others liked to call sitting pretty.

"Apparently Tradava invested a lot of money in a licensing agreement with Hedy London. She's a noir actress who started collecting costumes when she retired—"

"I know who Hedy London is," I said. Any self-respecting movie lover knew who Hedy London was. She was a legend, with the likes of Janet Leigh and Eva Marie Saint. The thing was, Hedy London didn't show up until thirty years after them.

"Hedy London's personal accessories are being sent here. Gloves, belts, stoles, and hats. That's the category the store's basing their projection on: the hats."

"Hats?"

"Hats. The guy you saw this morning, Dirk Engle, owns a third-generation hat store in Philadelphia." Eddie picked up a white thumb that had broken off the mannequin and tossed it across the floor like he was skipping stones on a lake. "Figures he'd bail on this thing. Now what am I going to do?"

"Why does that figure? You mean Thad was hostile toward him too?"

"Thad? He's not hostile. He's under a lot of pressure."

"Yes, but pressure doesn't excuse the need for manners."

I approached a row of bubble-wrapped heads sitting on the outskirts of the room. "Why would Tradava bring in a hat store owner to curate an exhibit with their name on it? Especially if they want to get all the retail credit. You would think that's a conflict of interest."

"Rumor has it they wanted him for more than his ability to merchandise millinery. He boasts the largest client list of hat collectors in the country. I'm pretty sure that client list is what Tradava thought they were buying when they offered him the job."

"Do I know his store?" I asked.

"What's On Your Mind."

"Nothing's on my mind except the name of the store."

"What's On Your Mind."

"Stop it! What's the name of the store?"

"Who's on first?" Eddie doubled over with laughter.

"And What's on second, and I Don't Know is on third. Why are we doing Abbot and Costello?"

"'What's On Your Mind' is the name of the hat store." This time Eddie used air quotes. "Christian made Dirk sign a nondisclosure agreement. I can't imagine what he was offered to make that happen."

"Maybe he made him an offer he couldn't refuse. Still, this is a pretty outside-the-box concept. I don't remember the Tradava executives being such forward thinkers."

I looked around at the building. It was bare-bones, the kind of blown-out interior that lacked architectural elements or character. The only thing it had going for it was that it was big. I hoped Eddie had access to lots of merchandise; otherwise, the exhibit would be dwarfed by the cavernous concrete shell.

"You were a buyer," Eddie said, referring to my past. "You know how all that stuff works better than I do. But you'd have to be living under a rock not to notice that every celebrity out there is wearing some kind of hat these days. Even if they don't know the difference between a fedora and a fascinator, hats are the last accessory to get the pop-culture treatment. They were all over the runways this season. It's a high-margin business, and apparently there's not a lot of competition. Even with the struggling economy, Engle's store gets national exposure."

A pretty woman climbed the stairs. She had platinum-blond hair and the eyebrows to match, framing a porcelain complexion half hidden behind square black glasses. Edith Head meets Lisa Loeb. The paleness of her face contrasted starkly with her black mock-turtleneck, tucked into boxy, hip-slung pants. And despite the low rise of her trousers, there was nary a muffin top in sight. If it weren't for square-toed loafers that bordered on orthopedic, I might have been jealous.

"Hat exhibit, heads up!" she said and giggled at her joke. "There's a delivery for you downstairs."

"The hats!" Eddie hopped up and jogged down the stairs two at a time.

"Hi, I'm Samantha," I said to the woman.

"I'm Rebecca," she answered with a smile. "I work in the gift shop downstairs. Are you part of Tradava's team?"

"You could say that," I said. I didn't add that it if you did say it, you'd be lying.

Eddie returned in the elevator with a cart piled high with matching brown boxes, each secured with packing tape. The corners were numbered. I spied two, five, and eleven and assumed the rest filled in the gaps. Number two had a crushed corner. Rebecca helped him maneuver the cart to the center of the room and then said, "Left."

"She's a perky one," I said.

"Tell me about it. She's here before me, and even after I've had three cups of coffee, she's still got me beat."

"Exactly how much coffee do you drink?"

He ignored the question and grabbed the box numbered five. "Help me open these." He handed me a box cutter.

I picked one of the boxes up, expecting it to be heavier than it was. I sliced through the packing tape and extracted a long piece of bubble wrap. I pulled it from the box, revealing nothing.

"This box is empty."

Eddie slid the blade from his Swiss Army knife through the brown tape on his box. "This one too."

We made it through half the boxes and had turned up little more than a hodgepodge of mismatched bubble wrap. When I picked up box number seven and shook it, something inside rattled. I sliced through the packing tape, folded the flaps back, and then pulled out an object wrapped in a long strip of clear bubble wrap. It took the better part of a minute to get to the item inside the packing material, and when I did, I wished I hadn't.

It was a forest-green fedora stabbed through the middle with a knife.

3

———

A 'TO WHOM' KIND OF GUY

I dropped the hat. Eddie snatched it from the floor and put it back in the box. He reached for a tape gun and resealed the box. "I'm not in charge, and that wasn't intended for me. I'm going to pretend I never saw it, and I'll tell Christian the hats are missing."

"Did I hear you correctly, Mr. Adams? Did you say the Hedy London hats are missing?" The man who had crept up on us without any clicking or clacking or elevator bells approached us slowly. Steely blue eyes glowed from a tanned face that was framed by highlighted, golden-brown hair. He wore a wrinkled white shirt with bold purple, black, and green stripes down the left side, dark jeans with wide cuffs, and black crocodile shoes that were both expensive and well cared for. His speech was proper and befitting the person to whom it belonged. And as weird as that sounded, he was a "to whom" kind of guy.

Eddie dropped the tape gun. It clattered against the marble. The man turned to me and held out a hand that flashed with a silver ring. "I don't believe we've met. Christian Jhanes, museum director." A spark of electricity bounced between our fingers when I grasped his hand.

"Samantha Kidd."

There was an air of electricity around Christian Jhanes. I tried my best to channel my old professional self. I brushed my hair away from my face and stood my full five feet, seven inches, but truth be told, his name had been an announcement; my name had been more of a mumble. I shrank under his (not particularly secret) assessment of my strapless jumpsuit, even though I'd defended its style integrity earlier.

His attention turned back to Eddie, who was paler than usual under his tan.

I stepped forward. "I think there was a mix-up with the shipment. These boxes are empty."

Christian's forehead wrinkled. He picked up an open box and checked the label. "Where did these come from?"

"I don't know," Eddie said. "Rebecca said there was a shipment for the exhibit. I assumed it was the hats."

"Have you gone through all them?"

"Only about half."

"Then I suggest you go through the rest before making an assertion of phantom hats, Mr. Adams." He smiled, though the smile didn't reach his eyes.

"Maybe there are more downstairs. I'll go check," I said. My ankle was still tender, so I rode the elevator to the first floor and headed to the gift outpost. A spinning metal rack that held books of designer paper dolls stood by the end of the counter. I spun the rack and hovered my hand by *Fashions of the Seventies.*

"Were you looking for me?" a voice asked from somewhere behind the display.

I stepped closer and saw Rebecca adjusting a tray of scarves behind the case. She refolded one of the Mondrian silk squares with right-angle precision befitting the De Stijl movement.

"Hi," I said. "I'm looking for the rest of the boxes. Are they down here?"

"There are no other boxes. Those were the only ones the woman dropped off."

"They were dropped off? Not delivered through the mail?"

"No. I mean yes. I mean, they were dropped off."

"By a woman, you said? Did you catch her name?"

Rebecca looked at me funny, like I was asking too many questions, which I was. "Is something wrong?"

"No, well, I don't know. Christian said there should be more hats."

"Christian—oh, you mean Dr. Jhanes. Yes, he's been anxious about the arrival of the hats. The woman who dropped them off works at a local hat store." She climbed a ladder behind the counter and adjusted a row of replicas of Rodin's *The Thinker*. "Are you excited about the exhibit?" she asked.

"I suppose. It's exciting to have this in Ribbon."

"With the attention surrounding this exhibit, we're all on our toes a little bit more. I don't know why, though. Dr. Jhanes is a genius. If everybody does what he asks, this'll be great."

"I thought he was new?"

"He's new to the museum. For the past seventeen years, he's been the chairman of the history of fashion curriculum at I-FAD."

"Eddie said something about him working at I-FAD. You mean he left there and works here now?"

She nodded. "Dr. Jhanes is going to shake things up around Ribbon. He's been hobnobbing with donors and members of the board. He's supposed to be collaborating with the former director, but he's not interested in the way things used to be done. He's high-energy, fast thinking. The last director was a dud. I don't think they see eye to eye."

"I thought Dr. Daum was the museum director," I said.

She bit her lower lip before nodding and then turned her attention back to the Thinker statues. "Dr. Daum retired. He still comes around a couple times a week, though."

I knew Dr. Daum well. I'd volunteered at the museum one day a week during my summers off from college. I did research, typed up labels, wrote grant proposals. Dr. Daum was the only person who wanted to walk around the museum with me and talk about the garments displayed in the rotating collections. Fortuny, Poiret, Norma Kamali. I spent the better part of my day in the basement updating files or working on the computer, but I'd spent my lunches learning about the collections from him.

Dr. Daum had written one of my two letters of recommendation to Bentley's New York department store, helping me land a job in their training program. After I'd been promoted to senior shoe buyer for them, he'd occasionally send me magazine clippings of shoes with notes in the margin. "Were you responsible for this?" he'd write, or sometimes, "Not my fave."

My favorite was after I'd had a particularly difficult season because the rest of the world didn't believe as strongly as I did that riding boots were just as fabulous in mauve as they'd been in black, brown, and tan. I'd taken a bloodbath on markdowns to liquidate my inventory and questioned my risk-taker instincts. A clipping from our catalog arrived in the store's mail along with a page from a glossy celebrity magazine that showed a young it-girl in the boots. Dr. Daum's comment said, "Everybody should own a pair of mauve riding boots." Despite the poor performance of the inventory, I agreed.

"I don't care how much of a mover and shaker Christian Jhanes is," I said. "If he doesn't appreciate Dr. Daum's experience, he's an idiot."

Rebecca's eyes grew wide, and she stared behind me from her perch halfway up the ladder.

"Ms. Kidd," Christian said from behind me.

I turned around. My hands fingered a pair of turquoise beaded moccasins from a large cylindrical container next to the register. It was more for distraction than necessity.

Christian ran a manicured hand through his golden-brown locks, and I was struck by how long it had been since I saw buffed nails on a man's hand.

Rebecca lost her balance on the ladder, and her knuckles went white as she caught her fall and reestablished her footing. Slowly she stepped on the rungs until her clunky shoe connected with the rubber mat behind the glass counter.

"What were you doing, Rebecca?" he asked.

"I was organizing the back stock of Thinkers," she said.

"You shouldn't waste your time on anything above eye level. Nobody looks up in a store. But your cases, your bookshelves, your displays that relate to the rotating collections should be immaculate. And always, always full."

"Of course, Dr. Jhanes."

"This isn't a formal environment. Call me Christian."

"Of course, Christian," she said softly.

"Come down to my office this evening after you close the shop. I have a special project to discuss with you."

Rebecca flushed. Christian paused and rested his hand on the spinning metal rack of paper dolls. "And should Samantha Kidd decide she wants the moccasins she's eyeing, give her a 30 percent discount. She's been helping with the exhibit and should get something for her troubles."

I stiffened at the use of my full name. He'd heard it once when I introduced myself to him. Using it now was less a formality than his way of letting me know he'd been paying attention.

"Speaking of the exhibit, I should be getting back," I said. I set my credit card on the counter. Christian stared again at the turquoise moccasins and left. I gave him a solid thirty-second lead and left the shop with the shoes tucked under my arm.

The elevator doors opened to a scowling Eddie juggling two large metal stands. He set them down and tugged at the bottom of his Frankie tee. "Dude, it's been, like, forty-five minutes. I thought you bailed."

"What is your major malfunction?"

"'Major malfunction?' What is this, a bad eighties movie? Did you find any of the hat samples?"

"No. Rebecca said some woman dropped off the packages. They were sent to the hat store by mistake. You don't think—"

"That Dirk Engle's screwing the exhibit by not delivering the merchandise? I don't know what to think. Maybe he'll cool down tonight and work things out with Christian tomorrow."

"Then what now?"

"New plan. We'll keep working for a couple of hours, give Christian time to leave. Take pictures of everything. I want proof of what I'm doing here. Next, research and copywriting. Go to the computer and look up whatever you can find on Hedy London. And make it good. Rumor has it Christian's trying to get her to come to the gala."

"She's coming? Here? To Ribbon, Pennsylvania?"

"That's what he said."

"Sounds like a publicity stunt. She'll probably cancel at the last minute. Good word of mouth, get people talking. Big letdown the night of the show, though."

"That's why we're not supposed to say anything until it's confirmed. She's working with an up-and-coming designer to produce a collection of hats based on her personal collection. Tradava got the whole thing as an exclusive. Supposed to be huge."

"A licensing deal? Hedy London accessories?"

"Just hats. She signed an agreement for her name to be used—"

"I know how a licensing deal works," I said. "Somebody puts her name on the product, and somebody else makes it. The perfect storm is to get a good name and good merchandise."

It was one thing to have Hedy London's name on the collection of merchandise that would be sold by Tradava. But if she showed up at the opening of the gala? It would put this collection on the map.

"Well, the name is Hedy London, and the merchandise is a limited-edition collection of hats based on the styles she wore in her most famous movie."

"*The Reaper Wears Red*?"

"No, the other one."

"*Murder After Midnight*?"

He nodded.

"What's in it for her?"

"Money and publicity, I'm guessing. You know who she is because you watch TCM. I know who she is because of this exhibit. Christian and Thad know who she is because they're cultured people. But if you asked most people, they probably wouldn't remember her."

"Hedy London was huge in the seventies. She was credited with bringing back the neo-noir."

"The seventies were a long time ago."

"Hedy London transcended the seventies."

"For the sake of this exhibit, I hope you're right," he said.

"Say she's doing it for publicity. What about Tradava? It's a big gamble for them. I doubt her name comes cheap. If it doesn't work, it'll be hard to land another licensing deal in the future. People like a sure thing. Just about the only person who isn't taking a big risk is the designer who she's collaborating with. A lot of designers get their start that way. Nick Taylor got his start that way."

Eddie paused and looked at me. "You know whenever you say his name, your voice changes."

"Does not."

"Does too."

There were battles worth fighting. This wasn't one of them because Eddie was probably right. Ever since my relationship with shoe designer Nick Taylor had shifted from a name on my vendor matrix to the person I was kind of dating, I felt butterflies when I said his name. And there was the teensiest possibility that I sought opportunities to say his name for that very reason.

"But it's true. An unknown designer sometimes gets their big break under a known label, and if the collection is a success, they can come out from behind the velvet curtain and take credit. Brian Atwood for Versace! Another example."

"Don't go off on one of your fashion tangents." Eddie said. He pointed to the computer. "Research. Hedy London. Hats. Go."

It felt good to get off my ankle. I dropped into the chair by the desk, propped my foot on a mannequin torso, and cued up a search engine, making notes of any relevant information. I made a list from IMDb of Hedy's better-known movies and added five of them to my Netflix queue. I watched several trailers on YouTube, joined the Facebook page for her fans, and learned about her background from Wikipedia.

Hours passed. The museum lights shut off automatically at eight o'clock. Once we were in the dark, the eerie quiet of our surroundings became evident. The only illumination came from an assortment of flashlights Eddie had scattered across the floor.

I shut down the computer. "You ready to go?"

"Sure. Can you give me a ride home? I rode my skateboard today."

I looked around for other signs that it was 1985. "Fine."

"Let me drop off the keys, and we can get out of here." Eddie took the stairs, and I took the elevator. I waited by the back doors. After a few minutes, I went looking for him. I found him standing in the doorway, his back to me. I crossed the vestibule. A ray of light from the office sliced through the otherwise dark museum foyer.

"Are you done? Can we leave?" I shuffled closer and saw that he was as white as a sheet of printer paper.

I was pretty sure I matched his shade when I saw the body behind the desk.

4

NO PULSE, NO NOTHING

A man's body lay on the floor. A piece of bubble wrap covered his bald head, distorting his features. A large pomegranate-colored stain pressed against the plastic. His vacant eyes stared through the pockets of air. His torso was wrapped in bubble wrap, and his arms were secured to his sides.

"Is he dead?" I asked, approaching the body. I dropped to my knees and put my hand on his wrist. There was no pulse, no nothing. The temperature of his skin was cool, like a chicken breast that had been left on the counter to defrost.

I shivered and looked around the office. The air conditioner was on high, even though it was October. On the floor by the base of the air conditioning unit sat a pair of royal blue reading glasses.

"This is Dirk Engle," I said, standing too quickly. I tipped forward at a dangerous angle and caught myself on the corner of the desk. The window was pushed open, and a breeze snapped the shades against the frame. A small lamp on the bookcase behind the desk was on, a single bulb shedding light on the scene.

"Look," Eddie said. He pointed inside the room, and I turned back around.

The forest-green felt fedora from the shipment of otherwise

empty boxes lay upside down on the floor next to the body. It looked more out of place than a brunette starring in a Hitchcock movie. The single light source glistened off the jewels on the hatpin. A thin trail of blood had escaped the bubble wrap covering Dirk Engle's head and made a slow but steady path toward the hat.

"That's the hat we had earlier, isn't it?" I asked.

I didn't need him to answer. We both knew it was. And here it was, sitting in the admissions office of the museum, next to a dead body wrapped in packing plastic.

Before I could stop him, Eddie picked up the hat. He turned it over in his hands and then dropped it. He squatted, his breathing heavy. "I'm responsible for this. I'm responsible for the hats and the exhibit and the museum. What am I going to do?"

"You're going to call the police."

Eddie looked as surprised as I felt by the voice of reason coming from my mouth. What I didn't tell him was the steady stream of thoughts that had led to that statement: no gloves, dead body, stolen memorabilia, wrong place, wrong time. I might be a lot of things, but I never said I was normal.

Eddie picked up the receiver and called 911. I heard the words "museum," "emergency," and "dead body." He hung up, and a door slammed at the back of the building.

"Who else is here?" Until I'd heard that door shut, I hadn't stopped to think the murderer might still be around.

Eddie's eyes widened his shoulders raised. "I thought it was just us."

"Me too. How long until the cops get here?"

"Soon, I hope."

Sirens wailed in the distance. There was nothing for us to do but wait.

Soon a mêlée of cars, ambulances, and crime scene investigators arrived. Eddie unlocked the back doors and doubled over by the flowerbeds. I looked in the other direction and tried not to think about the image in the office.

A stout man with a short buzz cut got out of a brown sedan and spoke to the female officer who had first arrived on the scene. He dropped his head down, cupping his ear to hear her better. The female officer pointed at me.

He looked up, and his face expression soured.

It had to figure that there was one homicide detective in Ribbon: Detective Loncar. He was tough and gruff, and the last time I'd seen him, he'd been losing the battle with the buttons that kept his shirt closed. Detective Loncar and I had a spotty relationship that started when I discovered my boss dead on my first day at Tradava and continued through a second homicide investigation at a different retailer in Ribbon. Before moving back to my old hometown, I'd researched the weather, the number of sandwich shops in the area, and the caliber of outlet shopping. It hadn't occurred to me to notice that the crime rate was on the rise.

Tonight, he wore a black suit and tie with a white button-down collar shirt. I wondered if his wife had started shopping for him. The shirt was too tight, the tie was too wide, and the pants were too short. Still, I applauded the effort.

He flipped through a small notepad and approached me. "Ms. Kidd. What are you doing here?"

"I'm helping Eddie with the exhibit."

"Who's Eddie?"

"Eddie Adams. Visual manager for Tradava. It was my idea for him to call you," I said, like I was trying to score brownie points with one of my parents by tattling on my sister.

He made a note in his notepad. "Is he around?"

"He's fertilizing the rosebushes."

The detective glanced at the back of the building, where Eddie was bent at the waist. Both of his hands were on the building for support. Lights blazed in the background. The parking lot was a collection of black and white cop cars parked at angles, like a pile of saddle shoes cast off at a sock hop. Lights pulsated in the background like a disco, completely confusing my dance-era metaphor.

"Were you with him when he found the body?"

"Sort of. I mean, yes. I mean, I was by the back door, and when he didn't catch up with me, I went to check on him."

"Because you were concerned."

"Yes."

"What was he doing that made you concerned?"

"He was dropping keys. It took him longer than it should have."

"You're saying Mr. Adams could have been doing something other than dropping off keys in the admissions office?"

"I'm not saying that. Eddie was with me the whole time."

"Except when he was dropping off keys."

"Yes—no!"

"Ms. Kidd, what am I going to find when I go into that office?"

"A cold, dead man wrapped up in plastic packing wrap." I didn't mention the identity of the corpse. They would figure that out soon enough. I told the detective what Eddie and I were doing at the museum and how we had come to find the body.

Loncar took notes, the kind that probably only made sense to him when he reviewed them later, and flipped the notepad shut. "Ms. Kidd, stay out of this. Don't make me lock you up to keep you from being a public nuisance."

"I'm not *in* this. I was just trying to help a friend."

"Okay, so consider me a friend too." He smiled a half smile that made his face resemble a jack-o'-lantern. "You'll be helping plenty if you let me do my job. You're not planning to leave town, are you? In case I have any follow-up questions to our interview?"

The detective's question gave me pause. We'd done the right thing by calling him, but this wasn't my first time at this particular rodeo. Word about homicides spread quickly, and my boyfriend and dinner date wasn't going to be pleased about my involvement.

"No, but you're going to keep this between us, right?"

He stared at me for a couple of seconds, made another note in his notepad, and walked away.

I stood off to the side, waiting for Eddie to give his statement to the detective too. After a couple of minutes, they shook hands and Eddie joined me.

By the time we left the museum, it was clear that with or without a skateboard, he was in no shape to drive.

A few minutes and a wall of silence later, I pulled up in front of his apartment.

"Dude, do you want to crash here tonight?" he asked.

"No, I have to be up early tomorrow, and it's better that I sleep at home. Are you going to be okay by yourself?"

"As okay as I can be, considering."

He got out of my car, and I waited by the curb until he'd made it to the front door and let himself in.

I backed out of the lot and drove home in a swirling cloud of thoughts. There was no escaping it. Dirk Engle was dead. And considering the hat left sitting next to him, it wasn't a stretch to think the murder was connected to the exhibit.

I couldn't—just couldn't—let myself be involved. No way. Just because Eddie and I found the body didn't mean anything. The cops would figure out who had committed the crime. But I couldn't help wondering why someone had murdered the curator of a hat exhibit.

If the cops needed any information from me, they would know where to find me, but right now, I had to push the memory out of my mind. Because if I wasn't going to be helping Eddie at the museum, then it was back to the job search for me. And while I didn't want to think about it, I knew there was one person who would employ me, no questions asked. I'd been turning down his offer for a month now because, after nine years of working together when I was a buyer and he was a shoe designer, I was finally in a place where work couldn't interfere with my interest in dating him. I knew his offer had more to do with helping me through a rough patch of employment cooties than an interest in my resume. Eddie's request that I help him at the museum had given me a temporary excuse to keep Nick in the boyfriend column, but after tonight, I didn't expect to be back at the museum anytime soon.

As much as I didn't want to do it, tomorrow morning I was going to see Nick about a job.

5

———

A SERIOUS TALK

THE NEXT MORNING, I ROSE WITH THE SUN, DRANK THREE CUPS OF coffee, and pulled into the parking lot to the strip mall where Nick kept a satellite office five minutes before he usually arrived. I'd chosen a black pinstriped pantsuit that I'd worn only once and a pair of polka-dotted ankle-wrap sandals I'd recently rediscovered thanks to my closet purge. My ankle was swollen thanks to yesterday's fall, so I secured the shoe to my foot with a roll of black electrical tape.

I approached the door to the showroom and yanked on the locked handles.

"Hey, Kidd," Nick called out from behind me.

I jumped so high I would have flown out of my shoes if one hadn't been secured with electrical tape. Nick wrapped his arms around me from behind and kissed my right cheek. I shrugged out of his embrace, adjusted my jacket, and turned. "We need to have a serious talk."

He looked confused. He unlocked the door and held it open. I crossed the blond-wood floor, trying not to favor my ankle. Halfway to the chair by the desk, my ankle rebelled, and I fell to the floor.

Nick helped me up. "Are you okay?"

"I'm fine." I tried to pretend the fall was intentional.

"Are you sure?"

"I said I'm fine."

"Then why is your shoe taped to the side of your foot?"

We both looked down. My shoe jutted out at a ninety-degree angle from my instep.

Nick wheeled a chair from behind the desk and faced me. He picked up my foot and moved the shoe back into place. His hands lingered on my ankle, slowly massaging the sore joint. The pain was quickly replaced with a different sensation that traveled from his fingertips to somewhere in the panty region.

"We haven't been together long enough to have a serious talk, have we? Is everything okay?"

"No. I mean, yes. I mean, this isn't about you and me."

"What's it about?"

"A job. I need you to give me a job." I almost couldn't believe I was asking for a pity paycheck from Nick.

He released me, picked up my foot, and set it on the ground next to my other foot. "You're asking me for a job."

"Yes."

"This... is an interview."

"Yes. You know my work history. You know what I'm capable of. You know I moved here for a job at Tradava."

He crossed his arms and tilted his head. "Refresh my memory. Why did you lose that job?"

"Mix-up."

"What kind of mix-up?"

"Suspicion of murdering my boss."

"Maybe I should take some time to think about this." The laugh lines by the corner of his eyes crinkled.

"I wasn't guilty, and you know it."

We stared at each other longer than I expected. Truthfully? I figured when after I choked on the words, he'd say "Fine, you're hired. Start work on Monday, and oh, by the way, I made dinner reservations at seven."

But he didn't. Working for Nick would give me experience to fill the gap on my resume, and it would keep me from returning to the museum. But Nick saying yes would make him my boss. And that would create some potential problems, considering my thoughts about Nick didn't involve performance reviews. Unless you consider a different kind of performance, and that wasn't the type of thing I hoped he'd review me on—

"Kidd? What do you want to do with your life?"

"I want to get a steady job. I don't care what it is."

"That's not a to-do. That's a side effect. You were a buyer. You were a good buyer. Why'd you give it up?"

"I don't know," I said. But I knew. I'd gotten good enough at my job that I'd gotten restless.

Retail buying involves a constant shifting of focus and priorities. Planning a business for today, tomorrow, three months, next year. You often buy sandals in winter and boots during a heat wave. You learn to take risks, at first calculated, until the calculations become second nature.

If you sell out of one hundred pairs of rain boots in the first week of February, how many could you sell by the end of April? What if a fashion director names them a seasonal trend? And then, advertising comes onboard and makes rain boots part of their print campaign: rain boots poolside in summer and as a gift item for the holidays. Can a pair of $100 rubber boots become hot enough to help you layer a million dollars of top-line sales to your year end?

Second nature.

By the time I'd pushed the boundaries of rain boots, mid-heel dancing shoes, and gladiator sandals, I'd become something of a tastemaker. (Cowboy boots may have been my downfall.)

In truth, I never had a light bulb moment that caused me to leave. My parents dangled that carrot in front of me: "We're selling the house and moving to California." The weekend I spent in Ribbon helping them empty out the house I'd known my whole life left me feeling like I'd lost touch with my grounding center.

I had a chance run-in with a wise man who might have become my next mentor if he hadn't gotten killed before my first day on the job. He gave me the encouragement I needed in the form of a job offer in the trend office of Tradava. Despite my experience with planning, projecting, and taking calculated risks, that didn't work out as I'd planned.

"You need a showroom manager, right?" I asked.

"Right."

"And I need an income stream."

"The pay's not that good," he said with a chuckle.

"This isn't funny."

"We should talk about this." His expression turned serious. "It'll change things."

An unexpected windfall in the form of a cash payout from my short-lived tenure at Heist, a competitor of Tradava that had barely been open a fortnight, had paid four months of bills and my car insurance and bought me a spectacular outfit that made me feel like Rosalind Russell in *His Girl Friday*. Did I mention the windfall paid for my Netflix addiction as well?

I looked away and fought to clear my head. Something—maybe the all-too-recent memory of Dirk Engle's bubble-wrapped body at the museum—told me this was the right thing.

"Hire me. I know you need help. I can do the work. Put me on your payroll, at least until I find something else."

"You're sure?"

"Yes."

"I'll hire you on one condition: it's temporary, and the second something better turns up, you'll either quit or I'll fire you. It'll be a big help working with someone who doesn't have a learning curve."

"Great. Thank you."

"You're welcome," Nick said and leaned down to kiss me.

I leaned out of range of his lips. "I think we should be professional while we're working. So it feels official."

He traced a line down my nose and onto my lips. His eyes focused on them. My heartbeat picked up and my palms got sweaty.

"Kidd, I kind of like having you as my girlfriend. I'm not sure I'm willing to trade that in. It would be a lot easier to find a showroom assistant than to find another you." His warm fingers cupped the side of my neck inside the collar of the white shirt I wore under the pinstriped suit, and he pulled me close. This time when he kissed me, I didn't pull away.

There was something about kissing Nick that made me feel like a teenager, not a thirty-something. I got butterflies in my stomach, and my knees went weak. We'd been taking our time over the past few months—silly since it had taken us nine years to get to our first date —but I didn't want to blow what we had by keeping secrets from him.

Job or no job, I had to tell him what happened.

I pulled away. "Nick, last night—" I paused. I put my fingertips on his lips and considered the consequences of lying versus the consequences of telling him the truth. He studied me with his root-beer-barrel colored eyes, and I knew there was only one option. "Last night there was a homicide at the Ribbon Museum of Art. I was there when Eddie made the 911 call."

6

HANGING AROUND THE DOCKS LOOKING FOR ACTION

DETAILS OF THE HOMICIDE HAD BEEN IN THE MORNING PAPER AND ON the local news. I knew because I'd gotten up early to see what the police knew. I wasn't going to tell Nick any of that.

"I was helping Eddie at the museum. He's working on an exhibit of Hedy London vintage costumes. When it was time to leave, he went to the admissions office to drop off the keys. He found a body."

Nick sat up straight. "If I put you on my payroll, will that keep you from getting involved?"

"With you? I'm already involved with you."

"With the homicide."

"I'm kind of involved in that too. Like I said, I'm the one who called the police. I told Detective Loncar what I saw. And then I drove Eddie to his apartment and went home."

"That's it?"

"That's it. It's not like I was hanging around the docks looking for action."

"There are no docks in Ribbon."

"You know what I mean. I wasn't looking for this. I was helping a friend. It's not my fault someone committed a murder while I was there."

"I don't like it when you put yourself in dangerous situations. You know that."

"Then give me a job. I can't be in two places at once. If I'm here with you during the day, and out with you at night, then I can't exactly be in any dangerous situations, can I?"

"If you weren't here right now, I would have hired some young college graduate and lost three months of my time teaching her how to run the office. Are you serious about this? Because I need someone who knows what goes on in a showroom, who can problem-solve and think fast, who can act on her own without having to ask my permission for every little thing. I need someone like you. I know it was your idea, but it would solve a problem for me too."

"Then it's decided?"

He held out his hand, and I shook it. "You're hired. You start on Monday."

"So if we go out tonight, you won't be my boss yet, right?"

"I sure hope not." He leaned forward and kissed me again. This time his hands went places that would have cost him a sexual harassment suit seventy-two hours later.

Later, I couldn't help wondering what it was about me that voluntarily made my life more difficult.

I arrived home shortly after two. Eddie was waiting on the porch. I unlocked the front door, and he followed me inside.

"I have a problem," I said.

"Join the club."

Logan, my slightly snobby black cat, met us in the living room and meowed loud enough to alert the neighbors across the street that it was time to be fed. I scooped him up and carried him into the kitchen, set him down, and fed him a few treats from a drawer that needed a new knob. Eddie scratched Logan's ears until he purred like a coffee percolator. He tipped his head and ran the length of his body against Eddie's faded jeans and then left us alone in search of something more interesting under the sofa.

"Are you hungry?" I asked.

"Sure. Do you have any fruit?"

I reached into the freezer and pulled out a carton of Neapolitan ice cream.

"I said fruit."

"It's Breyer's. It has strawberries." I pulled two bowls from the cabinet. I doled out the ice cream and pulled two spoons from the drawer and carried it all to the table before Eddie spoke.

"Dude, I think I bit off more than I can chew."

Yesterday, Eddie had presented the situation at the museum as an opportunity to get back in at Tradava coupled with the opportunity for him to become a director. Today, the story was different. The director was pressuring him with unreasonable demands. Hats had gone missing. Curators had been killed. Odd items had arrived in the mail.

"It's starting to sound like Lilac Inn over there," I said.

"What's that?"

"*Lilac Inn.* You know, Nancy Drew?"

He shook his head.

"Okay, Terror Castle."

"What?"

"The Three Investigators?" Still nothing. "Didn't you read as a kid?"

He ignored the question. "Christian called me at six this morning. He wants to open the exhibit this Thursday. This Thursday! That's less than a week. I can't make that deadline. Not now."

"You'd think he'd cancel the whole thing, considering a man was murdered."

"I asked him about that. He said it was too late to cancel. Collectors are scheduled to view the exhibit on Thursday afternoon. Christian only communicates the vaguest of details, and I don't know which way to turn. It's overwhelming." He repeatedly tapped his fingers against his sternum.

"You told Detective Loncar all of this, right?" I asked.

"Sort of."

"What does 'sort of' mean?"

"Wait here." Eddie left the room and returned with his black nylon backpack. He set it on the dining room table, reached inside, and pulled out a hat.

Not just a hat. *The* hat. The forest-green felt fedora that had been in the admissions office next to Dirk Engle's body. It was dusty on one side. He stared at it for seven seconds without moving. Then he set it on the center of the wooden table.

"This is the hat from the admissions office," he said, confirming my worst thoughts. "It was in my backpack when we left."

"How did it get in your backpack?"

"I put it there."

"You stole evidence from the crime scene?"

"I picked it up off the floor to keep the blood from getting on it, remember? I must have carried it outside with me when I got sick. I found it in my backpack this morning."

"You have two choices: call the detective or take the hat back to the museum."

"To the admissions office? It's a crime scene. I can't just waltz in there."

"You just said Christian moved up the deadline on the exhibit! How are you supposed to get anything done if you can't get into the museum?"

"I can get into the museum. I can't get into the admissions office."

"You also can't walk around with a hat that was found next to a corpse." From the way Eddie looked at me, I suspected he thought I was being less than supportive. "What about the gift shop? Can you leave it there? That's nowhere near the admissions office."

"Sure, yes, the gift shop is probably available."

"Too bad you left the keys on Thad's desk."

Eddie reached into the zippered pocket on the outside of his backpack and withdrew a set of keys. He set them on the table next to the hat.

"Well, that changes things, doesn't it?"

I leaned against the back of the sofa and looked up at the ceiling. There were a thousand things wrong with what Eddie had done and what I was thinking. But Eddie was my closest friend. He was the one who'd seen me through the murder of my boss when I first moved back to Ribbon. He was the one who trusted me when I shut him out and got involved in another shady situation. I'd known him since I was in high school, and with all of the change in my life over the past few years, his friendship felt stable. If he needed my help, I'd be there for him.

"Okay, here's what we'll do. We'll take the hat back to the museum while they're closed. You can leave it somewhere nobody would look, like the lost and found? After we leave, you'll call Loncar and tell him to look for the hat. Tell him you forgot about it until today. You remember it was there but don't remember where you left it. Let him go back to the crime scene and find it in an evidence sweep. Yes, that'll work. The sooner we get the hat back to the museum, the sooner you can wash your hands of any involvement."

THE DRIVE to the museum took less than fifteen minutes, and during fourteen and a half of them, I kept up a steady chatter so Eddie didn't have a chance to think about what we were about to do. Before long we were parked outside the Planetarium, making our way toward the museum.

"While we're here, look around and see if anything seems out of the ordinary. You can't do it when everyone else is around. There are too many distractions," I advised.

"What about you? Aren't you a distraction right now?"

"No. I'm like an extension of you."

"That's comforting."

We headed around to the back of the building.

"Look," Eddie said.

"What?"

"Two suspicious-looking characters making their way through the grounds."

I got excited. "Where?"

He pointed to our reflection in the glass doors.

"This is serious, Eddie. Can you see anything?"

He cupped his hands around his eyes and crept closer to the doors. "There's a stack of boxes inside, addressed to Hat Exhibit. There's a whole bunch. The return address labels are torn off."

"Let me see." I pressed my face up to the glass. I counted nine boxes. *Do not crush* had been printed in a cursive font on the adhesive labels stuck to the side of the boxes.

"Are those the boxes that were delivered yesterday?"

"They don't look the same. Look. There's an open one." He pointed to an empty carton. There was a small red number 2 on the corner. "I think there's something in it. An invoice or packing slip."

"Eddie, when did Thad give you the keys to the museum?" I asked suddenly.

He stared at the keys. "Yesterday. You were there, remember?"

I did. "He specifically asked you to leave them on his desk when you were done?"

"Yes. He said I should work late but to drop them off before I left."

"He arranged it so you'd have access, all by yourself, to the museum and the admissions office. And if you'd left the keys, he could say he knew you'd been there. Are you following me?"

"You don't think Thad—"

Again, I did. "Forget returning the hat. We have to leave."

But we didn't, because just then gunshots filled the air.

NOT EVIDENCE PER SE

EDDIE AND I DROPPED TO OUR HANDS AND KNEES. EDDIE'S HEAD WENT closer to the ground than mine. I looked toward the car but saw nothing suspicious. I pushed myself up until I was kneeling on the grass, and I strained to see into the darkness. If I hadn't heard the crackling of gunfire myself, I wouldn't have believed the sound had taken place.

When nothing happened after ten minutes of waiting, we ran to my car. I dropped Eddie off at his apartment and went home. It wasn't until I parked the car safely in the garage that I realized the hat was still in the backseat. I retrieved it and carried it into my house.

Sunlight filtered through the front windows and struck the jet bead that pierced the grosgrain band around the hat like the single bulb had in the office the night we first found the body. A pheasant feather stood up a full twelve inches. Logan jumped onto the table and swatted the feather. I scooped him up and set him on the floor and then picked up the phone and called Detective Loncar.

The call went into voice mail, and I left a message. "Hi, Detective, this is Samantha Kidd. I know you probably weren't expecting to hear from me, but I have something at my house that relates to your case, and I think you should see it. I mean, I think you should have it. I mean, it's not a gift, but it's from the exhibit. At least I think it is. I don't know. But probably you should figure that out, not me. Isn't that how this is supposed to work?" I paused for a moment, left my phone number so he wouldn't have to dig through my police file to find it, and hung up.

I wrapped the hat in tissue paper, nestled it in a shopping bag, and then carried it to the garage and set it on a top shelf between Logan's slate-blue cat carrier. I propped an old license plate ("You've Got a Friend in Pennsylvania") in front of the bag and stepped back. I wasn't sure what Eddie was going to say when I told him I'd called the detective, but I was fairly sure I'd done the right thing. The longer that hat stayed at my house, the more involved I'd be.

I changed into a satin caftan top that I'd gotten in Chinatown for seven dollars and a pair of black leggings. The top had a kaleidoscope pattern in shades of teal, yellow, black, and white. Logan liked it as much as I did, and now the thin band of black satin that bordered the collar, sleeves, and hem showed the effects of cat teeth and claws from a particularly eventful day of burrowing into the laundry pile.

I went outside and picked up the mail—a pet store ad and new catalog from Tom Sturgis Pretzels—and found a rubber-banded copy of the *Ribbon Times* on the grass halfway between my neighbor's and my house. Possession being nine-tenths of the law and all that, I took it. Not that I knew much about the law outside of what David E. Kelly had taught me in the nineties.

I'd been trying to block the visions of Dirk Engle wrapped in bubble wrap in the admissions office, but flashes of memory kept bleeding through. The gallery had been filled with packing materials, and it would have been easy for someone to get a piece from our trash.

I thought about the argument I'd overheard when I first arrived at the museum and the way Dirk had stormed out. I wish I knew who he'd argued with. Christian? Thad? I'd talked to them both, but neither rang a bell.

That was another thing. Why had Dirk returned to the museum? He'd quit earlier that day. Had he hoped to take something while no one was looking? Or had someone lured him to the admissions office? Maybe he'd been there to sabotage the exhibit he was no longer part of?

I turned my attention to the newspaper. Eventually, I reached a two-page fold-out dedicated to fashion and art. A feature story on a pair of local sisters turning quilts into jackets was sandwiched between a What's Hot/What's Not list and a sidebar on Hawaiian shirts. The rest of the page was littered with shopping ads and coupons. It was hard to believe local boutiques and retailers— Tradava included—expected these ads to generate business. The copy was boring, the ads were stale, and the placement was a waste of money. Why weren't they modernizing their approach with e-mail blasts and postcard mailings?

Because this was Ribbon, Pennsylvania, not Manhattan, New York. We were 130 miles west of the Big Apple, which some days felt like living at the fuzzy end of the lollipop.

I scanned the rest of the page. One ad stood out from the rest. A fifties-style cursive script was laid out next to a photo of a stylish woman with one hand touching the brim of her hat and another hand resting on her hip. The model stared at the copy:

"Cloche" call? Not at all! OVER YOUR HEAD carries the finest assortment of hats from around the world, including one-of-a-kind vintage selections in mint condition. Come Thursday to meet designer Milo Delaney and preview his collection. New merchandise arriving daily!

I tore the ad out. I flipped through the rest of the newspaper, looking for something a little deeper to sink my teeth into. Between the automotive and the sports pages, I found the arts section. New movie openings this weekend, a touring performance of *Romeo and Juliet* coming to town, and an article: "Hollywood Comes to Ribbon." It was about Hollywood memorabilia that had been tagged for local display.

Hollywood memorabilia.

I leaned forward and read the article with interest.

Few celebrities find themselves in Ribbon, Pennsylvania, but that is exactly where film star Hedy London plans to be next Thursday. London, 70, star of noir films The Reaper Wore Red *and* Murder After Midnight, *has entered a partnership with local retailer Tradava to license a collection of millinery under her name.*

London was discovered on the pages of a men's magazine in the early sixties. She pouted in a way that would have made a pin-up girl proud and caught the attention of an entrepreneurial film director who was casting roles in his homage to the noir Murder After Midnight. *The moment Hedy London appeared wearing a translucent silk negligee trimmed in marabou, the audience was enraptured.*

In the months following the movie's launch, she was never seen in anything other than vintage-inspired styles, thus launching a fashion frenzy for all things retro, and solidified London's ties to the fashion community.

Most people thought it was a publicity stunt. Cameras followed her to the grocery store, the mall, the dry cleaners, waiting for the inevitable photo opportunity of her with her guard dropped. They were disappointed. Hedy London was never out of character. Slowly but surely the public accepted that this was who she was. Soon after, the fashion magazines followed suit, styling models in her likeness to showcase the glamour.

I looked at the byline. *Ribbon Times* staff reporter Carl Collins's article was more of a love letter than a hard-hitting piece of investigative reporting. The rest of his article went on to say that London's style became bigger than her acting talent. Fashion designers sent homages to Hedy down the runways. In the fickle world of fashion and entertainment, she seemed untouchable.

It wasn't until she was paired to work with a renegade director who decided to use her for his own publicity stunt that the glamorous life of Hedy London encountered trouble. He cast her in a dystopian love story and dressed her in a set of pasties and a pair of torn, acid-washed jeans.

After a very public argument that culminated in a pricey lawsuit, Hedy London's name was removed from the picture. Her career trajectory reversed. She could have been the next Kim Novak, but instead, she never acted again.

Hedy London now resides in Hollywood, California, where she has become a respected member of the film preservationists' society. She is loaning a portion of her priceless collection to the Ribbon Museum of Art in an exhibit funded by Tradava, which will coincide with the launch of her collection of hats.

It didn't take Columbo to recognize that I had a piece of said priceless collection nestled behind a Pennsylvania license plate on a shelf in the garage.

It was shortly after four. I showered and dressed quickly in a Go-Gos concert T-shirt from their *Talk Show* tour and a pair of faded boot-cut jeans. I piled on several ropes of pearls, pulled on an olive-green army jacket and a beret, and stepped into olive suede boots. I drove to the grocery store and picked my way through the pet section for food for Logan.

Only one teenager, pierced on her eyebrow, nostril, and lip, worked the checkout counter. My cell rang while I stood in the line and I fished it out. The word "Detective" flashed up on the screen. *Mental note: edit Loncar's contact information to minimize anxiety attacks when he returns calls.*

"Hello?"

"Ms. Kidd? Detective Loncar."

"Did you get my message?" I asked.

"Are you at your house?" he asked.

"I'm at the grocery store."

"Let's see if I understand this. You have evidence to a murder investigation at your house, and you're at the grocery store. Is that right?"

"It's not evidence, per se," I said. I let two teenagers go ahead of me in line and turned around to see if anyone else was close by.

Someone was. Dante Lestes.

Dante was the brother of a local boutique owner. He had pale skin, dark brown eyes, juicy red lips, and tattoos of flames from his wrists to his elbows. He smelled like cinnamon and wore black leather like he'd been born in it. He'd recently taught me a few things about taking care of myself, and I'd recently pretended I wasn't attracted to him.

The grocery store checkout line got about ten degrees warmer.

Today, Dante wore a green bandana knotted over his head babushka-style. The last time I'd seen him, his hair had been cut into a buzz that made him look more like a security guard. He'd let it grow out since then. Black hair stuck out the back of the bandana. His face had a couple of days' beard growth. The motorcycle helmet that dangled from his wrist held a bottle of transmission fluid and a couple of canisters of film.

"Where did you come from?" I asked.

"Ms. Kidd? Who are you talking to?" the detective asked.

"Hold, please," I said into the phone and then held it against my chest so the detective couldn't eavesdrop. "Maybe you should go in front of me too."

Dante raised his eyebrows but stepped past me and put his stuff on the conveyor belt.

"Hello, Detective?" I dropped my voice. "Sorry about that. I'm here."

"At the grocery store."

"Yes."

"Does this have anything to do with my investigation?"

"The grocery store? No, I was out of cat food."

"Does the evidence have anything to do with my investigation?"

"We don't know if it's evidence."

There was a deep inhalation on the other end of the phone, followed by an exhalation of the same force.

Dante held out a hundred-dollar bill to pay for his purchases. I suspected by the way he ignored the cashier's subtle attempts to flirt with him that he was listening to my conversation.

"Ms. Kidd, what was it that you called me about?" the detective asked.

"A hat."

"Where did you get this hat?"

"The museum."

"Where in the museum?"

"The admissions office."

"When?"

"The night Dirk Engle was—" I looked at Dante. He made no secret of the fact that he was still watching me. The checkout girl scanned my three cartons of ice cream. I handed her a twenty and turned my back on Dante. There was a long pause on the other end of the phone.

"Are you still there?" I asked tentatively.

"Ms. Kidd, I think it's safe to call it evidence."

"Okay. I thought it was better to leave that up to you."

"You say you have it at your house? Same address that we have on file?"

As much as I didn't like knowing my address was on file with the police department, now didn't seem to be the time to quibble. "Same address," I confirmed.

"I'll send a car over," Loncar said.

I carried my bag out of the store. Dante leaned against my car. He scanned my outfit as I approached and then looked at my face. "Interesting conversation," he said.

"That was my uncle," I lied. "He's going to help me rearrange my garage."

He leaned forward and his lips brushed my ear. "Good luck with that," he whispered. He leaned back, studied me for a moment, and then turned and walked toward the motorcycle at the far end of the parking lot. I piled my bags into my trunk and slammed it shut. Dante pulled on his helmet and straddled his bike.

Was it a coincidence that Dante was shopping at the same grocery store as I was at that exact time? Or was it a sign, like the falling track lighting and the forest-green fedora with the knife through it? Was the universe sending me a message?

I hadn't seen Dante for months. Not since Nick returned from Italy, and I perfected my good girlfriend impersonation. What did it mean—if this was a sign, was it All Systems Go or Caution: Sharp Turns Ahead?

Nothing was random about Dante, which meant there was a reason he'd popped back up in my life. I wanted to know what it was. I flipped my hair, balled my fists, and closed half the distance between us before noticing the white pickup truck barreling in my direction.

8

MEOW

THE UNIVERSE WAS SERIOUSLY MESSING WITH MY MIND. THE DRIVER OF the truck was Nick. He slowed the truck and called out to me. "Yo, Kidd! Can you hold up a minute?"

I turned and looked for Dante and saw him disappear down the exit ramp. I turned back to Nick. He'd parked his truck and was leaning against the door. The sun danced in his amber brown eyes. When he smiled, his dimples deepened. Hmmm. Those dimples were going to be distracting during work hours. "I've been looking for you," he said.

"How did you know where to find me?" I asked.

"Hoagie store. It was a guess."

"I don't eat that many hoagies," I said, crossing my arms.

"I found you, didn't I?"

"I wasn't here for a hoagie. I was at the grocery store."

"Out of ice cream?"

Darn him. "Actually, I thought I would make you dinner tonight. To say thank you for the job. You know, before I start working for you on Monday?"

"You're cooking?"

"What? I can cook when I want."

He smiled. "That sounds great. There's only one problem—I need you to meet me at the showroom tomorrow morning."

"Tomorrow's Sunday!" I blurted before thinking.

"I know. A sample collection arrived today. I wasn't expecting it until Monday. If we can get everything unpacked, priced, tagged, organized, photographed, and set up online, I can book a couple of appointments for the end of the week. The sooner I get orders, the sooner I can submit them to Italy. Every day between now and then will cost me delivery time, and I can't afford that. Not when I'm starting out on my own."

About a year ago, Nick had bought his distribution rights from the company who had financially backed him. The retailers who stocked his collection had taken markdowns and liquidated what they owned in Nick Taylor inventory. He reduced the number of accounts he sold to and started from scratch.

During the time Nick was laying the groundwork for his business plan—establishing credibility and contacts with fashion editors and living in Italy for six months to establish contacts at the factories of his choice—he'd still found ways to help me out of unexpected (and dangerous) situations. This was my chance to reciprocate. *I can sit this one out*, I thought. *I can let Detective Loncar handle the murder of Dirk Engle, and I can pay Nick back for his understanding by helping him get his dreams off the ground.*

"What time to do you want me to be there?"

"Can you do noon?"

"Noon tomorrow. Anything I should know before then?"

He looked surprised that I'd asked. "I'll bring you up to speed when you get here. As for tonight, remember: you haven't started working for me yet." He kissed me goodbye and left.

I DROVE HOME, dropped off the (now soft) ice cream and assorted groceries and took the hat from the garage and sealed it in a cardboard box. I carried the box to the front porch. Logan joined me on the porch. He lowered his head and sniffed the corner of the box. A few seconds later, he hopped onto the porch swing next to me.

"I'm going to turn this hat over to Loncar and be done with this whole murder."

"Meow."

"And after tonight, I'm going to be professional and do a good job for Nick."

"Meow."

"And I'm not going to spend any time thinking about Dante."

"Meow."

"Maybe the universe is playing a cruel joke on me. Maybe the next man I talk to is going to lead to a long-lasting relationship."

Just then a brown sedan pulled into my driveway. I didn't recognize it. The driver's-side door opened, and Detective Loncar stepped out.

"Forget I said that," I said to Logan. He jumped down from the swing and meowed at the front door.

The detective wore a brown suit with a white shirt and another wide tie. If he'd asked my opinion, I would have suggested something a little more this century, but he hadn't, so I didn't. As he approached, I couldn't help but notice that he was favoring his left foot.

"Hi, Detective," I said brightly. "You look nice. Do you and your wife have a date?"

He glanced at the box. "Is that the evidence?" he asked.

"This? This is what I called you about."

"Ms. Kidd, did anyone overhear our conversation today?"

"At the grocery store?" I thought back to Dante. Had he seen the word "Detective" flash on my screen? I was going to have to reprogram my phone. And the pierced checkout girl? She didn't seem to be eavesdropping—

"Ms. Kidd?" Loncar prompted.

"No, I was alone. I mean, there were people around, but I wasn't with anybody."

He waited a few seconds but said nothing.

"You should take this," I added and tapped the top of the box. "I don't know what it has to do with anything, but it was in the admissions office next to the body."

"Why do you have it, Ms. Kidd?"

"Eddie picked it up to get it out of the way of the blood. When he got sick, he carried it outside. I don't think he realized he had it with him. He gave it to me, and I'm giving it to you."

Loncar took the box. I realized this was his way, letting me babble on with more information than I probably should have shared, but it was the truth.

"If you talk to your friend Mr. Adams, tell him to call me," he said and then headed back to his car.

"I can't imagine why he's avoiding you, considering how nice and friendly you are," I muttered as he walked away. I was fairly sure he didn't hear me.

I dumped my handbag on a chair inside the front door and headed straight for the freezer. The light on my answering machine mocked me, but before I had a chance to check my messages, someone pounded on the front door. The doorknob jiggled rapidly, and a key turned in the lock.

I grabbed a painting off the wall and held it like a shield in front of my body. The door opened, and Eddie came in. His eyes were wide; his face held terror. I dropped the painting, and it landed with a *thunk* and then tipped. A corner dug into my shin, and I hopped backward and swore. I hung it back on the wall, and Eddie rushed into the kitchen and shut all the blinds.

"Where's your remote?" he asked.

I handed him the clicker, and he turned on the news. A woman in a cream-colored turtleneck and pencil skirt stood in front of the museum.

"The body of Philadelphia retailer Dirk Engle was discovered last night at the Ribbon Museum of Art. Engle, owner of the hat store What's On Your Mind, had recently been consulting on a Hedy London millinery exhibit to be displayed at the Museum's Frowick Gallery. Engle's death has been classified a murder, and police are looking into possible suspects. This video of the museum grounds has given the police their only lead. If anyone has information regarding this crime, please call our toll-free hotline displayed on the screen. We'll have the full story tonight at six and eleven."

The footage was grainy, but there was no mistaking who or what it was: Eddie, making his way across the grounds in the back of the museum. He stopped, looked at the building, moved his lips, and continued. He disappeared around the back to the door. The footage jumped forward, and suddenly there he was, ducking behind the shrubbery, staring at the parking lot like we had when we'd heard the gunshots.

Even if I hadn't been right next to him at the time, I would have known it was Eddie. But as I watched the recording, I knew there was a much bigger problem than how easy it had been to recognize him.

If I had been beside him when this took place, why wasn't I in the video too?

9

CHUMMY

EDDIE SANK ONTO THE SOFA AND HELD HIS HEAD IN HIS HANDS. "WHAT am I going to do?"

I lowered myself to the floor and stretched my legs out in front of me. "There's got to be something the police aren't releasing because it's more significant than a couple of seconds of recorded security surveillance. This is probably why Detective Loncar wants to talk to you."

"How do you know Loncar wants to talk to me?"

"He told me. Did you call him? You should. He generally doesn't like it when people avoid him." (Spoken from experience.)

"When did this conversation take place?"

"He came here to pick up the forest-green fedora. We had a nice conversation about it when I was at the grocery store."

"You went grocery shopping with the detective? Since when are you two so chummy?"

"I wouldn't call us chummy, but it did look like he dressed up before he came over." Logan walked across my legs and continued through the room. "Somebody killed Dirk Engle because of that hat," I said. "I'm glad it's gone."

"We don't know that. There could be a hundred reasons why someone killed Dirk Engle."

"Name one. Aside from that hat, give me one reason why someone would want to kill him."

"Maybe he screwed someone over. Maybe he skipped out on a poker game. Maybe he jilted a lover. Maybe he—"

"Dude, he was killed at the museum. We don't even know why he was there. Did someone lure him back with the intention of murdering him? Was he trying to get something that belonged to him? Or did someone catch him trying to steal something?"

"Do you know what you're saying?"

"Yes. That his murder is connected to the exhibit."

Eddie's phone rang. He looked at the display, and the color drained from his face. He turned his ringer off and set his phone on my coffee table. A few seconds later, the screen announced a new voice mail. He picked up the phone and listened to the messages. When he set down the phone, he looked confused. "I got two messages. First one: detective. He wants me to come in for questioning."

Considering the detective's request for Eddie to call him and the highlights reel of the six o'clock news, I wasn't surprised. "Who was the other message from?"

"Christian. He says he can't beat publicity like this, and he's arranged for me to work on the exhibit during off hours. He wants to meet with me tomorrow."

"Did you erase that message?"

"No. Why?"

"Can I hear it?"

He tapped the screen a few times and handed me the phone. I held it up to my head, comparing it to the argument I'd heard through Dirk Engle's cell phone. After a few words, I was sure.

"Don't freak out, but I'm pretty sure Christian was the person fighting with Dirk Engle the morning I came to the museum."

"What does that have to do with the price of rice in China?"

"I don't know, but it might give him a motive. Or it was just an argument. All we know is that they had a fight the day Dirk was murdered." Eddie looked at me like I was explaining faggoting to a first-year sewing student. "One argument does not a killer make."

"It's a heck of a lot more suspicious than if he showed up with a tray of cupcakes."

"Detective Loncar doesn't take well to blind accusations. We can't even place Christian at the museum that night. The only thing we know is he was there during the day."

"So were a bunch of people! Thad was there. Maybe he was jealous of Dirk? Rebecca was there. Maybe she caught him shoplifting little Thinker statues. There was a delivery guy with hats from Dirk's store. Maybe he held a grudge? What about us? Somebody can say we had a motive."

"Hold on," I said. "Rebecca told me a woman from a hat store dropped off the boxes, not a man. Do you know who she was? Do you know where she works?"

"Over Your Head."

"No, it's not. It's pretty pertinent information if you ask me." I glared at him.

"No. It's Over Your Head."

"Fine, don't tell me. I'll find out on my own."

A smile tugged at Eddie's face. "The woman was Vera Sarlow, and her store is called Over Your Head. It's on Penn Avenue. I don't know why she had the hats. She's Dirk Engle's biggest competitor, and Tradava wants to take their business away."

"Over Your Head," I repeated, trying to place why it sounded familiar. I grabbed my handbag and pulled out the page I'd torn from the newspaper. "I wonder if Loncar knows she was there."

"Dude, call him. Tell him."

I hesitated. "I kind of promised Nick I'd have nothing to do with the homicide investigation. It was a condition of him hiring me."

"You took a job with Nick?"

"After what happened at the museum, I figured your opportunity was going to dry up."

"Fine. Don't tell him you're helping me on the side. How's he going to know?"

"He's not stupid." I glanced at the clock. "Besides, he's due here for dinner in a little more than an hour."

Eddie perked up. "You want to get a pizza? I'll order." He pulled out his phone and scrolled through his contacts with his thumb.

"Dude, it's Saturday night."

"So it'll take a little longer. No big deal."

"It's *date* night. My last date night with Nick before I start working for him." I needed a way to shorthand the importance of my alone time with Nick. "I was going to cook for him."

"You can't cook."

"Why does everybody make it sound like it's so hard to cook dinner?"

"What's on the menu? Spaghetti-Os and ice cream for dessert?"

"I think I can do better than that." I didn't mention that by "better," I meant pasta and a jar of sauce. I also didn't mention the box of Jell-O no-bake cheesecake I'd been saving for a special occasion.

Eddie walked into the kitchen. I heard cabinets open and close. Same with the freezer and the fridge. I moved to the sofa and scratched Logan's ears. A few minutes later, Eddie returned. "You got any wine?"

"A bottle of white, a bottle of red."

"When is Nick getting here?"

"Seven."

"You have an hour and a half to clean this place and get ready. I'll take care of your dinner."

"I already told you I had dinner under control."

Eddie held up the jar of Ragu. "I don't think so."

I did a few mental calculations. If Eddie took care of dinner, I'd have time to shower, redo my hair, and try on at least four different outfits before deciding which one I wanted to wear. I'd probably have time to hang the other three up just in case the night took an R-rated turn.

"We will never speak of this arrangement outside this house. Deal?"

"Counteroffer: I'll agree never to mention this outside your house if you agree to help me with the Dirk Engle thing."

"Not a word," I said, pointing at him.

"Who am I going to tell?"

In the end, it wasn't that hard of a deal to make. He needed my help more than I needed his, and we both knew I'd say yes. Maybe I couldn't make a decent dinner for Nick, but the signs were all there. I *could* help Eddie with the situation at the museum, and that's the kind of friend I was.

It was six forty-five when I came back downstairs. I'd decided on a beryl green knit dress and a lime cashmere cardigan. The dress had a low scoop neck and a full skirt. Sexy and feminine at the same time. I'd twirled my long brown hair around my fingers and let it mostly air dry and then used the drier to soften the curls. I slipped my feet into matte gold lizard pumps and slipped a pair of gold bow-shaped earrings into each of my lobes. I reached for an amber lipstick, remembered Nick's parking lot kiss, and went with a flavored lip gloss instead.

Tangy tomato and spice scents wafted from the kitchen. I found Eddie fitting candles into a holders that had formerly been stashed under the sink. "Table's set. Wine's open. Sinatra's singing. I loaded a movie in the player. You're good to go."

"What are we having?"

"Chicken Florentine. Surprisingly, you had four packages of frozen spinach in your freezer."

"I like to rest the packages on my eyes when they're puffy."

"Use the peas. You have a bunch of them too."

Eddie left me last-minute directions and left. I would have asked him to go out the back door in case Nick was early, but Eddie's VW Bug was in my driveway, so "covert" was out the window. When the doorbell rang, I was more nervous than if I'd made the dinner myself.

Nick stood on the other side of the door, dressed in a crisp white shirt under a navy blue blazer. The shirt was unbuttoned at the neck, revealing traces of the tan he'd picked up during his last trip to Italy. His jeans were a dark wash; his shoes were black wingtips. "I brought dessert." He handed me a small white box. It was cold. He leaned down and said, "In case I was wrong about you shopping for ice cream."

I turned my head to the side and caught his lips with mine. We stumbled backward until I was up against the hall closet door. I raised my right leg because the knob was jammed into the back of my thigh, and Nick reached down and ran his fingers along the underside of it.

"We should eat," I whispered between kisses.

"I'm not that hungry," he whispered back.

WE KEPT things at the PG-13 level. An hour later, we reheated the chicken Florentine in the microwave. Nick moved the coffee table, and we set up a picnic on the floor of the living room. I turned off the stereo and started the movie. The title shot for *Murder After Midnight,* Hedy London's most famous movie, filled my TV screen.

Eddie might have delivered a perfectly respectable meal for my date with Nick, but he was making sure I remembered our secret pact.

10

SEXY SECRETARY

SUNDAY MORNING, I WOKE EARLY AND DRESSED TO WORK FOR NICK. I went sexy secretary: brown wool challis skirt suit nipped in at the waist, sheer blouse that tied at the neck, leopard print peep-toe pumps. My hair was pinned up in a French twist, and my eyes were shaded with large framed glasses. I snapped on a pair of taupe leather driving gloves I bought in Italy three seasons ago and kept them on until after I was inside the showroom.

"Good morning, sunshine," Nick said. He wore a chocolate brown suit—more dark chocolate than milk chocolate—with a crème turtleneck underneath. Aside from his curly hair, he looked like James Coburn in *Our Man Flint*. He flashed his smile, and the similarities grew stronger.

"Put your stuff on my desk and join me. I want to go over what we're doing all week. I know you might be worried about fingerprints based on your recent work history, but you don't have to wear gloves around the showroom." He grinned.

I went to the office in the back and stuck my tongue out at him while taking off the gloves. I pulled a steno pad from a drawer and tested three different ballpoint pens until I found one that worked.

When I returned, there was a steaming hot cup of coffee waiting on the table for me.

Nick looked good. Nick looked *really* good. I blew on the coffee and took a tentative sip, trying not think about the forty-five minutes he'd spent at second base last night. Not succeeding, just trying.

"Why don't you tell me what you expect from me?" I asked.

"It should be pretty easy. I expect you to show up and help out. I expect you not to get involved in a murder investigation. If you can manage those two things, this'll work out fine."

I glanced at Nick for half a second before looking away and focusing on the corner of his desk. Did he know about my agreement with Eddie? No. Eddie was bound by our chicken Florentine pact. Were the police so eager to talk to Eddie that they'd widened their circle of contacts and reached out to Nick to find him? And what would Nick have said? If he was annoyed at my involvement, he sure was taking it in stride—

"Kidd?" Nick snapped his fingers in front of my face. "Where do you go when that happens?"

"I was thinking." I stared into his eyes. He didn't look away. My pulse picked up, and—for a split second—I considered clearing the surface of the table for non-working-for-your-boss activities. "I was thinking..." I bit my lip. Nick's eyes moved from my eyes to my lip. He stared at my lips, and his eyes darkened. "I think maybe we should take a break from dating."

He made eye contact again. "Did something happen last night? After I left?"

"No." Well, yes, I ate a good portion of the ice cream he'd brought, but I didn't think that's what he meant. "Nick, if I weren't starting to work for you today, I wouldn't have asked you to leave last night."

"I don't remember you asking me to leave."

"What I mean is, I would have asked you to stay."

"And that's a bad thing?"

"I can't be your girlfriend and your showroom manager. It feels too—dirty."

"Dirty?"

"Dirty. Like I'm taking money from you, and I'm... you know."

"But you're not. We're not."

"But we could be. But this way we won't. See why it's important for us to take a break?"

"Kidd, if I had any idea this would be the first conversation we'd have on your first day, I would have rethought the job offer."

"Not a break for good. Monday through Friday. The work week."

"On a break from Monday through Friday." He leaned back in his chair. "I guess I can handle that."

"You're not mad?" I asked, leaning forward. "I thought you might be mad."

"I'm not mad. We have a lot of work to do this week, and maybe your plan will help us both focus."

"Good." I uncapped my pen and lifted the steno pad, ready to make my to-do list. "Okay, boss, what's my assignment?"

"We need to get this place ready for appointments. Shelves up, visuals ready. Samples should arrive by Wednesday or Thursday, and I'll need line sheets before I can book appointments. Right now, it's my chicken scratch in a notebook."

"You have costs?"

"Initial costs. We have to land them and calculate markup."

"Sixty?"

"Fifty-five. I'm keeping tight margins on my first collection, so I'll have a competitive edge against the rest of the assortments out there."

"What about inspiration boards? Leather books?"

Nick stared at me, and unlike the lip-biting/eye-darkening moment, his expression was unreadable. "It's been a long time since I worked with someone who knew what she was doing," he said.

"It's been a long time since I felt like I knew what I was doing," I admitted.

The longer the silence between us grew, the more I sensed Nick's internal struggle. He needed me. He needed my expertise. He needed my ability to get the job done.

And my internal struggle. I needed to be appreciated for my knowledge. I needed Nick's trust that I could do a good job.

And I needed a paycheck.

"Kidd," he started.

"Maybe when we're in here, you should call me by my first name?"

"Samantha," he said.

The sound of his voice saying my name was like melted chocolate poured over cookies hot from the oven. It was hot and sweet and made me wonder about stealing third base in the stockroom. (At least I wasn't thinking about the homicide investigation.)

I hooked my finger inside the collar of my blouse. "Call me Kidd. I'll call you Taylor. Unless you want me to call you Mr. Taylor? Scratch that. Let's just leave things the way they are, okay?"

I was interrupted by the sound of a woman clearing her throat.

Nick stood and went around the partition to the front door. "May I help you?" he asked.

"I should think so. Mr. Taylor, I presume?"

"Yes, I'm Nick Taylor."

"I'm Hedy London."

I dropped the steno pad and pen on the floor. I bent to pick them up, and when I sat up again, Nick stood in front of me next to the famous noir actress. Her hair was more gray than blonde, and her frame held a few more pounds around the middle, but otherwise, there was no mistaking that I was in the presence of a star.

The first thing I should have noticed was the long feather that stood a good twelve inches higher than her head, barely piercing the band on her ginger-colored cloche. A lavender double-faced wool jacket nipped in at the waist and a pencil-thin, cordovan leather skirt that ended at her knees completed her ensemble. I had to admire the fact that, at her age, she was perched atop three-inch heels. I also had to admire the beautiful brown alligator pumps she was perched on. Those shoes had cost several thousand dollars, even if she had bought them on sale. And Hedy London did not appear to be the kind of woman who bought anything on sale.

"Ms. London, this is my—" Nick's expression changed as he decided how to best introduce me.

I stood up on my leopard-print peep-toe pumps and adjusted the hem of my jacket. "I'm Nick's showroom manager, Samantha Kidd." I held out my hand, and she shook it.

"Hedy London." She looked around the interior. It was far from ready for appointments, even further from ready for a visit from a living legend. I was curious why she was there on a Sunday morning. Judging from the look on Nick's face as he watched her take inventory —or the lack thereof—I could tell he hadn't been expecting her.

"I expected you to have samples," she said.

"Ms. London, may I offer you something to drink? Latte, cappuccino?" he asked.

She turned to me. "I'll take a no-foam latte."

I looked at Nick. Was there a Starbucks around here that I didn't know about?

"Samantha, the espresso machine is in the back. Ms. London, please have a seat."

Great. My (Eddie's) chicken Florentine skills must have led Nick to believe I knew how to operate other kitchen equipment. I went to the kitchenette area and stared at the giant black machine. Elaborate dials with numbers on them, silver switches, and handles for small pots of coffee grinds had this thing looking like a prop from *The Time Machine*. Coffee drinks were meant to be ordered, not made at home. And while I was back here launching bombs with this contraption, Nick was talking to Hedy London. About what, I didn't know.

(And I was back to thinking about the homicide investigation.)

I filled a demitasse cup with an inch of milk and microwaved it, then added another quarter cup of water. I added a glug of coffee for color, dumped a packet of sugar on top, and swirled a demitasse spoon around it. I set the mug on a saucer and carried it out front. Nick and Hedy stood by the front door. She held out a hand, and her bracelet, heavy with thick gold charms, created tinkling sounds. Nick held the door open, and she left.

"I thought she wanted a latte," I said.

Nick looked at me. "From the look on your face when she ordered it, I didn't think you knew how to make one."

"Did you tell her that?"

"No." He sat down. "Now, where were we?"

I set the cup and saucer on the table. "Hedy London just showed up at your showroom. *The* Hedy London. You're not going to tell me why?"

"Sit down, Kidd." I sat down. Not because he told me to but because my left shoe pinched my toes. "I have a small moral dilemma," he said. "My *girlfriend* likes old movies. In fact, last night, we watched a Hedy London movie. She'd probably like to know that Hedy London was just here. The problem is, I don't think I'm going to talk to my girlfriend all week."

"If Hedy London was here to talk to you about business, that's the kind of thing you should tell your *showroom manager.*"

"True. The problem with that is the nature of the business. She asked me to produce fifty pairs of shoes for an exhibit at the museum—the same museum where a murder took place two nights ago. My showroom manager specifically said she wouldn't get involved in that."

"I don't want to split hairs here, but I think your girlfriend was the one who said that."

Nick leaned back in his leather chair and stared at the ceiling. His hands were folded across his waist. Every once in a while, his eyes narrowed, and the crinkles by the sides of them deepened. It was like he was having his own internal conversation.

"She's lending her collection of costumes to the museum, right?" I asked. "And Eddie said she entered a licensing deal for a millinery collection. What's she going to do with fifty pairs of shoes?"

"She has something special in mind for the gala. Fifty models dressed up as her from *Murder After Midnight.* At the opening of the exhibit, she wants to flood the museum with look-alikes: fifty women dressed and styled like her most famous character."

He told me the rest: hat designer Milo Delaney was going to produce fifty hats, and she asked Nick to produce fifty pairs of shoes. I wondered who was going to supply fifty matching suits on such short notice but didn't ask. That, it appeared, wasn't my problem.

"I was hoping we'd be able to take it easy this week, but this is going to take up most of my time. I'll need you to handle the day to day."

A slow anxiety climbed my spine. "How are you going to get fifty pairs of shoes here by Thursday?" I asked.

"I designed the shoes for the Ignottia runway show last season. Ms. London saw the samples in their showroom. If I can call in a favor at a factory, they'll slot me in the production queue and overnight the inventory."

"That's a borderline impossible deadline."

"Kidd, this order would solve a very untimely cash flow problem. I'm not in a position to say no."

"Where are the clothes coming from?" I asked out of curiosity.

"I gave Hedy the name of a designer."

"Who?" I asked.

"You remember my friend Amanda Ries? I thought I'd do her a favor."

Yes, I remembered Amanda Ries. Up-and-coming fashion designer-slash-college friend of my boyfriend-slash-boss. She could be the nicest person in the world for all I knew. Our face-to-face encounters had been few and far between. What I knew was that she and Nick had the kind of special friendship that transcended girlfriends, murder investigations, and chicken Florentine.

Fine, I thought. We'd just established that favors for friends weren't subjected to rules.

Things were looking good for Eddie.

11

———

UNEXPECTED LEVEL OF MATURITY

While Nick was off doing whatever it was he did with Amanda Ries that I was going to pretend fell under the umbrella of shoe designer and not boyfriend-on-a-break, I got to work.

First things first: I called Eddie. He answered after three rings. Devo played in the background.

"About time you called. How was your date?"

"What? Oh, you mean dinner. It was good."

"I know dinner was good. I made it. I'm talking about the movie. Notice anything?"

"I was a little distracted," I said. I blushed. "But that's not why I called. You're not going to believe who just came to Nick's showroom."

"Who?"

"Hedy London." I waited for a response. None came. After a few seconds, I said, "Hello? Are you still there?"

The music in the background stopped. "I'm either delirious or distracted. I could have sworn you said Hedy London came to Nick's showroom."

"I did. Just walked up to the door and waltzed in. She ordered fifty pair of shoes. Something about models dressed as her character in *Murder After Midnight* at the gala. Do you know about this?"

"First I'm hearing. Is he there? Can I talk to him?"

"No, he's not here, and no, you can't talk to him. Remember our agreement."

"Where is he?"

"Meeting with Amanda Ries."

Eddie whistled. "You're showing an unexpected level of maturity here."

"It's my day for personal growth." I leaned back on the desk and scoped out the showroom. "There's about four hours of work here that I can kick out in three. If Nick isn't back by then, is there anything you need me to do?"

"Can you get to Over Your Head? We're still missing some of the hats, and Thad confirmed they were delivered there."

"Sure. I'll call you when I'm on my way."

I hung up and started working on Nick's line sheets. A few formulas in an Excel spreadsheet made the project go quickly. When that was finished and Nick still hadn't returned, I draped my jacket on the back of his chair, kicked off my shoes, and started on the display shelves.

I found the power drill and a small package of wall anchors and screws, measured out the placement of the shelves according to Nick's sketches of how he wanted the wall to look, and finished that project too. I borrowed a Handi-VAC from the comic book store next door and cleaned up the resulting mess. By lunch, I was aware of two things: I was a pretty good assistant, and I didn't like the whole employee-not-girlfriend thing.

Nick hadn't returned or called. I scribbled a note to Nick that pointed out the first thing (and made no mention of the second), taped it to the inside of the front door, and locked up behind me.

Over Your Head was in West Ribbon. It was located on Penn Avenue, across the street from a used record store, sandwiched between a nail salon and an art gallery. I missed the store the first time I drove past. The second time, I spotted a black and white sign featuring a derby off to the side of the O in the logo. I got lucky with a parking space right out front. It was a couple of minutes past one o'clock.

Large bay windows were filled with stands featuring hats from a bygone era. Jewel-toned cloches with gently moving feathers and sparkling jeweled pins were arranged on hat stands around the store. The base of each window display was lined in vintage black and white ads, and the hat stands were all a shade of high-gloss mint green.

I window-shopped the way Audrey Hepburn had at Tiffany's until a petite brunette in a mint-green smock waved at me to enter. As I pushed the door open, it struck me that this tiny shop had modeled its interior after the kind of millinery shops you often saw in old movies. Sitting stations, like vanities, painted the same shade of green as the hat stands in the window, lined the room. A plump woman admired her reflection in the mirror in front of her, while the brunette stood to the side, holding a backup selection for the customer to try on next. Her red-rimmed eyes belied her pleasant disposition. I imagined her personal life had spilled onto the hours of the workday, but she was doing her best to remain professional.

"Welcome to Over Your Head. I'm Vera. May I help you with anything today?" She sniffled quickly and ducked her chin to cover the action.

"Thank you." A fat tear leaked out of the woman's eyes. "Is everything okay?" I asked.

She pulled a monogrammed lace hanky out of her pocket and turned away from me. "I'm sorry. Family." She dried her cheeks and turned back.

I paused, unsure how to react. I was there to pick up hats for Eddie but took pity on the woman. "I saw your ad in the paper and wanted to see your selection of hats by Milo Delaney." It was the first thing that popped into my head.

"Of course. Right this way." She handed a mother-of-pearl hand mirror to the woman in the chair. "I'll be right back, Mrs. Willoughby."

I followed her to a locked glass case. She fumbled through a set of keys, found the one she wanted, and unlocked the case.

"That's not necessary," I started to say, but she shushed me with a wave of the hand.

"You can't come into a hat store and not try anything on." She seemed to have gotten control of her emotions. "You obviously have taste. The shape of this would be great on you."

Great taste notwithstanding, it was probably my interest in their most expensive vendor that inspired her customer service, not my outfit. I didn't want to lead her on thinking she was about to make a sale. Though she was right, this green felt cap was darn near close to perfection. The price tag dangled in the breeze. Did that say $250? No. She was definitely not making a sale.

She excused herself and went to check on Mrs. Willoughby, who it appeared had decided on not one but two hats. Vera escorted her to the register and tallied her sale before returning to me.

Despite her not-very-well-hidden recent tears, she chattered on in that expert manner of the best sales associates. "It's one of Milo's newest designs. He has an eye, don't you think? He's going to be here on Thursday. Would you like me to have him sign this for you?"

"I thought you specialized in vintage styles. Milo is a current designer, right?"

"Yes and yes. Vintage is our thing but acquiring quality inventory is sometimes a waiting game, if you know what I mean. Milo's designs are inspired by past styles but are new. We can cater to two customers now, those who are interested in the historical aspect of the styles and those who want something that's never been worn before. Are you a collector?" she asked.

She placed her index finger on her cheek and rested her elbow on the other hand that was across her waist. She turned her head, looked at my handbag, and then stood straight and looked me back in the eye.

"Not really. I'm helping on the Hedy London exhibit at the museum." I handed the green felt hat back to her. "I'm here for the hats."

Her face clouded, and she put a hand to her chest. "I didn't know anybody knew about that. I took them to the museum last night. Right now, Milo's is the best collection we carry, but we're all looking forward to the ones from Hedy. London. I've seen the samples, and they are spectacular. Did Tradava negotiate an exclusive?"

I saw my confusion in the reflection of the mirror over the try-on station: eyebrows scrunched, two small dimples on my forehead. I tipped my head back and tried to relax my expression but succeeded only in looking like Gloria Swanson in *Sunset Boulevard*.

"I don't know about Tradava's involvement," I asked. "You said you took them to the museum?"

Vera looked embarrassed. "I'll admit, I was hoping to see what's been done on the exhibit so far. It's a great concept." She dropped her voice and looked from side to side. "I would have liked to be more involved, but it wasn't meant to be."

A delivery man pushed a wheeled cart piled high with boxes through the front door. He approached Vera. "I've got about twenty more of these in the truck." He held out a black box on a cord and asked her to sign a small screen.

"Bring the rest to the back, please," she instructed him. "I'll let you in the stockroom through the back. The door is in front of the white Explorer."

My eyes darted to the boxes on the cart. Small handwritten numbers in red marked a few of the corners. One box was punctured, and bubble wrap peeked through the opening.

I looked away from the box to Vera's face and caught her watching me. She picked up a tablecloth and tossed it over the of boxes. "I'm sorry, but I have to ask you to leave. I'm closing the store for the day."

12

A LOT OF ACTIVITY

Vera turned her back on me. I left the store and sat in my car for a few minutes, thinking about our conversation. Something was missing. I was surprised at how much she'd known about Hedy London and how she'd reacted to my knowing about hats. She had admitted to being at the museum last night, and she said she had wanted to be a part of the exhibit. A *bigger* part, she'd said. So what part had she played? What exactly did she mean?

I left Eddie a message that Vera had delivered the hats to the museum last night and crossed the street to a pizza shop. It was after two, and I was hungry. The sign above the door read J&D in crisp black letters underneath a Pepsi logo. Both sides of the sign were painted on thick plastic that sandwiched neon tube lighting. The bottom corner of the plastic was broken off, and from the right angle, I could look into the sign and see the neon tubes, along with a pile of dead flies.

A fat man in a white T-shirt, dirty white apron, and tomato-stained painter's pants stood behind the counter.

"I was hoping you'd come in here. You working for the lady across the street? Model or somethin'?"

"No, just a customer."

"There's been a lot of activity over there lately," he continued. "Trucks coming and going, boxes being delivered, trash being hauled away."

"Is that normal?" I asked.

The man put his thumb on the bottom of his jaw and stretched his index finger out along his chin as if stroking an imaginary beard. "Not normal, not to me. It's only been a couple of days now, maybe a week. Last Thursday we couldn't fit our trash in the Dumpster because she filled the thing up with that packing stuff—"

"Bubble wrap?"

"Yeah." He chuckled. "I made the guy turn on the compactor, and the plastic popped like a firing squad. The girl in the record store next door called the cops. Reported hearing gunshots. She was pretty embarrassed when she found out what it was."

"Can you tell me anything else?"

He dropped his hand and crossed his arms over his chest. "Why you asking so many questions? Don't you want to order nothin'?"

"Oh, yeah, right. Can I get two slices with extra cheese? And do you mind if I wait at the table by the front window?"

While I waited for my pizza, I watched Vera's store. Nothing unusual happened. But already I knew Vera was connected to the exhibit. Eddie had sent me here, the designer who was producing Hedy London's hats for the exhibit was scheduled for an event at her store, and she'd said herself she wanted to be involved. Add in the activity the pizza man described and her rollercoaster of emotions, and I knew she was hiding something.

A young boy delivered the pizza to my table. I ate while watching the storefront, hoping to catch Vera up to something. The only thing I caught was another employee who set a wooden sandwich board in front of the store. I finished eating, bussed my table, and crossed the street to check out the sign. It advertised the upcoming appearance of Milo Delaney on Thursday afternoon. I drove back to Nick's showroom, full of pizza, thirsty for soda, and hungry for answers.

Nick was busy answering e-mail when I walked in. "Everything okay?" he asked.

I could hardly tell Nick that I'd been out at Vera's store looking for info for Eddie, not after I'd practically cross-stitched my work ethic onto a pillow so he'd take me seriously. "Yes. Why?"

"You've been gone for hours. You might want to tell me now if you plan on having issues with timekeeping."

"No issues here. One-time thing." I sniffed the air, recognizing the scent of cured lunchmeats.

"I ordered us hoagies from B&S. I hope you don't mind, but I ate without you. I didn't know you'd be gone so long. Yours is on my desk next to the bag of chips."

"Thank you. I'm going to get a little more work done first. Besides, I'm not really hungry."

I walked past him to the desk, where a sandwich was wrapped in white butcher paper. On the outside, written in wax pencil, it said "hard roll, no tomatoes, extra oregano." Darn Nick for knowing exactly how I liked my hoagies.

I moved the hoagie to the side of the desk and opened the sketchpad of Nick's designs. A lined sheet of paper with a bullet-pointed list fell out onto my lap.

Milo

London

Collectors

Amanda

Shelves

Line sheets

The last three items had been circled in red. The last two were crossed out in green. Nick had gone to see Amanda, so was this a new item on his list? Or had he failed to cross her out?

And since when was Amanda Ries my biggest concern?

I flipped through the sketchbook. The designs would have made Cinderella's sisters green with envy. He'd doodled a few designs on cocktail napkins and scrap paper and stapled them to blank pages with notes. I'd watched him do this before when we were out for business dinners. He'd see a detail—an orchid as a centerpiece, or a particular pinstripe on a man's suit—and get an idea. He'd sketch it out on whatever surface he could find. More often than not, those spontaneous design ideas turned into his best sellers.

I closed the sketchbook and ran my finger over the to-do list.

"What's up, Kidd?" Nick said. I hadn't heard him approach. I tried to hide the list and knocked the bag of chips to the floor. I stooped to pick them up and then stood up quickly when I became aware of the butt-side view I'd given him.

"Nothing's up. Why?" I asked.

"I've never known you to turn down a hoagie. What gives?"

"I'm trying to eat better, that's all. You know, salads and fruit and stuff."

"Really," he said, crossing his arms.

"Really."

"You didn't stop off for lunch somewhere, like maybe at a pizza place?"

"Are you having people spy on me?" I asked angrily.

"There's a tomato sauce stain on your lapel."

I looked down at my chest. A telltale stain had blossomed across the brown fabric. I looked around the desk for a napkin but saw none.

Nick held out a box of tissues. "It's no big deal, Kidd. I just didn't know."

I wiped at the stain and then gave up and took off my jacket. "I hung the shelves and typed up the line sheets. I printed a copy for you to approve. If you're good with them, I'll photograph the samples and then send the finished file to the print shop."

"I'll look at them tonight." He handed me a key. "I have an appointment tomorrow morning, so I'll be late getting here. Let yourself in." While I was gone, Nick had taken off his suit jacket, and the cuffs of his shirt were folded up twice, exposing his tanned forearms. I looked away to the four-foot square painting I'd hung earlier, an abstract lime-green canvas that popped against the otherwise white walls of his showroom.

"Who are you meeting?" I asked, afraid of the answer.

"Milo Delaney."

"Let me go. We can divide and conquer. I'll go to Milo; you do your stuff. Call London, visit Amanda."

He ignored my mention of Amanda. "As it turns out, you got more done than I expected." He picked up my hand and ran his thumb across my palm.

A rush of heat went through me, and I pulled my hand away. "Don't make me threaten you with a sexual harassment case," I joked.

He picked up a pen and wrote something inside his sketchpad. "I'll meet you at Milo's at nine tomorrow morning. Here's the address." He tapped the page with his pen.

"And do me a favor," he said, the playfulness returning to his voice this time. "If you want to avoid a sexual harassment situation, skip the sexy secretary look. It makes it hard to concentrate."

LOGAN MET me by the front door. I dumped my handbag on the chair and scooped him up. As I scratched his ears, I called out for Eddie. "Honey, I'm home!" I heard him in the kitchen. "Do you want burgers or hoagie? I'll order." I carried Logan into the kitchen and found Eddie setting the table. "Dinner's done. Steamed chicken and brown rice."

"Is that a joke?"

Eddie picked up a filled wine glass and handed it to me. "You started working for Nick today, and I'm in the middle of a thing. We could both use some power food."

I couldn't speak for anybody else, but what I really could use was ice cream.

Within minutes, we sat at the table with plates of beige food. Logan begged for scraps from under the table. I didn't have the heart to tell him he'd be disappointed.

"What do you know about Vera Sarlow?" I asked.

"The owner of Over Your Head?" Eddie shrugged. "Not much. Why?"

"I was at her store today and something was off. She looked like she'd been crying, and then she said she wished she was involved in the exhibit. She mentioned Tradava too. Isn't that confidential?"

"It's supposed to be, but these things always get out. From what Thad told me, a lot of people wanted to be involved. Volunteers came out of the woodwork, but Dirk refused any outside help. He said he was risking his store's performance and bottom line, and the only way he'd agree to work was if the entire thing was kept under wraps."

That made sense. "Tell me again about this contest you won. How did Tradava get him to agree to working with you if Dirk refused outside help?"

He set down his fork. "That's just it. I won the contest for designing windows. Dirk wasn't exactly amenable to my talents. He wanted me to do grunt work. You know, move this mannequin here, move that pedestal there."

"The stuff you wanted me to do."

"That's different, dude."

"Was Dirk planning to shuttle his staff in from Philly?"

"Philly's thirty miles from here, so that's a big negatory. It was the museum staff and me, and if he could have booted me out, he would have. The Tradava tie-in kept me there. What did Vera say to get you so twisted?"

"We were talking about Milo Delaney. She carries his hat collection. There was a large delivery while I was there, and the boxes were all marked the same way as the boxes we unpacked—numbers on the corner, packing bubble peeking out from inside the boxes. It seemed suspicious."

"If we're going to suspect every person with access to packing materials, we might need to stakeout Mailboxes Etc."

I ignored him. "When Vera saw me staring at the boxes, she covered them in a tablecloth. But after, when I was at the pizza store across the street—"

"Are you using my situation as a license to eat poorly?"

"Pizza is its own food group. But the owner said there's been a lot of activity at the hat store in the past week. He also said she threw out a significant amount of bubble wrap, so much that the trash compactor was filled. When they activated the compactor, it sounded like gunfire. Somebody called the police."

"Do you think that could be what we heard at the museum?"

"Maybe. Do you know how Dirk Engle was killed?"

"His head was wrapped in plastic. What more do you need to know?"

"There was blood. Remember, that's why you picked up the hat."

Eddie turned green. "Don't remind me."

"I'm just thinking out loud here, but if somebody shot him, maybe nobody heard it because there was another explanation for the sound. Like bubble wrap popping."

"I didn't hear anything that night. Did you?"

"No, but we were upstairs. Maybe the acoustics aren't so good up there?"

"It's a museum with marble floors and stairs. The only fabric in the whole building is from the T-shirts they sell in the gift area. If there had been a sound, we would have heard it."

"What about the light fixture? What if that was a distraction? We wouldn't have heard anything else when that fell."

Eddie's eyes moved to the left and the right as he thought about it. "That was a couple of hours before we found the body."

"But we don't know how long the body was there. And the air conditioning was on too. Like someone wanted to keep his body cold and confuse the time of death."

Eddie set his knife and fork down. "I'm done."

"You barely touched your food."

"Something about the conversation killed my appetite."

I looked at my plate. The chicken was gone, and the steamed rice was—well, the steamed rice was moved around enough to make it look like I'd eaten some of it. I set down my utensils too.

"What about Thad? He came to the museum to see what happened. What if he committed the murder, knowing he'd arranged for the light fixture to fall so he could join us and look like he wasn't anywhere near the admissions office?"

Eddie finished his wine. "Just yesterday Thad told me Dirk

wanted out of his contract. Dirk said urgent personal business came up and he couldn't fulfill his commitment."

"If that's true, then why was he fighting with Christian? Why did he storm out and say the exhibit was cursed? Why did Christian tell him he was fired?"

"Here's another question: why would Thad lie to me?" Eddie asked.

I could think of one very good reason.

13

——————

CHARMING GUY

Before I had a chance to answer, the sofa rang. I mean, the phone under the delicately placed white afghan that hid the bald spot on the sofa rang. I answered.

"This is Thad Thomas. May I speak with Eddie Adams, please?"

"He's not available," I said, using my best kill-them-with-kindness voice. "Can I give him a message?"

"I'm sure he *is* available. He's waiting for my call. I'm certain he would like to talk to me about museum matters. I'll hold while you find him and tell him that I'm waiting to speak to him."

What a charming guy.

I carried the phone back to the kitchen and held it out to Eddie. "It's Thad." I held my hand over the bottom of the phone. "Remember what you just asked me."

Eddie took the phone. "Hey. Yeah. Where? Okay. Later." He handed the phone back.

"Why is Thad calling you here? Why not your cell?"

"I told him I dropped my cell in water, and it's sitting in rice."

"Did you?"

"No, but I needed an excuse for why I'm not answering."

"What did he want?"

"He was checking on whether I still had the keys to the museum."

"And you said...?" I swear it was like pulling teeth.

"I said yes. I couldn't say no, could I?" There wasn't time to address Eddie's ignorance of the acceptable times to lie. I reached for my wine and took a sip. "The museum had the locks changed. He wants to give me a new set. Is that cool with you?"

I choked and set the glass back down. After I got the coughing under control, I said, "Five minutes ago. Here. We had a conversation. Were you not listening? Because I don't think you heard me. Thad. Could be. A. Murderer."

"I don't think so."

"You don't think so?" I put my hands on the table and leaned forward. "You don't *think* so?" I repeated. "He wants to get you back to the scene of the crime. Alone. At night. That doesn't sound suspicious to you?"

"He wants to help with the exhibit."

"Thad has been nothing but nasty since the first time I met him. He's hiding something."

"Or he's the assistant director of the museum, and he's under a lot of pressure."

I knew how Eddie felt, wanting to believe in the honesty of one person connected to his world so it felt a little less scary, but I also knew Thad wasn't above suspicion.

Back in high school, I'd stood up for Eddie when he was involved in a cheating scandal. We hadn't been close friends at the time, him having transferred in halfway through senior year. But I'd seen the whole thing from my seat in the back of the classroom. I'd watched a member of the football team copy Eddie's test, and when the allegations of cheating were investigated, I'd watched the football player accuse Eddie. He said/he said. It could have gone either way.

Until I made an appointment with the principal and told him what I'd seen. The football player lost his scholarship. Eddie kept his. Life went on.

I didn't know who had killed Dirk Engle, but I wouldn't let Eddie take the blame for something he didn't do.

"Call him back," I said. "Tell him you'll meet him. I don't care where, just pick a place that isn't the museum."

I handed the phone to Eddie, who stared at it like it was a newborn alien baby that had been dropped off on his doorstep. He finally took it and hit redial. "A little privacy, please?" he said, shooing me out of the room.

I carried Logan into the kitchen and fed him a piece of chicken from my plate. He bit down on the chicken breast and jumped onto the floor, then ran to the corner by the sink and set it down. He sniffed it and then carried it to the living room.

About a minute later, Eddie came back. "Done. I told him to meet me at Tradava in fifteen minutes. He's leaving now."

"Perfect." I left Eddie at the house and drove to the museum. The sun hovered above the horizon. I parked in a space at the back of the lot and entered through the back door.

With Thad away from the museum, it was the perfect time to snoop. I went down the stairs to the catacombs—the offices for the museum director and staff—to see what I could find.

Two solid wood doors intricately carved with flora and fauna separated the offices from the hallway. The doors were shut but not locked; someone had turned the bolt on one door, so it rested against its partner. I eased my way in and let my eyes adjust to the minimal light.

The last time I'd been in this office had been when Dr. Daum was the director of the museum. Dr. Daum was of the messy-desk-organized-mind category, but under Christian's leadership, the surface was neat. The wood surface had recently been oiled and held the faint scent of lemon. A miniature copy of Rodin's *The Thinker*, like the ones in the gift shop Rebecca had been straightening yesterday, served as a paperweight, holding down a pile of notes and memos.

I moved the statue and fanned out the papers. Two vacation requests. A grant proposal. A responsibility sheet for an upcoming luncheon. And—bingo. A list of names and addresses titled, "Interest in Hats."

The names were followed by a city and state: Edith Willoughby,

Philadelphia, Pennsylvania; Charlotte Mann, Princeton, New Jersey; Mildred Manners, Dover, Delaware; Paul Haines, Albany, New York. There were twenty names on the list.

I set the plaster statue on top of the other pages and made a copy of the list on the scanner. The doors swung opened. I grabbed the copy and ducked behind an A/V cart. There was no time to return the original list to the pile on his desk.

Christian crossed the room and sat. He changed out of a pair of dusty brown construction boots into the shiny black wingtips he'd worn the day I met him. The boots were tossed along the back wall. A clump of dirt tinted dark red fell from the waffle-stomper tread.

He opened the scanner and lifted the page I'd left behind. He turned back to his desk and glanced at *The Thinker*, pressed a button on his phone, and wedged the phone between his ear and his shoulder. "Have you been to the office recently?" He paused. "No, nothing. Thank you."

He set the receiver down, moved *The Thinker* from the pile of papers, and flipped through them. His forehead was creased in confusion. He added the list to the pile and replaced the paperweight, and then he made another call, this time using ten buttons.

"Everything is going according to plan. You'll be pleased. Quite." Pause. "We knew there would be challenges along the way, but I'm dealing with them discreetly. No. Yes. Of course. If she gets too close, I'll tell the police what I know. I don't want you to worry. Soon it will all be over, and the hiding and the lies can stop. It will be worth the sacrifice. I'm happy to do this for you. Until tomorrow."

It wasn't until he hung up that I realized I was a sitting duck. Who had Christian been talking to? And who was he talking about? *If she gets too close, I'll tell the police what I know.* Who was she—Hedy? Vera?

Me?

If I hadn't hidden to begin with, I could have stepped out from behind the racks and told Christian I'd been waiting for him, but I could hardly pop up from behind a row of books and pretend my presence was normal now.

But Christian showed no sign of leaving. I looked around the room, desperate for an escape plan. My eyes passed over his boots, a Louis Vuitton briefcase that sat next to his own tattered leather one, and a stack of dog-eared exhibit catalogs. The room was painfully silent. I needed a distraction and a way out. I was not going to become one of the challenges along the way that he would have to deal with. If he was the killer and thought wrapping someone in bubble wrap was discreet, what else he was capable of?

Jazz trickled from small speakers on either side of Christian's computer. The music was faint but enough to drown out ambient noise. Light from a streetlamp outside the museum shined through a small window above the shelving unit on the other side of the office. I crawled toward the door. I quietly tore a strip of paper from the sheet of collectors I'd printed and balled it up. I bowled it across the shiny concrete floor. It skidded past Christian's desk like a mouse. He looked up, startled. He stood and went to the shelving to investigate.

My pulse raced. I slipped through the double doors, through the hallway, and up three stairs toward the exit. I was steps away from the cloak of anonymity that night provides. But before I reached the door, Thad stepped out of the shadows.

"Thad!" I jumped. "You scared me." If my pulse was racing before, then now it was about to lap Mario Andretti. But the increased blood flow triggered a new synaptic fire. "Weren't you supposed to meet Eddie at Tradava?"

He glared at me with his unnaturally light eyes. Today they were lavender—confirming my suspicion of contacts. I wanted to look away, but Thad broke our eye contact first. (Victory!)

"What's that?" he asked. He snatched the paper from my hand. (Defeat.) "Where did you get this?"

"Isn't that Eddie's to-do list? He said he left it here and I told him I'd pick it up. Did I grab the wrong piece of paper?" I stood on my tiptoes and pretended to look at the page.

Thad folded the paper and ran his thumb and index finger over the crease. "Samantha, if you want to help Eddie, give him a message. Tell him to stay out of this before he gets in too deep."

14

———

MENSWEAR

I LEFT THAD IN THE DOORWAY TO THE MUSEUM WHILE I POWER-WALKED to my car. His message to Eddie was a borderline threat. Thad knew more than he was letting on, and I was going to find out what.

Another thing nagged at me—Christian's two phone calls. Only the second one used ten digits. That indicated the first was an internal call. Was he working with someone else on the inside?

Eddie was asleep in my bed when I got home. I didn't have the heart to wake him. I carried pajamas to the bathroom, washed my face and changed, and set up a makeshift bed on the sofa.

It wasn't the sunlight or the smell of coffee that woke me up Monday morning. It was the sound of my name being repeated over and over. (It was my name coupled with, "Don't you have to meet Nick in half an hour?" that finally did the trick.)

I opened one eye to a scary version of Eddie standing over me. Scary because he was in my terrycloth bathrobe. Second day of employment with Nick and show up late? Not a chance.

Today I went with the opposite of sexy secretary: menswear. When I returned to the kitchen, I was in a brown blazer and matching pants, light blue shirt, brown and navy paisley silk vest, and brown leather ghillies. I added an oblong scarf knotted as a necktie and topped it all with a pile of pearls.

"How did you do that in ten minutes?" Eddie asked with awe.

"It's a gift."

I grabbed my keys, pulled on Jackie O glasses, and left. Rush hour was thinning out, so I arrived at Milo Delaney's address in record time. I drove past a series of row homes, checking the numbers on the front of each house until I found the one that corresponded to the address Nick had given me. It was an odd place for a showroom.

Two kids bounced a ball on the street, and a pair of old men sat on a porch watching them. They turned their attention to me when I got out of the car. I suspected they didn't see women in menswear and seven strands of pears every day.

A thin man in a close-fitting T-shirt and faded ratty jeans approached. He held a cup of coffee in one hand and a leash attached to a very big dog in the other. I took a step backward to give him room to pass. He nodded at me and approached the address I intended to visit. He went inside. I looked around for Nick, spotting him a few feet from his white pickup truck parked farther down the street.

"You should have gone up without me," he said. "I didn't realize I was going to have to park so far away."

"I'm not sure this is the right address. I saw someone go inside, and he didn't look like a hat designer."

Just then a window above us opened, and the man with the large dog poked his head out. "Nick Taylor?" he asked.

"Yes."

"Come on in."

The door buzzed. Nick grabbed the handle and held it open for me. I stepped inside, and Nick followed. The man jogged halfway down a dark wood staircase. "I'm Milo. Showroom's up here." He turned away and scaled the stairs.

Nick jogged up after him. I climbed as quickly as I could, finding it unexpectedly difficult as I was wearing shoes not designed for stair-climbing. By the time we reached the room, only one of us looked professional. The black Labrador lay on a rug of colorful braided rope next to an antique wooden desk.

"Welcome to my temporary showroom," Milo said. "Sorry about the informality. I've been scrambling since my business manager left me."

"Nick Taylor," Nick said. "This is Samantha Kidd. She works for—with—for—me."

We all shook hands. A skylight from above flooded the showroom and samples with natural light, and I caught my reflection. Yikes.

Aside from my sub-par reflection, the mirror reflected Milo's samples. Hat stands similar in design to the green fixtures in the window of Over Your Head but unpainted held exquisite bits of feather and fluff.

I approached a forest-green fedora like the hat Eddie and I had found next to Dirk Engle's body. I ran my fingertips over the felt edge. "This is," I paused, searching for the right word.

"Fantastic, right?"

"Actually, 'familiar' is the word I was looking for. I've seen this hat before."

Milo glared at me. "Nobody has seen this collection." The phone rang in the background, but he made no move to answer it.

"Is that part of the Hedy London collection?"

"No," he snapped. "It's an original."

Nick stepped behind Milo and put his hand up to his throat and made a side-to-side gesture, signaling me to cut my questions. I smiled and went for complimentary. "I do like the nostalgic element to your collection. The styles remind me of the way people dressed in old movies."

"I'm not a copier; I'm a designer. I design." Milo said bitterly. The phone continued to ring. "My ideas are mine."

"I didn't mean to imply they're not." Clearly, this was not going well. "Do you handle your own marketing and publicity?"

"I have a team of experts hidden in the back room. You hear the phone ringing off the hook. What do you think?"

I tried to figure out what I'd said to trigger his animosity. "You're a successful designer, consistently getting awards for your contributions to the industry." The phone was driving me nuts. "Don't you need to answer that?"

Milo went to the phone. He glanced at the display, picked up the receiver, and turned his back to us. I strained to hear what he said, but he hung up before I had a chance. He lifted the receiver again, hit four numbers, and set the receiver back on the base.

"What were you saying?" he asked me.

"I'm impressed that you can handle all the aspects of your business by yourself. I didn't mean any disrespect."

"As far as business managers go, I've always found they're more trouble than they're worth. As for today's appointment, we're going to have to reschedule."

"Of course," Nick said. He held out his hand, and Milo shook it.

Nick and I left. My skin prickled from Milo's animosity. When we reached my car, I turned to Nick. "Did I say something wrong in there?"

"It's not you, it's him. Misplaced anger. Considering the circumstances, I can't say I'm all that surprised."

"What circumstances?"

"You don't know?" He looked surprised and then quickly recovered. "Nothing. He's had a turn of bad luck, that's all."

Nick was being evasive for a reason. "See you back at the showroom?" he asked.

"No. *I'm* going back to the showroom. You're going to get us something to eat."

"It's nine forty-five."

"I feel guilty for not eating your sandwich yesterday."

Nick looked at me like I was crazy. I adjusted my pearls and smoothed my necktie. He shook his head. "Bagels and cream cheese? Will that work for you?"

Considering the brown rice and chicken option Eddie had offered me yesterday, it sounded darn near perfect. "Works for me."

I waited until Nick got into his car and started the engine before I peeled out. Nick knew something I didn't but not for long. I ran a couple of yellow lights and possibly one red. After unlocking the showroom and dumping my handbag on the floor, I ran to his desk and booted his PC. When the search engine came up, I typed "Milo Delaney business manager."

No wonder Nick didn't tell me what he knew. Milo's former business manager had been Dirk Engle.

15

IT'S NOT WHAT YOU THINK

BY THE TIME NICK ARRIVED AT HIS SHOWROOM, I'D SCANNED IN HIS inspiration photos and mocked up four separate mood boards for his approval. He set a cup of coffee and a brown paper bag on the desk and sat down in the chair across from me.

"Did you honestly think I wouldn't find out that you're digging into Dirk Engle's murder while you're on the clock?"

"Nick, it's not what you think."

"You haven't been to the museum since the murder?"

I sat back in my chair and took a breath. Our voices had been steadily rising, and while we were very lucky that we were in the privacy of Nick's showroom and not a public arena, it did seem best not to go on shouting about things like dead bodies.

"I did the right thing, Nick. When Eddie and I found the body, I called the cops. I talked to Detective Loncar. When I found out Eddie had accidentally taken a hat from the crime scene, I arranged for Loncar to pick it up at my house. Inviting the detective to my house? That is so far from digging into Dirk Engle's murder that it's completely unlike anything I would have done under former circumstances."

"That doesn't make this any better."

"I think it makes it a *lot* better. I've been a normal upstanding citizen since we found Dirk Engle's body."

"You wanted to meet with Milo *after* you found the body. Why is that? I know you. You're trying to get involved."

"No, I'm not. You're the one who set up the meeting. And you knew—you knew! —Dirk Engle was Milo's business manager. You're guiltier of the lie of omission than I am. I went to the meeting because I'm working for—with—for—you."

"I didn't tell you Dirk Engle was Milo's business manager."

"Yes, you did. You said you weren't surprised, all things considered."

Nick's face went red. "Is that why you wanted me to get you food? You could have asked, Kidd. I would feel a lot better about all this if you had just asked what I meant. But you didn't. You came back here —raced back here is more like it because I saw how you blew through two red lights on Penn Avenue—because you wanted to do some research without my knowing."

"You don't know what you're talking about." I paused and clenched my jaw so hard I felt it in the filling in my back left molar. "It was *one* red light, and it was on *Perkiomen* Avenue, not Penn."

"I think what bothers me the most is that you lied to me. You said you wouldn't get involved, and you did."

Nick leaned back and put his hands on his armrests. He shook his head slowly. His temples pulsed as he clenched and re-clenched his teeth, and I wondered how many fillings he had and if he felt it too.

"Call Detective Loncar. You're friends with him, right? Ask him if I've been a help or a hindrance. Ask him if I've been bugging him about the case. Go ahead. Call him."

"I'm not going to call the detective to check up on you."

"Well, you could. He'd back me up." Nick shot me a look. "Are we done here?"

"Darn near close. Stay out of it, Kidd. Please. I can't handle—"

"You can't handle what?" Shock hit my face like a cold rag. "You're worried about your reputation? You don't want me to get involved because I'm working for you! This reaction has nothing to do with Eddie and nothing to do with me. I'm right, aren't I?"

He didn't answer.

I grabbed my bag and stood up. "I have to get to the printer to pick up your line sheets," I said and stormed out.

I HAVE this thing about approval. It comes from growing up as the kid in the family. My older sister had managed to out-do me my whole life: SAT scores, colleges, marriage, family. She'd become the adult she was intended to become, and I'd continued to be the kid. That's even what my parents still called me. The Kid. Vying for attention and positive feedback had gotten me a lucrative career in fashion. It had severed those close sisterly ties that other families maintained because I'd eventually tired of the feeling that I was never going to catch up. My attempts to rediscover my roots and get on a different path had changed the direction of my future. But my need for approval remained. Maybe that's why I drove to the museum in search of my mentor, Dr. Daum.

Dr. Daum and I had formed an unlikely friendship during the months I'd volunteered at the museum, him coming to me to share news of a new acquisition or a particularly frustrating meeting with board members who didn't see eye to eye with his outlook. I'd never questioned why he took me under his wing because asking would have undermined our relationship.

I circled through the parking lot, taking note of the cars in the lot: white SUV, burgundy Jaguar, and two unattended police cars. A man in a wrinkled suit and straw hat, camera on a strap around his neck, wandered the museum grounds. I drove past him and went around the block and parked in front of a large white brick colonial with a red front door and blue trim. I rang the bell and waited.

"Samantha! What a pleasant surprise." said the man who answered the door. He had white hair, blue eyes, sun-spotted skin, and the kind of smile that made people feel welcome.

"Dr. Daum," I said. We hugged. He pulled the front door closed behind him and gestured toward the two rocking chairs on his porch. We spent a few minutes catching up and discussing the weather before he questioned my presence. "I know you know the museum is closed on Monday. That leads me to think you're here for me. To what do I owe this visit?"

"It does have to do with the museum," I said. "The hat exhibit. Can you tell me anything about it?"

"Ah, the exhibit. Christian's masterpiece. I wonder, I've wondered all along, what would happen if we tried an exhibit on that scale, what would it do to our small town? We invited trouble into our backyard, and now we've been caught unprepared to handle it."

"What kind of trouble?"

"The kind of trouble that comes from too many secrets. Christian wanted to keep things under wraps, but the executives at Tradava who are footing the bill are eager to see what he has planned. There have been mishaps, theft, and now murder. Christian may believe there's no such thing as bad publicity, but I disagree."

"Mishaps—like when the light fixture fell?"

"That was the most recent, yes, but I'm afraid that was my fault. Your friend Eddie had asked if we could hide the normal lighting fixtures for the exhibit. He said he had an idea. I spoke to the engineer about it but failed to mention to anyone else that the fixtures were being removed. At least the gallery was empty when it fell."

"The gallery wasn't empty. I was there. The fixture almost fell on me."

Dr. Daum's eyes closed, and he took a deep breath that puffed out the narrow span of his chest. He exhaled and opened his eyes. "Samantha, I'm sorry for my negligence. Were you hurt?"

"No." I relented under his stare. "I twisted my ankle when I fell, and I picked up a couple of bruises nobody's going to see since it's not bathing suit weather."

"What were you doing there? The only person who should have been there at the time was Dirk Engle. Where was he?"

"You mean Dirk and Eddie, right? Eddie Adams is the visual manager for Tradava, and he's in charge of the exhibit."

"Yes, I know Eddie. Charming man. He mentioned you two were friends."

"The same day the lighting fixture dropped, Dirk quit and stormed out. Eddie and I were the only two people there." An awkward silence grew between us as I remembered how we'd found Dirk Engle's body and how we had realized that all along we had not been alone. New questions pooled in my head. "Except now I know we weren't."

Dr. Daum was quiet too. I didn't know how much he knew about the murder, but even without his museum connections, his house was close enough to the property to have woken him up with the lights and the noise.

"This exhibit is worth quite a bit of money," Dr. Daum said. "The insurance on Hedy London's hats is around several million dollars. The only people who knew about the insurance were Christian, Dirk, and me. Dirk went behind Christian's back and had the hats sent to his store. I'm not sure anybody knows his true motivation—gaining favor with his clients by giving them first view or copying the designs for his inventory—but it seemed as though he were taking advantage of the situation."

"If Christian knew Dirk was taking advantage of the situation, why didn't he fire him? Would that be a bigger risk to the exhibit than keeping him on board?"

"Christian confronted Dirk, who denied any such allegations. Your friend Eddie was called in to help run interference between Dirk and Christian. Dirk should have been fired, but his contract made terminating him difficult. A person without integrity has no right to be involved in the business of art, of preservation, or of style."

"The day I came to the museum to help Eddie, Dirk was there. He fought with someone. I think it was Thad or Christian."

"Christian was waiting for board approval to fire Dirk. The board was dragging their feet, afraid of poor publicity and potential legal repercussions. Dirk Engle fought with a lot of people about this exhibit. I think the only person he agreed with was the hat designer responsible for the samples."

"Milo Delaney."

Dr. Daum paused for a moment. "I've kept up with your activities since you moved back to Ribbon, and I know you've had success with this sort of thing. But Samantha, this is not our business. The police will investigate his murder and conclude that he was involved with unsavory characters. We're all in a much better place without his sort, but it's a shame that the museum will suffer."

"Not just the museum. Eddie will too. He's being pressured to pick up where Dirk left off, and his job security at Tradava is now riding on how well he pulls this off."

"Do you believe Eddie can handle the job ahead of him?"

I nodded.

"Wait here." Dr. Daum stood and entered his house. He returned with a set of keys. "This is a spare set of museum keys. Please give them back to him and apologize to Eddie on behalf of the museum. I'll make sure he has twenty-four-hour access to the Frowick Gallery, so he can continue working."

I stood and took the set of keys. "What about Thad?" I asked. "Do you think he's capable of murder?"

Dr. Daum's face clouded. He looked over my head and then back at me. "My dear, do you have any reason to suspect him?"

I shifted my eyes to Dr. Daum's left while I thought back over that first day when Thad had closed the door to the admissions office hours before Eddie and I found Dirk's body, and to last night when he'd caught me coming out of Christian's office. Despite his claims to be helping Eddie, he hadn't appeared happy to find me. What was the reason for his animosity?

The police must have questioned him. I'd all but told them to. And Dr. Daum was right—without anything concrete, I had no business going around casting suspicion on anybody, regardless of their disposition.

"No, I guess I don't have any reason to suspect him."

"Then I'd suggest you worry less about Thad and more about yourself."

"Why me?"

"Perhaps that man with the camera can tell you more than I can." Dr. Daum pointed over my shoulder to the parking lot, where a sizeable telephoto lens was pointed in our direction.

16

A CERTAIN FLAIR

I HAD CHALKED UP TO MY ENCOUNTER WITH DANTE IN THE GROCERY store as coincidence, but this was too much. I said goodbye to Dr. Daum and hiked across the grassy back lawn of the museum toward him. I didn't know why he was following me, but it was going to stop. Now.

My pearls swung back and forth as I picked up speed. Dante lowered his camera as I approached. He smiled and then stepped away from his motorcycle and crossed his arms over his black leather jacket.

"Why did you take my picture?" I demanded.

"That's an interesting question."

"No, it's not. It's probably the least interesting question I could ask."

"Then why did you ask it?"

"Why did you take my picture?" I asked again.

"I like your outfit. Shows a certain flair."

My face grew hot. "That's not what I mean."

"You asked why I took your picture. That's why I took your picture. If it were me asking the questions, I would have asked why I was following you."

"Why are you following me?"

He ducked out from under his camera strap and put the camera into a heavily padded equipment bag. "Now that is a good question. I wish I had a good answer."

"Why don't you tell me the truth?"

"The truth," he said, with a smile on his face. "I was asked to follow you."

"Why?"

"You're stuck on that question. If it were me, I would have asked *who*."

"Why?"

"Still with the why?" He secured the equipment bag to the back of his motorcycle with a stretchy cord.

"No. Why would you have asked who wanted you to follow me? If I know why you were asked to follow me, I can probably figure out who."

"You are an inquisitive woman. I'll give you that," he said.

"How did you know where I'd be?"

"Generally speaking, when someone is asked to follow someone else, they're given a location, or at least some ideas of where to find the subject. I don't know many instances where people say, 'Drive around town and find a woman in a necktie and pearls,' but in your case, that would have worked as well, because I think you're probably the only woman in Ribbon wearing that outfit."

"Enough about my outfit. I want answers."

"If you could decide what questions you want to ask, maybe we could work something out."

I felt like I was having a conversation with the Mad Hatter. I turned to see if Dr. Daum was watching us. He wasn't. When I turned back to Dante, his helmet was in his hand, and he was straddling the bike.

"Where are you going?" I asked.

Dante leaned forward, holding the helmet upside down in his two hands. "You're still not asking the right questions, Samantha." His breath smelled like cinnamon. He put on the flame-decorated helmet and started his bike. He nodded once and then rolled off the kickstand and pulled out of the lot.

I should have felt angry/concerned/nervous/creeped out, but I didn't. I felt annoyed. And excited, which triggered guilt. I turned back to the museum. I'd told Nick I wouldn't be involved, and here I was at the museum. Involved.

There had to be a reason Dante was following me. And then I realized something.

I was in a position to follow *him.*

As fast as I could, I unlocked my car, jumped inside, and revved the engine. The tires squealed as I backed out and threw the car into drive, hoping to catch up with Dante. I caught sight of his motorcycle making a left turn onto Penn Avenue. I made the same left, weaved in and out of cars on the two-lane road, and closed the distance between us.

It was almost too easy.

Within two blocks I was directly behind him. I kept on his tail as he pulled onto the highway, exited by the Ribbon Designer Outlets, and parked next to the loading dock. I parked next to him and slammed my door while he was unlocking the equipment bag from the back of his bike. He pulled off his helmet, slung the camera bag over one shoulder, and tipped his head toward the building.

"Not bad," he said. "Follow me."

"I'm not going anywhere with you."

"You followed me this far. What's ten more feet?" He turned around and walked into Catnip, his sister, Cat's, boutique.

For all the warning bells that might have sounded in a different person's mind, the only bells I heard were the ones that sounded when we entered the store. I'd shopped here before, soon after I moved back to Ribbon. The soft lighting showcased the boutique's merchandise, tables of cashmere sweaters, folded jeans, racks of last year's designer looks. Cat had great taste, and I would have been happy to become a regular customer if only we hadn't gotten off on the wrong foot. We'd since worked past most of our issues, but still, she didn't look happy to see me.

"Cat," I said.

"Samantha," she said back.

"You two need to talk," Dante added.

Though their coloring was different, Dante and Cat shared the same square face and wide-set eyes. Cat's hair, a vibrant red, could have come at the hands of an expert colorist, and Dante's jet-black hair could have come from a bottle of shoe polish, but confirmation of either point would have to wait because I had bigger questions on my mind than hair color.

Cat looked delightfully fresh in a lime-green taffeta jacket that was cinched at the waist over biscuit-colored skinny pants and spiked olive-green heels. "I guess you're wondering why I asked my brother to follow you around Ribbon."

"You? *You* asked him to follow me?" I asked, again feeling like Alice in Wonderland.

"Dante, go get me a latte. Samantha, would you like anything?"

I would have killed for a cup of coffee but wasn't ready to accept her hospitality. "No thank you," I said.

She held out a twenty, which he looked at but didn't take. "It was all her idea," he said to me.

After Dante left the store, Cat turned to me. "I don't know you very well, but after what happened at Heist, I feel like I can trust you." She was referring to a publicity contest we—Cat, Dante, Eddie, and I —had entered a few months ago. What had started as a contest with a sizeable cash prize had ended in three murders and my second failed employment in six months.

I waved my hand in front of her. "Water under the bridge," I said, not 100 percent sure the cliché fit the situation.

"I asked Dante to check you out. Follow you around, see the kind of people you spend time with. I know you're working on the Hedy London exhibit. That's one of the reasons I wanted to talk to you."

"I don't know anything about Hedy London. Or the exhibit. Tradava is the one who has the exclusive on the collection, and I don't work for them."

"No, that's not it. I have—had—a hat, a Lily Daché, and now it's gone."

"I don't have access to the sample collection either."

"Listen to me. I bought my hat on the secondary market a few years ago. My old boss has connections. With all the press surrounding this exhibit, I thought it would be fun to take it out and wear it."

"Cat, I'm not sure I understand what this has to do with me. Do you want me to see it?"

"No, I don't want you to see it. And even if I did, I can't. The day I wore it I was mugged, and the only thing they took was my hat."

17

———

FOR A GOOD TIME CALL

I HAD A STRANGE FEELING I KNEW WHY CAT HAD WANTED TO TALK TO me, and I wasn't sure I liked it.

"Cat, I'm flattered, but if you were mugged, you should be talking to the police."

"I called the police. They have a report. But they didn't seem all that interested in helping me. You can. I can't help but believe it's related to the exhibit."

"I don't know what you're asking me to do."

"I don't think the police care all that much about my missing hat, but I'm not willing to just accept that it's gone. Will you, I don't know, keep an ear to the ground?"

I hesitated. Could I make an argument that helping Cat find her hat wasn't related to the Hedy London exhibit and honor the promise I'd made to Nick? It was a little gray. "You said you got it from the secondary market. eBay?"

"Nothing that mainstream." Cat leaned in closer and dropped her voice. "My old boss, the previous owner of this store, collects Hedy London memorabilia. A few years ago, he invited me to go on one of his field trips. It was crazy cool. We had to dress down like bums. He had an address that led him to a driver who took us to a row home in the middle of Ribbon, where a guy met us on the street and ushered us into his loft. It was filled with the most amazing vintage fashion. I found a hat that Hedy London was supposed to wear in an early movie, but it ended up on the cutting room floor."

"They threw the hat on the floor?"

"The footage from the movie ended up on the floor. The hat ended up in this guy's collection. It's so yummy. It's a turquoise pillbox confection of felted wool, satin, and rhinestones!" She clapped her hands like a five-year-old at her first puppet show.

"At least you didn't pay retail," I muttered, half under my breath, remembering the style I'd tried on at Vera Sarlow's store. A thrift store find would have been a nice change of pace.

"I wish I'd paid retail. That hat probably cost about three dollars back in its day."

"What did inflation cost you?" I asked.

"Three thousand."

I was speechless. Cat's news had just let me know that as far as fashionistas go, she was in a whole other league.

I told her again I didn't know what I could do for her but promised to stay in touch. We were interrupted by a phone call. To me. From Nick.

"Kidd, do I need to find another showroom manager?" Nick asked.

"Hi! I'm waiting on the printer. I'll be back in about twenty minutes." I disconnected before he could get another word in and then said goodbye to Cat and left out the back door.

Dante leaned against the hood of my car. He held two coffee cups. "So that's it? You're back in Ribbon because your sister asked you to follow me around?" I asked.

"Philly's not all that far." He tipped his head to the side and then righted it, as though I was close enough to the situation that there was no point in adding to my reasoning. "Besides, it was an interesting proposition, so I said yes."

"I don't want to be rude, but I'm late for something."

"Work. You're late for work. With your boyfriend, who is now your boss," he finished.

"Exactly how much do you know about my life?"

"Not nearly enough." He held out a cup. "Coffee. Cream, no sugar. I'm fairly sure you wanted it even though you declined my sister's offer."

This time I took the cup.

"Call me if you want to talk about the questions you should be asking."

"What if I didn't keep your number?"

"If you look hard enough, I'm sure you'll find it."

"Ladies' room stall? 'For a good time call'?"

"Something like that. Bye, Samantha."

I DROVE to the print shop, picked up Nick's line sheets, and drove back to his showroom. I spent the twenty-minute drive concluding that I had to talk to somebody about what was going on. The person I trusted, the person I wanted to be my confidant, was waiting for me inside that showroom. It would be nice to talk to Nick. He'd have a different perspective, and in the past, he'd even been willing to help me out when I needed it.

It took about ten more minutes in the parking lot to work through all the reasons I shouldn't confide in Nick: lecture, warning, and accusations of broken promises. By the time I decided to go for it, I was more concerned about the voices in my head than anything Nick might say.

By the time I opened the door to his studio, I felt as though I'd played three sets of tennis with Novak Djokovic and was left with a tightening knot at the base of my neck. *Mental note: find an outlet for tension. Soon.*

Nick stood by the left wall of the showroom with a power drill in one hand and a screw in the other.

"We need to talk," I said. "Not like 'boss-employee.' I mean, I know I said we should be on a break while we were working together, but can we talk? Like boyfriend-girlfriend? Or is that not a good idea?"

Nick set the drill on the desk and studied me. A dull heat prickled my hairline. I didn't look away. For a few seconds, the attraction to Nick I'd felt on Saturday night lit up like the fuse on a stick of dynamite, and I wondered how long it would take until it exploded.

"Let's—" His voice cracked. He tucked his chin and coughed a couple of times into his fist. "Let's get out of here."

I followed Nick to his truck. He drove to a bakery about three miles from his showroom. I followed him inside. He gestured for me to sit in a booth while he went to the counter. He returned with two cups of coffee and two donuts.

"What's up, Kidd?"

I could have opened with an explanation, or an excuse, or a meandering path of events that had led me to breaking the promise I'd made. It all led to one undeniable fact that we both already knew.

"I'm involved," I said.

He reached across the table and set his hands on top of mine. For a few seconds, we didn't speak.

"I know you're concerned about what my involvement says about your showroom while I'm working there. I had no right to lie to you, but everything else I told you was true. Eddie needed—needs—my help."

"Kidd, I don't think you understand."

"I think I do. Your reputation is on the line. When you asked me not to get involved, I thought I could. Not get involved. I thought I could not get involved. But I already was involved, and I can't just walk away. You need to know that about me. You might not like that about me, but you need to know it because it's probably not going to change."

The heat from his hands felt good. I stared into his eyes, his soft, brown, root-beer-barrel colored eyes. I closed my own eyes and inhaled the scent of his cologne mixed with the scent of the bakery: dark and spicy with a glazed-sugar coating. I felt him staring at me and opened my eyes. He was. My thoughts took a less-than-appropriate turn involving a countertop in the kitchen. Abruptly, he pulled away and tucked his hands in his lap. Could he read my mind? And what was so inappropriate about a bakery-based fantasy anyway?

Someone cleared her throat. I looked up. Mrs. Aguan, the head of human resources at Tradava, approached our booth. She wore a white mandarin-collared shirt, a boxy, forest-green cardigan, and gray slacks. Her hair was short, gray, and spiky, and was the same color as her pants. A multi-strand necklace of rough-cut green stones filled in her neckline.

"Nick Taylor, what a pleasant surprise. We miss you coming through the store to check on your collection. How are things going with your new launch?"

"Fine. I'll start booking market appointments soon. How are things at Tradava?" he asked. I suspected the question was for my benefit.

"It seems everyone's overworked these days. We lifted the hiring freeze but can't find the right caliber employee." She looked at me briefly, as if gauging whether I could be trusted with the conversation.

"You remember Samantha Kidd, don't you?" Nick asked. "She was the trend special—"

I cut him off with a kick to the shin and a sudden fit of coughing. I took a sip of water to make the coughing fit look real.

"I'm his showroom manager," I said after I'd swallowed.

Mrs. Aguan studied me. "Samantha Kidd." She dragged out my name, as if trying to place where she'd heard it. I could tell the moment she figured it out, because she looked like someone had shot a pulse of electricity between her ears. Her eyes popped open a bit wider, and her mouth went into an O for a second before she recovered.

I held out my hand. "Pleasure seeing you again."

She took my hand in a limp handshake and forced a smile. "Likewise."

Mrs. Aguan said goodbye and left us. I didn't know if she'd heard any of our conversation before she approached us. If Nick was concerned about his reputation, holding hands with his showroom manager in a public bakery might not have been the way to go. And as far as *my* reputation went, my behavior was less than professional. She'd never recruit me back to Tradava. Even if I applied for a job, she'd see that as me having no loyalty to Nick. It wasn't the first time I found myself wondering if taking this job had been the right decision.

"Kidd, I know I asked you not to get involved, but all things considered—"

"All things considered, Eddie helped me out when I had similar problems last year. Put yourself in my shoes, Nick."

"I am. Eddie's my friend too. But this isn't about work. It isn't about my reputation, and it isn't about my showroom. It's about you. I want to protect you."

"I can take care of myself."

"I'm not always going to be your boss, Kidd, and when that day comes, I want you to still be in one piece."

The low flame that I'd felt earlier flickered inside me again. Nick turned his hand over and entwined his fingers with mine. The palm of his hand felt softer than I expected. He rubbed his thumb back and forth over my life line, my love line, and whatever other lines were etched into my flesh. The longer we sat there, the faster my pulse raced.

"I made a mistake," I said, my voice husky. I was willing to go out on that limb, to tell him that I should never have accepted this job. "I should have known better, but I didn't, and now things are complicated..." My voice trailed off.

He lifted my hand and pressed the fingers to his soft lips. "Kidd, don't apologize. It's not too late." His eyes deepened. I could drown in them.

I leaned my head back against the booth, my low ponytail pressing into the cushion. "But how do we—what do we—what's next?" I asked.

"Tell Eddie you're done. I'll come up with something."

"What does Eddie have to do with us?" I asked, with the slow realization that maybe we weren't talking about the same thing. Clarity pierced the fog of attraction that had clouded my mind only moments ago. "What are you talking about?"

"The homicide investigation. I'm glad you can see what a mistake it was to get involved, but it's for the best."

I pulled my hand away. "I wasn't talking about the homicide investigation."

"What were you talking about?"

My temperature rose for completely different reasons than it had only moments before. "That's what you got from this conversation? That I'm going to quit helping Eddie?"

"You said you should have known better."

"About working for you. I should have trusted my instincts all the times you offered to give me a job while I looked for something more suitable."

"Your instincts told you to say no to working for me but yes to getting mixed up in a murder investigation? I'm telling you I'll help you get out. What do your instincts say about that?"

"Nick, I don't want out. I want the person who killed Dirk Engle to get caught."

"The police are working on that."

"But they don't know any more than we do. They don't know about the collectors. They don't know about Cat's hat-jacking. They don't know about Thad—"

"Kidd, for someone who says she's been turning everything over to the police, you sure have a lot of information in your back pocket."

"I don't need a lecture, Nick."

He leaned back and ran his hand over his hair. "I think it's time we went back to the showroom."

"No, Nick, I think maybe I'm done for the day." I stormed out of the diner.

I DROVE HOME at breakneck speed. I tried to call Eddie, but there was no answer. I pulled into my driveway and ran to the front door. "Eddie?" I yelled.

I tossed my handbag onto the side table by the door like I always did. The table was missing, and my handbag landed on the floor. I took a couple of steps inside and tripped over a chair.

Everything had been moved; everything had been cleaned. It was as if I'd been ransacked by the Merry Maids, who'd left the place better looking than when they arrived.

"Eddie! Are you here?" He didn't answer. I looked for a note of explanation as to where he might be or tracks on my carpet indicating that he'd been dragged out against his will, but there was nothing.

I called him four times in a row. He didn't answer. I circled with nervous energy, not able to sit and relax. Every time a car turned onto my street, I hopped to the windows, hoping it was him. Between the drive-bys, I checked the answering machine and my cell phone, hoping I'd somehow missed a message. No such luck.

There was nothing left for me to do but dole out some ice cream and wait. I pulled the rocky road out of the freezer and retrieved a clean bowl from the dishwasher. When I opened the ice cream container, I found a piece of paper curled up inside. *Was going stir crazy. Had to get out. No worries. Am incognito.*

He was mocking me. He was mocking my cooking abilities. He was mocking my predictable ice cream cravings.

Mental note: find a way to indicate that I'm not domestically incompetent.

Additional Mental note: have some ice cream first.

I dropped into a dining chair and massaged my temples. I'd gotten distracted by Dante and Cat, by Nick and Tradava. But before all of that, I'd met with Dr. Daum. What had he said? Dirk Engle was dead because of the exhibit.

And Dirk Engle's death hadn't slowed the exhibit down. Whoever was behind the murder would either kill again or get whatever it was they wanted that Dirk had obstructed.

If someone were after Dirk Engle, it would have been easy to find him at his store. Why come after him at the museum? The fact that he was found at the museum was curious. As in not good. As in his death had less to do with his own business and more to do with the exhibit. And that meant Eddie was in trouble—especially since he'd been the one to find the body and remove a hat from the museum. Even though I'd made sure it had been turned over to the police, chances were the murderer didn't know that.

I grabbed a pen and scribbled notes across a fresh sheet of paper. *Dirk Engle: Victim. Milo Delaney Business Manager. Hat store owner.*
Christian Jhanes: I-FAD chairman. Museum director.
Hedy London: Film star. Costume collector. Hat designer.

Then I thought about Dr. Daum's casual mention of Milo Delaney and how he'd changed the subject after introducing it to our conversation. I remembered how angry Milo had gotten when asked about Hedy London. I wrote *Milo Delaney* again. It seemed as though he was the piece that sat squarely in the middle of the puzzle, even if some of the connecting puzzle pieces were missing.

I turned to my computer and searched *millinery exhibit, Ribbon, PA, curator*. It was on page three that I found an article in the *Ribbon Times* online edition credited to Carl Collins, the same reporter who had written about Hedy London's collection coming to town. "Local Boutique Owner to Consult on Hollywood Exhibit" was the headline.

"Local" was a generous description of the thirty miles between the cities of Philadelphia and Ribbon, but calling Dirk Engle a local boy gave the article a hometown spin. I clicked the link and discovered that "local" wasn't a generous description after all.

The picture and article were not of Dirk Engle. This article was about Vera from Over Your Head.

18

BURGLARIZED

"Ace" reporter Carl Collins seemed to have taken a special interest in Hedy London. I read the article.

Friends of the Ribbon Museum of Art were notified by private newsletter of an upcoming exhibit at the museum. The unnamed exhibit was described as "cinematic treasures on loan from a high-profile collector," and is to be funded by local retailer Tradava. Vera Sarlow, owner of the hat shop Over Your Head, was mentioned as a consultant, indicating that the exhibit features hats [editor note: Sarlow could not be reached to verify details about the exhibit]. Additional names mentioned in collaboration with the exhibit were Christian Jhanes, former I-FAD faculty member, and Thad Thomas, assistant director of the Ribbon Museum of Art. Dr. Daum, recently retired director of the Ribbon Museum of Art, will stay on in a consulting position per a unanimous vote by the board of directors. The exhibit is expected to open as part of the museum's fall calendar.

I wished I had that sheet of names I'd printed from Christian's computer, but, thanks to Thad, I didn't. I typed "Thad Thomas" into Google and searched. There were more than five million hits, seventeen alone on LinkedIn. I narrowed my search: "Thad Thomas director." That filtered the hits down to 4.9 million. I continued adding words: "assistant," "museum," and "Ribbon." By the time I layered in "Frowick Gallery," I was down to one.

It was a mention of his post as assistant director of the museum. I clicked on the link and found myself staring at a thumbnail image of Thad next to Christian Jhanes. Below the picture was the caption *Assistant Director and Former Chair of Fashion Marketing.* I returned to Google. There were no other hits for Thad Thomas. It was as though he'd appeared out of thin air.

I climbed the stairs and took a long bubble bath, during which I stared at the ceiling. After climbing out and drying off, I dressed in a cashmere hoodie and a pair of black leggings and flopped on the bed, no closer to answers.

Logan hopped up next to me, settled in next to my thigh, and purred. I'd been neglecting him. "What do you think is going on here?" I asked. "What am I missing?" He meowed.

I heard a faint sound from downstairs. Logan stood up and jumped off the bed, crouched low, his tail getting fat. He started toward the door. I followed him down the stairs. When I reached the bottom step, I froze. There was a man in my living room.

Afternoon sunlight bounced off his shiny, bald head. His arms held a large bag stuffed with objects. I was being burglarized.

A shiver ran down my spine. How long had he been there? How did he get in? Did he know I was there?

Logan rubbed against my ankles, and I stiffened, hoping our movement hadn't alerted the intruder to our presence.

I reached for a pillow from the sofa and eased it out of its case. I wrapped each end around a wrist and slowly, quietly, crept behind the intruder. He bent down. I threw the pillowcase over his head and pulled the cotton tight.

"Don't move!" I kneed the back of his legs. He dropped the bag and fell to the floor. His bag spilled open. Shoe boxes fell out.

"Dude, get off me!" He pulled the pillowcase off his head and looked around.

Eddie? I switched on a lamp and helped him up. "Why are you creeping around my living room?"

"I couldn't stand sitting around here anymore. I had to get out."

"You shaved your head."

He rubbed a hand against his scalp. "I told you I was incognito. The tapes from the museum showed a guy with floppy blond hair. This was easier than messing around with Ms. Clairol."

I leaned back against the sofa and took a longer look at him, noting the contrast between his smooth head and beard stubble. "What's all this?" I asked, glancing at the boxes on the floor.

"I went shopping."

"You bought shoes?"

"I bought Vans." One by one he opened the boxes and pulled out sneakers decorated with wild prints: checkered, plaid, camouflage, floral. "Eighteen pairs. I couldn't stop. I've never bought eighteen pairs of anything at one time before, and that counts boxers that are packaged in threes."

I hugged him.

"Dude," he said.

"Sit down. There are a couple of things you need to know."

I told him about Milo Delaney, Christian's telephone conversation, the list of collectors, and Vera's involvement with the exhibit. He let me speak, uninterrupted except for the occasional sigh, grunt, and "WTF." Only he didn't say the letters W-T-F. The Lord's name got invoked a couple of times too. I finished by telling him about Cat being mugged.

"Is she hurt?"

"No. She's angry."

He pulled his knees up to his chest and curled his arms around them, like he was trying to shrink himself down to the size of a bowling ball. He started to rock back and forth against the white crocheted afghan that I left on the back of the sofa. I didn't think he knew he was doing it.

"It goes back to the exhibit," he said.

"How is that possible? Cat said she bought that hat years ago. She'd been saving it for a special occasion, and the first time she wore it, she got mugged. Nobody even knew she had it, except for her boss, who apparently is a Hedy London collector, and whoever sold it to her."

"Do you know where she bought it?" Eddie asked.

"She said it was through back channels. I don't think they're listed in the phone book."

"So now she's a Cat without a hat."

"I don't think she took out an ad in the paper to tell people she was going to debut it. It seems like a random act of violence. Except who steals a hat?"

Conversation ceased while we pondered that. "What do you know about Milo Delaney, the hat designer?" I asked. "He's the one producing Hedy London's collection."

He scratched the side of his head. "Nobody mentioned him."

I was starting to wonder exactly how much Eddie had been told before being given the job. "Tell me how you found out you'd be working on the exhibit."

"Two weeks ago, the regional director of visual merchandising called me to his office. He congratulated me again on winning the contest and said the museum wanted me to work on this exhibit. I admitted I was surprised. When I won, I thought there would be a little fanfare, but the more time that passed, the more I thought it was one of those never-gonna-happen things."

"You said something about a promotion."

"Yes. He said if I could pull it off, I'd get a bump to director of visual merchandising. Nicer title, better pay."

"Not that you don't deserve it, but it seems like they sweetened the pot on top of the whole contest win. I mean, is that normal? Win a contest, get a great opportunity as your prize, and then get a raise and promotion too?"

Eddie pulled my white afghan around his shoulders like it was a superhero cape and walked into the kitchen. I followed him, and we sat at the table.

"When I told you about the promotion, I wanted to impress you. I didn't tell you the other part."

"There's more?"

"Or less. If I don't pull this thing off, I'm out of a job."

"They're going to fire you?" He nodded. "I think it's time someone rewrote Tradava's employee-relations handbook."

Eddie smiled, but it seemed as though the effort was almost more than he could manage.

"My boss told me a personality conflict at the museum was holding up progress on the exhibit. Tradava had a lot of money invested in the collection, and they'd been counting on the museum to give them national press."

"Before you were onboard, it was just Dirk Engle. Right?"

"Right." Eddie picked at a loose thread on the afghan.

"And now he's dead."

"Right."

"Tonight, I found out that before Dirk Engle, Vera Sarlow was involved."

"Vera from Over Your Head?" he asked with surprise.

"One and the same."

Eddie lowered his head to the table and rested his forehead on the placemat for a few seconds. When he lifted his head, the imprint of a grid remained on his skin. He burped and set his head back on the placemat.

Seeing Eddie's panic paralysis affected me on a level I hadn't expected. I'd told Nick that I wasn't going to let Eddie face this alone, and I meant it. Except for right now, because there was something I had to do, and I didn't think it was wise to ask Eddie to come with me.

"Are you in for the night?"

"Sure. I may never go out again."

"Then you don't mind if I borrow your car?"

I DROVE TO THE MUSEUM. Instead of pulling into the parking lot, I parked Eddie's Bug on a residential side street about half a mile from the museum and walked. I let myself in with the keys Dr. Daum had given me to give Eddie. A single light glowed from behind the counter by the gift outpost, casting weird shadows from the merchandising trinkets. I passed the gift shop and went down the stairs that led to Christian's office. Light glowed from the bottom of the door. I tiptoed across the marble, not making a sound (thanks to my wrestling sneakers) and listened for sounds. When I heard nothing, I put my hand on the knob and pulled the door open.

Christian stood by a fax machine that was spitting out paper. His back was to me. I slipped into the office, dropped to all fours, and crawled past his desk to the metal A/V cart I'd hidden behind yesterday.

Christian ran his fingers through his golden-brown hair, the same way he had the day we'd first met, and then turned to the desk and picked up the receiver. He pressed a button and spoke. "If you'd still like to talk, I'm available." There was a pause, and then he said, "I'll be waiting." He hung up and scanned the surface of his desk, moving papers into one of his desk drawers.

I shifted my weight, wondering who he'd called. I was disappointed when Rebecca peeked around the door into Christian's office. Today her blond ringlets had been brushed into soft, feminine waves. She smelled like Madonna's *Like A Prayer* album (patchouli had been infused into every pressing).

Christian waved toward the chair in front of his desk. "Have a seat."

The A/V cart blocked my view of Rebecca. I contorted from my position until I was able to see them over the top of a flat black DVD player. She sat away from the back of the chair, with erect posture, like she was balancing a book on her head.

"What did you want to see me about?" Christian asked.

"I wanted to see if there was anything I could do to help with the exhibit," she said in a soft voice.

He looked at her across the desk. I wasn't sure whether I should concentrate on Christian's expression or Rebecca's, but knew if I kept moving, there was a pretty good chance I'd be discovered.

"I do have a project for you," he said. He opened his desk drawer and pulled out a piece of paper. "These are the top millinery collectors in the area. They must be contacted about the upcoming exhibit. A few may have concerns that we're going to cancel, and they need to be reassured that we're not. They represent a great deal of exposure and a great opportunity for the museum to raise funds. Can you do that for me?"

Rebecca leaned forward, and her black silk blouse exposed a lace trimmed bra and cleavage created by padding. Christian's eyes flicked down to her chest for a split second, and then he looked up at her. "Each collector need only be told only the most salacious pieces of information about the exhibit. Their interest should be piqued to maximize the wow factor. Tell them about the murder if you think it will heighten the drama."

"Is that a good idea? Won't that tarnish the exhibit?"

Christian crossed his arms over his chest. "What happened can't be helped. Quite the opposite. We now have a unique opportunity to gain national coverage for the museum. It is better to seize this moment than to avoid it because of an unfortunate event. Can I count on you?"

She cocked her head to one side, and her curls fell over her shoulder. "Of course, Dr.—Christian."

"Thank you, Rebecca."

She looked at the piece of paper like it was a love note, folded it and then folded it again, and stood. I slouched lower, scared that she'd see me.

After a few seconds of silence, Christian spoke. "Is there anything else you wanted to discuss?"

"No, I don't think so," she said.

"Then please close the door behind you. I'll be leaving after I finish with some paperwork."

"Of course." Her chunky loafers made clunking noises against the concrete floor. The door opened and then swung shut. And once again, I was trapped. And this time, there was no way out.

19

YOU'RE EITHER IN OR YOU'RE OUT

I'D TAKEN A CHANCE SLIPPING IN WHILE CHRISTIAN'S BACK WAS TURNED, but there was no way I could get the door open and get out without him noticing. Not at night. I was either going to spend the night in his office, or I was going to have to figure out a way to get him to leave.

I pulled my phone out of my pocket and put it on mute, and then pressed *67 followed by the museum phone number. The shrill ring pierced the silence. Christian answered.

"Christian Jhanes," he said.

I'd forgotten that his voice would come through my phone! I pressed the phone between my palms to muffle the sound. He said hello a few times and hung up.

I called him again. The phone rang four times before he answered. Again with the hellos, again with the hang-up—this time harder than before. It was working.

The fifth time, he let the phone ring twenty-six times before answering.

The sixth, he got up from his desk and stormed out of the office.

As soon as he was gone, I snuck out. The ringing became muffled behind the wooden doors. I took the elevator to the Frowick Gallery, snatched two empty boxes, and slowly descended the stairs. Rebecca was in the gift shop pulling covers over the merchandise. I waved. She waved back and beckoned me inside.

"I had no idea you were here!" she said. She blushed and looked over one shoulder and then the other. "I thought Christian and I were alone."

"Christian's here? Are you sure?" I asked, trying out my clueless routine. "I thought he was long gone."

"He was. He left a few minutes ago." She stared longingly at the exit.

I remembered what it was like to work hard to impress the new boss and how it felt to go unappreciated. I put my hand on Rebecca's forearm. "If I were you, I wouldn't get too attached to Christian. I don't think he plans to stay in Ribbon for long."

"Yes, he does. He loves this museum. After this exhibit is over, just think what he'll do next." She opened her eyes wide and blinked, her curled lashes batting up and down like a little girl afraid of the dark. "I don't think he'll leave us for a long time."

"Maybe I'm wrong," I said. "It's been known to happen."

She picked up a large cardboard box filled with a plastic bag of trash and glanced at the boxes in my hands. "Do you want me to throw those away for you? I'm headed to the dumpster with the trash from the store."

"That's part of your job?"

"We take turns. Today's my day. It's not a big deal. We just line up the plastic bags behind the building. The trash man picks them up every Tuesday morning before we open."

"Thanks." I handed the boxes to her and pretended to leave. She'd just given me an idea, and as much as I dreaded it, I knew if I wanted to find out what someone was hiding, it was time to get my hands a little dirty.

***

I WAITED until the museum lights went out and crept toward the dumpster. In the dark, the exterior of the museum was horror-movie creepy. I lifted the lid and counted eight lumpy black garbage bags.

Eight garbage bags filled with potential clues. (Or half-eaten lunches.) I pulled three of the bags out and lined them up outside the dumpster. The others were out of reach. Already I was having second thoughts. I untied the bag next to me. It was filled with Eddie's sketches for the exhibit. I wasn't going to learn anything from that. I untied the second bag, and the scent of coffee grinds hit me. Accessing whatever was in there was going to require a lot more light. And industrial-grade rubber gloves.

You're either in or you're out. I'd already prioritized my relationship with Nick over this exhibit. I was in over my head. If I lost Eddie too, I'd be done. There was only one choice.

I threw a leg over the edge of the dumpster and climbed in. I tossed the remaining bags out of the trash unit and climbed out. I carried the bags to Eddie's car and stuffed them into the backseat, and then dropped into the driver's seat and pushed the VW key into the ignition.

It wasn't until I was inside the safety of my garage that I stopped to think about the trash I'd taken from the museum. I lined the bags up against the back wall. There were nine bags in all.

Nine? I'd only taken eight.

The last bag was light. I undid the knot. Inside, wrapped in a large sheet of bubble wrap, was a turquoise pillbox confection of felted wool, satin, and rhinestones.

While I'd been snooping around Christian's office, someone had broken into Eddie's car and returned Cat's missing hat.

20

LIKE TWINS

I left the hat in the bag and the bag in the garage. Eddie was asleep on the sofa, and I would have left him in that condition, too, if I didn't need to tell him what had happened.

"Wake up," I said, shaking his shoulder. He rolled into the back of the sofa and grunted something. "Eddie, come on." He flung a hand at me. I stepped backward, and he missed contact.

I went into the kitchen and opened a can of tuna, took a pinch, and set it by Eddie's collar. Logan jumped on him and licked it off. Eddie woke up.

"Good cat," I said. I moved Logan from Eddie to a bowl on the floor with the rest of the tuna.

"What time is it?" Eddie asked.

"It's something's-not-right-o'clock. Do you want some coffee?"

Eddie rubbed his eyes and sat up. He pulled a bottle of 6-Hour Energy out of a pocket on the side of his cargo pants. He downed the contents. "What's up?"

"I went to the museum and talked to Rebecca. She told me the garbage gets taken out every Monday night."

"I could have told you that. So what?"

"If the garbage has been sitting around the museum for a week, maybe we should look at it."

"The police collected the garbage the night of the murder. Even I know that's standard procedure."

"Yes, but what if the killer threw something out after the fact?"

"Sometimes you take this Columbo thing too far. You really want to take the museum garbage?"

"I already did." My feelings on the matter were somewhere between pride and nausea. "Eight of them. But when I got here, there were nine."

"You counted wrong?"

I opened the trash bag that sat by my feet and pulled out Cat's hat. "This was in the ninth."

"That doesn't make any sense. Why would Cat's hat be in the trash at the museum? That hat has nothing to do with my exhibit."

"I don't know. The way I see it, someone wanted to get rid of it, and they saw me put bags in your car, so they added it to that pile. Or someone knows Cat told me she was robbed. Or..." My voice trailed off. I remembered the ambulance speeding in the opposite direction. I'd been leaving the museum. The opposite direction was going toward it. "Or somebody wants to frame you for another crime."

"Eddie, listen to me. I have all those trash bags in my garage. If somebody saw me take them, and they don't know I'm me, they might think I'm you."

"Yeah, because we're like twins," he said sarcastically.

"I was driving your car. I was working on the exhibit. And I kind of led Rebecca to think you were there too."

"You told her we were working on the exhibit. There's nothing suspicious about that because I'm supposed to be working on the exhibit. It's more suspicious that I'm not."

He was right. Someone either thought Eddie had been at the museum last night, or they knew he wasn't. Both meant trouble for him.

THE NEXT MORNING, I maintained the menswear routine with a black and white tweed blazer over a white cotton shirt and black pinstriped pants. I threaded a red silk scarf through the collar and tied it like a necktie and then buckled my feet into black and white spectator d'Orsays on a three-inch heel. It had always been my conviction that pattern goes with pattern. I might be late, and I might be tired, but darn it if I wasn't going to look put together. I drove to the Ribbon Designer Outlets and found Cat straightening her shoe racks.

I carried the garbage bag with her hat into her store and set it on a display of jewelry. I pulled out the hat. "Does this look familiar?"

"It's my Hedy London hat! You should start a business. 'Missing Fashion' or 'Stolen Style,' something like that. Dante told me I was a fool for wearing it in public. He'll be impressed." She turned the hat over in her hands. "Where did you find it?"

"I didn't find it. It found me. Is there someplace we can go to talk?"

She looked at me funny. "My office. Follow me."

Cat's office was a closet-sized room that sat off to the side of the stockroom. She took the seat behind the desk, and I took the small folding chair in front of it. Nice power play for interviews.

"Have you been following the news about the exhibit?" I asked.

"A little. I know there's supposed to be a big show this Thursday, and I know the hats are missing."

"Do you know about the murder?"

"I heard about it, but to be honest, I don't know details."

"Dirk Engle, the owner of What's On Your Mind, was murdered at the museum a few nights ago. We—Eddie and I—know it has to do with the Hedy London hats, but we don't know how. When you were robbed two nights ago, it seemed like there was a connection. I was at the museum last night. I drove Eddie's car. Someone left your hat on the passenger-side seat. Someone put two and two together."

"Well, I'm thrilled that they did. Let me know if I can ever return the favor."

"There's one thing you can do for me."

"What? Oh, I know. Do you want a discount? Sure. How's thirty percent—"

"No. I mean, sure, but no, that's not what I was going to ask."

"You want more? I guess I could go to forty, but you can't tell anybody."

"Cat, slow down. I don't want a discount." Who was I kidding? Of course, I wanted a discount. "I, um, need you to hold on to something for me for a couple of days."

Her eyebrows pulled together, but she didn't say anything.

"I don't want to get into details here, but I have some trash in my car, and I need it to *not* be in my car for about twenty-four hours."

Her arms crossed over her leather jacket.

"It's normal trash. Nothing weird." Normal trash? What was I saying?

"Let me get this straight. You're asking me to hold on to trash—'normal trash'--that you took from the scene of a homicide. Did I get that right?"

"The police collected the trash after the homicide. This is not homicidal trash. I mean—like I said, it's normal. I gathered up Eddie's notes and sketches and threw them away, and now I think maybe there was something in there that shouldn't have been thrown out."

"Just give him the bag and be done with it."

"It's not that easy."

"Why not?"

"Because it's slightly more than just the one bag."

She opened a small fridge by her feet and pulled out a plastic bottle of water. She drained half of it and then set it down on her desk with a thud. By the time she looked at me, I'd tapped out half the alphabet in Morse code with the ball of my foot.

Finally, she looked at me and shook her head. "Normal people don't ask friends to hang on to their trash."

"Normal people don't pay $3,000 for a hat."

We stared at each other for a couple of seconds. I didn't know if I'd overstepped my bounds with that last statement, but if she was going to hit me below the belt, then I was going to hit her over the head. Seemed fair.

"Samantha, I appreciate that you found my hat. I owe you a big thank you." She leaned back against the register, looked at the wall over my head, and then back at my face. "Fifty percent."

"I don't want the discount, Cat."

I sat on the other side of her desk, not sure if we were at an impasse. She picked up a rose gold pen and wiggled it back and forth in her fingers.

"What do you remember about the afternoon when you were mugged?" I asked, changing the subject before she made me an offer too good to refuse.

"It's kind of a blur, you know? I was walking out to my car. Someone came up from behind and grabbed me with one arm and took my hat. I didn't get a good look at him. He shoved me down toward the back of my car, and when I turned around, he was running away from me."

"How do you know it was a guy? Did he say anything? Do you remember any other details?"

"I think he said, 'You can't have this yet.' His voice was low, and I can't place it, but it was familiar. I just keep going over what he said. 'You can't have this yet.' That's not what you say when you're mugging someone. You say, 'Give me your wallet.' What he said makes it sound like *I* was the one who took the hat from him."

"You said the voice was familiar?"

She nodded, and her red hair bounced off her shoulders.

"Do you know anybody from the museum? Christian Jhanes, Thad Thomas? Dr. Daum?"

"I don't know any of those names."

"What about Milo Delaney?"

She leaned forward and looked at the notebook on her desk for a few seconds. She pulled a leather agenda out of the top right drawer of her desk and flipped through pages from earlier in the year. She stopped on March and tapped one perfectly manicured fingertip on the second Friday.

"Yes. I mean, maybe. Maybe yes. I met Milo Delaney at the accessories market last year. We were next to each other in the airport security line, and he got into a fight with the woman at the counter because she said his bag was too heavy."

"He does seem to have a short fuse," I said, thinking back to how he'd treated me when I was at his showroom with Nick.

"But he's a hat designer. What would he want with my vintage hat?"

"You said you bought it on the secondary market, right? Can you introduce me to your contact?"

"I may have made it sound like I was more connected than I was. My boss was the one with the contact. He invited me to tag along because he thought he'd look less suspicious if he were with a woman. His contact—he didn't exactly put an ad in the paper. I wouldn't know where to begin to find him."

"I don't understand. Aren't these people in the business of selling something?"

"Collectors are different from people like us. You can't just walk into a store and buy a valuable piece of history. To get the real thing, to know it's been authenticated, but not pay a fortune, you can't go standard retail. You'd be amazed what's out there. Vintage Hermes, Stephen Sprouse, Pierre Cardin. You name it, somebody has one to sell. It's all hush-hush, and it'll cost you, but you can get it."

"You're saying that the sellers are protective of who gets their stuff?"

"Exactly. The people selling stuff love it as much as the people who want to buy it, and the sellers want to make sure it's going to someone who will truly appreciate what they bought. Remember Audrey Hepburn's dress from *Breakfast at Tiffany's*? Christie's predicted it would go for something like a hundred thousand. It sold for close to a million. And that Jean Louis dress that Marilyn Monroe wore to sing 'Happy Birthday' to President Kennedy? That went for *more* than a million. I know the economy's tough for the rest of the world, but collectors... well, they're still willing to shell out money when something rare becomes available. They're willing to accept that they might never be able to tell anyone that they have what they have. And most serious buyers know when they see the real thing. They're willing not to ask questions about provenance."

"You're saying they'll relax their ethics to get what they want."

"Most collectors don't even *have* ethics."

21

ASKING FOR HELP

I THOUGHT BACK TO THE LIST OF COLLECTORS I'D PRINTED OUT FROM Christian's computer and about Dirk Engle's coveted client list. *Those* were the people who would be most interested in this event. Christian even said so. I leaned back on the folding chair and ran my hands down over my pinstriped pants. There was one person I'd encountered who claimed not to have that kind of information but who would benefit from it if she did. Vera Sarlow.

Cat picked the hat up and used her hands to mold the smashed corner. "Give this to Eddie. Have him use it in his show. At least it's authentic."

"That's nice of you," I said, wary of her generosity.

Cat shrugged. "It's not worth getting killed over."

"None of this is. That's why I'm trying to help Eddie figure out what's going on. So it all stops."

I wasn't sure exactly where we stood on trash storage issue. After an awkward amount of time, I stood up. "I have to get to my job," I said. Assuming Nick hadn't fired me.

She stood up behind her desk, stepped around to the front, and then held the door open and followed me out.

"Good luck, Sam," she said.

"I don't need luck, Cat." I walked a few steps away from her and then turned back. "But if you won't help me, maybe you can tell me how to reach your brother?"

———

I DROVE to the edge of the outlet center parking lot and boosted my confidence with a vanilla shake from the drive-through on the corner. I was starting to believe there was a direct link between my mental acuity and the amount of ice cream I consumed. Now wasn't the time to test the theory.

I called Dante. He answered after two and a half rings.

"Hello, Samantha," he said.

"You don't happen to be in the area, do you?" I asked.

"It would help if I knew which area you meant."

"If you've been following me, you'd know."

"Today's my day off."

"Figures."

"To what do I owe this honor?" he asked. His voice was drawn out, as if I'd woken him from a nap.

"I have something that I don't think I should have, and I'm looking for someone willing to hold onto it for me for a day or two."

"Fine."

"It's nothing illegal, just so you know."

"I didn't expect it would be."

"Don't you want to know what it is?"

"No."

"Why not?"

"That's not the question that interests me."

"What is?"

"Why you waited this long to ask for my help."

I could have told Dante that he was the next person on my list, or that I'd asked his sister first because I made important decisions in alphabetical order. I could have told him he was reading too much into my request. I could have said never mind, tossed the trash into the dumpster at the edge of the outlet property, and driven away while enjoying the rest of my milkshake.

It didn't matter what I said to Dante. The person I had to answer to was myself.

"I'm going to drop the stuff off by your sister's house. Don't tell her. I want you to put it someplace nobody would look. Don't make contact. I'll arrange to get it when it's safe." I hung up.

The phone rang almost immediately.

"What part of 'don't make contact' don't you understand?" I asked.

The phone was silent. I pulled it away from my head and looked at the screen. It was Nick. The call disconnected.

When I reached Cat's house, there was a motorcycle parked in the driveway. Maybe I should have told Dante he'd need more than a backpack. I blocked him in with my car and got out. I didn't see him. I opened the back doors of my car and started unloading trash bags.

"Nice outfit. Who are you today, Banker Barbie?"

"Your fashion commentary is somewhat undermined by the fact that you're named Dante, and you cover yourself in flames." I unloaded the trash bags and stacked them next to his motorcycle. He moved them a few feet away. I knew none of them were heavy, but still, I couldn't help noticing the way his biceps flexed when he picked them up.

"You don't seem surprised that I called you," I said.

"Surprised? No. Interested is more like it."

"In what?"

"You. I'm interested in you." He glanced at the trash bags. "I just didn't expect you to come with so much baggage." He smiled.

I raised an eyebrow. "Your sister wants no part of this."

"She'll never know about it."

"Good."

"Anything else you want to ask me?" he asked.

"This isn't the beginning of some kind of working relationship."

"Are you sure about that?" he asked. "Because I could teach you some things."

"You think I don't know stuff?" I asked. "I know a thing or two."

"I'm sure you do, Samantha."

My phone rang. I glanced at the display. Nick again. "I have to take this. It's work."

"Still working for your boyfriend? I didn't expect that to last."

I wasn't sure if he was referring to my relationship with Nick or my employment status. Since both were tenuous (at best) I didn't ask him to clarify.

I hopped back into my car and called Nick back. He didn't answer. I texted him that I was finishing up with a late lunch and then drove to Over Your Head. (By now, even I would have fired me.)

Customers crowded the inside of the store. Quite a change from a few days ago. Most of the sitting stations were filled with women, many of them holding glasses of champagne. The sales staff was easily recognizable in their mint-green smocks. I asked one if Vera was available, and after nodding, she disappeared behind a green curtain.

Moments later Vera came out front. Unlike the first time I'd met her, today her eyes were clear and bright, and her attitude was more confident and less tragic. "Let me guess. You couldn't get your mind off the green Milo Delaney hat, right?" She turned to the locked case.

"I, uh, actually was more curious about the vintage items you mentioned in your ad. I forgot to ask about those when I was here last time."

She looked around the store at the bustling business. "We did recently score a large supply of vintage hats, but I don't have any on display at the moment."

"Where did the inventory come from?"

"What's On Your Mind. When the store closed, we took possession of their inventory. Word of mouth spread quickly. It's certainly helped business."

I couldn't believe my ears. Vera Sarlow just admitted that she'd benefitted financially from Dirk Engle's death. And she'd said it without a trace of sadness. It was the same thing Christian had advised Rebecca: use Dirk Engle's death as an opportunity.

Vera Sarlow had been the original consultant of the millinery exhibit, and thanks to the ad in the paper and the sign I'd seen in front of her store the day I stopped for pizza, I knew she had a relationship with Milo Delaney. I felt missing puzzle pieces dropping into place all around me. I had to keep her talking.

"Vera, considering you were competitors, did you and Dirk Engle have a good relationship?"

"We had a relationship, but I'd hardly call it good," she said in a low voice. She glanced over each of her shoulders and steered me away from her customers. "Dirk Engle was my brother."

22

—————

TWO HEADS ARE BETTER THAN ONE

Vera continued. "My grandfather was the first milliner in the family. He started the Philadelphia store. My dad took it from there, and Dirk and I helped him run it. But after Dad died, we didn't agree on what direction to take it. I wanted it to feel like an old millinery shop, welcoming as if you stepped into a time warp."

"What did your brother want?"

"Dirk wanted an exclusive boutique with a bell on the door and an invitation to enter. He had my dad's contacts of collectors who wished to buy rare items discreetly. He didn't want to deal with what he called the 'riffraff.'" She made air quotes around the word "riffraff," like it was a term to be credited exclusively to Engle. "I always thought hat shopping should feel like playing dress-up in Mother's closet."

I thought about Tradava wanting to enter the hat business at a retail level. "Your brother's store does very well, doesn't it?"

"Did. The shop is closed now."

"What will happen to it?"

She chuckled. "What's On Your Mind is going to be absorbed into Over Your Head. Maybe I should rename it: 'Two Heads Are Better Than One.' It would make him roll over in his grave."

Vera showed no grief over her brother's murder. He'd been deceased for less than a week, and already she was planning how to leverage the situation to her benefit. Apparently, the hat business was rather cutthroat.

"What about his client list?" I asked.

"If I can find it, I'll contact each person individually and let them know about the changes. Of course, I'll tell them that I'm his sister, that my store is a third-generation milliner, but it'll be up to them to decide if they want to shop with me."

"You don't have the list?"

"I've been through his desk and his computer, and it hasn't turned up yet."

I WAS ABOUT fifteen minutes from Nick's showroom, and I made it there in eleven. I scanned the parking lot for his truck. It wasn't there. I sat in the car for another minute and listened to his voice mail.

"Kidd, I'm not sure if you're coming to work or not. I'm headed out to Milo's. I left the keys to the showroom with the manager of the video store."

From an employer/employee standpoint, I didn't like what the message implied—that I was avoiding work because I'd gotten my feathers in a twist. I didn't like it, but I knew it was the truth. I liked that even less.

I'd been the one to demand that Nick hire me, and regardless of how I felt about his not-a-lecture lecture yesterday, I wasn't going to be the petty girlfriend who up and left him in the lurch. I was embarrassed by how I'd stormed off, but I couldn't change that now. What I could do was the job he needed me to do. I could prove my moral fiber was as fabulous as the tweed in my blazer.

And if he wasn't at the showroom, then I didn't have to worry about details like apologizing. Just think of the time I'd save.

I picked up the keys from the video store, and since I was all about proving my integrity, I emptied my wallet on a late fee I'd accrued from keeping Isaac Mizrahi's *Unzipped* past the due date. I let myself into the showroom and unpacked Nick's sample collection. I fought the urge to try on every style—even though I was a sample size—and printed up labels for each right foot with the style name and the suggested retail. I carried the empty shoe boxes to the storage area to the right of the powder room and arranged them in alphabetical order by style name.

I unpacked the line sheets that I'd picked up at the copy center and cleaned the espresso machine. I vacuumed the showroom. I dusted the shelves. I found the list Nick had been working off and completed everything on there too.

I left Nick a note asking him to call me. I locked up and returned the keys to the video store and figured as long as my account was up to date, I might as well rent something. I picked out every Hedy London movie they had—only available on VHS—and left.

I stopped at the gas station on the corner and filled up my tank, picked up a Slim Jim for protein, and drove home. My phone rang, and the display said, "Fuzz." I took me a couple of seconds to remember I'd reprogrammed Detective Loncar after the incident at the grocery store.

I answered and put the call on speaker. "Hi, Detective," I said.

"Ms. Kidd." A beat passed. "Where are you?"

"I'm driving. But I have you on speaker."

"Pull over. Someplace safe. Call me back."

"Why?"

"Just call me back when you're still."

I crossed two lanes of traffic, turned left into the lot outside of the Sunny Suds Laundromat, and then called Loncar back.

"Hi, Detective, I'm still."

"I understand you were at the museum last night."

"Yes, I was. Why?" Oh, no. Was this about the trash?

"Ms. Kidd, a museum employee was stabbed last night. Thomas Daum. Do you know him?"

23

CAMOUFLAGE

"Dr. Daum was stabbed at the museum?" I asked. "Is he okay?"

"He's in the hospital."

"I have to go." I disconnected and stumbled out of the car and into the laundromat. It was empty, though a few machines were running. I collapsed onto a green plastic chair in front of an industrial dryer and stared at the clothes as they tossed around in a circle.

This wasn't some random act of aggression I usually heard about on the news. Eddie's situation involved a murder and a stabbing, and neither one of us knew what else. I hadn't even seen Dr. Daum last night. If he'd been at the museum, then who else had been there? Why didn't I know about it? Did he know something? Confront someone? Been stabbed to keep quiet?

I felt sick. I left Eddie an urgent message, a text, and a couple of telepathic messages. I returned to my car and called Nick. My call dumped into his voicemail, and I asked him to call me back. There would be time for explanations later. I drove home in a fog.

I called out for Eddie as soon as I had the front door unlocked. I found him in the kitchen stirring a pot of something red.

"Dr. Daum was stabbed last night," I blurted.

Eddie dropped the spoon. Sauce spattered down the front of the cabinet and onto the legs of his concrete-colored cargo pants. He ran his hands over his face and then his head. Tiny bristles of blond hair had already started to grow in. "When? How?"

"At the museum."

He sank onto the kitchen floor. His back pocket sopped up more of the sauce spill. Logan padded into the kitchen and sniffed the fallen ladle. He patted it with his paw, licked the sauce, and followed with a *pfft* sound. He looked at Eddie, meowed, and slunk away.

"Thad called after you left last night. He said he saw my car at the museum and wanted to know how long I planned on working."

"I never saw Thad."

Eddie looked at the toes of his sneakers. "He was making sure he could pin something on me."

I thought back to last night. To Christian and Rebecca leaving, to me packing Eddie's car full of trash. To someone leaving Cat's hat inside. I'd been stupid to go by myself. I'd pretended Eddie was with me so it seemed like I had company, but my lie placed him at the scene of the crime.

I squatted next to him. "Detective Loncar said Dr. Daum is at the hospital."

"You talked to Detective Loncar?"

"Yes."

"What did he want?"

"He called to find out where I was last night. I told him I was at the museum. He asked if I saw anything suspicious. I thought it was about the trash, so I didn't say anything. And then he told me about Dr. Daum."

Eddie didn't move. My knee could only take so much squatting, so I stood and moved to a dining room chair.

"I can't believe Dr. Daum was stabbed. I can't believe someone wants it to look like I was there. I can't believe I'm involved in all of this." He hugged his knees to his chest.

"Do you have any idea what 'all of this' is?"

He shook his head. "Dude, I don't know what to do," he said.

"I think we need to go to the hospital."

He looked down at his outfit. "Do you have anything around here that doesn't look so much like me?"

"Wait here."

WHEN WE PULLED into the hospital parking lot, I was in an ivory fisherman's sweater, dark denim jeans with a wide cuff, and the turquoise suede moccasins I'd bought from the museum gift shop the first day I helped with the exhibit. Eddie wore a windbreaker and a pair of black jeans with seashells printed on them, both courtesy of a box of painting clothes my dad had left behind when he and my mom moved out. Camouflage Vans. Though it was too late for the sun to be an issue, half of his face was hidden behind a pair of blue blockers we found in a drawer in my kitchen.

We sat in the waiting area until the current visitors left. Eddie flipped through a gossip magazine that dished on celebrity marriages that had long since ended in divorce, and I lost myself in a two-year-old issue of *Harper's Bazaar*. In the middle of an article about orange being the new pink, Eddie folded his magazine shut and leaned over. "It had to be Thad. He's the one person who checked to make sure I was there. I'm not going to let him get away with this."

"What are you going to do?"

"I'm going to tell the police what I know. Maybe it's enough to help them catch Thad."

"Catch Thad doing what?" a voice behind us asked.

Dr. Daum stood in the doorway to the visiting area. His eyes were red, and his suit was rumpled like he'd worn it while sleeping in the backseat of a very small car.

I jumped up and, without thinking, threw my arms around him. "Dr. Daum! How are you—what are you—are you okay?"

Dr. Daum looked bad, worse than I'd ever seen him, but there was no way he'd been stabbed in the last twenty-four hours.

"It's wonderful of the two of you to be here. My son's had a hard time. It will be good for his spirits to see someone other than me."

"Your son?" I asked.

"That's why you're here, correct?"

If Dr. Daum wasn't in a hospital bed, then we didn't know why we were there.

"Come with me. I'll walk you to his room." Dr. Daum entered the room first and spoke. "Thomas, you've got some visitors I think you'll enjoy."

He moved aside, and Eddie rushed over to the bed. "Thad?"

24

NEPOTISM

THAD'S NORMALLY ALMOND-COLORED SKIN APPEARED BLANCHED. A respirator sat to the left of his bed. The bed itself was inclined enough to keep him from falling asleep. Rumpled sheets were bunched around his waist and covered his lower half. His white hospital gown had two small stains that had resisted bleach, and his normally clean-shaven head was dusted with the black stubble of hair growing in due to a life-threatening shift in priorities. Today his eyes were brown. This color seemed real.

I pulled Dr. Daum aside while Eddie and Thad hugged.

"Your son?" I asked in a low voice.

"Thomas requested I keep our relationship a secret at the museum." He rubbed his finger and thumb back and forth in his eye sockets, massaging away either a tension headache or the dried tears left behind from when he'd first heard the news. I couldn't tell which, though I suspected both had been present. "Let's get a cup of coffee and talk."

Dr. Daum and I left Eddie alone to visit with Thad. We followed the directions of a woman behind the reception desk, who advised us to order coffee from the machine in the lobby instead of paying the extra two dollars for a cup from the cafeteria. After emptying the bottom of my handbag for coins, we sat in opposite plastic chairs with a chipped wooden table between us.

"I adopted Thad when he was five. He was inspired by my life in museum work and chose the same path, but after years of schooling and achieving top honors, he only ever existed in my shadow."

"You never mentioned a son during the hours we spent together at the museum."

"Thad had a hard time of it. A long time ago he learned that being my son didn't give him instant respect in the eyes of fellow fine arts majors or museum employees. Quite the opposite. Most people thought nepotism was little more than an overly beneficial resume statistic."

"Did you get him the job at the museum?"

"I didn't even know he applied there. When he'd started at I-FAD, he changed his name to Thad Thomas, keeping his real last name under wraps so people wouldn't judge him based on his familial connections. He knew I was going to retire and had planned on that being his time to shine."

"You said I-FAD. Did Christian hire him?"

"Yes. But Thad hadn't counted on Christian leveraging Thad's connections for his own good."

I learned more from Dr. Daum over a cup of vending machine coffee than I'd found on the internet. Christian Jhanes had been the chair of the fashion marketing curriculum at I-FAD for close to seven years and then left abruptly and moved to the west coast. Only recently, when the newly designated Frowick Gallery had opened at the museum, had he returned to Ribbon in the role of acting director. Though Dr. Daum had started several programs and initiatives, when Christian started, he undid everything Dr. Daum had built.

"Thad expected to shine, but his efforts were overshadowed by Christian's demands."

"Has Thad told you anything about this particular exhibit?"

"My son has never liked to ask my advice when it comes to matters of art. I think it's his way of proving his self-worth. But a few nights ago, he came to me with concerns."

Dr. Daum shared what Thad had confided in him. Christian had pressured Thad to use stunts to create publicity for the exhibit. Initially, Thad obliged. He thought it was a chance to prove he was capable of being part of the new museum team. He leaked information to the press, changed the opening timetables, and limited the budget. His initial antics were met with resistance from the first consultant—Vera Sarlow. When she left, Christian replaced her with her brother, Dirk Engle. Dirk's one condition of hiring was that his sister's name never be mentioned in connection with the exhibit. He promised his client list in exchange for full credit.

I'd found that client list on Christian's desk. Had he obtained it rightfully? Or was that list the reason Dirk Engle had been killed?

I remembered another thing: Thad taking the copy of the client list from me. Was that why he'd been stabbed?

Who wanted that list enough to kill? Christian Jhanes. Vera Sarlow. Maybe even Hedy London.

"I heard Dirk and Christian argue the day Dirk was killed. He said he quit," I said.

"Dirk demanded to be included in the publicity stunts, and Thad had begrudgingly agreed to do so. Their shenanigans worked. A story about Hedy London coming to Ribbon was leaked to the *Ribbon Times* and picked up by the AP. The museum started getting phone calls to confirm the appearance. Answering the phones became a full-time job. Christian asked me to field questions from the media. Calls were redirected to Thad and Rebecca too."

"But she *is* coming—I mean, she's here. In Ribbon. I met her two days ago."

"That was Christian's doing. I don't know what he promised her: publicity? Fame? The spotlight?"

"How come nobody told Eddie any of this?"

"Eddie was not to be interrupted. He and Dirk had the important task of making the exhibit spectacular, with or without the presence of Hedy London."

"What happened?" I asked.

Dr. Daum crumbled his empty paper cup into his fist. "Soon our museum was getting national attention, as was Dirk Engle's store. He may have wanted to quit to capitalize on the business at his store, but he was bound by a contract."

"But he signed a non-compete clause, right? I mean, why would he agree to curate this exhibit if there was nothing in it for him? I can't figure that out."

"Dirk may have had his own agenda all along. We'll never know."

Dr. Daum stood and moved his crumpled cup to the trash. He excused himself and returned to Thad's room. I thought back to what had happened at the museum the day Dirk Engle had been murdered. I'd overheard the argument. Dirk had quit. And then, a light fixture had almost crashed onto my head. The forest-green fedora with the knife through it had arrived. Dirk's body was found behind the admissions desk. And Eddie, having only recently come onboard, was a solid scapegoat.

And then what? I'd started working for Nick in an attempt to steer clear of the exhibit and ended up smack in the middle of it. The hat designer Milo Delaney snapped at me when I showed up asking questions. Cat had been hat-jacked, Vera had taken possession of her brother's store's inventory, and Thad had been stabbed. Even Rebecca was more in the know than I was.

I would be willing to bet my next sandwich that Thad had never realized the publicity stunts at the museum were going to escalate to include murder. He probably never expected to be stabbed in the process of proving his loyalty, either, a result that would put a damper on his dedication to Christian. Nepotism was a small price to pay for a work environment devoid of stabbing coworkers.

I fell asleep in a chair in the visitor's lobby. Eddie called me a ride. There was a short list of people Eddie felt comfortable calling close to midnight on a weekday, even if it was only to ask to give me a ride home, and an even shorter list of people who would answer the phone and not ask questions. Eddie made the call, and Nick agreed to come get me.

We rode to my house in silence. He parked in my driveway. He helped me out of the truck and up to the front door, where we stood awkwardly as if it was the end of a first date and we didn't know if it was the right time to kiss.

"Nick," I said, "I'm sorry about yesterday. I'm sorry about today. I made a mess of things."

"Shhhhh."

I closed my eyes, absorbing the smell of him—oak and Irish Spring. We were close. I felt his breath against my mouth.

Screw the job.

I didn't like what had happened to us since I started working for him. If Nick wasn't going to fire me. I'd quit. Tomorrow. No. I didn't know if I'd be alive tomorrow. I'd quit tonight. Right after we kissed. I leaned forward and tipped my head up. Our bodies made full contact, and I brushed my lips against his.

I opened my eyes. His left hand circled my waist. I didn't care that we were standing in front of my house, or that Mrs. Iova who lived across the street might be watching us through her curtains. His lips were so soft, so tender, that I wanted him to kiss me again. Only, judging from the expression on his face, he hadn't kissed me at all.

I'd kissed Nick, and he hadn't kissed back.

Consumed with embarrassment, I turned away from him and reached into my handbag for my keys. I came up with a dry-cleaning ticket.

Nick gently pushed me to the left. He removed the doorbell placket and pulled a hidden key from inside the cubby. He unlocked the front door and held it open. I expected him to leave, but he followed me inside.

"Kidd, you're exhausted."

"I'm not exhausted. I'm hungry. And I'm angry. I'm hungry and angry and confused. And hungry."

I wouldn't make eye contact. I would not! I opened random cabinets, looking for something to eat. Why was he still there? Why hadn't he left? "Everything's going to be okay, Kidd."

"No, it's not, Nick! It's not. Am I your girlfriend, or am I your office assistant? I'm doing a pretty poor job of both. You didn't thank me for the work I finished, and you didn't kiss me out front. So I don't know. I don't know! What am I?"

"You're hungry, you're angry, and you're confused." He opened the cabinet next to me. "And you're hungry." I thought it was safe to look at him since the cabinet door separated us. He closed the cabinet and smiled at me. "And you're exhausted even if you don't want to admit it. You need to get some sleep."

He pushed my hair away from my face. He kissed my forehead. It would have been intimate if it hadn't followed up our sad, one-sided kiss out front. I looked away and concentrated on fire-starting the pile of Tradava catalogs that sat on the corner of the kitchen counter. It didn't work.

"I'm taking a personal day tomorrow," I said. I didn't ask if showroom managers who'd been on the job for less than a week were entitled to such things. He let himself out. When the door clicked into place, I ran over to it, threw the deadbolt and turned around and leaned against the door.

"I am so screwed," I said to Logan. He buzzed my ankles and agreed via meow.

Nick was right; I needed sleep.

I'd sleep when I was dead.

I plugged my phone into a port on my computer and nuked a package of frozen spinach. When the beeper went off, I carried the bowl to the table and burned my mouth on the first forkful. (That's what I get for eating vegetables?) I pushed the bowl to the side to cool, opened a bag of Splits Extra Dark Pretzels, and bit into one.

I tapped the keyboard as I crunched. Plugging in my phone had brought up a pop-up window in the middle of my screen asking what I should do with the files on the phone. I closed the window like I always did and then realized what I had on the phone.

Photos of the exhibit from the day I helped Eddie.

I cued up the photos and scrolled through them. The quality wasn't fantastic, but it was passable, and passable was good enough to see one important thing. On the desk, next to the computer monitor, was a small pile of papers. I enlarged the image and read the words INTEREST IN HATS across the top.

It didn't matter that Thad had taken my copy of that file after I swiped it from Christian's desk. Eddie and I had had a copy the whole time.

It also didn't matter that Eddie had cleaned up after us, because I had eight bags of trash from the museum, and maybe that sheet of paper was inside one.

I needed to get the garbage from Dante.

25

I NEED THE STUFF

I took off my tweed blazer and pinstriped pants and changed into a navy blue and red spandex yoga outfit I'd purchased a few years ago. At the time I thought I'd be more inclined to exercise if I had attractive workout wear. I tore off the tags, set them on my dresser, and rooted around for a pair of matching sneakers. I pulled my hair into a high ponytail and called Dante.

"Hey," I said when he answered.

"Hey yourself."

"I, um, I need the stuff."

"The stuff?"

"The stuff I asked you to hold."

"Is your phone tapped?"

"I don't think so, why?"

"Because I think you're talking about the garbage you took from the museum, but you're making it sound like you're looking for kilos of drugs. I would think, if your phone isn't tapped, that you would call it what it is."

"Is this part of my lesson plan?"

"You think I want to be your mentor?"

"I'm not sure what you want from me."

"That's funny. I thought I was pretty clear when you dropped off 'the stuff.'"

"Speaking of the stuff." I paused.

"You need it."

"Yes. Do you remember where I live?"

<hr>

I TRIED out two other hairstyles and applied tinted lip gloss before Dante arrived. Logan stared at me from the arm of the chair by the door.

"What?" I asked him while re-ponytailing my hair. He yawned.

Fourteen and a half minutes later, there was a knock on the door to the rhythm of "Shave and a Haircut." I tapped back twice, peeked through the peephole, and opened the door. Dante and Cat stood on my porch. They were surrounded by bulging black plastic bags.

"Don't look at me that way," Cat said. "Dante said he needed to borrow my car. As soon as I saw him shoving garbage into the trunk, I knew what he was doing."

"You could have said no," Dante said.

I looked back and forth between their faces. It wasn't the first time I'd been struck by the humor of their sibling relationship. More often than not since I'd met her, Cat was cool, aloof, and a little reserved. Dante was hot, forward, and ready to go. Yet there was something similar about them when they were together. It was as if a deeply rooted rivalry still existed. Like they were both still trying to prove themselves to each other.

I picked up a bag and set it on the floor next to me. Logan jumped down and buzzed around it and then started chewing on the bottom corner. I picked the bag up by the knot and held it above his head. He meowed at it and skulked away.

"I guess this means I don't get a discount?" I asked Cat as a joke.

"Sam, you're a fashion industry professional. You shouldn't be going through trash. If people found out—"

I interrupted her. "Remember when you mentioned the secondary market?"

"Yes."

"To some people, that's trash. It's old, used stuff."

"It's not the same."

"What if I told you there's something in one of these bags that someone was killed over?"

"If you think there's incriminating evidence in these bags, you should take them to the police."

I'd been completely bluffing, but she had a good point, and I didn't know how to counter it. Would Detective Loncar take me seriously if I showed up at the police station with eight bags of trash? And more to the point, what if something in one of these bags linked Eddie to Dirk Engle's murder? Delivering that to the police would do more harm than good. I had to know what was in there before anybody else did.

"I'm waiting in the car," Cat said. She turned around and left Dante and me facing each other.

I carried several bags into the kitchen. Something slimy that I didn't want to think about transferred to my hand, and I wiped it on my yoga pants. Dante followed me and set the rest of them next to the table.

"You don't agree with her," I said. "You don't think I should turn the trash over to the police."

"I think there are better ways to get dirty."

"I think you should go."

"You sure? I could stay, help you work off some tension."

Logan returned and sniffed the toe of Dante's black boot. Dante scooped him up and held him face to nose. Logan's head jutted out, and he sniffed Dante's face. Dante set him on the dining room table, and Logan stuck his nose in Dante's sleeve.

"I guess I'll get going," Dante said.

"Thank you."

"For bringing these here or for leaving you alone with them?"

"Both."

"Anytime." He let himself out.

I locked all three locks on the back of the door and headed into the kitchen. I washed my hands, grabbed a bottle of Pellegrino and the bag of pretzels I'd opened earlier, set them on the dining room chair, and eased myself onto the floor with my back against the floor-to-ceiling curtains that covered the sliding glass doors to the backyard. I ate two pretzels, guzzled Pellegrino directly from the bottle, and then opened the first bag.

It was slow going at first. I picked through wet newspaper and coffee cups, smashed brown paper bags with empty yogurt cartons inside, an unnatural amount of Diet Coke cans, and a stack of schedules that had been printed on a printer with a low toner. I'd lost a fair portion of my sleeping time, and the only thing I'd gained was a lovely smudge of something that smelled like bananas down the front of my formerly new yoga attire.

It was in the fourth bag that I found the yearbook.

More curious than the hunter green textured leatherette cover and the lack of signatures inside of it was the fact that someone at the museum would have taken the time to throw away a yearbook in the first place. My own yearbooks had been in the back of a closet in my tiny apartment in New York for years, at least until I started looking up friend requests from Facebook. When I moved, I'd pared down significantly, but my yearbooks made the cut of what I'd kept.

Why? Aside from the point-and-laugh, can-you-believe-I-wore-that? significance of most of the photos, yearbooks served little purpose. Most were presold so the school wouldn't over-order. A few copies were bought for the library. But if someone wanted to make a case for who my network of friends was at that time, they could easily use my yearbook as evidence.

Evidence.

I leaned back against the curtain and opened the front cover. I-FAD, 1992. I flipped the pages and looked at the pictures, unfamiliar except for the overall style-stamp of the early nineties. Flannel shirts opened over white undershirts, denim jackets with torn-off sleeves, baggy faded jeans worn with tight wide-necked bodysuits and wide belts that cinched in waists. Chokers. Peasant blouses. Square-toed chunky shoes. Grunge. I flipped the pages, not sure what I was looking for but confident that I'd know it when I saw it.

And there it was, on page seventy-nine.

A young blonde with soft ringlets and Lisa Loeb glasses, walking next to a man in a black leather jacket with flames on it.

Rebecca and Dante. Holding hands.

26

THE WRONG QUESTIONS

I flipped to the index of the yearbook and looked up Lestes. The only person listed was J. D. Lestes. The page number corresponded to the picture, and it was the only picture of him. But what about Rebecca? I didn't know her last name. I started going through every name in the index, looking for Rebecca as the first. My vision blurred before I'd finished the Cs.

I flipped back to the picture to make sure I hadn't imagined it. There was no mistaking the image. It was a younger Dante and a younger Rebecca, but neither had changed all that much since then.

I didn't trust my instincts to call Dante and demand to know why he hadn't told me. I considered calling Cat, but what good would that do? If I pressured her with questions about her brother, no doubt she'd defend him over me and my crazy implications. But still, I had the proof. Dante knew Rebecca. They'd both gone to I-FAD. Something was up.

By two in the morning, I'd worn a path in the nap of the carpet in the living room. I'd long since abandoned the trash project (washing my hands every time I wanted a pretzel was leaving me with pruney fingertips), showered once, tried to sleep twice, and watched four episodes of *The Fugitive* back to back. I'd started establishing parallels between Richard Kimball and Eddie. I wondered if I'd ever see my friend again.

It's possible that my paranoia was running at slightly high levels.

By the time Eddie returned, I'd hooked up the VCR and was halfway through the second of the four Hedy London movies I'd rented from the video store. It was 4:26. I grabbed Logan, kissed him on top of the head, and told him to save himself. Halfway up the stairs, his tail grew fat, and he hissed.

Eddie unlocked the three locks, shut the door, and locked them behind him. He was gray. The color had drained from his face; the spunk had eked out of his manner, the spring had long since left his step.

He dropped his keys onto the chair by the front door, took his windbreaker, and placed it on top of the keys. He walked past me into the kitchen. I followed a few steps behind. He rooted around the vegetable bins of my refrigerator and pulled out a carrot. He bit into it without washing it.

"I think you need something stronger than a carrot."

"What do you have?"

"Chips, pretzels, popcorn... spinach! I nuked some spinach." I expected him to be impressed. He wasn't. He snapped into the carrot again and then tossed it on the counter.

"After I visited with Thad, I got in the car and started driving."

"You've been gone for hours."

"I've been driving for hours."

"You didn't stop?"

"I stopped to fill up the tank."

"Where?"

"Delaware."

"You drove my car to Delaware?"

"I filled up the tank and realized how far gone I was. Not with Delaware"—he added before I could say it—"but with this exhibit. I can't get out now. Someone's trying to make it look like I'm involved in something I'm not. I don't know anything, except that someone's watching me. That feels a little creepy. If I knew who it was, if I knew how someone had taken me off the video surveillance, if I knew what was going on at the museum, I could deal with it. But I don't. I need answers."

"I've got one for you. Check this." I reached for the yearbook and opened it to the page marked with the empty pretzel bag. "Notice anything interesting?"

He scanned the black and white photos. "Aside from the fact that women were never supposed to wear construction worker boots, no. Wait!" He looked closer at the incriminating photo of Dante and Rebecca. "Well, goodness, gracious, great balls of fire."

"Exactly. Notice anyone else?"

Eddie looked at the photo again. "No way."

"Yes, way. It's Rebecca."

"You don't think—"

"That maybe she's involved? I didn't before I found this, but I sure do now. She was at the museum the day Dirk was murdered. She's the one who told us a woman dropped off the hats. Maybe she took the hats. Maybe she sealed the boxes back up and had empties delivered?"

"But why? She's like a mouse."

"It's always the ones you don't suspect."

"At the rate you're suspecting people, this must be a phantom crime because there's nobody you *don't* suspect."

"I just think it's smart not to trust people who might be murderers. Seems like a good idea."

"Have you told anybody about this?"

"Not yet." I tapped the page a few times.

"Where'd you find this, anyway?"

I looked over my shoulder at the bags of trash lining the wall. "It was in the museum trash. Ironic, right? That I trusted Dante to hold the trash for me when Cat said she wouldn't, and it turns out there was something in there that linked him to this whole thing?"

"Talk about coincidence," Eddie said.

"I don't believe in coincidence."

I thought back to what Dante had been saying all along. *You're asking the wrong questions, Samantha.* I couldn't wait to find him and try out a whole new set.

I LEFT Eddie watching *The Reaper Wore Red* and went to bed. The next morning, I left him asleep on the sofa, grabbed a breakfast sandwich and a coffee at a drive-through, and drove to Dante's house. I'd drawn a few conclusions before falling asleep. I just needed to hear him confirm them.

Dante stood on his balcony holding a white mug. I addressed him from the street level. Romeo and Juliet-style, role reversal. "You wanted me to find that yearbook," I said.

He raised his brows and closed his eyes at the same time, like he was acknowledging the truth of my statement.

"Why?"

He held up an index finger and shook it back and forth. "Try again."

"Why didn't you tell me you knew Rebecca?"

"Strike two."

I bit my tongue. He was toying with me, but there was something here I wasn't getting. My mind whirred with thoughts. I stared at the crack in the concrete on the landing halfway up the stairs to his front door and forcing my thoughts to quiet down.

"What can you tell me about the exhibit that I don't already know?"

"Brava."

"That's not an answer," I pressed.

"You want to come up? I have coffee."

"I want answers."

"Then come up. Answers go well with coffee." He went inside. I jogged up the thirty-nine steps and walked the narrow balcony to his front door. I stood in the door frame and watched him pour a second cup.

"One of these days I'm going to give up coffee," I said.

"But not today. You need it. It goes nicely with the breakfast sandwich you ate in the car."

"Why are you watching me?"

"Watching? No. Waiting? Yes."

"For what?"

"For this." He motioned back and forth between us. "For you to come to me with the right questions."

"You put the yearbook in the trash."

"Maybe."

"You knew if I went through the trash, I'd find it."

"Maybe."

"You wanted me to discover your connection to Rebecca."

"Maybe."

"Why go to the trouble? Why not just tell me?"

He held out his mug for a second, but instead of drinking, he set it on a table next to his futon. He sat on the futon and kicked his heels out in front of him. I leaned back against the doorframe, my hands behind me. I raised my eyebrows in an indication that it was his turn to talk.

"You want to know why I led you to that info? Because I needed to know how far you were willing to go for answers."

"It was fairly obvious. I didn't go that far."

"Samantha," he said and leaned forward, "in the past twenty-four hours you went through at least four bags of garbage. And the bag with the yearbook had coffee grinds and two-week-old bananas."

"That was on purpose?"

"I had to test your resolve."

"You should have tested my Tide with Stain Release Technology."

He stood up and walked closer until he was right in front of me. "Do you want to talk about this, or do you want to *talk about this*?"

His breath hit me on the T words, strong from the scent of coffee.

"I don't want to, you know, *not* talk about this," I said quietly.

He reached his hand around me and ran his fingertips down my arm. They left a hot trail. When he reached my palm, he gently pulled my hand out from behind me and braided his fingers through mine.

"Sit down, Samantha. We have lots to talk about." He led me to the futon.

I sat next to him. My heart pounded. I felt like I was back in high school on a second date with Tommy Cordoba. I reminded myself that a futon wasn't the same as the skateboard park after dark.

"Rebecca and I went to the same college," Dante started. "I dated her my freshman year. We spent a lot of time together because we were both art majors. I'd go to the photo lab late at night when nobody else was there, and she'd be in the studio working. Some nights we were the only two people around."

I bristled with an unexpected twinge of jealousy.

"We used to joke about how much we could learn about the students who left their stuff behind. She said I had a knack for observation. Hooked me up with an investigator who needed a cheap photographer."

"Like, to catch cheating spouses?"

He nodded. "Money's money, and it was easy. He taught me how much you can learn from people if you just watch them."

"Spying."

"Call it what you like. I called it an opportunity to pay my student loans back early and get a secondary education in human nature."

"How did Rebecca know an investigator?"

"He was her father."

"Did she work with you?"

"No. Rebecca and I broke up, but I freelanced for her dad every now and then. He had a heart attack some time after we broke up. Rebecca fell behind on her coursework and dropped out of school. I tried to contact her a couple of times, but she cut ties with everyone." He leaned back and stared at his hands. "And then she called me a couple of weeks ago. Out of the blue. Said she was working at the museum, and something strange was going on. She wanted to know if I was still investigating on the side and asked if I'd check things out."

"All this time, you popping up at the museum, taking pictures, following me around, it's because you're on the job?"

"Are you going to get all Philip Marlowe on me now?" He dropped his head and smiled. "I met with her because I was curious. Old girlfriend. You never know where you're going to find a spark."

"And?"

"And nothing. She's a nice girl. That's it."

"Not that 'and.' And what did she tell you when you met with her?"

"She said Dirk Engle told her he thought there was something up with the exhibit. He called the police before he was killed. He suspected the exhibit wasn't just an exhibit, that it was a front for something illegal."

Dr. Daum had said the same thing. "I heard the police have been watching the museum."

"For weeks. They arranged for the hats to be hijacked."

"The police have the Hedy London hats? Since when? And why? Those hats were supposed to arrive at the museum the day Dirk Engle quit. If anything, the hats not arriving made it look like Dirk took off with them. That's what I would have assumed if he hadn't been murdered. But something doesn't fit. Why would the police have intercepted the hat shipment before the murder? They must have suspected something. Is that what you told Rebecca?"

"I told her it was probably all her imagination."

"But you don't believe that. You're still around. How come?"

"Because once I found out you were involved, I knew things were going to get interesting."

"And have they?"

He tipped his head and looked me square in the face. "They're on the right track."

27

___

SEALED THE DEAL

"Yeah, well, speaking of tracks, I'd better be going. Lots of work to do. No time for skateboard parks." I set the coffee mug on the end table next to the Sharpies and stood.

"That didn't make any sense."

I backed toward the door. "Made perfect sense to me." Before Dante could reply, I was out the door and on my way down the stairs. Once I was in my car and on Duryea Drive, I called Eddie. "Rise and shine, sleepyhead. I have news. Rendezvous at the art park." I hung up.

The phone rang almost immediately. I put it on speaker. "You up?"

"Dude," he said. "'Rendezvous at the art park'?"

"Code."

"Bring me four dozen D-cell batteries and thirty yards of fishing wire. I'll meet you in twenty minutes." He hung up.

I stopped off at a drug store, cleaned out the battery aisle, and substituted dental floss for fishing wire. Even though rush hour was coming to an end, it still took twenty-five minutes to get the four miles to the museum. I parked in the space closest to the entrance.

Eddie was waiting outside. I slammed the door and jabbed a finger into his chest.

"You're not going to believe who has the hats," I said.

"Your friend?"

Considering how many/few friends I had at any given moment of this investigation, I had zero confidence trying to fill in the blank. "Which friend?"

"Detective Loncar."

"He's my friend?" I asked. "Since when?"

"Dude, it was only a matter of time before Loncar caught up with me." He ran his open hand over the blond bristles on his head. "When I woke up this morning, I called him."

"You called Loncar? Finally? What did he say?"

"Not much. He asked a lot of questions about who was in charge of the exhibit and who else was helping me. I kept your name out of it. He said for me to call him when I was at the museum again. The entire ride here, I've been trying to figure out a way to avoid making that call. But then I think of how exhausted I am but how I can't fall asleep. I think of Thad in the hospital, and I get mad. I don't know how to fix this. Got any ideas?"

"The obvious one. Call Loncar back. It's now or never. Or, you know, you can sleep when you're incarcerated. Your choice, of course."

Eddie handed me the keys to the back door and asked me to give him some privacy. I agreed to no such thing. The only concession I was willing to grant was to stand ten feet away after I watched him make the call. (I have remarkably good hearing.)

The conversation was brief. Eddie turned his head away from me and kept his voice low, but I heard occasional snippets—"museum," "hats," "tonight"—enough to know he kept up his end of the bargain.

We walked side by side to the back door. Eddie unlocked it and held it open.

"So?" I asked.

"The detective is on his way. He's bringing the hats."

I stopped walking and looked from side to side. "Does he know I'm here?"

"No."

"How are you going to know when he arrives?"

"He's going to call me."

We worked side by side in that way only people who really know each other can. Conversation consisted of Eddie's instructions and my occasional under-my-breath responses. Time passed. I was working up nerve to ask for a five-minute break when Eddie's phone rang.

He stared at the display. "It's Detective Loncar." He looked up at me on the fourth ring. "I can't answer it."

"I'll handle this." I grabbed his phone. "Hello?"

"I'd like to speak to Mr. Adams, please," the detective said.

"Detective, this is Samantha Kidd. Eddie asked me to take the call. Do you have the—" I caught myself before saying the word. "Do you have the merchandise?"

"Ms. Kidd, put Mr. Adams on the phone."

"He's currently indisposed. I'm at the—" Again, I caught myself. "I'm at the meeting point. Do you need access?"

"Ms. Kidd, I'm in the museum parking lot. I have a trunk filled with hats for Mr. Adams to use in his exhibit. If you're coming outside to meet me, bring a cart."

"Okay, great, thanks. I'll be right there." I hung up.

I found a small collapsible cart in the hallway outside Christian's office and carried it to the back door of the museum. Detective Loncar stood outside. I wasn't expecting to see him, and I jumped.

"Jeez, Detective. I thought you were going to wait in the parking lot."

"Ms. Kidd, what are you doing here?"

"I just told you I was here. On the phone. Thirty seconds ago. Weren't you paying attention?"

"Why are you at the museum?"

"I'm helping Eddie."

"Are you sure? You're not trying to figure out who killed Dirk

Engle or who attacked Thad Thomas? You're not interfering with my investigation?"

"I resent the implication." I paused. "Why don't you help me with the hats and come see for yourself?"

He grunted something and turned around. I followed him to his dusty gray sedan. He popped the trunk and pulled out two corrugated cardboard boxes with small red numbers on the corners.

"That sure was clever of Christian to arrange for you to take the hats. Or was it Dr. Daum? Or someone else?"

He glared at me.

"Let me guess. You intercepted these boxes after they were delivered to the museum. I saw them. You must have thought they had something to do with Dirk Engle's murder. But they're clean, right? Otherwise, you wouldn't let me have them for the exhibit."

"Ms. Kidd, these boxes have been in our possession for some time. I don't think you saw these."

"Yes, I did. The night Eddie and I came back here to find out what had happened."

Loncar stood up straight. "What night was that?"

"The night after we found Dirk's body. The night you have Eddie on film. The reason you've been after him."

"You weren't on that footage."

"I know, and I can't figure that out. I was next to him the whole time. How did someone delete me from the video? And why?"

"Maybe they didn't want you to be part of the investigation either."

I ignored his joke at my expense and pointed to the boxes. "These were in the museum. We saw them through the glass doors. And someplace else too." I tipped my head back and looked up. The sun was playing peek-a-boo with a couple of clouds, coloring the museum grounds in bright sunlight and then darkening them with shadow.

"Ms. Kidd, you were saying?" Loncar prompted.

I tipped my chin down and looked him in the face. "It's Over Your Head."

"Pardon me?"

"It's not an insult. It's a store. You must know it. Vera Sarlow's store on Penn Avenue. Over Your Head. She's Dirk Engle's sister."

"For someone who claims not to be trying to figure out who killed Dirk Engle, you seem to know a lot about the people who were recently involved with Dirk Engle."

"With all due respect, my boss asked me to go to her store. It had nothing to do with Dirk Engle's murder."

"Who's your boss?"

"Nick Taylor."

"I thought he was your boyfriend?"

"Detective, are you keeping tabs on me?"

Loncar removed the last box from his trunk and slammed it shut. "Are you going to be at the gala here tomorrow night?"

"Yes. Are you?"

"There will be a significant police presence here. But on behalf of the Ribbon Police Department, I'd like to ask you to stay home."

"Detective, I'm not going to stay home."

"Then try to stay out of trouble. It would make my job easier." He held out his hand. I shook it. I wasn't sure if we'd sealed some kind of deal, and if we had, I wasn't sure how much control I had over my end of the bargain.

28

SEXUAL HARASSMENT

When I returned to the Frowick Gallery, Eddie was on his hands and knees smoothing a vintage poster into an oversized frame. Cardboard tubes were lined up along the back wall of the exhibit. I knelt on the floor and helped him secure the corners. He picked up the frame and set it on an easel. I moved the boxes of hats from the cart to the floor and told him about my conversation with the detective and my meeting with Dante earlier that morning.

Eddie bumped the easel forward a few inches with the instep of his sneaker and reassessed its placement. "Do you believe him?"

"I don't know. He seemed sincere, but something's still off."

"Now you suspect Rebecca."

"Not sure. Has she been much help on this exhibit?"

"Rebecca? I don't think she's ever been up here."

"That's funny," I said. On the desk, sitting on a pile of paper next to the monitor, was a pair of square black Lisa Loeb eyeglasses.

I tucked the glasses into the pocket of my sweatshirt. "Will you be okay for a little while if I go talk to her?"

"Fine, just don't take too long. It'll take two people to hang the posters."

Rebecca was inside the gift shop. She was back on the ladder that put her within reach of the sculptures on the top shelf. Her boot-cut pants and collared shirt almost made the smock she wore over her clothes look like designer apparel. When she saw me, she climbed down the ladder and started to unpack a box of umbrellas made of fabric inspired by the Impressionist masters. I recognized the goldfish print as Matisse and the water lilies as Monet. She was about halfway done unpacking the box, and worry tugged at the sides of her mouth.

I helped sort the various umbrella patterns as she unpacked them. "Why didn't you tell me you were working on the exhibit?"

She knocked three of the umbrellas to the floor and quickly scooped them up. "Me? I'm not. I don't even know what's going on up there."

When she stood back up, I noticed the layer of makeup she had used to mask the redness around her eyes. For an instant, I questioned my suspicions. She'd worked at the museum every day for years, with people she knew and trusted. She was probably the one who organized the Secret Santa at Christmas.

I put my hand in my pocket and closed my fingers around the glasses frames. I couldn't accept her innocence at face value. "I know you were upstairs. I found your glasses." I pulled them out of the pocket and set them on the top of the display case between us.

Rebecca started to cry. "When Christian asked me to stay late, I thought he wanted—I didn't think he wanted me to work. I thought he saw me differently. He asked if I thought the setup was exciting enough. If it had sex appeal. I thought he was dropping hints."

By now her face was a pinkish red, darker around her eyes. She'd smeared her eyebrow pencil by her right eye, leaving a stripe that faded off into her hairline. It made her appear Romulan. I looked around for a tissue but didn't see any.

"Rebecca, if you think Christian is expecting a certain kind of behavior from you, well, that's sexual harassment. You can talk to someone about that."

She looked up. There was a sadness to her smile. "It's not like that.

I—I'm the one who expected something. I took off my glasses and my cardigan and unclipped my hair. I told him I thought the exhibit was sexy, that I thought he was sexy. He looked at me—just looked at me! —and told me to get dressed. I've never been so embarrassed." This time, when she put her face into her hands, her shoulders shook with sobs. "I've never done anything like that before!" she squeaked between breaths.

I was shocked at her confession and slightly more shocked that Christian hadn't taken advantage of the situation. "Rebecca, Christian is a jerk for leading you on."

"I never expected anything like this. I thought I wanted to be part of his team. I thought he would notice me. Now I don't want to work here anymore."

I nodded and searched for something to say to change the subject. Bits of the conversation that I'd overheard between Christian and her popped into my head like a collection of sound bites.

"I don't think he'd ask for your help if he wasn't interested in what you have to say. I heard Dirk Engle was Christian's connection to the collectors. Is that your job now that Dirk's gone?"

A fresh wave of tears filled her eyes. "How do you know Christian asked me for help?"

Uh-oh. "Eddie must have mentioned it," I said. I studied her face and hoped she wouldn't ask why Eddie and I were talking about her.

"It was so stupid of me. I volunteered to do whatever he wanted. I wanted to make sure he knew I don't want to run the gift shop forever. But now, this—" She waved her hands by her eyes and blinked a few times. "He didn't even say good morning when he got here today."

"He's here already?"

"Sure, he gets here really early. It's my favorite time of the day because we're the only two here. But lately, every time we start to have a meaningful conversation, that woman calls, and he has to leave."

"What woman?"

"Hedy London." Rebecca waved her hand in front of me. "I

shouldn't talk about her. He doesn't even know she's manipulating him."

I searched her face for signs of something other than sadness but discovered nothing.

Being inside the museum shop, surrounded by merchandise, my retail instincts kicked in. I flipped through a rack of aprons printed with scenes from pop-art paintings and sorted them on autopilot. "Lichtenstein in the front, Rauschenberg in the middle, Warhol in the back," Rebecca said as she reached in for a fresh handful of umbrellas. This time I spotted the décolleté of the barkeep on Manet's *A Bar at the Folies-Bergère.*

"I thought museum gift shops were leased by an independent museum store association?" I asked.

"Most are, but we're an independent shop that's attached to the museum. We have some flexibility. Christian terminated the contracts with the last suppliers, and what they wouldn't take back he put on clearance."

"Like my moccasins?" I looked around the store but didn't see them. "Did they sell out?"

"No, they're in the back. Christian hates them. He wants me to find a buyer for the whole lot. You're lucky you bought a pair when you did." She peered over the counter at my feet. "You have small feet. I wanted to buy a pair, but I could only fit into the men's size."

"You're the lucky one. You can probably balance on super-high heels if you wanted. I tip over." I grinned. "Back to the store, the profits now feed the bottom line of the museum?" She looked at me suspiciously, so I added, "My background is in retail buying. I find this fascinating."

Rebecca nodded and moved from Gauguin to Matisse. "I'm not sure how Christian convinced the board to approve the money, but he ordered a lot of merchandise—all inspired by the museum catalog of holdings in the rotating collection—and plans to keep the profits to fund future exhibits and add to the acquisition funds."

I stopped sorting T-shirts for a second. "He's been licensing apparel and home goods based on the art the museum owns. He thinks there's money in that?"

"He's counting on it." She held up an umbrella that featured a Van Gogh in the second-floor exhibit. "He said if we focus on the collector market, we'll make a fortune. This hat exhibit is the test. The hats from Hedy London's collection are going to be on display, and we're going to sell duplicates."

"I thought Tradava was producing a collection based on the Hedy London samples," I said, confused. "That's why they're funding the exhibit. Why would they agree to let you sell the copies?"

"I don't know." She looked as confused as I felt.

I looked at the stack of boxes building up behind her counter. "You told me the trash got picked up on Tuesday mornings. What do you do with it during the week? I don't think I've seen it sitting around back, but you can't keep it here."

"We recycle what we can, but everything else gets carried downstairs to the basement outside of Christian's office."

I thought about the boxes with the little red numbers on the corners. "So if there were empty boxes here, someone might have reused them?"

"Sure. Dr. Daum started an initiative for us to go green before he retired. Christian hasn't stopped it, so we're still trying to keep it up."

"Why are you so certain Christian is going to stay in Ribbon after this exhibit?"

She chewed the inside of her mouth, which caused her lips to purse and wiggle off to one side. "This exhibit is just the beginning. I guess it's normal that he would obsess over his first show. He's trying to make sure it's not a disaster. If Eddie hadn't left such a mess, everything would be different."

"Eddie didn't leave a mess. He's working on the installation right now."

"That's great news!" She said, suddenly happy. "Does Christian know? Because if Eddie's finishing the exhibit, then maybe everything will be okay after all."

I RETURNED UPSTAIRS. Eddie stood on the top of a ladder tying a piece of dental floss to the end of a sleek silver flashlight. I picked up a beanie and spun it around my finger like a Harlem Globetrotter spinning a basketball.

"I was just talking to Rebecca. She said the gift shop is planning on selling duplicates of the Hedy London hats. All Christian's plan. But isn't that Tradava's role?" I asked.

"That's what I heard."

"And now that I think of it, Vera Sarlow said something funny back when I first met her. She asked if Tradava had negotiated an exclusive. Was she talking about the copies too?"

"You're back to Vera?"

"I don't know. The other day we were talking about the exhibit, I think, or at least I was. I'm starting to think she might have been rambling. She said she hadn't found her brother's client list." I used the inside of my foot to shift the base of a mannequin stand until it was lined up with the first three Eddie had already placed. "That's a strange thing to be concerned with when she's dealing with the death of her brother, don't you think?"

"Yep," Eddie agreed. "Go another inch to the left."

I shifted the mannequin to his specifications. "Maybe those collectors Christian's trying so hard to woo are the clients she wants to get hold of."

"Is she planning a memorial for Dirk?"

"She didn't mention it. The only thing she wanted to talk about was his client list."

"Did you find it in the trash? Hold this flashlight."

I steadied a dangling silver light while Eddie measured out a length of dental floss and tied it onto the end. "Once I found the yearbook I forgot about the list. I know I cleaned up that night, and I know I carried a bag of trash downstairs and left it where Rebecca told me to leave it. So where did it go?"

"Good question. Start unwrapping the hats."

Eddie scribbled measurements in a notepad while I removed the tape from the ends of the bubble wrap that protected each hat. Occasionally Eddie picked up a hat and set it on a mannequin or a pedestal. He'd step back and survey the result, then either swap it out with a different hat or move on to the next mannequin. We continued for hours, stopping only for shots of espresso and bathroom breaks. Finally, Eddie and I had the exhibit looking like an exhibit.

Mannequins were arranged in conversational stances grouped by like eras of fashion from the twenties to the seventies. I'd been surprised by the breadth of the hat collection Hedy London had provided, but Eddie explained she'd not only loaned items from the movies she starred in but had also become a collector in her own right, obtaining costumes from studio sales and friend-of-friend bequeaths.

In Eddie's exhibit, mannequins were positioned around the perimeter of the room, interspersed with pedestals and columns that showcased hats, shoes, gloves, and other period-specific accessories. Cat's turquoise pillbox hat, the only one that wasn't on loan from Hedy London's collection, was worn by a mannequin dressed in a snug turquoise velvet dress with a deep V-neck and broad shoulders. The femme fatale was surrounded with others dressed in vintage trench coats, with colorful fedoras on their heads. Eddie had hooked up a smoke machine and positioned it behind that corner, piping in a soft layer of atmosphere.

Small flashlights had been loaded with batteries, secured to dental floss, and suspended from the rafters. As long as the exhibit remained free from breezes and seven-foot-tall people who could reach up and grab them, gravity would keep the lights aimed at the hats below directly below them.

I swept the floor and filled trash bins with scraps of paper, snippets of dental floss, empty battery packages, and packing materials. I nestled the empty cardboard boxes inside of each other. The last box I picked up wasn't empty.

"What's in here?" I asked, shaking it. I opened the flaps. A videotape sat inside. A sheet of white paper was doubled over it and secured with a rubber band. I pulled at the rubber band, and it broke and snapped my fingers. "Ouch!" I dropped the box.

The paper fell away from the video. Eddie picked up both. The paper was a lobby card from *The Reaper Wore Red.* He turned the tape over in his hands. It was unmarked.

"There's an A/V cart in Christian's office," I said. "It has a TV and a VCR."

"Let's go."

We ran down the stairs. I put out my arm and stopped Eddie from moving forward. As I listened for sounds that we weren't alone, I heard Dr. Daum's voice coming from the front of the museum.

"Stay here," I whispered at Eddie. I jogged back up three stairs and joined the former director.

"Dr. Daum, is there a VCR around here?" I held the black tape up. "Research. Small detail. Eddie and I can't agree over which movie Hedy London wore the banded beret in. If we can't move past this, we're going to be here all night."

"Research is important, even with a millinery exhibit. There's an audiovisual cart behind the door of Christian's office. You can take it upstairs. Just please return it before tomorrow."

"Is Christian there?"

Dr. Daum checked his watch. "No, I believe he's entertaining out-of-town collectors."

"Okay, thanks!" I called out. I returned to the hallway where Eddie stood and held my finger up to my mouth.

"Dr. Daum says we can take the A/V cart upstairs."

Eddie looked confused. I dropped my voice to a whisper. "This is our chance. Unlock the door. We have permission to get in there. You get the cart behind the door and make a big production of getting it upstairs on the elevator. I'll see if I can find a copy of the collectors in Christian's files. Go." I pushed him toward the door.

It took Eddie a couple of minutes to realize the wheels on the cart were in the lock position. When he released them, he pushed the cart out of the office and into the hallway. One of the wheels squeaked out an *eeeeee-eeeeee-eeeeee*, alerting anyone within a five-block radius that the equipment cart was on the move. Big production, minimal effort.

Christian's desk was clean. Any piles of paper I'd seen earlier had been filed. His monitor, computer, and printer were off, and his chair was tucked under his desk. The only sign that he was planning to return were the construction worker boots along the back wall. The soles had been cleaned, but traces of dirt still clung to the toes.

"Samantha?" Dr. Daum said from the doorway.

I jumped. "Dr. Daum! You scared me."

"Did you and Eddie find the equipment?"

"I think so. I wasn't sure if we had all the cords."

"I'm quite sure everything is on the cart. I must lock up for the night, so if you don't mind..." He held his hand toward the door, palm-side up. I walked past him to the elevator. Any chance I'd had at rifling through Christian's files was gone.

When I caught up with Eddie, he stood in front of the TV with the video in his hand. He popped the tape into the machine. A black-and-white image of Hedy London replaced static. She rested on the arm of an overstuffed sofa, and her smile lit up the screen. She wore a striped boat-neck sweater and sailor pants. One leg dangled while the other supported her. The date stamp on the bottom right corner of the video said December 12, 1998.

"Ms. London, would you like to introduce this footage?" an off-camera voice said.

"Yes, what we are about to see is a series of outtakes from my earlier pictures."

"And how did this footage become available?"

"Through the generosity of my lover," she said, smiling at the camera with darkly painted lips. One could only wonder if the cameraman was embarrassed by her admission.

Eddie and I stood transfixed as formerly unseen footage replaced the image of the star. There she was in a pegged skirt and matching fitted jacket. A fox stole was clamped around her neck, and a pillbox hat sat on top of her head. She walked down the street, hips swaying ever so slightly. It was Hedy London, the starlet, the woman who had first captured the attention of moviegoers decades earlier. As much of a fan of old movies that I was, it wasn't the familiarity of the movie that struck me. It was the familiarity of the hat on her head.

"Recognize anything?" I asked Eddie.

"No, and I thought I saw all of her movies."

"I'm not talking about the movie; I'm talking about the hat. I know the hat. You know that hat. It's the one someone mugged Cat to get."

29

A BETTER IDEA

"But Cat said her hat wasn't in any Hedy London movies. The only way someone would recognize Cat's hat as a Hedy hat was to watch this video."

"I think we should go back to the exhibit and take a closer look at that hat."

We returned to the gallery. Eddie reached past the dental floss and picked up Cat's hat. He flipped it over, and together we stared at the label. It was a small rectangular tag, frayed on one edge from the passage of time. The hat maker's logo was on a diagonal, stitched on in red thread. One corner had become unattached and curled up, making it hard to read the decorative font.

I picked up another hat from the grouping of fedoras and looked at the label. This one was in much better condition. We compared the two. It seemed as though they were by the same maker. After checking an additional three of the hats, we concluded one thing: Cat's hat had seen more action than the others. Maybe that's what happens when a hat finds its way onto the black market.

"Who do you think the video was meant for?" Eddie asked.

"I've been wondering about that. It seems to me it was intended for someone in charge of the exhibit, and that leaves a couple of people."

"Two, right? Dirk Engle and Christian Jhanes."

"And Vera Sarlow," Eddie said. "She was the original curator of this exhibit. She said she wished she'd been more involved, but it wasn't meant to be. Nobody's talking about the fact that she had access to the entire exhibit, that she has a connection to Milo Delaney, that she is a little bitter about not being here anymore. You know what? I think I need to know more about that."

"What are you going to do, march into her store and ask her why she was fired?"

"No, not exactly. I have a better idea."

I drove Eddie to his apartment. Sooner or later he was going to remember he paid rent, and I wanted to reacquaint him with the concept of our own independent lives. He got out of the car and leaned over the passenger-side door before shutting it.

"You headed home?" he asked.

"No, I'm heading to Nick's showroom."

"Dude, there are these things called phones. You can talk to people who aren't in the room. They're very high-tech. Some of them don't even have cords. They're especially useful for people who look like you look right now."

I glared at Eddie. "You're no spring daisy yourself."

He slammed the door and left.

I pulled around the block and headed back toward the highway. Before I hit the entrance ramp, I pulled off into a parking lot and called Nick. I wasn't sure if I was calling him in the role of girlfriend or showroom manager. No matter which role I chose, I was only marginally performing the duties.

The phone rang three times before he answered. "Nick Taylor," he said.

"Samantha Kidd," I replied. It was the same way we'd answered the phone back when he was one of my vendors, on the off-limits list of men to consider dating, though years of not acting on the attraction had somehow allowed the flirtation to filter into the way we said our names. For the first time since I'd taken the job with him, I felt like it was old times.

"Samantha Kidd," Nick repeated. "It's been a long time since I heard you answer the phone that way."

"Nick." I hesitated. I wasn't sure what I was going to say, but now there was only one way I could see the conversation going. "This isn't working out as I'd hoped." I bit my lip and waited out his silence.

He finally said, "Are you breaking up with me or quitting?"

"I'm talking about the job. Only I'm not talking about the job."

"Then what are you talking about?"

I sighed. "I think maybe we should talk about this in person."

"This sounds serious."

"Can you meet me at J&D Pizza on Penn Avenue in half an hour?"

"J&D Pizza? Not Brothers?"

"I'm branching out."

"Half an hour. I'll see you there."

I looked in the rearview mirror and realized how right Eddie had been about my appearance. Circles from a lack of sleep colored my under-eye area, and my hair had flattened from being pulled up in a ponytail. I'd chewed my lipstick off somewhere during the hours at the museum and had little other than a ring of red around the outside of my lips.

Half an hour wasn't enough time to go home to freshen up or change. It was barely enough time to stop at the mall, pick out a new outfit, change in a fitting room, spritz myself with a tester from cosmetics, and brush on a sweep of blush to my cheeks, which is what I did. I pulled my hair into a low ponytail and secured it with a multicolored scarf I kept in the trunk for accessorizing emergencies.

I'd been impressed with J&D's Pizza when I stopped here a couple of days ago and not just because they were across the street from Vera Sarlow's hat store. I drove past the restaurant, parked on a side street, and walked back up Penn Avenue, checking out the front of the store. Like the last time I was here, the sandwich board out front advertised the Milo Delaney public appearance tomorrow.

Oh, come on. Nick and I could talk anywhere. Why shouldn't we talk and conduct surveillance on a suspect at the same time? (And by "we" I mean "me," but don't tell him.)

Nick was already seated at a table inside the pizza shop when I entered. He stood. "Kidd."

"Taylor." I looked around. The table by the front window with the clear view across the street was available. "Can we sit over here?"

"I thought this would be a little more private—" he started but stopped when I held up my hand.

"The sun's going to be in one of our eyes if we sit there," I said. "This one in the front is perfect."

He carried a bottle of water and two glasses to the front table. "What's this about?"

"We should order first." I went to the counter. "Large round." I looked at Nick and then back at the pizza man. "Pepperoni on one half, anchovies on the other. Do *not* let them touch."

The man tapped a few keys on the register, and I handed him a twenty. I stuffed the change into a large mayo container that had "Tips" written on it in red marker and rejoined Nick.

"Did you get the shoes for the Hedy London exhibit?" I asked.

"Yes. They arrived this morning."

"And what about Milo? Did he finish with the hats?"

"I imagine so. I haven't heard otherwise. What's up, Kidd?"

"Nick, for the rest of this conversation, can we pretend I don't work for you?"

"I think that should be pretty easy."

I looked out the front window. "I know we need to talk about all kinds of things, and I'm not avoiding you, but I can't—I don't—" I sought the right words but couldn't find them.

"Kidd, you've been burning the candle at both ends. Trying to help me and trying to help Eddie. I don't like how distant we are right now. It wasn't fair for me to snap at you like I did."

Exhaustion kept me from replying. I closed my eyes. I nodded off for a second and then snapped to attention when my chin hit my chest.

"Are you okay?" he asked.

I took a swig of water directly from the bottle and then was immediately embarrassed by my poor table manners. Nick smiled at my faux pas, and the creases around his eyes deepened.

"Here comes the pizza. Have a slice. It's okay if you want to drink Pellegrino from the bottle. I kind of like that about you."

For a moment, I forgot about the hat store across the street and the exhibit at the museum and the video in my handbag. I forgot about everything but the connection I felt with Nick, the mutual attraction I knew was there underneath the don't-get-involved advice and the haven't-you-learned-anything lectures. The promise of something in the future and the smell of mozzarella and cheese and oregano. I was going to have to stop allowing food to distract me from the important things in life.

We finished off half the pizza before talking. I tore a piece of crust from a remaining slice and looked out the window. Vera picked up the wooden tent sign from in front of her shop and carried it inside.

I was instantly alert. "Did you see what that sign said?" I asked Nick.

"What sign?" Nick followed my pointed finger, and I could almost see the light bulb go off over his head.

Uh-oh.

"Is that why you asked me to meet you here? You wanted to check out Vera's store, didn't you?"

"I like their pizza," I said.

Nick shook his head. "I want to believe you. Really, I do. But you're hiding something, I can tell."

"After this exhibit is over, I won't have to hide anything."

Nick stood up and tossed his napkin on the table. "Take the leftovers. Eddie might be hungry. Don't worry about the showroom tomorrow. I'll pick you up at five?"

"Do we have plans for tomorrow night?"

"The opening gala for the exhibit?"

"Oh. Yes. Sure. Right."

"Then I'll see you this time tomorrow. And Kidd?" He put his palms on the table and leaned down close. "To be clear, this is a date.

Not work. I'm not particularly happy with my showroom manager at the moment, and I'm looking forward to spending some time away from her." He left.

I ate half a third slice and asked for a box for the rest. I carried it to my car and drove home. Eddie's VW Bug was in my driveway. I parked next to his car and approached the front door. A cardboard box sat on my doorstep.

It was way too early for UPS. The box had a white rectangular mailing label attached over the clear packing tape. My name and address were printed on the label. And on the side of the box was a small red number three.

The return address was from the designer showroom where I *didn't* claim to work.

Milo Delaney, the hat designer.

30

FOREST-GREEN FEDORA REDUX

I used my car key to slice through the tape. Inside the box was the forest-green fedora Eddie had taken from the museum the night Dirk Engle had been killed. It was wrapped in a large piece of plastic —the same kind of bubble wrap that had encased Dirk Engle's head. I shuddered at the memory.

I'd turned this hat over to Detective Loncar days ago. I hadn't wrapped it in bubble wrap, and I hadn't sealed it in a box with a small red number three on the corner. But I'd seen the hat again since then. The hat designer had gotten mad when I'd said it seemed familiar. What had he said? *I'm not a copier. I'm a designer. I design.* I turned the hat over in my hands and checked the label. It was a white rectangle, like the ones at the museum, only this one had Milo Delaney's logo in the center.

I carried the box inside and found Eddie in the kitchen rooting around in the refrigerator.

"Look at this." I held out the box. Eddie looked inside and then quickly looked up at me when he realized what it was. "It was sent from Milo Delaney's showroom."

I turned the box over and showed him the small red number three on the bottom corner. I extracted the hat and handed it to him.

He set it on the kitchen table and stepped away from it like it was going to bite.

"Were you expecting Milo to send you something?" he asked.

"No! I haven't thought about him since the day he snapped at me at his showroom." I stopped to think for a second. "I don't even know how he has my address."

"You could ask." Eddie held out the phone.

I didn't want to tell Eddie that I wanted to call Milo Delaney about as much as I would have wanted to trade out my collection of candy-colored T-strap sandals for Birkenstocks. I followed Logan into the living room. Instead of calling Milo, I called Nick.

"Hi," I said when he answered, not giving him a chance to mention our recent conversation. "Did you give Milo Delaney my address?"

"Why would I give him your address?"

"I got a package from him. A hat. I have no idea why he'd send it to me."

"Maybe it's a gift. Designers do that on occasion, remember?"

Oh, I remembered. Receiving shoes from designers had been a perk of my job. Receiving shoes from Nick had been like getting unexpected and off-season valentines.

"Was there a note?" he asked.

"I don't know. I didn't look."

"Check it out. He knows you're helping, and he probably feels bad about the way he treated you."

"Are you going to give me shoes?" I asked suddenly.

"No, why?"

"Because I'm helping you, and if designers are in the business of giving things away, I'd much prefer a pair of your shoes to one of Milo's hats."

"Nice try, Kidd."

"So no free shoes?"

"Not for staff members. Tell you what. I'll pay you in benefits."

"Benefits don't pay the mortgage," I said.

"Neither do shoes."

I hung up.

"Trouble in paradise?" Eddie asked. He stood by the front door with keys in his hand.

"We're in a weird place right now," I said. "Are you leaving?"

"Thad was released from the hospital today."

"Ask him why he didn't want me to go into the admissions office the first day I was at the museum. And why he took the list of collectors from me. And why he's rude to me for no apparent reason —" I stopped talking when I saw the expression on Eddie's face. "Forget it. Tell him to take it easy."

After Eddie left, I took a much-needed shower. Twenty-five minutes later I was loofahed within an inch of my life. I dried off and moisturized with a rose-scented lotion I kept for special occasions. I dressed in a soft green cashmere sweater and a pair of worn-in jeans and walked across the hallway to the spare bedroom.

I had to come at this from another angle. If I tried, I could think like a collector. I pulled a large aqua plastic tub down from the shelf in the closet. I hadn't paid much attention to this box since moving in. It was my collection of designer Barbie dolls.

I sat on the carpet and opened the tub. Inside were more than a dozen long white boxes, each holding exquisite Barbie dolls in their high-fashion glory. Opaque white tissue protected each doll inside the box in the manner they'd left the factory.

I hadn't planned to collect Barbie dolls. I'd planned to buy just one. But after the first purchase came a second. After the third and fourth came a fifth. Each doll was viewed, admired, coveted, and then packed up and tucked safely into this bin. Preserved for safe keeping. It was a little sad if you thought about it. Aside from the day they arrived from Mattel, these beautiful dolls were never seen again.

The doorbell rang. By the time I reached the stairs, I heard a fist pounding on the door. "Sam! It's Cat. C'mon, open up!"

"I'm coming!" I opened the door, and Cat pushed past me. She held a cream garment bag over one finger and a black plastic garbage bag in the other.

"We have to talk." She went directly to my kitchen. "You went through it, didn't you?" she asked, pointing to the trash.

"Cat—"

She pushed her hand palm-side out to shut me up. "Listen. You were all intense when you brought my hat to my store. I felt bad about saying no. I wanted to do something to say thank you. So I picked out an outfit that I thought you might like to wear to the exhibit tonight. It's an outfit your shoe designer boyfriend might like appreciate as well. It's my way of saying thank you for returning my hat, and I'm sorry for saying no."

I reached for the bag, but she pulled it away from my range. "And then I find out you gave the trash to my brother. You involved me even though I didn't want to be involved."

"I already told you I made arrangements with your brother. You were never supposed to know." My eyes flickered down to the black plastic garbage bag that rested by her feet. "What's that?"

"He left one behind." She held both hands up, trash in one and garment bag in the other. "You get one. Choose."

"That's not fair."

She stamped her foot. "Samantha, you're a fashion person! You're supposed to like garments, not garbage. This should be a no-brainer."

"I might spend a disproportionate amount of money on my wardrobe, but that doesn't change who I am. I got into this because I'm helping a friend. A pretty outfit isn't going to change my mind about seeing him through the mess he's in."

She handed me the garbage bag. I untied the knot and looked inside. My eyes watered when a rank chemical odor hit me in the face. I waved my hand back and forth to clear the air.

Cat picked up a copy of *Vogue* from the coffee table and used it to fan the air. "Eww. It smells like developing fluid."

I reached inside and pulled out a piece of wet paper. Along the top, it said INTEREST IN HATS. It tore at the corner, and the soggy sheet stuck to the leg of my jeans.

"How do you know what developing fluid smells like?" I asked while I peeled the paper from my leg.

"Dante's a photographer. He turned his closet into a darkroom once and stank up the whole house."

"Why would someone at the museum be using developing fluid?"

"Maybe Dante knows. Let me ask him. He's waiting outside."

I grabbed her arm. "I don't want Dante to see me going through the trash."

"Here's a tip. If you don't want people to see you going through the trash, then stop going through the trash."

If only it were that simple. I folded my hands in front of me in a *please?* gesture.

"Okay, I'm not going to tell him. But if that list is as important as you think it is, don't you think it's crazy how fate got it to you? Weird, right?"

"Yeah, weird. It's like someone up there is looking out for me."

We raised our eyes to the ceiling. Something scraped the ceiling over our heads. Cat screamed.

There should have been no one else in the house. The idea that someone was in the room over the kitchen was too much to take. I rummaged around in a kitchen drawer for a weapon.

The front door opened, and Dante charged in. "What's wrong? What happened?" He looked back and forth between our faces and then rested his gaze on my weapon. "What's that?"

I gripped a rolling pin. My mom had left it behind for me, along with her notions that one day I might learn how to bake pies. The rolling pin was my starter kit to pie domesticity. Or self-defense, depending on the circumstance.

"There's someone upstairs," I whispered.

"Are you going to roll him to death?"

"Dante, will you check it out?" Cat asked.

It was one thing for Cat to ask her brother to check out the situation but a completely different one for me to sit back like a helpless female while he went to the front lines. The helpless-female gene was one that didn't exist in my DNA. (Unless you count spiders.)

"I'm coming with you."

"No."

"Yes."

I followed him up the stairs. We reached the door to my old bedroom—the room directly above the kitchen. Logan sat outside the door, a low growl coming from his throat and his tail fat with anticipation of a fight. "Is this where the noise came from?"

I nodded.

"Are you sure you want to keep going?"

I nodded again but felt it was somehow less convincing.

He opened the door. A flight of stairs covered in green shag carpeting led to my childhood attic-bedroom. There was no mistaking the noise this time: hands desperately clawing against the window screen, trying to get away. Logan stalked his way up the stairs past us.

I clutched the rolling pin. Dante's knuckles were white on the banister. Four steps up, he whispered for me to stay put; this time I didn't argue. He climbed the rest of the stairs, but the chains hanging from his jeans caught on the banister and held him back. He unclipped the chain from his belt loop and handed me his wallet. He reached the top of the stairs and then disappeared into the room.

"What are you doing up here? How'd you get in?" He was silent for a few seconds. "You're scaring everybody. Calm down. I'll get you out."

Dante knew my intruder. That was one coincidence too many. I raised the rolling pin in the air and pulled myself up the remaining stairs. I found myself face to face with a pair of beady brown eyes.

31

SAW A SQUIRREL

THE SQUIRREL THAT STARED AT ME DID NOT SEEM ESPECIALLY HAPPY that I stood between him and the stairway. Neither of us moved. He turned suddenly and charged toward the window.

The light in the room was minimal, but after my eyes adjusted, I was able to see that the closet door was open, the attic stairs were unfolded, and there were a few small piles of, shall we say, droppings in the room. On the opposite side of the room, the window was raised, and the screen had a squirrel-sized hole.

The squirrel went through the screen-door hole, onto a branch of a nearby crabapple tree, and raced away. Dante shut the window before the squirrel could change his mind and then crossed the room and disappeared into the attic.

Minutes later he reappeared. "You need an exterminator."

"How did he get into my attic?"

"There's some sunlight coming from the wall on the other side of the attic. I think he came through there. I pushed a trunk over to the wall, so he can't get back in. How long have you lived here?"

"About a year. But I know the previous owners pretty well..." I grabbed the phone and called my parents in California.

I STOOD in the kitchen making small talk with my mom while waiting for my dad to came to the phone. Cat and Dante were in the living room. My mom rattled on about a basketball game while I watched Dante clip his chains back to his jeans and tuck his wallet into his pocket. He looked up, caught me watching him, and came into the kitchen.

I hoisted myself onto the counter and swung my legs. Dante reached out for my hand and slowly traced his index finger along the lines of my palm.

I blushed and balled my hand into a fist without thinking. He turned it over, held it up to his lips, and kissed it.

"Always a pleasure seeing you, Samantha."

I was searching for an appropriate response when I heard my name repeated in my ear.

"Hello, Kid. Kid? Hello? Are you there? Samantha!"

"Hi, Dad," I said. I pulled my hand away from Dante, who walked out of the room. Cat peeked in and waved, and then the front door opened and closed. "I saw a squirrel," I said.

"Your ADD kicking in?"

"No, I saw a squirrel. In the attic. Do you know something about that?"

"Oh, that squirrel. I thought he was gone. An exterminator cut a hole in the side of the house, so he could get out."

I already knew the answer to the question I was about to ask. "Dad, what happened to the hole?"

"It's probably still there. Come to think of it, you might want to get someone out there to patch it, or Rocky might come back."

"Rocky?"

"The squirrel."

"You named him?"

"Consider yourself lucky he didn't show up with a moose," he joked.

Yeah, lucky, that was me.

I asked several pointed questions about other potential house problems that hadn't been disclosed when I bought the house at a price they'd argue was far below market value, and then we moved into chitchat. We talked about their new life on the west coast and my job search in Ribbon. I told my dad I was working for a local designer, and he told me he was happy I'd found something steady. He handed the phone off to my mom, who asked about my love life. I told her Nick and I were seeing each other on a regular basis. She mentioned something about free milk and cows, and I told her I had to go because dinner was burning.

———

THE NEXT MORNING, I woke, finally well rested. I found Eddie in the kitchen pouring two cups of coffee.

"What time did you get back?" I asked. I followed the question with a yawn.

He handed me a mug. "Around eleven. I had a brainstorm while I was out. I went to the twenty-four-hour print shop after I visited Thad and had some last-minute banners done. Do you still have that video from Hedy London?"

"It's in my handbag."

"Thad told me about a projector in the basement of the museum. I'm going to project the video on the main wall inside right behind the check-in desk. There won't be any sound, but still, it's all about her image, right?"

"That and the fact that you might be able to figure out who it was sent to."

"I've been thinking about that. I'm pretty sure it was sent to Dirk. Who else could it be?"

"I don't know. It seemed like she was flirting with the cameraman."

I was about to take a drink when I saw the coffee was the color of motor oil. Eddie took a long pull on his cup and didn't wince. Now that's commitment to caffeine.

"Do you think the exhibit will open tonight?" I asked.

"If it doesn't, it won't be because of me. There are a few last-minute things to tend to, but everything's doable. I mean, I Plan B'd the whole exhibit, but let's face it, this week hasn't exactly gone according to plan." He took another drink. "Did you call Milo? Do you know why he sent you the hat?"

"No, but I keep thinking about the box. It had the same small red number in the corner that we saw on the boxes at the museum." I took a sip of my coffee. "Rebecca said the museum recycles boxes. That might explain the box."

"But why would Milo have a box from the museum?"

"If he's part of the problem…"

He made a silent O and nodded. We stood there in shared silence, digesting this latest theory.

"Let's review what we know," I said. "Dirk Engle was Milo's business manager until Dirk left Milo high and dry. Would Milo kill him over that? And why would Milo edit me out of the surveillance footage—to make you look guilty? How would he even get the surveillance footage? Why would he stab Thad? And even if he did those things, when did he do them? We've never seen Milo at the museum."

"None of it makes sense."

I found a stale muffin and picked the cranberries out of it. "If you count everybody, including Dirk, we have two store owners, a hat designer, a Hollywood icon, and a bunch of museum employees. What about the collectors? We need to know the why."

"The Y?" Eddie asked.

"The why. The motive. The reason someone would want to kill Dirk Engle."

"What's your theory?"

"Someone wanted his client list. Vera could double her business. Milo could seek out financial backing. Christian could approach them as donors. I'm pretty sure that's why Hedy London agreed to be a part of the exhibit. Just about anybody involved could leverage her name for their benefit, and she wanted to make sure if someone was going to be in the limelight, it might as well be her. She's coming to the exhibit. What time is she supposed to arrive?"

"This afternoon," Eddie said. He rocked back on his chair legs. I had to fight the adult urge to tell him to bring it down on all fours. I scooted back on my barstool until my legs were dangling.

Eddie picked up the now-dry list of collectors from the table. The developing fluid had warped the paper, and a faint pinkish-brown stain covered two-thirds of the writing. He used his index finger to trace down the list. "A couple of these names are in the program. The Willoughbys are known costume collectors. There was an article in the paper about them last year when they bought some costumes from one of those thirties husband-wife detective-team mysteries. Remember? The costumes came up at auction in New York?"

"There was a Mrs. Willoughby at Over Your Head the day I first went there. Maybe she wasn't there for a hat. Maybe she was feeling Vera out for information." I remembered someone else. "Some guy in a wrinkled seersucker suit and straw hat has been hanging around outside of the museum. Have you seen him?"

"That's Carl Collins. He's a reporter for the *Ribbon Times.*"

I recognized the name from the article I'd read. "On one hand, I should have known there would be a reporter snooping around the museum. But on the other, only one? There was a homicide. Where's the rest of the press?"

"Restricted access. The police aren't letting the press get close."

"According to you, Carl Collins got close. He was feeding the ducks across from the main entrance."

"Carl's harmless. They put him on puff pieces."

I thought about things from a different angle. "What if Christian is planning to resell the hats on the collector's market? What if he had a set of fakes made up by Milo, and he replaced the originals with the phonies?" I thought back to the samples I saw at Milo's showroom, how familiar they looked, and how upset he'd gotten when I asked about his inspiration. "The twelve people on this list represent money for the museum. If these people are rabid collectors, wouldn't they be interested in seeing the Hedy London hats first?"

"You think the hats at the exhibit are fakes?"

"It would explain the different labels. It would also explain how we have two of the same hat—the one we found next to Dirk Engle's body and the one Milo sent here. Detective Loncar isn't exactly a style expert. He might not know he gave you the replicas and not the originals."

Eddie flattened the paper against the table with the side of his hand. "If he did, then somebody better get the real hats to the museum for the gala. Collectors know their stuff. They'll be able to spot a fake a mile away."

"Maybe the police don't know they had fakes. Maybe the real hats went missing from the beginning."

He folded the paper in half and then in half again. "I'm going to spend the day at the museum. You wanna come?"

"No, I'm going to see Milo. His public appearance is today, and I want to thank him for sending me a hat for tonight." At least that's how I was going to interpret the unexpected shipment until I learned he had other intentions.

After Eddie left, I dressed in a black-and-white-checkered strapless dress layered over a mint-green cotton poplin shirt. I fed French knots through the cufflink holes, pulled on a pair of pointy-toed black ankle booties, filled a houndstooth handbag with my wallet, sunglasses, phone, and lip-gloss, and left.

The ad for Milo's event said he'd be available between noon and two. I arrived at twelve thirty, figuring it was better to be early than late, surprised to find a Closed sign in the window. Next to that was a smaller sign taped to the inside of the glass. *Milo Delaney event canceled until further notice.*

Interesting. If someone involved in the homicide were looking for a good day to skip town, today would rank right up there.

32

HYPOCRITICAL

I sat in the car out front and called information for the store's number. The answering service clicked on after five rings. Vera Sarlow's voice confirmed what the sign said: the Milo Delaney public appearance was canceled, and Over Your Head was closed until further notice.

I drove around back, hoping to find a crew quietly smuggling her inventory out of the store, but I found nothing. The building was locked up as tight as a drum. I hopped out of the car and glanced in the Dumpster. It was empty. Trash pickup had been that morning.

Curses.

It was after two by the time I pulled into my driveway. There was little else for me to do but get ready for the gala. Nick was due to pick me up at three thirty, which left me an hour and a half. Despite the drama surrounding the event, my excitement over attending the soiree colored my expectations. The risk of spending time at the museum was barely a thought.

I surveyed the contents of my closet, narrowing my choices down to a strapless cocktail dress with full skirt and built-in crinoline and a burnt sienna backless jersey gown cut on the bias.

Both were favorites.

Both had been worn only once.

Both held promise.

Neither felt right.

I went downstairs for a glass of water and saw the ivory plastic garment bag draped over one of the dining room chairs. The logo on the bag read Catnip. It was the other bag Cat had brought when she delivered the last bag of garbage.

It seemed Cat wasn't a very good negotiator. Even though I'd chosen the garbage, she left me an outfit anyway. I carried the bag to my room while wondering what was behind door number three.

I pulled out the dress. It was a Mandarin-inspired style, straight out of *The World of Susie Wong*. A subtle black-on-black jacquard print of bamboo decorated the silk. The neckline and sleeves were piped in red. I had a sneaking suspicion it wouldn't hide my recent ice cream or pizza indulgences. It was knee-length with slits on the side that made it borderline inappropriate for a work function. Good thing Nick said he didn't want to spend time with his showroom manager.

I rooted around the bottom of the bag and found a pair of black patent Mary Janes with a red lacquer heel. Cat had also included a pair of black fishnet stockings, a corset and matching panties (apparently, she had concerns about my ice cream and pizza indulgences showing too), a pair of gold shoulder-duster earrings, and a black satin bag with gold metal handles.

She'd omitted nothing. There was no way she figured I'd choose the garbage over this.

I showered, shaved, moisturized, perfumed, blow-dried, flat-ironed, up-twisted, and made-up before putting on the lingerie. The corset was a snug fit, boosting me in the right places. I pulled the fishnets over the panties, slipped on the shoes, and checked out the Moulin Rouge effect in the mirror.

A horn beeped out front. I peeked out the window and saw Nick's truck pulling into my driveway. He was early! Not cool. I traded the shoes for slippers, knotted my silk kimono over my underwear, and ran downstairs. The door opened, and Eddie came in.

"What are you doing here? Where's Nick?"

"Probably getting dressed."

"Why are you driving Nick's truck?"

"He said I could use it. More undercover than my Volkswagen, plus I needed more space to move a few extra mannequins from Tradava."

"He has your Bug?"

"Yes. I left it at his house when I went to pick this up."

Eddie wore a fitted tux, white shirt, and white necktie. He looked like Daniel Craig's version of Bond, I thought, until I noticed the checkered Vans on his feet.

I pointed to them. "Dude."

"This is going to be a stressful night, you know? I know I don't completely look the part, and I know I should either abandon the whole dress code or go all-in on formal wear, but I don't feel right doing either. I don't want to feel like I'm trying to be somebody that I'm not, so I compromised. It's not too bad, right?"

"It looks like you. Only not."

"The police are going to be watching me. They agreed to let me go about my business launching the exhibit as though nothing were wrong. After the evening is over, I'm out of this whole thing." He smacked the palms of his hands together twice like a baker dusting off the flour. "*Basta!*"

"Have you talked to the detective recently? About the exhibit, or security, or anything like that?" I asked.

"Detective Loncar met with the museum staff this morning. He said police would be everywhere, but he told us to act normal. Christian and I walked him through the whole thing: the entrance, the exhibit, the exits. Dr. Daum is going to greet guests. Rebecca is going to work the check-in desk."

"Who's going to run the gift shop?"

"Christian wants it closed."

"And pass up a perfectly good opportunity to peddle Thinker

statues? That doesn't sound like him." I thought back to the day he found me in the gift shop, and it hit me. I dragged Eddie to the kitchen table, and we both sat down.

"Christian told Rebecca to leave the Thinker statues alone. She was trying to straighten them, and he told her to get down and focus on keeping the inside of the store neat. Not just that one time but twice. He said nobody ever looks above eye level. What if he's hiding something up there?"

Eddie tipped his head back and stared directly at the ceiling. I didn't think he was looking for anything, just trying to think. "We have to get in and look."

"No, we have to call the cops. Christian's already at the museum, I'm sure. You can't show up and demand to go looking around."

So we did. Call the cops, that is. Yes, we were learning from our mistakes. I let Eddie take credit for the information and the call. He identified himself and asked to speak to Detective Loncar. Eddie had common sense after all and was setting a nice example for the kids out there.

His second phone call was to Dr. Daum. Eddie had asked for privacy when making his phone call, so I left the room but hovered just close enough on the other side of the wall to hear him tell the former director about his arrangements with the police. You didn't think I was going to let him conduct all this business without my knowledge, did you?

"Everything's under control?" I asked.

"Yep. The law's in the hands of the law, and the fashion-y stuff is in the hands of the fashion people. I worked hard on this exhibit. I deserve the credit."

I squeezed his hand. "You're going to be great tonight. You know that, right?"

He squeezed back. "I hope so. I'd better get going—last-minute touches and all."

EDDIE LEFT, and I changed out of my kimono and into my dress. Forty-five minutes later I swapped the dress back out for my silk kimono so I could comfortably sit while cursing Nick out. I had long since moved into if-you're-not-coming-just-say-so mode. I touched up my makeup and considered loosening the corset when Eddie's VW Bug careened down the street. When I opened the front door, Nick stood on my doorstep.

He wore a vintage black 1940s satin roll-collar tuxedo, white shirt, and black tie. The waning sunlight flashed on his ebony cuff links and off the shiny patent of his shoes. Where Eddie had gone modern formalwear with a side of surfer dude, Nick had gone Cary Grant all the way.

He held up his hands. "Before you say anything, I'm sorry I'm late." His expression was serious. He pointed over his shoulder. "Go for a walk?"

I checked the locks to make sure the door wouldn't lock behind us and then followed him onto the porch and down my driveway. The air was cooling down now that the sun had dropped. We made it halfway down the block before he spoke.

"I don't think this is working out," he said.

"I know."

A thin veil of mist surrounded us, typical of the evenings in Ribbon. I took a few steps back to where he was standing and stood in front of him.

"Let me explain something." He looked down at the sidewalk, using the toe of his shiny tuxedo shoe to play with loose gravel. There was a childish quality to his body language. "I'm worried about you, Kidd. Like it or not, your involvement with this exhibit put you right in the crosshairs of this thing."

"Nick—"

He held a finger to my lips to shush me. "I care about you. I want to protect you. And the only way I know how to is to keep you from going tonight."

"But Eddie's counting on me. I can't let him go through this alone."

"Whatever this is, it's not just about Eddie anymore. This time neither of you has to be involved." He put his fingers under my chin and tipped my head back. "Spend the night with me," he said softly.

My eyes widened.

"That's not a proposition. It's... it's an alternative." He took my hands in his. "Let's stay away from the exhibit together. Go to dinner, see a movie."

"But Eddie needs me."

"Eddie's got the Ribbon Police to watch over him. He doesn't need you."

What I didn't say out loud was that deep down, I knew Nick was right. Eddie might not need me, but I needed him. I needed his confidence in my friendship and loyalty. I needed to be there to support him, because being there for him said something about me. I needed to watch him get through the night without a hitch to know that he was going to be okay, and I needed to see the killer get his due.

When I finally spoke, it was a mere hint of a whisper. "I need to go to the museum."

He stepped away from me and dropped my hands. "I can't watch you do this."

"I know."

The mist swirled around us. He ran a finger along the side of my face and twisted it around a tendril of hair that had escaped my fancy up-do and turned curly.

"You look beautiful."

"I'm not even ready yet." I flushed and looked down at my slippered feet with embarrassment.

"If I were a different kind of boss, I might take advantage of a moment like this," he said with a smile, his fingertip now tracing a line down my neck. His palm opened up, and he wrapped his hand around the side of my neck, his thumb stroking the spot under my ear. I tipped my head to the side, and he leaned forward and kissed my neck.

"If I were a different kind of employee, I'd want you to," I whispered.

He moved from my neck to my lips. This time, the kiss wasn't one-sided. The mist turned into a sudden rain that pasted my kimono to my body. Nick pulled his hand away, took off his jacket, and draped it over my shoulders.

We ran through newly formed puddles on the way back to my house. As quickly as the shower had started, it stopped, just before we reached my front door.

"I think I should be leaving," he said.

"Don't leave. You're already dressed. Think of the visibility for your business."

"I can't do this with you." He took my hands in his and kissed me on the cheek. "And it would be hypocritical to do it without you. Be careful, Kidd."

I didn't want to think about what he meant. Sometimes a woman has to know how to take care of herself, and this felt like one of those times. I dried off, fixed my hair, changed into my dress, and stepped into my shoes. I was ready. For what, I still didn't know.

33

A CLONING EXPERIMENT GONE WRONG

I FILLED THE SMALL BLACK SATIN BAG WITH ESSENTIALS: TWENTY-DOLLAR bill, fully charged cell phone, identification, lipstick, powder, keys, breath mints, nail file, painkillers, moisturizer, small notepad and pen, Swiss Army knife, and emergency sewing kit. I snagged a second twenty to cover what-ifs and left.

The sun was setting behind the museum, giving the sky a romantic orangey-gold tone. It was the perfect backdrop for the event. I pulled up in front of the museum, handed my keys to a valet attendant, and adjusted the slit in my dress to be slightly less revealing. Shiny black limos dropped off well-dressed patrons. I scanned the crowd for police and spotted three uniformed officers standing to the left of the entrance and two more on the right. Good. They weren't taking any chances here tonight.

The last time I had been at the museum for a formal event, I had not been on the guest list. There'd been no thrill of being one of the partygoers. In fact, I had been dropped off a few blocks away and walked to the event, watching by the pond and conducting surveillance before being threatened, hiding in a tree, and being chased from the premises by a figure that bore a passing resemblance to Michael Myers (at least in my memories).

Tonight was different.

I felt every bit the glamorous socialite as I stepped onto the red carpet. Nice touch, I thought. Eddie had never mentioned the final details, so I didn't know if he was responsible. Either way, it made for a dramatic entrance.

I felt anonymous. I wished someone would be waiting to meet me at the entrance, but after realizing that I hadn't planned to arrive alone, I thought twice about that wish. Lost in thought, I made my way through the crowd to the massive front doors, propped open for the evening with large urns that held topiaries shaped to resemble pillbox hats on hat stands.

The sunlight painted the foyer gold. Chic volunteers, dressed in matching belted camel skirt suits and long brown gloves, greeted guests. They were all modeled after a scene from *Murder after Midnight*. Stylistically, it was a home run. It was like a cloning experiment gone wrong.

Two guards were at the entrance. Another stood off to the side, radio in hand, watching the crowd as they entered the museum. They weren't the museum guards who had ushered patrons from one wing to the next, keeping viewers a safe distance from the paintings. These officers were police, I guessed, dressed in less obvious uniforms than the men out front but armed all the same, radios in hand. Detective Loncar must have coordinated that as part of his plan to keep Eddie and the other patrons safe tonight. I was curious about the detective's possible take on formal attire (Walter Matthau in *Plaza Suite?*). I didn't see him.

Blondes with carefully coiffed French twists peeking out of camel and brown trilby hats bustled around, checking invitations and directing guests here and there. Invitations! Of all the things I remembered to pack in my bag, I suddenly realized I had left that vital piece of paper on the counter at home.

I stepped to the side of the line, pretending to search through my purse, all the while knowing I could be bounced out before even getting a glimpse of Eddie's work.

"Samantha! I'm delighted to see you this evening," a voice called to me.

Dr. Daum stood beside one of the volunteers. He held out his elbow, and I hooked my hand under it. Together we walked past the faux Hedy Londons into the museum lobby.

"How's Thad?" I asked as we walked past the coat check line.

"He's doing fine, just fine. He was released today. He was hoping to be here tonight, which I think was a little presumptuous on his part, considering his multiple wounds. He was quite a lucky young man, though. Quite lucky." His voice drifted off.

"Multiple wounds? I thought he was stabbed."

"Three times, three shallow wounds." The former director guided me toward the elevator. "But now's not the time to talk about it. He'll recover, and that's what counts."

We arrived on the second floor amidst a crowd of people buzzing about Eddie's exhibit. Twelve hats had been positioned on sculpted white bust forms and perched on Ionic pedestals. Twelve pencil-thin flashlights were suspended from the ceiling, directly over each hat, to shine on them from above. The dental floss was invisible; the flashlights appeared to be hanging in midair and only added to the design concept. Behind the hat displays were mannequins dressed in shades of camel, brown, ivory, and taupe. Nipped-in waists on jackets and skirts full with accordion pleats of netting recalled Dior's New Look that had launched in the late forties and defined the fifties. I walked from one mannequin to the next, wondering how the city of Ribbon was going to react to such strikingly feminine—yet retro— fashion. That is if the fashionistas weren't going to buy it out first as they'd done with the latest designer collaboration at Target.

While a large portion of the crowd *oohed* and *ahhed*, a throng of partygoers stood off to the side sipping champagne and munching hors d'oeuvres. I saw mini quiches and cocktail shrimp. I cursed the corset that would keep me from eating.

"Your friend Eddie has turned out to be precisely what we needed for this exhibit," Dr. Daum said. "He managed extraordinary work during what must have been a trying time.

In fact, he kept much of his exhibit under wraps. Even though we're viewing it now, he and Christian still planned for an unveiling."

"Eddie said something special was happening tonight, but he didn't tell me what."

"Yes, Christian said the same thing."

"Dr. Daum, there's something I think you should know about Christian—"

"An interesting approach, I think, considering this is a crowd that expects a lot to be impressed." He checked his watch. "In fact, it's almost that time. Have you seen him yet?"

"Christian? No, not yet. But Dr. Daum—"

"Then I must go and see if Eddie requires any help. Until later, Samantha."

Once again, I was by myself. I glanced around, looking for someone else who might provide a conversational escape but found nothing more than well-dressed couples walking around, nodding in my direction. I suddenly became aware that someone was standing close behind me, breathing on my neck.

"Hello, gorgeous." Arms wrapped around my waist and pulled me backward into his body. "You didn't think I was going to leave you all alone, did you?"

I closed my eyes and leaned back. "I knew you wouldn't stand me up," I said.

"Stand you up? I wasn't even sure if you'd show."

I whirled around and stood face to face with Dante. Heat shot through my body and face and a few other unmentionable places.

"What are you doing here?" I asked.

He raised his eyebrows. "Expecting someone else?"

A volunteer approached us with a silver tray of champagne flutes. Dante took two from the tray and offered me one. I took it and sipped (swigged).

"Aren't you going to tell me how nice I look?" he asked.

He cleaned up nicely. That was for sure. Still the rebel, though, he sported a black shirt under his peak lapel tuxedo and a black tie with green flames that looked like they'd been lifted from a motorcycle with a custom paint job.

"What did you do, call ahead to find out the dress code?"

"You think I don't know how to dress?"

"No." I stared him straight in the eyes. I wasn't going to let him get to me. "I think you probably know more than you let on. What brings you here tonight?" I asked.

He leaned in close, and once again, I felt his breath next to my ear. "What do you think brought me here?"

He was evasive on purpose, and I finally understood what he meant about the questions I asked. Mine were polite. Innocuous. They were reactive, based on our encounters, and he knew it. My questions deflected attention. He had come to expect the expected from me. As long as he kept me on my toes, he'd be the one controlling what I knew and what I didn't. It was time to turn the tables.

"What's your connection to the exhibit tonight?" I asked.

Passing couples looked in our direction. Part of me was looking for Nick, still expecting him to arrive, and the other was looking for Christian. And there was that murderer to consider too. The rest of the guests in attendance had the luxury of relaxing into party mode. I knew too much to relax.

Dante leaned against the wall and poured half his champagne down his throat. "I know the guy who's running the show—Christian Jhanes. He had me do some dirty jobs back in my college days." He scanned the crowd. "Plus there's this woman I was hoping to run into..." His voice trailed off.

I'd done it. I'd gotten him to admit to a connection between himself and Christian. And despite his attempt to distract me with innuendo, I knew I'd scored a point. I thought over what I wanted to ask next but didn't get the chance. Cat approached us.

"Samantha, Dante, you found each other," she said. She was one of the few people to pay proper homage to the exhibit, and her signature red hair was topped with a green satin turban. It was trimmed with white feathers that spiked a foot over her head. It was the perfect complement to her white silk skirt suit. If she'd paid $3,000 for the last one, I didn't want to ask about the price tag on this one. She cocked her head to one side and touched her finger to her cheek. "You like?"

"Won't lose you in the crowd, that's for sure," Dante answered.

She caught her reflection in the glass doors of the gift shop and adjusted the pleated satin over her shoulder-length bob. "It's almost better than the last one. It was designed by Lily Dache's assistant. You know who that was, right?"

Dante stuffed his hands in his pockets and looked across the room. I tried to follow his gaze to see who or what he was watching. "Who was Lily Dache's assistant?" he asked mechanically.

"Halston!" Cat and I said in unison.

She giggled at me and then turned back to Dante. "What are you still doing here? I thought you had someplace to go."

"I do."

She rolled her eyes and tipped her head conspiratorially. "Dante's got a thing for Hedy London—ever since he first saw one of her movies. Then she spoke at his graduation. I think that meant more to him than the diploma."

"You know Hedy London?" I asked.

He raised an eyebrow and then dropped it.

Cat leaned in. "He keeps telling this ridiculous story that she made a pass at him before she gave the speech at his commencement. I told him he could come tonight if he were on his best behavior."

I looked back and forth between their faces. Cat's invite and enthusiasm appeared completely genuine.

"What do you think? Did I keep up my end of the bargain?"

She eyed the details of his tuxedo. "I thought I told you not to go with the black shirt. I like the tie, though. I mean, if you insist on wearing flames everywhere you go."

He flipped a lock of her hair. "I don't think you want to finish that sentence, Red."

Neither spoke for a moment. I turned my back on their brother/sister tiff and scrutinized the crowd.

A variety of dress code interpretations wandered the room. There were cocktail dresses, gowns, sequined tops paired with skinny jeans and stilettos, and at least one purple velvet tuxedo. The few Tradava faces that I recognized played it safe: classic tuxedos on the men and little black dresses on the women. They needed someone on their team to shake things up.

Cat and I shared critiques of some of the more unique outfits that circled the room. She pointed out what I didn't know: designers and critics who had made the extra effort to come to the exhibit to grab a piece of Eddie's limelight.

And then I saw Milo Delaney.

It made sense he'd be here. Tonight's opening was a hat exhibit and a cross-promotional event for Tradava, and I knew from working with Nick that Milo was the designer behind the Hedy London hats even if he didn't want to admit it.

What if Milo had knocked off the hat collection and produced two sets of samples? And kept the originals for himself? His connections with Vera at Over Your Head would provide the channels for resale. Was that why he'd canceled his appearance at her store?

If nothing else, I wanted to ask him why he sent me the forest-green fedora. He caught me staring at him. I smiled feebly and tipped my champagne flute in his direction. He turned and walked the other way.

Out of the corner of my eye, I caught Dante waving too. But it was Vera Sarlow who'd stepped in his path. They hugged briefly, and he kissed her on the cheek. Her black chiffon dress had a fitted bodice and a sweetheart neckline that showed off a figure I didn't know she had. A small wafer of felt with black net and a pheasant feather perched on her head.

The fact that Dante knew Vera raised questions I hadn't considered only minutes before.

I turned to Cat. "Dante went to I-FAD, didn't he?" I asked.

"Yes."

"That's where Christian worked."

"I know. He was Dante's photography professor. Christian gave him a couple of jobs on the side between classes."

"Can Dante do film editing?" I asked.

"Sure. His junior year, he duplicated our home movies and edited me out of the footage."

Warning bells sounded in my head. "Is that hard?"

"I don't know, but I remember he was mad because he didn't get an A." She looked around the crowd. "Where did he go?"

"He's over there." I pointed toward her brother and Vera.

"Is that Vera Engle?"

"It's Sarlow now. Vera Sarlow. How do you know her?"

"She went to school with me. I haven't seen her in years. I should say hello. Are you okay if I leave you alone?"

"Sure."

Cat approached Vera, and Dante broke away. He stopped by a tray of champagne flutes, picked up two more, and returned to my side.

"Your boss not coming?"

"He's running late."

"For his sake, I hope he finds you soon. Otherwise I might monopolize you for the rest of the evening." He moved closer to me and placed his hand on the small of my back.

Just then, the lights went out.

34

———

STABBED

A COLLECTIVE GASP ESCAPED FROM THE CROWD. PEOPLE RUSTLED about, wavering between excitement and nervousness over what to do next. I searched for the security guards I'd seen out front. In the dark, it was hard to differentiate between partygoers and police officers.

Soft emergency lights glowed by the exits. A rush of air overhead ruffled my hair, punctuated by a loud clank. A power outage would have been too much of a coincidence on a night like this.

Footsteps sounded behind us, followed by a second clank. A light sliced through the darkness and threw a spotlight on a cloaked twenty-foot-long banner hanging from the balcony of the upstairs galleries.

The silhouette of a woman appeared behind the cloak. She raised a microphone to her lips, and her sexy voice teased the audience with a song.

The singer was Hedy London. She worked the stage with a thick feather boa and a dress of sequins. Catcalls and wolf whistles accompanied her singing. She stepped out from behind the white cloak and made her way down the spiral staircase. She reached the bottom step and punctuated the final words of her song with hip thrusts. I stood, mesmerized. I hoped I had half that much sex appeal when I was her age.

Applause met her performance. The white cloak dropped and unveiled the banner promoting the exhibit. It was a blown-up fake movie poster modeled after her most famous movie, with *"Millinery" After Midnight* in the title space instead. This must be what Eddie had picked up from the sign shop. I had to hand it to him; he'd created a great opening for what I hoped was a great exhibit.

My heartbeat was still racing from the panic when the museum went dark, and my proximity to Dante didn't help matters. He, on the other hand, was completely oblivious to my presence now that Hedy London was in the house. I guess Cat had been telling the truth about that crush.

"I'm going to look for Eddie," I whispered.

I weaved through the crowd. Before I got far, Eddie appeared at the top of the stairs by a podium I hadn't noticed earlier.

"Friends, patrons, and guests of the museum, welcome to our tribute to the iconic nature of the chapeau. As we've worked on this exhibit, we've come to view this collection of memorabilia as more than a collection of hats from different movie sets but as pieces of a different sort of artistic history, unique with their intrinsic value. Join us in the Frowick Gallery to view our collective ideas of millinery as memorabilia, of fashion as art. We hope you enjoy what we've assembled for you. A special thank you to Ms. London for her presence here this evening." He paused while the crowd applauded the film star. "Now, I know it's only eight o'clock in Ribbon, but it's midnight somewhere. Enjoy your private viewing of 'Millinery After Midnight.'"

Applause once again rang out through the foyer of the museum, this time for Eddie. No one in the room would have suspected that the speaker who addressed them so eloquently had been in hiding for most of the week. Within minutes, he was engulfed in adoration. There was no point trying to reach him now.

The fact that no one had formally introduced him only added to his cachet—as if his identity transcended his name. I couldn't believe

Christian hadn't even bothered to be there to give him formal credit for what he'd accomplished.

Then it struck me. The publicity-obsessed crafty museum director who'd kept maniacal deadlines in place to open this exhibit wasn't present. But surely he was here somewhere. Was he watching us right now? Or had that been the real motivation behind getting the exhibit to open on time—that it was the perfect chance to make a clean getaway with a trunk filled with collectibles?

I sipped the last of my champagne and watched the crowd overtake the massive marble staircase. Others stood in line by the elevator. The lobby had thinned out. All was under control. I could relax. I took a deep breath and exhaled.

"Pssst," Eddie hissed from behind me. "Come with me."

He held a finger to his lips to indicate silence and pushed me toward the gift shop. I wasn't prepared to be pushed anywhere, and I took an awkward step back, shifted my weight at an unpredictable angle, and felt a shooting pain through my ankle. I turned to face him. His eyes darted back and forth.

"Christian never showed up, and Hedy London appeared out of nowhere. It's like I'm trapped in the middle of someone else's funhouse, and I don't know which direction to go."

"Still, that was a nice opening," I said. "Cutting the lights for her musical number."

"The lights? I wouldn't know how to cut the lights. Your friend, the detective, is supposed to be around somewhere, but I checked in when I got here, and he hasn't made contact." He pulled a key from his pocket and unlocked the door to the gift shop. "Get behind the display cases." He shut the door and ducked behind the register. I followed.

"Is that why no one introduced you?"

"Hedy London was here when I arrived. She said she and Christian had this whole opening act planned, not to worry, and if he didn't appear at the end, I was supposed to address the crowd."

"Sounds more like they planned a massive distraction, don't you think? She shows up and does a little number, and he's gone? Like maybe she gave him a head start out of town?"

"I thought he was the one controlling the lights and that he probably couldn't get back upstairs in time."

I was bothered by Hedy London's pop-up appearance and the fact that Dante knew her, Christian, and Vera. Plus, it wasn't sitting well with me that Loncar hadn't approached Eddie after he'd checked in. Any number of people had access to our plans, and some of those people knew our plans because we'd told them. It was starting to look like we'd better watch our backs.

I didn't ask Eddie why he wasn't mingling with the crowd. There was a good chance that he wanted to ask me why I wasn't with Nick. The good thing about friends is that sometimes you can hang out in an off-limits gift shop together and respect each other's secrets without a second thought.

I flopped (as best I could in a Susie Wong dress, corset, and fishnets) onto the rubber mat behind the register, pushing my legs out in front of me. The hem of my dress rode up to near-peek-a-boo levels. I pulled a scarf from a pile on the floor and set it on my lap like a dinner napkin.

"I ran into Dr. Daum when I got here. He said Thad wanted to be here tonight."

"You don't suspect him again, do you?"

"I can't justify the stabbing if Thad's involved. But he did take that list of collectors from me, which means someone might have attacked him over that."

"Dude, I'd feel a lot better about tonight if I knew the detective was out there."

"I don't know where Loncar is, but there are cops all over this joint. Vera Sarlow is here too. So is Milo Delaney." I put my hand on top of the pile of scarves and pushed myself up. Something sharp pierced the palm of my hand, and I screamed.

A security guard came into the gift shop. I held my hands over my head, looking very much like a guilty partygoer. Blood trickled from my palm from three small puncture wounds.

"Ma'am?" the security officer said. "Are you okay?"

Eddie scooted out behind his back unnoticed. "I was hoping to find a first aid kit in here." It didn't take much to convince the officer, considering the red droplets spidering down my arm.

"How did you get in?" His flashlight danced around the store for a few more moments. "This store was supposed to be locked. Come with me."

He pulled the door shut and turned a key in the lock. "Are you alone? I thought I saw two people."

"Must have been my shadow. My date didn't realize I'd left."

He eyed my outfit but said nothing. I followed him to a table tucked into a corner, where he pulled out a first aid kit and dressed my wounds.

"Are you a cop?"

"Security officer. Don't get me wrong—there are cops all over this place tonight. A bunch of us were hired for general security. You know, take care of small problems."

"Like what?"

He wound my hand with an adhesive bandage. "Like this."

"Gotcha. Have you had any other small emergencies tonight?"

"Just the lights going out, but the guy in charge said that was supposed to happen. Shoulda told us ahead of time. Coulda caused some panic."

"You saw the guy in charge? Golden hair, deep tan?"

"Yeah, that's him." He secured the bandage with white medical tape and turned my hand over. "He's upstairs in the exhibit. The elevator will take you back to the party. Don't let me catch you in the gift shop again."

"Thank you, officer," I said. I adjusted my slit and felt the boning from the corset dig into my ribs.

"Ma'am? That would be a shame if your date didn't notice you were gone. If my date wore a dress like that, you can bet I'd never let her out of my sight."

I smiled and crossed the lobby to the elevator. My ankle—the same one I'd hurt when I jumped to avoid being hit by the light fixture—throbbed, my hand throbbed, and my head throbbed. I wasn't sure which direction to turn. The elevator doors opened, and I got on. I pressed the button for the second level. The doors closed, but the car descended instead.

When it stopped, and the doors opened, a very angry, very blonde woman in a beaded dress stood in front of me.

"You're coming with me," she said. She grabbed my arm with unexpected forcefulness and pulled me out of the elevator.

And just like that, Hedy London kidnapped me from the gala.

35

DON'T PLAY THE VICTIM

Her hand landed on the fresh puncture wounds on my palm, and I cried out and doubled over. Blood seeped through the bandages the security officer had applied.

"Ow! Please, let go. My hand is hurt," I said.

"Don't play the victim," Hedy London snapped. She repositioned her hand to my wrist and yanked me forward. "I've known for a long time that you and your friend are trying to sabotage my launch. I'm not giving you a chance to undermine what we've accomplished."

We turned down a dark hallway that ran under the gallery. I'd never been in this area before. There were no offices here, only concrete floors below our feet and exposed pipes above our heads. I yanked my hand back, but her grip on me tightened. This woman was twice my age. How strong could she be?

"Let me go," I said.

"Not until you tell me what you did with Christian."

"I don't know what you're talking about."

"You and your friend have been trouble from the start. I will not allow you to get in the way of this opportunity. I know you've been spying on us and listening to our plans. I'll ask you again. What did you do with him?"

As lost as I was between both our location and the conversation, her accusation meant one thing: Christian Jhanes was missing.

"Eddie hasn't been trying to do anything other than pull off—I mean establish—this exhibit, Ms. London. I've been helping. I don't know where Christian is. Eddie's been working here night and day to make sure everything was properly installed." I paused, gauging whether or not my panicked stream-of-consciousness was having any impact on the hostile environment.

"For God's sake, stop calling me Ms. London. You're making me feel ancient."

No way to interpret that other than hostile. That's how I reacted to "ma'am."

She pushed me along the underground path in the dark. My eyes sought something—anything—familiar. We passed metal shut-off valves attached to pipes on the wall, square-cut openings above us that dangled ropes over our heads, and supply closets labeled in stenciling that had faded and chipped over the years. We turned a corner, and she pushed me toward a flight of stairs. I stumbled, falling. She pulled me back up and kept going. Hedy London may have been an aging film star, but she was proving to be a tough old broad in a lot better shape than I was. Maybe Eddie was on to something with the steamed chicken and the brown rice.

We reached a metal door. Hedy put both hands on a vertical bar and moved it from flush against the door to out at an angle. I heard the locking mechanism of the door shift. She threw her hip into the door and pushed on the spring-loaded bar in the center. It swung open. I smelled rather than saw the grounds behind the museum: freshly cut grass and faint notes of exhaust fumes. We'd traveled through an underground passage and exited through the groundkeeper shed.

"Where are we going?" I asked.

She flung me past her. I stumbled in too-high heels, lost my balance, and landed on my hands and knees on the grass. Pain seared through my palm. I felt a breeze on my shoulder and high up on my hip and knew my dress had torn.

"It'll take you time to get back to the front of the museum, past security. Time is what I need to find Christian and make our announcement to the media. Once we do that, you can't stop us."

"I'm not trying to stop you. I'm trying to help Eddie. I'm trying to impress somebody at Tradava enough to get a job." I'd given up on trying to find a killer, but she may have found me.

Hedy leaned down, her face very close to mine. "Christian and I were lovers before we were partners, and this collaboration will make it official. He's finally ready to announce our engagement to the world. I will not let you take this moment away from me."

She stood back, smoothed her dress with gloved hands, and stepped into the dark interior of the museum. I pushed myself up and reached for the door. My fingernails scraped against the metal as it closed.

I pounded my fist on it. There was no answer. I turned and leaned against the utilitarian door, bending forward with my hands on my thighs. My ribs felt cold. I wrapped one arm around my body and felt a split in the fabric along the side seam of the dress.

My handbag was a few feet away from where I'd left a Samantha-shaped depression in the grass. The contents had scattered.

Hedy London and Christian were announcing their engagement? What did that have to do with anything? And why would it have to be kept a secret?

Worse, the film star had acted like *I* was the one who was causing *her* trouble, not the other way around. She had shown genuine concern over Christian's absence. If she'd been behind any of this, I doubted she would have sounded so sincere. And if she was in love with Christian, was she blind to the fact that he was taking advantage of her?

Or what if he simply was a man in love, who knew the day was coming soon when he could let the world know how he felt? That he was helping the love of his life realize a new set of dreams that included him?

And if all of that was the case, then who would be the person to sabotage those plans?

I patted the grass and crawled in a slightly larger circle, making sure I'd found everything. I felt something sharp jab into my shin. I rolled over and felt the area, revealing a set of keys.

But I already had my keys. Whose keys were these?

I hooked the ring over my index finger and held the keys up against the moonlight. They were museum keys, like the ones Eddie had clamped onto his waistband the first day I'd helped him.

It was a sign.

I didn't have to go around front. I could let myself back in the way Hedy had brought me. I had to get back into the museum.

I stumbled forward and dusted off pieces of cut grass from my fishnets. The fourth key I tried fit the lock. I turned it and pulled on the handle. Something clicked, and the door opened.

I tried to remember the path Hedy London had pulled me through. Three right turns and some serious pain later, I was back where I'd started. I sat on the steps again and massaged my ankle.

I pulled myself up and rested against a valve cover. The electrical panel was only a few feet ahead of me. A screwdriver protruded from it, the occasional spark snapping from it like a Fourth of July sparkler. Otherwise, the catacombs of the museum were dark.

I crept toward the sparks, feeling my way along the wall. A figure stepped out from the shadows. His face was distorted by a mask made from bubble wrap, with cut-out openings by his eyes and nose. He swung something cold and thick at my midsection. I fell.

My face hit the floor. Fabric ripped. I gulped for air. I lifted my head and stared at a pair of dusty brown construction-worker boots in front of me. A fire extinguisher dropped on the concrete next to my head. The clang echoed through the dark hollow passageways. The tank rolled in a semicircle and came to a stop next to my head.

I couldn't move—or didn't want to. I blinked back tears of pain. Through blurry vision I watched the boots turn around and jog away from me into the darkness. The last thing I thought was, *There's only one person I know who would wear those boots to this event...*

Then I passed out.

36

THAT WOMAN

I woke in the darkness of the gift shop. The museum was empty and silent. My left cheek was swollen, making it hard to see. My tongue flicked over my upper lip, and I tasted blood. My hands were bound behind my back, and my ankles were taped together in front of me. The only thing I could do was tip over.

I didn't know how I'd gotten here. Or how long I'd been here. Or what had brought me back to consciousness.

"Come on, Samantha, wake up. Come on," said an urgent whisper behind me. I tried to turn my head, but I felt bruises everywhere. The pain kept me still.

"Samantha, wake up. Please."

"Rebecca?" I tensed.

"Shhhhh. Be quiet. I don't know if we're alone," she said.

"What happened? Where is everybody?"

"The party's over." I heard a *glug-glug-glug* sound behind me, and Rebecca held a Dixie cup of water to my lips. "Here," she said.

I tried to drink. Water dribbled down my chin and the front of my dress. I struggled to hold my head up. I felt like a rag doll with too little stuffing.

"It's been you all along, hasn't it?" I asked quietly. When she didn't answer, I continued. "The boots. I saw them when you knocked me down with the fire extinguisher. They're the ones from Christian's office. You told me you wore a man's size shoe when we were talking about the moccasins. You wore his boots so nobody would ever suspect a woman."

She stood up straight and backed away from me. In addition to the boots I'd recognized in the catacombs, she wore a nondescript navy blue jumpsuit.

She reached inside one of the deep pockets of the shapeless garment and pulled out a gun. It couldn't have appeared bigger if it had been designed by Claes Oldenburg.

"You don't want to do this," I said. "No matter what you've done already, you can stop it here. Now."

Rebecca's blonde curls framed her face in a frizz of platinum. "You would have been found in the morning," she said, "but now I have to kill you too. If I leave you alive, you'll tell the police that I killed Dirk and stabbed Thad. I sold off two of the collectible hats, and I have enough cash to get to Canada tonight. To start over. There isn't any other way." Tears streaming down her face belied her tough-girl talk.

"Rebecca, this isn't the only way." I forced myself to look at her and not at the gun. "You won't get away with it." I wondered if I had the energy for a fight if that's what it came to.

"Hedy London will get her publicity." She spat out the actress's name, and spittle flew from her mouth. "That's what she wanted. She won't come after me."

"That's what this is about, isn't it? Christian and Hedy. And your relationship with Christian in college."

Rebecca set the gun on the glass counter. She unzipped the jumpsuit and stepped out. She was wearing a camel suit like the rest of the Hedy London impersonators. With her platinum-blonde hair, she had probably blended in with the crowd. Nobody had noticed her being anywhere unexpected. She balled up the overalls and shoved them into the depths of a camel handbag and picked the gun back up.

"He was one of your professors, wasn't he?" I asked softly.

"He was more than that. He was my mentor. He saw what I went through when my father died. I hated being at college, and my father told me if I applied myself, everything was going to be okay. He died from a heart attack the next month. Christian was the only person at I-FAD who cared about what I was going through. We had a brief..." Her voice trailed off.

"You slept with your teacher?" It flew out of my mouth before I could stop myself.

"He was my first." Tears flowed down her cheeks. "I almost failed out of school when my dad died. My advisor told me to take a year off and get my head together. Christian encouraged me. When I excelled in his film-editing courses, he taught me things. Special skills. He knew what I was capable of. He saw in me what my father saw in me, and I paid him back the only way I knew how."

The surveillance video. It made sense. She'd learned the same skills Dante had learned. I didn't know what she was saying about her relationship with older men, but whatever had happened, the repercussions had left her with a lot of damage and had left me with a very large gun pointed at my chest.

"Rebecca, having a crush on your college professor is normal. It's not a reason to kill."

"The money ran out, and I had to drop out anyway. Christian promised me everything was going to be okay. He told me to get myself together and come back to the college, and he'd make sure I got back on track and graduated. He was going to wait for me and give me a future."

Dante and Rebecca had been at I-FAD at the same time, and I pieced together the timing. "Christian left the college before you returned."

"He met *that woman* at the graduation ceremonies. He never looked back. I followed his career and tried to keep in touch with him, but he never returned my calls or e-mails. They tried to keep their relationship a secret, but I found out." Her head bent down, and tears dripped onto the floor.

"Why would they keep it a secret? If two people are in love, wouldn't they want the world to know it?"

"He wanted his own identity. He wanted to be known as Christian Jhanes, not the man who married Hedy London."

"Did he tell you that?"

She put her left hand on top of her right, steadying the gun. "He didn't have to. I understand him. I know what he needs."

"What happened in the admissions office with Dirk Engle?"

"When Dirk found me in the admissions office with the hats, he tried to—he thought I was interested in him. I turned him down, told him I was with Christian. He called me a stupid girl and said Christian was only in Ribbon to do this exhibit for Hedy. He said Christian and Hedy were together, and if I wanted to get back at Christian, maybe I should get together with Dirk. He said Christian was a two-bit hack, and only a desperate loser would waste her time pining away after him." Her face twisted as if she'd bitten into rotten fruit.

"Rebecca, I think Dirk was telling the truth. Christian *was* using Hedy London. That's why he wanted their relationship to stay a secret."

"No! I knew if I could destroy the exhibit, I could make Christian see Hedy London wasn't worth it, but I had to get rid of Dirk first. It was easier than I thought. I made things go wrong around here. Accidents. And I took the hats out of their boxes and resealed the empty boxes and sent them up to the exhibit so it would look like Dirk stole them."

"What about the hat with the knife through it?"

"He saw me slash the hat with the knife. He said he'd go to Christian and have me fired if I didn't—if I didn't—" She struggled with the words. "I told him I changed my mind. I asked him to come back, to meet me in the admissions office that night after everybody left. I had to shut him up. I had to make him go away. I asked him to turn around while I undressed. I hit him over the head with a gardening tool, and he collapsed."

"That's what I stabbed my hand on tonight. You hid it in the gift shop. You were always remerchandising the store so you could keep track of the murder weapon. You used it to stab Thad. That's why he had three stab puncture wounds, not one."

Her eyes glossed over, and she seemed far removed from the interior of the gift shop. "All that blood—I couldn't look at all that blood." She started to shake. "I had to stop the bleeding. I covered Dirk's head with bubble wrap and hid when I heard you and Eddie."

Cold came over me, a chill that seemed to grow from inside my bones and swallow any warmth in my body. "Rebecca, where's Christian now?"

"He's gone," she said quietly. "I told him to leave while he could. I couldn't hurt him."

Her words hung in the air, surrounded by silence that magnified them. She'd let Christian leave. Had he gone for help or taken the chicken's chance to save himself?

Seconds felt like an eternity. The gun dropped slightly.

Rage propelled me head-first into her. I knocked her down. The gun fired. I yanked on the tape that bound my wrists. It stretched. I freed my right hand and pinned Rebecca to the floor, my dress now all but destroyed.

She didn't fight back.

I pulled the phone cord until the phone fell to the floor, and I called the police. "This is Samantha Kidd. I'm at the museum. In the gift shop. It's an emergency." I dropped the phone to my side.

I looked at the beanbag chair where I'd sat. A bullet had torn through the plastic, somewhere between where my collarbone and heart would have been. A trail of white Styrofoam pebbles spilled onto the floor. I shivered, no smart comeback sounding off in my head, only the notion that Rebecca had come close to either killing me or fixing it so I could never wear strapless again.

For the second time that night, the museum exploded with the sounds of activity. Overhead lights switched on, blinding me until my eyes adjusted. Uniformed police officers flooded through the front doors and came to my rescue.

I was afraid to move. Afraid to leave Rebecca alone. It wasn't until

Detective Loncar had her cuffed on the floor that I climbed off her. The sweat that dripped from my face was gray with dirt, mascara, and survival. A din of white noise in the background. Loncar pulled Rebecca to her feet and pushed her toward the door.

All I cared about was getting sleep. Tomorrow was Saturday, and I wanted nothing more than to hide in my bed. The police maneuvered around, taking pictures, taping off areas that required further investigation, and jotting notes in notepads. Someone bandaged my hand again. Someone wrapped me in a blanket.

An officer walked me through the museum to an ambulance. A few police cars remained, red and blue lights cutting through the darkness, washing the scene with their strobes. I closed my eyes as the ambulance drove me to the hospital. It was hard to believe it was over.

37

EFFECTIVE IMMEDIATELY

Sunlight streamed through my windows, the kind of bright, uninterrupted rays that can only follow a Pennsylvania rainstorm in autumn. It was the kind of day where indoor cats ventured outside, sniffing the green grass and investigating the sidewalks. I'd spent almost thirty hours in bed, getting up only twice: once to feed Logan, the other to chat with Eddie on the phone.

I had enough muscle aches to know that my museum activities came with a price. My cheeks and ribs were bruised, and I had muscles I never knew existed. All of them were crying for attention.

I might have stayed in that bed all day, but when Logan jumped on my ankle, I flinched and sent him flying across the room. I apologized with a can of tuna. The September heat wave had broken, and a cool breeze led me to pull on socks, my new turquoise suede moccasins, and a large fringed poncho atop a turtleneck and jeans. I found a soggy newspaper lying on the street. I scanned the front page while I followed the sidewalk back to my house.

Hollywood Hat Exhibit Turns to Homicide, by Carl Collins.

I suspected Carl Collins would soon be writing more than puff pieces.

Most of the article was old news, considering I'd been at the museum until the bitter end and Mr. Collins had not. Rebecca confessed to stealing the collection of hats when they first arrived at the museum and hiding them in the shop behind the row of Thinker statues. What she'd wanted was Christian's attention, but when she learned about him and Hedy London, she set out to destroy the exhibit. She'd taken the hats out of the museum one by one, hidden in boxes that she carried to the trash. When asked at the time, she claimed she was moving and needed to take the boxes home. She was innocence personified, with her soft curly blond hair and nondescript wardrobe. She was a mouse. No one had suspected her of the theft or the murder. The thought still gave me chills.

Whether or not Christian had truly loved Hedy London would remain a mystery. The police caught up with him at his apartment, packing to leave town. It sounded to me like he realized he didn't want to lie in the bed he'd made for himself.

An opportunist like Christian would have made a poor role model, and I wondered how that had impacted Rebecca. I didn't know if she'd been seeking a lover or a father figure, but either way, she came up empty. What I did know was that my life in Ribbon, living in the house where I grew up, had only been important to me because I had the love and support of a family. She didn't.

Vera Sarlow reached out to her brother's clients and found a surprising number didn't really care who supplied them with hats as long as they were supplied.

Milo Delaney was the person who'd hat-jacked Cat. He didn't know her hat had been legitimately bought in the somewhat shady fashion underground and thought it was one of the stolen samples. He put it in Eddie's VW Bug the night I'd been at the museum— never knowing it was me, not Eddie, who'd discovered it.

Mrs. Willoughby bought the forest-green fedora for an undisclosed sum. I suspected it would have paid my mortgage for at least six months.

Dr. Daum resigned from the board of directors to remove any claims of nepotism that could be made about his son.

Thad made a full recovery.

Eddie got his promotion.

And me?

I called my parents and told them I loved them and forgave them for not telling me about the squirrel in the attic. I told my dad I'd been unemployed for eleven of the twelve months since I'd bought the house, and I told my mom that Nick and I had broken up. I told them both that I'd be okay because I knew I would.

I informed Nick's answering service that I needed three days to recover. When my black eye turned to an attractive shade of yellow and the swelling went down in my lips, it was time to face him. I drove slowly, half because I couldn't turn my head to the left without pain and half because I wasn't sure what I was going to say when I got to the showroom.

When I arrived, I found a college-age girl sitting at the reception desk, sorting through the mail.

"Is Nick here?" I asked.

"He isn't coming in today."

"Oh." I scanned the interior. Samples had been placed on the shelves I'd hung, lit by almost-invisible threads of filament. It was better than he'd planned and bore a striking resemblance to the lighting situation at the museum. I wondered if Eddie had had a hand in it but didn't ask.

"Are you Samantha?" she asked.

"Yes. How did you know?"

"Nick told me you might show up." She stepped out from behind the desk and picked something off the floor. It was a pink gift bag. "He asked me to give you this."

I didn't look inside until I'd made it back to my car. I unwrapped the paper from a first-edition hardbound copy of *Barbie Solves a Mystery*, published in 1963. I opened the front cover of the slightly worn book and found another piece of paper, folded into fourths. It was a letter of termination, addressed to me, effective immediately. Under the official-looking, typed note was a handwritten postscript: *Kidd, I'm sorry it worked out this way.*

I folded the paper and looked at the sky. A storm was on its way. A fat droplet of rain hit the windshield. I rolled up the windows and closed my eyes. I relaxed into the seat and listened to the sudden storm pelt the car. Like most storms, this one would pass in a matter of minutes.

When the rain subsided, I opened my eyes and looked back at the letter from Nick. I reread it and noticed a second note, written on the back. *S: I figure I owe you a job lead. Amanda Ries, my friend from design school, needs help putting together a runway show. I gave her your name. —xo, N*

I crumpled the page and threw it into the back seat. Three seconds later, I retrieved it and smoothed the paper out. I ran my fingers over the X and the O and felt ... something. Loss? Regret? Hope? The truth was I couldn't put a name to my emotions. I put the paper in my handbag and started the car.

Halfway home, I saw Dante's motorcycle two cars behind me. I parked in front of my house and waited for him to catch up. Seconds later he pulled into my driveway. He flipped the visor of his helmet up, exposing his face. The rain had stopped, leaving a film of mist in its place.

"You don't look surprised to see me," he said. His leather jacket was wet, the water beading and running down into the flames.

"Should I be? Oh, you think I didn't see you in my rearview mirror." I shrugged. "I could pretend to be surprised, but really, what's the point?"

"Interesting."

"What?"

"That I'm finally on your radar." He flipped his visor back into place. "Call me when you're ready, Samantha. I'll be waiting."

ABOUT THE AUTHOR

After two decades working for a top luxury retailer, Diane Vallere traded fashion accessories for accessories to murder. She is a national bestselling author and a past president of Sisters in Crime. She started her own detective agency at age ten and has maintained a passion for shoes, clues, and clothes ever since.

Sign up for her newsletter at www.dianevallere.com/weekly-diva and receive girl talk, book talk, and life talk.

ALSO BY

Teacher's Threat

The Kill of It All

Love Me or Grieve Me

Please Don't Push Up the Daisies

The Glass Bottom Hoax

<u>Sylvia Stryker Outer Space Mysteries</u>

Murder on a Moon Trek

Scandal on a Moon Trek

Hijacked on a Moon Trek

Framed on a Moon Trek

Warped on a Moon Trek

<u>Material Witness Mysteries</u>

Suede to Rest

Crushed Velvet

Silk Stalkings

Tulle Death Do Us Part

<u>Costume Shop Mystery Series</u>

A Disguise to Die For

Masking for Trouble

Dressed to Confess

<u>Mermaid Mysteries</u>

Dead in the Water

<u>Non-Fiction</u>

Bonbons for your Brain